Dorothy Gilman

Three Complete Mrs. Pollifax Mysteries

The Unexpected Mrs. Pollifax

The Amazing Mrs. Pollifax

The Elusive Mrs. Pollifax

BARNES
&NOBLE
BOOKS
NEW YORK

This edition published by Barnes & Noble, Inc.,
by arrangement with Doubleday & Company, Inc.

1993 Barnes & Noble Books

ISBN 1-56619-008-8

Printed and bound in the United States of America

M 9 8 7 6 5 4 3 2 1

Contents

The Unexpected Mrs. Pollifax

To Dr. Robert Vidor,
with thanks

Chapter One

The nurse walked out of the room, closing the door behind her, and Mrs. Pollifax looked at the doctor and he in turn looked at her. He was a very *nice* young man, with black hair, very white teeth and horn-rimmed glasses that he removed now, placing the stem of the earpiece between his teeth. "Well, Mrs. Pollifax," he said pleasantly, "I don't know how you manage it, but for a woman of your age you're in fantastically good health. I congratulate you."

"Oh," said Mrs. Pollifax flatly, and the doctor glanced at her with such a peculiar expression that she added brightly, for his benefit, "Oh!"

He smiled and returned his glasses to his nose. "Which brings me to the fact that, although I find you in excellent health physically, I do note certain signs of depression. You're not quite the same Mrs. Pollifax I saw last year. Anything in particular troubling you?"

She hesitated, wondering if he could possibly understand. He looked so absurdly young—he *was* young.

He added pointedly, "I had the distinct feeling that you were disappointed at being in such excellent health."

She said guardedly, "I don't believe I've ever cared about outliving my contemporaries, you know. I've never regarded life as a competition to see who can hold out the longest. I think one can sometimes have too *much* time." She paused and then added recklessly, "I daresay it sounds terribly frivolous when people are starving in India, but I can't help feeling I've outlived my usefulness." There, she thought firmly, she had said it, the words were out and curdling the air.

"I see. Your children, Mrs. Pollifax, are . . . ?"

"Grown and far away. And visits aren't the same, you know. One can never *enter* their lives."

He was listening attentively—yes, he was a very nice young doctor. "I think you said you do a great deal of volunteer work?"

In a precise voice she ticked off the list of charities to which she gave her time; it was a long and sensible list.

The doctor nodded. "Yes, but do you enjoy volunteer work?"

Mrs. Pollifax blinked at the unexpectedness of his question. "That's odd," she said, and suddenly smiled at him. "Actually I suppose I loathe it."

He could not help smiling back at her; there was something contagious about her smile, something conspiratorial and twinkling. "Then perhaps it's time you looked for more congenial outlets," he suggested.

Mrs. Pollifax said slowly, with a little frown, "I enjoy meeting the people, you know, it's just that so often nothing more is needed for volunteer work than a good set of teeth."

"I beg your pardon?"

"Teeth—for smiling. There are rules, too. You can't imagine how regimented some of the volunteer work can be. It's very impersonal—not yours, somehow, because of all the restrictions."

"Do you feel you're a particularly creative person?"

Mrs. Pollifax smiled. "Goodness, I don't know. I'm just—me."

He ignored that, saying very seriously, "It's terribly important for everyone, at any age, to live to his full potential. Otherwise a kind of dry rot sets in, a rust, a disintegration of personality."

"Yes," she said simply. "Yes, I agree with you whole-heartedly on that, but what is one to do? After my husband died I set out to make a very sensible life for myself—I always intended to, you see —so that I would never be a nuisance to my children. It's just that—"

"It's too sensible, perhaps?" Caught by something in her eyes that did not match the light mockery of her voice, he said, "But isn't there something you've always longed to do, something you've never had either the time or the freedom for until now?"

Mrs. Pollifax looked at him. "When I was growing up—oh for years—I planned to become a spy," she admitted.

The doctor threw back his head and laughed, and Mrs. Pollifax wondered why, when she was being her most serious, people found her so amusing. She supposed that her tastes always had been somewhat peculiar. Her husband's favorite form of endearment for her had been "lovable little goose," which was his way of forgiving the odd bent in her that he didn't quite understand, and as they grew older the children, too, had acquired the habit of thinking her just a little absurd. She could hear Jane now: "But mother, why on earth—why on *earth*—a dozen antimacassars? Nobody's used antimacassars since Queen Victoria died!" How futile it had seemed even to explain the woman selling crochetwork at the door that morning, a dear, mangy little woman with a most fascinating story of being abandoned six years earlier on McGovern Street. With no husband and four babies to support she had turned in desperation to the handwork learned as a child at a convent, and Mrs. Pollifax had listened with rapt attention, enjoying every minute of it. After buying the antimacassars, however, she had felt it only kind to make a suggestion. "When you go to the next house," she had said tactfully, "it would be much wiser to call it McGivern Street, not McGovern. Strangers invariably make this mistake, but there has never been a McGovern Street here, and if you'd lived on it for six years you'd have known this. Although otherwise," she added warmly, "it's a terribly good story. The tears came to my eyes, they really did."

The woman had looked astonished, then confused, then badly frightened until she saw the twinkle in Mrs. Pollifax's eye. "Well, if you aren't the surprise," she said, beginning to laugh. "I certainly had you down as an easy mark."

They'd had a lovely talk over a cup of tea in the kitchen, and the woman's real story had proven even more fascinating than her false one, and just to prove her basic honesty the woman had offered to sell Mrs. Pollifax the antimacassars at list price—they'd been made in Japan. But Mrs. Pollifax had firmly refused, feeling the morning was well worth the price. Jane would never have understood, however; Jane had sensible Pollifax blood flowing in her veins and Jane would have been deeply shocked. "What, you didn't call the police?" she would have demanded. "Mother, honestly! That would have been the sensible thing to do."

Mrs. Pollifax thought with astonishment, "I don't suppose

that I *am* a very sensible person actually. Perhaps the doctor's right, I can't be happy trying to be what I'm not."

The doctor was still chuckling, his glasses off again as he polished them with his handkerchief, but the mood of confessional had ended with his roar of laughter and was not to be recaptured. He wrote out a prescription for antidepressant pills, they chatted a few minutes longer but without further rapport, and Mrs. Pollifax left his office.

"But I wasn't joking," she thought indignantly as she walked down the street. "I really was going to be a spy." She had worked hard at it, too, going to the town dump every Saturday morning with her cousin John to watch him shoot rats, and proving such a persistent tag-along that he had condescended to show her how guns worked. On several glorious occasions he had allowed her to shoot with him. There were the maps, too, that she had pored over in her room year after year, and with such scholarly devotion that when the second world war began she was able instantly to announce the longitude and latitude of obscure little islands nobody else had ever heard of. What a funny child she had been, she thought with affection, a lonely but very happy child. She was lonely now but so—so *unused*, so *purposeless*, she realized; and at the back of her mind lay the memory of last Monday when she had carried her geraniums to the roof of the apartment building and had stood at the edge of the parapet looking down, her mind searching for one good reason why she should not take a step forward into oblivion. And she had found none. Even now she was not sure what would have happened if young Mr. Garbor hadn't seen her and called out, "Mrs. Pollifax! For heaven's sake step back!" When she obeyed him she saw that he was trembling.

She hadn't told the doctor this. Obviously she must find a way to instill novelty into her life or she would be afraid to carry her geraniums to the roof, and she was very fond of geraniums.

She walked up the steps to her apartment house and pushed aside the heavy glass door. Her mailbox produced an assortment of circulars, but no letters today. She stuffed them into her purse and unlocked the inner door to discover that Miss Hartshorne had preceded her to the elevator and was standing guard beside it. Immediately Mrs. Pollifax felt herself and her intentions shrivel. It was not Miss Hartshorne's fault that she reminded Mrs. Pollifax of the algebra teacher who had nearly blighted her life at thirteen, but Mrs. Pollifax illogically blamed her for it nevertheless.

"Mrs. Pollifax," boomed Miss Hartshorne in her quartermaster's voice.

"Lovely day, isn't it?" said Mrs. Pollifax, trembling a little. The elevator arrived and they stepped inside. Thoroughly cowed, Mrs. Pollifax let Miss Hartshorne press the floor button and received a pitying glance in return. ("You have forgotten pi again, Emily").

"It's warm," Miss Hartshorne announced as the elevator began to rise.

"Yes, warm. Quite humid, too," contributed Mrs. Pollifax, and pulling herself together added, "Planning a trip this summer, Miss Hartshorne?" It was not so much a question as an exploratory statement, because Miss Hartshorne was always planning a trip and when she was not planning one she was showing colored slides of previous trips. Sometimes Mrs. Pollifax felt that her neighbor did not really see the countries through which she traveled until she came home to view them on a screen in her living room.

"In September," said Miss Hartshorne crisply. "It's the only month for the knowledgeable traveler."

"Oh, I see," replied Mrs. Pollifax humbly.

The door opened and Miss Hartshorne moved toward apartment 4-C and Mrs. Pollifax to 4-A. "Good day," Miss Hartshorne said dismissingly.

"Yes—that is, to you, too," mumbled Mrs. Pollifax, and opened the door of her apartment with a feeling of escape.

Nothing had changed in her three rooms except the slant of the sun, and Mrs. Pollifax adjusted the venetian blinds before removing her hat. As she passed the desk the engagement calendar caught her eye and she stopped to glance at it with a sense of *ennui*. This was Monday; on Tuesday she wheeled the bookcart at the hospital, on Wednesday she rolled bandages, on Thursday morning there was a meeting of the Art Association and in the afternoon she worked in the gift shop of the hospital. On Friday the Garden Club met, on Saturday morning she would have her hair trimmed, and in the afternoon Elise Wiggin would come for tea—but Elise talked of nothing but her grandchildren and how joyously they embraced toilet training.

The doctor had said, "Isn't there something you've always wanted to do but never had the time or freedom for?"

Mrs. Pollifax tossed the day's newspaper on the couch, and then on second thought picked it up and leafed through its pages because it was important to be well informed and in touch with the world. On page three the photograph of a woman caught her eye. FINDS CAREER AT 63, said the words over the photograph, and Mrs. Pollifax, captured, immediately sat down to read. It was about a woman named Magda Carroll who had turned to "Little Theater" groups after her children married, and following only two plays she had been discovered by a Broadway casting director. Now she was performing in a play that had opened to rave reviews in New York. "I owe it all to my age," she told the interviewer. "The theater world is teeming with bright and talented young things, but there is a dearth of sixty-three-year-old character actresses. They needed me—I was unexpected."

Mrs. Pollifax let the paper slide to the floor. " 'They needed me—I was unexpected.' How perfectly wonderful," she whispered, but the words made her wistful. She stood up and walked to the mirror in the hall and stared at the woman reflected there: small, feminine, somewhat cushiony in figure, hair nearly white, eyes blue, a nice little woman unsuited for almost everything practical. But wasn't there any area at all, she wondered, in which she, too, might be unexpected?

Nonsense, she told herself; what she was thinking was absolutely out of the question.

"You could always try," she reminded herself timidly. "After all, nothing ventured, nothing gained—and you're a taxpayer, aren't you?"

Preposterous. Unthinkable.

But at the back of her mind there remained the rooftop and how very nearly her right foot had moved into space.

"Isn't there something you've always longed to do?" the doctor had asked.

"Of course it wouldn't hurt to ask," she began again, feeling her way cautiously toward the idea once more. "Just looking into the idea would be a nice little vacation from volunteer work."

Now she was rationalizing because it was insane, utterly.

"But I haven't visited Washington, D.C., since I was eleven years old," she thought. "Think of the new buildings I've not seen except in pictures. Everyone should remain in touch with their own Capitol."

She would go. "I'll go!" she announced out loud, and feeling positively giddy at her recklessness she walked to the closet and pulled down her suitcase.

On the following morning Mrs. Pollifax left by train for Washington. The first thing she did after registering at a hotel was to go by taxi to the Capitol building and visit her congressman. The next day was spent in sight-seeing and in restoring her courage, which had a tendency to rise in her like a tide and then ebb, leaving behind tattered weeds of doubt. But on Thursday, after lunch, she resolutely boarded the bus for the twenty-minute ride to Langley, Virginia, where the new headquarters of the Central Intelligence Agency had been built. Its address and location had been discovered by Mrs. Pollifax in the public library, where she had exercised a great deal of discretion, even glancing over her shoulder several times as she copied it into her memo pad. Now she was astonished—even shocked—to see sign after sign along the road directing everyone, presumably Russians, too, to the Central Intelligence Agency. Nor was there anything discreet about the building itself. It was enormous—"covers nine acres," growled the bus driver—and with its towers, penthouses and floors of glass it fairly screamed for attention. Mrs. Pollifax realized that she ought to feel intimidated, but her courage was on the rise today—she was here now, and in such a glorious mood that only Miss Hartshorne could have squashed her, and Miss Hartshorne was several hundred miles away. Mrs. Pollifax walked through the gates and approached the guards inside with her head high. "I would like," she said, consulting her memo pad, "to see Mr. Jaspar Mason."

She was given a form to fill out on which she listed her name, her address and the name of Mr. Mason, and then a guard in uniform escorted her down the corridor. Mrs. Pollifax walked slowly, reading all the signs posted on how classified wastepaper should be prepared for disposal, and at what hours it would be

collected, and she decided that at the very least this was something
that would impress Miss Hartshorne.

The room into which Mrs. Pollifax was ushered proved to be
small, bright and impersonal. It was empty of Mr. Mason, however,
and from its contents—several chairs, a striped couch and a mosaic
coffee table—Mrs. Pollifax deduced that it was a repository for
those visitors who penetrated the walls of the citadel without invitation. Mr. Mason contributed further to this impression when he
joined her. He carried himself like a man capable of classifying and
disposing of people as well as wastepaper but with tact, skill and
efficiency. He briskly shook her hand, glanced at his watch and
motioned her to a chair. "I'm afraid I can give you only ten minutes," he said. "This room is needed at two o'clock. But tell me
how I can help you."

With equal efficiency Mrs. Pollifax handed him the introduction that she had extracted from her congressman; she had not told
the congressman her real reason for wishing to interview someone
in this building, but she had been compelling. The young man read
the note, frowned, glanced at Mrs. Pollifax and frowned again. He
seemed particularly disapproving when he looked at her hat, and
Mrs. Pollifax guessed that the single fuchsia-pink rose that adorned
it must be leaning again like a broken reed.

"Ah—yes, Mrs. Politflack," he murmured, obviously baffled
by the contents of the introduction—which sounded in awe of Mrs.
Pollifax—and by Mrs. Pollifax herself, who did not strike him as
awesome at all.

"Pollifax," she pointed out gently.

"Oh—sorry. Now just what is it I can do for you, Mrs. Pollifax? It says here that you are a member of a garden club of your
city, and are gathering facts and information—"

Mrs. Pollifax brushed this aside impatiently. "No, no, not
really," she confided, and glancing around to be sure that the door
was closed, she leaned toward him. In a low voice she said, "Actually I've come to inquire about your spies."

The young man's jaw dropped. "I beg your pardon?"

Mrs. Pollifax nodded. "I was wondering if you needed any."

He continued staring at her and she wished that he would
close his mouth. Apparently he was very obtuse—perhaps he was
hard of hearing. Taking care to enunciate clearly, she said in a

louder voice, "I would like to apply for work as a spy. That's why I'm here, you see."

The young man closed his mouth. "You can't possibly—you're not serious," he said blankly.

"Yes, of course," she told him warmly. "I've come to volunteer. I'm quite alone, you see, with no encumbrances or responsibilities. It's true that my only qualifications are those of character, but when you reach my age character is what you have the most of. I've raised two children and run a home, I drive a car and know first aid, I never shrink from the sight of blood and I'm very good in emergencies."

Mr. Mason looked oddly stricken. He said in a dazed voice, "But really, you know, spying these days is not bloody at all, Mrs. —Mrs.—"

"Pollifax," she reminded him. "I'm terribly relieved to hear that, Mr. Mason. But still I hoped that you might find use for someone—someone expendable, you know—if only to preserve the lives of your younger, better-trained people. I don't mean to sound melodramatic, but I am quite prepared to offer you my life or I would not have come."

Mr. Mason looked shocked. "But Mrs. Politick," he protested, "this is simply not the way in which spies are recruited. Not at *all*. I appreciate the spirit in which you—"

"Then how?" asked Mrs. Pollifax reasonably. "Where do I present myself?"

"It's—well, it's not a matter of *presenting* oneself, it's a matter of your country looking for *you*."

Mrs. Pollifax's glance was gently reproving. "That's all very well," she said, "but how on earth could my country find me in New Brunswick, New Jersey? And have they tried?"

Mr. Mason looked wan. "No, I don't suppose—"

"There, you see?"

Someone tapped on the door and a young woman appeared, smiled at them both and said, "Mr. Mason, I'm sorry to interrupt, but there's an urgent telephone call for you in your office. It's Miss Webster."

"Miss Webster," murmured Mr. Mason dazedly, and then, "Good heavens yes, Miss Webster. Where *is* Miss Webster?" He jumped to his feet and said hastily, "I must excuse myself, I'm so sorry, Mrs. Politick."

"Pollifax," she reminded him forgivingly, and leaned back in her chair to wait for his return.

Chapter Two

Carstairs was lean, tall, with a crew-cut head of gray hair and a tanned, weather-beaten face. He looked an outdoor man although his secretary, Bishop, had no idea how he managed to maintain such a façade. He spent long hours in his office, which was a very special room equipped to bring him into contact with any part of the world in only a few seconds time. He often worked until midnight, and when something unusual was going on he would stay the night. Bishop didn't envy him his job. He knew that Carstairs was OSS-trained, and that presumably his nerves had long ago been hammered into steel, but it was inhuman the way he kept his calm—Bishop was apt to hit the ceiling if his pencil point broke.

"Anything from Tirpak?" asked Carstairs right away, as Bishop handed him reports that had been filtering in since midnight.

"Nothing from him since Nicaragua."

"That was two days ago. No word from Costa Rica, either?" Bishop shook his head.

"Damn." Carstairs leaned back in his chair and thought about it, not liking it very much. "Well, business as usual," he told Bishop. "It's time I made arrangements for Tirpak at the Mexico City end. One must be optimistic. I'll be in Higgins' office."

"Right."

"And keep the wires open for any news from Tirpak; he's overdue and if there's any word I want to hear immediately."

Carstairs opened and closed the door of his soundproof office and joined the life of the humming building. Higgins was in charge of what Carstairs—humorously but never aloud—called "Personnel": those thousands of paper faces locked up in top-secret steel files and presided over by Higgins of the cherubic face and fantastic memory. "Good morning," said Carstairs, peering into Higgins' room.

"Actually it's cloudy outside," Higgins said mildly. "That's the trouble with this modern architecture. But come in anyway, Bill. Coffee?"

"You're saving my life."

Higgins looked doubtful. "You'd better taste the swill before you say that, and you'll have to manage your own carton, I've already lost a fingernail prying open the lid of mine. What can I do for you?"

"I need a tourist."

"Well, name your type," Higgins said dolefully, and lifting his coffee high murmured, "*Skoal.*"

"I want," said Carstairs, "a very particular type of tourist."

Higgins put down his coffee and sighed. "I was afraid of that. Tourists I can supply by the droves, but a particular type—well, go ahead, I'm free for half an hour."

"He or she will have to come from your inactive list. This tourist must be someone absolutely unknown, Higgins, and that's vital."

"Go on. For what type of job, by the way?"

Carstairs hesitated. He always hated divulging information, a feeling bred into him during the war years, but Higgins was not likely to meet with torture during the next twenty-four hours. "There's a package coming into Mexico City. This particular tourist is to be nothing but a tourist for several weeks but on a certain date stop in at a specified place and pick up said package—rendered innocuous for customs, of course—and bring it into the United States."

Higgins lifted an eyebrow. "A regular courier won't do?"

"Couriers are pretty well known to them," pointed out Carstairs gently.

"And to mail it . . . ?"

"Far, far too risky."

Higgins' gaze grew speculative. "I see. I gather, then, that this package of yours is dynamite—not literally, of course, but figuratively—and that you are therefore reduced to being terribly ingenious and circumspect, but that the job is not dangerous so long as said tourist is utterly unknown to *them.*"

"Bless you for saving us both precious minutes," said Carstairs fondly.

"Have you considered someone not inactive but absolutely new—a fresh face?"

Surprised, Carstairs said, "No I hadn't—that would mean someone totally unseasoned, wouldn't it?"

Higgins shrugged. "If there's no point of contact would it matter?"

"Mmmm," murmured Carstairs thoughtfully.

"One has to sacrifice something for said tourist's being unknown to anyone I mean, that's what you want to avoid, isn't it—someone met in Vienna in 1935 suddenly popping up in Mexico City years later?"

Carstairs smiled faintly—he doubted if Higgins had even been born in 1935. "Suppose you show me the possibilities," he suggested. "Very little is demanded of my tourist except accuracy, but he or she must look exactly right."

They walked back into the files where photograph after photograph was drawn out, sometimes to be instantly withdrawn with a "Oh dear no, he won't do, he broke his tibia in the Balkans," or "Oops, sorry, this lady's been loaned to the Orient." When Carstairs left it was with five photographs and a soggy carton of cold coffee.

"Nothing yet," said Bishop, glancing up from his typewriter.

"Damn," said Carstairs again, checked his watch—it was just half-past nine—and went into the office. Bishop, bless his heart, had left a fresh carton of coffee on his desk and Carstairs peeled it open, brought a cube of sugar from his desk drawer and dropped it into the coffee. He reminded himself that Tirpak was good, one of his best men, but if Tirpak had reported from Nicaragua two days ago he should have been in Costa Rica by now. For eight months Tirpak had been on this job, and from the bits and pieces he'd sent out of South America by wireless and coded mail his eight months had been extremely fruitful. Visually Tirpak was only a photograph in the top-secret files, but Carstairs knew his mind very well—it was that of a computer, a statistician, a jurist. Months ago he had been fed all the tips, stories and rumors that reached the department and from these he was bringing back neat, cold, irrefutable facts on all of Castro's secret operations in the hemisphere. But alone the facts were nothing; what was most vital of all was the proof that Tirpak was carrying with him out of South America, proof so concrete and detailed that each nation in the Alliance for Progress would know once and for all the face of its enemy and in exactly what form the Trojan horse of communism would appear in its country.

Coffee in hand Carstairs walked to the ceiling-high map on the wall and stared at it moodily. One might say that Tirpak's job of work was finished now, and so it was in the literal sense, but actually it was only beginning. This was "phase two," the most difficult of all, the getting of the proof into the right hands, moving it north, country by country, until it would arrive here on Carstairs' desk to be forwarded upstairs. That was the difference between this particular job and the others, that it entailed quantities of documents, photographs, dossiers and descriptions of operating methods. It could only be expected that eventually the wrong people would get wind of Tirpak's job, and it was no coincidence that several of Tirpak's informants had begun disappearing. The wonder of it was that Tirpak had worked for so long in secrecy. Now time was against him and Carstairs realized that he was worried. He knew the shape that phase two ought to take if everything went off perfectly . . . the shabby photographic studio in Costa Rica where Tirpak's bulky packages of material would be reduced to microfilm, and then the trip into Mexico to leave the microfilm with DeGamez, for Tirpak was *persona non grata* in the United States, a myth that had to be perpetuated for his safety. Once the microfilm reached Mexico City it would be out of Tirpak's hands and the rest would be up to Carstairs and his tourist—but Tirpak ought to have reached Costa Rica before now.

Restlessly, Carstairs lit a cigarette. This was when he sweated, this was when his own war experience went against him because he knew what it was like to be on the run. He wondered where Tirpak was on this humid July morning, whether he was running scared or still had the situation well in hand. If he couldn't reach Costa Rica would he try to push through to Mexico? Was he being followed? Had he been killed, and all that documentation scattered and lost? This had happened before too.

The door opened and Carstairs immediately rearranged his features into their habitual mask. "Yes, Bishop," he said.

Bishop was smiling. "Tirpak has reached Costa Rica."

Carstairs' reaction was fervent and brief. "Thank God," he said, and then added savagely, "What took him so long?"

"They're decoding the message now," Bishop said. "It'll be here in exactly five minutes."

Five minutes later Carstairs was frowning over the message from Tirpak. It was the longest one that Tirpak had permitted himself, but Costa Rica was the safest place he had visited in eight months. In essence Tirpak said that it was Castro's Red Chinese friends who were interested in him, and he had decided it was time for him to go into hiding. All the documents were being processed as planned, and would be forwarded to Mexico City, suitably camouflaged. Tirpak planned to throw them off the scent by remaining in Costa Rica for a week or two. Carstairs could absolutely (repeat, *absolutely*) count on the microfilms arriving in Mexico City between August 12 and August 18.

When he had finished reading the decoded words a third time Carstairs put down the sheet and lit a cigarette. Tirpak had obviously been having a rough time or he wouldn't be planning to stay in Costa Rica to "throw them off the scent." In a word, things were getting very hot for him. He must have been closely watched and followed, so closely that for him to travel any further would jeopardize both the documents and any other agents he contacted.

But Tirpak was a seasoned man, and not a giver of reckless promises. Carstairs had unalterable faith in Tirpak's ingenuity, and if Tirpak said the microfilms would arrive in Mexico City between the twelfth and the eighteenth then the microfilms would be there. It was time for Carstairs to get his tourist moving.

"Bishop," he said, arranging the five photographs on his desk, "Bishop, you know the setup. Which one?"

Bishop sat down and carefully scrutinized the five photos. "I'm afraid I lack your imagination, you know. They all look like authentic, true-blue American tourists to me."

Carstairs sighed. "Heaven knows that nobody should be judged by face alone, but this chap's expression is too damn eager for me. Retired businessman, excellent background, but personality a bit—ingratiating, shall we say? Might get carried away in a foreign country and do some bragging—it's amazing the loss of identity some people suffer in a strange country. This man might do except that he was in on some behind-the-line work in China during World War Two. If it's the Red Chinese that have been hotly pursuing Tirpak we certainly can't risk him."

"And the woman?" Bishop asked only from curiosity. Carstairs had an uncanny knack for assessing people; he was astonishingly perceptive and of course he was a perfectionist or he would never have gotten away with the outrageous operations he launched.

"Too young. I want someone over forty-five for this, especially if they're inexperienced. This tourist must be absolutely *right.*"

Bishop stabbed the fourth picture with a finger. "How about this woman?"

"Mmm." Carstairs studied the face. "Humorless, but not bad. Compulsive type. She'll do the job, won't mix, probably won't talk to a soul." His glance dropped to the data beneath the photo. "Charlotte Webster, age fifty-eight—" He frowned. "She's not precisely what I had in mind, but she's passable. Bishop, I'd like to take a look at Miss Webster without committing myself. Is there some way in which I could see her without being seen, so to speak?"

Bishop said promptly, "Yes, sir. I can ask Mason downstairs to set up an appointment to review her credentials. He can meet her in his first-floor interviewing room and you can stop in and look her over."

"Absolutely inspired, Bishop. Excellent. Contact Mason and ask him to take over. Tell him he's to handle it completely and without involving me. Tell him I'd like to see her today if it's possible. I've a hectic afternoon ahead but I'm free for a few minutes at two o'clock. See if he can set up an appointment with her for two this afternoon."

"Right, sir."

When Bishop had gone Carstairs took a last look at the photograph, frowned, sighed heavily and then resolutely put it aside.

Carstairs went to lunch at forty minutes past one. The table-service rooms were filled and so he walked on to the cafeteria and picked up a tray instead. He finished eating at two, and after consulting his watch he hurried toward the first-floor interviewing room. To the guard stationed outside he said briefly, "Mason's appointment in there?"

"Yes, sir. A woman."

"Good."

Carstairs opened the door. The woman was seated alone in the room, waiting, and she was at once so utterly and astonishingly right for the job that Carstairs could scarcely believe his eyes. He had always been extremely intuitive about his people: it was almost a psychic quality that enabled him to separate pretense from authenticity. His glance first noted the really absurd hat—it was difficult to overlook—with one fuchsia-colored rose completely askew; it then traveled over the wisps of white hair that refused to be confined, marked the cheerful mouth, and when it met a glance that was as interested and curious as his own he felt the triumph of a casting director who discovers the perfect actress for a pivotal role. He strode across the room with hand outstretched. "I'm Carstairs," he said warmly. "I wanted to meet you while you're here. We're not really interested in your qualifications, you see, we want you for a job. Have you been talking with Mason?"

"Mr. Mason?" For just a moment she appeared bewildered. "Oh yes, but he was called to the telephone, and—"

"It doesn't matter, I'll take over now." He sat down beside her on the couch. "I realize that you're inexperienced but this is the very simplest of jobs. The important thing from the very beginning has been that I find someone absolutely right. I think you'll do. I think you'll do very well indeed."

"I will?" Her cheeks turned pink with pleasure.

"Yes. Are you free to work for us from August 3 to August 22?"

"Why—oh yes," she gasped. "Yes, I'm quite free—I'd be delighted!"

"Excellent. Have you ever visited Mexico?"

"Mexico!" She looked positively radiant. "No, never. You'd like me to go to Mexico?"

He appreciated the quick response; there had been no hesitation at all. "Yes. You'll be paid the usual fee for courier work, and of course all your expenses will be taken care of while you are there. It's quite simple. You'll be an American tourist and use your own name. The job consists of visiting a specific place in Mexico

City at a specific date, and for the rest of the time you'll be on your own." She was listening with a look of wonder, as if she could not believe her good fortune. He reflected that an extremely bad photographer had taken her picture; Miss Webster was not only right but perfect. "You can handle this?" he added with a smile.

She drew a deep breath and nodded. "That's why I came, you see—because I thought I could." She added quickly, "Yes, I'm sure I can handle it. I will do my very, *very* best."

"I think you will, too," he said. "Look here, do you mind coming up to my office for a moment? I won't have time to brief you this afternoon, and only my secretary can tell me when I'm free, but I'll want to arrange an appointment with you as soon as possible." With a nod Carstairs dismissed the guard outside the door and guided his companion toward the bank of elevators. "I'd like to wrap this up without delay. I'll need you for at least an hour and my schedule this afternoon is quite hopeless. I could see you this evening but I think tomorrow morning would be better. Would that be convenient?"

"It would be perfect," she assured him, beaming. As they entered the elevator she had been fumbling in her purse; now she extracted a small white card and held it out to him. "I don't believe you know my name," she told him. "I always carry these with me."

Carstairs was amused, but he dropped the card into his pocket. The doors slid open at his floor and he grasped the woman's arm to escort her down the hall. "Here we are," he said. "Bishop? Ah, there you are. Am I free tomorrow from nine to ten?"

Bishop sighed. "Are you ever? Yes, technically you're free."

"Good. Nine it is then." He held out his hand. "I'm terribly sorry to bring you back again but I always insist on very thorough briefings."

"I think you should," she told him approvingly. "And really, you have been so kind. So *unexpectedly* kind. Thank you."

"Kind," echoed Carstairs when she had gone. "She's not only perfect but she appreciates my finer qualities. Well, Bishop, what do you think? I found my innocent tourist, didn't I? In fact one so congenitally innocent that she'd baffle Mao Tse-tung himself."

Bishop's jaw dropped. He said in a hollow voice, "Sir—"

"What is it, Bishop, are you feeling ill?"

"That was your *tourist?*"

"Yes, isn't she marvelous?"

Bishop swallowed. He said, "As you entered this office, sir, I was just putting down the receiver of the telephone. It was Mason calling to tell you that Miss Webster has just arrived."

Carstairs frowned. "Webster? Webster?"

"He sent a message up earlier, telling of Miss Webster's delay. I forwarded it to the table-service room."

"I ate in the cafeteria."

"Now Miss Webster is here."

"Nonsense," said Carstairs, "Miss Webster has just left."

"No, sir, Miss Webster has just arrived."

Carstairs began, softly and vehemently, to swear. "Then will you do me the kindness, Bishop, of asking Mason just who the hell was waiting for me down there in his interviewing room at two o'clock, and who the devil I've just engaged for this job? On the double, Bishop. I'll be in my office."

He strode into his office and sat down. Gingerly, reluctantly, he drew from his pocket the calling card that he had been given and placed it on the desk before him. He read it and frowned. He read it again and reached for the photograph of Miss Webster. There was a very superficial physical resemblance between her and his tourist but he knew now that Miss Webster was not going to do at all. Miss Webster was a dehydrated and flavorless copy of the original. "Well?" he growled as Bishop returned.

"Her name was Politick or Politflack, Mason can't remember which, but they'd know in the lobby."

"Pollifax," said Carstairs. "Go on. What brought her here?"

Without expression Bishop said carefully, "Mason says that she came here to apply for work as a secret agent."

Carstairs opened his mouth, closed it and stared incredulously at Bishop. "Impossible," he said at last. "Nobody just walks in asking to be an agent."

"Mason was most emphatic—and still quite shaken by the incident."

A full minute passed, and then the corners of Carstairs' mouth began to twitch and he threw back his head and roared. When his laughter had subsided to a chuckle he said, "Unbelievable. Preposterous." But he had reached a decision and he knew it. "Bishop," he said, "it's unorthodox even for this unorthodox department, but damn it—order an immediate, top-priority security check run on"—he consulted the chaste white card on his desk— "on Mrs. Virgil Pollifax of the Hemlock Apartments in New Brunswick, New Jersey. I want the results before eight o'clock tomorrow morning. And when you've done that, Bishop, start praying."

"Praying, sir?"

"Yes, Bishop. Pray that she's never unwittingly contributed to subversive organizations, voted Socialist or entertained a Red bishop for dinner. After that," he added flatly, "you can tell Mason to send Miss Webster home."

Chapter Three

"Flight Number 51 loading at Gate Four. . . . Flight Number 51 . . . to Mexico City loading at Gate Four. . . ."

Mrs. Pollifax found her seat on the plane and sat down feeling suffused with an almost unbearable excitement. For days she had been practicing the inscrutable look of a secret agent, but now she found it impossible to sustain; she was far too enraptured by the thought of her first visit to Mexico and her first trip anywhere by jet. And it was just as well, she told herself sternly, for Mr. Carstairs had emphasized that she was not a secret agent but an American tourist. "You are to be yourself," he had told her firmly, and had added, with a faint smile, "If I thought you capable of being anyone else I would never have given you this job to do."

Mrs. Pollifax had listened to him with shining eyes.

"You will arrive in Mexico City on the third of August and you will check in at the Hotel Reforma Intercontinental. The reservations were made an hour ago, in your name. You will be Mrs. Virgil Pollifax, visiting Mexico for three weeks, and you will behave like any other tourist. Where you go is entirely up to you. You will be on your own completely, and I assume you'll visit the usual tourist places, Taxco, Xochimilco, Acapulco, and so on—whatever is of interest to Mrs. Virgil Pollifax. But on August 19, without fail, you will visit this book store on the Calle el Siglo in Mexico City."

He had handed Mrs. Pollifax a slip of paper. "I want you to memorize this address before you leave the building," he said quietly, and Mrs. Pollifax's heart beat a little faster.

"You will not see me again but you will be visited once before you leave by one of the men in my department who will make certain you've forgotten nothing."

Mrs. Pollifax had looked at the words on the piece of paper.

El Papagayo Librerí (The Parrot Bookstore)
Calle el Siglo 14,
Mexico City

Senor R. DeGamez, Proprietor—Fine Books Bought & Sold

Carstairs had continued. "On the nineteenth of August you will walk into the bookshop and ask for Dickens' *A Tale of Two Cities.*"

"The nineteenth," Mrs. Pollifax repeated eagerly.

"The gentleman there, whose name as you can see is Senor DeGamez, will say with regret that he is very sorry but he does not have a copy at the moment."

Mrs. Pollifax waited breathlessly.

"Whereupon you will tell him—with the proper apology for contradicting him—that there is a copy in his window. You will then go to the window with him and he will find the book there and you will say, 'I think Madame Defarge is simply gruesome, don't you?'"

Mrs. Pollifax repeated the words under her breath.

"These identifying phrases are a nuisance," Carstairs told her. "The gentleman will be expecting you about ten o'clock in the morning, but it is always wiser to have a double check set up for you both. Your asking for *A Tale of Two Cities* and your reference to Madame Defarge are the important things to remember."

Mrs. Pollifax nodded. "And that's all?"

"That is all."

"And whatever I'm to bring you will be in the book?" she asked, and instantly covered her mouth with her hand. "Oh dear, I should never have asked that, should I."

Carstairs smiled. "No, and I would not in any case tell you. Although actually," he added dryly, "I can in all honesty say at this particular moment that I don't know myself what he will give you. You will of course—as soon as you have paid for the book—leave and not return again. There will be nothing more asked of you but to continue your sight-seeing for two more days and return by jet on the twenty-first. You will receive your tickets and reservations by mail within the next few days, as well as the tourist card necessary for entering Mexico."

She nodded. "What happens when I come home? What about Customs?"

Carstairs smiled, saying gently, "That need not concern you. Let's just say that we will be aware of your arrival in this country, and there will be no problems for you. None at all."

"Oh."

"In the meantime I must emphasize that you are a tourist who happens merely to be dropping in at the Parrot Bookstore. I want you to think of it that way."

"Oh," Mrs. Pollifax said sadly, and as Carstairs lifted his brows inquiringly she added, "It doesn't sound dangerous in the least."

Carstairs looked shocked. "My dear Mrs. Pollifax, there is always risk—we discussed that—but if there was the slightest element of real danger involved I can assure you that I would never allow an amateur to be sitting here in my office. This is what we call simple courier work, and in this case your amateur status is especially useful. I know that I can trust you to follow directions intelligently—"

"Oh yes," gasped Mrs. Pollifax.

"And out of it you will have a very nice little vacation in Mexico. We will both be satisfied." He stood up, smiling lest he might have sounded reproving, and added, "Bishop will now show you to a quiet corner where you can memorize that address. I hope you weren't insulted at taking a lie detector test?"

"Oh no, it was terribly interesting," she told him, beaming.

"Good. Nothing personal, you understand, it's routine for everyone, even our clerks." He had held out his hand and shaken hers. "I won't be seeing you again, Mrs. Pollifax—have lots of fun."

She shrewdly suspected that he had used the word *fun* deliberately, to rid her of any lingering fancies concerning her trip. Well, she didn't mind; she was going to have fun. Her suitcase was fairly bursting with tourist literature on Mexico City and its environs, and Miss Hartshorne had insisted upon giving her three rolls of color film. "As a bon voyage gift," she explained, "because you will just adore having slides of your trip, they're the perfect souvenir for your Memory Book." Miss Hartshorne had insisted also upon coming to her apartment to instruct her, and had left telling

Mrs. Pollifax she just knew she would come home with perfectly marvelous pictures of Mexico that everyone in the apartment house would enjoy viewing.

Mrs. Pollifax's daughter had received the news with dismay. "But Mother," Jane had wailed over the long-distance wires, "if you wanted to do some traveling why didn't you tell us? You could have come out here to Arizona. I've hired Mrs. Blair to take care of the children while John and I are in Canada. If I'd only known— we'd feel so much better if it could be you, and the children just love it when you come."

"It's just a little trip I thought I'd take for myself," Mrs. Pollifax told her gently, and wished her daughter a happy vacation in Canada.

Her son, Roger, on the other hand, had visited Mexico in his student days, and he told her that she must eat no green stuff and be terribly careful about the water. But there was a great deal more of his mother in him than in Jane, and he had added, "I was getting worried about you, Mother, you haven't erupted in years. God-speed and all that. See you at Christmas and if you get in a jam send me a wire."

Dear Roger, she thought as she fastened her seat belt. She leaned forward to glance out of the window and saw a great many hands waving from the deck, and she fluttered her own with animation. As the plane began to taxi toward the runway Mrs. Pollifax thought with jarring abruptness, "I do hope I'm going to like this." Sunlight caught a wing of the plane and the glare momentarily blinded her; then with a nearly overwhelming burst of sound the landscape beyond Mrs. Pollifax's window began to move with dizzying speed, it blurred into a streak and dropped away. We're in the air, she realized, and felt an enormous and very personal feeling of accomplishment.

"We're airborne," said the man sitting next to her.

Airborne . . . she must remember that. People like Miss Hartshorne knew these things without being told, and, after all, nothing was an experience unless there was a name for it. She smiled and nodded and brought out the latest copy of *Ladies Home Journal* and placed it in her lap. Presently, because she had not slept at all well the night before, Mrs. Pollifax dozed. . . .

As the plane banked and turned over Mexico City, Mrs. Pollifax peered down at its glittering whiteness and thought how flat the city looked, horizontal rather than vertical, and so different from New York with its skyscrapers rising like cliffs out of the shadows. A moment later Mrs. Pollifax was infinitely relieved to discover that landings were more comfortable than takeoffs, and presently she was breathing Mexico City's thin, rarefied mountain air. All the way to the hotel she kept her face pressed to the window of the taxi, but when she spied her first sombrero she gave a sigh of contentment and leaned back. Never mind if most of the women looked sleek and Parisian and the men dressed exactly like Americans—this was Mexico because she had seen a sombrero.

The hotel proved luxurious beyond Mrs. Pollifax's dreams— almost too much so, thought Mrs. Pollifax, who would personally have preferred something native, but she recalled that the choice was not hers, and that this was where tourists stayed. "And I am a tourist," she reminded herself.

Mrs. Pollifax had arrived in the late afternoon. She dined early at the hotel, had a lukewarm bath and, sensibly, retired at nine. The next morning she was first in line for the tour bus that promised to introduce her to Mexico City. On the tour she fell into conversation with two American schoolteachers, Miss Lambert and Mrs. Donahue, but in spite of exchanging pleasantries during the trip she was careful to note each street sign they passed. When the tour ended Mrs. Pollifax had learned the location of the Paseo de la Reforma, the Palacio de Bellas Artes, the Palace of Justice, the National Pawnshop and the Zocalo; she had made two new friends and learned a great deal of Mexico's history, but she had not discovered the whereabouts of the Calle el Siglo. Both Miss Lambert and Mrs. Donahue warned her of the change in altitude and the necessity of adjusting gradually to it. She therefore went no further than Sanborne's that evening, where she ate dinner, admired the lavish gifts in their showcases, and went to bed early again.

The next day Mrs. Pollifax bought a map and after an hour's study set out to find the Calle el Siglo and the Parrot Bookstore, for she was conscientious by nature and did not feel she could relax and really enjoy herself until she knew precisely where she must present herself on August 19. To her surprise she discovered that the street was in walking distance of the hotel, and that it was a perfectly respectable side street already found by the tourists, whom she could identify by the cameras strung about their necks on leather thongs. She wandered almost the length of it, and when she saw the Parrot Bookstore across the street she blushed and quickly averted her eyes. But that one swift glance told her that it was neither shabby nor neglected, as she had somewhat romantically imagined, but a very smart and modern store, small and narrow in width but with a very striking mosaic of a parrot set into its glittering cement façade.

On the following afternoon, returning to the hotel with her two friends after a visit to the National Palace, they found themselves momentarily lost and Mrs. Pollifax steered them all up the Calle el Siglo, saying with a ruthless lack of conscience that it was a direct route to the hotel. This time they passed the door of the Parrot, and Mrs. Pollifax glanced inside and took note of the man behind the counter. She thought he looked very pleasant: about her age, with white hair and a white moustache that was very striking against the Spanish swarthiness of his skin. Like a grandee, she decided.

During the week that Mrs. Pollifax spent sight-seeing in Mexico City she found the opportunity nearly every day to pass the Parrot Bookstore. She did not seek it out deliberately, but if it proved a convenient way to return to her hotel—and it often did— she did not avoid it. Once she passed it in the evening, when it was closed, in the company of Miss Lambert and Mrs. Donahue. Once she and Miss Lambert passed it in the morning when Senor DeGamez was just inserting the key in the door, and twice Mrs. Pollifax passed on the other side without giving it more than a glance. She realized that she was beginning to think of it as *her* shop, and to feel a proprietary interest in it.

When Mrs. Pollifax had enjoyed Mexico City for a week she bid her new friends adios and went by bus to Taxco, where for several days she wandered its crooked, cobblestoned alleys, looked over bargains in silver, and sunned herself in the market plaza. She then returned by way of Acapulco, stopping there overnight. Everywhere she went Mrs. Pollifax found people charming and friendly, and this spared her some of the loneliness of traveling alone. On the bus returning to Mexico City she was entertained by a widower from Chicago who showed her pictures of his six grandchildren, and in turn Mrs. Pollifax showed him pictures of Jane's two children and Roger's one. From the gentleman's conversation Mrs. Pollifax guessed that he was a professional gambler, but this in no way curtailed her interest—she had never before met a professional gambler.

As soon as she returned to Mexico City—it was August 15 on the day she came back—she found it convenient to walk down the Calle el Siglo and reassure herself about her store. It was still there, and Senor DeGamez looked just as elegant as ever. He really looked so pleasant that she thought, "Surely it wouldn't hurt just to step inside for a minute and buy something? Other tourists do, and I pass here so often, and I haven't a thing to read tonight." As she paused, considering, a party of tourists came out of the Parrot laughing and talking and carrying packages that could only be books tied up in white paper. On impulse Mrs. Pollifax crossed the street and went inside.

Chapter Four

After the briefest of glances around her—Senor DeGamez was busy at the counter—Mrs. Pollifax hurried to a corner table that bore the placard LATEST BOOKS FROM USA, and plucked one from the pile. The only sounds in the shop were the crackling of fresh paper, as Senor DeGamez wrapped books, and the sound of his voice as he spoke to his customer. Unfortunately, however, he was speaking the language of his country and so Mrs. Pollifax could not eavesdrop. She selected a volume of memoirs by a well-known American actress and groped in her purse for currency; she was mentally translating dollars into pesos when a strident voice broke the hushed, literary atmosphere. "Old books, new books, read a book," screeched the voice, and Mrs. Pollifax turned in astonishment to see a live parrot addressing her from a cage nearby.

"Well, for heaven's sake," she gasped.

"You like my parrot?" asked Senor DeGamez from the counter. His customer had departed and they were alone. "But he startled you, I think. My customers, they are used to him, but Olé surprises the new ones. Come see," he said, walking over to the cage. "You know parrots? Not many do—this one is exceptionally fine. Have you ever seen such color?"

"Beautiful," said Mrs. Pollifax in a hushed voice. "But seeing him was what startled me, rather than hearing him. He is so brilliantly colored, like a sunset—or are parrots she's rather than he's?"

Senor DeGamez smiled, and with courtly, old-fashioned humor said, "Well, some are he's and some are she's, no? And so it must always be."

Mrs. Pollifax smiled back at him. "Of course, I wasn't thinking, was I? I do say things without thinking, it's a very bad habit.

And of course the name of your store is the Parrot. The bird adds just the right touch."

He lifted a hand. "No, no, my store is named after Olé, not the other way around. My Olé came first—she has been with me twelve years. What I do when she dies I don't know."

Mrs. Pollifax nodded sympathetically. "What *will* you do—exactly! Of course *they* would say find another parrot, but it's never the same, is it?"

He said gently, "That is so, never. You are very wise."

"No," said Mrs. Pollifax reflectively, "only experienced, which comes from living a good many years. Wisdom is something else, I think." Her eyes returned admiringly to the gaudy bird. "She is company for you?" When he looked blank she said, "Your parrot keeps you from being lonely?"

"Oh—*si,*" he said, nodding in understanding. "Yes. My wife she is dead five years now, and my sons, they are grown and in business. When I wish to hear talk I uncover Olé's cage and we speak together. She says a few words in English, a few in Spanish, and when we are finished speaking I cover her cage again and she stops."

Mrs. Pollifax laughed. "The perfect companion!"

"Exactly. And you—you have children too perhaps?" Senor DeGamez was smiling.

Mrs. Pollifax gave her book and her money to him and they moved toward the counter. "Two," she told him, "a boy and girl, both grown up now. I've been a widow for eight years."

He at once looked compassionate. "I am so sorry. But you have surely not come to Mexico alone?"

Mrs. Pollifax nodded.

"Then you are courageous. That is good, very good."

"It's sometimes a little lonely," admitted Mrs. Pollifax.

"Yes, but like me with my Olé you can be alone when you choose. Some of these American women, they are like swarms of—you will forgive me—swarms of geese, always together, always making cackling noises." Here the senor stepped back and did a very humorous imitation of chattering women.

Mrs. Pollifax burst out laughing. "I'm afraid you're too good!"

"But think—when you are lonely you need only find some

American geese and join them. And when you tire"—he snapped his fingers—"off you go. To read. You like to read? I understand that, or you would not be here. Solitaire? Do you play solitaire?"

Mrs. Pollifax shook her head.

"But senora," he cried, "you are missing a delight. I myself treasure the solitary cards." He tapped his forehead. "It clears the brain, it clears the thought, it is mentally sound, mentally healthy."

Mrs. Pollifax said doubtfully, "I remember trying a few games when I was a child—"

"*Si*, but you are a grown-up lady now," he told her, smiling. "Please—you are buying this book? Allow me then to add another as a small gift. No, no," he said, putting up a hand to cut off her protests, and he walked to a shelf, fingered a few titles and chose one with a bright blue jacket. "This one," he said, handing it to her with a flourish. "*77 Ways to Play Solitaire.*"

"Well," murmured Mrs. Pollifax, charmed but not sure what to say.

"For the loneliness, *si?* Because you like my parrot and you are not a geese."

"Goose," said Mrs. Pollifax and began to laugh. "All right, I'll try it, I really will."

"Good, you accept my gift then. Better yet you read it and use it. Remember," he said as he finished tying up the book she had purchased, "remember you are not a child now, you will appreciate better the enjoyment." He nodded affably to a man and a woman who had entered the store. "This has been a pleasure to me, senora, may you have a beautiful visit."

Mrs. Pollifax felt deeply touched and warmed by his friendliness. "Thank you so much," she said, "and thank you for the book."

She had reached the door when he called across the store, "Oh, American senora . . ."

Mrs. Pollifax turned.

He was smiling. "How can you play seventy-seven games of solitaire without cards?" He had picked up a deck from below the counter and now he tossed the pack of playing cards the length of the room to her.

Mrs. Pollifax said, "Oh but . . ." and reached up and caught the cards in midair. Her son, Roger, would have been proud of her.

"How do you Americans say it—'on the house!' " he called out gaily.

How nice he was. Mrs. Pollifax gave in graciously—after all, he had other customers waiting. She held up the playing cards to show that she had caught them, dropped them into her purse and with a wave of her hand walked out.

Mrs. Pollifax had gone less than a block when she stopped, aghast, her mouth forming a stricken O. She had just realized that the charming gentleman with whom she had been chatting for half an hour was no other than Mr. Carstairs' Senor DeGamez. She had not intended to speak to him at all, she had meant only to walk in and very discreetly make a purchase and leave. How could she have allowed herself to be carried away like that? What on earth would Mr. Carstairs think of her now? For that matter what would Senor DeGamez think when on the nineteenth of August he looked for Mr. Carstairs' courier and it turned out to be the American tourist lady who was not a geese.

"How awful," she thought, hurrying along with burning cheeks. "How terribly undignified of me. This is not the way secret agents behave at all."

Thoroughly penitent, Mrs. Pollifax returned to her hotel, and as punishment resolved not to go near the Calle el Siglo again until the nineteenth. To further punish herself she made a list of *Things To Do* during the next four days: souvenirs to be found for Roger, Jane and the grandchildren, postcards to be sent to friends at home, and she even went as far as to carry her camera with her to Xochimilco and take a few pictures. *Dear Miss Hartshorne,* she wrote without enthusiasm, *Mexico is lovely. I have visited . . ."* and she listed some of the places she had seen. *I hope you are having a pleasant August. Sincerely, your neighbor, Emily Pollifax.* All of this seemed to her exceedingly dull because it deprived her of the opportunity to observe the Parrot, toward which she felt an almost maternal solicitude after this length of time. It was this frustration that led her to open the book that Senor DeGamez had given her, and to her surprise she discovered that she really could enjoy solitaire. Instead of going to bed with a book each night she invested in a tray upon which she could spread out her playing cards. The first ten games in the book were quite easy and she quickly mastered them; as the nineteenth of August drew nearer and she became increasingly restless she went on to more difficult games, sometimes playing them in the hotel lobby after breakfast or carrying the cards in her purse to spread out on a park bench or a cafe table. She found that solitaire not only relaxed her nerves but entertained her mind, and she wondered if she ought to mention this to Senor DeGamez when they met again.

"Better not," she decided regretfully; this time she really must play the part of secret agent to perfection. She would be cool, impersonal, businesslike.

On the eighteenth Mrs. Pollifax ventured out to complete her shopping for the family and when she retired that night there were serapes draped across desk, bureau and chairs. "Not the very best serapes," reflected Mrs. Pollifax as she turned out the lights, "but buying six is so expensive and of course I'm paying for these myself." She had kept a conscientious account of every dollar spent, recalling how grimly Jane's husband talked of waste in Washington. She had the distinct feeling that as a taxpayer Jane's husband would not enjoy contributing to her three-week holiday in Mexico. For the first time it occurred to Mrs. Pollifax to wonder why Mr. Carstairs had sent her here for three weeks. Why not one week, she wondered, or two at the most, and for a fleeting moment she toyed with the idea that her visit to the Parrot Bookstore might be more important than Mr. Carstairs had led her to believe.

Nonsense, she thought, he wanted to be sure everyone knew her as a tourist. Nothing was worth doing unless doing well, she added piously.

She fell asleep thinking of serapes and dreamed of serapes spread across chairs, desk and bureau with a talking parrot guarding them.

Chapter Five

When Mrs. Pollifax opened her eyes the next morning she knew it was *The Day* she had been waiting for, but she felt no flicker of excitement. She had waited too long, and during the last few days—she had to admit this—she had been quite bored. In fact nothing but her games of solitaire had kept her amused, and remembering this she tucked the playing cards into her purse to carry with her for the day. Glancing into the interior of the purse she noted that again it had become the repository of an astonishing assortment of odds and ends: a pocket knife for her grandson's birthday, two chocolate bars, a package of paper handkerchiefs, a tin of Band-Aids, stubs of travelers' checks, two new lipsticks and one old tube that was worn flat—she would have to clear this out soon. But not now. She zipped up the back of her best navy-blue dress, and because it was cool this morning she added the gorgeous hand-loomed Guatemalan wool jacket that she had given herself as a gift.

She ate a small breakfast in the hotel dining room and passed the hour that followed in playing solitaire in the lobby. At 9:45 she was walking up the Calle el Siglo and repeating to herself the words *A Tale of Two Cities* and Madame Defarge. The door of the Parrot Bookstore was open. Mrs. Pollifax walked in with what she believed to be exquisite casualness, blinked a little at the sudden change from sunlight to shadow and nervously cleared her throat.

"*Buenos dias,*" said the man behind the counter, looking up with a smile, and after a second glance he added, "Good morning."

Mrs. Pollifax glanced uncertainly around the room, but there was no one else there. "Good morning," she said. This was not her friend Senor DeGamez whom she had met on her earlier visit. This man was small and dapper, with black hair, spectacles and no moustache at all; when he smiled a gold tooth gleamed at one side of his lip. To cover her confusion she gave him a bright smile in return and moved to the table on which the books from America were displayed. She began picking up one volume after another.

"May I be of help?" suggested the man with a bow.

Mrs. Pollifax had gained a moment to reflect. She decided there was no alternative but to ask just when Senor DeGamez would be back. Perhaps he had been taken suddenly ill, or had run out for cigarettes. "When I was here before," she told the man confidingly, "the proprietor was so helpful, he chose just the right book for me. Will he be in soon?"

The man looked surprised. "But I am the proprietor, senora. I am Senor DeGamez."

Mrs. Pollifax, taken aback, said, "Oh."

Smiling, the man added, "That would have been my cousin, I think, who comes in to the store to help when I am away on business. It happens that way, you know? He is Senor DeGamez too. But he is not here."

"He was so extremely charming and kind," explained Mrs. Pollifax eagerly. "He gave me a book on solitaire—77 *Ways to Play*, and—" She gasped. "Oh dear, perhaps I shouldn't have mentioned that. After all, it's your shop—but I would be happy to pay you for it, indeed I insisted at the time—"

"Yes, that is José," said the man with a rueful smile. "Definitely that is José, but what is one to do with him?" He shrugged, his gold tooth gleaming. "José is always implusive; if the store were his he would be bankrupt in one month. Still . . ." His second shrug was even more eloquent. "Still, it is José's charm that brought you back, no?"

"Yes indeed—and for *A Tale of Two Cities*," she told him boldly.

"*A Tale of Two Cities*," he mused. He returned to the counter to thumb through a pile of papers. Extracting one, he ran a finger down its list. "That book we do not have, I am so sorry."

"I believe there's a copy in your window," she told him breathlessly.

"*Si?*" He said it with just the proper note of surprise and she walked with him to the low curtain that divided the window from the store.

"Yes." They both looked, but Mrs. Pollifax could see no copy of *A Tale of Two Cities* and with a sinking sensation she realized that she ought to have looked for it before coming inside. Nothing seemed to be going well; it was as if fate was putting up little barriers everywhere to test her. She said with a frown, "It was here the other day, I ought to have stopped then. Or perhaps I have the wrong store. I think Madame Defarge is simply gruesome, don't you?" She waited now for him to say something, her eyes alert.

Senor DeGamez continued to lean over the curtain and study the books in the window. When he stood erect he looked at Mrs. Pollifax and his eyes behind the glasses had grown thoughtful. She thought that he, too, appeared to be assessing. "It is not there," he said, watching her.

"No, it is not there."

He said quietly, "But I think that we understand each other nevertheless, you and I."

"I beg your pardon?"

"I mean that we have something in common, no? I have been expecting you. Please—a cup of tea while I get for you what you have come for. I was just brewing the tea in my little back room."

Mrs. Pollifax said cautiously, "I'm sure that's very nice of you." She wasn't sure that it was nice of him at all; the absence of the book in the window was a jarring note and made her feel like a fool. Yet the man said he had been expecting her. Perhaps the book had been accidentally sold or mislaid—even spies must have their bad days. "Very kind indeed," she added more firmly, and since he was holding the curtain that separated the back room from the shop, she walked past him into the rear. There seemed nothing else to do.

"Please forgive the untidiness," he said with a sweeping gesture.

It was indeed untidy, with cartons of books piled to the ceiling and the floor littered with scraps of wrapping paper. But Senor DeGamez had not lied, he really had been brewing tea on a Sterno and was not luring her behind the curtain to hit her over the head. The tea was here and visible, and at sight of this domestic detail— there was something so cozy about tea-making and all its accouterments—her confidence returned.

"Milk, lemon, sugar?" he asked, leading her to the desk and clearing a place for her.

"Milk and one sugar, please," she said, sitting down in the swivel chair and looking around her with interest. "Although really I mustn't stop more than a minute."

"No, of course not, that would be most unwise," he agreed, bringing her a steaming cup. "I will not take long. Tea is my breakfast. I often share it with early customers." He placed a paper napkin before her. "Please relax, I will be back in a minute."

He disappeared behind the curtain and Mrs. Pollifax obediently relaxed by slipping off one shoe and sipping the tea. He was certainly a very polite man, she decided, but he lacked the warmth of his cousin. She wondered what he would bring her, another book or something in a package? Tiring of the calendars on the wall in front of her, she turned in the chair to regard the room behind her. Her glance roamed over the cartons, a smock hanging on a peg, a sink in the corner—a very dirty sink, she noted disapprovingly—and she thought what a hot and stuffy room this was. Very hot. She drained the cup of tea, wriggled into her shoe again and stood up. It was kind of him to have invited her back here, but it would have been kinder of him to open a window; she would wait for him in the shop. An odd but vaguely familiar shape caught her eye; it was domelike and mounted on a pedestal and covered with a cloth. She walked over to it and pulled the cloth aside. It was a large bird cage, empty now of all but one vivid blue feather.

"The parrot!" she thought in astonishment.

In her confusion she had forgotten the parrot, and remembering Olé she at once recalled the first Senor DeGamez with great clarity. "My store is named after Olé, not the other way around," he had said. "My Olé came first, she has been with me twelve years."

My store. . . . *my* Olé . . . yes, he had definitely referred to both of them as his. It was not so much that she had forgotten this as that today's Senor DeGamez had not given her the time to think. Nor could she think clearly now for it was very close in this room and her head was beginning to ache. She stared at the cage and forced herself to think about it. The cage was here. The parrot was not here. "But if this is the Parrot Bookstore, and if the parrot belonged to the first Senor DeGamez . . ."

There was something else, too, and she struggled to think of it. If the parrot belonged to the first Senor DeGamez, and the shop belonged to the first Senor DeGamez—there was a conclusion that ought to be drawn but Mrs. Pollifax found that she could not draw it. Something was terribly wrong, and not only with this shop but with herself, for her mind felt dazed, groggy, unable to reason or to reach conclusions. And it *wasn't* the heat, she realized, it wasn't the heat at all. It was the tea. Mrs. Pollifax had been drinking tea for years and it had never before left such a very peculiar taste in her mouth.

"There was something in that tea," cried Mrs. Pollifax, taking a step toward the door, but her words made no sound, her cry was only a whisper, and she took no more than the one step before she sank, unconscious, to the floor.

Mrs. Pollifax opened one eye, dimly aware that someone was methodically slapping her face, first the left cheek and then the right. She closed her eye and the rhythmic slapping began again. When she next roused Mrs. Pollifax made an attempt to focus on the face that loomed only a few inches away. "Fu Manchu," she murmured wittily, and giggled a little.

"You will wake up now, pliss," said a disembodied voice.

Mrs. Pollifax sighed. "Very well—except I don't really want to, and certainly not when you keep slapping my face." This time she made a distinct effort to open her eyes and keep them open, but the dismal sight that confronted her was not rewarding. She and the cheek slapper appeared to be sharing a small tar-paper shack that listed slightly to one side. A kerosene lamp hung from a rafter and sent grotesque shadows over the earthen floor and rough walls. There was a smell of kerosene and mustiness and wet earth. She saw no windows in the shack and the only bright new piece of equipment in the room was the lock on its door. Her eyes arrived at the cheek slapper and as she pondered him, too, she saw why she had burbled in her sleep about Fu Manchu: the man was Chinese. There the resemblance ended, however, because he was neatly dressed in Western clothes and looked like a serious and kindly young student.

Then Mrs. Pollifax realized that her hands were bound tightly behind her with wire and she decided that the young man was not so kind after all. "Where am I, anyway?" she asked indignantly.

"I wouldn't bother asking if I were you," said a voice behind her. The voice was male and very definitely American, and Mrs. Pollifax squirmed in her chair to look but discovered that she couldn't.

"We're tied together," explained the voice. "Back to back, wrist to wrist—very chummy. Farrell's my name, by the way. Nice to meet you."

"Nice?" said Mrs. Pollifax weakly.

"I was only being polite, actually. Who the devil are you, anyway?"

She said stiffly, "Mrs. Virgil Pollifax from New Brunswick, New Jersey. Look here, young man," she told their guard firmly, "I know enough about first aid to tell you that you will presently have to amputate my left hand if you don't allow it some circulation."

The man said calmly, "Soon you will eat and be given an opportunity to exercise the hands."

As he said this the door opened and a man walked in, and Mrs. Pollifax, glancing beyond him, saw that it was dark outside. Night already! "Then I've been unconscious all afternoon," she thought in astonishment. Her eyes fell to the tray the man carried and she realized how hungry she was. The cheek slapper brought a pair of pliers from his pocket, and while he leaned over to free her wrists Mrs. Pollifax kept her eyes on the food, which consisted of tired-looking tortillas, two slices of dry gray bread and two cups of either coffee or soup. It was just as well that she had this to divert her because her captor was none too gentle; tears rose in Mrs. Pollifax's eyes as he worked, and when her numbed hands were free she placed them in her lap and tried not to notice the blood trickling into her palms.

The young Chinese said, "Eat," and he and the other man walked to the door, glanced back at them once, and went out. Mrs. Pollifax could hear the grate of the key in the lock. She turned at once to look for the man behind her and found him staring at her incredulously. "Bless my soul," he said, his jaw dropping.

"What's the matter?" asked Mrs. Pollifax.

"I've never seen you before in my life. Damn it, where do you fit into this? No, don't touch the coffee," he added quickly, "it's probably drugged."

Mrs. Pollifax regarded him with suspicion, his reference to

drugs reminding her that not so long ago she had drunk tea with Senor DeGamez. Now she was less inclined to trust strangers. Nor was this man a type that she could approve of even though he was American; he had a lean, hard-bitten face—very hard, she thought severely, with a Hollywood kind of handsomeness about it that had grown worn from careless living. It was such a *type* face—such a ladies' man's face, she amended disapprovingly—that it lent itself to caricature. You could draw a perfect, deeply tanned oval for the face, square it a little at the jaw, cap it with an almost horizontal line of straight black hair, add an exquisitely slender black moustache to the upper lip and there was Mr. Farrell—tough, hard and an inhabitant of a world that Mrs. Pollifax knew would shock her: perhaps he even dealt in the drugs that he was mentioning so lightly. "But why?" she demanded. "Where are we, and who are these dreadful people?" The circulation was returning to her raw, chafed wrists and the pain of it brought fresh tears to her eyes. She picked up a tortilla and resolutely chewed on it.

"These are Mao Tse-tung's boys," said Farrell. "Cuba is full of them now, you know." He put a finger warningly to his lips and tiptoed to a corner of the room where he pressed his face against the boards. He came back shaking his head. "Too dark. But I definitely heard a plane land outside while they were trying to bring you back to consciousness."

"A plane?" said Mrs. Pollifax falteringly. "Then we're at an airport? But what airport can this be?"

He shrugged and sat down to resume eating his tortilla. "If the stars had been out I could have done some figuring. I think they've brought us to some remote part of Mexico where the Reds have staked out a secret airfield. I've heard they have them."

Mrs. Pollifax said stiffly, "You certainly seem well informed. How do you know all this unless you're one of them?"

He grinned. "Don't trust me? Now that makes me suspicious of you for the very first time, Duchess. But I'm being abducted, too, in case you hadn't noticed. Whisked away from a theater date with the beautiful Miss Willow Lee—the bitch."

"I *beg* your pardon!" gasped Mrs. Pollifax.

"Sorry," he said after one swift amused glance at her face. "But she is, you know. Very high connections in Peking."

Mrs. Pollifax was astonished. "And you were going to take her to the theater?"

He grinned. "My dear lady, I knew all about her when I met her. What I didn't realize until now—at least it's beginning to dawn on me slowly here—is that she knew all about me too. Now just how did *you* land in this?"

The question startled Mrs. Pollifax. She thought to herself, "I'm here because I carried geraniums to the rooftop one day, and because there seemed no purpose in my life." And Mrs. Pollifax, who had been feeling a little frightened and very small, suddenly laughed. She thought, "I have no right to complain, I don't even have the right to be afraid. It's true that I haven't the slightest idea of what's ahead for me—and at my age this can be especially disconcerting—but I asked for a little adventure and it's precisely what I'm having." She felt at once calmed and unafraid. "I don't think it really matters how I got here," she pointed out to Farrell. "But I think I'm here because I walked into a little shop in Mexico City to buy a book."

Farrell was looking at her strangely. "Not El Papagayo," he said slowly. "Not the Parrot Bookstore!"

His face swam toward her and then receded. She heard him say in a thick voice, "Damn it, they must have put it in the tortillas."

Mrs. Pollifax nodded wisely. Just enough food to keep them alive, and then new drugs in the food to dope them again. Very clever, she thought, and this time took the precaution of carefully sitting down so that she would not fall to the floor. "I'm becoming quite experienced," she thought proudly, and even smiled a little as the familiar blackness descended, blotting out Farrell and all consciousness.

Chapter Six

Carstairs had spent most of the morning of August 20 conferring with a State Department official about a revolution that had erupted in one of the small South American countries. His was the only department with a comprehensive file on the very obscure young man who had emerged overnight as head of the junta. He was able to tell the official that this young man was not a Communist. He was not particularly democratic either, but he was definitely not a Communist.

Then Bishop brought him a carton of black coffee and a slip of paper from the teletype marked CARSTAIRS, URGENT. "Better have the coffee first," he said dryly, and Carstairs gave him a quick glance before he picked up the message.

It said simply:

BODY IDENTIFIED AS RAFAEL DEGAMEZ PROPRIETOR PARROT BOOKSTORE, CALLE EL SIGLO, MEXICO CITY, FOUND DEAD IN CANAL LAST NIGHT AUGUST 19 OF KNIFE WOUNDS AND/OR DROWNING STOP POLICE ESTIMATE DEATH OCCURED TWO DAYS EARLIER ON AUGUST 17 STOP INVESTIGATION UNDERWAY.

Carstairs stared at the impersonal black letters and felt a hot rage grow in him. He knew that in time this rage in him would pass and that it would be supplanted, as it always was, by a cold and ruthless efficiency, but now he allowed himself this brief moment to mourn DeGamez, whom he had known personally. It was no way for any man to die and it was not always enough to remind himself that his people knew the risks.

When he was under control again Carstairs lifted his head and said coldly, "I want the complete file on this. And the message

—did it come from the Mexico City police or from our friend in Monterey?"

"Monterey," said Bishop, and slipped the file on DeGamez under Carstairs' hand.

"I want a direct wire to Mexico City immediately to get this verified by the police. You know who to contact there."

"Yes, sir."

"Tell them we have a definite interest in the man and want to be kept in touch. Oh God," he added suddenly and explosively.

"Yes, sir?"

"Mrs. Pollifax."

"I beg your pardon?"

"She was to visit DeGamez yesterday." He picked up the telephone and barked an order for a connection to the Hotel Reforma Intercontinental, and Bishop went out, marveling at Carstairs' memory. The man must have nursed along half a dozen intricate operations since first meeting Mrs. Pollifax and yet he had remembered precisely the date on which she was to pick up Tirpak's microfilm at the Parrot.

Five minutes later Bishop returned to verify the murder of DeGamez. Carstairs was still on the line to Mexico City, listening, giving orders in fluent Spanish and listening again. "Mrs. Pollifax is being paged at the hotel," he told Bishop, hanging up. "Now get me Johnny at the Galeria de Artes in Mexico City."

Bishop presently came back with the report that he had talked with the man who swept the floors at the Galeria de Artes and Johnny had not come in to open the gallery that morning. Carstairs picked up the connection and began speaking. Had this happened before? When had the sweeper last seen the owner of the Galeria? Carstairs began looking grim.

"Trouble," said Bishop. He did not bother to make a question of it.

"Trouble," repeated Carstairs flatly. He deliberated a moment, and then said, "Take this down. TEMPERATURE 102 IN MEXICO CITY WORRIED ABOUT HEALTH OF AUNT JOSEPHINE SUGGEST COMPLETE REST IN HOSPITAL." He wrote names on a sheet of paper. "Translate and send out at once, top priority, to these people."

"Right," said Bishop, and hurried out. No lunch today, he

was thinking, and wondered how stale the peanut butter crackers were that he kept in his desk for such emergencies.

By two o'clock messages had begun filtering in from various points. Mrs. Pollifax had been paged but there was no answer. She was not in the hotel. She had not been seen in the hotel since the morning of the nineteenth when she had played solitaire in the lobby after breakfast.

"Damn," said Carstairs. "Bishop, get me the hotel again—I want her room checked by the hotel detective, everything in it gone over thoroughly. And try the Galeria de Artes again, I've got to reach Johnny." He could not face the thought yet that they might have snatched Johnny too. Damn it, if that had happened then the whole thing had blown higher than a kite.

The police in Mexico City called in to report that it was only by a freak accident that DeGamez' body had been discovered at all. It had been weighted with cement and tossed into an abandoned canal which the sanitation department had just last week earmarked for drainage under a newly launched insect-control drive. DeGamez' shop had been thoroughly checked. The peculiar thing there was that, although DeGamez had been murdered on the seventeenth, the Parrot Bookstore had been kept open until noon of August 19. They were looking into this and checking out descriptions of the man who had continued selling books there.

There was still nothing from the Galeria de Artes.

"Get me the police again," he told Bishop. "I want Johnny's apartment searched too. Tell them he lives behind the Galeria."

More reports came in. The hotel detective had done a competent job at the Hotel Reforma Intercontinental. The chambermaid reported that on August 19, at her usual hour of eleven, she had arrived to clean the room that Mrs. Pollifax occupied. There had been a number of serapes hung over chairs, and there had been two books on the bureau that the maid remembered picking up to dust. The hotel detective, checking it today, found the books and the serapes gone. Clothes belonging to Mrs. Pollifax still hung in the closet but linings had been slit open in two coats and the clothes ruined. Her suitcase, the mattress of her bed and the pillow on it had also been slit with a knife and hurriedly searched.

"Hell," said Carstairs, looking haggard.

At four o'clock the police reported again. They had searched

Johnny's apartment behind the Galeria de Artes. Nothing had been touched except a small safe in the kitchen. This had been tidily blown open with nitroglycerine.

Carstairs swore savagely. "They've got Johnny then," he said. "Johnny and the code as well. More telegrams—take them down. REGRET TO INFORM YOU AUNT JOSEPHINE DIED . . ." He paused. "Bishop, Code Five is clear, isn't it? All right, REGRET TO INFORM YOU AUNT JOSEPHINE DIED 5 O'CLOCK KINDLY VERIFY ACKNOWLEDG-MENT OF THIS AT ONCE.

He now had to face the fact that they might have caught Tirpak too. "Get Costa Rica," he told Bishop. "There must have been some kind of contact set up between Tirpak and our chap in San José. Someone's got to know where Tirpak is. We've got to break silence and locate him."

"Yes, sir."

The Mexico City police were back on the wires at five o'clock to report that they now had descriptions of the man who had been running DeGamez' shop for two days. He was short, of Spanish extraction, had receding black hair, was clean-shaven, well dressed, wore glasses and showed a gold tooth on the left side of his jaw when he smiled. No one in the neighborhood had ever seen him before.

The description made Carstairs thoughtful.

"Recognize him?" asked Bishop.

"God, I only hope I'm wrong. Get me File 6X." It arrived and Carstairs scowled at two pictures of the same man, one an enlargement showing him standing in a crowd next to Mao Tse-tung, and the other a candid snapshot taken secretly in Cuba. "We'll teletype these to Mexico City and have them shown for identification. Take away the glasses," he said, holding a picture up to Bishop, "and who do we have?"

Bishop whistled. "Good God!"

Carstairs nodded. "Our brilliant and ruthless old friend General Perdido. Mao's hand-picked man for his South American operations—the one person who's responsible for bringing Castro closer to Red China than to Red Russia." Now he knew they must have found Tirpak; he could feel it in his bones. "There's only one very feeble hope," he said at last. "General Perdido was in Cuba last week, wasn't he?"

Bishop was glancing through innumerable reports. "Seen there on August 15."

Carstairs said slowly, "He just might take one of them—Johnny or Tirpak or Mrs. Pollifax—back to Cuba with him. General Perdido has always enjoyed his little trophies. I'll shortwave descriptions to agents in Cuba." He glanced at Bishop and smiled faintly. "For heaven's sake, go and have lunch or dinner or breakfast or whatever it's time for, Bishop. You can bring me back some fresh coffee and a chocolate bar." The door closed behind Bishop and Carstairs lit a cigarette, relieved at being alone for a few moments. Tirpak . . . DeGamez . . . Johnny . . . he thought about them, his face like granite as he weighed all the angles. From the point of view of the department it meant failure, of course—a clean sweep for the other side, an utter rout, eight months of invaluable work gone up in smoke, no microfilms and three top agents missing and presumed dead. But it was in the broader sense that it cut more deeply. He thought of the years that DeGamez and Johnny had spent in carefully building up their respective reputations in Mexico City as cover for their real work. They had been good, very good. All of this was gone now, swept away overnight, the work of years wiped out.

But in this game these things happened and Carstairs could accept the failure. One started all over again every day—Tirpak, DeGamez and Johnny had been aware of this. They had all—he was already using the past tense, he realized—been seasoned agents. They were trained and knowledgeable; once in trouble they would weigh the odds against themselves and the odds in their favor; they knew the tricks of the enemy, they had their own tricks and if all else failed they knew how to kill themselves quickly and efficiently. It was Mrs. Pollifax who must be on his conscience. He had misjudged the job he had given her. She had been exactly right for it and he had taken ruthless advantage of that rightness. He had not been able to resist the unexpected twinkle, the preposterous hat, the little absurdities that gave her so much character. Who would suspect her as anything but a tourist? She had been given the simplest, most routine job that any agent could be given. Nothing had been asked of her but accuracy, yet the fact remained that even as a courier he had sent her off totally unprepared and untrained for emergencies. She had not even been given a cyanide pill. She was not a woman of the world, nor was she even aware of General Perdido's kind of world, and although he did not want to be ungallant she was an old woman, with neither the stamina nor the nerves to withstand these ruthless people. He had unwittingly sent a lamb into a wolves' den—a fluffy, innocent, trusting white lamb, and the wolves would make short work of devouring his lamb.

God help her, Carstairs thought devoutly.

Chapter Seven

I'm wondering if they'll try to brainwash us," Mrs. Pollifax was saying cheerfully. "Do you know anything about brainwashing, Mr. Farrell?"

"Uh—no," Farrell said politely.

"It might prove rather interesting." She was remembering the lie detector test she had been given in Washington, and she wondered if there were similarities. Life was really very scientific these days. She looked at Farrell because there was nothing else to look at. She had been alert for an hour now, and it was still night, and they were still flying through the air, and once she had examined the seats and the floor of the plane she had exhausted the possibilities. There was at least one blessing in being airborne, however—her wrists were no longer bound. Instead there was a very medieval-looking shackle around each of her ankles with a chain that led to a ring set into the seat. It was not uncomfortable but it did give her a perverse longing to cross her legs now that she couldn't.

"Feeling better now?" she asked Farrell sympathetically. She had opened her eyes at least half an hour before he did.

"You didn't answer my question," he said suddenly. "About that bookstore you walked into."

"I don't believe I heard you," lied Mrs. Pollifax smoothly.

"I asked if it was El Papagayo."

"I'm afraid I didn't notice its name. I seldom do, you know. Of course I know when I'm in Bam's or Macy's or Gimbels but this was a very little store. *Very* little."

There was a glimmer of amusement in Farrell's eyes. "I get the point—a very little store. And what happened there?"

"I went in," said Mrs. Pollifax, "and I asked for a book and this man seemed very friendly. He invited me into his back room for tea, he said it was his breakfast and he often offered it to early customers. And I drank it and began to feel rather peculiar. That's when I saw the—I mean, I suddenly realized the tea had left a very strange taste in my mouth. The next thing I knew I was tied up with you back in that dirty little shack." Mrs. Pollifax suddenly remembered that the best defense was an offense and she said, "How did *you* come to be here?"

He shrugged. "I, too, entered a bookshop."

"Are you a tourist then?"

He shook his head. "I've lived in Mexico since '45." He reached into his pocket, searched and swore. "I did have a card," he explained. "I run the Galeria de Artes in downtown Mexico City. John Sebastian Farrell's the name, Galeria de Artes."

Mrs. Pollifax, relieved, said, "Oh, I thought at first you might be a dope peddler, or—or . . ."

He grinned. "I've done some rum things in my life, and some of them outside the law, but I'll be damned if anybody's ever taken me for a dope peddler before."

Mrs. Pollifax at once apologized. "I've lived a very sheltered life," she explained, "and you do have a rather—well, I don't think I've known anyone—I mean, you look as if you'd done some rum things, you see."

"It's beginning to show? Well, at forty-one I daresay it's bound to—a pity." He said it with mock despair.

Mrs. Pollifax paid his mockery no attention. "What are some of the rum things you've done?"

"Good heavens, should you be interested? I hope you're not planning to write a book on your travels." He was still grinning at her.

She considered this seriously and shook her head. "No, it had never occurred to me, although I'll be very interested in seeing Cuba. You still believe it's where they're taking us?"

Farrell said irritably, "By all rights it's where we ought to land, but it's taking us a hell of a long time to get there. Sorry— what were you asking?"

"You were going to tell me what a rum life consists of."

He grinned. "You don't think I'd dare give you an un-laundered version, do you? After all, I've bummed around Mexico since '45, ever since I was discharged from the Marines, and that's a long time. I used to run a charter boat out of Acapulco—at least until I lost the boat in a poker game. I've given painting lessons to debutantes—you may not believe it but I do occasionally move in the best circles."

"As well as the worst?" asked Mrs. Pollifax, hoping he wasn't going to disappoint her.

"As well as the worst. For a year I smuggled guns in to Castro before he won his revolution. Rather a good friend of mine although I've not seen him lately," he added with a roguish glint. "And I might add modestly that women constantly fall at my feet. I have that effect on them."

Mrs. Pollifax could not allow this weakness in her sex to go undefended. She said very blandly, "Like the Chinese woman you were going to take to the theater tonight?"

Farrell gazed at her for a moment and then said frankly, "Duchess—and I hope you don't mind my calling you that—you interest and surprise me. I've decided you're not a member of the D.A.R. after all."

"No, I've never joined that one," mused Mrs. Pollifax. "Do you think I should? But I *am* a member of the Garden Club, the Art Association, the Woman's Hospital Auxiliary, the—"

"Good God, spare me," he said, throwing up his hands. "If General Perdido knew these things he'd turn pale."

"General who?"

He turned his glance to the window. "Just someone I know." He leaned forward. "We're still flying very high but I thought I saw some lights down there." He added savagely, "You do understand what you've gotten yourself into, don't you? You do know what the odds are?"

Mrs. Pollifax blinked. She thought of expressing ignorance of what he meant, but to feign innocence indefinitely was tiresome. She said very quietly, "Yes."

"Yes what?" he demanded.

She did hope he wasn't going to shout at her. She added with dignity, "I am quite aware that I have been abducted by dangerous people, and that it's possible I may never see Mexico City again."

"*Or* your Garden Club *or* your Hospital Auxiliary *or* your Art Association," he told her flatly. "It doesn't bother you?"

Mrs. Pollifax wanted to tell him that of course it bothered

her. She had enjoyed herself very much in Mexico City and she had enjoyed being a secret agent and now she would like very much to be flying home to New Brunswick, New Jersey, to bandage her torn wrists and soak her bruises in a hot tub. There was, after all, a distinct difference between nearly deciding to step from the roof of an apartment house and in having such a decision wrested from her by men who appeared to be quite brutal. She did not want to die in a strange country and she did not labor under any illusions about Mr. Carstairs or her country coming to her rescue. If life was like a body of water, she had asked that she be allowed to walk again in its shallows; instead she had been abruptly seized by strong currents and pushed into deep water. It was a lonely situation, but Mrs. Pollifax was well acquainted with loneliness and it did not frighten her. What did frighten her was the thought of losing her dignity. The limits of her endurance had never been tested, and she had never met with cruelty before. If her life had to end soon she only hoped that it could end with dignity.

But she saw no point in saying these things to the man who shared her predicament and who must also be thinking of these matters. He had more to lose than she; his life was only half completed and he would be thinking of the women he would never make love to again, and the children he would never have. A pity about the children, she mused . . . but in any case she must be very careful not to display any unsteadiness; it was the very least that the old could do for the young. "There's no point in your being angry at *me*," she said calmly. Her gaze fell to the seat beside Farrell and she gasped. "Look—my purse! They haven't taken it away, it's squashed down between your seat and the next."

"Thoroughly searched, of course," he said, handing it to her. "What's in it?" He leaned forward to watch as she opened the clasp.

She, too, felt as if she were opening a Christmas grab bag. "It's a good deal emptier," she agreed, peering inside. "Yes, they've taken things. Oh dear, my aspirin's gone," she said mournfully.

"Extremely suspect."

"And they've taken Bobby's pocket knife—he's my eleven-year-old grandson," she exclaimed.

"No, they wouldn't approve of that at all."

"But the Band-Aids are here, and my wallet and coin purse

and lipsticks—oh, and look," she cried happily, "they've left me my playing cards!" She greeted them as old friends, slipping them tenderly out of their box.

"Small comfort," growled Farrell.

"Oh, but you don't know how comforting they can be," she told him with the enthusiasm of a convert. "I already know twenty-two games. It's true there are fifty-five more to learn—I have a book on it, you see—but it's so relaxing and it will give me something to do." She was already laying out cards in a circle on the seat beside her for a game of Clock Solitaire. "They left the chocolate bars too," she said absently. "You can eat one if you'd like."

"You're not particularly hungry, either?" he asked.

She shook her head, her eyes on the cards.

He said in a funny voice, "We ought to be hungry, you know. We ought to be terribly hungry."

Mrs. Pollifax put down a card and looked at him. "Why, yes, that's true, we should be," she said wonderingly. She frowned. "I had breakfast, and then that man's tea, and nothing until night, and then I had only a slice of bread and a stale tortilla—I ought to be ravenous."

He hesitated and then said quietly, rolling up his sleeve, "I'm wondering if you have needle marks on your arm, too."

"Marks?" faltered Mrs. Pollifax, and stared in dismay at the arm he showed her. There were several angry red dots there, and a faint outline of gum where adhesive tape had been affixed and then removed. It was all the more unnerving to Mrs. Pollifax because she had been idly scratching at her arm since she awoke. She slipped out of her jacket and stared at her arm. "What are they?" she asked at last.

"I think we've been fed intravenously."

"Intravenously!" she gasped. "But *why?*"

"To keep us alive." He leaned forward and said in a low voice, "That's not all, there's something else. The plane I heard landing back there in Mexico was a propeller job. The plane we're traveling in now is a jet."

In astonishment Mrs. Pollifax took note of the sound of the engines. "Why so it is!" She stared at him with incredulous eyes. "Wh-what does it mean, do you think?"

He said quietly, "I think we've been unconscious for a longer time than we realized. I think we've been unconscious for a whole day instead of a few hours. I think this must be *another* night, and we met *yesterday* in that shack, not today. I think they must have landed us somewhere during the day where they switched planes and took the precaution of feeding us intravenously so that we wouldn't die on their hands."

Mrs. Pollifax put down her cards with finality. It was not difficult to follow his reasoning to its obvious conclusion. "But jets travel very fast," she said, her eyes fastened on his face. "And if we have been traveling for such a long time—"

He nodded. "Exactly. I don't think that you are going to see Cuba after all."

"Not see Cuba," she echoed, and then, "but where . . . ?" On second thought Mrs. Pollifax stifled this question; it was much better left unsaid. Instead she said in a voice that trembled only a little, "I do hope Miss Hartshorne is remembering to water my geraniums."

Chapter Eight

It was still night when they began their descent through the clouds—through the very stars, seemingly—and Mrs. Pollifax felt a flutter of excited dread such as she had often felt as a child when the dentist beckoned her into his office, saying it was her turn now. She pressed her face to the glass, staring in amazement at the unearthly convolutions and formations below.

"Mountains," said Farrell, frowning. "High ones, some of them snow-covered." His gaze went from them to the stars, assessing, appraising, judging, his eyes narrowed.

Mrs. Pollifax watched him hopefully, but he did not say what he was thinking or on what continent such mountains might be. The flight continued, with Farrell's glance constantly moving from earth to sky. "We're going to land," he said suddenly.

Mrs. Pollifax leaned forward. A scattering of lights increased in density, the plane wheeled and began its approach to the runway. Mrs. Pollifax braced herself—there were no seat belts on this plane—and suddenly the earth was rushing past her with dizzying speed, they touched land and taxied to a very bumpy stop. Mrs. Pollifax gathered up her playing cards and put them in her purse. The door to the cockpit opened and two men they had not seen before walked in, one of them carrying a revolver. The other drew out keys and unshackled their ankles. Both were Chinese. The door was pulled away and by gestures it was indicated that Mrs. Pollifax and Farrell were to get out. This was accomplished only with difficulty because there was nothing more than a wooden ladder propped against the side of the plane, and for illumination a flashlight was shone on its rungs. Mrs. Pollifax descended into an oppressively warm night that gave the feeling of new heat lying in wait for sunrise. The two men waiting for them at the bottom of the ladder were not Orientals and she saw Farrell stare intently

into their faces. To Mrs. Pollifax they looked—perhaps Greek, she
decided, recalling an evening spent in Miss Hartshorne's apartment viewing slides on Greece; at least to Mrs. Pollifax their skin
had that same similarity to the skin of an olive, moist and supple
and smooth. She saw Farrell glance from them to the mountains
behind the plane and then again at the stars in the sky. She said
anxiously, "It's not Cuba, is it."

He shook his head.

"Do you know—have you any idea *where* we may be?"

His eyes narrowed. He said grimly, "If my guess is right,
Duchess—I hope to God it's not—I should now turn to you and
say, 'Welcome to Albania.' "

"Albania!" gasped Mrs. Pollifax, and peering incredulously
into his face she repeated blankly, "*Albania?*"

"Albania."

"But I don't *want* to be in Albania," Mrs. Pollifax told him
despairingly. "I don't know anything *about* Albania, I've scarcely
even heard of the place, the idea's preposterous!"

"Nevertheless," said Farrell, "I think it's where we are."

A long car, once black but nearly white with dust now, drew
into the periphery of the flashlights and they were ushered to its
door and prodded into the rear. "A Rolls," Farrell said out of the
corner of his mouth, and Mrs. Pollifax nodded politely. The two
men with Grecian profiles climbed in and sat down on a drop seat
facing them, guns in hand, and the car began to move at reckless
speed over incredibly bumpy ground. Mrs. Pollifax clung to its
sides and longed for an aspirin. The headlights of the car illuminated the road onto which they turned but the road held as many
ruts as the airfield. They appeared to be entering a town, and
presently they were threading narrow streets where garbage flowed
sluggishly in gutters. They passed cobbled alleys and shuttered
cafes and what appeared to be a bazaar. They met no other cars
and saw no people. Even the homes that showed briefly in the glare
of the headlights looked inhospitable, their rooftops barely seen
over the tops of high walls that surrounded them. The walls were
guarded by huge gateways with iron-studded doors—clearly not a
trusting neighborhood, thought Mrs. Pollifax—and then they had
left the town behind. Looking out of the window at her side Mrs.
Pollifax saw the mountains again silhouetted against the night-blue

sky; not comfortable-looking mountains at all, but harsh craggy ones with jutting peaks and cliffs and towering, rocky summits. The mountains, decided Mrs. Pollifax, looked even less hospitable than the homes. It was toward these mountains that they appeared to be heading.

Their guards stared at them impassively and without curiosity. Mrs. Pollifax turned to Farrell and said, "But why Albania? Surely you're wrong!"

"Well, this isn't Cuba."

"No," responded Mrs. Pollifax sadly, "it isn't Cuba."

"I thought at first these mountains might be the Himalayas, but this isn't China. The mountains aren't high enough, there aren't enough of them and the whole topography is wrong."

"I shouldn't care at all for China," Mrs. Pollifax agreed.

"One has to think of the few parts of the world where the Red Chinese are welcome. There aren't many, you know. That town we passed through was definitely not Chinese, it was Balkan in flavor. These mountains must belong to the Albanian Alps, and certainly these men are Europeans."

Mrs. Pollifax nodded. "I thought they looked Greek."

"If this is Albania then Greece is only a few hundred miles away," he pointed out. "You saw how primitive the airport was, and you see how primitive the country is. If we're in Europe there's no other country but Albania where the Red Chinese can come and go at will."

"I didn't know they could come and go *anywhere* in Europe," said Mrs. Pollifax indignantly.

"It happened about 1960," he mused, his brow furrowed. "Until then Russia was Albania's big brother and pretty much in control of the country. Then Stalin was denounced—that was a surprise to the world, you must remember that. It rocked Albania, too—they're Stalinists here, you see. I don't recall the details, it happened at one of their Big Party Congresses, but there was rather ugly name-calling, with China and Albania siding against Khrushchev. Russia punished Albania by withdrawing all its aid, all its technicians, all its military, and China very happily moved in to help. The chance of a lifetime, giving Red China a toehold in Europe."

"I didn't know," faltered Mrs. Pollifax. "The very idea—and

to think that I subscribe to *Time* magazine. I really *must* stop skipping the Balkan news. But why bring us here? Why go to such a great deal of trouble?"

Farrell gave her a quick glance and looked away. "Perhaps they feel we're worth the trouble," he pointed out gently.

"Oh," said Mrs. Pollifax in a small voice and was silent.

The car had been climbing steeply for the past twenty minutes on a road that appeared to be carved out of the side of the mountain. On the left the car lights picked out weird rock shapes, on the right side nothing, and Mrs. Pollifax had a terrible suspicion that there really was nothing there, and that any nervous turning of the wheel would send them hurtling through space into the valley. Higher and higher they climbed until at last the car came to a stop and their two guards came to life and jumped out. They spoke rapidly to the driver in a strange, oddly nasal language, and gestured to Farrell and Mrs. Pollifax to leave the car. Once outside they found themselves in a vast basin of desolate gray rock, and noting this, Mrs. Pollifax realized the darkness was dissolving and that dawn must be near. Another day, she thought wonderingly, and suddenly, quite absurdly, recalled her son Roger telling her to wire him if she found herself in a jam.

"This is extremely sticky jam I'm in," she reflected. "Treacly, oozy black raspberry, I think. And no Western Unions."

One of the guards had disappeared behind a rock. Now he reappeared leading four donkeys, and to Mrs. Pollifax's consternation the man signaled that she mount one of them. "I can't," she said in a low voice to Farrell, and to the guard she said in a louder voice, "I can't."

"I believe you're going to have to," Farrell pointed out in amusement.

She eyed the animal with distaste and in turn it eyed her with suspicion. Farrell moved forward to help; it was only with his intercession that a truce was accomplished between the two, and this was mainly because, once upon its back, the donkey could no longer see Mrs. Pollifax. When Farrell and the guards had also mounted donkeys they formed a procession and moved on.

The wilderness path along which they moved was desolate beyond belief. This was a country where all life had been extinguished, to be supplanted by rocks of every color, shape and formation. The air was thin but only a little cooler than the valley. There was no shade of any kind. Slowly, as they traveled, the sunrise spread a golden light across the valley and Mrs. Pollifax could look down upon green slopes and occasional trees, but the rising of the sun brought warmth as well, followed by heat, and between this and the donkey Mrs. Pollifax was soon extremely uncomfortable. Horseback riding had never been her métier, and sitting sidesaddle on a donkey was taxing; it took a great deal of energy simply to keep from falling off, and the donkey moved with unexpected lurches. They had traveled for perhaps an hour when Farrell said suddenly, "Psst—look."

Mrs. Pollifax reluctantly lifted her eyes. They had left behind the bleak gray rocks and cliffs of the first leg of their journey and had come out upon a small plateau literally carpeted with stones. The ground was like a brook bed that had been emptied of silt and water—the stones were scattered everywhere in such profusion that not a blade of grass could grow. The sun beat down mercilessly on the landscape, turning everything into a tawny color of yellow dust. At the edge of the cliff overlooking the valley stood a square, fortresslike building made of stone piled upon stone, with only black slits for windows. It stood at the very edge of the precipice, and after a drop of a hundred or so feet the earth formed a rock-strewn terrace, and below this another, showing tentative signs of green, and then the earth flowed like a green river down to the floor of the valley. As her donkey picked its way over the stones Mrs. Pollifax saw a second, smaller building at some distance from the first, also built of rocks and precisely like the other except in size. If she were a tourist, thought Mrs. Pollifax wistfully, this would be a wild and romantic scene; one could imagine bandit chieftains holing up in these impregnable buildings, completely safe against attack. But unfortunately she was not a tourist, she was an American spy who had been abducted—no, captured, she thought uneasily—and no one on God's green earth knew where she was except the people who had brought her here. For just the briefest of moments she allowed herself to think of her children, of Jane having a safe and happy vacation in Canada, of Roger, who had told her to wire him if she got into a jam. "If it just didn't seem so *unreal*," thought Mrs. Pollifax unhappily. "I mean—what on earth am I doing *here*? I'm in Albania—at least Farrell *thinks* it's

Albania." And again she felt it was preposterous, her being in Albania. Why, she didn't even own a passport.

"Journey's end," commented Farrell dryly, with a nod at the smaller building toward which they were heading.

She said crossly, "I really don't think you need put it in just that manner." But as they approached the second of the two buildings she realized that unconsciously she had begun bracing herself for the worst. She drew herself up to her full height—it was a little difficult on a donkey—and said primly, "I have always found that in painful situations it is a sensible idea to take each hour as it comes and not to anticipate beyond. But oh how I wish I could have a bath!"

Someone must have noted their approach through the slits in the wall because the iron door of the building opened as they drew near. A man stepped out into the blazing sun with a rifle under his arm but Mrs. Pollifax was too busy to pay him any attention; she was involved in separating herself from the animal to which she had become welded during the past hour. No sooner did she stand upright, all her bones protesting, when the guard grasped her arm and led her into the building.

"Journey's end," she thought bleakly, looking around her at more stone—really she was growing very tired of stones. In shape the building was a rectangle about thirty feet long. The door through which they entered was set at one end of the long rectangle, and as they entered they faced a room that occupied the precipice end of the structure. On their left was a dark hall that ran across the front, and looking down it Mrs. Pollifax saw two iron cell doors opening from it. She quickly turned her gaze back to the room, which contained a desk, a chair, a water cooler, a well-stocked gun rack, a small switchboard and a gray-haired man dressed in a uniform. He greeted them curtly in English.

"I am Major Vassovic." With this announcement he took a huge iron key from the wall and led them down the hall to the first door and opened it. "In, please," he said.

"I don't suppose you have an aspirin," Mrs. Pollifax told him hopefully. "I've had the most ridiculous headache for hours. I don't often get them, you know, and I don't mean to complain, but I've been doped twice and apparently fed intravenously, and it's been a rather exhausting plane ride—"

The major looked at her in astonishment, and then carefully wiped all expression from his face. "I have no orders to give you anything," he told her stiffly.

Farrell gently pulled her into the room, the door clanged shut behind them and Mrs. Pollifax said, "I don't see how one aspirin could . . ." Her voice died away at sight of their prison. It was quite decent in size, but so dark—lighted only by the two slits in the wall—that it was twilight inside. There was to be no privacy for her or Farrell, she noted; none at all except for the dimness. There was an iron cot at each end of the room, with a night chamber under each; there were two small tables and that was all. No chairs, no screens, no lavatory, no clothespegs, nothing else except the oppressive stone walls and floor.

"Well," said Farrell, and sat down on a cot.

"Well," said Mrs. Pollifax, and sat down on the other cot. They stared at each other through the gloom, a distance of perhaps twelve feet, and Mrs. Pollifax realized that the silence was becoming long and much too dismal. "Well," she said again, briskly, and getting up she carried one of the tables to the cot, reached into her purse and began spreading out her deck of playing cards.

"Not again," groaned Farrell. "Not *here.*"

"Whyever not?" said Mrs. Pollifax and was glad to see him diverted.

She had played three games when the door was unlocked and opened and a guard gestured that she come with him. Farrell also stood up but the guard shook his head. Farrell said lightly, "Well— I do feel snubbed. Good luck, Duchess."

Mrs. Pollifax did not look back. Her knees were trembling, and this unexpected separation from Farrell—on whom she had once looked askance—left her feeling very lonely. She was led out into the blazing sun to stumble over the stones to the other, larger building. The door was opened from inside and Mrs. Pollifax was led into a large cool room of whitewashed stone. The room was furnished like Major Vassovic's office except that everything was larger. There were two men in the room, both in uniform, but Mrs. Pollifax's glance flew to the man seated at the desk.

"Why, Senor DeGamez," she gasped. "How did you get here?"

His gold tooth flashed in a brief smile. "In the same manner that you did, Mrs. Pollifax. Allow me to present General Hoong, who is in charge of the—uh—buildings here."

"How do you do," Mrs. Pollifax said politely to the Chinese. He bowed, his expression remote, and Mrs. Pollifax immediately forgot him. "Except that of course you're not the real Senor DeGamez, I know that now," she went on. "I realized it as soon as I saw the empty parrot cage. It had one feather in it."

"Actually I am General Raoul Perdido," he said, motioning her to take the chair beside his desk. "Do sit down, Mrs. Pollifax, we have a few things to discuss. Pleasantly or unpleasantly, depending upon your attitude."

Brainwashing, thought Mrs. Pollifax contemptuously, and suddenly realized that she was not afraid. She had endured other crises without losing her dignity—births, widowhood, illnesses—and she was experienced enough to know now that everything worthwhile took time and loneliness, perhaps even one's death as well. "I don't mean to be morbid," she told herself. "It's just that I refuse to be frightened by a man whose only weapon over me is the cessation of life. After all, I have nothing to hide. I only wish I did. I'm not even a spy. I almost was, but then this horrid man rushed in to spoil everything." She sat down and faced him with growing indignation. Aloud she said, "May I ask, General Perdido, just why you had to abduct me like this?"

He leaned back in his chair, lit a cigar and suddenly impaled her with a sharp glance. "I had hoped for a more intelligent question from you than this, Mrs. Pollifax. I abhor pretended innocence."

"And I have a great deal to complain about," she retorted, "and no consul to whom I can complain. I was having a very pleasant vacation in Mexico, and now I am informed that I am in Albania. Is this true?"

"I am in charge of the questioning," said General Perdido.

"Then you have been very extravagant," she told him coldly. "You have flown me thousands of miles across the world to ask questions that could have been very easily asked in Mexico. I don't know what country you work for, General Perdido, but your taxpayers would certainly have every right to be furious if they knew."

The general's face darkened. "I see that you are going to deny you are an American spy."

"*Spy?*" said Mrs. Pollifax scornfully. "Is that what you take me for? This is one more grievance I must hold against you, General."

"Fool," spat the general. "You are not in the United States now, and you are not in Mexico, Mrs. Pollifax, and—"

"Then I wish that you would tell me where I *am*," she reminded him.

"Never mind," he shouted. "Wherever it is, you are far from home and no one knows where you are. No one, do you understand? You are removed from all influence and all hope of rescue. I have methods for extracting the truth—very refined or very brutal but all of them painful. I am extremely accomplished in all of them."

"I'm sure you are at the very top of your profession," she said tartly, "but I do not find it a very admirable profession."

General Hoong turned from the window and spoke rapidly to General Perdido. There was silence and then General Perdido said reluctantly, "Let us try to be reasonable, Mrs. Pollifax."

"Yes, let's," she agreed.

"You visited the Parrot Bookstore a few days ago, did you not?"

"Yes, of course."

"For what purpose?"

"To buy a book. Naturally."

"At this time you confided in me that you had visited the Parrot Bookstore on a previous day, is this not correct?"

Mrs. Pollifax nodded.

"Also at this time you inquired of me where the other Senor DeGamez was. You told me you had talked with him at some length, is this not so, Mrs. Pollifax?"

"But of course," said Mrs. Pollifax warmly. "He was most enjoyable, a thoroughly charming man."

The general said patiently, "You said he made you the gift of a book?"

"Yes, he did, it was very kind of him." In this matter Mrs. Pollifax could be completely frank. "We began talking, you see— about his parrot, and then about grandchildren and traveling alone. That's when he gave me the book. He told me that solitaire was something I would enjoy very much. Have you tried it, General? He was quite right, I have found it enormously stimulating."

The general opened a desk drawer and brought out two books. "Then it is the book on solitaire that he gave you," he said triumphantly.

He held up the books and Mrs. Pollifax gasped. "Why—you have both of them! You *stole* them from my hotel room."

"But of course," replied the general with a flash of gold tooth. "We are very thorough."

Mrs. Pollifax said indignantly, "Of course it's your conscience and you'll have to live with it, but I would like to point out that those are *my* books."

He nodded. "Yes, but one of them was presented to you by an extremely dangerous man."

"Was he really?" said Mrs. Pollifax.

The general leaned back in his chair and studied her. "I think you are being a little ingenuous, Mrs. Pollifax, I do not know. We have gone through these books with what you Americans call a fine-toothed comb and we have not found anything. For the moment it is sufficiently rewarding to learn that it is this particular book that he gave you. 77 *Ways to Play Solitaire*," he read with distaste, and pushed it away from him. "We shall examine it many more times."

Mrs. Pollifax said stiffly, "Really, General, don't you think you can become too devious, too suspicious? That book was given to me out of kindness, I can assure you of that. If you insist that it is full of secret messages written in invisible ink—"

"Please," said the general, looking pained.

"Well, whatever you people use these days," she pointed out. "At any rate, his gift of a book to me a few weeks ago seems a very feeble reason for my abduction."

The general stared at her with dislike. "If you are innocent you chose a most inauspicious morning to visit the Parrot Bookstore, Mrs. Pollifax."

"On the contrary, I chose a most auspicious morning," she said coldly. "The sun was shining and I wanted a book to read."

"What is more you behaved very suspiciously when the book was not in the window."

"I did not behave suspiciously at all," replied Mrs. Pollifax. "I was in hopes that you might prove just as charming as the earlier Senor DeGamez. You didn't," she reminded him sternly.

"You did not so much as demur when I suggested I had something to give you."

"I was allowing you every opportunity to be as hospitable as the first Senor DeGamez," she snapped. "After all, he gave me a book."

"Why did you accept tea from me?" he demanded. "Just what were you expecting?"

"A chat," said Mrs. Pollifax firmly.

"A what?"

"A little chat," she said. "Is that so difficult for you to believe? My government expects each and every one of us to be traveling ambassadors when we go abroad. I was *trying*," she added piously, "to know you better."

General Perdido exploded in what sounded like an oath. He and General Hoong exchanged glances and General Perdido said bitterly, "You may go back to your cell."

Mrs. Pollifax nodded and arose. "There is one other matter," she said. "Please could I be given one aspirin?"

Chapter Nine

The guard inserted the huge, comic-opera key in the lock and opened the door for Mrs. Pollifax, slamming it shut behind her. At once Farrell sprang to his feet. "Are you all right?"

Mrs. Pollifax was deeply touched by his concern. "Yes, I really am," she told him. "I was asked questions by that man I met in a bookstore in Mexico City, except now he's here in Albania. Imagine." She sat down on her cot and picked up her playing cards and shuffled them. In a low voice she said, "Farrell, I must apologize to you for something quite dreadful."

"Good heavens, what can that be?"

Mrs. Pollifax tried to think of the word the professionals used. "Are we being bugged?" she asked.

Farrell walked over and sat down beside her on the cot. "If you mean are there microphones hidden in here I don't know, but there must be some kind of listening device. I'm sure it's why they put us together—but where on earth did you pick up that word bugging, Duchess?"

"At the hairdresser's. One learns a great deal there about life."

"And the apology?" Farrell whispered the question.

She turned and faced him. "It's really quite terrible," she whispered back. "It seems the reason they brought us here is that they believe I'm a dangerous American spy."

"You?" The corners of his mouth twitched a little at this revelation. "You're not, are you?"

Mrs. Pollifax hesitated. "In one sense, no," she admitted. "In another, yes. But certainly not *dangerous*."

Farrell said flatly, "I don't like the way you say that, Duchess, you'd better be much more specific. Do you trust me?"

Mrs. Pollifax nodded.

"Good. Then for heaven's sake, are you or aren't you?"

Still whispering, Mrs. Pollifax plunged into her confession, beginning with her visit to CIA headquarters, describing the simple courier work that she was to do and how this man with the gold tooth had totally ruined her assignment. "And he's the same man who questioned me here, but now he calls himself General Raoul Perdido."

"Oh God," said Farrell.

"You mentioned his name once—quite lightly—on the plane. Do you know him too?"

He said grimly, "Nobody mentions Perdido lightly, and if I did I ought to have my head examined. Yes, I've heard of him, and he's a cruel, vicious bas—sorry," he added, and glancing at her face a smile lit up his eyes, "You of all people, Duchess!" The smile abruptly left his eyes and he became thoughtful. "You've certainly outflanked the general for the moment at least." He frowned. "You've bought yourself more time, which is the most important concession, but I only wish—I'm very much afraid—"

"It's all right," she told him gently. "I know what you're thinking. Even if they believe everything I've told them they can't afford to let me go home again."

He smiled wryly. "You continue to surprise me, Duchess, but let's not be gloomy, they may save you for an international incident and trade you for one of their own." Glancing up he said, "Oh-oh, we have company again."

The door swung wide and a man walked in carrying a tray of food, followed by a guard who insisted upon dramatically covering them with his rifle. Mrs. Pollifax thought it extremely ill-bred of him and turned her back on him, ignoring him just as she would have ignored a rude waiter. "Can you explain this odd-looking food?" she asked Farrell conversationally, hoping he knew what lay on her dish like a piece of melted rubber. "And is it drugged, do you think?"

Farrell said evenly, "Not likely. They'll be questioning me soon and I'd be no good to them drugged. It's some sort of cheese dish," he added, pushing a spoon into it. "Go ahead and try it. Not bad."

"It just looks such a mess," said Mrs. Pollifax with a sigh.

"Rather like Welsh rarebit," he told her, nodding approvingly. "Cheese and milk cooked together."

They ate quietly. There was coffee, very strong, and cakes drenched in honey. When they had finished Farrell brought out a crumpled pack of cigarettes, extracted one and lighted it, saying dryly, "The condemned man ate a hearty meal. And now, Duchess, there is something I believe I should tell *you.*"

Mrs. Pollifax was feeling much more cheerful now, and her headache was virtually gone. "Fire ahead," she said gaily.

"You've been frank with me. I think it only politic to tell you what General Perdido already knows about me—namely that I, too, work for Carstairs."

Mrs. Pollifax drew in her breath sharply.

"I've been an agent since '47 when the CIA was formed," he went on. "You might say that I'm their man in Mexico City. Or one of them," he added absently. "A long time ago I did a job with DeGamez, so I knew what his real work was, and therein lies the rub, as old Billy Shakespeare would say. I hadn't seen DeGamez for years, not that we had to avoid each other, we just didn't move in the same circles. But on the nineteenth, just after I'd finished lunch, I received a crazy, garbled message from him and I went off at once to his bookstore. You see, the message had a code word inserted into it, a word meaning SOS. All the words in the message should have been in code—I knew that when I set out—but when a friend sounds in trouble how can a guy hang back? I should have been more cautious; I was impulsive instead. I went to see what the hell DeGamez meant and walked right into their trap. I realize now that Perdido must have pried just that one word out of DeGamez or some poor soul who knew it, but there's no use crying over spilt milk. By going to the bookstore—by reacting to that code word—I proved I was just who they thought I was, an agent they'd been looking for since '47." He was silent, smiling a twisted smile as he looked into his thoughts. "It takes only one goof and the others follow like one-two-three. The first thing they took from me was the cyanide pill I'm never without. The second thing they took from me was my identity, and then my freedom. So here I am, as full of information for them as Santa's knapsack. A real Christmas present in August for General Perdido."

Mrs. Pollifax stared at him in astonishment, understanding

for the first time the hardness in him. "I thought him a reckless adventurer," she remembered. "I thought him a philanderer and a professional charmer and a man of no scruples, and he is perhaps all of these things, but I completely missed the truth in him: namely that he is all of these things and yet none of them."

To Farrell she said simply, "You are very brave."

He lifted an eyebrow mockingly. "Not at the moment, Duchess, not at the moment. You see, I can't allow General Perdido to question me. You understand what I've got to do, don't you?"

"What do you mean?" faltered Mrs. Pollifax.

"I mean that no one can hold out indefinitely against their methods of torture, and the general is considered an expert in the field. I mustn't be taken alive into that building."

As the meaning of his words penetrated Mrs. Pollifax became very still.

Farrell got to his feet and began pacing the floor. "For me it's part of the job," he said, "but I hate leaving you in the lurch. It's not very gallant of me, but under the circumstances—"

Mrs. Pollifax said breathlessly, "You mustn't concern yourself with me at all. *Please*. But what do you intend to do?"

He shrugged. "Whatever presents itself. Try to break away between here and the other building and hope they'll shoot me. Throw a rock at somebody." He shrugged again. "*Que sera, sera*, as they say—except I must not enter that building and meet General Perdido."

"You can't think of any other way?" she asked anxiously. "You don't think the general . . . ?"

He smiled cryptically. "Not on your life, Duchess, not on your life."

She averted her eyes so that she need not embarrass him with her compassion. She thought of her son Roger and daughter Jane, of Miss Hartshorne in apartment 4-C, and of the simple life she herself had lived, and then she thought of men like Farrell who for years must have been dying in queer parts of the world without her ever knowing of their existence. Life was certainly very strange, she reflected, but in spite of its uncertainty she was extremely grateful to have known Farrell.

"I don't know how to advise you," he continued, pacing and frowning. "There's no possibility of your getting away or being rescued. I hate deserting you. If I just didn't know so much—but Carstairs would never approve of my staying alive, there's too much at stake." Hearing the guard at the door he stamped his cigarette out on the floor. "Take what's left of them," he said, handing her the flattened pack. "You never know who's bribable in this world."

"Thank you," said Mrs. Pollifax, standing up, and as the door opened she and Farrell gravely shook hands.

This time the two guards were heavily armed. Major Vassovic had come as well to superintend Farrell's removal. "It's been so nice meeting you, Major," said Farrell as he went out.

"God go with you," whispered Mrs. Pollifax, staring after him.

Major Vassovic pointedly coughed. "The—uh—order has been received now. One aspirin for you, to be taken in my presence. Come."

Mrs. Pollifax realized that her headache had returned doublefold. She humbly followed the man into the guardroom and stood patiently while he brought her a cup of water and the pill. As she placed the tablet on her tongue her gaze came to rest on the collection of weapons on the wall, a number of guns and knives beautifully decorated with carved-silver ornamentation. They were works of art belonging in a museum and she told the major so.

"The long guns are called *pushkas*," he said gruffly. "The sabres we call *yataghans* in this country."

There were also an assortment of undecorated and very lethal-looking pistols and revolvers but she ignored these, her glance falling to the three drawers set into the base of the gun rack. One of them held a key in its lock; a small brass key, really quite distinctive. She kept her glance riveted to this, every nerve in her body waiting. "I am admiring a brass key," she told herself. "I am in Albania and presently Farrell will be killed and I mustn't think about it." She did not have long to wait. Her concentration was interrupted by harsh shouts from outside the building, and then by the sound of guns being fired. Mrs. Pollifax very carefully placed the cup of water on the major's desk and was pleased to see that her hand was not trembling. "I mustn't look," she told herself. "I don't want to look. There was nothing else for him to do."

At the sound of firing Major Vassovic uttered an explosive

oath. After one glance from the window he said, "Back—back," and roughly pushed Mrs. Pollifax down the hall to her cell and slammed the door upon her. The firing had not continued beyond that one frenzied burst. There was only silence now in the building. Mrs. Pollifax sat down on Farrell's cot and said in a quiet voice, "I didn't look." For some reason this was very important to her. "I didn't look," she repeated in a louder voice, and fumbling in her purse she brought out a handkerchief and angrily blew her nose. Then she resolutely shuffled her deck of cards and laid them out for a game of Spider.

Mrs. Pollifax had played for several minutes, the silence like a shroud in the stone cell—like Farrell's shroud, she thought bitterly —when slowly her thoughts became diverted by a small sound emanating from the wall behind her. She turned her head to hear it better. It was not a metallic noise, it was more like a clenched fist rhythmically striking the stone wall. Recalling the second iron door set into the hall outside Mrs. Pollifax frowned. Kneeling on Farrell's cot she tapped with both hands. Immediately the sound stopped, as if in astonishment, and just when Mrs. Pollifax decided it must be someone repairing a drain, the fist beat an excited staccato reply. This fist had a personality all its own, thought Mrs. Pollifax in surprise; at first it had seemed to be hitting the wall in a monotonous rhythm of despair, then finding itself answered the Fist had panicked and stopped, afraid. But perhaps the Fist had remembered that another cell stood between it and Major Vassovic, for after its hesitation it had replied with joy.

"Yes with joy," repeated Mrs. Pollifax firmly, and reflected that if this were anything but real life they would now exchange urgent messages in Morse code. Unfortunately Mrs. Pollifax knew no Morse. She tapped again once more and received a reply, but it was a little like communicating with a newly born infant or someone who spoke only Swahili; once the initial greeting had been made there was really not much more to manage. Besides, her mind was on Farrell and she returned sadly to her game of solitaire.

It seemed a long time later when the building filled with noise again. A number of booted feet tramped down the hall and Mrs. Pollifax heard Major Vassovic issuing orders in an irritable voice. He sounded like a frustrated and angry man. Mrs. Pollifax placed a

black ace on a red two and waited for the inevitable grating of the
key in the lock—it was a sound she was beginning to dread. The
door swung open. Mrs. Pollifax looked up and the cards slipped
from her hand to the floor.

"*Farrell!*" she gasped.

He was propped between two guards, one leg dangling uselessly, his clothes smeared with blood. At her cry he lifted his head
and opened one eye. "Goofed again, Duchess," he said, and as the
men lowered him none too gently to the cot he added peevishly,
"Damn cliff. If *you* jumped from a hundred-foot cliff wouldn't *you*
bloody well expect to be killed?" Having delivered himself of this
diatribe he fell back unconscious on the bed.

Chapter Ten

The two slits in the wall of the cell gradually darkened as night fell. Mrs. Pollifax sat beside Farrell and listened to his ravings as he slipped in and out of feverish dreams. She knew his leg was broken in two places and she had neither water nor bandages for him. There was a great deal of blood all over him, but as far as she could see only one bullet had entered his body and this was embedded in his right arm above the elbow. She had staunched the bleeding by removing the coarse blanket from her cot and using it as a tourniquet. When General Perdido arrived she had worked herself into a cold fury over the cruelty of the situation and her own helplessness. "Good evening," she said icily.

The guard accompanying Perdido carried a candle which he inserted into a metal ring set into the wall for this purpose. The general walked over to Farrell and looked down at him contemptuously. Clearly he, too, was furious.

Mrs. Pollifax said coldly, "I have asked for water and bandages and no one brings them. If I may be so presumptuous as to make a suggestion, General, why don't you shoot Mr. Farrell? It would be much more efficient because he is making a great deal of bothersome noise and what's worse he is bleeding all over your furniture."

General Perdido turned on her angrily. "I find you insolent, Mrs. Pollifax."

"I *feel* insolent," retorted Mrs. Pollifax. "Perhaps you would like to shoot me as well."

For a moment she thought that General Perdido was going to strike her. She almost hoped that he would for her rage was nearly uncontainable and she would have welcomed violence, even if directed at herself. But his hand fell. He glared again at the moaning Farrell and turned on his heel. At the door he said to Major Vassovic, "Give the woman the water and bandages she asks for. Perhaps she can revive the prisoner for questioning." He turned and gave Mrs. Pollifax a tight, sadistic smile. "For questioning and other things." With this he marched out.

Major Vassovic looked doubtfully at Mrs. Pollifax. "Water? Bandages? You are a nurse?"

"No, a human being," she snapped, and sat down again beside Farrell's cot.

The major returned with strips of cloth and a pitcher of water. He stood and watched while Mrs. Pollifax moistened Farrell's lips and untied the tourniquet. "You have been loosening it?" he asked.

She nodded. The bleeding had stopped; Mrs. Pollifax placed the blanket to one side and walked over to her cot and rolled back the mattress. The cot was made of wood, with rough slats to support the thin hard mattress. She removed two of the slats and carried them back to Farrell's bed.

"What do you do now?" asked Major Vassovic curiously.

"I intend to set his leg."

Major Vassovic looked astonished. "*Zott!* You know how?"

"No," replied Mrs. Pollifax, "but someone has to. I'm hoping you will help me."

He said stiffly, "I have no orders."

"But you are here, and you are a man and he is a man, and do you think any leg should look like that?"

"I have no orders," he repeated, and went out.

Mrs. Pollifax felt suddenly very tired. She looked at Farrell and she looked at his leg and she knew that she would bungle the job alone. Gritting her teeth she leaned over him and began ripping away his trouser leg. "I will not faint," she told herself, "I will not, I will not. Surely I can push one of those bones back myself. It certainly ought to be done now, while he's unconscious." She stood back and looked at the leg, already swollen and red and turning black and blue, and she thought forlornly, "I wish I had another aspirin."

The door behind her opened so quietly that Mrs. Pollifax started when a low voice said, "Lulash."

She turned. One of the guards stood there, his finger to his lips, nodding and smiling nervously. "My name is Lulash."

"I see," said Mrs. Pollifax blankly. "Lulash. Well, how do you do, Mr. Lulash."

He tiptoed back to the door, listened a moment and gently closed it. "The major has gone for the night. He sleeps." He walked to the cot and stared down at Farrell. "I have worked in hospital," he said suddenly. "I can set this man's leg. *Zott*, but it looks bad."

Mrs. Pollifax's eyes weakly filled with tears at this offer of help. "He jumped from the cliff," she explained in a strangled voice. "He was trying to kill himself."

Lulash only nodded. "I wish him better good fortune the next time." He leaned over to examine Farrell's leg more closely. "*Zott*, but this is not good."

"But you can do something?"

"Something, yes. Better a doctor, but they will not bring a doctor. I do my best." His eyes fell to the slats that Mrs. Pollifax still held in her arms. He took them from her and leaned them against the wall. "Later," he said. "Now you must sit on the man's chest and hold him down. I bid you do it." Numbly Mrs. Pollifax obeyed.

Ten minutes later Farrell's leg was set and Mrs. Pollifax, feeling shaken and a little ill, sat on her cot and watched Lulash bind the slats against Farrell's straightened leg. After one enraged scream Farrell had lost consciousness again, and he was still unconscious. Lulash placed a hand on Farrell's heart and then on his pulse, counting the beat. With a nod he came to sit down beside Mrs. Pollifax and mop his brow with a soiled handkerchief.

"Would you like an American cigarette?" asked Mrs. Pollifax humbly. She brought from her purse the crumpled pack that Farrell had given her.

"Thank you."

"We are both Americans," said Mrs. Pollifax, with a nod toward Farrell. "Do you think—that is, is it all right for me to ask if this is Albania?"

The guard shrugged. "We call it Shkyperi, which in your language would mean Land of the Mountain Eagle. But yes, it is called Albania."

"Where did you learn to speak such fine English? Do all the Albanians speak it? Major Vassovic does, and you."

"I was brought here two days ago because I speak the English. Before then I was in Sarande. It was the same with Major Vassovic, who came from Tirana. They went searching for those of us in the Sigurimi who speak your language."

"The Sigur—what?" asked Mrs. Pollifax.

"That is the name of the secret police in this country."

Mrs. Pollifax gasped. "That means that you—I mean—"

He shrugged. "The time is very difficult here. Those of us who can read and write have two choices, to join the Sigurimi or not to join. Those who do not join can usually be seen on the roads any day. They smash rock. They carry rock. They have no hope."

"I'm sorry," said Mrs. Pollifax. "It sounds quite sad." She looked at him with curiosity, studying him carefully because of his extraordinary kindness to Farrell, but unable to find anything in his face to explain him. It was a dark, secretive face with pointed features: black brows, a long, thin nose, a sharp thin jaw, a thin sharp mouth. She would not have taken him for a kind man or an unselfish one, and yet he had flouted orders to help a sick man.

"It was not always this way," he said. "Albanians are a proud, fiercely independent people. But without luck," he added. "First the Turks ruled us, then the Russians, now the Chinese. Whatever the master the country stays the same. Poor, primitive, frightened too."

"You speak English so well," she pointed out.

His face brightened. "My cousin and I learned the English as children from a man who had come here to write a book about the country. He was a travel man, you know. He wrote the book the year I was born but each year he came back to visit my father. It pleased him to teach us. He was friend to all the tribes, a very good man."

"Tribes?" said Mrs. Pollifax.

He nodded. "You know nothing of our country?"

"Nothing at all, I'm afraid," she admitted.

"The most beautiful country in the world," he said firmly. "Here the rocks and the high mountains, below the flatlands, the valley, the rivers. And oh, the sea," he added with nostalgia. "Patrolled now, of course. But the Adriatic is the most beautiful sea in the world."

"Yes, I've heard that," said Mrs. Pollifax quietly.

"This man, this Mr. Allistair, gave us the book he wrote of my country. He loved it too." He pinched out the cigarette and placed the butt carefully in the pocket of his shirt. "Your friend is stirring, I will find for him one aspirin."

He got up and opened the door to the hall and stood there, waiting. Mrs. Pollifax realized that he was waiting for her to accompany him. Surprised, she followed him out, quite touched by his trust. Once in the guardroom he began opening and closing drawers of the desk while Mrs. Pollifax stood beside him. She heard his murmur of satisfaction as he brought up a flask containing what looked to be brandy. While he attacked a new drawer Mrs. Pollifax's glance wandered and came to rest, mesmerized, upon the gun rack behind the desk.

The little brass key to the drawer in the gun rack was still there in its lock.

What, she wondered, would people keep in the drawer of a gun rack?

"If they put ammunition there they certainly wouldn't be so careless as to leave the key in the lock," she reflected. "It's probably filled with paper clips or something idiotic. Except, why paper clips in a gun rack?"

It was an interesting thought. If it *was* a drawer for ammunition a person could steal the key and hide it and later hope to come back and remove whatever was there. Then perhaps some use could be made of it, or a gun taken from the rack—

She looked at Lulash, at his narrow back bent over the bottom drawer. Still watching him she took several steps backward, until she felt the gun rack between her shoulder blades. Fumblingly she tugged at the drawer and felt it slide open. Lulash was still leaning over the desk and she quickly turned and glanced down. She had been right about its holding ammunition: the drawer was filled with neat stacks of bullets, cartridges and clips, all of them unwrapped and accessible. She slid the drawer closed and placed her fingers around the key. Then she hesitated.

"I can't," she thought bleakly. "I just can't."

"Lulash would be blamed," she realized. "It wouldn't be fair. He would be blamed for its loss and punished and he has just set Farrell's leg and now he is going to give him brandy and an aspirin.

"I am an utter failure as an agent," she decided with anger.

"It should have occurred to me before that I would have to be
ruthless and unscrupulous. These people are planning to kill me
and still I can't steal this key or so much as a bullet because this
man has helped me and would be blamed for it."

Lulash stood erect, brandishing a bottle of white pills and
smiling at her. Automatically she smiled back, her mind totally
occupied with her defeat. Lulash found a paper cup and drew water
from the cooler and she accompanied him back to her cell.

"What goes?" asked Farrell shakily.

"This gentleman set your leg," she told him, patting his arm.
"We've brought you some brandy for your nerves, and aspirin for
your fever. Could you manage to sit up just a little if I help?"

Farrell struggled to one elbow. "I hope I haven't given away
any state secrets. I have the feeling I've been talking like an idiot."

She smiled faintly. "Exactly like an idiot, but not like any
friend of Mr. Carstairs."

"Thank God for that." He swallowed some brandy, winced,
and saluted Lulash with a wave of a hand. "Does he speak English?"

"Yes."

"The brandy isn't bad. More?"

"Aspirin next," she said firmly, and placed one tablet on his
tongue. "If you prefer washing it down with brandy we can dis-
pense with the water."

"Loathe water," he said, and gulped down two aspirin with
huge draughts of brandy. "What are the prospects?" he gasped,
lying back.

"Dim," replied Mrs. Pollifax dryly. "General Perdido has
been in to look you over. You have considerably frustrated him by
injuring yourself so badly, and he left in disgust." She added in a
low voice that Lulash could not hear, "It might be wise of you,
when anyone comes in again, to continue talking as wildly as possible, and to see things crawling up and down the walls."

He whispered back, "That's delirium tremens, not fever.
You'll make a bloody alcoholic out of me."

In a louder voice, and tartly, she said, "In your weakened
condition, and with all the brandy you've just consumed, you will
soon be in precisely that state."

Lulash slipped the aspirin bottle into his pocket and showed signs of leaving. Mrs. Pollifax arose and reached for his hand. "Thank you," she said warmly, shaking it. "We both thank you very much."

"Is all right," he said, nodding and smiling.

When he had gone Mrs. Pollifax sat down abruptly on her cot, realizing how terribly tired she was. Farrell, watching her, said, "You look exhausted, Duchess, for God's sake get some sleep. I'll try to limit my ravings for a while."

Mrs. Pollifax looked at him in the flickering eerie light of the candle and realized how very fond of him she was becoming. "It *is* comforting not to be alone," she thought. She stood up and rolled back the mattress to arrange the slats around the two that were missing. "It has been rather a long day," she admitted aloud, and lying down she fell at once into an exhausted sleep.

Chapter Eleven

On the twenty-third of August Carstairs sat down in his office to review the Mexico City fiasco with a man named Thaddeus Peattie. Peattie came from another department; he was extremely interested in all matters concerning Mao Tse-tung and he was one of the few Americans to have personally known Rauol Perdido—they had met frequently in China during the war when Perdido was a member of Mao's guerrillas and Peattie was a liaison officer between Chiang Kaishek and the guerrillas.

"There hasn't been a sign of Farrell or Mrs. Pollifax being smuggled into Cuba," Carstairs said, offering Peattie and Bishop cigarettes. "This doesn't for a moment exclude their being there. They could have landed at night in some secluded area and been whisked into solitary confinement or killed at once. But General Perdido hasn't been sighted in Cuba, either. I think we can say without any doubt at all that Perdido is not in Cuba at the moment."

"South America?" suggested Peattie. "Mexico? Perdido is a Mexican by birth, after all. Need he have left Mexico at all?"

"He's not particularly welcome there," pointed out Carstairs. "If he's still there he would certainly be in hiding. What we want to know is where he would go if he left the country. Where's that report from Belmonte?" he asked of Bishop.

Bishop riffled through the pile of papers on his lap and efficiently extracted the needed sheet. Carstairs handed it over to Peattie. "It's common knowledge that the Russians have used Mexico as a takeoff point for spies and defectors in this hemisphere. We know of two secret landing strips used by the Reds for smuggling people out. These strips," he added pointedly, "are not entirely unobserved, as you will see by this report from—an observer, shall we say?"

Peattie picked up the report.

"As you will note," continued Carstairs, "there has been some activity observed in this lower California landing strip. A plane—a four-engine prop—was reported landing there on the night of August 19. It was on this day that General Perdido closed the doors of the Parrot Bookstore and vanished from sight. It is also on this day that Farrell and Mrs. Pollifax visited the Parrot Bookstore and vanished."

"Mmm," murmured Peattie, frowning. "This report says that two people were carried aboard this plane."

"Yes, carried. On stretchers."

"Definitely a Russian-made plane," read Peattie aloud. "Markings thought to be Cuban." He returned the sheet to Carstairs. "You say that our beautiful Miss Willow Lee has also left Mexico City?"

Carstairs nodded. "Yes, but she left on a registered flight, destination Peking, and has already arrived in Hong Kong."

"Then it's not likely that she and General Perdido were the passengers taken aboard that plane," mused Peattie.

"Not on stretchers," remarked Carstairs dryly.

"No, not on stretchers," agreed Peattie with a quick smile. "Perdido is of course the key to this. If he's involved—and from what you've implied this whole affair is big enough to interest him —then he's the man to trace, of course. The two others, dead or alive, could be anywhere but are doubtless with him. Or were." He stood up and walked to the map on the wall and stood before it, his hands locked behind his back. "I hate to say this," he remarked. "At least I assume you're grimly hoping to regain or trace these two agents of yours. But if General Perdido is not in Cuba—and surely by now he would have been seen there by someone—then I fear the general would have headed for Red China."

"This department does not grimly hope," said Carstairs in a hard voice. "No, my dear Peattie, the names of Farrell and Pollifax have been crossed off all earthly lists as far as we are concerned."

"Then I don't think I understand," said Peattie, returning to his chair and sitting down.

Carstairs hesitated. "You might call our investigation fifty per cent precaution and fifty per cent conscience. We don't want any international incidents growing out of it, for instance."

"You mean like the U-2 affair," cut in Peattie dryly.

"Right. We want to"—his voice softened apologetically—"we *have* to be sure these two people are dead. We have to have *proof*."

Peattie nodded. "I'll send out feelers at once, of course. I think that within four days—a week at the most—I can tell you whether General Perdido is or has been in China." He gave Carstairs a curious glance and said, "And the fifty per cent conscience —or isn't that any of my business?"

Carstairs sighed. "I'm thinking of Mrs. Pollifax. The late Mrs. Pollifax, I fear. You didn't know her, of course. Perhaps I can give you a capsule picture of her if I tell you that she strolled in here one day and asked if we needed any spies."

Peattie looked at Carstairs in open-mouthed astonishment.

Carstairs nodded. "A comfortable little woman in her sixties, with a charmingly direct way of going about things. Asked Mason if there was something she could do for us. Rather like volunteering for work at a charity fete. Hellishly innocent and naïve, but so patently right for the tourist I needed that I gobbled her up, so to speak."

Peattie gave him a sympathetic glance. "I see," he said quietly. "She knew the risks?"

"Oh yes, she knew the risks. But she left without indoctrination, without training, without a cyanide pill."

"Fortunes of war," pointed out Peattie softly. "Necessity is a ruthless mistress."

Carstairs sighed. "No one knows that better than I, but I haven't been sleeping too well these past three nights. From a practical viewpoint it's she who could become the international incident—she is so clearly usable, because of her innocence. But what is far more likely—"

He stopped and Peattie said wryly, "Don't torture yourself, my friend—don't."

"I try not to," Carstairs said with a bitter smile. "Let us say very simply that I must now think of plausible telegrams to send to the woman's relatives explaining why she is not en route home from Mexico at this moment, and that eventually—once her death is substantiated—I must arrange some plausible death for her in Mexico."

"Stevens is working on that now," put in Bishop. "A boating

accident has been suggested, with no body recovered. Either a chartered boat off Acapulco or a freak drowning at Xochimilco. Mexico is being very helpful."

"How nice," said Carstairs sourly. "Then her son and daughter will hold a memorial service for her and have her name cut on a stone in the family plot and say 'What a way for Mother to go' and they will never guess how their mother did die, or for what purpose, or know that half a dozen people in Washington, D.C., and Mexico City worked over the details, making their mother's death palatable and acceptable to them."

"I get the point, you needn't labor it," said Peattie gently. "But you must know by now that inevitably there's one person for whom one feels unusually responsible."

Carstairs nodded, a faint smile on his lips. "I ought to know that by now, Peattie. Rum job, what?"

"Rum job," agreed Peattie, and stood up. "I've got the picture now. I can promise you information, positive or negative, within the week. I wish it could be sooner but China still moves pretty much by oxcart in spite of Mao's boasts to the contrary."

"Thanks—we'll take anything we can get."

When he had gone Carstairs lit a cigarette, leaned back in his chair and gave Bishop a weary smile. "I don't know whether you saw the message that came in late last evening or not. Tirpak is dead. A knife in the back in Guatemala about a week ago, the identification just made."

Bishop sighed. "What you'd call a clean sweep then. No, I haven't had time to catch up on last night's communiques."

"They make lively reading—there's even more," added Carstairs wryly. "Our photographic-supply friend in Costa Rica processed all the information that Tirpak brought him, and duly burned the papers. It took three days to get all of Tirpak's documents on film. There were six microfilms, but here's the sad news: Tirpak gave no indication of how these films were going to be conveyed to Mexico City, or in what form. Whatever he did next with them was done secretly. According to our friend in Costa Rica Tirpak picked up each microfilm with a pair of tweezers, dropped them one by one into a plain white envelope, and left."

"Ouch," said Bishop.

Carstairs nodded. "Three days later he was murdered, but he

must have started moving them toward Mexico City before then.
What he did with them is anybody's guess but I would assume he
planned to insert them into something printed—say a letter or a
book."

"You do think the microfilms reached Mexico City then."

Carstairs nodded. "Tirpak would have seen to that even at the
cost of his life. He was that kind of man. What he couldn't have
realized was just how closely he was being followed and watched—
and just how closely those microfilms were being watched. Yes, I
believe they reached Mexico City. They reached the Parrot Bookstore and DeGamez was killed because of them."

"So General Perdido has the microfilms then."

Carstairs frowned. "They're lost to us in any case, Bishop, but
I'm not so sure that General Perdido has them, either. Take a close
look at this timetable of events I've written out—see if it suggests
anything to you."

Bishop took the memo and read:

August 17: probable date of DeGamez' murder
August 17: General Perdido poses as DeGamez and installs
           himself at the Parrot Bookstore
August 19: Mrs. Pollifax visits the Parrot Bookstore to pick
           up microfilms and vanishes
August 19: Farrell visits the Parrot Bookstore for unknown
           reasons, and also vanishes
August 19 Mrs. Pollifax's room at the Hotel Reforma Inter-
or 20:   continental entered and searched.

Bishop was thoughtful. "I see what you mean. Why go to the
bother of keeping the bookstore open after DeGamez' demise, and
why search Mrs. Pollifax's room, if they'd gotten what they
wanted."

Carstairs nodded. "Exactly. It implies a certain lack of success. If General Perdido had gotten the microfilms from DeGamez
before DeGamez was killed, then I don't really see what purpose
was served by his turning into a bookstore clerk to set a trap for
Mrs. Pollifax and Farrell. And that's another thing: their including
Farrell bothers me very much. Farrell's only link with the Chinese
Reds was the friendship with Miss Willow Lee that he was busy

cultivating at our orders. He had no knowledge of either Tirpak or Mrs. Pollifax, and as to the microfilms, he didn't even know of their existence."

Bishop nodded. "Snatching him *does* imply desperation on the part of General Perdido."

"Yes. And that's why I'm reasonably sure that he chose to keep Farrell and Mrs. Pollifax alive—at least for a day or two. And that, my dear Bishop, is why I am not sleeping well these nights, because General Perdido's methods of extracting information are neither polite nor pretty."

"But Mrs. Pollifax had no information to extract," pointed out Bishop.

Carstairs gave him a hard look. "Let's not be naïve, Bishop. Do you think Perdido would believe that?"

There was a long silence during which Bishop tried to think of something tactful to say. Finally, with a forced brightness, he concluded, "Well if Perdido doesn't have the microfilms, that's something, isn't it?"

Carstairs gave a short laugh. "Oh yes—yes, indeed. It means they're lost to everyone, floating in space, so to speak, and of no use to anyone. If they were appended to a book sold in DeGamez' shop then someone at this very moment may be reading that book, never realizing that it's the repository of secrets costing eight months work and the lives of innumerable people who would otherwise be alive today. And that is what I call waste. Where is the telegram sent to Mrs. Pollifax's next of kin?"

Bishop drew copies from his file. "Here they are, sir. They went off late yesterday from Mexico City; this one to Mr. Roger Pollifax in Chicago, this one to Mrs. Conrad Kempf in Arizona."

Carstairs read them with irony:

HAVING WONDERFUL TIME STOP POSTPONING RETURN A WEEK OR MORE STOP MEXICO CHARMING STOP LOVE TO ALL MOTHER

Chapter Twelve

General Perdido returned to the cell the next afternoon, but Mrs. Pollifax had been forewarned by the sound of his voice in the hall. The general, entering, found Mrs. Pollifax playing a quiet game of solitaire and Farrell tossing feverishly on his cot.

"Good afternoon," said Mrs. Pollifax coldly.

"Where?" shouted Farrell, thrashing feebly. "Take the green ones away, for God's sake!"

Both the general and Mrs. Pollifax turned to look at Farrell, one with exasperation, the other with admiration. To the general Mrs. Pollifax said bitingly, "I have set his leg but he still has a bullet in his arm and I am *not* Dr. Schweitzer. The wound is infected."

General Perdido crossed the cell to Farrell and looked down at him. "Senor Farrell," he said harshly.

Farrell opened his eyes and stared into the face above him.

"Carmelita?" he said tenderly, and then, hopefully, "My darling?"

General Perdido drew back his arm and sent his fist crashing against Farrell's cheekbone. There was a sickening sound of bone meeting bone. Mrs. Pollifax turned away and thought, "I really can't bear this."

There was, for the next few minutes, a great deal more to bear. The general was a thorough man, a determined and an intelligent man, and he intended to leave no stone unturned in his search to learn whether Farrell was shamming or if his mind could still be reached. Mrs. Pollifax moved to the attenuated window and forced herself to look beyond it to the narrow rectangle of stones glittering in the sun, and the thin slice of bleached white sky. "I won't listen," she thought. "I will detach myself forever from this room and this moment." It was an exercise in deception that she had practiced before but never so desperately as now. But when at last the general desisted she was more calm than he—the general's face was distorted with fury. Pausing with his hand on the cell door he said stiffly, "I will be going away until I am informed that Mr. Farrell is well enough to be questioned. You may tell him so. You may also tell him that I will look forward to his speedy recovery." He opened the door and turned back dramatically. "As for you, Mrs. Pollifax, you have inconvenienced me so greatly that I resent your very existence." The door slammed behind him and she heard the bolt drawn outside. Only then did she dare look at Farrell. "I think General Perdido has been seeing too many B movies," she said lightly, and wanted to cry at the sight of Farrell's battered face.

Farrell said evenly, his words slurred by two very puffy lips, "Let's give him to Hollywood then with our compliments." He sat up. "Did he break my nose, damn him?"

Mrs. Pollifax sat down beside him and for the next few minutes they took inventory. The list was encouraging: it consisted of bruises, two loosened teeth—both molars—and a split upper lip; but there appeared to be no bones broken and Mrs. Pollifax felt it was reasonable to hope there was no concussion of the cheekbone. She said gently, "You managed very well. Have you had to endure this sort of thing before?"

He glanced away. "Once, during the war. That was when I knew Carstairs." He looked at her thoughtfully. "There are limitations, you know, especially after the first time. The second time the mind knows what to expect. It anticipates. Actually the mind can become a worse enemy than the person inflicting the pain. But this was brief—mercifully."

Mrs. Pollifax considered his words and nodded. "Yes, I see how that can be." She felt his forehead and sighed. "You still have a fever, you know. About a hundred and one, I'd guess."

"But not the raving kind," he said, and winced as he tried to smile.

"No, not the raving kind—you put on a very good act." She brought from her purse the package of cigarettes he had given her and held out the last one to him. "Could you manage this with your torn lip?"

"Pure nectar," he said longingly. He took it and began stabbing his mouth with it to find a comfortable corner for it. She lighted it for him and he inhaled deeply. "Duchess," he said gratefully, "I've known an incredible number of young, beautiful and nubile women—more than any one man deserves—but I would have to nominate you as the Woman I Would Most Like to Be Captured with in Albania. You are a true blessing to me in my old age—and I feel I'm aging pretty damn fast in this place."

"Ah, you are feeling better, I'm delighted," said Mrs. Pollifax with a twinkle. She returned to her own cot, carrying her small table with her, and laid out her playing cards for a game of Clock Solitaire. "How did you fall into this preposterous sort of life?" she asked, thinking he might like to talk now. "This preposterous life with beautiful nubile women and General Perdidos in it. You're American, aren't you?"

"As American as San Francisco," he said, sending streams of blue smoke toward the ceiling from his horizontal position. "My mother was Spanish—I learned to speak Spanish before I knew English. And I got the wandering bug from them. They were both vaudeville people—dancers."

"How very nice," said Mrs. Pollifax, charmed by the thought. "I always did enjoy the flamenco. Did you live out of a suitcase?"

"Mmm, just about."

"Do you dance?"

"Only a waltz," he said cheerfully. "In me the talent came out in art. I was in the war very early, and when I got out I headed for Mexico to paint. It may surprise you to hear that I really do paint—off and on. By the time Carstairs found me I had already acquired just the reputation he wanted: half playboy, half adventurer, half artist."

"You have too many halves there," pointed out Mrs. Pollifax primly.

"You don't feel that exaggeration adds flavor?" he inquired.

Mrs. Pollifax struggled and lost. "Actually, I have been guilty of a small amount of exaggeration myself at times."

He chuckled. "I'll bet you have, Duchess, I'll bet you have. But lived a very quiet and respectable life in spite of it?"

"Oh yes," she said. "Very quiet and very respectable. My husband was a lawyer, a very fine one. My son is a lawyer, too," she added, and thinking back added with nostalgia, "Yes, it was a very pleasant and peaceful life."

Farrell turned his head to look at her through the gloom. He said tactfully, "Think I'll have a little nap now, Duchess." Carefully adjusting his position to his wounded arm he left Mrs. Pollifax to her thoughts and pretended to fall asleep.

It was at mealtime that the new prisoner arrived. He was pushed in ahead of the trays and kicked ungenerously by Major Vassovic and apparently sworn at in the language of the country. A third cot was then brought in and placed along the third wall. Mrs. Pollifax was too busy feeding Farrell with a spoon to pay much attention, but while she ate her own meal—reluctantly putting away her playing cards to make room for it—she eyed the man curiously. He lay on his side, with his face resting on his two hands, but all that she could really see of him was a bristling, white, walrus moustache jutting up, and the top of a bald pink head fringed with white about the ears. It was a very elegant, splendidly Victorian moustache—she hadn't seen one like it since she was a child. She realized that Farrell, propped against the opposite wall, was also studying the man. He said suddenly, "My name's Farrell, what is yours, sir?"

The man's head shifted, aware of Farrell's voice, but his face remained blank and he said nothing.

"Speak English?" asked Farrell.

"Inglese?" repeated the man, and with a shake of his head added a jumble of words in a language that neither of them understood.

"He doesn't speak English—that's good," said Mrs. Pollifax. "What did we eat tonight, by the way?"

Farrell said broodingly, "Heaven only knows." He was still watching the stranger. He said suddenly, in a particularly meaningful voice, "Look at the candle!"

Mrs. Pollifax's glance went at once to the candle over the newcomer's head, and she frowned because there was nothing wrong with it, nothing to see but the one sputtering flame that gave little more than an illusion of lighting the shadows. Then she realized that the new man, who had been lying on his side, had thrown back his head so that he, too, was looking at the candle.

How very curious, she thought, he had understood perfectly what
Farrell said. It occurred to her that he was arriving in their cell just
as General Perdido had announced that he was leaving for a few
days, and she pondered the connection. Yes, it was quite possible; it
would be very inefficient of the general to leave without making
some arrangements to learn more about her and Farrell. The general would not care to waste time, and what better way to make
time work for him than to place a spy in their cell to eavesdrop on
them while he was gone? Apparently the general had unearthed
another English-speaking member of the Sigurimi. She smiled at
Farrell to show him that she understood his warning.

Tonight it was Lulash who came to remove their trays and he
went first to Mrs. Pollifax after directing a quick glance at the new
prisoner. "We are late tonight in collecting your tray. General
Perdido had to be driven to his airplane."

Mrs. Pollifax saw that he had deposited two aspirins on her
table and she gave him a grateful glance.

"Also for you, to read in the English about my country." He
spoke in a very low voice, and with his back still to the new prisoner he leaned over and slipped a book under her pillow. "It is *the*
book, the one I told you about," he added reverently. "I carry it
everywhere with me, it is even inscribed to me."

Mrs. Pollifax had to content herself with another grateful
glance, for she dared not speak. Lulash moved away to Farrell's
table and after removing his tray went out. With her table again
empty Mrs. Pollifax arranged her cards for a new game of solitaire
and played doggedly for an hour. Farrell was the first to fall into a
restless sleep. Soon the stranger turned his back to the room and
filled the air with rhythmic snores, and Mrs. Pollifax, growing
drowsy herself, put away the cards and lay down.

The book that Lulash had placed beneath her pillow proved
uncomfortable to lie upon—she had forgotten its existence as soon
as Lulash went away. Since no one was awake to see her she
brought out the book and opened it. It was an old volume; the first
thing she noted was its copyright date—1919—and at sight of this
Mrs. Pollifax was touched that it was still such a treasure to Lulash,
and then she was disappointed because a book written forty-five
years ago could not possibly be informative; too many wars had
been fought since then, too many political parties gone from the

scene, making the book a virtual antique. She thumbed through it, however, with a feeling of nostalgia, recalling books in her childhood with the same gray, sunless photographs, the same pictures of people in national costume, with the author himself posed artfully beside monuments and graves and on horseback. The book was entitled *Albania: Land of Primitive Beauty*, and it was written in the florid verbiage of the day. The plainest sentence in the book stated simply that in size the country was equal to the state of Maryland. Its last chapter ended with the words, "And so I bade farewell to the head of the clan of Trijepsi, leaving him by the leaping flames of his campfire, a real friend whom I must always cherish. Rough, yes; but a pearl among men, truly a chief among men." Mrs. Pollifax winced at the style and turned a few more pages to come face to face with a very clearly rendered black and white map. A map . . . she idly turned another page and then came quickly back to the map. It was a very good, clear map. There was Albania fitted neatly between Greece to the south and what would now be Yugoslavia on the north, and there was the Adriatic Sea. . . . Water, thought Mrs. Pollifax, feeling her way toward a thought not yet expressible. Thoughtfully she turned the map closer to the light and began looking for mountains, wondering just where they might be at this moment. In the south there was a thin line of mountain range facing the sea, but according to the description these were hardly fifteen hundred feet in height—the ones they had traveled through were higher and so she ignored these for the time being. The central part of the country was flat and open with the exception of one mountain rising out of the plains, but she and Farrell had been brought to a very long, high range of mountains and she dismissed this solitary peak. Her glance fastened on the north, narrowing as she spied the words *North Albanian Alps*. Farrell had said something about Alps, and the mountains to which they had been brought resembled Switzerland in their naked ruggedness. These mountains ran from east to west across the top of the country like a necklace—a necklace extremely close to Yugoslavia, she noticed—and, if the country was no larger than Maryland, they were not excessively far from the Adriatic Sea, either.

"We have to be somewhere in these mountains," she mused. She would have to begin reading the book tomorrow because in forty-five years the topography would remain the same. But still she lingered over the map. They had landed by plane in a town that was plainly old and well established, and after driving toward the mountains they had traveled for one or two hours by donkey. Would it be possible to figure out in what direction they had traveled?

"The sun," gasped Mrs. Pollifax. From the heaving, slippery back of her donkey she had watched the sun rise and spread across the valley in a flood of gold. Sleep left her as she concentrated on remembering. Yes, the sun had definitely risen in front of her and slightly to the right. Therefore they had been traveling eastward. If she reversed this, moving her finger westward, there was only one city, named Scutari, printed in bold print, that would be large enough to sustain a crude airfield. The other towns were all in small print—villages, no doubt, none of them large enough to drive through for a period of ten minutes. If it was Scutari where they had landed then they must be about *here*, she decided, scratching an X with her fingernail. It was a point astonishingly close to Yugoslavia, and surprisingly near the Adriatic, and across the Adriatic lay Italy. . . .

She placed the book carefully under the mattress at her feet and lay down, almost frightened by the thought that the map engendered. "But how very difficult it is to dismiss an idea once it has presented itself to the mind," she mused. She would have to look at the map again more carefully tomorrow and read about the North Albanian Alps. Perhaps Farrell would have noticed landmarks she had missed. She tried to tame her thoughts, but it was a long time before she fell asleep.

Chapter Thirteen

Y ou may come out," said Lulash the next afternoon, standing in the doorway and speaking to Mrs. Pollifax. "General Hoong has said you may have a little walk for the exercise."

"How very kind," gasped Mrs. Pollifax.

Lulash said cheerfully, "General Hoong has wired for instructions about you. Everyone has wired for instructions about you. Now with General Perdido gone we only wait."

Mrs. Pollifax nodded and went to look at Farrell. During the night his temperature had flared dangerously and she was very worried about him. If he was to survive at all the bullet would have to be removed from his arm; for what purpose he must survive she did not know, but it went against all of her instincts to let a man die without making every effort to save him. He was flushed and drowsy and his appetite had vanished; his temperature must be 104 or 105, she judged, and he was not always lucid. Mrs. Pollifax leaned over him and said gently, "I will be back in a few minutes."

Farrell opened one eye and grinned weakly. "Have fun."

Before leaving Mrs. Pollifax went to her cot and picked up the Guatemalan jacket which an eternity ago she had worn when she left her Mexico City hotel room. She had lived in the same dress for six days and nights, and had passed the point of fastidiousness; but the jacket she guarded with feminine illogic. During the day it was spread carefully atop her pillow; at night it was folded across the table on which she played her card games—it had become almost a fetish with her. As she plucked it now from the pillow her left hand groped underneath for the book on Albania. She slipped it under the jacket and without even a glance at the Gremlin—this nickname had been bestowed upon their stool pigeon by Farrell— she walked out.

"Did you like my book, will you read it?" asked Lulash once they gained the hall.

She nodded with vivacity. She had already done much reading and she was in the process of assimilating some extremely interesting information. She had been wrong to think that a book written in 1919 could yield nothing pertinent; she had entirely overlooked the fact that political parties and wars could sweep like clouds across a country but leave its terrain untouched. Mrs. Pollifax was becoming very interested in Albania's topography and she eagerly welcomed a few minutes outside her prison to view it.

In the guardroom, as she passed through it, the key to the ammunition drawer had again been left in the lock.

Lulash led her outside. The sun, dazzling even to a normal eye, had an almost searing effect upon Mrs. Pollifax's eyeballs after the darkness of the cell, and she covered both eyes with her hands, gasping at the pain.

"Here," said Lulash, and gravely handed her his pair of dark glasses.

"Really you are so kind," said Mrs. Pollifax, and found that a few seconds after putting them on she was able to look around her without discomfort. They were not a great distance from the precipice from which Farrell had jumped. From here to its edge there were nothing but yellow rocks—boulders, stones, pebbles of every possible shape and size and texture, some worn smooth, others sharp and jagged. On their left the larger stone building cast a sharp black shadow across the stones, its edges as precise as if they were lines drawn with a ruler. On Mrs. Pollifax's right, not too far away, stood a hill of rock lightly screened by fir trees—it was from this direction that they had come. But Mrs. Pollifax was more interested in what lay in front of her. "I am to walk?" she asked of Lulash.

He nodded, and lowering himself to the bench beside the door he explained, "Better today if you walk within my eye, you understand? From there to there." With his hands he indicated boundaries.

Mrs. Pollifax nodded, and limping over the uneven stones made her way to the edge of the cliff. There she began what she hoped looked like an aimless stroll back and forth but was in reality a reconnaissance. The valley especially interested her, and from this height she could look far across it. Some distance away she traced with her eyes the winding skein of a riverbed that ran from east to west across the plain. Between herself and the river she could see four small towns, clusters of buildings baking in the brutal heat. The floor of the valley was almost a checkerboard of symmetrical lines dividing field after field—or possibly rice paddies, decided Mrs. Pollifax, having already dipped into four chapters of the book. Off to her right—or to the west, if her reasoning was correct—a road ran toward her into the mountains, and on its surface she could see men at work, so tiny they resembled little black insects. Mrs. Pollifax turned to look at what lay behind her, beyond Lulash and the stone house, and her head had to go up and far back before her eyes found the sky—the mountain towered above her. She concluded that this stony cut upon which she stood, and into which the two fortresslike buildings had been inserted, was an accident of nature, the path of some long-ago landslide or avalanche that had killed the soil for every growing thing. But of one fact she was certain: there could be no efficient escape over the peak above them into Yugoslavia, the only possibilities lay to the west, along the route they had come, or below, through the valley.

Escape . . . for the first time she acknowledged the direction of her thoughts, and having at last formed the word in her mind she took it out and examined it. Escape . . . the idea was quite mad—she admitted this cheerfully—but surely some effort had to be made? It struck her as extremely characterless for any human being to sit around waiting for execution. It wasn't that she had so much character, thought Mrs. Pollifax, but rather that always in her life she had found it difficult to *submit*. The list of her small rebellions was endless. Surely there was room for one more?

She smiled and waved at Lulash and sat down on a rock near the cliff's edge, her back to him as she carefully removed the book from under her arm. She had already marked the map's page and now she opened to it at once. A valley, an alp and a river . . . yes, there *was* a river in exactly the right place. On the assumption that her directions were correct she quickly compared its location on the valley's floor with its location on the map.

"The River Drin," she exclaimed in a pleased voice, memorizing the name, "Drin . . ." About fifteen miles away, according

to the scale of the map, and if her sense of direction was accurate
then it flowed westward into the Adriatic Sea.

Walking back to Lulash she said pleasantly, "The city with
the airport, is that Scutari, your capital?"

His face lit up. "Ah, you really did read my book. No, it is not
the capital any longer, nor is it called Scutari now," he said. "Its
name is Shkoder. But yes, that is where the airport is, in the
north."

"You are a mine of information about your interesting country," Mrs. Pollifax told him with complete honesty. "I shall hope to
learn much more from your book. Forgive me, but I think I will go
inside now, this sun—this heat . . ." She placed a hand daintily on
her brow, impatient to get inside and begin new calculations on her
map.

Lulash jumped to open the door for her before he sat down
again on his bench.

Considerably refreshed by her small excursion Mrs. Pollifax
walked back into the ice-house coolness of the stone building, and
closed the door behind her. "Oh—I do beg your pardon!" she said,
discovering Major Vassovic kneeling in a corner on the floor. For
one fleeting moment Mrs. Pollifax wondered if she had interrupted
the major in prayer, but then she remembered where she was and
put this thought aside. Curiosity drew her closer. "Is that some
form of Yogi you're practicing?" she asked.

"*Zott*, no," he said heavily.

Mrs. Pollifax knew by now that *Zott* was a derivative of Zeus
and a favored exclamation of the country; this much had not
changed since 1919; and she nodded.

"The electric wire, there is only the one—ah! I have it!" The
major climbed laboriously to his feet, and finding her still watching
him he added, "For my heat brick. The electric is difficult here."

"Yes, it would be," she agreed. "How on earth do you get
electricity? Surely not from the valley."

"*Zott*, no," he said, untangling the wire that ran from the
floor to his desk. "We have, what do you call it, a big machine in
the other building. But here, only the one wire."

Mrs. Pollifax brightened. "Oh yes, a generator. That's clever.

And this is your heat brick?" She reached out and touched it. "Why, this is what we call a heating pad at home."

"Yes, for the back," he said, nodding. "These stones are hard to live with."

"Back?" repeated Mrs. Pollifax, puzzled.

"My back. Very cold, very sore."

Mrs. Pollifax understood at last. "You mean a cold has settled in your back!"

He nodded morosely. "To get up, to get down, it hurts."

"You poor man," said Mrs. Pollifax, genuinely concerned. "I know exactly what that's like. How long has it been bothering you?"

"Since they moved me here."

Mrs. Pollifax frowned. "Have you tried any deep heat, have you tried massage?"

He only stared at her, uncomprehending, and Mrs. Pollifax made an exasperated sound. "Take off your shirt," she said firmly. "Yes, take it off, I won't hurt you, it's the only thing that really helps. Have you rubbing alcohol?"

"Alcohol?" He reached into a drawer of the desk and dubiously held up a flask of brandy.

"Yes, why not?" she said cheerfully. "Now the shirt, please, and if you would be so kind as to lie across your desk—"

He retreated in alarm.

"No, no, you don't understand, I will rub your back. Massage it. This has . . ." She was making no headway with him. She went to the door and opened it. "Mr. Lulash," she called, "could you please come and translate for me? I want to rub the major's back."

"You want to what?" said Lulash, entering.

"His heating pad will do very little for him, he needs a sound back rub. Please ask him to remove his shirt and lie across his desk."

With a grin Lulash translated the words. Major Vassovic said, "Ah!" and then, "Oh?"

"He did not understand you," said Lulash. "He thought you were insisting he lie down and drink the alcohol and his instructions are to never drink while on duty."

"I see." The major was removing his shirt.

"He says," translated Lulash, "that he did not bring long

winter underwear here because it is summer. He did not expect a stone house."

"Nor did any of us," murmured Mrs. Pollifax, her eyes running expertly over his back. Once the major had lowered himself to the desk she rolled up her sleeves, poured brandy into the palm of one hand, and approached him. She was a knowledgeable back-rubber; at one period in her life she had visited a Swedish masseur and had seen no reason why she should not apply the same principles to the backs of her family. Experience added a special fillip to her technique, and now she pummeled, pushed, kneaded and slapped the major's back with enthusiasm. His small shrieks of protest presently became sighs of joy.

"He will need a blanket now," Mrs. Pollifax told Lulash. "He must lie still for several minutes before getting up." Lulash nodded and returned with a blanket. Mrs. Pollifax threw it over the major and collapsed into the desk chair. "Now that was good exercise," she said happily. "I haven't done it in years."

"Was good, good," grunted the major from the desk.

"You must be extremely careful in getting up," she told him sternly. "When the muscles are inflamed and swollen they push little bones out of place. This is what hurts you."

Lulash went to the water cooler and brought back two paper cups. "Allow me," he said, and with a bow poured brandy into each cup.

Mrs. Pollifax said doubtfully, "I suppose I could call it a late afternoon cocktail?" She accepted the drink with her right hand. Very casually she dangled her left hand in the vicinity of the ammunition drawer and felt for the protruding brass key.

"Half-past three," said Lulash, and seated himself in the chair on the other side of the desk. He and Mrs. Pollifax exchanged friendly smiles across the lumpy, prostrate form of Major Vassovic. "*Skoal!*" called Lulash, lifting his cup.

"*Skoal,*" returned Mrs. Pollifax gaily, pulling open the drawer behind her. In the comfortable silence that followed she filled her hand with gun cartridges and pushed the drawer closed again.

The lumpy figure stirred and sat up. "But that was delicious," gasped the major. "You do that for my back again sometime?"

Mrs. Pollifax beamed at him. She now had four gun clips in

her lap and was feeling congenial indeed. "Of course, Major. At least until they decide how to dispose of me."

Lulash said in surprise, "Dispose? Dispose?"

She said cheerfully, "Oh yes, I'm sure they'll eventually have to kill me. What else can they do with me?"

"But you cannot be dangerous," protested Lulash.

Mrs. Pollifax shrugged. "Does anyone care? This isn't a democracy, you know."

"They do not shoot people in a democracy?"

"Oh dear, no. Not unless they've committed a murder, and even then—no, really, people do not get shot as punishment in a democracy." She sipped her brandy appreciatively. "And then it's in the hands of a jury, you know. It takes twelve people to decide on a person's guilt."

Major Vassovic stared at her. "Twelve officers, you mean."

"Oh no," said Mrs. Pollifax. "Twelve people. Citizens. Ordinary people. Working people."

The two men stared at her incredulously. Major Vassovic said, "But then no one would ever be found guilty. Who instructs them?"

Mrs. Pollifax smiled forgivingly. "They are free to make up their own minds from the evidence that's presented."

Major Vassovic looked thoroughly alarmed; Lulash looked interested. "Explain to me how it works," he said.

Mrs. Pollifax hesitated, not from any lack of articulateness but because she was holding four gun cartridges in her lap. She said, "First I must put on my jacket, I'm cold." She left her chair and walked over to the stool upon which she had arranged her jacket so that it would conceal *Albania: Land of Primitive Beauty*. Slipping the gun clips into the pocket she shrugged on her jacket and managed to squeeze the book tightly under one arm. Her activity reminded Major Vassovic of his own condition and he started buttoning on his tunic.

"It works like this," Mrs. Pollifax said, and returning to the desk drew pencil and paper toward her and began diagraming a courtroom. "The judge sits here," she announced, drawing a circle, "and we will call this the jury box and put twelve circles here. You will be one of them, and I will be another, and the major will be a third."

"Please no," said the major in alarm.

"It's only on paper," she told him soothingly. "And we will pretend that you, Mr. Lulash, are a farmer, and I am a housewife, and Major Vassovic sells ties in a store."

"What are our political affiliations?" asked Lulash quickly.

"Oh, but that doesn't matter at all."

"But it must."

She shook her head. "No, because this is a court of law and justice. We would be concerned only with truth."

Lulash said, "But surely the jury would have been appointed by party officials?"

"No," said Mrs. Pollifax firmly. "Not appointed at all. No commitments, no ties, no obligations. Absolute freedom to decide."

"*Zott,*" cried Major Vassovic despairingly.

"Then surely the judge is appointed?"

"Yes," said Mrs. Pollifax.

"Ah!" cried Lulash triumphantly.

"But the judge has nothing to do with the verdict," emphasized Mrs. Pollifax. "He cannot decide whether a man is guilty or innocent. That responsibility rests with the twelve jurors."

Lulash looked bewildered. "He cannot tell the twelve jurors they're wrong? He cannot punish them if they bring in the wrong verdict?"

"Absolutely not," replied Mrs. Pollifax.

From the doorway General Hoong said coldly, "Good afternoon, Mrs. Pollifax."

Mrs. Pollifax turned. She had not realized before how very much the general's face resembled a fresh brown egg. The skin fitted his bones so snugly that she could not find a single line of laughter or of sadness, and she wondered if he could have had his face lifted. There was something very sinister about a man of forty or fifty who looked so remote and untouched by life. "Good afternoon," she said.

His nostrils quivered fastidiously. "There is a smell of alcohol in this room. Private Lulash, Major Vassovic, have you been drinking?"

"It's entirely my fault," intervened Mrs. Pollifax. "I was allowed a small walk and I had a touch of sunstroke. They offered me the brandy for medicinal purposes."

Seeing the general's gaze drift from Lulash to Major Vassovic she continued in a firmer voice. "I'm glad you are here, General Hoong. I would like permission to extract the bullet from Mr. Farrell's arm. You have seen Mr. Farrell today?"

The general's glance rested upon her and his left eyebrow lifted. Mrs. Pollifax was relieved to see that this caused two lines above the brow without cracking the surface of his face.

"It is obvious to me," she said in her most imperious Woman's Club voice, "that he will die if the bullet is not removed. This will make General Perdido quite angry, don't you think? I don't believe he will appreciate his dying at all. Not at all."

The general's gaze lingered on her face. He might have been pondering a piece of rare jade, a beautiful sunset or the fish he was to eat for dinner.

"I will need a knife," she went on recklessly. "A knife and some boiling water to sterilize it, and a bandage. This is possible?"

The general's right eyebrow was lifted this time. His lips moved. "It is possible, yes."

"Good."

Gradually something resembling an expression stirred the shell-like surface of his face. "There is nothing else?" His voice was brushed with the most delicate sarcasm.

"I don't believe so," Mrs. Pollifax told him, ignoring the sarcasm. "Your food is quite good and I'm growing accustomed to the mattress. It's not exactly posturpedic, but it's firm. No, I think this is all."

He bowed slightly. "I am so glad."

"And now I believe I'd like to go back to my cell and lie down," she finished. "If you will excuse me?"

Major Vassovic at once produced the key and led her down the hall. As he swung the cell door open for her he whispered, "Tomorrow, same time?"

Feeling like a paramour making an assignation Mrs. Pollifax told him gravely, "Tomorrow, yes." She entered the cell to discover that the Gremlin had disappeared and Farrell was asleep. As soon as the door closed behind her she hurried to her cot and hid the book on Albania under the mattress. Only then did she bring from the pocket of her Guatemalan jacket the items she had stolen from the ammunition drawer. It was a little like opening up a mystery prize, she reflected, as she held them up to the light to see what she had won. Carrying them to the nearest window slit for a closer scrutiny she found that two belonged to a Beretta pistol, and two to something called a Nambu. Very good, she thought, nodding. Next she wondered where to hide them and she decided at last upon diversification; she placed one in her purse, another inside her underclothes in a time-honored place of concealment, a third she trusted to a hole in her mattress and the fourth she hid in Farrell's mattress. Since Farrell was still asleep she took out Lulash's book and turned again to the map.

"What, no solitaire?" asked Farrell suddenly from across the room, turning his head toward her.

"For the moment I have something better to do," she told him absently. "Lulash has loaned me a book on Albania, much prized by him in spite of its being published in 1919. What is particularly interesting is that it has a very good map of the country. He really should have remembered it was there and removed it."

Farrell's mouth dropped open. "Good God," he gasped, "you can't possibly be thinking of escape!"

She thought it tactless to mention the alternative. Instead she said calmly, "But why not? You don't think I want to spend my sunset years in Albania, do you? The winters are extremely cold, the book says so, as cold as the summers are hot. If I only apply myself there must be a way to get us out, preferably before General Perdido returns."

"Us?" echoed Farrell in astonishment. "You said 'us'?"

Mrs. Pollifax looked up from her map in surprise. "You can't possibly think I'd leave you behind!"

Farrell shook his head. "My dear Duchess, it must have escaped your notice that for most of today I've been off my rocker with fever. I also have a broken right leg and a bullet in my right arm."

Mrs. Pollifax nodded indifferently. "Yes, I'd noticed. But I've asked for permission to cut the bullet out of your arm, and if you can bear another operation—I know it won't be pleasant—then your temperature ought to go down, and that will leave only the healing leg."

"That's right—only a broken leg," rasped Farrell.

Mrs. Pollifax returned impatiently to her book. "It isn't clear to me yet, but I'm hoping it will come. The simplest way would be lowering you over the cliff, but we would need at least a hundred feet of rope for that. We ought to have a gun, too, and some sort of clothes for disguise, and food, and I suppose to be really efficient we ought to have a compass, although if the stars are out—"

She found that Farrell was regarding her as if she had gone mad. He said with sarcasm, "A rope, a gun, a disguise, food and a compass—anything else? How about ordering a limousine?"

"I don't think you're being at all receptive," she told him stiffly.

It was their first quarrel. He said scornfully, "I think you've gone off your rocker, too, Duchess, but if it gives you something to keep your mind occupied—well, have lots and lots of fun. And now if you'll forgive me I'll go back to sleep, which is the best escape *I* can think of. You know—'sleep that knits the raveled sleeve of care' and all that?"

"Coward," said Mrs. Pollifax with a sniff, and then was sorry for the word as soon as it left her lips. But it was too late; Farrell's eyes were closed and a kind of gentle snore was issuing from his half-open mouth. Mrs. Pollifax, watching him, wondered if he knew how becoming a beard would be to the shape of his face. A few more days, she mused, and he would have a very striking one, and then with a start she went back to *Albania: Land of Primitive Beauty.*

The boiling water, a penknife and a towel arrived at dusk, brought in by Major Vassovic, who looked disapproving and then somewhat distraught as he added that he had been ordered to remain behind to help with the operation. In a gruff, nervous voice he addressed the walrus-moustached man who now shared their cell. "His name is Adhem Nexdhet," he told Mrs. Pollifax. "I have asked him to hold the candle for you, Lulash is not on duty tonight."

"For me," thought Mrs. Pollifax, "he means hold the candle for me," and her knees suddenly felt very wobbly. She put down

the pack of playing cards and stood up, trying to recall the dozens
of splinters and the broken glass she had extracted from small
knees and fingers in her lifetime, but finding little comfort in the
thought. She remembered only one bit of advice given her by a
doctor: never bleed for the patient, let him do the bleeding, you
just get the job done.

Mrs. Pollifax took the knife from Major Vassovic, saw to its
sterilization, glanced just once at Farrell, whose eyes were open,
and proceeded to go about getting the job done. She mentally
granted to Farrell his own right to dignity, assuming he could
manage his own hell just as she must somehow manage hers.
Quickly and ruthlessly, knowing that speed was kinder than gentle-
ness, she probed the rotting flesh for the bullet. When the knife
met its hard resistance she thanked heaven that it was not embedded in a muscle and with one swift, cruel turning of the knife she
lifted the pellet to the surface and heard it drop to the stone floor.
Not knowing how else to complete the job she poured the hot
water over the infected skin, and this at last brought from Farrell a
yelp of pain.

"I wondered when we'd hear from you," she told him.

"They'd never hire you at Mount Sinai, Duchess." His face
glistened with perspiration.

"Really? And I was planning to apply next week—what a
pity."

He grinned weakly. "Just can't keep you from volunteering
for things, can we. Have you finished your butchery?"

"Quite."

Farrell nodded and turned his face to the wall, and Mrs. Pollifax realized what he had already endured and must still face, and
the resolve to escape hardened in her. She would not, *must* not,
save Farrell only for General Perdido. Even if an escape attempt
brought only death it was certainly a cleaner way to die than by
whatever means the general was planning. In that moment she
realized they were going to have to try it, and with this all her
doubts ended; it was no longer a matter of *whether* but *when* and
how.

Major Vassovic had disappeared, leaving her the basin of water and several towels. Mrs. Pollifax dipped a towel into the water
and began swabbing blood from Farrell's mattress.

"You did that well," said Adhem Nexdhet suddenly. "Without emotion."

Mrs. Pollifax stepped back in surprise. "You really do speak English," she said accusingly.

He smiled wryly. "But you already knew this, did you not? I am not unaware of the little trick Mr. Farrell played on me. Allow me," he said, taking the towel from her. "You are not young, you must be tired."

Mrs. Pollifax backed to her cot and sat down. "I suppose you're also in the secret police then!"

"Yes, I am Colonel Nexdhet of the Sigurimi."

Mrs. Pollifax winced. "I see. That makes you the major's superior then." She sighed. "It also makes it especially kind of you to help. Thank you."

He shrugged. "A good officer knows when to break rules here and there. Major Vassovic is not a good officer, except for his rigid obedience, which is the mark of a follower, not a leader. He is afraid of life." The colonel wrung out one towel and picked up another, saying over his shoulder, "There is one thing that General Perdido does not know about you, Mrs. Pollifax."

Startled, she said, "Oh? What is that?"

He turned to look at her. "He does not know how well you perform under pressure."

There was a long silence. Nexdhet's words were ambiguous, but the man's stare made Mrs. Pollifax feel distinctly uneasy. Until now the comic moustache had obscured the fact that his eyes were both penetrating and intelligent. As pleasantly as possible Mrs. Pollifax said, "I'm glad to hear that."

"You are more than you appear to be," he said, smiling.

"Really?" He was clearly testing her, she decided. "I have no idea how I appear."

"It is very interesting to me," continued Nexdhet. "I underestimated you at first glance. To General Perdido you are an embarrassing mistake. Now I wonder if he may not have underestimated you as well."

"What you have underestimated," retorted Mrs. Pollifax firmly, "is my experience in first aid. However, if it pleases you to think otherwise—"

The cell door opened. The guard who did not speak English

came in to collect the dinner trays and the conversation was mercifully ended. Mrs. Pollifax spread out her playing cards for a last game of solitaire, but whenever she glanced up she was aware of Colonel Nexdhet watching her with a mixture of speculation and amusement.

Chapter Fourteen

The next morning Mrs. Pollifax began to plan in earnest. When Colonel Nexdhet was removed from their cell, presumably for his exercise, she brought from her purse everything that could be used as a bribe or trade, and spread the items across the little table. There were three lipsticks, two of them brand-new and in smart bejeweled gold cases; a tin of Band-Aids, her wallet containing five dollars and thirteen cents; traveler's checks amounting to fifty dollars (the rest were in her suitcase in Mexico City) and a small memo pad with gold pencil. To these she reluctantly added her Guatemalan jacket, and distributed the small items between the two pockets of the jacket, keeping only the memo pad. On one of its pages she had jotted down the few Albanian words with which the author of *Land of Primitive Beauty* had salted his book. The words were as follows:

dunti—hope chest
shkep—rock
zee—voice
rhea—cloud
gjumë—sleep
bjer—bring
pesë—five
zgarm—fire
natë—night

It was meager fare for her purposes, but after an hour spent in arranging and rearranging the words she had selected four of them for the message she wished to write in Albanian. It was a crude affair but it was the best that she could manage, and now she carefully copied out the four words on a fresh sheet of memo paper. *Night—Sleep—Bring Voice.* To this she added hopefully in English, since everyone else here seemed to speak it, "We are two Americans here, who are you?"

"What's up?" asked Farrell from his cot, watching her.

"Nothing, nothing at all," said Mrs. Pollifax hastily, and slipped the memo into her pocket. "How are you feeling?"

"Weak but human at last."

She nodded. "Your temperature is almost normal, I felt your forehead while you were asleep." She stood up as the cell door groaned open and a guard appeared. "I believe it's time for my walk now," she told Farrell.

From his cot he said dryly, "You look like a cat planning to swallow the canary, Duchess. Whatever you're up to it won't work, you know. This is Albania."

"Yes, Albania, land of primitive beauty," she told him, and swept from the cell.

She had no more than closed the door behind her, however, when a familiar voice said, "There you are, Mrs. Pollifax, I have been waiting for you."

It was Colonel Nexdhet, the very man she would have preferred to avoid. He wore a pair of binoculars around his neck and carried a book under his arm. "We can walk together," he said.

"You are to guard me?" she inquired coldly, and then as they entered the guardroom she said warmly, "Good morning, Major Vassovic, and how is your back today?"

"Ah, Zoje Pollifax," said the major, beaming. "It is still sore, yes, but last night I sleep like the baby."

"Mrs. Pollifax," cried Lulash, coming in from outside and holding the door open for her. "You have good walk before the sun climbs high?"

"Thank you, I hope to," replied Mrs. Pollifax.

"Take my sunglasses, please," insisted Lulash, peeling them from his eyes. He winked. "Remember we are jurors, you and I."

"What did that mean?" asked Colonel Nexdhet as they emerged into the brilliant sun.

"Nothing important," Mrs. Pollifax assured him airily. She stopped a moment, adjusting to the bright tawny landscape, and then moved on. "There are so many of you here to guard so few of us, it seems such waste."

"We will go in this direction," said Colonel Nexdhet, gesturing to the east. "No, it is not waste. There are other prisoners in the larger building."

"I didn't know that. How long have you been here, Colonel?"

"Oh, for several months. I was brought here to be second in command to General Hoong."

"You must find it bleak?"

"At times. I take many walks, I fancy myself as a bird watcher." He gestured toward the binoculars around his neck. "I enjoy walks."

"So I gather," she said dryly.

He helped her across a deep cut in the earth, and they began to climb a little, toward the forest.

"And do you enjoy being a colonel in the Sigurimi?" she asked.

He shrugged. "It is my job." He looked at her and smiled. "You question everything, and this is good. But you doubt nobody, and this is bad. We are neither of us young, you and I, we are each nearing the end of long lives and so can speak frankly. I observe in you the desire to trust, even here. This is weakness in a human being, a foolish thing, the desire to lean."

Mrs. Pollifax followed him among the trees, her face thoughtful. She had already forgotten that he made her uneasy. "No," she said honestly, "no, I don't think I agree with you. I don't lean on people, as you put it. It only comforts me to know that people are there. You don't find this to be so?"

He looked at her and again she was aware of the tired wisdom in his eyes. "Then it is because you are a woman."

"Perhaps. You mean you trust no one at all?"

"No one but myself."

"Why?" asked Mrs. Pollifax.

He shrugged, and helped her over a fallen log. "That is only common sense. Perhaps I have seen too much of life, I don't know. I am sixty-three, I have perhaps watched too many knives in the back, too many sudden changes of the face. Nothing endures except the *idea*, the *mind*. I served Albania under the Turks, I served her under King Zog. We were friends with Mussolini and then Mussolini turned on us and conquered us and I fought in the resistance then, for communism. After the war it was Hoxher who came to power and ruled, with Russia our friend. Now we have quarreled with Russia and it is the Red Chinese who help us." He shrugged again. "It is the way life is. Nothing endures except the idea. This alone is clear, pure, not soiled by change."

Mrs. Pollifax nodded. "Yes, you have seen too much of life— the bitter side, at least."

"In the Balkans, in Albania, life *is* bitter," he said.

Mrs. Pollifax considered. "Of course by the idea you mean the political idea—communism—but aren't you wrong to say it never changes? There is this matter of Stalinism—"

"One adapts," he said. With a wry smile twisting his preposterous moustache he asked, "Politically you are what?"

"Republican," acknowledged Mrs. Pollifax. "Although twice I voted for Adlai Stevenson—*such* a charming man."

He smiled. "Then you, too, adapt." He touched her arm and directed her to the right. "We have gone far enough," he said. "We will follow the cliff back. There is a good view here, you will see the valley from a new angle."

There was indeed an excellent view, and she was grateful to stop walking for a minute. "Beautiful, is it not?" said Colonel Nexdhet, standing beside her. "And those men below, how small, like ants."

"Yes, I just noticed them," said Mrs. Pollifax. "What on earth are they building down there?"

"A missile site," he said without interest. "Seeing Man like this reminds me always of Man's fragileness, don't you agree?"

A missile site, he had said. *A missile site?* A shock of excitement moved down Mrs. Pollifax's spine disc by disc. The Chinese were building a missile site in Albania? She forgot her failure in Mexico; if she could bring news of a missile site to Mr. Carstairs then she would not have failed as a spy at all. It was obvious that Colonel Nexdhet would not have mentioned such a thing if he was not absolutely sure that both his secret and Mrs. Pollifax would remain in Albania, but this was only a new goad. Aloud she said disapprovingly, "They would do better to build roads, why do you need a missile site?"

Colonel Nexdhet gave her his arm. "Shall we start back? The Chinese are very patient, Mrs. Pollifax, they build for the future. They are not taken seriously yet as a major power, but see what they have already accomplished! They have fought and won a small slice of India. They have their finger in a dozen pies in southeast Asia. They are proving extremely successful in infiltrating Latin America—every Communist party there has its Mao-ist wing. They now have trade relations with most of western Europe and with Canada, Australia and Japan. They have exploded a primitive atom bomb. But most of all they are here to help and to protect my country, which you must not forget is a European country. The Chinese have arrived in Europe."

"Good heavens," said Mrs. Pollifax as she absorbed the meaning of all that he said. "It's really quite shocking."

"If you are an American, yes," he said with a shrug. "As for the Chinese—they look ahead."

"Very enterprising of them," she said weakly, and wondered how to change the subject before she gave away her profound interest. "But I have not seen any of your birds, Colonel Nexdhet."

He said gravely, "That is what makes bird-watching so fascinating, Mrs. Pollifax. There are so few of them up here along the cliffs."

Presently they came out into the hot sun again, and the stone buildings lay ahead.

Mrs. Pollifax had left her cell at half-past nine in the morning. It was quarter-past five when she returned, flushed from the sun and a string of small, happy accomplishments. She found Farrell livid.

"Don't you ever do this to me again," he sputtered, sitting up on his cot and glaring at her. "Don't you dare."

"Do what?" she said in astonishment.

"Go off for a whole day like this. I've been nearly out of my mind picturing you in front of a firing squad or being stretched on a rack somewhere being tortured. And now you have the audacity, the unmitigated gall to walk in here looking happy."

She walked over and kissed him fondly on the top of his head. "Bless you for worrying. I'm sorry."

"Then try to look sorry," he snapped. "I'm a very sick man. Where have you been?"

"Oh, here and there," she said airily. "Walking with Colonel Nexdhet, picnicking on the cliff with Lulash, rubbing Major Vas-

sovic's back. We have even been discussing holding a small party in
the guardroom tomorrow night."

"Party!" exploded Farrell.

"Yes, you see Lulash knows some old Albanian mountain
songs and he wants to sing them to me, and Colonel Nexdhet will
bring a musical instrument and Major Vassovic went so far as to
volunteer something alcoholic for the occasion, and one thing led
to another, and now it's to be a party."

Farrell stared at her open-mouthed. After a minute he closed
his mouth with a snap. "All right," he said crossly, "what exactly
have you been up to, Duchess?"

She sat down beside him and drew from the pocket of her
jacket a sheet of onionskin paper and placed it in his lap. "For
tracing the map in Lulash's book," she whispered. Drawing out a
flat, round, metal case she added it to the sheet of paper. "And I
won't have to tell you what this is."

He pried open its lid and whistled. "A compass! But how on
earth—and who—"

"I traded with the major after I rubbed his back. I said I was
getting rid of my effects early. It cost two new lipsticks, one Petal
Pink and one Hug Me."

"Yes, but didn't he wonder at a *compass?*"

She smiled reminiscently. "He gave me several things to
choose from in return, it was quite fun. He offered an old watch, a
pen and this surveyor's compass that has been in the guardroom
for years, he said. Does it work?"

"It moves," Farrell said, frowning over it.

"East," she told him, "would be in the direction of the guardroom, and west behind the wall you're leaning against."

He looked up. "And just how do you know that?"

"Because we traveled into the rising sun when we came here,"
she said. "We arrived from the west, from the city of Shkoder,
where our plane landed. And according to the map the River Drin,
which I see from the precipice, flows from east to west, into the
Adriatic, which places Yugoslavia just behind us."

She had captured his attention at last. He closed the lid of the
compass with a snap and said quietly, "Perhaps you'd better tell me
exactly what you're thinking of, Duchess, if it's not too late to ask.
You really *have* been busy."

"Of course I'll tell you," she said warmly. "I'm only an amateur, you know—although a very determined one, I warn you—and I desperately need your professional advice. Have you been trained in escape procedures?"

"Afraid not," he said in amusement.

"Oh, what a pity. Well, I guess that can't be helped."

"Good of you to see it that way."

"What I do think I ought to tell you, though—and I would have sooner if you hadn't been in such a state—is about the person in the cell next to us." She described in a whisper the rappings on the wall that had taken place on the day that Farrell jumped from the cliff. "I've heard nothing since, you understand, but this afternoon, walking around the building, I dropped a note through the window slit of the cell next to us."

"A note?" echoed Farrell. "But this is Albania, and an Albanian jail. I really doubt that whoever it is would speak English, you know."

"Well, it wasn't the most articulate message, but I made it up out of scraps of Albanian from Lulash's book," explained Mrs. Pollifax. "It said *night—sleep—bring voice*, if I remember correctly, but I did rather hope our neighbor would get the point that we'd like to hear from him again somehow." Footsteps echoed in the hall and Mrs. Pollifax seized compass and paper, stuffed them into her purse and moved back to her cot. She was seated on it fingering her deck of cards when the door opened and Adhem Nexdhet—no, Colonel Nexdhet, she remembered—walked in. "Have a good walk?" she inquired pleasantly, and was suddenly all too conscious of the contraband book under her mattress, the gun cartridges distributed around the cell, the food and compass in her purse.

"What is this game you always play?" he asked, stopping beside her table.

"Different kinds," she told him. "All sorts of solitaire. Very healthy for the mind and the nerves, I enjoy it. Has General Perdido returned yet?" she added casually.

"He comes late Thursday, in the evening," Adhem Nexdhet said absently, his eyes on the cards she was arranging.

Mrs. Pollifax managed a rueful laugh. "And I don't even know what day it is today!"

"Tuesday." Nexdhet abruptly sat down beside her. "Show me," he said. "The cards in a circle, what is the key to this?"

"It's called Clock Solitaire," replied Mrs. Pollifax, and began to explain the rules. But her heart was thudding at the realization that General Perdido would return on Thursday, and already this was Tuesday. . . . At once the general's face came very clearly to her mind: impassive and observant with only the eyes, sans spectacles, betraying shrewdness and cruelty. Over the cards she glanced at Farrell and saw him chewing reflectively on the moustache that would in time resemble Adhem Nexdhet's walrus-type adornment —if ever given the time. Haste makes waste, she thought a little wildly; escape in haste, repent in leisure; she wondered if Farrell remembered any of General Perdido's parting promises; he had been feverish and in pain and she hoped he did not recall them. It was far kinder for him not to know what lay ahead of him.

But only two more days, and they had made almost no arrangements . . . !

Then something else occurred to her and she said in shocked astonishment, "But why is he coming back so soon? Is it you who told him Farrell is well enough to be questioned by then?"

Colonel Nexdhet met her glance with a faint smile. "I believe I warned you that you must trust no one," he pointed out gently.

On Wednesday morning during her walk along the cliff Mrs. Pollifax selected two round, fist-sized rocks from the ground and took them back to the cell and hid them. She then borrowed Lulash's sunglasses and walked a little farther, toward the clusters of fir through which she and Farrell had ridden on donkeys. What they needed most of all, she knew, was a crutch for Farrell; a very stout crutch or walking stick. Without this they might as well abandon all hope of reaching the valley.

"Lulash," she called across the rocks. He was sunning himself on the bench outside while he cleaned his gun. "Lulash, I've had the nicest idea." She walked up to him, smiling. "But first I'll need your permission and your help."

"What is that?" asked Lulash.

"It's Mr. Farrell," she explained. "He cannot take walks, as I do—"

"He would not be allowed," Lulash said bluntly.

"I know that, and it's very difficult for him, shut up all day in that cell. Lulash, I should so like to hang some branches in the cell. Fresh green branches."

"Branches?" repeated Lulash, scowling.

"Yes, branches. Surely it would be all right? Surely no one would mind?"

Lulash's brow cleared and he smiled indulgently. "Every woman, she likes to make things pretty, eh?"

"Uh, yes," said Mrs. Pollifax. "You do understand, I'm so glad. Should I ask the major's permission, too?"

"That I can do for you," Lulash said gallantly.

Major Vassovic not only gave permission but announced that he would come too, and they set out for the line of scattered firs together, with Mrs. Pollifax pointing out the beauties of the sky—a horrid bleached blue—the uniqueness of the rocks, and the wild scenery above them. She talked mercilessly until they reached the trees, whereupon she became reverently silent, and for such a long time that the men became restive.

"This one—or this one?" she asked at last, touching first one branch and then another. She stood still, struck with apparently spontaneous inspiration. "Or do you suppose we could take back a very small tree?"

"Tree?" echoed Major Vassovic in astonishment.

"Tree?" repeated Lulash.

"This little one, for instance. It looks just like a Christmas tree."

"But this is summer," pointed out Major Vassovic.

"Yes," Mrs. Pollifax said, nodding, and then, ruthlessly, she delivered the *coup de grace*. "But I will not—I will not be here—I will not see another Christmas."

That did it. Lulash angrily tightened his lips. "She will have the little tree," he told Major Vassovic.

"Of course," nodded the major, and at once twisted the tree to test the depth of its roots. Lulash gave a small assist and the young tree was uprooted.

"Lovely," murmured Mrs. Pollifax with feeling, and with the tree between them like a fourth member of the party they marched back to the stone building.

* * *

"What on earth!" exclaimed Farrell as Lulash leaned the tree against the wall of the cell.

"Isn't it beautiful? Christmas in August," said Mrs. Pollifax, and added a warning frown because Colonel Nexdhet was seated on his cot reading a newspaper on which the banner head proclaimed the words ZERI I POPULIT. But he had already begun folding up his paper, and presently, with a nod, he went out wearing his binoculars.

When he had gone Mrs. Pollifax sat down on her cot and said tartly, "I loathe myself. I have just given the most nauseating performance of my life—I, Emily Pollifax! I was girlish, I was kittenish, I very nearly fluttered my eyelashes at those two men, and at my age! Sickening."

"You didn't," exclaimed Farrell, grinning.

She nodded. "I pulled out all the stops. I nearly had them weeping for me."

"Not over this—this ragged specimen of evergreen, I hope."

Mrs. Pollifax said crossly, "That ragged-looking specimen of evergreen, my dear Farrell, is shortly going to be transformed into the crutch that is going to help you walk across Albania to the Adriatic Sea."

Farrell whistled. "I've done it again, Duchess—my apologies." His glance ran appraisingly over the trunk and he nodded. "Yes, the shape is there all right."

"No crosspiece," she explained, "but we can use pieces of mattress and blanket to wad the top and protect the arm. Did you finish tracing the map?"

"Yes, in spite of Nexdhet. That man wanders in and out—if he has to keep up the pretense of being a fellow prisoner I wish he'd put his heart into it and suffer along with me. He obviously has bathroom privileges, a discrimination I deeply resent, and he never speaks to me, he only grunts."

"But you finished the tracing!"

"Oh yes. And something else happened, fortunately while Nexdhet wasn't here. About half an hour ago *this* fluttered through the window." He brought from his pocket a slip of paper.

"Our neighbor!" gasped Mrs. Pollifax. "He did reply after all!"

"In a fashion," said Farrell, and watched with ironic eyes as she held the slip of paper up to the light.

On it had been printed in beautiful script the following message:

天
言
林
右
人
好
不
好

Chapter Fifteen

That evening Colonel Nexdhet followed their dinner trays out of the cell, and as soon as he had gone Mrs. Pollifax crossed the room to Farrell and sat down on the cot beside him. She had spent the afternoon in playing solitaire and doing some private assessing which had definitely not aided her digestive juices. She was also beginning to scratch and she feared that she had lice, but this did not concern her nearly so much as the knowledge that within twenty-four hours General Perdido would be appearing. The general, she reflected, was the more compelling irritant.

"He's gone?" whispered Farrell, sitting up. They did little talking at all while Adhem Nexdhet was with them.

"He may not be gone long," Mrs. Pollifax reminded him. She thought that Farrell was no less haggard, but he looked brighter-eyed and more interested than she had seen him in a long time.

"All right, let's go over the list."

Mrs. Pollifax nodded. "We have one tree." She gave it a reproachful glance. "But no earthly way of cutting it down to a crutch."

On her memo pad he wrote *knife or facsimile*. "Go on."

She continued gloomily. "We have four magazine clips, apparently for Beretta or Nambu pistols but unfortunately we have no Beretta or Nambu pistols."

Farrell winced as he made a note of this.

"We have enough cheese and stale bread for two people—two pygmies, really—for two days. But no water."

"Mmm."

"We have one compass that works—we think. And one tracing of a 1919 map of Albania. And two rocks."

"Ah—rocks!" Farrell brightened. "But let's take the items

one by one. The tree first of all: they'd never allow us a saw or a knife. I don't suppose you've seen one lying around that you could, uh, pinch? Make off with?"

"There are at least half a dozen knives in the gun rack in the guardroom," Mrs. Pollifax told him. "But they're under glass and locked up. There's always someone with me, and I doubt if they'd trade a knife."

"No, not likely. I could always ask to shave—"

"I'm sure they'd want the razor blade back."

He nodded, but without appearing in the least discouraged, which pleased Mrs. Pollifax because she was beginning to feel very discouraged indeed. He said, "The branches we can tear off at the last minute with our hands, but we do need a cutting edge to shape the top."

"How do we manage all this with Colonel Nexdhet here in the cell with us?" asked Mrs. Pollifax. "I thought—I mean I picked up one of those rocks thinking we could hit him over the head at the proper time but . . ." She shivered. "I couldn't, you know, could you?"

"Yes."

"But you can't even walk yet."

Farrell smiled faintly. "No, but I haven't been completely idle, Duchess. At night while you and our spy friend are asleep I've been trying to get my strength back. I stand. I do crazy exercises. Look." He got laboriously to his feet and stood, his weight on the good leg. "I don't get dizzy any more. I nearly fell over the first time, I was so lightheaded. I've been exercising my hands and arms, too. Yes, I could hit our friend over the head, at least I can if he gets close enough to me. Let's see those rocks, by the way, and whatever's left of your trading goods."

"Trading goods," repeated Mrs. Pollifax, smiling. "You mean for friendly natives?" She brought out the diminished contents of her pocket. "One lipstick, one handkerchief . . ."

He was examining both as if he had never seen either. "Always use men's handkerchiefs?" he asked with amusement.

"For a number of years, yes. They were my husband's, and so much more substantial."

"Excellent gag," he pointed out.

Mrs. Pollifax brightened. "I didn't think of that."

"One must," he murmured. He had taken apart her lipstick case and was studying it. He ran a finger over the rim of the metal tube and said quickly, "Let's see those rocks, are any of them rough?"

Mrs. Pollifax leaned eagerly over his shoulder. "You mean we may have found a cutting edge?"

"Only a peeling edge, I fear. I'll see if I can chisel a sharper point with the rock. Try to bring back a few more rocks if you're allowed a walk tomorrow. Except that without a gun . . ."

Mrs. Pollifax said reasonably, "But if we escape as far as the guardroom we can steal as many guns as we want."

"Yes, and a knife, too, except we can't leave the crutch until the last minute. It would take too long to make. We're going to have to manage it somehow during the last hour we're here, preferably after our spy has been rendered unconscious."

"And he's so pleasant, I like him," mourned Mrs. Pollifax. "You *will* hit him gently, won't you?"

"Gently, yes, but very thoroughly."

"When should we—that is, what hour tomorrow should we plan on?" asked Mrs. Pollifax timidly. "It will have to be a time when someone unlocks the cell and comes in, Lulash with a tray or whoever's on duty. We hit him over the head, too, I suppose?"

"Everybody. Major Vassovic, too—somehow."

"I could scream or do something like that to bring him in," suggested Mrs. Pollifax, getting into the spirit of the thing. "About six o'clock, do you think?"

Farrell shook his head. "Dinnertime's too early. Too light outside. We don't know how many people are left in the other building, the big one. They might see us stumbling around on the rocks."

Mrs. Pollifax said anxiously, "But if we wait until later, when they bring in the candle, that might be too late. General Perdido may have returned, and I'm sure he'll want to see us right away."

Farrell said firmly, "I'll think of something. I'm better now, trust me. Just don't worry."

"Not worry," echoed Mrs. Pollifax, and at once felt a trembling begin deep down inside her and run along her nerves until she began to shiver uncontrollably. Really this was madness, she realized—absolute madness, none of it could be real, neither Albania nor Farrell nor General Perdido nor this ridiculous cell in which she had been placed as a prisoner—and tomorrow evening they were going to try to escape with two rocks and a Christmas tree turned into a crutch. It was the final touch of madness.

The spasm passed, and Mrs. Pollifax regained her poise and was relieved to see that Farrell had not noticed her moment of weakness. He was staring at their pathetic heap of treasures and saying, "Not bad, really, not bad at all. Their letting you out for walks, and these rocks you picked up, are the two real miracles allowed us. Nobody can ask for more than two miracles, the rest is up to us."

"*I* could ask for another," said Mrs. Pollifax tartly.

He grinned. "Then go ahead, maybe you have more influence than I. But don't turn gloomy on me suddenly. Thanks to that map you spotted in Lulash's book we know fairly well where we are—"

"We think," added Mrs. Pollifax warningly.

"And thanks to your ingeniousness we have weapons, a bit primitive but no less effective."

"Yes, but if only we had a *knife!*"

Farrell said flippantly, "Maybe someone will start throwing knives at that party of yours and you can deftly catch one between your teeth and hide it in your pocket."

Unfortunately there was not a knife to be seen at the party. There were forks—Mrs. Pollifax at once secreted two of them—and various-sized spoons, but no knives, not even dull ones. Mrs. Pollifax might have become despondent again if it were not for the *raki* that Lulash had filched from the wine cellar in the larger building. He and Major Vassovic had obviously begun sampling it already. "Join us," said Lulash with shining eyes.

"I believe I will," said Mrs. Pollifax, and startled them by emptying her glass. "It is extremely sweet of you to have a party for me," she told him with feeling.

"Have an olive," said Lulash, embarrassed. "Have more *raki.*"

"But you have no knives," pointed out Mrs. Pollifax.

"Why do you need a knife?"

"I always eat olives with a knife," Mrs. Pollifax told him hopefully. "A sharp knife."

"Americans do this?"

"Always."

Major Vassovic shook his head. "We have no knives. Try a fork."

Mrs. Pollifax philosophically accepted a second glass of *raki* instead, and was sipping it when Colonel Nexdhet arrived bearing a dish of cheese and what looked like a zither. Mrs. Pollifax's reaction to his arrival was ambivalent: she felt extremely wary of him and yet as a human being she liked him.

"General Hoong will be coming too," said the colonel. "It seems that he enjoys parties."

"Then I will sing before he comes," said Lulash, and promptly sat down on the floor and crossed his legs. "Please," he told Mrs. Pollifax, gesturing her toward the desk chair. The colonel plucked a few strings of his peculiar-looking instrument and Lulash began to sing a song filled with weird half notes and pauses.

How beautiful is the month of May
When we go with the flocks to the mountains!
On the mountains we heard the voice of the wind.
Do you remember how happy we were?

In the month of May, through the blossoming trees,
The sound of song is abroad on the mountains.
The song of the nightingale, ge re ge re ge re.
Do you remember how happy we were?

I would I had died in that month of May
When you leaned on my breast and kissed me, saying,
"I do not wish to live without you."
Do you remember how happy we were?

I wish again the month of May
That again we might be on the mountains,
That again we might hear the mountain voices.
Have you forgotten those days of beauty?

There was a long silence when he had finished. With his head still bowed Lulash said sadly, "There was a Russian engineer in Tirana, she once said to me those same words. Where is she now?"

Why was it, wondered Mrs. Pollifax crossly, that love songs everywhere had to be so terribly sad? Major Vassovic was noisily blowing his nose and Mrs. Pollifax realized that something was needed to cut the treacly sentiment that was submerging them. She herself did not feel sad; on the contrary the *raki* had left her light-headed and a little belligerent. She turned to Colonel Nexdhet and said with unsteady dignity, "Colonel Nexdhet, I have been thinking about your country and I have decided it was immoral of you to give it to China."

Lulash looked appalled. *"He* gave us to China?"

The colonel said firmly, "Not personally, Private Lulash."

"Then who did? That's what I'd like to know, who did give us to China?"

The colonel shrugged. "Russia moved out, China moved in."

Major Vassovic looked up and said piously, "We needed and wanted China to help us. We gave ourselves to her gratefully, willingly."

Lulash looked insulted. "I didn't have anything to say about it, Major—did you? What this country needs is a George, a George . . ." He turned to Mrs. Pollifax. "Whoever he was you told me about."

"Washington."

"Tha's right, George Washington. And let me tell you something else, Colonel, if anybody was to ask me who to give this country to, I'd say, give it to Mrs. Pollifax."

"Why, thank you, Lulash," she said warmly.

Colonel Nexdhet said mildly, "Lulash, you have had too much *raki.*"

"I? Too much? It is a lie. I will sing to you another song."

"Yes, please do," said Mrs. Pollifax.

"An old song," announced Lulash defiantly. "Full of old heroes who belong to Albanians and nobody else. I will dedicate it to—"

The door opened and General Hoong entered in full dress uniform, medals pinned to his chest, a pistol strapped to his belt.

"To democracy!" shouted Lulash, standing and emptying his glass of *raki.*

General Hoong looked around him and focused at last upon Lulash. He said distastefully, "Private Lulash, you are drunk." To

Mrs. Pollifax he bowed and said, "I have come to your party. I have
brought for it a bottle of vodka."

Mrs. Pollifax said eagerly, "Did you bring a knife with you to
open the bottle?"

"A knife? No, a corkscrew," said the general reprovingly.
"Vassovic, open the vodka."

"At once, General," cried Major Vassovic.

General Hoong removed the pistol from his side, held it at
arm's length and fired six shots into the ceiling. "The party may
begin now," he announced. Seating himself next to Mrs. Pollifax
he said, "I like noise with a party."

"Yes, it is so convivial," she admitted, her eyes on the pistol
which rested upon his knee. "What an interesting-looking gun,
General," she said.

"Since it is empty you may look at it," he said condescend-
ingly. "It is a Japanese pistol, called a Nambu."

"How very odd," murmured Mrs. Pollifax, and held it to the
light admiringly. When she had finished admiring it she placed it
carefully on the top of the desk between them.

"Some vodka?" suggested General Hoong.

"Oh, a very little," she said, and as he leaned forward she
neatly slid the Nambu into her pocket.

"I sing my next song," cried Lulash, and reaching over to
pluck the strings of the instrument on Nexdhet's lap he began
chanting loudly,

>
> *Ahmet Bey, the Beautiful! O! O! Ahmet Bey!*
> *Ahmet, the son of the Mountain Eagle . . .*

From the stricken look on Major Vassovic's face Mrs. Pollifax
at once deduced that this was a subversive song. She moved closer
to General Hoong and said, "It really is so very kind of you to join
us. Very considerate."

His empty eyes turned to look at her. "A general is always
alone," he said.

"But soon General Perdido will be back and you can be alone
together."

He said fastidiously, "Perdido is a barbarian."

Mrs. Pollifax thought about this and nodded, "Yes, he is."

General Hoong sighed. "I am not the happiest of men."

"I'm sorry," Mrs. Pollifax told him with sincerity. "I can quite understand why, of course. You live a very isolated life up here. Have you hobbies?"

"I have a mistress."

Mrs. Pollifax considered this frank statement and gamely nodded. "Yes, that would help to pass the time."

"And I write poetry."

"Do you really! I wish that I might hear some."

"My most recent one I have committed to memory. I will recite it for you."

"Please do," said Mrs. Pollifax, and wished that Lulash would end his interminable song about Ahmet Bey.

Closing his eyes General Hoong recited in a sonorous voice:

> *Pale moon torn by white clouds:*
> *Spool of purest light.*
> *Enchanted. Timeless.*
> *Without heart, lacking grief.*
> *I gaze, and wish my soul*
> *Lacked heart and bore no grief.*

"But that is charming," said Mrs. Pollifax.

"Yes," he said simply.

"I had no idea you were so sensitive, General Hoong. I had no idea you suffered so. You seem so—so impervious to the demands of your job."

"I suffer," he announced firmly.

"Then you really must find another job," she urged him sympathetically. "You certainly must be qualified for some work where you don't have to shoot people, or beat them, or torture them to death."

"Job?" he said, frowning. "Job?" He sighed and drained his glass of vodka. "There is nothing wrong with my job. It is my mistress who causes me torment." He stopped talking and began staring broodingly into space.

Lulash had reached the end of his song. He said to Mrs. Pollifax, "Now you must take a turn and sing to us a song of your country."

"I?" said Mrs. Pollifax.

"Yes, yes, for it must be a beautiful country, a country of justice," cried Lulash exuberantly. "Maybe one day Albania too will be like that, let us all drink a toast to that hope."

Major Vassovic gently belched. "Shplendid idea." He lifted his glass.

Colonel Nexdhet was smiling mockingly. "Well, Mrs. Pollifax?"

Mrs. Pollifax accepted the challenge, arose and bowed to General Hoong. "We have your permission to drink Lulash's toast, General Hoong?"

General Hoong roused a little from his reverie. "What? Oh yes, I like noise with a party."

"To the United States of America," said Mrs. Pollifax in a ringing voice. Remaining on her feet, however unsteadily, she sang one chorus of "God Bless America." It was on this note, carrying with her the general's Nambu pistol but still lacking a knife, that Mrs. Pollifax withdrew from the party, pleading weariness.

"I tried," said Mrs. Pollifax, sitting on the edge of her cot and staring sadly at Farrell. "I tried to steal a knife, but all I could bring back was the pistol."

Farrell was still admiring it. "At this moment, Duchess, the odds against our escaping have just shrunken by about five hundred."

"But it isn't a knife," she pointed out. "It's true that you could blow the top of the tree off with a pistol but you can't make a crutch with a pistol."

"Nevertheless, you can't imagine how much more secure I feel," said Farrell. "Get me the cartridges and I'll load it." She gave him the two Nambu clips and he grinned. "You're turning into quite a scavenger, you know. How was the party?"

"Quite dismal, really. Except for Lulash." Mrs. Pollifax smiled reminiscently. "Lulash would like a George Washington for Albania."

"You haven't been planting seeds of insurrection, have you, Duchess?"

"Well, it's a change from planting geraniums," she retorted.

He finished loading the pistol, patted it lovingly and slipped it beneath his mattress. "I strongly advise getting some sleep now, considering what's ahead of us."

The effects of the *raki* were wearing off, leaving Mrs. Pollifax depressed. "Sleep?" she said resentfully. "Why?"

"Because if we're going to be shot tomorrow trying to escape I'd much prefer dying with someone who can say something jaunty, like 'I regret that I have only one life to give for my country,' or—"

"Jaunty!" exclaimed Mrs. Pollifax, but she was smiling. "That's all very well but I didn't bring *Bartlett's Quotations* with me, you know."

"A pity. Do come up with something magnificent, though, will you? Surprise me," he suggested with mischief in his eyes.

At that moment Colonel Nexdhet walked in, but Mrs. Pollifax's sense of humor had returned—Farrell had seen to this—and she realized that she could face the next day, if not with equanimity, at least with a philosophic stoicism. Then she realized that Farrell was pointedly staring at her and she raised her eyebrows questioningly. Slowly and deliberately his glance moved to Nexdhet, who was removing his jacket in preparation for a night's sleep. Mrs. Pollifax's eyes followed and abruptly widened. Colonel Nexdhet was wearing a knife strapped to a sheath on his belt.

"Our third miracle," said Farrell quietly.

Mrs. Pollifax could scarcely believe it, but being of a practical mind she at once said, "You or me?"

Farrell gestured ruefully toward his leg. "You, I'm afraid."

Mrs. Pollifax nodded. She put away her table, yawned elaborately, scratched her leg—lice, obviously—and lay down. "Good night, Colonel Nexdhet," she said sweetly. "It was a lovely party, wasn't it?"

"Oh?" He looked surprised. "Oh yes, good night." He nodded curtly to Farrell and stretched himself full length on his cot. It really was a pity, thought Mrs. Pollifax, that he had to continue sleeping in the cell with them; at his age he must long for clean pajamas, a comfortable mattress and a private room. Then she remembered that at least he had bathroom privileges, and this cut short her pity and she lay on her side with her eyes fixed upon the knife and tried, through the gloom, to figure just how it was affixed to his belt.

Farrell began to snore gently—she did not believe for a moment that he was sleeping—and Nexdhet began to snore loudly.
There were no sounds from the hall or the guardroom. Mrs. Pollifax slowly sat up, the mattress producing even more ominous
rustlings than usual, which only substantiated her suspicion that it
was filled with corn husks. Once in a sitting position she remained
so for a few minutes to make certain the snores continued. She
stood up and waited again before moving slowly toward Nexdhet's
cot. She was nearly there when she was attacked by an almost
irrepressible urge to giggle; she had just remembered that when
she was a child she had been given a part in a school play where she
had to glide like a wraith. After it had been explained to her just
what a wraith was the result had been this same gliding, tight-
hipped movement. Firmly she controlled herself and leaned over
Nexdhet. Neither his breathing nor his snores changed. Her hands
moved to his belt and she fumbled with the strap on the sheath,
gently drawing it up and out. When this had been accomplished
she sank to one knee, and with one hand steadying the bottom of
the sheath she placed the other on the handle of the knife and
pulled. The knife came out easily. Still Nexdhet had not stirred,
and after a moment's hesitation Mrs. Pollifax glided, still wraith-
like, to Farrell's cot.

He was still snoring softly but his left hand reached out,
open-palmed, to accept the knife that she placed in it; then he
turned on his side, his back to her, and Mrs. Pollifax knew he was
hiding it under his mattress. She returned to her own cot and sank
upon it with relief, corn husks and all. Two minutes later she was
asleep.

Chapter Sixteen

In the morning when Mrs. Pollifax awoke she realized at once that a fateful day was beginning. She lay and thought about this dispassionately, almost wonderingly, because to every life there eventually came a moment when one had to accept the fact that the shape, the pattern, the direction of the future was entirely out of one's hands, to be decided unalterably by chance, by fate or by God. There was nothing to do but accept, and from this to proceed, doing the very best that could be done. Without knowing the end, reflected Mrs. Pollifax; like being wheeled into an operating room and wondering if one would ever see this or any other ceiling again. Twenty-four hours from now would she and Farrell be staring at these same stone walls, or would they be free, or would they even have survived to see that next day?

Farrell was sleeping soundly. She momentarily begrudged him such discipline until she remembered that he did his exercising at night. Colonel Nexdhet was sleeping too, and suddenly she remembered the knife she had taken from him and was afraid. He would wake up soon and find it gone and know at once that she or Farrell had taken it—who else could have stolen it from him while he was asleep in a locked cell? She wondered why on earth they hadn't thought of this last night. They had so badly wanted a knife and Nexdhet had walked in wearing a knife and it had seemed like their third miracle.

"When actually it may prove our undoing," she thought.

As if he had felt her thoughts Nexdhet sat up and yawned and rubbed his eyes. Meeting her gaze he nodded, and one hand went to his sweeping white moustache to smooth it. Mrs. Pollifax fought to keep her eyes from dropping to the empty knife sheath; she prayed that Colonel Nexdhet's talents did not include mind reading. Nexdhet's second move was to stand up and stretch, and then his hand went out to his jacket at the foot of the bed. While Mrs. Pollifax watched with alarm he lifted the jacket, patted one pocket and shrugged his arms into the sleeves. At least he had not *seen* the empty sheath, she thought wildly, and waited next for him to feel for the knife's presence. But he didn't. He leaned over and began tying his shoes.

Farrell sat upright. He, too, glanced quickly at Colonel Nexdhet and then anxiously at Mrs. Pollifax, who shook her head. At the same moment steps echoed in the hall, keys rattled, the door opened and the guard named Stefan walked in carrying breakfast trays. Nexdhet spoke curtly to him in Albanian, and then walked out.

"Bathroom privileges," muttered Farrell darkly.

"You don't suppose there's a bathtub on the premises?" asked Mrs. Pollifax breathlessly.

"A shower maybe."

Mrs. Pollifax closed her eyes and thought yearningly of hot water coursing down her body and taking with it the accumulation of dirt and dust, and then, most voluptuous of all, the feeling of being clean again and not itching. Life was incredibly simple when stripped to its essentials, she reflected, and for a moment her thoughts lingered on luxuries taken for granted during a long life. Except it was not really a long life, she amended, certainly not if it was to end today, and she began to feel quite angry with these people for wanting to kill her. "After all, it's my life, not theirs," she thought peevishly, "and all I did was . . ."

All she had done, she added more reasonably, and with a faint wry smile, was to walk into CIA headquarters and offer her services as a spy. This made her at once feel better, since it was obviously a spy they would wish to kill rather than Emily Pollifax of New Brunswick, New Jersey. Somehow this knowledge made it less personal; women were always so sensitive to snubs.

Stefan backed out, leaving the trays. Farrell whispered, "He doesn't know it's missing?"

"No, not yet. And now that he's out of here he can't blame it on *us*."

"Hooray for our side." Farrell stood up, wobbled dangerously but waved her away. "Let me show you what I did last night while you were sleeping." He half crawled, half limped to the tree that leaned so idiotically against the wall. Grasping it at the top he neatly removed the last twelve inches like a magician pulling a rabbit from a hat.

"Why, for heaven's sake," Mrs. Pollifax said in pleased surprise.

"I hollowed one end and sharpened the other so the two pieces fit into each other. It's a beginning, anyway, and just the right height now to fit under my arm. Later we'll rip and cut the branches off. Think you can collect some padding?"

Mrs. Pollifax nodded. "There's a very nice hole in my mattress. Not nice for sleeping but nice for taking out what's inside. Did you know we've been sleeping on horsehair? It may be why I itch." She was already extracting it from the mattress and making a bundle to fit the top of his crutch-stick.

"What will you wrap it in?"

"My petticoat—and therein lies a tale."

"I beg your pardon?"

"Pins," said Mrs. Pollifax. "I never was good at sewing and both straps are pinned together."

"I bless your sloppiness," said Farrell reverently.

"If you're going to call me sloppy I refuse to lend them to you," she told him indignantly.

"All right then, your charming lack of housewifery."

"Much better. Now if you'll turn your head I'll remove my petticoat."

"My head is turned. Better give me the stuff to work with, though, you may be summoned for your walk at any time."

"You can turn around now," said Mrs. Pollifax, and she presented him with slip, pins and horsehair, whereupon they both sat down to eat their breakfast, the bread and cheese disappearing automatically into Mrs. Pollifax's handbag, leaving them only a thin porridge with which to begin their day. What was most nourishing, however—to Mrs. Pollifax at least—was the realization that this was the day they were going to do something about their fate. They were going to act. Her fears had evaporated now. She had faced them, made her obeisance to them and now she could dismiss them. Anything was preferable to submission, and now she began to feel almost reckless at the thought of their attempt at freedom. She cleared her throat. "You still feel we should wait for dark?"

"From what I remember of the terrain it struck me that anything else would be suicidal."

Mrs. Pollifax put down her spoon and nodded. "Quite true. But in which direction should we head? Right away, I mean. They'll expect us to leave the way we came, won't they?"

"Yes, but can you think of anything better?" asked Farrell, and there was irony in his voice.

Mrs. Pollifax concentrated firmly on prospects she had entertained only lightly before, and she began to understand his irony. It would be very clever of them to head east, away from the sea, and throw General Perdido off the scent for a while, but eventually they would have to double back, either this way or through the valley, and in the end they would only have added extra miles to their journey. Farrell could never endure this. In fact it was doubtful whether he had the stamina to go anywhere at all, but the thought of leaving him behind was untenable; they had to try together or not at all. Then there was the mountain behind them, and the forest in which they could hide, but here, too, Farrell's condition prevented them from going far and General Perdido would be very aware of this.

She said sadly, "No, I can't think of anything better."

"So all we need is darkness and a great deal of luck." He smiled at her. "It's not too late to change your mind, you know—about including me in this wild venture, I mean. I would feel a great deal of relief if you left me behind."

"Absolutely not," said Mrs. Pollifax flatly. "If I made it alone, which I doubt, I would only be extremely unhappy when I got there, which would defeat the whole purpose." She rose to her feet as the door swung open and Lulash walked in. "Good morning, Lulash, I may go outside now?"

"Yes, Zoje Pollifax. It was a good party last night, was it not?"

"Every minute of it," she told him with more cheerfulness than she possessed. "And you're looking very well in spite of so much *raki*."

"You make all of us feel like human beings again, Mrs. Pollifax."

From his cot Farrell said, "Beware, Lulash, that is a very bad way to feel in a place like this."

* * *

There was no one to guard her this morning, and it occurred to Mrs. Pollifax that she might try to find the missile site again and observe more closely how it fitted into the cliff. In some ways it made her uneasy to be given such freedom; it was pleasant to be considered harmless, but it also proved how secure her captors felt. She wondered whether she or her captors were the more naïve, but unfortunately this would not be discovered until the escape had been committed. Life had never looked better than when death was imminent, and Mrs. Pollifax found herself looking long and ardently at earth, sky and clouds.

She cut across the seam in the rocks and climbed doggedly toward the slanting pines in the wood. Once she had reached the trees she stopped to recapture both her breath and her sense of direction; she and the colonel had entered the woods at this point, and gradually made their way downhill to meet the cliff again a half mile beyond; she would therefore follow the course that Colonel Nexdhet had set. Patting her moist temples with her handkerchief Mrs. Pollifax resumed her walk. She had moved only a few hundred yards deeper into the trees when she began hearing a very peculiar noise ahead. It was a familiar sound, but not customarily heard in a forest, so that she could not for the life of her identify its source. The feverish crackling sound came from between two large boulders that leaned toward each other up ahead.

Deeply curious, Mrs. Pollifax hesitated and then tiptoed across the fallen pine needles to the rocks. At once a voice broke the stillness of the woods but the crackling sounds continued without interruption.

"*Static!*" thought Mrs. Pollifax, brightening. Of course, it was static and someone had carried a radio here into the woods.

The canned voice stopped speaking, and to Mrs. Pollifax's amazement a live voice began talking from behind the rock. Mrs. Pollifax poked her head between the two rocks and stared through the gloom at the man seated on the ground facing her in the small cavity there. "Why, Colonel Nexdhet!" she faltered. He was speaking into a telephone—no, a walkie-talkie, she recalled—and at the sound of her voice he dropped the mechanism as if it were a live coal.

"*Mrs. Pollifax!*" There was no doubt but that she was interrupting something clandestine; his eyes were blazing. He picked up the fallen walkie-talkie, spoke a stream of foreign words into it, and then placed the instrument in a hole of the rock.

"What are you doing here? Why are you allowed in the woods this morning?" he barked, crawling from the hole and standing beside her.

She said scornfully, "So this is how you report to General Perdido! And if you come out here to do it secretly then you must inform not only on Mr. Farrell and myself but on General Hoong as well. You're nothing but a paid informer, Colonel Nexdhet! Shame."

He glanced back once among the rocks and then firmly grasped Mrs. Pollifax by the arm. "I will take you back to your cell," he said firmly.

"I trust you told General Perdido that Mr. Farrell is in glowing health, and can scarcely wait to see the general again? And that a party took place last night, with subversive songs being sung under the influence of *raki?* You quite disillusion me, Colonel Nexdhet!"

He remained silent, his mouth in a grim line. They reached the edge of the wood and emerged into the blinding sunshine. He helped her over the stones toward the two buildings, his hand tight on her arm. Both Lulash and Major Vassovic were in the guardroom but he did not so much as look at them. He marched Mrs. Pollifax straight to her cell, closed the door behind her and turned the key in the lock. She heard him issuing curt orders in the guardroom.

"He sounds peeved about something," said Farrell pleasantly.

Mrs. Pollifax said indignantly, "Colonel Nexdhet is nothing more than a paid informer. A spy on his own men. An informer on everyone."

Farrell said mildly, "What on earth makes you say that?"

"Never mind, just beware of him. He's not to be trusted." She added in a kinder voice, "I'll tell you about it when we get out of here—if ever we do. Just remember he's not to be trusted."

"But I never did trust him," pointed out Farrell logically. "He's a colonel in their secret police, isn't he?"

"Yes," said Mrs. Pollifax forlornly. She sat down on her cot and stared into the long, desolate and nerve-racking day that lay ahead of them and she wanted to cry. Instead she brought out her deck of playing cards and shuffled them.

At noon it was not Lulash who brought lunch to them but the guard who did not speak English, and when he left he carefully locked the door behind him. Nor did anyone else come. The afternoon wore on, hour by hour. Mrs. Pollifax played every game of solitaire that she had learned, and then played each one again, and then chose her favorites and played them until she was tired to death of cards. She reflected that Senor DeGamez could certainly not have foreseen the conditions under which she would play his cherished game, and remembering his kindness she thought of him for a moment. He had been a spy too; perhaps he had played his games of solitaire under precisely such conditions. She did hope he was in good health because obviously Mr. Carstairs' friends proved very poor insurance risks.

The dinner trays arrived, and with them Colonel Nexdhet. "Good evening," he said in a pleasant voice, as if nothing unusual had happened. "We are getting ready for General Perdido's return, he arrives by plane about half-past eight and should be with us by nine or half past."

"That's interesting," said Mrs. Pollifax politely. It would be quite dark by then—good! "What time is it now, Colonel Nexdhet?"

"Half-past six."

She looked at him in surprise. "I always thought we ate at five although I never really knew. Is it really so late?"

He said primly, "Usually the trays are brought to you by five, yes. We are late tonight because we are understaffed. General Hoong and Lulash have gone to meet General Perdido, leaving only myself, Major Vassovic and Stefan here, and two guards in the other building."

Mrs. Pollifax met Farrell's glance; the colonel was a veritable mine of information.

Nexdhet added casually, "And when you have completed the crutch you are making—and I advise you to finish it at once—I would appreciate your returning my knife to me. I am very fond of it and would prefer that you not take it with you."

They stared at him incredulously—it was a full minute before his words were absorbed. Mrs. Pollifax gasped, "I beg your pardon?"

"You know?" said Farrell in a stunned voice.

"Of course."

"But how?"

Colonel Nexdhet shrugged. "It is my business to know."

Mrs. Pollifax was staring at him in astonishment. "You know and yet you're not going to give us away?"

"Give you away?" He frowned. "Like a bride?"

Farrell was studying the man intently. "She means you're not going to inform on us, you're not going to prevent us from this absolutely wild escape idea?"

"But how can I?" he inquired blandly. "I know nothing of such plans. And if I did I am quite weaponless, as you see, whereas you have my knife as well as a loaded Nambu pistol."

"You know that, too?" gasped Farrell.

Mrs. Pollifax's eyes narrowed. She took a deep breath. "Colonel Nexdhet," she said, "just what *were* you doing in the woods this morning?"

"I am extremely sorry you saw that, Mrs. Pollifax, it would have been much safer for all of us if you had not."

Farrell said, "What *did* you see in the woods this morning, Duchess?"

"I don't know," she faltered, watching the colonel. "That is, I must have leaped to the wrong conclusion. I thought—he was in the woods listening to a voice on the radio, and then he talked back into the radio. He was very upset when I saw him, he escorted me back here and locked the cell."

"He was in the woods—secretly?"

She nodded. "Hidden under two rocks."

Farrell drew in his breath sharply. "Over these mountains lies Yugoslavia, and to the east is Bulgaria; they're both within reach of radio." Farrell stared at Nexdhet and suddenly began laughing. "My God," he gasped, "you're a Russian agent!"

"He's a what?" echoed Mrs. Pollifax in a shocked voice.

"Of course! They left him behind to report on the Red Chinese!"

Colonel Nexdhet walked to the door, placed his ear against it and listened. "No one is there," he said, coming back, "but would you do me the kindness to speak in a lower voice?"

"My apologies," said Farrell, his eyes still brimming with laughter. "Don't you see, Duchess? He's the only one here who goes for walks. Bird-watching, you said. He has radio contact with someone across the mountains." To Nexdhet he said, "But why help *us?*"

Nexdhet sighed. "I strongly dislike the word help. I am *not* helping you."

"All right, you're not helping us."

Mrs. Pollifax suddenly blurted out, "But you *have* been helping, Colonel Nexdhet! That knife—you deliberately wore that knife in here last night, you've never worn one before. And you showed up wearing it just after we'd been talking about how badly we needed one!"

The colonel winced. "Please, Mrs. Pollifax . . ."

"And it was you who told us General Perdido was coming on Thursday night, we'd never have known, otherwise."

"Duchess," said Farrell firmly, "don't look a gift horse in the mouth. He has told us he is *not* helping us."

"And a Russian agent shouldn't be helping us," she added indignantly. "Why?"

"Yes, why?" asked Farrell. "Considering all we know about you already—"

The colonel sighed. "Far too much, I agree. Very well, I will say this much." He hesitated, choosing his words carefully. "You were brought to Albania because you are suspected of knowing the whereabouts of a missing report—well-documented—of Communist activities in Latin America."

"Oh?" said Mrs. Pollifax with interest.

"Red China is extremely interested in seizing that report. Red China will do anything to prevent the United States from learning how heavily involved it has become in Latin America. Red China has still another interest in that report: she would like to learn what Russia is up to in Latin America."

"Ah," said Farrell.

"Russia in turn would enjoy knowing what Red China is secretly doing in Latin America."

"Mmmm," murmured Farrell.

"But if there is a choice between Red China reading that report, or the United States reading that report, Russia would infinitely prefer the United States to have it."

Startled, Mrs. Pollifax said, "But you are both Communist countries!"

Colonel Nexdhet's voice was dry. "You bring up a subject that is—uh—very tender, Mrs. Pollifax, and one that I could wish we not explore. Let us simply say that between Red China and Russia there are certain conflicts. On the part of Russia, a certain amount of alarm, certain suspicions—"

"Russia is more afraid of Red China than of America!" gasped Mrs. Pollifax.

"In some areas, yes. There is something called the balance of power that must be preserved at all costs."

Farrell nodded. "This I understand, yes. But what guarantee have we that Russians aren't waiting somewhere to recapture us and throw us into a Russian prison?"

Nexdhet shrugged. "There are no guarantees at all, Mr. Farrell."

Farrell considered for a long moment. "I'm afraid we'll have to trust him," he told Mrs. Pollifax.

She smiled. "Should we trust you, Colonel? You have repeatedly advised me to trust no one here."

His answering smile was grave. "Nor should you even now, Mrs. Pollifax, for you must remember that I will be in the party that hunts you down after your escape."

Mrs. Pollifax thought about this and nodded. "Then could you do one more thing for us—shoot to kill?"

He said simply, "If you are caught I could not afford to let you survive."

"Thank you, that is all we can hope for."

Nexdhet stood up. "I help you no further. In return I ask only that when you hit me with your rock you do not hit me here." He pointed to the back of his skull. "I have already a small steel plate here from an old wound."

"Better than that we will only gag you," promised Farrell, taking out the knife and beginning to slash branches from the tree.

"With the male handkerchief?"

Farrell grinned. "No secrets at all. You have your own microphone in here?"

"Hidden in my cot, yes. You need not worry, however, I destroyed the tapes this afternoon."

But Mrs. Pollifax's mind was still fixed upon Colonel Nexdhet and she suddenly burst out again. "There's the missile site, too!" She turned to Farrell. "I didn't tell you about that because you still had a fever and might have babbled in your sleep, but the colonel took me for a walk a few days ago, a walk that just happened to include a missile site." To the colonel she said, "You *wanted* me to see it!"

"See *what?*" exploded Farrell.

She nodded. "The Red Chinese are building a missile site only a mile away from here."

"Good God," gasped Farrell.

Nexdhet looked apologetic. "A small detail, but a vital one lest your country underestimate Red China." He smiled wryly. "Russia no longer underestimates Red China."

"You've known our plans that long then?" asked Farrell.

Nexdhet smiled. "I had no interest in your possibilities at all when I first met you. A badly wounded man, a woman no longer young—I thought your escape plans hopelessly naïve, as they still are. It was after observing Mrs. Pollifax remove the bullet from your arm that I decided to do what I could for you. You were worth the risk." Turning to Mrs. Pollifax he said with a smile. "Wherever there is violence there is absurdity, also. And now is there anything else you would like to mention as reminder to me of how dangerous you both are becoming? Certainly it will be to my benefit to see that neither of you is ever questioned by Perdido."

Mrs. Pollifax shook her head. "I can't think of anything else, except . . ." She frowned. "I am wondering if it is quite ethical to let you help us. It feels terribly unpatriotic."

Farrell grinned. "World politics make strange bedfellows, Duchess. Do try to manage a small sense of expediency, will you?"

"If you think it's proper," she said doubtfully. Her eyes fell on the window slit and she jumped to her feet. "It's already twilight," she told Farrell in a shocked voice, and was suddenly struck by the meagerness of their preparations. "Is the crutch finished?"

"I'm just padding it," he told her, and stood up and tested it. "Not bad."

Mrs. Pollifax opened her purse and brought out the rocks and the gag. She collected the Beretta gun cartridges, the map and the compass from their various hiding places and added the cheese from tonight's dinner. She was contemplating them with a frown when Farrell said quietly, "Psst, they're coming for the empty trays, I think."

The trays. . . . She wondered what time it was, and at what hour the candle would be brought. To conceal the rocks she sat down on top of them just as Major Vassovic walked in rattling his keys. "Evening," he said.

Nexdhet grunted; he had brought out a newspaper in which to bury his head. Farrell nodded; he had hidden his crutch under the bed but the tree's absence was conspicuous, and Mrs. Pollifax decided she must divert the major's attention. "How is your back?" she asked, and then saw the candle he was carrying and her eyes widened. "But you're not—not going to light our cell so early?" she faltered.

"Busy tonight," said Major Vassovic, and struck the candle in its round metal ring. "No time for it later."

Farrell looked up, appalled, while Nexdhet put down his paper and regarded Mrs. Pollifax with a sardonic, challenging amusement. Mrs. Pollifax realized with a sinking heart that she was sitting on the rocks that were to knock their guard unconscious; the moment had come and neither of them was prepared. A fretful anger rose in her over changed plans, broken routines, unpredictable guards. It wasn't dark yet. The candle had never before been brought in so early. It could not be more that eight o'clock but the cell door would not be opened again unless to admit General Perdido, and she was sitting here like a brood hen on the rocks that Farrell ought to have if he was to hit Major Vassovic over the head.

"Farrell has to do it," she reminded herself. "He's the only one who knows how." But Farrell was across the room and without the rocks.

"I can't," she told herself fiercely—what on earth would the Garden Club think of her, or the pastor of her church?

Major Vassovic was bringing a match from his shirt pocket, his back turned to the room. In a moment he would strike that match against the wall, light the candle and then turn around. "I can't," she repeated to herself stubbornly.

He struck the match against the wall and Mrs. Pollifax watched it flame into life. "I've never hit anybody in my life," she remembered. "Never," she repeated. "Never never *never*."

Quietly, rock in hand, Mrs. Pollifax rose from her cot, walked up to Major Vassovic and hit him on the head. To her utter astonishment he collapsed at once, falling to the ground to lie there like a suit of old clothes. "For heaven's sake," she said, staring down at him in fascinated horror.

"Good girl," said Farrell, and reaching under the cot for his crutch he hobbled over to look at the major. "Out like a light."

"I do hope I didn't hurt his back again," said Mrs. Pollifax anxiously. "It was coming along so well."

Nexdhet said politely, "Not at all, I'm sure. What next?"

Farrell plucked Vassovic's huge, comic-opera keys from the floor and dropped them into Mrs. Pollifax's purse. "What next?" he repeated. "We call the other one in—Stefan—and to spare the Duchess I'll try *my* skill with the rock."

"Oh?" said Mrs. Pollifax wistfully. "Actually it was rather interesting."

"Then you'll jolly well have to sublimate, I'll be damned if I'm going to encourage you to hit men over the head. Here, help me arrange Major Vassovic in a more sprawling position. We'll say he's fainted. I do beg your pardon, Nexdhet," he added with a smile. "Damn funny doing all this in front of you."

"But he isn't helping, he's just overlooking," Mrs. Pollifax reminded them both. "Now?" Farrell had taken a position behind the cell door, a rock in his good hand. When he nodded, Mrs. Pollifax gave a squeal, held her breath and followed this with a penetrating scream. "Guard! Guard!" She ran to the door and pounded on it.

Footsteps hurried down the hall and the unlocked cell door was pushed open. Stefan walked in and Farrell stepped forward and hit him. Stefan also sank into a heap. "You're quite right, it *is* fun," Farrell said.

"I'll go out and look for rope to tie them with," said Mrs. Pollifax, and hurried up the hall to the guardroom. It was not until she arrived there that she realized it might not have been empty;

she made a mental note to develop more cunning, and at once
locked the outside door so that no new guards could surprise them.
Rummaging through the desk drawers she found a few lengths of
rope and carried them back to Farrell.

Nexdhet said, "I really think you had better tie me up now,
too, before I am tempted to change my mind or before General
Perdido walks in. It surprises me, how alarmed I am beginning to
feel."

"Frankly, I'm a little alarmed myself," said Farrell with a grin.
"It's the Duchess who gives this such an amateur quality. Delightful but alarming. Lie down, chum."

Nexdhet gratefully lay down and Farrell began linking him by
rope to Major Vassovic and Stefan. "I'll gag you but not hit you.
You'll have to play dead," explained Farrell. "Are you a good ac-
tor?"

"No, but I'm known as a very good Sigurimi man."

Farrell gave a bleat of a laugh. "Let's hope it protects you
then. And Nexdhet—thanks."

The colonel smiled faintly. "Just spare me the trouble of
shooting you, that's all."

The gag went into his mouth and Farrell knotted it securely.
Over his shoulder he asked of Mrs. Pollifax, "Where are you off to
now?"

"To look for a Beretta. And it's nearly dark!" With this Mrs.
Pollifax left again, this time with her purse, to return to the guardroom and strip it. With the major's keys she found a Beretta pistol
and a second Nambu, and she double-checked both to be perfectly
sure that her stolen gun clips fitted. Then she decided to load up
on cartridges for them and reached down to the drawer beneath.
This time it did not budge to her fingers. The drawer that for a
week had held a key in its lock was now firmly closed and not a one
of the major's keys fitted. "What a pity," she murmured, and
turned back to the hall.

But first she had something else to do, something that had
occupied her thoughts quite tantalizingly from time to time. This
was her curiosity about their next-door neighbor who had rapped
upon the wall. Mrs. Pollifax tiptoed past her own cell and down the
hall, not at all sure that Farrell would approve of this side excur-

sion. She inserted keys into the lock and opened the door upon a dark closet of a room. She stood there uncertainly, peering inside.

From the farthest corner there came a rustling sound, and Mrs. Pollifax's instincts told her that something was moving. Suddenly the darkness expelled a form, a wraith, a gray genie of a man in flowing gray robes who began a repeated bowing of his head as he chattered to her eagerly in a melodic, singsong voice.

Mrs. Pollifax interrupted him. "Not now, please. We are going to try to escape. Escape," she told him. "Would you like to come along with us?"

He stopped speaking and regarded her with great interest. His face was surprisingly long and Gothic for an Oriental; the mouth was thin and turned up at the corners into a fixed, sweet smile; his eyes were large and bright and childlike, with only a faint suggestion of an Oriental pouch above the lids. Between the pursed lips and the twinkling eyes he looked—well, not quite responsible, thought Mrs. Pollifax; rather like a happy child in the guise of a man, all twinkles, smiles and curiosity.

"Come," she said, as if to a child, and pulled him by the sleeve. He followed without protest, his eyes lively and curious. When they reached the cell Mrs. Pollifax said in a voice whose confidence was spurious, "Look what I found."

"Good heavens," said Farrell, staring at the little man beside her. "Who on earth is this birdlike creature?"

"The man next door. Colonel Nexdhet can tell us who he is, I'm sure." They both glanced at the colonel and saw that he was straining at his gag and ropes. Farrell bent over and slipped the gag from his mouth.

"No," said Nexdhet harshly. "No, I will not tell you who he is. No, you must not take him, absolutely not."

"Take him!" Comprehension was dawning upon Farrell, leaving him inarticulate. "You can't possibly—you're not thinking—?"

"Why not?" asked Mrs. Pollifax.

"But who is he? You don't know a damn thing about him. For heaven's sake, Duchess, he may be a Commie worse than General Perdido."

"Then why would he be in jail?"

"Who knows? He may have seduced somebody's mistress or

tried to organize a *coup d'état*. He's Chinese, isn't he? He had to *be* somebody to get here."

"I refuse to listen to you," Mrs. Pollifax said indignantly.

"Trusting, always trusting," pointed out Colonel Nexdhet from the floor. "Now you are crazy."

Farrell's lips thinned in exasperation. "There's another point, Duchess. If he doesn't speak English he doesn't understand that we're escaping. When he does realize it he's likely to let out one long bloody yell at the wrong moment. He may not *want* to escape."

"Nonsense, everybody wants to escape," said Mrs. Pollifax scornfully.

"Have you explained the odds to him? He just may not want to end up in front of a firing squad," pointed out Farrell.

"Defeatist."

"Her conscience again," Farrell explained wearily to Nexdhet.

"You must put him back in his cell at once," warned Nexdhet. "And remember, I know who he is."

"You won't tell us?"

"Absolutely not." On this matter Nexdhet sounded unequivocal.

Both regarded him thoughtfully until Farrell, rousing, said, "Oh, to hell with it, Duchess, this whole thing is insane, anyway. Bring him along, damn it, we haven't all the time in the world."

Mrs. Pollifax wordlessly handed him the two pistols and helped him tie the last knot and stuff the gag in the colonel's mouth. "Okay, let's go," Farrell said crisply, and they moved out into the hall with Mrs. Pollifax hanging onto the sleeve of her genie. Carefully Farrell locked the door of the cell behind them and restored the keys to Mrs. Pollifax's purse. "Get rid of them later," he told her, and limped into the guardroom. "What do we call this—this lamentable mistake of yours?"

"Our Genie," said Mrs. Pollifax at once. "He reminds me of the one in Aladdin. Smaller, of course."

"Our Genie with the light-brown hair," quipped Farrell and ignored her cross glance. Leaning on his crutch he unlocked and pulled open the door to the outside. "Only two lights shining in the big building," he said. "Shall we go?"

With charming gallantry he held open the door for Mrs. Pollifax and her charge, and they walked past him into the sultry night air. "We're outside, we're free, we're no longer prisoners," thought Mrs. Pollifax, and she drew a long deep breath. She was in the process of expelling it when a voice to her right said unpleasantly, "Well, well, my three prisoners, and no guard in sight! It seems that I have returned from Peking just in time."

General Perdido had come back.

Chapter Seventeen

Back—into the guardroom!" barked General Perdido, drawing the gun from his belt holster. "I'll have Vassovic's head for this. Lulash, see what they've done with Vassovic. At once."

As the general shouted orders, his attention distracted for a second, Mrs. Pollifax lifted her arm and threw the cell keys far into the night. She thought somewhat hysterically, "I shot an arrow into the air, it fell to earth I know not where," and she tried not to wince as she heard the sound of metal against rock. But neither her gesture nor the noise appeared to have been noticed by anyone, and Mrs. Pollifax began to feel more confident. She could not have said exactly why her courage revived except that two such unusual occurrences really ought to have been noticed by the general, and somehow this proved that he was not superhuman. A man who barked and shouted and popped up out of the dark could easily acquire such a reputation, she reflected; but these particular keys to the cells he would not get, and if there were duplicate keys they would require time to find.

And so, quite ignominiously, they were back in the guardroom, the three of them standing like naughty children before the desk at which the general had seated himself. Desperately Mrs. Pollifax tried to think: the electricity was primitive—only one line, the major had told her; it would be marvelous if she could hurl herself at the one power line and plunge the building into darkness. Unfortunately she was again without a knife, and totally without knowledge of power lines.

"What fools you are," hissed the general. "I would never have believed it of you. I will take great delight, Mr. Farrell, in punishing you for this. As for you, Mrs. Pollifax—yes, what is it, Lulash?"

Lulash appeared in the hall, his eyes anxious as they encountered Mrs. Pollifax's glance. "I can't get in," he said. "The doors to the cells are locked."

The general muttered an oath and irritably opened one desk drawer after another. "They're not here, one of these three must have them. Search them!"

Mrs. Pollifax's heart sank, because a search of their persons would reveal two pistols. She said defiantly, "I was carrying the keys, but I threw them away. Outside, in the dark."

The general stood up and walked around the desk to Mrs. Pollifax. He slowly lifted one arm and with precision struck her across the cheekbone.

Lulash looked stricken. Farrell cried angrily, "Hey!"

Mrs. Pollifax, reeling and a little faint, heard the general promise that this was only the beginning of what lay in store for them. The Genie spoke then, too, his eyes darting with interest from Mrs. Pollifax to the general. The general answered him in fluent Chinese, the Genie appeared satisfied and nodded.

"Go ahead, Private Lulash—search them," said General Perdido harshly.

Lulash exchanged a long glance with Mrs. Pollifax, but she could not tell whether she read apology or a plea in that glance. He moved carefully to Farrell and stood before him. "Turn to the wall, please, and place your hands against the wall."

It took a second before Mrs. Pollifax realized that Lulash stood squarely in front of Farrell, concealing him from General Perdido as well as protecting him from the general's gun. There was a curious smile on Lulash's lips as he looked into Farrell's eyes. "Faster," he said, "or I will shoot you."

Farrell understood. One hand moved swiftly to his pocket, the other seized Lulash. Over Lulash's shoulder he fired his pistol at the general, and then lightly tapped the guard on the head with the butt. The sound of the pistol's discharge in the small room was deafening. Both Lulash and the general had fallen to the floor.

"Let's go," said Farrell, and headed for the door on his crutch. But the Genie reached it first and the three of them fled into the night. Or perhaps fled was not precisely the word, thought Mrs. Pollifax, as Farrell stumbled and tripped over the uneven rocks, muttering a variety of oaths at his clumsiness. She went back and took his arm and they struggled toward the fir trees. "I'm afraid I only winged him," Farrell said furiously through his teeth. "I meant to kill him, but damn it I think I only got his shoulder or his arm."

"He fell to the floor," Mrs. Pollifax reminded him. "He disappeared behind the desk."

"Pure instinct. Self-preservation. Give him a few minutes to stop the bleeding and catch his breath and he'll be after us."

"Yes," Mrs. Pollifax said grimly, and realized that without Farrell to deter them they would already have reached the sanctuary of the fir trees. She took a long glance at this thought, examined it with brutal honesty, measured the difference this would make in both their small chance of escape and in their lives, and allowed herself one brief pang at being who and what she was. Then she put aside the thought forever. "Here we are," she said with relief as they reached the thin cover of firs.

"My God, the donkeys," gasped Farrell. "Look!"

Now that her eyes had adjusted themselves to the darkness Mrs. Pollifax could see at what he pointed: two donkeys were tied to a tree and were nibbling at the slender thread of green that separated the rocks from the forest of boulders beyond. "Luck," she whispered.

"Plain bloody miracle," growled Farrell, hobbling toward the animals. "Except of course with the general just arriving the donkeys had to be somewhere."

"But we don't have a knife to untie them," wailed Mrs. Pollifax.

"Feels like a square knot," murmured Farrell, working at it. "Tackle the center."

The Genie stood back, not helping. When the donkeys were freed he stepped forward and put out his hand for the two ropes, gesturing to Mrs. Pollifax and Farrell to mount. At the same moment Mrs. Pollifax heard the sound of a gunshot behind them and she froze. "They're after us!"

"Don't panic, it could be someone signaling for help from the main building. For God's sake jump on and let's go."

Mrs. Pollifax unfroze. She heard herself say calmly, "No, I will not mount one of these dreadful beasts again, I refuse. I believe the path or whatever it is lies to our right so we mustn't go that way and how could I ever make the Genie understand this? *He* must climb on, I'll do the leading. We have to find the edge of the cliff and follow it—it's our only hope." She was already tugging at the ropes and telling the Genie in frenzied sign language that he was to take her place. He climbed on at last, and with the two lead ropes in her hand Mrs. Pollifax set out to find the cliff and orient herself. There was now very little time left them—she could already hear shouts being exchanged behind them. The donkeys moved with maddening slowness. Without a flashlight Mrs. Pollifax could distinguish only the larger boulders, and her feet kept stumbling over those half buried in the earth. There was no moon; the stars covering the sky did no more than give her the ability to distinguish between a rock and a tree. Mrs. Pollifax was painfully aware of this, and of the fact that behind them a chase was being efficiently organized. The precipice, which they certainly ought to have reached by now, failed to materialize, and the rocks proved so abortive, so inconveniently placed, that Mrs. Pollifax soon wondered if in skirting the large boulders she might have begun circling back toward their starting point. It was not a happy thought.

No one spoke. At best they were only a few thousand yards from the main building and recklessly moving at right angles to it instead of away from it. "Where *was* that damn edge," thought Mrs. Pollifax, and was appalled at her choice of language. She tugged mercilessly on the donkeys' halters and quickened her step. It proved an ill-timed moment to increase her speed. Mrs. Pollifax's right foot moved out into space, sought reassurance, came down in anticipation of solid earth or rock and found neither. With a startled gasp Mrs. Pollifax pitched forward, guide ropes still in her hand, and meeting no resistance that would save her she catapulted into space, the men and donkeys dragged with her.

It was not a long fall. Just as she assumed that the end had come, her jacket was seized by something knifelike, her fall suddenly broken and Mrs. Pollifax discovered that she was ignominiously straddling a creaking, groaning tree branch that threatened to break at any moment. Mrs. Pollifax had found her cliff and walked over it. Mercifully she had also found a stunted tree branch that had grown perpendicular to the sides of the precipice. But where she was to go from here, and where Farrell, the Genie and the donkeys had gone, she had no idea.

"*Well!*" exclaimed a voice nearby.

"F-F-Farrell?" gasped Mrs. Pollifax in astonishment.

"Good God, you're here too?"

At the same moment she heard both the melodious voice of the Genie, a trifle reproachful, and the faint, anguished bray of a donkey. "But where are we?" cried Mrs. Pollifax.

"I don't think we should try to find out," Farrell told her fervently. "And I think the first thing you'd better do is join us. There's rock under me but what's under you?"

Mrs. Pollifax said nervously, "A tree branch and—and really I don't think there's anything else. Only air."

"Keep talking. Let me find you—this damn darkness—and I'll see what I can do."

Mrs. Pollifax began reciting poetry, first Wordsworth's "Daffodils" and then "The Rhyme of the Ancient Mariner," and tried not to consider her predicament if the branch broke or Farrell could not rescue her. When she felt a hand clutch her ankle a little sob of relief escaped her.

"You're lying straight out on a branch," he told her, as if she didn't already know this. "I want you to very carefully, very gingerly, start shinnying in the direction of my voice. Don't try to sit up and don't move hastily. I'm going to keep my hands on your ankles and very gently pull. If the branch starts to go I think I can still hang on to you."

"Think?" repeated Mrs. Pollifax, and felt like laughing hysterically because, of course, if the branch went, taking her with it, her brains would be dashed against the rock below no matter how tightly her ankles were held. But she obeyed, and thereby learned how subtly and sinuously a person could lift and move his hips if life depended upon it. After what seemed like hours her toes met the solid rock platform on which Farrell was kneeling. When at last she knelt beside him she allowed herself the luxury of feeling faint.

"It *seems* to be a small ledge we fell onto," Farrell explained.

"You didn't hurt your leg again?" she dared ask.

"I fell on one of the donkeys. The Genie wasn't so lucky, he fell on the first donkey and then the second donkey fell on *him*, but he's all right. Crazy. But from the feel of our fall I'd say we fell only about twenty feet or so."

"Only that," marveled Mrs. Pollifax, and then stiffened as she heard voices above.

"Back," whispered Farrell urgently. "There's a shallow overhang, and a hollow in the cliff. Find one of the donkeys and hold his mouth together, or whatever donkeys bray with. I'll take the other."

"The Genie?"

"Blast him, he doesn't understand English so he can't help. If we could see him I'm sure we'd find him bowing and scraping again."

Mrs. Pollifax found a donkey and by the touch system managed also to find its lips and encircle them with both hands. The two donkeys had crawled into the shallow indentation of rock, leaving no room for humans; Mrs. Pollifax did all but climb on top of them for shelter as she heard the general's voice querulously shouting orders. So Perdido was still alive—Farrell had been right about that. A powerful searchlight was turned on from above, and directed downward, and Mrs. Pollifax closed her eyes, hoping this would make her even smaller as she pressed against the donkeys. Then the light moved farther along the cliff's edge and the voices of the men diminished as they moved away. Mrs. Pollifax relaxed, and presently fell sound asleep.

It was the Genie who awakened her with a tap on the shoulder. Her head had been pillowed on the abdomen of a donkey, and when she lifted it she was startled to discover that she had slept through the whole night—the sky was perceptibly lightening in the east. In this first light of dawn she could see the appalling smallness of the ledge upon which they had fallen: it was no more than a lip on the side of the precipice, extending a bare seven feet from side to side. Below her, virtually at the edge of her shoes, lay a drop into the valley that turned her blood cold. Even the tree branch that had caught her looked no sturdier than an arm, and Farrell, noting her face, grinned. "The gods were with us, eh?"

Mrs. Pollifax replied with a shudder.

"The Genie donated his sleeves to tie up the donkeys' mouths," he pointed out. "Voices were heard now and then until about an hour ago. They're probably wirelessing the news of our escape all over Albania now. We'd better move in a hurry, before it gets light and the search begins again."

"Move!" repeated Mrs. Pollifax incredulously. "Move? Move *where?*"

He said mockingly, "Well, we absolutely can't move *up*. Did you really plan to spend the rest of your life here? Besides, I'm getting hungry."

"Hungry?" Mrs. Pollifax automatically groped for her purse, but stopped when she saw Farrell shaking his head.

"Your purse wasn't so lucky," he told her. "I've already looked, it's gone. Down *there*, presumably."

"I wish I could brush my teeth," Mrs. Pollifax said suddenly and fretfully, thereby expressing her complete dissatisfaction with the situation. She leaned forward just a trifle—heights always made her dizzy—and looked down into the valley. Her first thought was that Farrell was feeling suicidal to believe they could ever negotiate such a cliff, but her resistance to the idea was inevitably overcome by curiosity and then interest. The cliff did not drop to the valley like a plumb line; it slanted almost imperceptibly, with avalanche-like beds of gravel and rock, then short drops, then more beds of stone gravel until it reached a green terrace below, the same pasture where on her walks she had seen goats grazing. "But you couldn't make it with your leg," she protested. "Absolutely not."

Farrell smiled. "Look, you've forgotten something. Walking's hard for me, but nobody walks down a cliff. One slides down backward, using arms and hands, not legs. Come on, let's go."

"Oh, these happy morning people," thought Mrs. Pollifax, and then she realized that it was not simply a matter of temperament but of age; Farrell was younger and more flexible; Mrs. Pollifax at this moment felt unutterably weary and ancient. To be shot by a firing squad appeared absolute luxury compared to crawling down a precipice, even if it did slant. She had left a cell which from this distance appeared a haven of safety, had stumbled into space from the top of a cliff, been mercifully caught by good luck and a slender tree branch, and had endured the suspense of creeping inch by inch to this cliff ledge. What she wanted now was a great deal of reassurance, a hot bath, clean clothes and sleep. What Farrell wanted of her was more.

Very coldly she said, "All right, who leads the way, you or the Genie?"

Farrell said casually, "Neither, which brings up another subject. I don't trust the Genie."

"Oh, for heaven's sake!"

Farrell shook his head. "He jolly well may have come along as a spy, and I won't have you trusting him, either. I don't speak his language, I don't know what he said to General Perdido back there in the guardroom, I don't know anything about him. All I know is, he's here and we're stuck with him. You go first, then the Genie, and I'll go last because I still have the gun."

Preposterous, absurd, decided Mrs. Pollifax furiously. Gritting her teeth she inched her body forward and dangled her feet over the edge of the cliff.

"Not that way, backward," Farrell told her just as coldly. "Hang from the tree branch with your face to the cliff and reach with your feet for a toehold on the jut below."

She said bitterly, "Great—I can join the circus when I get home."

"If you get home," Farrell pointed out curtly, and this had a galvanizing effect. She told herself that scarcely anyone died as dramatically as they wished and that her being shot by a firing squad had been no more than a wistful dream after all. Her anger gave her the recklessness to place both hands around the tree branch and to anxiously let her body swing in space—and there was a great deal of space. There she hung for a sickening moment, with Farrell hissing directions to her from the ledge. "There—now you've got it," he said.

What she had gotten, as Farrell put it, was one foot on an outcropping of rock below her, but she could not share his jubilance over this. She glanced under her at the rock, then below to the valley, thought of depending upon that rock for her life and clung harder to the tree branch. "No, no, you've got to let go," he told her.

"That rock will *not* support me," she said furiously.

"It will if you move your hands to that stubby little root growing out of the rock over there."

"I prefer staying with this tree branch, thank you."

Farrell said nastily, "For how many years, Duchess?"

She saw his point; she had to go up or she had to go down, and since either course could bring about her violent demise she might as well try going down. She felt for the root with one hand, the other still grasping the branch, and closed her eyes. "One for the money," she whispered, "two for the show, three to make ready and four to. . . ." She dropped her left hand from the branch, stoically endured that ghastly second when her weight was neither here nor there, and then she was clinging with both hands to the root, her feet braced on the rock jut below. Cautiously she opened her eyes to discover that she was still safe. What was more, her position had vastly improved, for instead of hanging from the branch, with nothing below her but ugly space, her body was now pressed tightly against the face of the cliff wall, which was just diagonal enough to give her some reassurance. She was even able to note a small hole in the cliff into which her hands could fit for the next move. Mrs. Pollifax was beginning to understand the mechanics of cliff-scaling.

In this manner the three of them descended inch by inch toward the valley, their cliff gradually changing in color from the luminous gray of dawn to a tawny gold as the sun discovered them. It was growing embarrassingly light when they reached the last slope, a charming easy hill of pebbles. They stopped here to catch their breath and to take stock of their surroundings.

This was the rocky pasture, usually alive with goats, that Mrs. Pollifax had seen on her walks along the top of the cliff. It lay just above another pasture, and then another, each terrace tipping a little drunkenly toward the floor of the flat dry valley. There were no goats now, and Mrs. Pollifax's gaze moved westward, to the right, and she saw what had gone unnoticed before, the home of the man who tended the goats. She recalled from Lulash's book that in this country a hovel like this was called a *han*. It was a small, primitive building built of rocks taken from the hillside; there were no windows. Then she drew in her breath sharply, for a woman stood in the doorway of the *han* watching them, her figure almost lost in the shadows cast by the cliff.

"What is it?" demanded Farrell.

Wordlessly Mrs. Pollifax pointed.

Farrell leaned on his crutch and slipped one hand into his pocket.

"No," Mrs. Pollifax said slowly, "you mustn't shoot her. Anyway, she can't be alone at this hour, there must be others inside."

"She's seen us," growled Farrell. "It's her or us, Duchess."

"At least let's be sure she's alone," begged Mrs. Pollifax. "Then we could just tie and gag her if she's by herself, couldn't we? A gunshot would be heard for miles." Her sympathy for the woman staring at them was instinctive and, in these circumstances, irrational. Still she could not help herself.

Farrell's hand left his pocket and he sighed. "Woman to woman, eh? Have it your way, Duchess—in for a penny, in for a pound."

Nervously Mrs. Pollifax led the way toward the *han*.

Chapter Eighteen

The woman looked as ageless and stoic as the rocks around her, nothing but her eyes alive in a watchful, sunburned face. When she was perhaps two feet from the doorway Mrs. Pollifax stopped, smiled wanly and pointed to the top of the precipice. Then she pointed to herself and to Farrell. *"Inglese,"* she said.

The woman's impassive glance moved to the cliff above, returned to Mrs. Pollifax to examine her torn dress and Guatemalan jacket, roamed briefly over Farrell's crutch and the Genie's flowing garments. She made a sudden turn back into the *han* and Mrs. Pollifax's heart constricted. Then the woman paused, holding back the goatskin at the door, and gestured to them to follow. Again Mrs. Pollifax led the way, aware that Farrell's hand had slipped back into the pocket that held his pistol. It was like twilight inside, with a small fire burning in the center of the earthen floor. The first object that caught Mrs. Pollifax's eye was her purse lying on the ground beside the fire, and she realized that their progress down the cliff must have been observed for some time. The woman spoke to the two men squatting near the fire: the younger was a boy of fifteen or so, the elder a tall, well-built man with a fierce-looking moustache and smoldering eyes. The three spoke together for several minutes, not heatedly, but in disjointed sentences interspersed with reflective pauses. Mrs. Pollifax wondered if Farrell and the Genie felt as edgy as she did standing there and being discussed with no knowledge of what was being said. There were no chains holding them here and yet the fact that they had been seen by the woman gave her the power of life or death over them. Were they going to have to kill the woman and her family? "I'm too old and too soft for all this," she thought.

Suddenly the man of the *han* stood up and went to the door, pushed aside the goatskin and went out, causing Mrs. Pollifax and Farrell to exchange alarmed glances. The boy also jumped to his feet and brought stools from the shadows, gesturing to them to sit. "What do you think?" asked Mrs. Pollifax in a low voice.

"I don't know," Farrell said, and limped to the door and glanced outside.

The woman had gathered up three wooden bowls and was dishing into them something that resembled lumpy oatmeal drowned in oil. With a polite smile Mrs. Pollifax accepted hers and sat down. Farrell, too, came back and sat down beside the Genie. "I don't know," he repeated.

Mrs. Pollifax nodded, spooning up the honeyed grain but scarcely aware of its taste as her mind worried over the man's disappearance. He had consulted and then left. Where had he gone? What had been decided by these three people? She felt again that her fate was no more than a slender thread loosely held by indifferent strangers, yet there was nothing to do but wait. She sat and waited, having no idea what to expect. It was the woman who made the next move. She walked to a chest in the corner of the room and began pulling from it an assortment of clothes. Astonished, Mrs. Pollifax wondered if possibly these people were going to help them. She turned to Farrell and saw the same look reflected in his face: the confusion of a suspicious and desperate man confronted by hope. The woman had taken out a shabby, cone-shaped felt hat that she now clapped on the Genie's head; then she held against Farrell the loose-flowing clothes and sash of an Albanian mountain man. To Mrs. Pollifax she handed two petticoats and a voluminous woolen dress with inserts of handmade lace. She gestured toward the blanket hung across one corner of the room.

"Well!" exclaimed Mrs. Pollifax, beaming at Farrell.

"Could still be a trap," Farrell said.

"I refuse to think so," she told him loftily, and retired behind the blanket to wrestle with the voluminous skirts.

A few minutes later they reassembled around the fire, their appearances strikingly changed. Because of his unshaven jaw, Farrell was clearly the most authentic of the three, looking as fierce and dangerous as a bandit. The Genie appeared much the same: small, birdlike, somehow transcending the absurdity of his costume. Mrs. Pollifax had no idea how she looked but she knew she felt very warm indeed under so many layers.

The woman held out Mrs. Pollifax's purse to her, her fingers stroking the soft dark-blue calfskin. On impulse Mrs. Pollifax opened it, extracted the pistol and its clips, the compass, the map, the food and her pack of playing cards, and gave the purse back to the woman. "Keep it," she said, smiling. "It doesn't go with these new clothes. I'll use the pockets instead, there are so many of them. One in each petticoat," she told Farrell in an aside. She showed the woman how to zip and unzip the purse, a feat that brought surprise and then delight to the woman's face. Her smile was beautiful and Mrs. Pollifax realized that in years she was still only a young woman. She also pressed the Guatemalan jacket on her, hoping she would not wear it outside the *han* for a good many months.

Now it was the boy who flung back the goatskin at the door, and Mrs. Pollifax saw that his father had not gone to report them but to assemble his goats for the day. He had driven them to the door, where they were milling about bleating rudely and with no sense of direction or intelligence. With his shepherd's crook the man prodded them even closer to the door. The boy turned to the three of them and with an eager face began explaining in panto-mime what the family had decided. First he pointed to the cliff and crossed himself, grimacing, so that Mrs. Pollifax understood that General Perdido's mountain eyrie was known and disliked in the neighborhood. Then he pointed to the sun and appeared to be emphasizing the need for them to go quickly, before men came to the *han*. In their new clothes—he pointed to them and rubbed a piece of Mrs. Pollifax's skirt between his fingers to prove he meant clothes—they might be able to reach the road unaccosted.

"Road?" said Farrell, startled.

Mrs. Pollifax nodded. "It can't be seen from here but I've spotted it from the cliff. It runs across the plain from south to north about five miles from here, I'd say."

The problem was in getting unobserved to the floor of the valley but the boy had not finished. The pastures around them could all be seen very clearly from the buildings above—a fact to which Mrs. Pollifax could testify—and someone might be watch-ing, perhaps even with binoculars. Here the boy made circles with his fingers and squinted through them. Today his father had decided to drive his goats beyond this pasture and down to the one nearest the valley. If Mrs. Pollifax and the Genie would become goats they could move with the herd and not be seen from above.

"Become goats," said Mrs. Pollifax dazedly—obviously she had misunderstood his gestures. But again he dropped to his hands and knees, this time crawling into the center of the thickly clustered herd.

"Good heavens," said Mrs. Pollifax faintly.

Scrambling to his feet again the boy pointed to Farrell's leg and shook his head, seized his father's crook and placed it in Farrell's hand. The father in reply got down on his hands and knees.

"Well, I never," breathed Mrs. Pollifax.

Farrell was grinning. "You really ought to see your face, Duchess. Do you get the same message I do? From the cliff above it will appear that Mac here and his son are taking their herd of goats out, as they do every morning at this hour. One man and a boy going out, one man and a boy coming home. But going out I will be the goatherder while he joins you and the Genie and the goats—pretty damn noble of him, I have to add—and in some convenient place we are left behind."

Mrs. Pollifax found herself wishing she were back on the ledge. On the ledge she had wished herself back in her cell. What, she wondered crossly, must she endure next? She made only one comment and it was succinct. She said clearly and irritably, "Damn."

"Acquiring some downright bad habits, Duchess," grinned Farrell. "They'll be blackballing you at the Garden Club this winter, won't they? Hurry now, I think they're waiting for you."

The Genie was already crouched down among the goats, apparently undismayed by this new development; he glanced once over his shoulder, his eyes bright, twinkling and as interested as usual. Gingerly Mrs. Pollifax sank to her knees and crawled in among the beasts. "For heaven's sake move them slowly," she cautioned.

Farrell grasped the shepherd's crook and the boy called out something in the high clear air and prodded the goats in the front. The herd, with Mrs. Pollifax, the Genie and the shepherd as its nucleus, began to move slowly out into the pasture.

The boy did most of the work, running backward and forward

to keep the goats in a tight cluster. But it was the tightness of the cluster that soon became Mrs. Pollifax's major concern, for although she had not crawled on hands and knees since she was a child—and never for any distance—it was the goats that proved especially unnerving. They stepped on her, they bleated alarmingly in first her left ear and then her right ear, they playfully nipped her, and over and above these hardships there was their smell. She had never thought of goats as smelling; she had never thought of goats at all, but of course no one bathed goats and this was the dry season. They had a particularly obnoxious odor, and she was surrounded by, and distressingly intimate with, an entire herd of them. From time to time Farrell and the boy would halt the procession so that the three humans in their midst could catch their breath, but Mrs. Pollifax found that catching her breath was the very last thing she wished to do. It was during these resting intervals that the goats butted her, licked her and stumbled over her. Nor was this all, for as the ground slanted more and more perceptibly the soft grass became thinner, to be replaced by pebbles that cut her knees, and once they left the shadow of the cliffs the sun beat down on them mercilessly. To walk on all fours was difficult enough for a child, but for a woman of her age it was quite mad. Yet as their queer progress continued and the time spent on hands and knees grew longer and less bearable all early reactions faded, even thought faded as Mrs. Pollifax's mind fixed itself upon the next rest when she could throw herself full-length on the earth, indifferent at last to how many goats stepped on her. The slow, gradual descent into the valley must have taken them an hour, but after a long time Mrs. Pollifax became aware that the herd had come to a standstill and that she was being lightly touched by a shepherd's crook. She looked up to see Farrell standing over her. "You can stand up now, Duchess," he told her. "We're hidden from the top of the cliff, we've reached the valley."

He looked drained and white and Mrs. Pollifax realized that a shepherd's crook was not the same as a crutch; he must have had to place his weight on a leg broken in two places, poorly set and unmended yet, and all this on a rocky downhill terrain. Pity brought her to her feet. "Where's your crutch?"

"The man has it."

The Genie's head popped up from among the goats and he

joined them looking so untouched and cheerful that Mrs. Pollifax began to feel almost hostile toward him. She took a step forward and almost fell, regained her balance and glanced furiously at her knees. But she had always been a gracious hostess; she tottered forward to wring the hand of the boy and his father who had helped them at so much risk to themselves.

"*Det,*" the man kept saying over and over again, pointing westward.

Mrs. Pollifax recalled that this word meant sea, and nodded, smiling. Farrell also shook their hands and the Genie, odd little man that he was, went into his bowing and nodding routine. Then the man and the boy strolled away toward the goats that had fanned out across the pasture, and Mrs. Pollifax, Farrell and the Genie were alone.

They were standing in the center of a dried-up brook bed at the base of the last terrace. Behind them rose scallop after scallop of rocky pasture culminating in the towering cliff above. In front of them stretched the flat dry valley, already shimmering in the morning heat. To the south, barely visible, lay a cluster of objects that might be tall rocks or a village. There were almost no trees. "Well," said Mrs. Pollifax doubtfully, and then because it all seemed so overwhelming she suggested they sit down and rest.

"Not on your life," said Farrell flatly. "They must be combing the mountains for us, they'll be getting to the valley next."

She nodded wearily. There seemed nowhere to hide in this naked countryside and she was bone-tired but they had come this far and somewhere to the west lay a road. She glanced at the Genie and he vivaciously smiled at her. Farrell, following her glance, sighed heavily. "Not a brain in his head, is there? You certainly picked a lemon, Duchess."

She frowned. "I don't know, sometimes there seem to be flashes of intelligence there."

"An intelligent man would be tired or scared stiff. All this guy does is smile."

"But the Chinese are always polite, aren't they?" pointed out Mrs. Pollifax. "He may be just a little eccentric."

"Eccentric!" barked Farrell. "Well, we're stuck with him, anyway. Let's get moving."

They clung to the security of the creek bed, knowing without mentioning it that although they wore native clothes they were still three in number, and it was three for whom the general would be searching. The sun was searingly hot, for it was at least midmorning, and Mrs. Pollifax's knees did not grow any more reliable. She stumbled along in the prison of her woolen dress and two petticoats, the old numbness reasserting itself. She longed for water—they had none—and for something green to look at, anything but this tawny, rocky, dusty hot August landscape around them. She was aware, too, of Farrell's hobbling as she plodded. Only the Genie had the resilience to give the appearance of a man out for a morning stroll. She was beginning to feel very sorry that she had liberated this annoyingly tireless man.

They came in sight of the road very suddenly, so suddenly that Farrell, glancing up, gave a sibilant hiss through his teeth and dropped quickly to the ground behind a rock. The Genie promptly imitated him and Mrs. Pollifax gratefully sat down beside them. The road was still some distance away, perhaps half a mile, but it was overrun by men. These men, wearing the striped suits of prisoners, were spread out along the road for nearly a mile, listlessly splitting rocks and carrying them to the roadbed. What was most alarming was the number of guards posted near them; she could identify them because they were seated on the rocks with rifles across their knees, and several of them were sprawled in the shade of a large black car. The road ran in a straight line across their path, vanishing in the south against the horizon, while in the north it lifted gradually to begin a spiraling toward the cliffs from which they had escaped. This was the road by which the general had come from the airport, but with so many people rimming it the road might as well have been an unsurmountable wall. "What can we do?" whispered Mrs. Pollifax helplessly.

Farrell ran a dusty hand across his eyes. He was terrible to look at with his week's growth of beard, bloodshot eyes and a dreadful pallor that was new today. Mrs. Pollifax noted that his hand trembled and she shuddered at what he must be enduring. He said in a cracked, furious voice, "What rotten luck, we'll have to wait until dark to cross the road. Spend a whole bloody day here without water? God."

Dear Farrell, she thought, poor Farrell, and then she glanced beyond him and stiffened. Her look of horror caused both Farrell and the Genie to look too. Men—half a dozen of them—were crossing the plain behind them, clearly visible in the brilliant sun and less than a mile away. What had first caught her eye, however, was the flash of a mirror that was shortly answered from a tree-lined foothill up on their right. The search for them was underway, obviously a methodical daylight search leaving no margins for error, one group combing the cliffs, the pastures and the foothills, another group taking the valley. She wondered if they had already been seen, she wondered if the message flashed from the hill was in fact reporting three suspicious shapes crouched beside a rock.

The Genie suddenly stood up.

"Hey," yelped Farrell, reaching for him.

"Down—get down!" cried Mrs. Pollifax, forgetting that he couldn't understand.

But the Genie backed away from their groping hands, jumped over the rock and began running toward the road and the men there. "What on earth," faltered Mrs. Pollifax.

"I told you I didn't trust him," snarled Farrell. With an oath he fumbled in his pocket for the pistol and drew it out. His shaky hands fumbled with the safety catch and Mrs. Pollifax, befuddled by sun, thirst, exhaustion and panic, watched him steady the gun on the top of the rock. Dimly she realized that she ought to stop him; they were already trapped on three sides and it was senseless to take the man's life now. Yet she made no move to halt Farrell. The Genie was racing to betray them, he was running over to the enemy and because it had been her idea to bring the Genie with them it made his betrayal the more personal. She had no right to halt his execution; she could even share some of Farrell's rage and frustration that all their suffering came to nothing. All wasted.

Farrell swore again and dropped the pistol. "Too late," he groaned. "My hand shakes, damn it, damn it, damn it."

She thought from his voice that he might be crying, so she was careful not to look at him. Instead she stared out across the dust and the heat at the Genie, who had slowed to a walk as he approached the guards. He was in conversation with them now. "Of course—he's Chinese," she remembered bleakly. This was a country controlled by the Chinese, naturally the guards would treat him with respect; perhaps they were Chinese too. She glanced behind her and saw the men in the valley walking with more purpose now, a few of them running. Her eyes moved to the hillside and she could see the men who had flashed the message; they, too, were hurrying down the slope toward the valley. She realized that within a few minutes the two groups would converge upon them.

"Well?" said Farrell grimly, holding up the pistol in a meaningful way and lifting his brows at her.

She said steadily, "Yes—yes, it's really the only thing left to do, isn't it. Except—I'm sorry but I'm afraid I couldn't, you'll have to be the one to—the one to—"

He said harshly, "I understand. But for God's sake, Duchess, you realize it's only to spare you worse. Tell me you understand that."

"I do realize it, of course I do."

"Because I've grown damnably fond of you, you know."

"Thank you," she said gravely. The Genie and a guard with a rifle were climbing into the big dusty black car parked beside the road, the guard taking the driver's seat, the Genie sitting beside him. The car started with a jerk, turned and left the road to bounce over the dry earth toward the rock that sheltered them. "They're coming," she said quietly. "They're coming in the car, the Genie and another man. I think you'd better hurry."

Farrell nodded and ran his tongue over parched dry lips. With one hand he lifted his gun, trying to steady it as he aimed at Mrs. Pollifax's heart. "Is that really the best place?" she asked curiously. "Isn't the brain faster?"

"Oh for heaven's sake," groaned Farrell, the pistol wobbling. "Just don't talk, will you do me that favor please?"

Mrs. Pollifax sat up straight and primly folded her hands in her lap—as if she were about to be photographed, she thought—and waited patiently for oblivion. Again Farrell lifted the pistol and took aim. She did wish he would hurry because the car was racing toward them in a cloud of dust, but she feared reminding him of this lest she disconcert him again. Farrell carefully steadied his shaking hand and his lips thinned with the concentration this took. She could see the perspiration beading his nose and brow and watched a drop fall from his temple. Farrell lifted an elbow to clear his eyes and patiently took aim a third time.

But it was too late. The car was already upon them, and the Genie leaped from the opened door and knocked the pistol out of

Farrell's grasp. It fell into the dust, to be retrieved in an instant by the Genie. With a low moan Farrell hid his face in his hands, utterly drained and exhausted. It was the Genie who brandished the pistol now, gesturing them both into the car.

Mrs. Pollifax sat and regarded him without expression, her mind sifting a thousand reproaches and a few epithets, but if he was Chinese he would understand none of them. And if he was Chinese he could not really be called a traitor either, nor could she call him a fool when she had proven the greater fool. Silently and wearily she climbed to her feet and bent over Farrell. "Come, they want us in the car," she said, and then in a whisper, "I still have the Beretta, you know." Without looking at the Genie she walked past him and climbed into the back seat. It was a Rolls, she noticed, looking over the accouterments that reminded her of childhood rides in the park with an aunt. "A very ancient one," she amended. "Highly appropriate for funerals."

Farrell sank down beside her in the rear seat and the guard slammed the door. This time the Genie slid behind the wheel of the car and started the engine while the guard climbed in beside him and propped his rifle between his legs. With the motor idling the Genie turned his head and smiled at the guard, his eyes bright and fathomless.

"Snake-in-the-grass," thought Mrs. Pollifax, watching him.

With one smooth and effortless movement the Genie lifted the pistol he had taken from Farrell and astonished Mrs. Pollifax by shooting the guard between the eyes. As the guard slumped in his seat the Genie leaned across him, opened the door and pushed the man's body into the dust. Slipping back behind the wheel he said over his shoulder in clipped, perfect English, "I think we'd better get the hell out of here, don't you?"

Chapter Nineteen

Their shock was so complete that for a moment neither Mrs. Pollifax nor Farrell could utter a word. Then something like a small gasp escaped Mrs. Pollifax, and from Farrell came a brief, violent grunt. The Genie abruptly backed and turned the car and the sudden movement brought them to life. "Who the devil are you?" demanded Farrell.

"And why didn't you tell us you speak English?" asked Mrs. Pollifax.

"Didn't dare trust you—sorry," the Genie said over his shoulder, and as the car regained the road he added, "I don't know how long we can stick with this car. There are only something like four hundred cars in the whole country but there are wirelesses and things like roadblocks. And I'm not very good at driving the bloody thing, had to watch what buttons the guard pushed to learn how it started. Whole dashboard is full of buttons."

He was leaning grimly over the wheel as he spoke, and noting the speedometer Mrs. Pollifax reached for Farrell's arm. "We're going one hundred miles an hour," she told him in horror.

"That's kilometers, not miles, Duchess. We're in Europe now."

It still felt alarmingly fast. Mrs. Pollifax turned to look out of the rear window, and the men who were scattered all over the landscape—guards, working prisoners and search party—were already receding into the distance.

Farrell said with his old briskness, "This road leads into Shkoder. Hell, we don't want to go there, do we?"

Mrs. Pollifax, surrounded by so much masculine profanity, said firmly, "Hell, no."

Farrell turned to stare at her and his old debonair smile

crossed his face. Gently he said, "No, Duchess, absolutely no more swearing. Absolutely."

"All right," said Mrs. Pollifax meekly. To the Genie she said, "We have a map, you know. There look to be two villages between us and Shkoder, and to the west of us there's a huge lake called Lake Scutari. Shkoder lies at the southern tip of it. Would you like to see the map?"

"They're following us," interrupted Farrell savagely. "Damn it, they've found one of those four hundred cars the country owns." He had turned around to look through the rear window and Mrs. Pollifax turned too. It was all too true: she saw first the cloud of dust and then the small gray car racing in front of it.

"Three, maybe four miles behind us," said the Genie, his eyes on the rearview mirror. "No time for maps. I say we stick to the car as long as we can. A car moves faster than six legs, one of them broken."

"They must have wirelessed—"

"I know, I know." The Genie was peering at the panel in front of him. "There's plenty of gas, thank heaven." He shoved the accelerator to the floor and the car surged ahead in a burst of speed.

"One hundred kilometers an hour," thought Mrs. Pollifax in dismay, and wished that she dared close her eyes. The landscape moved past them like a projector that had run wild: olive trees, scattered farms and wells all blurred together. Ahead of them Mrs. Pollifax saw the outlines of a village and had no sooner seen it than they were upon it and the Genie was braking to avoid an oxcart plodding through its street. The next obstacle was a sheep that stood its ground in the center of the narrow road and baa-ed at them indignantly. They swerved around it and through a cobble-stoned main street with stone houses on either side, and then the village was behind them and the Rolls resumed its breakneck speed. Mrs. Pollifax wondered how the Genie managed to hold tight to the wheel, for the ruts in the road, which could at best be called primitive, produced a strange undercurrent of jolts that not even the magnificent upholstery of a Rolls could overcome. At the same moment she heard a growing, indefinable noise and looked out and up in time to see a small plane zoom over them, bank and fly over them again at low altitude. Farrell said grimly, "They've heard about us in Shkoder, too."

"We'll have to ditch the car," the Genie said. "But where and how I don't know."

Mrs. Pollifax didn't know either, but her mind grasped at once that just ditching it wouldn't be enough, not with a car following behind them and their progress observed from the air. They wouldn't have a chance of getting away, not with Farrell unable to run. "An accident," she said suddenly.

"What?"

"An accident. Isn't there some way to tip over the car and set it on fire? They would think for at least a few minutes that we were still inside."

Both men were silent, fumbling with the idea, and then the Genie said, "You haven't any matches, have you?"

"Two," said Farrell.

"You said there's a lake to the west of us, to the right?"

"Yes."

The Genie had seen a cart track branching from the road into Shkoder and with a squeal of brakes the car slowed enough to turn its wheels down the track and head west. The car bounced hideously, and Mrs. Pollifax's head hit the ceiling. "They'll see our dust, won't they?" she gasped. She had no sooner spoken than they left the cart track to plunge toward a copse of trees.

"In there looks the place," said the Genie. "The trees will be cover for getting away. You'll have to have a head start, Farrell—that's your name, isn't it? I doubt if any one of us has the strength to tip the car over but I'll try to ram it into a tree. Start running as soon as we stop."

As soon as they were in among the trees he braked the Rolls and jerked open the door next to Farrell, "Out," he said. "Out and hurry in a straight line that way." He pointed. "Go as fast as you can."

"Me too?" asked Mrs. Pollifax.

The Genie shook his head. "Out, but wait for me. I'll need your help."

They left the car, Mrs. Pollifax to stand uncertain and nervous as she watched Farrell hobble away for dear life. Dear *dear* life, she reflected, and how tenaciously people held on to it and what things they did to remain alive!—that is, physically alive, she amended, for to remain alive inside was far more intricate and difficult and defeating. Her thoughts were interrupted by the roar of the Rolls engine as the Genie pressed his foot to the accelerator. Aghast, she watched the car pass her at top speed, the Genie leaning half out of the door. Faster and faster it went, heading inexorably toward the largest of trees, and then the tree and the Rolls met with such force that the front of the Rolls crumpled like an accordian and the tree shuddered to its roots. Then Mrs. Pollifax saw the Genie, shaken but entirely whole. He had leaped at the last minute and now was fumbling for the matches Farrell had given him. She ran to help. "How? Where?" she cried.

He was wrestling with the cover to the gas tank, his hands trembling. Mrs. Pollifax gave it a twist and lifted it off. "Start running," said the Genie as he lighted one of the matches.

Mrs. Pollifax obeyed, too numb to protest. She did not look back until she heard the explosion, and then it was only to see if the Genie was still alive. He was both alive and running, with more vitality than she possessed, and she envied him. Together they came out into the open country beyond the copse of trees, and there they discovered Farrell leaning on his crutch and looking very ill again. It was obvious that he could go no farther.

The landscape offered no hope of concealment, and when it was discovered that their bodies were not in the Rolls General Perdido would expect to find them nearby. Mrs. Pollifax could see the roof of a *han* some distance away, a good many rocks, another dried-up creek bed, and a pen of some kind where goats or sheep were kept at night. Her eyes moved over and then swerved back to an object in the corner of that pen: a two-wheeled primitive wooden cart filled to the brim with hay.

"Look," she whispered, and without a word they moved toward it, recognizing it as only a slim hope and not at all sure what to do with it. But it did have the advantage of being out of sight of the *han*, which presumably housed the owners of the farm, and it was the only object in sight that could possibly shield them. They stood and looked at it; rather stupidly, thought Mrs. Pollifax, until she realized that both Farrell and the Genie were exhausted and that as the senior member of the party—rather like a Scout leader, she thought with blurred, semihysterical humor—she was going to have to assume command whether she was exhausted or not. At that moment, as if to emphasize the need for decisiveness, she heard the plane returning. It was still some distance away but obviously it was flying back to scour the countryside for signs of life.

"Into the cart," she cried, pulling out tufts of hay. "Quickly, both of you." There was barely room for the two; both Farrell and the Genie had to curl up in womblike positions and she prodded them mercilessly.

"What about you?" demanded Farrell.

"They don't know I'm in peasant clothes," she pointed out, devoutly hoping this was true. "And they're looking for three people." She was recklessly piling the hay back on top of them. "For heaven's sake don't move."

One of them replied by sneezing.

"And don't sneeze either," she added crossly. The plane was circling now over the woods where they had abandoned the car and she saw what she had not noticed before—a plume of fading black smoke above the trees. The Rolls was still burning then, or had been until a moment ago, and presently the remains of it would be cool enough to examine. Hadn't she read somewhere that bodies, turned to char, still held their shape until breathed upon or touched? She supposed it depended upon the heat of the fire. At any rate they couldn't remain here indefinitely. The first time she was seen from the air she might be mistaken for the farmer's wife contemplating clouds or earth, but if she was seen a second time in the same place such rootedness would be suspicious. Mrs. Pollifax regarded the cart speculatively, glanced over the terrain and then kicked the rock from under the wheels. Bracing herself she picked up the tongue of the axle, moved between its two shafts and tugged. Oddly enough the cart moved quite easily, being high enough from the ground to balance the weight of two grown men, and the earth sloped conveniently downward to aid momentum. With a squeak of wood against wood the cart began to make progress toward the next copse of trees with Mrs. Pollifax feeling rather like a ricksha boy. At any moment she expected to hear shouts from the direction of the *han*, but none occurred. Without any challenge, and having achieved a precarious speed, Mrs. Pollifax marched sturdily on, the cart at times pushing her in front of it. It was rough pastureland they crossed now, but a wood lay less than half a mile away. The noon-hot sun glared down but there was grass—green grass—in this pastureland and it led Mrs. Pollifax to hope that they were nearing the coast. She was in the middle of the pasture when another plane passed overhead. Its presence ought to have alarmed her, but as it roared over them and then headed west Mrs. Pollifax saw its pontoons and her heart quickened. "It's a seaplane, and where there are seaplanes," she thought with a flicker of excitement, "there has to be water."

Water!

Chapter Twenty

After ten minutes of being pushed by the cart, and another ten minutes of pulling it, Mrs. Pollifax had to concede that she was neither an ox nor young enough to imitate one. The ground was rough, and after thoughtfully slanting downhill it had begun to slant uphill, but what was most discouraging was the field of maize that lay ahead directly in their path. She could not pull such a broad cart through narrow corn rows, and the field stretched from left to right almost as far as the eye could see: the thought of walking around it utterly dismayed her. Mrs. Pollifax stopped and laid down the shafts, wiped the sweat from her brow with a sleeve and said aloud, in an anguished voice, "I just can't pull you any more."

It was the Genie who emerged first from the straw. "Quite so," he said in his clipped British voice. "Farrell badly needs a rest too. I suggest we crawl into the corn and rest a few minutes."

It was a very bad idea. Mrs. Pollifax knew it and the Genie must have known it too, for if the burning Rolls had confused and diverted General Perdido it would not be for long. Ashes would be sifted: for rings—her wedding ring, for instance—or teeth or gold fillings or bone fragments. Even if the general remained in doubt he would be compelled to assume they had gotten away because he was not a man who could afford doubts; his reputation and his pride were too valuable and both would be at stake.

Yet Mrs. Pollifax conceded there was nothing else for them to do. Certainly she could not go on much longer in such an exhausted state, and what was worst of all her mind felt battered and senseless. It was a major effort even to weigh what the Genie was suggesting, and all of her instincts told her that a mind was needed to compete against the general's cunning. "Yes," she said simply, and stood back and let the Genie help Farrell out of the hay.

Farrell looked utterly ghastly but his mind at least was unaffected, for he took in the situation at a glance and said, "We'll have to be careful not to break off any stalks as we enter. And the cart can't be left here."

The Genie's eyes shone with their usual birdlike brightness, half mockery, half inquisitiveness. He bowed with his hands tucked into his sleeves and said, "I, too, have read your Leather-stocking tales. You go, I'll move the cart and cover your trail as I join you."

Together Farrell and Mrs. Pollifax tottered in among the cornstalks, each helping the other, but neither of them impressively secure. They did not stop until the rows of corn neared an end and then they fell apart and sank wordlessly to the ground. Here in the shade of the tall stalks there was at least shelter from the blazing sun and the illusion of a faint breeze as the stalks rustled and creaked and whispered. With a groan Farrell stretched out his damaged leg and studied it with bloodshot, menacing eyes. "Damn thing," he growled. "Never gave it a thought before, but damned if legs aren't pretty useful appendages. I'm hungry, by the way."

Mrs. Pollifax roused enough to explore the capacious pocket of her first petticoat. She drew out the pistol, the map, the compass, and then one slice of stale bread and a small amount of cheese. "There isn't much and we have to save some for later," she reminded him.

"Later," mused Farrell. "I can't imagine anything more distant than 'later.'"

They could hear the Genie looking for them, his footsteps stopping and then starting again as he peered into each aisle of corn without finding them. Mrs. Pollifax carefully put aside his portion of food, returned the remaining cheese and bread to her pocket, picked up the pistol to put it away, and hearing the Genie's footsteps virtually at their door she glanced up smiling.

But it was not the Genie standing there and looking down at them, it was the guard Stefan who had accompanied General Perdido. He was staring at them with his mouth half open, his eyes incredulous and a look of blank stupidity on his face. For just the fraction of a second Mrs. Pollifax shared his stupidity, and then she realized that she was holding the pistol in her hand and without thinking she lifted the pistol, aimed it as her cousin John had

taught her years ago and squeezed the trigger. The noise was deafening in the stillness of that hot, quiet, summer afternoon. The
look of stupidity on Stefan's face increased and Mrs. Pollifax realized with a feeling of nausea that she was going to have to shoot
him again. She lifted the pistol but Farrell rolled over and clasped
her wrist with his hand, deterring her, and that was when she saw
the blood slowly spreading across Stefan's chest. She watched with
horrified fascination as he began to crumple, his knees carrying
him steadily downward until they struck the earth and his hips and
shoulders following. Farrell was already reaching for his crutch and
struggling to get to his feet. Mrs. Pollifax said blankly, "I've killed
him. I've killed a man."

"He'd have gladly killed both of us in another minute,"
gasped Farrell, standing upright. "For heaven's sake, don't just sit
there, Duchess, they must have heard that shot for miles."

Certainly the Genie had heard it. Mrs. Pollifax became aware
that he was with them again; he was kneeling beside the dead guard
removing his pistol and checking his pockets. She stuffed pistol,
map and compass away and stood up, curious as to whether her
knees would hold her or if she would slowly sink to the ground as
Stefan had done; Stefan, the man she had killed—*she*, Emily Pollifax of New Brunswick, New Jersey. "Madness," she muttered
under her breath. "Madness, every bit of this."

"They certainly know we're alive now," Farrell was saying
grimly. "God how I wish I could run."

"I saw him and had to hide," the Genie said in a stunned
voice. "There wasn't a chance of warning you." He was tugging at
Mrs. Pollifax's arm to get her moving, and Mrs. Pollifax automatically took a few steps, then turned to look back at the dead man,
but Farrell reached over and forced her face to the west. "Don't
ever look back," he told her harshly.

So he understood in his rough, compassionate way. With an
effort Mrs. Pollifax pulled herself together, lightheaded enough by
now to see the three of them, blood-smeared, exhausted and
harassed, as absurdities pitted against the whims of fate. They entered the forest of pines that lay beyond the cornfield but the
shadows brought only meager relief and this was from the sun
rather than the heat. Yet it was lovely among the pines, the earth
soft and springy with layer after layer of pine needles, some old and

brown, others freshly green. It seemed very peaceful and Mrs. Pollifax yearned to forget General Perdido and sink to the ground to rest.

The Genie said suddenly, "I smell water," and he began hobbling stiffly ahead, leaving Mrs. Pollifax to wonder how anybody could smell water. She stayed with Farrell, whose pallor alarmed her; he looked already dead, she thought, like someone embalmed and strung up on wires by a fiendish mortician. Then she realized that she, too, smelled water, except that smell was not quite the word, it was a change in the air, a freshness new to her nostrils. "Something's ahead," she gasped to Farrell, but he only grunted, not lifting his head. If it was the lake—and it could be nothing else from the look of the map—they must be very near Yugoslavia and very near to freedom. "Bless Tito and foreign aid," she thought reverently, hope rising in her. The Genie was ahead of them waving his arms, but it seemed an eternity before they reached him. "Look," he said.

Mrs. Pollifax lifted her head to see water glittering in the sunshine, water to bathe in, water to drink, water to cool overheated flesh and relax parched dry throats. Water—she wanted to stumble through the scrub to the shore and bury herself in it, but as she started forward the Genie clutched her arm and she heard the sound of the plane again. "This way," he said, and led them back in among the pines to head north along the shore of the lake.

Lake Scutari, she remembered from the book . . . two hundred square miles in size, a large lake, half of it in Yugoslavia. . . . The plane roared over the lake at low altitude and it gave her a queer sense of panic to realize that it must be looking for them. Of course—she had shot a guard and advertised their aliveness. In this quiet, pastoral countryside the sound of a gunshot would be heard for miles. Not many natives would own guns, the country was too poor, too barren of life to supply money for such a luxury. There would be no explaining away such a provocative noise.

The plane disappeared to the north and the Genie stopped, one finger on his lips, one hand on Mrs. Pollifax's arm. She and Farrell halted. The floor of the forest had been sloping upward so that it was higher than the water on their left, causing a drop that made it less accessible from land. Apparently the Genie had thought of something, for removing his shoes and tying them

around his neck he began retracing their steps. Mrs. Pollifax
waited. She wanted to sit, she wanted to fall to the ground, but she
knew instinctively that Farrell couldn't sit down—mustn't, in fact,
lest he never get up again—and an innate courtesy kept her upright. Presently, much to her surprise, she saw the Genie wading
toward them along the shallows of the lake. He appeared to be
searching for something and she looked away without interest, all
curiosity deadened by the stupor of her body. Minutes or hours
later the Genie was touching her arm, and she and Farrell followed
him to the bank. He gestured toward the water, directing them to
sit down on the bank and then jump into the shallows. Mrs. Pollifax did so, obediently and humbly. Then he was guiding them
back a few yards toward an old tree that hung over the lake, its
roots exposed and rotting. There was no beach here; the water
lapped the eroded banking and over the years had brought to it an
accumulation of debris. The Genie parted the branches of a sumac
that had grown from the gnarled roots and said in a low voice, "It's
not particularly dry but there's room here for three people."

"There is?" and then, "Will they think of it too?" Mrs. Pollifax asked anxiously, and then was sorry she had said this, for there
was no safety anywhere in life, except as illusion, and she was surprised at herself for wanting a guarantee from the Genie. Perhaps
it was her American blood, Americans were so very security-
minded, or perhaps she was just too tired and stiff and afraid. But
the Genie did not reply and she was grateful that he didn't. Instead
he pushed aside a stout log that had been caught in the flotsam and
helped Farrell to kneel and crawl into the tiny cave under the bank.
She followed, and the Genie squeezed in after her, taking care to
bend back the branches of the sumac and to pull the log back to its
original position.

The little cave was not dry. The earth was wet but at least
there were no puddles. The ceiling was too low for sitting; they
had to lie on their stomachs, Farrell pressed against the earth, Mrs.
Pollifax in the middle and the Genie nearest the outside. It was a
curiously womblike place: dark, quiet and blessed cool. Mrs. Pollifax felt her eyes closing. She knew there were questions unasked
and things undone and yet her eyes simply would not remain open.
Fatigue won and Mrs. Pollifax slept, not deeply and certainly not

comfortably, but with a fitful, twitching, feverish need from exhaustion.

She was awakened not so much by sound as by the awareness of danger that emanated from Farrell and the Genie, a stiffening of their bodies and a lifting of heads. She, too, stiffened and lifted her head from her arms to hear the roar of a motor nearby. Straining, she realized it wasn't a plane but a motorboat, and running so near to the shore that it was a wonder its propeller cleared the bottom. She lay inert, terrified that at any moment some trace of them be seen. The boat drew level with their hiding place, passed them by and in its wake came the waves. Mrs. Pollifax had not thought of waves and in any case would not have considered them a threat. All motorboats caused waves, some large, some small. Waves rippled charmingly as they swept toward shore, and always they made lovely sounds as they met the beach. She had forgotten that here there was no beach.

The water came with a rush, lifting the debris outside their hole and flinging twigs and leaves aside to sweep inside their tiny earthen cave. One moment Mrs. Pollifax was gazing at the entrance and the next moment she was totally submerged and without hope of escape as the water filled their cave from floor to ceiling. "This at last is the end," she thought as she fought to hold her breath. As her lungs gasped for air she drew in the first water through her nostrils, found no sustenance in it and during the brief moment of panic that precedes drowning she arched her body for one last fight. The struggle brought her head up, and suddenly there came the near alien sensation of air entering her lungs again. Sputtering, choking and gasping she realized that the water had receded. She had just time enough to fill her lungs before the next wave entered. All in all there were six waves, three of them that filled the cave and three that came only to her shoulders before retiring. Then the surge of water desisted.

They were still alive. Farrell lay on his side, with only a weak smile to show that he survived. The Genie was vomiting water, his shoulders heaving, and she brought up one arm—it was difficult in so confined a space—and patted his shoulder in commiseration. The Genie gagged once and rolled over on his back, an arm across his face.

"Close," said Mrs. Pollifax.

The Genie only nodded.

From far away came the sound of the airplane, its noise steadily increasing, and from above they heard the sound of men's voices shouting, and Mrs. Pollifax conceded that the chase was on in earnest. Men called unintelligible orders above their heads, the launch came back, slowed for an exchange of shouts, then sped away sending fresh waves to torture them in their cave. The men along the shore moved away, their voices growing distant as they shouted back and forth in the forest, and as Mrs. Pollifax lifted a tired and dripping head a small lull occurred.

"I'm hungry," said the Genie.

Slowly and stupidly Mrs. Pollifax realized that he had not shared in the small meal that she and Farrell had divided in the cornfield and she fumbled in her petticoats for food. Sadly she drew out a sodden piece of cheese and handed it to the Genie—the bread had completely disintegrated and not a crumb of it was found. The pistol, too, was wet, and drearily she remembered that pistols did not usually function after being submerged in water. She turned her head and watched the Genie munch his cheese, very slowly, to make it last, and then her attention was distracted by the sound of gunshots from far away. This confused her tired mind; she wondered if only a part of herself and of Farrell and the Genie had hidden here in the cave while their physical selves had gone on and on through the pines and if somewhere along the shores of the lake the general was capturing them now. She pinched herself experimentally and it hurt, and this reassured her that she had not become disembodied after all.

"Must have caught some other poor devil in hiding," Farrell said in a low voice.

Mentally Mrs. Pollifax thanked him for reassuring her.

The plane was returning, and the launch with it, and for the next ten minutes each of them fought mutely and individually to keep from drowning. Nor were there any lulls following, for it became obvious that a number of police launches had begun to patrol the shores of the lake. Whole centuries passed—what time had they crawled in here, wondered Mrs. Pollifax, at one o'clock in the afternoon, two o'clock?—and each century left her colder and wetter. In what other world had she yearned for cool water to drink and bathe in? Now she was sated with it, and she kept recalling an old saying that one should never wish too hard for something lest the gods bestow it.

"Rubbish," she thought with a sniff, and wondered if next she might become delirious.

Then where patches of sunshine had illuminated the log outside and filtered through to the cave there was a deepening twilight. Farrell leaned across her and said to the Genie, "We have to leave soon."

She could no longer see the Genie's face but his voice said blankly, "Leave?"

Mrs. Pollifax turned her head back to Farrell. He said flatly, "Absolutely. I suggest we float that log that's outside, and hang on to it all the way across Lake Scutari. If we're lucky, if the wind isn't against us, if we have enough strength, we might land in Yugoslavia."

Mrs. Pollifax marveled at his resilience, that he could make plans after being so nearly embalmed, and then she realized that ever since this journey had begun there had been one of them to carry them a step farther when the other two could manage nothing more. How very surprising this was, she reflected, and again she pulled herself together to help and heard herself say, "Yes, of course, that's what we must do." Eight words and each of them labored, but at least she had said them.

"Police boats," pointed out the Genie wanly.

"We'll have to watch out for them, that's all. And if they have powerful searchlights—can you swim, Duchess?"

"Feebly."

"The same here," contributed the Genie.

"Then we either hide behind the log, or under it, or—"

Or be seen and captured, finished Mrs. Pollifax silently, and asked, "How far?"

"Who knows?"

Mrs. Pollifax turned to the Genie. "We still know nothing at all about you, you haven't told us even your name."

"Smith will do nicely if you'd like a name."

Mrs. Pollifax found herself reviving and bristling at such an insult. She said coldly, "I don't think it will do at all unless your name really is Smith."

"Nobody's named Smith," growled Farrell. "Not in my circle."

"Much, *much* better if you don't know my name," replied the Genie. "Better for you if you meet General Perdido again. Safer. He'd never appreciate your knowing."

"Can't think why," Farrell retorted.

"I was thinking of next of kin," Mrs. Pollifax told the Genie reproachfully.

Something like a chuckle came from the Genie. "Bless you, they would have held the funeral for me two years ago. I've been dead a long, long time, Mrs.—Pollifax, is it?"

"Yes," she said, thoroughly puzzled by now. "Well, no point in arguing."

"Right, it's time we go," Farrell reminded them. "You want to stick your head out?"

The Genie began pushing at the twigs and branches and dead leaves that had returned to the bank after the last wave, and presently he crawled out. Mrs. Pollifax knew when he left because he kicked her in the face as he went. She heard him stand up outside, dripping only a little, and a few minutes later he reached in to place an icy hand on her shoulder. "All clear," he whispered. "There are a few lights on the opposite shore but that's a distance of miles. No police boats to be heard or seen at the moment."

Mrs. Pollifax grimly began the job of moving a body that had lain on its stomach for half a day, and after considerable manipulation and experimentation she managed to climb to her knees and then to squeeze through the opening under the bank. Farrell followed slowly, pushing his damaged leg and homemade crutch ahead of him. The darkness they met was dark and opaque, broken only by a scattering of stars in the sky and half a dozen lights shining across the lake. The air was soft as velvet. The faintly abrasive murmur of a motorboat came to them from a great distance and as they stood there, listening, a fish jumped in the lake and drops of water scattered behind it. There were no other sounds.

The Genie was wrestling with the log. It had the advantage of being large enough and high enough out of the water to give them sufficient cover, but on other hand this had the disadvantage of making it harder for them to cling to it from the water. "Straddle it for now," suggested the Genie. "We can paddle with our hands or feet and if a boat comes we can slip off and hide behind it."

But for three exhausted people to mount a wet, round log proved not only difficult but nearly impossible; Mrs. Pollifax began to understand the problems of the logroller. No sooner had one of them climbed on than the others fell off, and they finally brought it back to shallow water and climbed on at the same moment.

"Everybody ready to set sail?" asked the Genie.

"As ready as we'll ever be," sighed Mrs. Pollifax, thinking how hungry she was, how sleepy, how cold and bone-tired.

"Damn it, let's go," Farrell said fiercely.

Gingerly they paddled the log out from the shadows and into the breeze that had sprung up from the north, their destination Yugoslavia.

Chapter Twenty-One

In Washington, D.C., on the morning of that same day, Peattie notified Carstairs that he had received information from Peking concerning General Perdido. He would bring in the messages personally whenever Carstairs had the time to see him.

"Come along now," said Carstairs, and hung up. As he sat back and lit a cigarette his eyes fell on the calendar and he realized it was now eight days since what he called the "Pollifax Affair" had erupted. Eight days was a long, long time in the life of his department, and he reviewed the facts. They did not cheer him and when Peattie was ushered in he had to forcibly remove the frown from his brow in order to appear civilized. "Good to see you," he murmured, half rising to shake his hand. "Dropping in doesn't inconvenience you, I hope."

"Lord, no. The Operations Department always fascinates me. I suppose I'm hoping you'll drop a few clues about how this is turning out."

"Badly," said Carstairs dryly. "What have you come up with?"

"Yes. Well." Peattie put on his reading glasses. "It seems that General Perdido has been in Peking, yes, but he did not arrive there until August 24, five days after the kidnapping of your Mrs. Pollifax and Mr. Farrell."

"Five days after," mused Carstairs, frowning. "Was anyone with him?"

"No one, he arrived quite alone."

"Hmmm. So presumably Mrs. Pollifax and Farrell were not taken to Cuba and not taken to China, either."

"Also, and this you may find interesting," went on Peattie, "he arrived in China on a jet that collected him in Athens."

"Athens!" exclaimed Carstairs, visibly electrified. "Athens?"

He leaned forward and briefly swore. "The Mediterranean—the Balkans—I never thought of Albania, although why on earth he'd take them so far—"

Peattie nodded and went on. "He remained in Peking until the middle of the week, leaving yesterday in a private plane, destination unknown except that a very reliable informant tells us the plane was heading for—care to guess?"

"*Albania?*"

"Right. But your friends were not with him, and have apparently not been in Peking at all."

Carstairs stubbed out his cigarette. "No, obviously not. Albania . . ." he repeated with a shake of his head. "Anything else?"

Peattie smiled with the pleasure of someone holding a very interesting card up his sleeve. "Yes, a little something more. I took the liberty of—well, after all, since Albania has become the prodigy of the Chinese Reds it has naturally fallen into my province and so I went ahead, that is—"

"That is, what?"

"I made inquiries. General Perdido *did* land in Albania last night, his plane came in at Shkoder, whereupon the car that met him took off immediately for the mountains."

"Very interesting indeed," said Carstairs. "So on the twenty-fourth, five days after the kidnaping, the general flies from Athens to Peking, remains a few days and then flies to Albania." He frowned. "It could mean a great deal, it could mean nothing."

Peattie nodded. "We know frustratingly little about Albania since the Red Chinese moved in, but there have been rumors that somewhere in the North Albanian Alps there is a building, a very primitive stone fortress originally built by bandits, where a few very top-secret political prisoners are kept. The countryside is almost inaccessible: cliffs, gorges, crags, landslides, you name it, and the mountain people are a clannish bunch. Still, the rumor persists that such a place exists, and it was into these same mountains that the general disappeared."

"Who's the informant?" asked Carstairs idly. "Reliable?"

"An Orthodox Christian priest," said Peattie. "You may or may not know that the churches have been closed and desecrated in Albania. Our friend's mosque, for instance, has been turned into a bar and his own existence is precarious. Not too long ago he was

put to work for a month on a road gang that repairs and builds
roads in the north, and it's there he heard stories about this place."

"Any chance of pinpointing its whereabouts?" Carstairs was
already out of his chair and crossing the room to the wall map.

With a shrug Peattie joined him. "Anywhere from here to
there," he said, tracing the line of the mountains in the north. "We
know the road ends about *here*," he added, "but of course that
doesn't mean anything, the roads are constantly coming to a crashing halt in these countries and life still goes on, by mule, donkey,
bicycle, oxcart, et cetera, et cetera."

Carstairs shook his head. "There's not a chance in the world
they could still be alive, not a chance, but is there any way of
confirming the fact that they were taken there? That they were
killed there?"

"Very difficult making inquiries," Peattie said. "Take weeks,
I'm afraid. Foreigners, of course, are immediately suspect and the
few allowed into the country as tourists see very little. A good
many Albanians are connected with the secret police, by member-
ship, through relatives or marriage—the usual trick, you know, to
keep the citizenry terrorized. I'm not sure . . ." He hesitated and
then said firmly, "I'm *very* sure the agents we have over there
wouldn't be allowed to endanger themselves for the sake of—"

Carstairs bluntly completed the thought. "For the sake of two
agents who have been at the mercy of General Perdido for more
than a week. Quite right, I wouldn't allow it myself."

Peattie very pointedly looked away and added, "I think I
should tell you that this mountain eyrie has a most unsavory reputation. My informant tells us that those who are Catholics cross
themselves when it's mentioned. It's spoken of in whispers, and
said that no one has ever left it alive."

"I get the point," Carstairs told him harshly, and then, more
gently, "I wonder . . ."

"Wonder what?"

"I'm curious about that mountain fortress." He got up, excus-
ing himself, and went out to confer with Bishop. He returned a few
minutes later. "I had an idea," he explained. "I've asked for a private seaplane to get lost over the Albanian Alps. They should have
it there in an hour."

"Reconnaissance?"

Carstairs nodded. "Strictly unofficial, of course—we'll share any information we get with you people, but if Perdido's going to go on snatching Americans we'd jolly well better find out if he's tucking them in there for the night."

Peattie stood up. "You'll keep me posted then. Good."

Carstairs also stood. "And thank you for stopping in. Let's get together for a drink one of these days."

"Yes, let's," said Peattie with his wry smile. "One of these days or years . . ."

When he had gone Carstairs went back to his paper work, made a few telephone calls, went to lunch and conferred for an hour with his chief upstairs. It was after two o'clock when he returned to his office to be handed a radiogram by Bishop. It was a report from the pilot of the seaplane that had made a sortie over the Albanian Alps. No building of Carstairs' description had been seen with the naked eye but the reconnaissance photographs would be dispatched as soon as they were developed. What had intrigued the pilot, however, was the activity going on in the area bounded by the Alps in the east, Shkoder in the south and Lake Scutari in the west. He had seen a large number of men scouring the area on foot, a stream of very black smoke rising from a wood—obviously something containing oil or gasoline had been set afire—and an unusual concentration of police launches patrolling Lake Scutari.

Carstairs frowned, wondering what the devil this would mean, if anything. He wished he knew more about Albania, he wondered if Peattie would have knowledge of whether this type of activity was normal or irregular for that country and he was about to pick up the phone when Peattie himself was ushered in again.

"This just came through," Peattie said without preamble. "Something's up all right in the north of Albania. One of our agents broke silence to send it—damned risky of him. Here, read it yourself, it's fresh from the decoding room."

Carstairs picked up the sheet and scanned it. It read:

GENERAL PERDIDO ARRIVED ALBANIA YESTERDAY, MYSTERIOUSLY SHOT AND WOUNDED DURING NIGHT, TODAY DIRECTING LARGE SEARCH PARTY FOR ENEMIES OF STATE ESCAPED MOUNTAIN HIDEAWAY IN CAR, NUMBER IN PARTY UNCERTAIN STOP TWO GUARDS

DEAD, ONE ESCAPEE RUMORED AMERICAN, GROUP ASSUMED STILL
ALIVE AND HEADING WEST OR NORTHWEST TO COAST STOP

Carstairs leaped to his feet to look at the map. "Whoever
these people are we've got to give them every possible help," he
sputtered. "If one of them's rumored to be American there's always
a chance it could be Farrell, but even if it isn't these people can
give us valuable information. Look at this map, see how damn close
they are to Yugoslavia, that's where they'll head, it's their only
chance. Bishop," he bellowed into the intercom, "get me Fiersted
in the State Department." To Peattie he said, "If Fiersted will clear
the way for us with the Yugoslavian Government we can scatter a
few of our men along their border to watch for them. We can have
men there by midnight—by midnight at the very *latest*," he vowed.

By midnight Mrs. Pollifax, Farrell and the Genie were no
longer adrift upon the waters of Lake Scutari. They were not in
Yugoslavia, either. They had been blown by an ill wind in the
opposite direction—south, and deeper into Albania—and at the
stroke of midnight they were huddled behind a stone wall in the
city of Shkoder at the southern tip of Lake Scutari. High above
their heads stood the walls of a grim-looking, medieval castle. A
fuzzy, heat-stricken pink moon shed a faint light on the scraps of
wet paper that had once been their map, and by this light Mrs.
Pollifax was trying to make some sense of the lines that had not
been obliterated.

"The damn thing looks like a river," the Genie was saying,
regarding the water in front of them angrily. "It can't belong to
Lake Scutari. There's a current, we felt it, and anything but a real
river would have dried up in this heat a month ago."

It had felt like a real river, too; in fact if the moon had not
emerged from wisps of cloud their log would have sailed right out
of Lake Scutari, past the castle on the hill and down this unidentifi-
able body of water. They had barely managed to propel the log
toward land, and they were now hiding in the shadows of an ancient, cobbled alley while they desperately tried to think what to
do. Their log had been lost in the darkness and they were back in
the city where they had first met Albania. It was difficult to decide
whether they had made progress or not.

"There *is* a line," said Mrs. Pollifax, peering nearsightedly at the map. "The line goes from Shkoder to the Adriatic Sea but it has no label, nothing *says* it's a river."

"I copied every single word there was," Farrell informed her stiffly.

"Of course you did, it's just such a small map. But there *is* a line, see?" She passed the scrap of paper around, and the two men took turns squinting at the line and pondering its significance. Mrs. Pollifax added hopefully, "The only other lines like that on the map are rivers. It even says they're rivers."

"And this does appear to be a river," the Genie said, nodding. "Even if we didn't expect a river here."

"A very good river, too," put in Farrell.

"But nameless, unknown and confusing," said the Genie.

Mrs. Pollifax took back the wet piece of paper to study again. "There's this to be considered," she told them softly. "To go by land from Lake Scutari to the coast looks quite a distance, between ten and twenty miles, I'd say, and all of it to be done on foot. This funny line meanders a bit, but this line, if it really is a river, ends at the Adriatic. If one had a boat—"

"If one had a boat, and if this truly is a river, and if it should empty into the Adriatic—"

The Genie broke off without finishing his sentence and they were all silent, contemplating the succession of hazards. "So many *ifs*," sighed Mrs. Pollifax at last. "A gamble in the most terrifying sense of the word."

The Genie said soberly, "But that is precisely what life is, wouldn't you agree? Everything is a matter of choice, and when we choose are we not gambling on the unknown and its being a wise choice? And isn't it free choice that makes individuals of us? We are eternally free to choose ourselves and our futures. I believe myself that life is quite comparable to a map like this, a constant choice of direction and route." He was silent a moment. "Stay here," he added, standing up. "I will try to find a boat for us."

Mrs. Pollifax nodded, feeling a very deep relief that someone had told her to remain sitting. It was bliss not to move, and even greater bliss to be ordered not to move since this immediately eliminated all sense of guilt and responsibility. She closed her eyes, then opened them to see that Farrell was already asleep and with a sigh she forced her eyelids to remain open, knowing that someone had to remain on guard or all their previous efforts would come to nothing. To occupy herself she began figuring how many hours ago they had escaped. They had left their prison around nine o'clock Thursday night, hadn't they? It had been roughly dusk, or nine of this day, when they had set their log afloat on Lake Scutari. This meant they had escaped only a little more than twenty-four hours ago, which was incredible because it already seemed a lifetime of nightmares. She then began figuring when they or she had last slept and when they had last eaten, but this was even more arduous and numbers kept slipping from her mind and her lids were just closing, her will power diminishing, when she heard the quiet drip-drip of an oar or paddle in the water nearby. She put out a hand to waken Farrell and when his eyes jerked open she placed a warning finger across her lips. They both turned to watch the silhouette of a long boat move across the path of weak moonlight. The boat looked a little like a Venetian gondola, its prow and stern sharp-pointed and high out of the water. A man stood in the center facing the bow, an oar in each hand, but Mrs. Pollifax couldn't be sure it was the Genie until the boat drew in to the shore. She and Farrell went to meet it.

"Come aboard," said the Genie, bowing as had been his custom, and Mrs. Pollifax could even see his old twinkle in the moonlight. The Genie was feeling pleased with himself, and quite rightly, she thought, wondering how he had found the *londra* and hoping he hadn't been forced to kill for it. She moved to help Farrell—it was necessary for him to sit on the side of the boat and tumble in backward because of his bad leg. She, too, half fell into the boat and lay on the floor too exhausted to move or speak. It was the Genie who was taking over now, it had become his turn, and she lay on her back and stared up at the clouded moon and hoped her turn would never come. The Genie was at work with the oars again, giving the water quick, short jabs. Mrs. Pollifax said in a low, dreamy voice, "You found a boat."

"Tied up, not far away," the Genie whispered over his shoulder. "Sleep a little, the current helps. With this moon I'll keep close to the shore."

Mrs. Pollifax's gaze traveled from him to the shape of Shkoder's castle set high above them, its sides almost perpendicular, the lines of its buildings outlined black against the deep-blue night sky. There was a solitary star, and with her eyes upon it Mrs. Pollifax fell softly asleep. When she awoke both the castle and the star had disappeared and she thought the sky looked a shade lighter. Then she realized that what had awakened her was the sharp crack of a pistol shot from somewhere along the shore. She sat up at once.

"Down," whispered the Genie violently.

Farrell, too, fell back, his eyes alarmed. "But what was it, who is it?"

"Someone on the shore. I think he wants us to stop."

"Are we going to?" asked Mrs. Pollifax weakly.

"I haven't seen him, it's too dark," the Genie said, speaking without moving his lips. "I heard something and glanced toward the shore. I could dimly make out a man waving his arms but I looked away. I am still looking away, I see nothing."

"He may fire again and hit you the next time," Farrell pointed out.

The Genie said pleasantly, "Yes, I know. But we are moving faster now, can you feel it? You mustn't look but the river has been growing wider in the last ten minutes, and the earth flatter. These are rice paddies we are passing now. There is a definite change in the air, too—smell it?"

Both Farrell and Mrs. Pollifax sniffed. "Salt," said Farrell wonderingly. "Salt? Am I right?"

"Yes."

The pistol was fired again and something plunked against the sides of the boat. "Above water line, I hope," said Farrell. "He's a damn good shot in this light."

"He's running away now," the Genie said casually. "He has begun thinking."

"Thinking?"

"That he can't question a man going toward the sea in a boat if the man in the boat refuses to stop. He will either find a boat himself or find a telephone and talk to people on the coast who will stop us."

"May I sit up now?" asked Mrs. Pollifax.

"Yes, he's gone."

She sat up and looked around her. The darkness was rolling

back to uncover a very charming scene of springlike tender green, flat to the eye and stretching as far as the horizon. Ahead—Mrs. Pollifax wondered what lay ahead and beyond. From the boat she could see only a floor of water, a huge ceiling of brightening sky, and a number of birds. "But those are sea gulls!" cried Mrs. Pollifax.

"We've got to know what to do," Farrell said in a brooding, nearly desperate voice. "Where we're going, what we're going to do. My God, to keep playing it by ear—"

"Yugoslavia is north," Mrs. Pollifax reminded him. "We know that."

"But we don't even have a gun that's dry!"

The Genie said, "Yes, we have." The two turned to stare at him and he said, "The guard Stefan, do you remember my taking his pistol? His holster was the waterproof type. Remove it from my pocket and check it. There may be time, too, to clean the others. Know how?"

"No, damn it," said Farrell. "You?"

The Genie shook his head. "Not my cup of tea, I'm afraid. Got the gun?"

Farrell was holding it and breaking it open. "Five cartridges."

The Genie nodded. "And you?" he asked of Mrs. Pollifax.

She began emptying the various pockets in her petticoats. Out came the playing cards and Farrell exclaimed, "Not those! My God, Duchess, I won't be able to see a deck of cards for the rest of my life—if I have a life—without thinking of you."

"Well, that's one form of immortality," she retorted, and drew out the pistol, the magazine clip, the dried shreds of map, the compass. "And if I'm captured again perhaps they'll spare me a few minutes for a game of solitaire instead of the usual last meal or cigarette. That's all I have," she added, gesturing toward the small pile. "No food. Not a crumb."

"That damn lake," sighed Farrell.

"Actually I've stopped feeling weak," said Mrs. Pollifax. "Rather like catching one's second wind, I suppose, except of course we've had drinking water to sustain us."

"The kind that will bring on dysentery in a week," contributed Farrell gloomily. "It's getting lighter."

"Too light," said the Genie.

Mrs. Pollifax roused herself again. She said to the Genie, "You've been standing there all night, would you like me to take a turn? The current's so strong now there's really no need to row, is there?"

"There's still need for steering," he pointed out dryly. "And I think we're very near the Adriatic, near enough to walk to it if this river decides to turn and go elsewhere."

Farrell said thoughtfully, "If they should know by now there's a boat on this river, and be waiting to stop it, perhaps we *should* walk to the Adriatic."

The Genie shrugged. "Maybe."

Mrs. Pollifax said gently, "No, Farrell. I mean, your leg. I mean—"

"Then let me take my chances with the boat and *you* walk," he said, and Mrs. Pollifax knew by the suppressed fury in his voice that his pride was quivering. On the other hand her amateur work in hospitals had taught her when a patient was on the verge of collapse, and Farrell's nerves had reached a breaking point, gone beyond and returned. He had more stamina than most men, but even a Hercules would have had to admit that the past thirty-six hours were enervating.

Suddenly the gaudy, blood-red sun cleared the high cliffs behind them and the misty landscape lost its oriental quality and Mrs. Pollifax thought, "Why, this is the dawn I was sure I'd never see!" For a moment she was caught by the magic of life, its brevity and unpredictability, and she stared at this world as if just born into it. The distant mountains were snow-capped, the nearer cliffs tawny with deep-purple shadows. Around her the ground mist that only a few minutes ago had been gray and tattered was transformed by light into silky clouds of pearl-white and palest pink. The air was cool, and smelled of damp earth and wet grass, and the river flowing around and past them contained in it mosaic patterns of sky and sun and shore. Mrs. Pollifax felt a stirring in her that was almost mystical; an exhilarating sense of freedom that she had never known before, as if in this moment all the rules and habits of a lifetime fell from her and she stood at the very core of life and felt its heartbeat. It came of experiencing dawn in this strange country a continent away from her own, it came of being still alive when she ought to have been dead; it was compounded of surprise, ap-

preciation, exhaustion, hunger, the effects of danger and an un-
quenchability of the human spirit.

She heard Farrell say, "You all right, Duchess?"

She started. "Yes. Yes, I'm fine, thank you."

At that moment ahead of them the ground mist rolled away
and they saw the sun shining on the clear, sparkling water of the
Adriatic. Almost simultaneously Farrell cried, "Oh, God—look!"
and Mrs. Pollifax glanced to the shore of the river on their right
and saw a police boat setting out to intercept them, flags flying
from its bow and stern, the spray rising majestically in an arc behind it.

Chapter Twenty-Two

There were two men in the boat, each of them faceless silhouettes from this distance, but it could be assumed they were well armed—police usually were—and each man was leaning forward with an intensity that suggested fixity of purpose. Their boat was too old and too broad in the beam to move with speed, but it took the waves like a sedate and experienced old dowager, and even a motor that kept missing and cutting out would make progress against a *londra* with one man at its oars. Mrs. Pollifax said anxiously, "They can't possibly know who we are, they know only that we came down the river."

"They'll find out who we are soon enough," pointed out Farrell dryly, and he began to swear quietly and thoroughly at their impotence while the Genie frantically churned the water with the oars, his face grim.

Mrs. Pollifax glanced around, hoping for some wild improvisation or concealment to present itself but behind them the river was empty, and ahead of them the sea was open and boundless, furnished only with buoys noting the river's entrance. Buoys . . . no, nothing could be done with buoys . . . Mrs. Pollifax's gaze swerved to the left bank of the river and she gave an exclamation. "Look! There's a wharf and a boat—a sailboat!"

"So?" growled Farrell, snapping the safety on the gun.

"But sailboats go fast!" Mrs. Pollifax leaned forward and clutched the Genie's arm. "Do look," she begged. "The man's getting ready to take the boat out, the sail's already up, we have that gun and we can make him sail us out to sea, it's our only chance!" She found herself standing and helping the Genie push and pull at the oars. "Faster," she whispered. "Faster, faster, faster." The Genie had backed one oar to change their direction but they were rowing against the current now and the police launch, coughing and sputtering, was nevertheless gaining on them with shocking speed. The wharf was a small one, a float, really, with a narrow catwalk leading over the water to it. The boat moored beside it looked heavy but certainly seaworthy; it was roughly twenty-five feet in length, with a sunlit white sail flapping gently in the wind as the man secured the halyards. Behind them the asthmatic whine of the motor launch grew louder, and now Mrs. Pollifax could see the two men clearly, one thin and dark-faced, the other fleshy and bald. Mrs. Pollifax began to tremble.

"Faster," Farrell was saying sharply. "For God's sake faster, we're almost there and so are they."

The fisherman wore a red jersey and a pair of tattered trousers. He seemed completely oblivious to the race being run nearby. In a leisurely fashion he reached from his boat to the dock, picked up a bucket and stowed it away, walked forward to untie the mooring lines, returned aft and pulled in the stern lines. Grasping the tiller he gave it a thrust, the sails filled with wind and the boat swung free of the wharf. The Genie had been aiming for the wharf; now he swerved to follow the sailboat out to sea, and both he and Mrs. Pollifax began shouting to the man at the helm. "Wait—wait for us," cried Mrs. Pollifax, and the startled fisherman turned to look at them. They were very close to him now, and the motorboat was even closer behind them. "Wait," shouted Mrs. Pollifax, waving violently. The fisherman scowled. Undecided, watchful, he gave the tiller a jerk and brought his boat about into the wind, sails luffing, bow pointed directly at them as he regarded them with suspicious curiosity. The Genie viciously thrust one oar back through the water and the *londra* shot across the bow of the fishing boat. Dropping both oars the Genie leaped over Mrs. Pollifax and jumped aboard the sailboat.

"*Zott,*" gasped the fisherman. He stood up and roared his indignation but the Genie ignored him and leaned over the water to pull the *londra* against the sailboat.

To Farrell the Genie shouted, "For heaven's sake aim your gun at this man! And climb aboard before he kills me with his bare hands!" His voice mingled with shouts from the policemen behind them. Their launch was heading straight for the sailboat to ram it, but the Genie had now pulled the *londra* between the two boats as a buffer. "Hurry," he told Mrs. Pollifax, and she stumbled toward Farrell to help him drag his useless leg over the side.

The fisherman had stopped bawling his indignation. He stood watching them with opened mouth, his stare moving ponderously from the gun in Farrell's hand to Mrs. Pollifax. He glowered briefly at the Genie and then his eyes came to rest on the men in the launch and narrowed as he recognized their uniforms. Startled, confused, he glanced back at Farrell climbing aboard, looked again at the policemen and then decided that he was caught in an insoluble situation, and very sensibly chose a prudent course. He jumped overboard and began swimming toward the wharf.

"No, no, come back," implored Mrs. Pollifax, seeing him slip through their fingers.

The tiller that he had deserted moved idly to one side and hung there a moment, then abruptly, savagely, the sails filled with a wind that sent the boom crashing, lifted one side of the boat and sent buckets skidding across the deck.

"Grab the tiller!" screamed Farrell from the bow.

"What's a tiller?" screamed back Mrs. Pollifax hysterically.

"That thing—for God's sake hold it steady!"

Mrs. Pollifax retrieved the long arm of smooth wood that jutted from the deck and clung to it, the boom nearly decapitating the Genie before it settled, the sails flapping erratically, the boat threatening to turn over on its side before it steadied. What saved them was the *londra*, which the Genie held captive with both hands, and which the two policemen also held captive, having attached themselves to the other side of it like barnacles. Only a second earlier the bald man had started to climb across it to reach the sailboat—he was caught with one foot in the *londra* and one still in the police boat; jerking upright he waved both arms wildly in a fight for balance, lost the fight and fell ignobly to the floor of the *londra*.

At once the thin man behind the wheel of the launch pulled out a revolver and fired across the boat at the Genie. Farrell returned the fire and the policeman slumped over the wheel. Mrs. Pollifax screamed, not because Farrell had shot the thin man but because the bald one in the bottom of the *londra* had climbed to his knees and was aiming a gun at Farrell. "Shoot," she screamed at

Farrell, pointing, and Farrell and the bald policeman exchanged shots simultaneously.

But the Genie's clutch on the *londra* had weakened during the melee and it was the *londra* that had acted as a sea anchor. With nothing to hold them now the rigging tightened, the sails went taut and the wind carried them zooming off across the water with an abruptness that sent Farrell sprawling across the Genie on the deck. Mrs. Pollifax, holding tightly to the tiller, screamed for help.

"Let the tiller go! Drop it!" shouted Farrell, thereby totally confusing Mrs. Pollifax because earlier he had insisted that she grab it. She was further mystified when she let it go and the boat came about into the wind and ceased its reckless caroming. She said with interest, "Why does it . . ." and then stopped because Farrell had lifted himself from the Genie and was staring at him in horror. "Oh no," she whispered, and both hands flew to her mouth to keep her lips from trembling. She understood now why the Genie had stopped holding the *londra*. Creeping over the coils of line she knelt beside him. "Is he dead?"

Farrell very gently placed the Genie's head in his lap. "Not dead but very *very* badly hurt."

"Oh God, you're hurt too," she told him, seeing blood well out of Farrell's sleeve at the shoulder.

He nodded. "Not badly but I can't risk moving and I don't think it would be very healthy for the Genie, either. Duchess, you're going to have to sail this boat."

"I?" gasped Mrs. Pollifax in a shocked voice. "Me?"

"I can tell you what to do," he pointed out. "Duchess, you've got to, you can't fall apart now, you realize how far we've come, don't you?"

She thought back to the night on the precipice, to the goats and the wild chase in the Rolls Royce and the guard shot in the cornfield, to the day spent in being periodically submerged by motorboat waves, and the night floating across Scutari on a log. She nodded wearily. There came a time when a person wanted desperately to give up; she supposed it was as good a time as any to rally; surely there must be a few ounces of overlooked iron in her soul. "I'll try," she said, and wiped a tear from what must be a very raddled cheek by now. "I can't help crying," she told Farrell. "I'm tired."

"Can't imagine why," he said dryly. As she crawled drearily back toward the tiller he added casually, "Have any idea whether I winged that bald chap in the *londra?*"

Mrs. Pollifax looked back. "The boats are still there, bobbing around at some distance from each other. No head showing in the *londra.* You must have hit him a *little.*"

Farrell nodded. "There may not be much time before they're discovered, and two boats, each with a wounded or dead policeman in them, will set off a merry chase. Duchess, before you take the tiller, do three things."

"Yes?"

"Look for fresh water. Hand me that tarp over there so I can make a tent to keep the sun off the Genie. See if the fisherman packed a lunch."

"Lunch?" said Mrs. Pollifax, brightening. "You mean *food?*"

"Naturally I mean food—the stuff we haven't had since heaven knows when."

Mrs. Pollifax, foraging around, was staggered by her success. She could not remember any triumph in her life that could possibly equal what she felt as she carried to Farrell the goatskin bag containing the fisherman's noon meal. She brought from it a slab of cornbread, six olives and a square of cheese. From a smaller goatskin bag she poured a cup of goat's milk. When she crept back to the tiller it was with her mouth full of flaky, exquisitely flavored cornbread and her heart filled with a faint hope that if the gods were smiling on them now their smiles might linger just a little longer.

"Okay, Duchess, full speed ahead."

"But speed is what I'm afraid of," admitted Mrs. Pollifax ruefully.

He paid this no attention. "Wind from the north. We can't risk heading north to Yugoslavia, we might run into more police launches. We'll have to head straight out to sea."

Mrs. Pollifax gaped at him. "Out to sea!"

Farrell grinned weakly. "We've been doing everything else the hard way, Duchess, why stop now? Give me that compass and turn the tiller to starboard—the right, I mean. And brace yourself first," he added.

Mrs. Pollifax tossed him the compass and turned the tiller to the right. At once the boat came to life; the wind seized them like a gigantic hand, the sail tightened, the rigging creaked and Mrs. Pollifax was overwhelmed by a feeling of total helplessness as wind, sail and boat combined to send them skimming the waves. "But how do you *stop* this thing!" she wailed. She had the feeling of being on a roller coaster, idle one moment, the next moment hurtling at breath-taking speed.

"Easy does it," Farrell shouted to her over the wind. "Keep the tiller in the center. You're broad-reaching now, the wind on your starboard side."

"Like this?"

"Excellent."

"Yes—oh *yes,*" gasped Mrs. Pollifax. She had just felt the boat steady itself in response to a subtle turn of the tiller, had felt the boat under her become disciplined, the sails taut but not under strain, and she was delighted.

"Keep it that way," Farrell told her. "If you hit a squall and get scared let the tiller go, the boat'll come about by itself. If the wind increases but you're not scared then move the tiller slightly left or slightly right—you'll be tacking then. The important thing for now, though, is to get the hell out of sight of land as fast as possible." With his one useful arm he was pulling the tarp over his head and shrugging it into position so that it would shade the Genie.

Mrs. Pollifax, tiller in hand, dedicated herself to getting them the hell out of sight of Albania as fast as possible.

Toward five o'clock that afternoon the *Persephone,* a seagoing tug returning to its home port of Otranto from Port of Venice, was making its way southward when the first mate sighted a sailboat with someone waving what looked to be a white petticoat. "Another damned tourist," he growled, mentally and savagely condemning those pleasure-loving hordes that descended upon the Adriatic believing anybody could sail a boat. He reported it to the captain, who ordered their course slowed, and presently the small boat drew alongside the *Persephone.*

The first mate looked down into the boat and gasped. "*Mon Dieu,*" he whispered, for seated at the tiller was one of the wildest-looking women he had ever seen, white hair in shreds, face filthy and blistering from the hot sun. Yards of voluminous skirt surrounded her, but although he recognized the clothes as Greek or Albanian the woman's features did not match them. Then he saw the tarpaulin lift and his eyes widened, his memory flashing back to the war years and to lifeboats found in the Mediterranean. Both men looked as if they'd had it but the bearded one at least was in motion; he was grinning broadly and waving an arm, although it was plain from the blood-stained cloth strapped around his other arm that he badly needed a doctor. The first mate gave a brief thought to the type of gunfighters they might be escaping, and hurried to report to the captain.

Mrs. Pollifax, gazing up at the ship from below, wondered why on earth the sailors along the rail were staring at her with horrified fascination. She had naïvely pictured them being welcomed back to civilization with delighted smiles and shouts of joy. Now it occurred to her that in the eyes of civilization she and Farrell and the Genie might just as well be returning from a trip to the moon: their experiences of the past fortnight were too exotic, too melodramatic for a prosaic world to digest. It was the three of them who must adapt now; it was they whom violence had made foreign, and for the first time she conceded how tattered and bizarre they must appear to these well-scrubbed sailors just finished with their tea.

"We're curiosities," she realized.

Then the spell broke; a sailor shouted, *"Inglese!* Welcome!" Cheering broke out along the deck rail, and Mrs. Pollifax had to look away to conceal the tears in her eyes.

"Well, Duchess," said Farrell, smiling at her.

"Well, Farrell," she said, smiling back at him, and lifted a petticoat to wipe her eyes.

"You look like hell, Duchess," he said fondly, "but you're safe."

"Safe," repeated Mrs. Pollifax, tasting the word on her tongue as if it was a rare wine.

A rope ladder was flung over the side and an officer with a medical kit descended hand over hand to their boat. He went at once to the Genie and bent over him. Two sailors followed down the ladder and in broken English instructed Mrs. Pollifax in the rudiments of rope climbing. With their help she began the ascent, a dozen men shouting words of encouragement from the rail. She would have preferred waiting for Farrell but an officer in a starched, white uniform insisted upon escorting her at once to the captain.

"I must request identification," said the captain, and then, unbending a little at sight of her face he added, "There must be people you would like to notify?"

Mrs. Pollifax thought of her son and daughter and reluctantly put them aside. "If you would be so kind as to contact Mr. Carstairs at the Central Intelligence Agency in Washington," she said.

The captain's eyes flickered. "It's that way, is it?" He looked at her with open curiosity. "Suppose you write the message. I ask only that it not be in code and that I see it before it is sent."

Mrs. Pollifax sat down gratefully at his desk and tried to pull her thoughts together. After chewing on her pencil for a moment she wrote the following:

SIR: RESCUED FROM ADRIATIC SEA THIS AFTERNOON BY . . .

She looked up. "What ship is this, and where are you going?"

"The *Persephone*, due to land at Otranto in two hours, or at 1900 hours."

Mrs. Pollifax began again:

SIR: RESCUED FROM ADRIATIC SEA THIS AFTERNOON BY S.S. PERSEPHONE ARRIVING OTRANTO AT 1900 HOURS. FARRELL AND SECOND COMPANION IN NEED OF MEDICAL ATTENTION. HAVE NO PASSPORT OR MONEY AND MUST REQUEST SOME HELP OTHERWISE IT HAS BEEN A MOST INTERESTING TRIP. SINCERELY YOURS, EMILY POLLIFAX.

The captain read it through and nodded. "It will be sent immediately," he said. "I will also send word to Otranto that a doctor will be urgently needed. We do not have one aboard, unfortunately." He looked at her and smiled faintly. "And you," he added, "you would perhaps like to wash a little and comb the hair?"

Mrs. Pollifax's eyes widened. "Wash a little," she repeated. "Wash a little? Yes, that would be very nice," she said politely, and suddenly began to laugh.

* * *

The boat had not yet docked when a harbor launch drew up beside the *Persephone* and requested permission for two passengers to come aboard. Both men wore business suits; one carried an attache case up the rope ladder and the other a medical bag. They were escorted at once to the cabin where Mrs. Pollifax, Farrell and the Genie were resting, and without a word the doctor hurried to the berth where the Genie lay. The second man stood and looked appraisingly at Farrell and Mrs. Pollifax. Completing his scrutiny he said, "Ben Halstead's my name, I believe we have a mutual friend named Carstairs."

Mrs. Pollifax brightened. "Yes indeed," she said, rising from her chair. "I am Emily Pollifax and this is Mr. Farrell, who has a broken leg and a fresh bullet wound in his shoulder and an old one in his arm; and this man . . ." She glanced toward the Genie, whose eyes were open now but vacant as he gazed at the doctor. "We don't know who he is but we brought him along anyway. He's a very peculiar but resourceful Chinese man who speaks English, except that he preferred keeping it a secret for quite a long time."

"Oh? That's interesting." Halstead moved to the berth and over the doctor's shoulder looked down at the Genie. "He dropped no clues at all, you don't know anything at all about him?"

"Actually I didn't trust him at first," put in Farrell. "Nor did he trust us, which is provocative. But he's not a Red, and he rescued us from a very sticky situation."

Mrs. Pollifax said slowly, "Yes, and when I asked him yesterday about next of kin, in case anything happened, he gave a little chuckle and said nobody would miss him, they would have held his funeral two years ago. He'd been dead a long time, he said."

Halstead frowned. "There's something damn familiar about the look of him. What's his condition, Bill, can he be questioned?"

The doctor removed the stethoscope from his ears. "Not for a day or two, sorry. He needs immediate attention and the best of care, but he can be moved. Stretchers, an ambulance, then blood transfusions and straight to the operating room."

"Will he survive?" asked Mrs. Pollifax anxiously.

"The vital thing is removing the bullet and that'll be a bit tricky. After that I could answer with more certainty. Some signs of malnutrition, of course; considerable patchwork needed after removal of the bullet, but the odds are in his favor. Barring anything unforeseen—yes, he'll survive."

"I'm so glad," Mrs. Pollifax said warmly.

The doctor, standing erect, only nodded. "From the sound of it we're docking now." He pulled the blanket from the top berth and tucked it around the Genie. "The ambulance is waiting at the pier, I'll send them word to hurry along with a stretcher and then I'll take a look at you, Mr.—Farrell, is it?"

Farrell said cheerfully, "That's me, but no need to hurry. I simply wouldn't feel comfortable without a bullet in me somewhere." He was watching Halstead, who kept staring at the Genie. "You recognize him, don't you." It was a statement, not a question.

"Very astute of you," said Halstead, not turning. "Except recognize isn't precisely the word; it's more a feeling of familiarity. If I could only—good grief!" He exclaimed, snapping his fingers. "Dr. Lee Tsung Howell!"

"I beg your pardon?" faltered Mrs. Pollifax.

"Considerably thinner, of course, that's what fooled me. Good heavens, and it was exactly two years ago that he disappeared—that ties in—and a memorial service really was held for him. Every bit of evidence pointed to his murder by the Red Chinese. There were even two reputable witnesses to testify he was killed and his body carried off by his assassins."

Mrs. Pollifax and Farrell glanced in astonishment at the Genie. "*Who* is he?" asked Mrs. Pollifax.

"And *what?*" asked Farrell.

"Dr. Howell, the scientist. Brilliant man. Born in China; father English, mother Chinese. English citizen. Made the mistake of traveling to Hong Kong two years ago. That's when they murdered—except they didn't murder him, did they? Snatched him."

Farrell said incredulously, "You mean he's *the* Dr. Howell? The protein man?"

"Please," said Mrs. Pollifax despairingly, "please can someone tell me what we're talking about, and why on earth a protein man would be locked up in a cell in Albania for two years?"

"Food," said Halstead. "Can you think of anything China needs more desperately for her underfed millions? She needs food more than communism, guns, armies, factories. If I tell you that at the time of his disappearance Dr. Howell was at work on a method for extracting protein from a common weed—a protein that would feed hundreds of people for only a few pennies—does that explain Red China's interest in him?"

Farrell whistled.

"Except," added Halstead, glancing at the Genie, "except they did a fantastic job of covering their tracks. We knew they tried to kidnap him but we believed he fought for his life and was killed."

"Except there was no body," pointed out Farrell.

"No, two witnesses instead, each highly placed and of impeccable reputation."

"Not so impeccable now," said Mrs. Pollifax.

"No indeed."

"Do you think they tortured him?"

"Possibly at first, but he'd be no good to them dead. They probably settled for solitary confinement, or slow starvation." He shook his head. "What a break for the world that you found him! The presses will be humming all night long."

"Will they hum for us, too?" inquired Mrs. Pollifax.

Both men turned to look at her. "Good God, no," said Farrell. "The Genie—that is, Dr. Howell—will have escaped by himself against impossible odds. As for Emily Pollifax of New Brunswick, New Jersey, who on earth is she?"

"But I feel like *such* a heroine," confessed Mrs. Pollifax sadly.

"And so you are, Duchess, so you are. But you have never left Mexico City, remember? As for Albania, where is it? You haven't even read about it in *Time* magazine, let alone visited it."

"Oh," said Mrs. Pollifax.

Farrell grinned. "Cheer up, Duchess. Do you recall—and it pains me to do so—my suggesting that the Genie was mentally retarded?"

She smiled back. "Yes I do remember, and I believe I said there were flashes of intelligence now and then."

Halstead laughed. "Just to be charitable I might add that he's known as quite an eccentric. Would that help?" The stretcher was brought in by two orderlies and they were silent as the Genie was lifted very gently onto it. As he was carried out of the stateroom Mrs. Pollifax said suddenly, "Will I be able to send him get-well cards? I should like to very much if you'll give me the name of the hospital here."

Halstead said, "Actually you can learn the hospital's name simply by reading your newspaper tomorrow morning in Washington, D.C."

"Washington!" exclaimed Mrs. Pollifax.

"My orders are to fly you at once, nonstop, to Washington." Seeing their stunned faces he added, "Sorry. You can eat and sleep on the plane, you know, but Carstairs has to see for himself that you're alive." He gave them a crooked half-smile. "Apparently he can't believe it. At any rate immediate questioning is in order. We leave as soon as Bill has taken a look at that arm and pumped Farrell full of anti-infection and anti-pain shots."

Mrs. Pollifax groaned. "But I'm still wearing the clothes of a goatherder's wife and I still haven't had a bath—only a facewash— and the lice are back and I think they've multiplied. Is there no rest at all for the weary?"

"Never. Not in this job, anyway." He added with a grin, "You may never be in the newspapers, but it isn't everybody who has a jet plane specially commandeered for them." He glanced at his watch. "It's seven o'clock now, European time. There's a car and a plane waiting, you'll be in the air within the hour and land in America shortly before midnight—losing a few hours on the ocean, of course. Looks like Walter Reed Hospital for you, old chap."

Farrell nodded. "Afraid so, yes."

"America," repeated Mrs. Pollifax nostalgically. "I feel like singing the national anthem."

"Better not," suggested Farrell mildly, and visibly braced himself as the doctor joined them.

Chapter Twenty-Three

They sat in Carstairs' office, each of them facing him across his broad desk. The lights had been turned low and there were cigarettes for Farrell and hot soup and coffee for them both. Farrell's arm was in a sling and he had been given four injections and seven hours of drugged sleep on the plane, but still he looked white and frail. After one glance at him Carstairs said flatly, "I won't keep you long. The important thing is to put the frame of this on tape before you forget; it will surprise you how unreal your adventures will seem to you once you reach a fairly normal state of recovery. At the moment it is only too fresh to you. We need that freshness. You've seen General Perdido—he's important to us. You've been in Albania—you've experienced a country we know too little about." His face softened. "And may I congratulate you both on rescuing Dr. Lee Tsung Howell?"

"You may," said Farrell with a grin.

"And on coming back yourselves," added Carstairs. "I don't mind telling you that I gave you both up long ago."

"Did you really!" exclaimed Mrs. Pollifax in a pleased voice.

"I'm going to call in Bishop now," went on Carstairs. "He'll take a few notes but the bulk of it will be put on tape tonight, the rest of the picture can be filled in tomorrow. I hope a tape recorder doesn't make you self-conscious?"

"Too tired," said Mrs. Pollifax.

He nodded. "I think we might give Johnny the rest he needs by letting you do most of the talking, Mrs. Pollifax. Johnny, you join in when it suits you, agreed?"

Bishop had come in, and Mrs. Pollifax noticed that his nostrils looked pinched during the introductions. "It's the goats," she told him forgivingly. "Just don't sit too near me." Half a day in the waters of Lake Scutari had subdued the smell but it was obvious that only a complete change of clothes and a vast amount of hot water and soap would ever make her acceptable to society again.

"*Goats?*" said Carstairs, startled.

She nodded. "Goats. Where would you like me to begin?"

"With your abduction—the rest can be filled in later," said Carstairs. "Begin with your meeting Johnny. That would be the nineteenth of August?"

She nodded. "*They* gave us soup and coffee too—the men in the shack." Awkwardly, and then with increasing absorption, she told of their flight to Albania and their subsequent days there, Farrell joining in occasionally to emphasize a point. Carstairs did not interrupt until Mrs. Pollifax mentioned the missile site.

"Missile site!" he exploded. "Missile site?"

"You didn't already know about this?" asked Mrs. Pollifax demurely.

"Albania is not a country where the CIA is given much scope," he said dryly. "No, we did not know about this, Mrs. Pollifax. Are you *sure* it was a missile site?"

"No," she said, "but Colonel Nexdhet was."

"Who . . . ?"

Farrell grinned. "Let her go on, it gets more and more interesting."

Mrs. Pollifax continued, eventually concluding, ". . . and we think the two men were left dead in their boats so we sailed west, straight out to sea, and by that time the Genie—that is, Dr. Howell —was more unconscious than conscious. At first we avoided any boats we saw in the distance but when we finally decided it was safe to be rescued nobody paid the slightest attention to us. We'd wave at them and they'd just wave back."

"Thought we were out for pleasure," added Farrell wryly.

Carstairs smiled and flicked off the switch of the tape recorder. "Quite a story. . . . Let's let it rest there for the moment. It's a good place to stop. There'll be many more details to clear up, more information on General Perdido, for instance, and I'd like that missile site pinpointed on a map if humanly possible. Those stone buildings, too. All this can wait, though. The important item —and after hearing what's happened to you the most surprising item—is that you're both alive."

Farrell said soberly, "You've very carefully avoided the beginning of all this, haven't you? Mexico City, I mean. I take it the whole thing blew up like a bomb and turned into a disaster area for us. They got DeGamez?"

Carstairs sighed. "I'm sorry you ask." He bent over a cigarette and a lighter, carefully avoiding Farrell's eye. "One thing lost, one thing found," he said. "Let's not underestimate what you accomplished in getting Dr. Lee Tsung Howell back, as well as yourselves." He put down the lighter and looked directly at Farrell. "Yes, Johnny, DeGamez is dead. He was murdered on the seventeenth of August."

"Damn," said Farrell savagely.

Mrs. Pollifax felt a tremor of shock run through her. She said quietly, "I'm terribly, terribly sorry. General Perdido did this?"

Carstairs nodded. "Fortunes of war, Mrs. Pollifax. All our agents know the risk."

She shivered. "Yes, but he was so kind, he was such a good man, he was such a *gentleman.*"

Carstairs suddenly became very still. Slowly he turned his head to stare at Mrs. Pollifax and his silence had a stunned quality. He said at last, very softly, "But how could you possibly know that, Mrs. Pollifax, when you never met the real Senor DeGamez?"

"Oh, but you see I did," she told him eagerly. "Not on the nineteenth, of course, but a few days after arriving in Mexico City —well, I had to be sure I could locate the shop, don't you see? And after finding it I passed it nearly every day. I really grew to think of it as *my* shop," she confessed with a rueful laugh. "And that's why —well, after passing it so many times and seeing him there I thought I would stop in one morning and browse around a little. I didn't think it would hurt," she added anxiously, suddenly noticing the intensity of Carstairs' gaze.

"Go on," he said in a stifled voice.

"So I went inside and we had a lovely chat, Senor DeGamez and I."

"When? What date?" The voice had urgency behind it.

"When? Why, it must have been—let's see, it was four days before the nineteenth, I believe. That would make it August 15 when I stopped in. Yes, it was definitely the fifteenth."

"What exactly did you 'chat' about?" demanded Carstairs,

and so harshly that Farrell gave him a second glance and narrowed
his eyes.

"Why, mostly about traveling alone, and the grandchildren
we had, and did I play solitaire. He gave me a book called 77 *Ways
to Play Solitaire*, and although at the time I didn't warm to the
idea—"

"Mrs. Pollifax," interrupted Carstairs in a strangled voice.

"Yes?"

"Mrs. Pollifax, DeGamez was given your photograph on the
ninth of August."

"My *what?*"

"Mrs. Pollifax, when you walked into the Parrot Bookstore on
August 15 DeGamez knew who you were. Do you understand, *he
knew who you were?*"

A small gasp escaped Mrs. Pollifax.

"He must also have had very strong suspicions by that date
that he was being closely watched. Mrs. Pollifax, I want you to tell
me every word he said, and just where I can find that book."

"Oh, but there was nothing in the book," she assured him.
"They thought there was, I forgot to tell you that, but General
Perdido spent days somewhere having it tested. They found noth-
ing."

Carstairs sat back and looked at her. He said carefully, "If
DeGamez had received the microfilms, Mrs. Pollifax, I know that
he would have found some way to give them to you on the fifteenth. I want you to think. I want you to go back and reconstruct
that visit as closely as possible."

Very soberly Mrs. Pollifax sent her thoughts back to that
morning.

"Describe it, tell me everything that happened."

Patiently and carefully Mrs. Pollifax began speaking of the
morning when she first entered the shop. The book of memoirs.
The parrot's shout. The conversation about Olé, about traveling
alone, about American geese, and the presentation of the book on
solitaire. "He wrapped both books together in white paper," she
added, frowning. "But by that time two other customers had come
in and so I left."

"Try again," said Carstairs.

Again Mrs. Pollifax described her visit, and once again uncovered nothing. "The two other customers had walked in, and he said something to me—in a more public voice, you understand—about wishing me a beautiful visit in his country. And then I—*oh*," she cried, "the *cards!*"

"Cards," repeated Carstairs, and leaned forward.

"Yes, of course," she said in a stunned voice. "How on earth could I have forgotten! It was just as I reached the door. He called out, 'But how can you play solitaire without the cards, senora'—yes, those were his words—and he threw them to me. Just threw them to me across the store. And he said, 'How do you Americans call it, on the house?' and I caught them. I held up two hands and caught them like a ball and tucked them into my purse. But surely he wouldn't throw anything of value like that, so casually, so impulsively, you don't think . . . ?"

Carstairs' voice was filled with suppressed excitement. "That is precisely the way a man who is under surveillance would dispose of something dangerous. Mrs. Pollifax, what happened to those playing cards?"

Farrell said incredulously, "Duchess, that deck you played with in Albania, that's surely not—?"

"But of course," she told Farrell. To Carstairs she said, "I have them right here in my pocket."

Carstairs stared at her in astonishment. "You mean you carried them *with* you? You mean they're with you *now?* You still *have* them?"

Farrell began to laugh. "Have them! Carstairs, the Duchess here played solitaire with those playing cards day in and day out, endlessly, right under the guards' noses, and in front of General Perdido, too. Have them! She drove everybody nearly crazy with them."

Mrs. Pollifax gave him a reproachful glance. Reaching down to her second petticoat she brought out the deck of cards and placed them on the desk. For a long moment Carstairs stared at them as if he could not quite believe they were there. Then he reached out and picked them up and ran his fingers over them. "Plasticized," he said softly. "They're enclosed in plastic. Bishop," he said in a strange voice, "Bishop, take these to the lab on the double. On the double, Bishop—it's microfilms we're after."

"Yes sir," gasped Bishop, and the door closed behind him.

Carstairs sat back and stared at Mrs. Pollifax with a look of incredulity.

"I know just how you feel," said Farrell, grinning. "She's full of surprises, what?"

"Rather, yes." Carstairs shook his head, a little smile tugging at the corner of his lips. "And ten days ago I believed I had sent an innocent lamb into a den of wolves. You seem to have great resources, Mrs. Pollifax."

"It's my age," said Mrs. Pollifax modestly.

"And if those cards should turn out to be . . ." Again Carstairs shook his head. "Why, then, nothing would have blown up in Mexico at all. It's incredible, absolutely incredible."

"But I simply can't think why I didn't remember about those cards," said Mrs. Pollifax. "In my mind I always identified them with Senor DeGamez, yet I completely overlooked his tossing them to me like that. Is this what's called a mental block?"

The phone buzzed and Carstairs picked it up. "Carstairs." He listened and grinned. "Right. Thanks, Bishop." Hanging up, he smiled at both Farrell and Mrs. Pollifax. "They've found the first microfilm. Tirpak used two packs of very thin playing cards. He cemented the back of one card to the front of another, with the film between, and enclosed each in special plastic." He added fervently, "If that was a mental block, Mrs. Pollifax, then bless it. Perdido would have sensed at once that you were concealing something—if you had consciously recalled how you received those cards. It very definitely saved your life when you were questioned, and it's certainly recovered for this country a great amount of invaluable information." He shook his head. "Mrs. Pollifax, we are in your debt."

She smiled and said gently, "If I could just have a bath and a change of clothes . . . I can't think of anything I'd enjoy more."

Carstairs laughed. "I'll make certain you have both within the hour. And for you, Johnny—a bevy of beautiful nurses."

Farrell stumbled to his feet and walked to Mrs. Pollifax. He bent over and kissed her. "I won't say good-bye, Duchess, I couldn't. Just don't you dare leave town without coming to see me on my bed of pain."

Mrs. Pollifax looked up at him and beamed. "I'll bring roses, I promise you, my dear Farrell, and just to prove how opinionated and shortsighted you've been I'll also bring a deck of playing cards and teach you one or two games of solitaire."

He didn't smile. He said gravely, "A very small price to pay for my life, Duchess. . . . God bless you and have a *wonderful* bath."

Mrs. Pollifax put down her suitcase in front of the door to apartment 4-A and groped in her purse for the key. It seemed a long, long time since she had last stood here, and it filled her with a sense of awe that the externals of life could remain so unchanged when she felt so different. Like a kaleidoscope, she thought, her imagination captured by the simile: one swift turn of the cylinder and all the little bits and pieces of colored glass fell into a different pattern. As she inserted her key into the lock a door across the hall flew open, spilling sunlight across the black and white tiles of the floor. "Mrs. Pollifax, you're back at last!" cried Miss Hartshorne.

Mrs. Pollifax stiffened. She said, turning, "Yes I'm home again, and how have you been, Miss Hartshorne?"

"As well as can be expected, thank you. You must have had a marvelous trip to stay so long."

"Yes, marvelous," agreed Mrs. Pollifax with a faint smile.

"I've a package for you, it came this morning and I signed for it." Miss Hartshorne held up one hand dramatically. "Don't go away, don't even move, I'll be right back."

Mrs. Pollifax waited, and presently her neighbor reappeared carrying a box wrapped in brown paper and covered with seals. "It came special delivery all the way from Mexico City! I'm giving you last night's newspaper, too, so you can catch up on our news here."

"How very kind of you," said Mrs. Pollifax. "Won't you come in and have a cup of tea with me?"

Miss Hartshorne looked shocked. "Oh, I wouldn't dream of bothering you now. As an experienced traveler myself I know how utterly exhausted you must be. But I hope you'll invite me in soon to see your slides. I trust you don't mind, I took it upon myself to tell the Lukes and Mrs. Ohrbach that they could see them too. We're all looking forward to them so much."

Mrs. Pollifax said quietly, "I'm afraid there'll be no slides, Miss Hartshorne."

Her neighbor's jaw dropped. "No slides? You mean your pic-

tures didn't come out?" Her glance was stern. "Didn't you study
the lighting charts I gave you?"

You've forgotten pi again, Emily. . . . Mrs. Pollifax smiled and
said gently, "I didn't take any snapshots, I was too busy."

"Too busy?" Miss Hartshorne looked horrified.

"Yes, too busy. In fact it might surprise you how busy I really
was, Miss Hartshorne." She added firmly, "I believe I'll insist that
you come in for a cup of tea now if you have the time. I don't
believe we've ever had a cup of tea together, have we?"

Miss Hartshorne looked shaken. "Why—why, no," she said
in an astonished voice. "No, I don't believe we have."

Mrs. Pollifax pushed wide the door and walked inside. "Do sit
down, I'll put some water on to boil and then I'll join you." Leaving package and newspaper on the couch she hurried out to the
kitchen to fill the tea kettle. "There," she said, returning, "that
won't take but a minute." From where she sat she could see the
headline on the newspaper that Miss Hartshorne had given her:
RESCUED SCIENTIST GAINS STRENGTH, DR. HOWELL TO MEET PRESS TO-
MORROW. Mrs. Pollifax smiled contentedly.

"Your package," pointed out Miss Hartshorne.

"I beg your pardon?"

"The package. Aren't you dying of curiosity or is it something
you ordered from Mexico?"

Startled, Mrs. Pollifax turned to eye the box beside her. "No,
I didn't order it and yes, I *am* curious. Would you hand me the
scissors on the table beside you, Miss Hartshorne? I'll attack this
right now."

Scissors in hand she cut the strings. The box inside bore the
label of a very expensive shop near the Hotel Reforma Intercontinental. "What on earth," she murmured, and eagerly tore it open.
"Serapes!" she gasped.

"How beautiful," said Miss Hartshorne in a hushed voice. "A
gift? How many friends you must have made, Mrs. Pollifax."

Mrs. Pollifax lifted out first one and then another until the
couch was aflame with their brilliant colors.

"Six!" cried Miss Hartshorne.

"Why so there are," beamed Mrs. Pollifax. "One for each
grandchild, one for Roger, one for Jane and one for myself. Isn't
that lovely?" Then she saw the card that had been slipped between

the folds of the last serape. It read very simply, "With mingled gratitude and apologies, Carstairs."

Carstairs. . . . A great warmth filled Mrs. Pollifax at the thoughtfulness of such a busy man. She glanced around her apartment at the familiar furniture, the sunshine striping the rugs, the atmosphere of quiet security, and just for a moment a procession of unusual people trouped through her thoughts: a goatherder and his wife, a Genie who talked of life's choices being like intersections on a road map, Colonel Nexdhet of the walrus moustache, Lulash, Major Vassovic and a man named John Sebastian Farrell who faced pain with gaiety. She said with a smile, "I met a great many unforgettable people on my trip, Miss Hartshorne. Somewhat eccentric people, perhaps, but extremely unforgettable, all of them."

Simultaneously the tea kettle began to sing and the telephone rang. Mrs. Pollifax said hastily, "Oh, Miss Hartshorne, would you pour the tea? The tea bags are in the cupboard over the stove and so are the cups. Do you mind?"

Miss Hartshorne laughed. It was the first time that Mrs. Pollifax had ever heard her laugh. "How casually you live, Mrs. Pollifax. This takes me back to my college days. No, of course I don't mind, this is really quite fun." Over her shoulder she called, "Call me Grace, won't you?"

But Mrs. Pollifax had already picked up the telephone. "Why Roger!" she exclaimed with pleasure. "How wonderful to hear from you, dear. Yes, I got in only a moment ago." She listened attentively to her son. "Worried?" she repeated. "You worried about me when I telegraphed I was staying longer? Yes, I fully intended to write but I was so busy." Mrs. Pollifax laughed suddenly and delightedly. "Roger dear, what possible trouble could I have gotten into at my age and in Mexico of all places. . . ." Her gaze fell to the serapes lying on the couch. With a small, very private smile Mrs. Pollifax picked up the card that had arrived with them and slipped it into her pocket.

The Amazing
Mrs. Pollifax

For Christopher and Jonathan Butters

Chapter One

Mrs. Pollifax had attended church that Sunday morning, and her hat—a garden of pale pink roses and green leaves—still sat on her head as she ate lunch in the sunny kitchen of her apartment. She had a tendency to be absent-minded lately about hats—in fact since beginning karate lessons she had become forgetful about a number of things—and since she would be going out again soon she had anticipated the problem by placing her hat where it could not possibly be left behind. This freed her mind for more important matters, such as a review of pressure points, or how to unbalance an assailant with an elbow-upward strike.

But Mrs. Pollifax was conscientious by nature, and if her karate textbook lay to the right of the sugar bowl, the Sunday edition of the *Times* lay on its left. She sighed faintly over her choice but it was the *Times* to which she turned first, carefully unfolding its front page for a quick scanning of the headlines. ENEMY AGENT DEFECTS IN ISTANBUL, THEN VANISHES, she read. *Woman Had Sought Sanctuary in British Consulate, Mysteriously Disappears.*

"Well!" exclaimed Mrs. Pollifax delightedly, and promptly forgot both lunch and karate.

Some months earlier a small episode of espionage had inserted itself like an exclamation point in Mrs. Pollifax's long, serene and unpunctuated life. Once it had ended—and she had enjoyed every moment of it—she had resumed her quiet existence with a sense of enrichment, of having added a dimension to her thoughts that could only be described as a chuckle. That chuckle was present now as she plunged into the newsstory, for not only was the defecting agent a woman but her past was so lengthy that Mrs. Pollifax guessed that fewer than six years separated them in age.

How very astonishing, she thought, reacting with the fascination of an amateur confronted by her professional counterpart. The news account promised a biography of the woman—Mrs. Pollifax's glance longingly caressed it—but with an exercise of will she saved it for the last.

The woman had leaped into the news by suddenly and mysteriously arriving at the British Consulate in Istanbul, breathless and ragged, to beg for help. After identifying herself as Magda Ferenci-Sabo she had been put to bed at once—at ten o'clock on a summer evening—with a sedative and a cup of tea. In the morning she had vanished, and this was all that the consul—tight-lipped and shaken—allowed himself to say, but rumors swept Istanbul that she had been abducted.

This in itself was front page news, and Mrs. Pollifax eagerly turned to the details of Magda Ferenci-Sabo's life. There were a surprising number, for an enterprising journalist had pieced together a great many old news items, adding suppositions and conclusions that alternately shocked and educated Mrs. Pollifax, who had been a spy quite by accident and for only a few brief weeks. "As an international beauty of the thirties, Ferenci-Sabo appeared at all the right places with the wrong people," commented the author of the article, and there was a blurred picture of her—all teeth and long hair—laughing on a beach with Mussolini. Then there were the marriages: first a French playboy mysteriously killed a year after the honeymoon (the journalist managed to suggest that he had been murdered by his bride); a wealthy German who later became a high official in the Nazi party, and at length a Hungarian Communist writer named Ferenci-Sabo, who was murdered in 1956 by freedom fighters. Following this the woman had disappeared—into Russia, it was believed, where it was rumored that she was actively involved in the INU.

"What an extraordinary woman," mused Mrs. Pollifax; and obviously a ruthless one as well. She wondered what such a woman thought about when the lovers and husbands had departed, leaving her alone with her thoughts, and she wondered what her motives might be in defecting now. It seemed a curious moment for such a leap. What could possibly have filled her with revulsion *now?*

Reluctantly Mrs. Pollifax put aside both speculations and newspaper because it was—she glanced at the clock on the wall—

almost two o'clock of a Sunday afternoon, and before leaving for the Garden Club film *(Gardens of the Mediterranean)* she wanted to compose a grocery list for the week. She reached for pencil and notebook and had just begun to concentrate when the telephone rang. List in hand she walked into the livingroom and before picking up the receiver added EGGS, ORANGE JUICE. "Hello," she said absently, and suddenly remembered that she had promised cookies for the Art Association tea next Sunday.

"Mrs. Pollifax?" said a bright young voice. "Mrs. Emily Pollifax?"

"Speaking," said Mrs. Pollifax, and carefully wrote *sugar, vanilla, walnuts.*

"One moment please . . ."

A man's voice said, "Good afternoon, Mrs. Pollifax, I'm certainly glad to have found you at home."

The point of Mrs. Pollifax's pencil snapped as she caught her breath sharply. This was a voice that she recognized at once, and a voice she had not expected to hear again. "Why, Mr. Carstairs!" she cried warmly. "How very nice to hear from you!"

"Thank you," he said graciously. "You've been well?"

"Yes—very, thank you."

"Good. I wonder if I might ask two questions of you then that will save us both invaluable time."

"Why not?" said Mrs. Pollifax reasonably. "Except I can't think of anything you don't already know about me."

Carstairs said pleasantly, "I don't know, for instance, if you would be immediately available—or even interested—in doing another job of work for me."

Mrs. Pollifax's heart began to beat very quickly. Split second decisions had never been her forte and she did not want to say yes without first remembering what Mr. Carstairs' work involved but on the other hand if a split second decision was necessary she did not want to say no, either. "Yes," she said recklessly, and promised herself the luxury of thinking about it later.

"Good," said Carstairs. "Question number two: are you free to leave immediately?"

"Immediately?" repeated Mrs. Pollifax, stung by the urgency of the words. "Immediately!" Of course he wasn't serious.

"I can give you thirty minutes."

"To decide whether I can leave immediately?"

"No, to leave."

Mrs. Pollifax was incredulous. Her glance fell to her grocery list, and then moved to the unwashed dishes on the counter in the kitchen; they at least were real. They would also, she remembered, take at least ten minutes to wash and put away. "But where?" she gasped. "For how long?"

Carstairs' voice was patient as if he realized the shock engendered by any such staggering rearrangements of a person's time concepts. "Put it this way," he suggested. "Have you any absolutely vital commitments during the next few days, say between today—Sunday—and Sunday a week?"

"Only my karate lessons," said Mrs. Pollifax. "And then of course I'm to pour at the Art Association tea next Sunday."

"An interesting combination," said Carstairs dryly. "You did say karate?"

"Yes indeed," admitted Mrs. Pollifax with a rush of enthusiasm. "I've been enjoying it enormously and I rather think that Lorvale—retired police sergeant Lorvale Brown—is quite shaken by my success." She stopped, appalled. "What on earth would I *tell* people? How would I explain my—just dashing off?"

"Your daughter-in-law in Chicago will have to be ill," said Carstairs. "We can, for instance, monitor any long-distance calls that your son might get from New Brunswick, New Jersey—but that's a problem we'll work out. Count on us."

"Yes," said Mrs. Pollifax, and took a deep breath. "Then I daresay I'd better hang up and get started. I'd better do something. *Something*," she added wanly.

"There will be a police car at your door in precisely twenty-two minutes. The call went through to them the moment you said yes—"

"How *is* Bishop?" asked Mrs. Pollifax fondly.

"—and in the meantime pack a small bag for a few days of travel. You'll be getting briefed within the hour. And now Godspeed, I leave you with twenty minutes in which to get ready."

"Yes," gasped Mrs. Pollifax, and to her first mental list—knit suit, pink dress—added: cancel newspaper and milk deliveries, notify janitor, Lorvale, Miss Hartshorne . . .

"Goodbye, Mrs. Pollifax," said Carstairs, and abruptly rang off.

Mrs. Pollifax slowly put down the receiver and stared at it. "Well!" she exclaimed softly, reflecting upon how quickly life could change, and then in a surprised voice, *"Well!"* Her gaze fell on the clock and she jumped to her feet and began clearing away the lunch dishes: it gave her something to do. By the time that she had rinsed the dishes there was suddenly a great deal to do. She changed quickly into her navy blue knit suit, immediately placed the flowered hat on her head again, and packed walking shoes, cold cream and travel kit. She telephoned the dairy and then the newsman, and last of all Lorvale.

"I'm off on a little trip, Lorvale," she explained. "My daughter-in-law in Chicago needs me for a few days. I'm terribly sorry but I shall have to miss my Thursday lesson."

"I'm sorry, too," he said reproachfully. "You won't have a chance to practice your omo-tude, will you."

"No, Lorvale," she agreed solemnly.

Her note to Miss Hartshorne was the more difficult because Miss Hartshorne lived across the hall and had met Mrs. Pollifax's son and daughter-in-law at Christmas. The note had to be couched in dramatic enough terms to explain Mrs. Pollifax's precipitous departure—thus canceling a lunch date with her—yet contain just enough information so that Miss Hartshorne would not unduly worry over Roger's wife and telephone Chicago to express her concern.

When the knock came upon her door Mrs. Pollifax was at the telephone again, having nearly forgotten the Art Association tea on Sunday. "Come in, it's unlocked," she called, and turned to nod at the young man who entered her livingroom—he was undoubtedly the plainclothes policeman sent by Mr. Carstairs. "It's my taxi," she blandly told the president of the Art Association. "Goodbye, dear."

"You're Mrs. Pollifax?" said the young man as she hung up.

"Yes, and you're—"

"Lieutenant Mullin. The car's outside. This your bag?"

"Oh—thank you." Mrs. Pollifax picked up her purse, hesitated and turned to glance with finality at her dear, familiar apartment. For the first time she allowed herself to compare the world

that she was leaving—safe, secure and predictable—with the world
she was about to enter, and about the latter she could know nothing at all except that it was certain to prove insecure, difficult and
totally unpredictable. "At my age," she murmured doubtfully, and
then she recalled that at her age, less than a year ago, she had been
held captive in an Albanian prison for a week, and before she led an
escape party to the Adriatic those seven days had proven extremely
informative and lively: she had met two Red Chinese generals, a
Russian spy, and a rogue of an American agent. It was quite unlikely that she would have met them in New Brunswick, New
Jersey. It was the quality of a life that mattered, not its quantity,
she reflected; and recalling this she straightened her shoulders.

"We're in a hurry," Mullin reminded her.

"Yes," said Mrs. Pollifax, took a deep breath and followed him
out into the hall, closing the door firmly behind her. She slipped
her note to Miss Hartshorne under the door of apartment 4-C and
with this act, at once so final and so irrevocable, all doubts fell from
her and she experienced a sudden exhilaration. She had committed
herself to another small adventure: something was going to happen.

The elevator door slid open at the first floor, Mullin hastened
ahead to hold the outer glass door for her, and they walked into the
sticky heat of a July afternoon. The unmarked police car was
parked at the curb, next to the NO PARKING sign, with a second man
at the wheel. Mrs. Pollifax was no sooner seated, with Mullin beside her, when the driver's foot hit the accelerator, a hidden siren
began to scream, and Mrs. Pollifax, clinging to her flowered hat,
was startled into delight. How marvelous to be involved in so much
haste, she thought, and was not even dismayed when she found
herself suddenly gazing into the eyes of her astonished pastor, who
barely escaped the racing car by jumping back to the curb. "C'est la
vie," she called out gaily, fluttering her hand at him, and then they
were leaving the city behind, cars scattering to right and left at the
sound of the siren. Moments later they entered the gates of the
small local airport. The police car bounced across the field and
came to a screaming halt in front of a helicopter whose blades were
already beating the air. Mrs. Pollifax, clinging desperately to her
hat now, was boosted into the copter, and almost before she had

reworked her hatpins the helicopter was landing at a very busy and much larger airfield.

They appeared to be expected: a man in a wrinkled beige suit left a waiting car and raced toward them. "Mrs. Pollifax?" he shouted up at her.

"Yes," she screamed back, and was dropped from the cockpit into his arms.

"Over here," he said, grasping her elbow. "They're holding the plane. Jamison's my name."

"Yes, but where am I going?" she gasped.

"Later." He hurried her into the car, which immediately tore off with a squeal of tires.

"Then where am I now?" demanded Mrs. Pollifax.

"Kennedy International," he told her. "You did very well time-wise, but that plane over there is waiting just for us and they've already held up the flight five minutes."

"Flight for where?" asked Mrs. Pollifax again.

"Washington. Carstairs wants to brief you personally before you leave the country."

So she was to leave the country; Mrs. Pollifax felt that shiver of the irrevocable again, of forces in motion that could no longer be halted, and then the reaction passed as swiftly as it had arrived. The car stopped, the door was thrown open and Mrs. Pollifax was hurried up steps and into the plane, where she and Jamison were belted into their seats at once. Before Mrs. Pollifax had sufficiently caught her breath they were landing again.

"Dulles Airport," contributed Jamison with authority, and once they had reached the terminal he guided her through the building to the parking area. "Here we are," he said, pointing to a long black limousine, and from it emerged Carstairs, tall, thin, his shock of crew-cut hair pure white against his tanned face.

"Good afternoon, Mrs. Pollifax," he said gravely, as if they had met only yesterday and she had not been spirited to his side in less than an hour.

"I'm delighted to see you," said Mrs. Pollifax, clasping his hand warmly. "It's seemed such a long time. How have things been going?"

Carstairs said cheerfully, "Abominably, as always." He gestured toward a stolid-looking young man in a dark suit and black tie. "I'd like you to meet Henry Miles first."

"How do you do," said Mrs. Pollifax politely.

"Henry is going to be traveling behind you but not with you, and it's important you know what the other looks like."

"Behind me?" echoed Mrs. Pollifax as they shook hands.

"He's keeping an eye on you," explained Carstairs, and added with a faint smile, "This time I'm taking no chances with you. All right, Jamison, take Henry off to seat 22 and make sure that plane doesn't get away!" To Mrs. Pollifax he said, "You're about to depart for the Near East. Come and sit in my car, we've only fifteen minutes in which to talk."

Chapter Two

The Near East!" echoed Mrs. Pollifax.

"Yes, on a ticklish courier assignment, and a risky one, the necessity of which became obvious only thirty minutes before I telephoned you." They were seated now in the rear of the limousine and he brought his attaché case to his lap. "I'm sending you to Istanbul," he said.

"Istanbul!" exclaimed Mrs. Pollifax, and in an astonished voice added, "Do you know, I was reading a news story from Istanbul only a few minutes before you telephoned!" She looked at him doubtfully. "Are you—that is, does this have anything to do with the Ferenci-Sabo woman, the Communist spy who tried to defect?"

"A great deal to do with it," Carstairs said. He unzipped the attaché case to expose an interior bulging with papers. Glancing up at her he said, "Except that rather a lot has happened since that news story you read."

"She's been found?" said Mrs. Pollifax eagerly.

"No." He shook his head. "If you take a second look at the dateline on your news story you'll discover the story was held up for twenty-four hours—Ferenci-Sabo reached the consulate Friday night, God knows how, and was taken in. No, she's not been found. This is Sunday afternoon—already late evening in Istanbul because of the time difference—and during these hours Istanbul has turned into a hotbed of intrigue, with agents pouring into the city from every point of the globe, all with one hope: either to find Ferenci-Sabo and offer her sanctuary in their country, or find Ferenci-Sabo and silence her, depending upon their political stance."

"She really was abducted then," said Mrs. Pollifax. "I thought —because of her importance—she might have been hidden away somewhere by the British."

"She was abducted all right," Carstairs said grimly. "Very cleverly, too, and it's believed she was abducted by Communists. The curious point is that she was abducted and not murdered. If it was silence her captors wanted, they need only have killed her in her bed at the consulate—the devils seemed to have had no problem entering the building! It leaves the implication that Ferenci-Sabo still has more value alive than dead—a conclusion," he added dryly, "that many other intelligence agencies have also reached. Ferenci-Sabo has now become fair game for everybody—and a great number of ruthless people have entered the game. A woman of Ferenci-Sabo's background was bound to be coveted but since she's been abducted, and is presumably still in Istanbul, there are high hopes that what one country has accomplished can be neatly done by another."

"I see," said Mrs. Pollifax, and waited patiently for the explanation that might make some sense of her being here. At the moment she could see no light at all.

As if reading her thoughts he said gravely, "I've called upon you, Mrs. Pollifax—with Miles to keep an eye on you—because in a city teeming with professionals you lack the slightest aura of corruption or professionalism yet at the same time"—his mouth curved wryly—"at the same time you give every evidence of being a resourceful courier."

"Thank you," said Mrs. Pollifax, "but a courier for what? I don't understand."

He said quietly. "We have heard from Ferenci-Sabo."

"You?" she said in astonishment. "The CIA? But how? When? Why?"

He held up his hand. "Please, we know almost nothing except that in a situation where we're technically only innocent bystanders we suddenly find ourselves in the position of being like the recipient of a ransom note in a kidnap case. No, that's misleading: she's apparently eluded her kidnappers and is alive and in hiding in Istanbul."

"How incredible," said Mrs. Pollifax.

He nodded. "The message, received late this morning, said only that Ferenci-Sabo would go each evening at eight o'clock to the lobby of the Hotel Itep—a small Turkish hotel in the old section—and look for someone carrying a copy of *Gone with the Wind.*"

"*Gone with the Wind!*" echoed Mrs. Pollifax, suppressing a laugh.

"In Istanbul it's now almost Sunday midnight," went on Carstairs. "We had time to immediately notify our agent in Istanbul, who presented himself at eight o'clock at the Hotel Itep." Carstairs' mouth tightened. "Word of his death reached us thirty minutes before I telephoned you, Mrs. Pollifax. I *cannot* regard it as an accident."

Mrs. Pollifax expelled her breath slowly. "Oh," she said soberly. "Oh dear!"

"Yes. At eight-fifteen he walked out of the hotel with a woman companion—and a car suddenly went berserk in the street, pinning him to the wall and killing him instantly. The woman seen with him vanished into the crowd."

"I'm terribly sorry," Mrs. Pollifax said. "You think he met Ferenci-Sabo there?"

Carstairs shrugged. "It's quite possible, in which case she must be even more desperate after seeing her contact killed before her very eyes. You are in effect replacing a dead man, Mrs. Pollifax —but with one difference."

"Yes?"

"There may be a leak somewhere—or with so damn many agents in Istanbul they may be keeping one another under surveillance—but no one could possibly recognize you, or suspect you of being an agent. I intend that no one outside of this building know of your departure. In the world of espionage there are only two living people who have ever met you—John Sebastian Farrell, currently in South America, and General Perdido, now recovering from a heart attack in Peking. And this is the way I plan to keep it. Henry Miles knows nothing except that you are to be kept under surveillance—I'm sure that not even in his wildest dreams would he guess that a novice is being sent into such a maelstrom, even if he should know the situation—which he doesn't. In turn you are to send no cables nor contact me at all. You are to trust no one and above all," he concluded grimly, "you're to watch for reckless drivers when crossing streets in Istanbul. Now I think you will be happy to learn that this time you travel with a passport—a bona fide one accomplished for you in an hour's time."

"How nice," said Mrs. Pollifax, as he handed it to her. "Even my photograph!"

"Yes, we took one for our files, you may remember."

"Very efficient."

"Also money," he said, drawing a manila envelope from the attaché case and handing it to her. "Rather a lot of money because of the unpredictability of the—er—situation. And in this second envelope is money for Ferenci-Sabo, as well as a passport for her in another name. It lacks a photograph, of course, and this she will have to supply but it has all the necessary stampings proving that she entered Turkey legally a week ago, and as an American citizen. Here are your plane tickets," he added, "as well as an especially gaudy edition of *Gone with the Wind*. A reservation has been made for you at the Hotel Itep—there wasn't time to be devious—and Henry Miles will have a room there too, but you are to avoid Henry, you understand? I don't want you linked with a professional under any circumstances—we've already lost one. And on Saturday morning you are to fly back whether you have made contact or not."

"All the way to Asia and back in six days?" said Mrs. Pollifax. "My dear Mr. Carstairs I shall almost be back in time for the Art Association tea on Sunday."

"As a matter of fact by American time you will be," he said. "You will experience the uncanny sensation of arriving here long after the tea should have ended, only to discover that they're putting up the folding tables in New Brunswick. Ah here it is!" he exclaimed, and drew out another slip of paper. "I can't foresee what will be needed, Mrs. Pollifax. All this has happened too quickly to consider possibilities, but I'm giving you the name of a man in Istanbul who can be trusted in case of emergency. He's lived in Istanbul for a number of years, and you can rely on him to advise and help—but only if you have absolutely no other recourse. He's very highly placed so for God's sake be discreet if you go to him."

"An agent?" inquired Mrs. Pollifax cheerfully.

Carstairs looked pained. "My dear Mrs. Pollifax, I do wish you'd not leap to such dramatic conclusions. He's a noted criminologist, retired now, who writes and teaches. His name is Dr. Guillaume Belleaux. You will find the name of the university with which he is connected on this slip of paper, as well as his home address. There's no need to destroy or hide this address, Dr. Belleaux is highly respected by the Turkish government as well as ours, and any tourist might legitimately carry his name. Now." He smiled. "Got it all?"

Mrs. Pollifax was stuffing the envelopes into her fat purse. The book she placed under her arm. "I'm to register at the Hotel Itep," she said, "and to present myself in the lobby at eight o'clock each evening until—hopefully—Ferenci-Sabo appears; I'm to give her passport and money, remember the name of Dr. Belleaux, and help Ferenci-Sabo in whatever way is needed."

"Right—and then vanish." Carstairs glanced quickly at his watch. "Now before we wrap this up are there questions?"

"Yes." She said slowly, "You say there may be a leak somewhere, Mr. Carstairs. You've also—somehow and very mysteriously —set up a meeting with a woman who is a notorious Communist agent." She hesitated. "Yet nobody has seen her, and your Istanbul agent was killed trying to meet her." She looked at him. "Don't you suspect a trap? Do you really trust this woman?"

Carstairs smiled faintly. "Quite true, Mrs. Pollifax, and this is why I insisted on briefing you personally." He removed a slip of yellow paper from the attaché case and handed it to her. "This is how we were advised about the rendezvous at the Hotel Itep."

Mrs. Pollifax took the proffered paper and read:

ISTANBUL: ARRIVED AT SIX STOP HAVE ENJOYED EIGHT HOURS ITEP OTELI STOP WISH YOU COULD JOIN ME STOP WHY NOT SEND RED QUEEN OR BLACK JACK BEFORE FRIDAY STOP LOVE ALICE DEXTER WHITE.

Mrs. Pollifax frowned. "Should I know what this means?"

Carstairs laughed. "On the contrary it took the coding department a number of trips to the archives to identify it and I don't believe they would have decoded it yet if the names of Red Queen and Black Jack hadn't been included. This was a code—a very simple one invented for rendezvous purposes—used by a small group of agents working in Occupied Paris during World War Two."

"World War Two," echoed Mrs. Pollifax, utterly lost. "But this has the flavor of a period piece!"

"Exactly. Code 6—this one, if you note the time of arrival—automatically stood for rendezvousing in a hotel lobby, with a copy of *Gone with the Wind* if identification was necessary. Code 5 stood for a metro station—I believe a Bible was used there—and seven, if I remember correctly, meant a church, and always the seventh pew on the left. And so on—there were eight in all. Red Queen was an agent named Agatha Simms, unfortunately killed several years ago in Hong Kong, and Black Jack was the code name of another agent in that group."

"And Alice Dexter White?" asked Mrs. Pollifax.

Carstairs looked at her and then he looked down at the unlighted cigarette he held. "A very dear friend of mine which is how I come into this," he said quietly. "A very remarkable woman to whom I twice owe my life, and with whom I worked during those war years." He lifted his glance and regarded her with level eyes. "You are now about to join a very small and exclusive club, Mrs. Pollifax—only four living people know what I am about to tell you." He tapped the yellow cable with a finger. "This woman is one of our most valued agents but Alice Dexter White is only her code name. Her real name is Magda Ferenci-Sabo."

Mrs. Pollifax caught her breath sharply. "Good heavens," she gasped, "but this turns everything upside down!"

Chapter Three

During the first hour of her transatlantic flight Mrs. Pollifax had time to consider the events of the afternoon, but she was not at all certain that this was to her advantage. Her head still spun from her briefing with Carstairs, and it was difficult to find some graspable point of view with which to organize all that he had told her. "You remain, principally, a courier," he had said, "because I'm working on the assumption that once she has passport and money Ferenci-Sabo will know what to do. You may be called upon to help with a disguise, but she should be able to manage the rest herself. If by any chance it proves too 'hot' for her to leave the country legally, this is when I recommend your approaching Dr. Belleaux."

"Why did she use such an ancient code?" Mrs. Pollifax had asked, understanding better now the choice of *Gone with the Wind*.

"Probably it's the only one she could recall from memory," he'd said. "Codes were simpler, more primitive, then. In those days she was Frau Wetzelmann," he added reminiscently.

"And you were Black Jack," guessed Mrs. Pollifax.

"Yes," he said quietly, and then, "Mrs. Pollifax, we don't know why Ferenci-Sabo came to Istanbul, or how, but this is one 'notorious Communist agent,' who must be allowed to defect. Must," he emphasized fiercely. "Not only for her sake—and what we owe her—but for ours as well, because if ever she were forced to talk—" He shuddered.

Mrs. Pollifax shivered a little too now, and opened up the copy of *House Beautiful* on her lap. Up and down the aisle passengers were studiously reading about the woman that Mrs. Pollifax was en route to meet. What was even more unnerving she now knew a great deal more about Ferenci-Sabo than the New York *Times*, and this in itself awed Mrs. Pollifax. But on the whole, as

material for reflection, it was all too overwhelming and after a
while Mrs. Pollifax sensibly decided to stop thinking about it. Since
by European time she would not arrive in Istanbul until late tomorrow afternoon she closed her eyes and presently slept.

Monday's dawn had arrived when they reached London, and
as Mrs. Pollifax disembarked from the plane she set her watch
ahead, noting that at home she would be listening to the eleven
o'clock news before retiring for the night—how very odd traveling
was! After purchasing a small travel guide to Turkey she made her
way into the waiting room to await the departure of her plane to
Istanbul. She noticed that Henry Miles wandered about for a little
while and then found a seat nearby, sat down and lighted a cigarette. They exchanged impersonal glances and then Miles endeared
himself to Mrs. Pollifax by slowly, wickedly closing one eyelid and
winking at her. Until that wink he had appeared curiously invisible,
totally lacking in personality and content, as if he drew himself in
flat chalk and then erased all but the outline. Now Mrs. Pollifax
realized that a second Henry Miles walked, sat, stood and breathed
inside that first Henry Miles, although a few seconds later, her
glance returning, it was impossible to believe in that other person-
age, he looked so buttoned-up again.

The flight to Istanbul was announced, and Mrs. Pollifax
boarded the plane and took her seat near the wing, with Miles
several rows in front of her. This time she acquired a seat companion, and one who arrived breathlessly, with every male including
Henry turning his head to stare at her. Mrs. Pollifax stared, too—
she had never seen anyone quite like her before, which made the
encounter educational as well. The girl was very young; she was
dressed in an incredible outfit of dramatic greens and purples
crowned with a brilliant green stovepipe hat which she removed
almost at once, displaying a flawless profile. Her eyelids and her
lips had been painted white, her long eyelashes were ink black, and
she wore her straight red-gold hair to the waist. Once she had
settled her bag and her magazines she turned to look at Mrs. Pollifax with equal interest, gazed frankly at the wisps of hair escaping
Mrs. Pollifax's flowered hat, met her admiring and startled glance
and smiled.

"Hello," she said, adding with a burst of candor. "Do I
frighten you? I do some of my mother's friends—not that Mother

has many pious friends but she does have tons of pious acquaintances, Daddy being an M.P."

"Parliament!" said Mrs. Pollifax rapturously.

"You're American!" exclaimed the girl. "What fun! Yes, Daddy's in Parliament, and I've just become a model, isn't it wonderful? It's terribly exciting. I hope to be an actress, but I think modeling's a marv way to begin. I'm on my way to Athens for a job. Tony and the cameras are already there— they're doing me in autumn clothes against the Acropolis and all that."

"Oh yes," said Mrs. Pollifax, beaming, and then, "I'd forgotten we stop at Athens. I'm going all the way through to Istanbul."

The girl's face lit up. "I say, that's wonderful! My brother's there. If I've time after the assignment I'm hoping to fly over and see him." A faint shadow dimmed her preposterously radiant face. "At least I hope he's still there," she added darkly. "He has such an awful time with just—well, just the *mechanics* of living. It's unbelievable." She sighed and tucked her young chin in the palm of her hand.

"What does he do in Istanbul?" asked Mrs. Pollifax, intrigued by her concern.

"Well, he's been given a job with Uncle Hubert," she explained. "But of course you wouldn't know what that means unless you knew my family. It means, translated, that everybody's simply given up on Colin—my brother—and nobody knows what else to do with him." She frowned. "I suppose every large family has one."

"One what?" asked Mrs. Pollifax.

The girl hesitated, and then said angrily, "Somebody who just doesn't fit, you know? And that person knows it and grows up— well, grows up feeling *invisible*. And it turns into a vicious circle because it's so desperately easy not to notice someone invisible, but nobody understands this."

Mrs. Pollifax smiled faintly. She decided she liked this girl. "You're fond of him then. But being fond is a form of understanding."

"Oh I understand what's wrong," the girl said earnestly. "But not how to help. Colin has no confidence, just no confidence at all, and because of this he absolutely bristles with hostility. He's gotten battered, you know? He's very precise by nature but he can't find anything to be precise about, if you know what I mean, and this is infuriating for him and he loathes himself. But although I understand all this I'm very bad for him because he brings out the maternal in me. I'm a Moon Child, you see—born under the sign of Cancer, and simply seething with motherly instincts. He hates that. Quite rightly, too—he's terribly intelligent, of course. Oh I do hope I'll have time to stop and see him, but I despair," she explained dramatically. "There's never enough time. It'll rain, and the filming get held up for days—things always happen like that in this business."

"You could write to your brother then," suggested Mrs. Pollifax comfortingly.

The girl turned her head and stared wonderingly at Mrs. Pollifax. "Write?" she repeated blankly, and Mrs. Pollifax understood that she had stumbled upon a word utterly foreign to this girl and her generation.

"It's a way to keep in touch."

"In touch," repeated the girl musingly. "Yes, we do rocket about a great deal, my friends and I. But still I know what you mean. I think 'in touch' is a beautiful expression, don't you? And yet I do feel in touch with Colin always, even when I never see him."

"Then you have something very rare and wonderful," pointed out Mrs. Pollifax. "A bond."

The girl nodded, beaming now. "You do see it, don't you. But what takes you to Istanbul, and why Istanbul?"

Why indeed, thought Mrs. Pollifax, and announced that she was going to do a little sightseeing, and also meet a friend there. "An old friend who has been exploring the Middle East," she added firmly.

"But that's marv," said the girl. "Oh I do wonder if—how long will you be in Istanbul?"

"Until Saturday morning," said Mrs. Pollifax calmly. "I wonder if I can guess what you're thinking."

The girl laughed delightedly. "Of course you can because you're a dear, I can tell, and probably psychic as well. But you know, Colin just *might* be useful to you, having been in Istanbul for four months. And if I shouldn't have the time to fly over and see him—it's so vital Colin feel that somebody cares—"

"Being a Moon Child," said Mrs. Pollifax gravely.

"Well, I truly can't help it, can I? And nobody else cares, not really, except in a generalized family sense, and only when something goes hideously *wrong*, if you know what I mean. Of course I shouldn't want to burden you—"

Mrs. Pollifax smiled. "If you'll give me his address I'll try. I can't promise anything but there might be time."

"Oh you *are* a dear," the girl said, and removing a ring from her finger handed it to Mrs. Pollifax. "Give him this, that's the important thing. It's his, really, he gave it to me when he left. It's a game we've played for years, handing it back and forth for luck. I wore it when he went off to Oxford—except he flunked out," she explained with a sigh. "Then he wore it when he sold vacuum cleaners—but Mother was the only one who bought one—and then he sold encyclopedias, or did he work at Fortnum's next? Oh brother I can't remember. Anyway, give him this and my love."

"But this is a valuable signet ring," pointed out Mrs. Pollifax. "And really there may be no time at all—"

"Then you can just tuck it into an envelope and mail it back to me—I'll give you my address as well," she said. She had begun laboriously printing on a sheet of memo with a small address book propped on her knee. When she handed it to Mrs. Pollifax it read:

> COLIN RAMSEY,
> RAMSEY ENTERPRISES LTD.
> 23 ZIKZAK DAR SOKAK, STAMBOUL.

To this she had added,

> MISS MIA RAMSEY
> C/O HEATHERTON AGENCY,
> PICCADILLY CIRCUS, LONDON W.I

"And I am Emily Pollifax," said Mrs. Pollifax, feeling that introductions were being made, if half of them on paper. "Also a Moon Child," she added with a twinkle.

"No! Are you really?" demanded Mia breathlessly. "Then that's what I felt at once. Colin's Capricorn, you know, that's why he's so inherently precise."

"My husband was a Libra," put in Mrs. Pollifax.

"But how marv," breathed the girl. "Charm? Diplomacy? Harmony?"

"Oh yes," said Mrs. Pollifax, nodding.

"Most of my family's Gemini," Mia added broodingly. "A very restless sign to be born under, you know. Tony's Libra," she confided. "He wants to marry me."

"Tony?"

"The man in charge of all this," she said with a sweeping gesture that apparently included her outrageous costume. "The one waiting for me in Athens. He's a marv photographer."

"And do you love him?" asked Mrs. Pollifax with interest.

Mia turned thoughtful. "I'm only eighteen, you know. Do you think it possible to love at eighteen?"

"In general no," said Mrs. Pollifax.

Mia nodded. "That's what I think, too. It's tempting—and terribly romantic—but I do want to find out who I am first. I don't want to be married umpteen times. It's so unstable."

At this point they were interrupted by lunch—the meals were growing very confusing—and then they were nearing Athens, and Mrs. Pollifax watched Mia reline her lips and eyelids with white, and comb her long hair. As the plane touched earth and taxied down the runway Mia looked at Mrs. Pollifax with huge eyes. "Do you realize we may never meet again?" she said in dismay, and was suddenly a very young child.

Mrs. Pollifax smiled. "But it's so very nice that we've met at all," she said warmly.

Mia laughed. "There I go, being greedy again—you're much the wiser." Standing, she leaned over and impulsively kissed Mrs. Pollifax on the cheek. "God bless," she said warmly, and placing her stovepipe hat securely on the top of her head she walked down the aisle, every eye on the plane fastened just as securely upon her receding figure.

Mrs. Pollifax watched her go. She thought she left behind her a very definite fragrance—not of an orchid in spite of her exotic green and purple appearance, she reflected, but something rather sturdy and British, like a primrose. Yes, a primrose, decided Mrs. Pollifax, and with a little smile brought out her travel guide on Turkey again, and settled down to read it.

Chapter Four

Mrs. Pollifax landed at an airport whose name she could not pronounce, and went through Customs in a state of numbness. Not even a glimpse of her first mosque or the delicate spire of a minaret roused her from this alarming sense of detachment; she was experiencing now the effect of crossing two continents and an ocean in the space of a day. She remembered that she had been contacted by Carstairs at two o'clock on a quiet Sunday afternoon, she had left the United States less than two hours later, and she had been in flight for seventeen hours, with a brief stopover in London. In America it would be Monday morning and she would be preparing to shop at the A&P, but instead she was in Istanbul and it was four o'clock Monday afternoon, all of which produced a bewildered weightless and unattached feeling: it was difficult to realize that she had reached Istanbul, or how, or for what purpose. As the airline bus carried her toward the city there was added to her blurredness a steady cacophony of noise: horns honking, donkeys braying, and vendors shouting.

When Mrs. Pollifax reached the Oteli Itep and registered at the desk, showing her passport, it was five o'clock. There was no sign of Henry, which reminded her that they were in Istanbul now and there would be no more reassuring winks. The desk clerk himself showed her to her room on the second floor and left her there staring, mesmerized, at the bed.

And the bed really was enchanting. It was mounted on a platform that made it the focal point of the room, it was covered with a brilliant scarlet afghan and what was more it looked voluptuously soft. Mrs. Pollifax moved toward it with longing, every bone of her body still in protest against the reclining seats into which she had been fitted for so long. She reached up to her flowered hat, fumbled for its hatpin and then hesitated. She remembered that in

fewer than three hours she must take up her post in the lobby with
her copy of *Gone with the Wind*—it was why she was here—and by
that hour she must be alert and rested. She had already done a
great deal of sleeping on the plane, and another nap could only
leave her woolly-headed. A more sensible idea would be to find
something to occupy and clear her mind. She thought of food but
she was not hungry enough to spend the next hour in dining, and
in any case she would prefer breakfast to dinner, her appestat being
still on American time. Yet somehow before eight o'clock she had
to recover a degree of perception and awareness, and enough vitality to think clearly.

"A walk!" she thought. "A good brisk walk!" It was the perfect idea, jewel-like in its simplicity and wisdom after so many
hours of tedium. She wondered if the bazaars would be open at this
hour, doubted, and immediately suffered a loss of motivation until
she remembered Mia Ramsey's brother.

"What a very nice idea, and it shouldn't take long!" she exclaimed aloud, and at once felt a leap of interest and purpose. She
dug the brother's address out of her purse, noted that they were
both in the old part of the city but decided nevertheless to take a
taxi there and do her walking on the way back.

Washing her face in very cold water she left the room without
opening her suitcase, walked down the heavily carpeted stairs to
the lobby, nodded cheerfully to the desk clerk and strolled out into
the bustling life of the streets.

According to her map Istanbul was a city divided by bridges,
water and the geographical coincidence of existing upon two continents, Europe and Asia. Mrs. Pollifax assessed the character of it
with a certain feminine casualness: the newer section, called
Beyoglu, contained the Hilton Istanbul, and therefore must also
contain the newer residences, the higher priced hotels, and most of
the tourists. The older section, called Stamboul, appeared to hold
most of the minarets, mosques, bazaars, native hotels as well as
herself and Mia Ramsey's brother. With this settled she hailed a
taxi. The driver greeted her effusively, swore by Allah that Zikzak
was not far, that his taxi was the best in Stamboul, he was a fine
driver and it was a beautiful evening, and they started out.

Delighted by her resourcefulness and already reviving at the thought of exchanging words with an authentic resident of the city, Mrs. Pollifax sat back in anticipation. What struck her forcibly as she looked around her was the patina of antiquity everywhere that went beyond old age; there was a grandeur in the shabbiness of Stamboul's flaking walls, peeling stucco, faded paint and eroded columns. It rested the eye: this city was thousands of years old. Istanbul also impressed her now as being a surprisingly gay place, and her ears began to sort out the sounds that had dismayed her earlier. A great deal of commerce appeared to be transacted from the sides and backs of donkeys, upon which were carried baskets of flowers, bread, tinware, bales of cloth, jugs of water, herbs and sweets, all of which had to be advertised incessantly and vocally, the louder the better. Children played and shouted. Strange weird music drifted out of shuttered windows and open doors. The light itself was purest Mediterranean—why had she assumed Istanbul would be gloomy?—and as they drove up and down unbelievably steep streets Mrs. Pollifax was reminded of San Francisco.

But gradually the streets grew narrower, darker and less traveled, and Mrs. Pollifax began to experience a growing sense of alarm. After all, they were in search of a business called Ramsey Enterprises Ltd., which had a solid, respectable and undeniably British ring to it, whereas this was old Istanbul, and growing older and older at each turn. For the first time she remembered the two envelopes in her purse, each of them bulging with money, and when the taxi turned into a cul-de-sac, a dead end alley with a high wall running along one side, Mrs. Pollifax was certain that she was going to be held up and robbed. She was wondering if she dared try out her karate—and which blow to deliver—when the driver brought the cab to a stop, jerked his head toward a ramshackle building on the left which leaned precariously to one side, and turning to her said, "Twenty-three Zikzak."

"Are you sure?" she asked doubtfully. She handed the printed address to the driver for verification.

"*Evet, evet*," he said, nodding indignantly, and jumped out and opened the door for her.

Mrs. Pollifax climbed out, paid the man—or over-paid him, she reflected wryly, having still no firm grasp of the country's lira and kurush—and when she walked across the alley to the lopsided door experienced the small shock of relief at discovering all her suspicions unfounded. The man was reliable and she was indeed in the correct place. But what an astonishingly unprepossessing place it was! A neat sign over the bell said RAMSEY ENTERPRISES LTD. A small dusty sign below it read RAMSEY DOCUMENTARIES IN REAR (Documentaries! thought Mrs. Pollifax); a third sign read HUBERT LUDLOW RAMSEY, ESQ. Mrs. Pollifax pushed the bell. Nothing happened. Sounds of traffic came dimly to her ears, and among the wilting bougainvillea a bee droned monotonously. From the other side of the alley's wall came shouts of muffled argument, and from a distance the sound of a muezzin's chant. Mrs. Pollifax turned her back on the front door and walked firmly down the narrow, beaten-earth driveway toward RAMSEY DOCU-MENTARIES IN REAR.

She came out upon a small cobbled courtyard walled with bougainvillea. A dusty van was parked here beside an equally dusty old jeep, and beyond them lay a series of small cement-block buildings, obviously quite new: a garage, a building with two skylights, and a small office bearing a sign, *RAMSEY ENTERPRISES*. The door to this office stood open, and as Mrs. Pollifax approached it she heard someone swearing—steadily and scathingly—in English.

"Good afternoon," called out Mrs. Pollifax cheerfully.

The swearing immediately broke off, and a round, owlish face peered around the door. "What the devil!" exclaimed the young man in baffled astonishment, and then, "I say—I'm awfully sorry, you overheard the swearing?"

"Every word," said Mrs. Pollifax amiably. "Is it a habit of yours?"

"It's rapidly becoming one," he said crossly from somewhere inside ("I'm putting on a shirt," he explained in an aside). "I'm swearing because I've been doing some filming while my uncle's away and not one damned frame has come out yet. My uncle will have my head for it. No, he'll probably fire me."

"Why didn't the pictures come out?" inquired Mrs. Pollifax curiously.

His voice drew closer. "Because yesterday I left the lens cap on, and today they're all light-struck." He suddenly appeared in the door, a small, compact young man wearing a fierce scowl, dusty khaki shorts, dusty shirt and dusty boots.

"Then you must be Colin Ramsey," said Mrs. Pollifax warmly, extending her hand. "You have to be Colin Ramsey."

"I don't have to be but I am," he said suspiciously. "Are you a friend of Uncle Hu's?"

"No, of your sister's," she told him. "That is, I flew from London to Athens with her today—my name's Mrs. Pollifax—and if I had time she asked me to stop in and give you both her love and this ring."

His face brightened. "Did she really! I say, that's decent of her." He took the ring and looked at it. "Beautiful Mia—what on earth is she doing in Athens! I suppose she's left school again?"

"I didn't hear anything about school; she's modeling."

He nodded, still staring down at the ring. "Funny," he mused, "this came from Uncle Hu when we were still in the nursery, I'd forgotten its source until this minute. He gave it me, said it was magic or some such bit of whimsy, and for years I wore it faithfully on a string around my neck. That's how it all started, and here I am working for Uncle Hu now, and the ring's here, too." His laugh was so bitter it startled him as well as Mrs. Pollifax and he glanced up. "It's really decent of you to have bothered with this, and I'm being terribly rude, boring you with my blighted life. May I offer you a lemonade?"

"You weren't being rude, you were feeling sorry for yourself," pointed out Mrs. Pollifax firmly. "And yes it *was* decent of me, except that I had too much time for just eating and not enough time for sleeping because of having to be back at the hotel before eight. Also I was curious. Yes, I will have a lemonade, thank you."

"Curious because of Mia?" he asked.

"Not entirely. I thought it restful—soothing, you know—to have a small errand to run, and the name and address of someone here, in a strange city and strange country." She stopped and suddenly smiled. "It just occurs to me: I'm probably feeling a touch of homesickness. Or rather of not-at-homeness."

He nodded. "Your first trip abroad?"

Mrs. Pollifax smiled faintly. "Yes and no," she said adroitly. "The first alone, at least."

"Then do come and have that lemonade," he suggested understandingly. "Although if you're traveling alone who's the chap with you, your driver? Guide?"

Mrs. Pollifax looked at him blankly. "There's no one with me. I came in a taxi but the driver went away." She turned, following Colin's glance up the driveway to the alley. "What is it?"

He grinned. "Some tourist—a chap in a dark suit with a camera. He's strolled past twice, trying not to look too interested in us. Tourists don't usually get this far."

Henry, thought Mrs. Pollifax warmly. But how absolutely astute of him, she reflected, he had not for a moment forsaken his post, he had seen her leave and followed. A rush of gratitude flooded her at such touching protectiveness, and then she put the thought aside and turned and followed Colin toward the house. "But how do you happen to notice such things?" she asked of Colin, responding at once to such an active imagination.

He smiled ruefully as he held open the door to the house. "Compensation, I guess—observation is my only talent. I'm a complete embarrassment to a brilliant family—it's why they've shipped me out here to Turkey."

Mrs. Pollifax entered a bleak, cheerless kitchen dominated by a very old refrigerator with coils on the top. "Purest Soho, circa 1920," commented Colin with a gesture toward the room. "Do have a seat."

Mrs. Pollifax slid gratefully onto a bench beside a long trestle table. "But what kind of brilliant family?" she asked. "That is, if you could use just one word—"

"That's easy," said Colin, removing ice cube trays from the antique refrigerator. "Successful."

Mrs. Pollifax nodded. "But in what way? What values?"

He scowled. "Well, they climb mountains. Big ones," he added angrily. "They excel at rugby and take honors at Oxford and rather tend to get knighted. They go into the Army and win medals, that sort of thing. My father's an M.P. My two brothers went to Sandhurst and they'll either be generals or M.P.'s, wait and see. You met my sister. She's the baby of the family, but if she's taken up modeling she'll be a top model on all the magazine covers by Christmas. My mother's a poet and the last time I saw a London *Times* she was in jail for picketing—some kind of labor protest. That's being a success these days too, you know." He gloomily handed Mrs. Pollifax a frosty glass of lemonade and sat down across the table from her.

Mrs. Pollifax said tartly, "I think someone in your family read far too much Halliburton in their youth. But if they're active and extroverted and like heights, that's their prerogative. What do *you* like best?"

He looked thoughtful. "It's hard to say, you know. I'm an absolute physical coward. I daresay that's something most people don't have to learn about themselves by the age of eight, but living with my family I learned it early. Alpine climbing absolutely terrifies me, boxing appalls me and fencing scares the hell out of me. The Army didn't turn out to be my cup of tea and I flunked out of Oxford." He brightened. "Frankly I like it *here*. It's a joy having nobody care that I'm a Ramsey, and Uncle Hu doesn't care tuppence about climbing mountains, he's too busy running this rum outfit. But damn it I'm desperately afraid that just when I've found the right nook I shall blow it. Failure *can* get to be a habit, you know."

"Nonsense," put in Mrs. Pollifax flatly.

"But just see what's happened. Uncle Hu goes off to Erzurum with his projection man for a week, and after showing me the work for four months he leaves me with just ten minutes of filming, the first assignment he's given me, and I'm already blowing the whole thing. He runs a shoestring operation; I ask you, how long can he afford me?"

Mrs. Pollifax glanced curiously around the barren room. "You mean this address is all there is to Ramsey Enterprises Ltd.?"

Colin nodded. "Mostly it's a matter of traveling around the country—he comes back here to splice and develop film and pick up his mail. He has a tie-in with the British Council. Winters he puts chains and a snowplow on the van and goes on tour, as he calls it. Shows Turkish films in the *hata series*—the council houses in the villages—and occasionally shows films from England. There are thousands of little villages in Turkey and for some of them it's the only contact they have with the outside world except for the traveling schoolteacher. But his real passion is making documentaries about Turkey—he really loves the place. In the summer he drops everything for this, he'll take on any assignment he can get—travelogs, industrial films, commercials, short subjects, that sort of thing."

"And works all alone!" exclaimed Mrs. Pollifax.

Colin smiled wryly. "There's scarcely enough money in it for
a crowd, but he does all right. As you can see, he picks up people
like me when it pleases him, and then there are students in the
summer, and in the winter there are mechanics and out-of-work
seasonal people. It's all very casual but it functions."

"And your family like him?"

Colin wrinkled his nose. "Everything's relative, isn't it? He
used to be *Sir* Hubert, with all the usual Ramsey accomplishments.
Medals. Honors. Came out of World War Two loaded with that
sort of thing, was knighted by the King and then one day took all
the medals, flushed 'em down the toilet, packed a duffel bag and
left England. A woman, my mother said. No, they don't *like* him
but they leave him alone." He sighed. "It's hard to explain my
family, they're not monsters, you know, they're marvelous really.
Colorful, competitive, uninhibited, uncomplicated. I'd have absolutely no problems at all if—well, if—"

"If you were also colorful, competitive, uninhibited and uncomplicated," said Mrs. Pollifax, nodding.

"Yes." He grinned at her appreciatively. "But what brings you
to Turkey?" he asked.

Mrs. Pollifax suddenly remembered why she was in Turkey
and a sense of dismay chilled her. "The time!" she gasped, and
looked at her watch only to discover that it had stopped. "Have
you the correct time? I'm to meet a woman at eight o'clock in the
lobby of my hotel."

Colin at once came to life. "I say—I'll take you back in the
jeep! It's the least I can do after your bringing Mia's message, and
it'll take my mind off my disasters." He glanced at his watch. "It's
not quite seven—three minutes lacking. I wish there were more
time, I could show you St. Sophia's on the way. Are you meeting
your friend for dinner?"

"Friend?" Mrs. Pollifax was caught off guard. "Oh no—that
is, I would like to take her to dinner but I don't know her. I mean, I
don't know that she'll have the time for it. I'm only delivering—"
She stopped, utterly appalled at the words she was letting slip.
Really she must be more tired than she'd realized.

Colin Ramsey was smiling at her. "You know, you act just the way I do sometimes, but I can't think when or why. You stammered."

"I'm tired."

He shook his head. "No, you're nervous."

"Well, I shall be very nervous indeed if I'm late," she said, regaining control. "How long will it take us to reach the Itep?"

"The Itep!" he said. "Not the Hilton?"

Mrs. Pollifax suddenly and overwhelmingly realized why she was drawn to Colin, and she felt a small sense of alarm. They were alike. They had each lived quiet lives in the shadow of more dazzling personalities so that, somewhat submerged but no less intelligent, they had become observers. Acute observers. She recognized at once from Colin's question—so very akin to what she too would have noted—that he was weighing the Oteli Itep against what he saw and guessed of her, and the Itep did not fit, it introduced an unguessed facet of character that entertained and alerted him.

"The Itep, yes," she said firmly.

He looked amused. He arose and rinsed the two glasses under the faucet automatically, as if he were accustomed to looking after himself, probably over hot plates and wash basins in grubby London rooms, she guessed. "Ever ridden in a jeep before?" he asked as he led her across the courtyard.

"Never."

"All you have to do is hang on tight," he explained. "Hold your skirt down and your hat on." He glanced at her hat and smiled faintly. "It will be an experience for you."

"Yes," agreed Mrs. Pollifax, realizing that he believed he was giving her an event in an uneventful life.

"But I still hope you'll dine with me, which is what I was leading up to," he confided. "Blast it, I've eaten alone for three days now, and if you don't mind awfully, I'll wait and see what plans you make with your friend." He added wistfully, "I could show you both something of Istanbul, you know—it's beautiful at night. The Galata Bridge, the moon over the Golden Horn, and St. Sophia's at night is unbelievable. We could eat at Pierre Loti's, and—"

She felt the undercurrent of his eagerness: he was lonely. She said gently, "We'll see, shall we?"

"I'll park outside the hotel and wait until quarter past the hour," he said. "It's no hardship, you know, the streets of Istanbul are never boring." He shifted gears and they were off, sending up clouds of dust, and Mrs. Pollifax became too busy clinging to her hat to exchange further comments.

Chapter Five

It was 7:35 when Mrs. Pollifax entered the lobby of the Oteli Itep, leaving Colin behind to look for a parking space and wait his allotted span of moments. She went upstairs, again washed her face in cold water, removed *Gone with the Wind* from her suitcase and locked her door behind her. Her mind was now functioning without blurredness; she was suddenly a courier, a secret agent, and she arranged the expression on her face accordingly. She realized that she ought to have taken the time earlier to explore the hotel—it would have been the professional thing to do—and so she walked upstairs instead of down—the hotel had no elevator—and discovered that the third floor was the top one. There was an interesting metal door to the roof: she tested it, looked out upon an expanse of flat tile, nodded approvingly and chose the narrow back stairs for her descent, virtually tiptoeing lest anyone point out that they were reserved for hotel personnel. The stairs ended in a shabby first floor landing with three exits: one into the lobby, one to the street, and the last to the basement. Pleased with her tour, Mrs. Pollifax walked into the lobby and sat down, book in hand, at precisely ten minutes before the hour.

It was a very Turkish lobby, its floor glowing with the colors and design of an unusually fine Turkish rug. The remainder of it was furnished with baroque statuary and old leather couches. Mrs. Pollifax had taken the couch near the back stairs, at some distance from the front, so that she was well out of the traffic between the main entrance and the larger staircase, and prominently displayed against the only window in the lobby. In fact she judged it to be the most conspicuous place possible, and she carefully arranged her book so that it was equally as conspicuous. With considerable suspense she watched the hands of the clock move slowly toward eight. The lobby was small, and there were only a few people

waiting. Henry Miles had come in and was seated in a corner looking nearly invisible again, his eyes half-closed as if he were dozing.
A young couple held hands in another corner and two men smoked
and gossiped along the other wall.

It was when Henry glanced up that Mrs. Pollifax also looked
to the entrance and became alert. It was precisely eight o'clock and
a woman had entered the hotel. She brought with her a quality that
changed the lobby so forcibly that Mrs. Pollifax wondered how
people continued to walk and talk without awareness of it. What
she brought with her—and to Mrs. Pollifax it pervaded the lobby—
was fear. No, not fear but terror, amended Mrs. Pollifax: a primitive, palpable terror so real that it could almost be smelled and
touched. The woman stood at the edge of the lobby, desperately
trying not to be seen as her glance searched the room. Did her eyes
ever so subtly drop to the gaudy book that Mrs. Pollifax held upright in her lap?

She cannot bear exposure, thought Mrs. Pollifax in astonishment; yet as she stood there, lacking the decisiveness to move, she
was accomplishing exactly what she did not want: people were beginning to look at her. And certainly she was not a logical person
to have entered a hotel lobby. Her dress was torn, old and shabby,
the castoff plaid house dress of a European, and she was thin to the
point of emaciation. But her face—what a beauty she must have
been once, thought Mrs. Pollifax, seeing those deepset haunted
dark eyes. Even her clothes, even the irresolution and exhaustion
could not conceal the intelligence in those eyes. That head went up
now, and the woman moved like a sleepwalker across the lobby
until she came to Mrs. Pollifax. "Your book," she said in a low
voice, only lightly accented. "You are—?"

"Sit down," Mrs. Pollifax said quickly. "You'll be less conspicuous and you do look exhausted."

The woman sank down beside her on the couch. "Who are
you?"

"Emily Pollifax. Are you being followed?" Beyond the
woman, on the other side of the window, Mrs. Pollifax saw Colin
Ramsey sitting in his jeep. He had found his parking space and was
patiently waiting for dinner companions. She felt that she had met
and talked to him in another world, a world of innocence that had
abruptly vanished at sight of this poor creature.

"I don't know, but—it is possible," whispered Ferenci-Sabo. "I should never have chosen this place—so far, so public, so open." She looked utterly wrung out, drained.

Mrs. Pollifax said crisply, "I've brought you money and a passport but obviously you need rest and food before you can use either. There's a rear exit on my left, do you see it? There are also stairs going up to the second floor. My room number is—" She broke off, startled. The woman beside her on the couch was staring across the lobby in horror. At once she jumped to her feet. "Oh please," she gasped.

Automatically Mrs. Pollifax glanced at the entrance to see what had frightened her; when her glance returned to the couch the woman was gone. She had vanished completely.

Two men in the uniform of the Turkish police were crossing the lobby, and one of them suddenly increased his pace, heading for the rear exit. His companion continued inexorably toward Mrs. Pollifax, and as he loomed above her—he looked surprisingly high —she doubtfully rose to meet him.

"*Pasaport, luften,*" he said, holding out a hand.

"Passport?" faltered Mrs. Pollifax. "But what has happened? Do you speak English?"

"You are American? English?"

"American." She opened her purse, careful not to touch the second passport.

He opened and scanned the passport, glancing from face to photograph and back again. "You arrived here only this afternoon, I see." He frowned. "Your business in Istanbul?"

"Why—tourist," she faltered.

"The woman to whom you spoke—the one who fled—" He broke off as his comrade entered the lobby through the side door. His friend shook his head, pointed to the ceiling and disappeared again, presumably to search the hotel. Mrs. Pollifax's inquisitor nodded. "You will come with me please to headquarters, to Santral Odasi." His request lacked the courtesy of an invitation; his voice was authoritative, as was the hand he placed beneath Mrs. Pollifax's elbow. He had also retained her passport, which he placed now in his pocket. She had no recourse but to go. As they walked out, leaving by the side door, she was just in time to see Colin shift gears, maneuver out of his parking space and drive away, his profile without any expression except boredom, as if he had at last relinquished all hope of dinner companions. He did not even see her.

The officer behind the desk was in uniform; the second man, seated beyond him and introduced as Mr. Piskopos, was not. As Mrs. Pollifax seated herself she was aware that both men studied her coldly and clinically, as if to wrest from her who and what she was by psychic divination. She had the feeling that neither of them noticed her hat or her suit, or even the expression on her face, but looked beyond and inside, into motivation, into why her hands remained in her lap, why she gazed at them imperturbably and what she had to be concealing. Since at the moment she was concealing a great deal, Mrs. Pollifax practiced exorcising all memory of Carstairs and Alice Dexter White. She was an American tourist, she reminded herself, an American tourist . . .

"I am an American tourist," she said aloud in reply to the police officer.

Her passport lay open in front of him. He said dryly, "We have suddenly this week so many visitors to Istanbul. All tourists. This woman you were speaking to in the lobby of the Hotel Itep . . . you were there to meet her?"

"No," said Mrs. Pollifax calmly. "I was sitting in the lobby of the Hotel Itep resting before dinner."

"But you were speaking with this woman, were you not?"

"Oh yes."

"But you did not know the woman to whom you were speaking?"

Mrs. Pollifax said truthfully, "I had never seen her before in my life."

"That is not the point," said the police officer quietly. "Had you an arrangement to meet her, to speak to her?"

"She came up to me and asked for money," said Mrs. Pollifax firmly, "and I must say she looked as if she needed it."

"In what language did she accost you?"

"English," said Mrs. Pollifax, and suddenly realized the trap that had been set for her.

"English," he repeated politely. "In a Turkish hotel run by Turks, in the old section of Istanbul where few tourists lodge, a woman beggar comes up to you and speaks in English?"

"She must have guessed I was American," pointed out Mrs. Pollifax.

"Still, if she was only a beggar it is unusual that she could speak your language, is it not?"

Mrs. Pollifax sighed. "If you say so, but why is all this all so important? Who is she?"

He looked faintly amused. He removed a square of cardboard from beneath his desk blotter and handed it across the desk to her, saying smoothly, "This is the woman to whom you were speaking." It was a question, yet stated so artfully that it was also a statement; he left it up to her to dispute or accept.

Looking at the snapshot he gave her Mrs. Pollifax saw that Mr. Carstairs and the New York *Times* might lack a photograph of Ferenci-Sabo, but that a very up-to-date one had begun circulating through Istanbul. It was certainly a picture of the woman she had met at the Itep, and a very recent one of her too. The eyes were half-closed, the face haggard and thin. Then Mrs. Pollifax noticed the dress Ferenci-Sabo was wearing, the same faded plaid, and she realized with astonishment that this snapshot had been taken of Ferenci-Sabo since she had reached Istanbul on Friday.

Had it been taken at the consulate? she wondered. In the confusion of the woman's arrival had someone really snapped her picture—or had it been taken of her *after* her abduction?

She looked at the police officer curiously. Was it possible that the Turkish government could have arranged Magda Ferenci-Sabo's abduction from the British consulate? For the first time she realized how important a defecting Communist agent must be to *them*. Russia was Turkey's next-door neighbor, their frontiers met and their guards faced each other for several hundred miles in the east. A great deal of practical information could be extracted from a knowledgeable Communist defector, and why should they share her when it was they who lived virtually under Russia's guns?

"Well?" demanded the police officer. "Is that the woman?"

"There's a resemblance certainly but beyond that—she left so suddenly! Who is she?" Mrs. Pollifax inquired again. When he ignored this she said quietly, "I really think I must refuse to answer your questions until I am told precisely why I am here, or am allowed to telephone someone who can inform me why I am here."

She added severely, "I had understood Turkey was a country friendly to Americans—"

"To Americans, yes," the man said flatly.

She was surprised. "You don't believe that I'm American?"

The officer turned and exchanged a swift glance with the civilian behind him. "That is a possibility," he said.

"But my passport—"

He looked at her pityingly. "Passports can be forged." He hesitated and then he leaned forward, frankly watching her face as he said with deliberation. "The woman to whom you were speaking is a woman wanted by the Turkish police, and one whom Officer Bey almost captured this evening. Her friends are of much interest to us—they may be our enemies. You arrived in Istanbul several hours ago, flying here directly without any tourist stops in between, and you meet this woman. A coincidence? We shall see." He touched her passport with a finger. "In the meantime—while we very thoroughly investigate your identity—we shall keep your passport."

She said indignantly, "I really must protest—"

He interrupted with a shrug. "You will, of course, notify your consul—we shall do this as well—but you are not to leave Istanbul, or the Hotel Itep, until you have been cleared to the satisfaction of all concerned." His expression lightened. "We should be able to return to you the passport by late tomorrow afternoon—if your credentials, how do you call it, check out. You may return now to your hotel, please." He did not shake hands; the other man, Mr. Piskopos, nodded curtly, and Mrs. Pollifax left.

In the police car, as it carried her back to her hotel, Mrs. Pollifax experienced something of the loneliness of the outcast. She had successfully met Ferenci-Sabo—this much was now obvious—only to see the woman frightened away; and now she had ignominiously lost her passport for twenty-four hours. What did she do next? What *could* she do? Did she go again tomorrow night to the lobby at the same hour? She could imagine Officer Bey's face should he see her there a second time at the same hour and clutching the same copy of *Gone with the Wind*. She did not concede failure as yet but she did admit to a deep discouragement and a certain amount of frustration.

She saw the hotel ahead, its exterior no longer nondescript at night under a blaze of neon color; somewhere along the pavement that other, nameless American agent had been pinned to a wall by an automobile. Mrs. Pollifax leaned forward. The taxi ahead of them slowed, turned, and pulled into the only empty space in front of the Itep to discharge Henry Miles—dear Henry, she thought fondly, and wondered what significance he had attached to her visit to police headquarters. His taxi drove away and as the police car in which she rode headed into the narrow opening another taxi suddenly cut in ahead of them, almost sideswiping them; a man leaped from it in a great hurry, pulled bills from his pockets, shoved them at the driver through the window and turned to run into the hotel. But something arrested him; he stopped, put his hands into his pockets and very casually sauntered across the pavement to the hotel. What he had seen, realized Mrs. Pollifax, was the back of Henry Miles disappearing into the lobby.

He was following Henry! thought Mrs. Pollifax in astonishment. It was no more than an impression but it was a vivid one: the haste, the panic, the fear of having lost sight of the subject, followed by the abrupt halt and even more abrupt change to casualness.

Only a few yards from here—somewhere beyond the front entrance, Carstairs had said—that other agent had been killed on Sunday night.

I can't let that happen to Henry—there must be some way to warn him, she thought in horror. Carstairs had said, *There may be a leak somewhere, or with so damn many agents in Istanbul they may be keeping one another under surveillance;* but what if Henry didn't know he had acquired a shadow?

She thanked her driver and walked into the hotel. There was no sign of Henry in the empty lobby. To the man at the desk she said. "There is an Englishman staying here, I saw him drop this earlier." She held up her small travel guide to Turkey and smiled at the man. "If you tell me his room number I should like to return it to him."

The translations took a few minutes and drew in the manager's son, who was fourteen and "took the English" in school, but had apparently not ventured yet beyond nouns and pronouns, and very few of those. A dictionary was produced and each word spelled out before it was understood what she wanted, and then the boy offered to take the book himself to room 214.

"No, no—thank you," said Mrs. Pollifax, and then with another look at the dictionary added, *"Tesekkur edehim,* no."

She walked up the stairs, ignored her own door and continued down the hall. The door to room 214 stood ajar and the lights were on. She tapped lightly. When there was neither reply nor movement she tapped again and then swung the door wide and peered inside. "Henry?" she called in a low voice. She recognized his green suitcase on the bed, its contents scattered all over the coverlet as if it had been unpacked by the simple expedient of turning it upside down. Then she saw that every drawer in the tall chest along the wall had been left open, and his trenchcoat lay on the floor in shreds. She realized that while Henry had waited patiently for her outside the police station someone had been searching his room. But who? And where was Henry?

The curtains opening to the balcony trembled slightly, catching Mrs. Pollifax's eye, and her glance moved from the curtains to the open window and then to the darkness beyond. She shivered suddenly. *I'm not supposed to be here,* she thought. *I'm not even supposed to know Henry, and certainly I mustn't be found here calling out his name.* His absence was alarming. Had he unlocked his door, switched on the light and retreated when he saw the state of his room? Was he even now down in the lobby complaining to the manager she had just left? Or had he stopped first in the public lavatory at the end of the hall?

She backed out of the room, touching nothing, and walked down the hall to the bathroom, but the door stood open and the room was empty. Mrs. Pollifax unlocked the door of her own room and flicked on the lights. Everything was in order, nothing had changed here except that a slip of white paper had been inserted under her door and glimmered white on the rug. "Henry!" she whispered in relief and picked it up, went to her window to check the lock, pulled the curtains and then unfolded the slip of paper.

But it was not from Henry, it was a message from the desk clerk on lined paper with the name of the hotel printed at the top. She read:

"9:02 Mr. Remsee fone. You lost pkge in his ownership. He bid you stop before—" The clerk had written *before tiring* but she judged the

word was meant to be *retiring*. She read it a second time, frowning. What on earth did it mean? It seemed hours since she had seen Colin Ramsey, and with her mind on Henry it was difficult to think what package she could have left behind when she visited Colin that afternoon. She tried to remember what she'd carried with her to Ramsey Studios but aside from the signet ring, which belonged to Colin, there had been only her purse. Lost package! She'd lost nothing today.

Nothing except a defecting counteragent, she thought in horror, and forgetting Henry she snatched up her purse and fled the room, almost overturning several people on the stairs in her haste to reach the street and find a taxi.

Chapter Six

By night Zikzak alley looked desolate and sinister, its buildings ghost-haunted. No light at all came from number twenty-three. A little worldlier now, however, Mrs. Pollifax walked down the narrow drive to the courtyard and was relieved to see thin stripes of light showing through the shutters of the kitchen window. She knocked on the door and it was opened at once by Colin. "What lost package?" demanded Mrs. Pollifax breathlessly.

Colin held the door wide and beckoned her in. "I say—I do hope they didn't give you a hard time!"

"Who?" she said, blinking at him.

"The police."

"You *saw?*" she flung at him accusingly. "You *knew* I was picked up by the police and you left? Just *left?*"

He was bolting the door behind him. "Of course," he said. "I was afraid you'd head for the jeep and talk to me. In that case the police would have headed for the jeep too, and would have noticed your friend—that woman who was sitting with you in the hotel window."

Mrs. Pollifax stared at him incredulously.

"I had her hidden in the back seat of the jeep, covered with a sheepskin," he explained calmly. "She was in a spot of trouble, wasn't she? Running out like that, looking like death itself—"

Appalled, Mrs. Pollifax stared at him. "You mean she was in your jeep when you drove *away?*"

He said patiently, "It's what I've been trying to tell you, yes. She came flying out, I leaned over and opened the door, said, 'Hop in—I'm Mrs. Pollifax's driver' or some such words. She fell in, I dropped the robe over her and that was that. A few seconds later the policeman followed and asked me if I'd seen a woman run from the hotel. I pointed out that I couldn't possibly see the entrance from where I was sitting without turning my head, but that no one had run up the street *past* me. So he went the other way."

Mrs. Pollifax faltered, "But then—what did you do with her?"

He looked surprised. "Nothing at all—she's here. She's still in the jeep."

"Still in the jeep!"

"I couldn't rouse her so I simply locked the garage and left her there, and—what's the matter?"

Mrs. Pollifax had sat down very suddenly in the nearest chair. "You mean she's here? In that garage in back? In your jeep?"

Puzzled, Colin said, "Yes, of course. She *is* your friend, isn't she? I saw you together in the lobby and—"

Mrs. Pollifax began to laugh, she couldn't help herself. The laugh was a mixture of relief and hysteria but if it had a disquieting effect on Colin it was extremely therapeutic for her. As she wiped her eyes and blew her nose she said, "I simply can't thank you enough, Colin."

"Yes you can—you can tell me what the hell this is all about," he said, sitting down and looking at her sternly.

"About?" she echoed.

"That woman is no tourist. She needs blood transfusions at a hospital, not shish kabob at Pierre Loti's. What did the police want of you?"

"My passport," said Mrs. Pollifax sadly.

"Passport! You mean they took it away from you?"

"Yes, but only until they've investigated me."

He looked appalled. "But good heavens, you can't do anything without a passport—this isn't America, you know. You can't even change hotels without your passport!" He stared at her incredulously. "Doesn't the seriousness of this seep through to you at all? What on earth do the police think you've done? What reason did they give for taking your passport?"

Mrs. Pollifax sighed—she was beginning to feel very tired. "They seem to feel that I might have come to Istanbul to meet a notorious Communist agent."

His jaw dropped. "They *what? You?*"

"Yes," she said, and stood up. "Now I really must speak to my friend—speak to her at once—and then I'll remove her as soon as possible. I don't want to involve you—"

"Involve me?" he said angrily. "I'm already involved. What I'm trying to discover is what I'm involved *in*. You do know you're being followed, don't you?"

"You keep noticing things," she said with a sigh.

"Of course. I saw that chap walking up and down the alley when you were here this afternoon, but when I left you at the door of your hotel damned if he didn't follow you directly inside, and for all I know he's followed you here again, and is outside right now."

Mrs. Pollifax brightened. "Oh I do hope so," she said eagerly. "I tried to find him only half an hour ago at the hotel but I couldn't. That's Henry."

Colin looked taken aback. "Henry," he repeated blankly. "You know him then. Look here, who the devil are you? Or to put it more succinctly, *what* are you?"

She said sympathetically, "I'm Emily Pollifax, truly I am. I live in New Brunswick, New Jersey, and I'm an American citizen and I have two grown children and three grandchildren, and that's more than the Turkish police believe at this moment but it's absolutely true."

He put his hand to his head. "All right. Oddly enough I believe you, although I can't think of any *logical* reason why I do. But why did you come to Istanbul then?"

"To meet a notorious Communist agent," she told him cheerfully. "Now do please show me where the jeep is."

"You insist on being facetious," he told her bitterly. He removed a key from the shelf over the sink, opened the door for her and closed it behind them both. "This way," he said, and they walked in silence across the courtyard. A bright moon had turned the whitewashed buildings into ghost-silver and the bougainvillea threw jagged shadows over the cobbles. The sounds of the city were muted in this enclosure. Colin unlocked the door to the office and beckoned her inside. "She's in here," he said, and opened still another door and turned on the lights with a flick of his hand.

Mrs. Pollifax entered a double garage, at the moment containing only the jeep, a pile of abandoned tires and an orange crate. A shapeless bundle in the rear of the jeep stirred and lifted a head, shedding a sheepskin rug, and Magda Ferenci-Sabo blinked at the sudden light.

"Good evening," said Mrs. Pollifax amiably. "It seems that Mr. Ramsey has reunited us!"

Magda's glance moved from Mrs. Pollifax to Colin. "He is also—?"

Mrs. Pollifax sighed. "No, he is not," and for a moment both of them looked dubiously at Colin, who gazed stolidly back at them. "Colin," she said, "I wonder if you would mind—"

"No," he said crossly.

Mrs. Pollifax regarded him with interest. "You won't allow us a few minutes—?"

"No."

"What a difficult young man," said Magda.

Mrs. Pollifax smiled. "Yes, but he hid you from the police, this is his jeep you're occupying and this is his uncle's garage. Now we must think how to get you out of here. You *are* the woman I was sent to meet, aren't you?"

The woman looked at Colin. "It's better not to mention names, but there was a cable—"

Mrs. Pollifax nodded. "Yes, it was shown to me. Can you quote it?"

"I think so." Magda closed her eyes. "It read: Arrived six P.M., have enjoyed eight hours Oteli Itep, wish—" She opened her eyes. "If you were shown it perhaps you would be so kind as to complete it so that I too can be sure."

"Of course," said Mrs. Pollifax. "Wish you could join me why not send Red Queen or Black Jack before Friday."

"Look here," said Colin, regarding them uneasily.

"And the identity of Red Queen?" asked Mrs. Pollifax.

"I say," broke in Colin again, looking increasingly alarmed.

"Red Queen was Agatha Simms. I thought at first you might be she but you're not. For my benefit—because you know so much about it—can you identify Black Jack?" asked Magda, and Mrs. Pollifax complied by bending over her and whispering the name of Carstairs. Magda nodded. "We understand each other—good. Now you must help me get to Yozgat, please."

Mrs. Pollifax looked at her blankly. "I beg your pardon?"

"Yozgat."

"Who on earth is Yozgat?"

Colin said testily, "It's a town, a Turkish town off beyond Ankara somewhere."

Mrs. Pollifax stared at Magda in astonishment. "But that's out of the question. I'm carrying a passport for you, all very legal and made out in the name of Alice Dexter White, and sufficient funds for you to get to America. You're to leave Turkey at once—and really you can, I think, in spite of all the furor because I've thought about it, and if I dye your hair and bring you some fashionable American clothes—"

A strangled gasp came from Colin but they paid it no attention. Magda sat up and said flatly, "I cannot leave this country yet, not even if it costs me my life."

"But you must," cried Mrs. Pollifax. "The police are looking for you—"

"I know, I know," admitted Magda, "and so are the Russians and the Bulgarians—"

An outright groan issued from Colin.

"—not to mention the people who kidnapped me from the British consulate and who are far more dangerous than any police." She edged her feet over the seat and dangled them. "But my life is of no significance at all if I leave without what I brought with me, and I *must* get to Yozgat. What is the trouble?" she asked of Colin, turning toward him. "Are you ill?"

He was sitting on the orange crate staring at them in open-mouthed horror. "My God," he gasped, "I'm harboring a bloody pair of spies! The two of you!"

"You insisted on listening," Mrs. Pollifax reminded him patiently.

"But she's that woman everybody's looking for!" He looked haggard. "And she's sitting right here in my uncle's garage!"

"Yes, she is," admitted Mrs. Pollifax, "but really I'm trying very hard to think of where to take her, I *don't* want to involve you in this, you've already been so very kind—"

"Kind!" he said in a stricken voice. "Kind! You seemed like such a nice elderly lady!" He stopped, appalled. "I say, I'm terribly sorry, I didn't mean that the way it sounded." He looked even more appalled to discover himself apologizing. "Oh, hang it all," he said fiercely, and turning to Magda, "Do you know of somewhere to go?"

"Yes, to Yozgat," she said firmly.

"Magda—"

She turned to Mrs. Pollifax impatiently. "Why do you think they not kill me?" she demanded. "They want what I brought with me; I cross the Bulgarian frontier—do not ask me how—and I know I am followed so I separate myself from what I brought with me and I go instead to Istanbul for help. Now I must get to Yozgat, to recover what I bring. Do you not understand that—" She stopped uncertainly. "I hear someone."

"It must be Henry," said Mrs. Pollifax and turned toward the door expectantly.

But it was not Henry. Two square-shouldered bulky young men in trenchcoats stood in the door regarding them and the interior of the garage with interest. Magda caught her breath sharply. Mrs. Pollifax pulled herself together and said in a steady voice, "And who are you?"

The bulkier of the two men casually pulled a gun from his pocket.

"Police?" said Colin hopefully.

"I don't think so," Mrs. Pollifax told him regretfully.

Magda sighed. "Stefan and Otto, I grow tired with you. For what do you want to follow an old woman like me, hmm?"

Stefan grinned; it was a joke he appeared to appreciate and in such a stolid Slavic face his mirth was almost indecent. "We do not follow you—it is this one leads us here." He pointed at Mrs. Pollifax, who stared at him uncomprehendingly. "Who would have guessed the plump American partridge would know the wily Russian fox?" As he spoke his eyes continued to roam over the garage, mercilessly assessing the possibilities of the situation. Now he moved to Colin. "You will give the keys to the jeep, please," he said, and extended his left hand, palm up, to Colin. Behind him his friend Otto also pulled out a gun.

"I say—it's not your jeep," Colin said indignantly. "It's not even mine, and you've absolutely no right—"

"The key," said Stefan, pressing the gun into Colin's stomach. "Otto, open the garage doors, and quickly."

Reluctantly, glaringly, Colin fumbled in his pocket and brought out a key that he placed in the palm of the man's hand. "You are wise," said Stefan. "Stay wise and you will live." Carefully he backed up until he reached the jeep, where Madame Ferenci-Sabo had begun making feeble attempts to climb out. With one arm he shoved her down. "Sit! Did you really think we wanted only a jeep?" he said mockingly. He opened the door and slid into the front seat, his head still turned to watch them. Only when the garage doors stood wide open did he insert the key into the ignition. Over his shoulder he called, "Don't forget our little souvenir, Otto!" To Mrs. Pollifax he said with a smile, "We do not wish to leave you emptyhanded. That would be quite unfair. We are like your pack rat, preferring always to leave something behind."

Mrs. Pollifax turned in alarm and looked toward the courtyard. From the shadow of the bougainvillea along the left wall Otto was dragging an inert and heavy bundle. She heard Colin, near the door, say, "Good God!" and she guessed by his whitened face that the burden Otto wrestled with was human. She watched in horror as Otto dragged a man into the garage; he placed the man at Mrs. Pollifax's feet and turned him over, and Mrs. Pollifax found herself staring into the vacant, unseeing eyes of Henry Miles. Dimly she heard Colin say, "You brutes," but his voice sounded miles away. She stared stupidly down at Henry, tears filling her eyes as she saw the small round bullet hole in his shirt. Henry had winked at her in the London air terminal, Henry had valiantly followed her since her arrival and now he was dead at her feet.

She looked up as the engine of the jeep roared into life; Stefan thrust the gears into reverse and she jumped back as the car virtually catapulted from the garage carrying a Magda who sat with eyes closed, her face unbelievably white. The jeep neatly turned around in the courtyard, Otto leaped in beside Magda, and the car shot up the driveway and disappeared.

"At least the petrol tank's almost empty," Colin said in a choked voice.

Mrs. Pollifax sank down beside Henry and looked into his face. "He's dead," she said in a trembling voice, and placed her hand over his heart but she could not change him. She felt a million years old and deeply shocked. It had all happened so quickly. Four minutes earlier there had been only the three of them here, talking about Yozgat. Now the jeep was gone, Henry lay dead at her feet and Magda Ferenci-Sabo had vanished a second time. Mrs. Pollifax looked across the empty garage at Colin. He was standing in the same spot, his mouth a little open in astonishment, his hand still extended to give the man the key. He closed his mouth now with a snap. "Do you know him?" he asked.

"It's Henry."

He nodded dumbly. "It was like a raid," he said, and then, blinking, "They've taken your friend."

"Yes. And killed Henry." Neither of them were sensibly communicating yet.

"And stolen my uncle's jeep." His lips thinned and he said peevishly, "Damn it, I absolutely loathe being pushed around." He walked to her side and leaned over Henry. "He's really dead?"

"Yes."

"What are you going to do with him?"

It was an interesting question, delivered with the detachment born of shock, but it served to bring Mrs. Pollifax to her senses, which had been badly jarred. "Why—I don't know," she said in astonishment, and at once understood that Henry dead could prove an almost insurmountable embarrassment, which was undoubtedly why Stefan had presented him to them. "Good heavens!" she gasped, and stood up.

"We ought to have followed them," Colin said. "There's still the van in the other garage but now it's too late. If they go far they're bound to empty the tank, there was less than five miles' worth left. We ought to have followed them. We can't keep Henry here," he added.

"No, we can't," said Mrs. Pollifax.

"Because you don't have a passport," he said, as if this explained everything.

She nodded. "I realize that. But I believe I know what to do with Henry. It's just struck me. I can take him to Dr. Belleaux."

"Who?"

"I was given the name of a man—a retired professor—to contact in an emergency."

"But with a body?"

Mrs. Pollifax thought about this. "I daresay it's unorthodox," she admitted, "but if he's equipped to handle emergencies can you think of any graver emergency than being presented with the body of a man who's been murdered? We have to consider your uncle, too; this is his garage."

"Yes," Colin said, nodding solemnly.

"Also," continued Mrs. Pollifax feverishly, "what else can we do with Henry? Stefan need only make one anonymous phone call to the police and I shall never get my passport back. And I have Dr. Belleaux's address right here in my purse. He's highly respected by the Turkish government—"

"Do you mean Dr. Guillaume Belleaux?" said Colin in surprise.

"Yes, do you know him?"

"I've heard of him. Everyone has."

"Well, I hadn't. But don't you see, he can vouch for me to the Turkish police! Of course we can't tell the police about Magda, but this time there's your jeep, with a registration number and a traceable license, and I can certainly describe to the police the two men who stole it. With this information the police may very well find both the jeep and the men by morning, and I shall have a clue as to where Magda may be!"

"Let's go then," Colin said, nodding. "The van's in the other garage. I'll back it up and we can put—uh—Henry inside." He disappeared through the door to the office and she heard an engine starting, garage doors open, and then a cumbersome van backed into the courtyard and Colin leaped out. "I think I'll turn the lights out for this," he said nervously and pulled the switch, leaving moonlight their only illumination. "You take his feet, will you? I'll take his shoulders."

Clumsily, slowly, they carried Henry to the van and inserted him into it. This proved extremely difficult because the van's rear doors had been welded closed—to gain more space inside, Colin explained breathlessly—and Henry had to be lifted up to the high cab of the van. Then it proved impossible to lift him between the two seats and they were forced to let him remain sprawled between the seats in a rather abandoned, drunken pose.

"I hope Henry doesn't mind," Mrs. Pollifax said breathlessly. "I mean his spirit, or whatever lingers behind."

"I suppose he's a spy, too," Colin said.

"Probably," said Mrs. Pollifax with a sigh, "although he was here only to keep an eye on me, to look after me, so to speak. Oh, if only I could have warned him!"

The van was moving ponderously up the driveway and now

turned down Zikzak alley. "You said you have Dr. Belleaux's address?" asked Colin.

She disentangled it from the other papers in her purse and handed it to him. "The bottom one is the home address," she pointed out.

He glanced at it, memorized it and handed it back to her. "That's in the Taksim area. At this hour it won't take long. I know that street—very posh." He glanced down at Henry briefly. "Did you know him well?"

"No," said Mrs. Pollifax. "I was introduced to him in Washington just before I boarded the plane. But in London he winked at me, and he was one of the men who kept staring in fascination at my seat companion—why that was your sister," she recalled in surprise.

"He liked Mia," Colin said soberly, and Mrs. Pollifax realized that they were giving Henry the nearest thing to a wake possible.

They lapsed into silence, each of them involved in their own thoughts as the van negotiated the dark streets. Doubtless Colin was thinking of his uncle's jeep—another disaster for him, she mused—while she tried not to think of what might be happening to Magda, or what had already happened to Henry. It must have been his murder that she had interrupted when she entered his room at the Oteli Itep to warn him. She recalled the curtains fluttering at the balcony window and shivered: his body must have lain behind those curtains. It was rather obvious now that Stefan had also hidden behind those curtains, and heard her call to Henry— and then she had led the murderers straight to Magda. *I should never have gone to Henry's room,* she thought sadly. *Mr. Carstairs warned me—no, ordered me—to have no contact with him at all. How could I have forgotten? One softhearted moment and I betray Magda.*

And Magda, she remembered, had been her assignment. Not Henry. In retrospect all kinds of ingenious little ideas came to her: she could have sent the manager's son to room 214 carrying the guide book as well as a note for Henry, whom she had believed to be alive then. Or she could have slipped an anonymous warning under his door and fled. But no, she had gone instead to his room and entered, calling out his name, and now his enemies knew that Emily Pollifax, too, was not what she appeared to be.

They were passing over the Galata Bridge now, and the lights of moving tugs and boats slashed the glistening inky water with long ribbons of gold. Even at midnight the bridge was filled with traffic: mules, trucks and donkeys bearing fruits and vegetables to the markets and merchandise to the bazaars. Pale moonlight etched out the silhouette of the mosque at the foot of the bridge and touched each passerby with a high light of silver. Mrs. Pollifax sighed and forced herself back to the moment, and to arranging explanations for the Dr.Belleaux whom she would presently meet. "How is it that you've heard of Dr. Belleaux?" she asked Colin. "Is he really that well-known?"

"To live in Istanbul is to hear of him," he said. "The police consult him on murders—he writes and lectures about criminology, you know—and the archaeologists consult him on bones, that sort of thing. He's quite lionized as an author and scholar. Goes to all the 'in' parties."

"What does he look like?"

"My impression is that he's fiftyish, or early sixtyish, with a pointed white goatee. Rather thin, talkative, elegant."

"I do hope he's of a practical nature."

"You mean practical enough to dispose of a body?" commented Colin dryly. "Ah, here's the street, I told you it was an impressive one."

"Indeed yes," she said, looking out upon well-spaced villas surrounded by charming gardens. The homes on the street were dark except for one in the center of the block that blazed with light. It was at this house that Colin applied the brakes. "You're in luck," he said. "Dr. Belleaux is not only up but from the look of all the cars parked here he's giving a party as well—and they've not left much space to get through, damn it." He leaned out and swore, maneuvered the van through the line of cars, turned around and came back, cutting the ignition and the lights. "Here we are," he said. "What do you plan to do?"

"I'd not expected a party," she said. "I shall have to ask to speak privately to Dr. Belleaux. I think I shall tell them at the door I'm from the American embassy—is there one?"

"They're all consulates here."

"All right, then I'm from the American consulate. That will do until I can get Dr. Belleaux aside and explain myself and *try* to explain Henry."

"Would you rather I pull into the drive?" he asked. "A bit awkward unloading in the front."

"Later—I want to be able to find you again," Mrs. Pollifax confessed. "This may take a little time. Would you care to come too?" She was growing rather attached to Colin, she realized.

"I don't feel I should leave Henry, do you? If anyone walked past and happened to glance in—"

His voice trailed off as a car rattled up the avenue, sputtering and backfiring, to turn into Dr. Belleaux's driveway a few feet away from them. At the crest of the drive the car shuddered to a halt, a man jumped from the rear seat and gave it a push—it was a jeep—and then leaped in as the car coasted down the driveway to the rear.

Mrs. Pollifax drew in her breath sharply. "Colin," she said incredulously. "Colin—"

"I saw it," he said in a stunned voice.

"I'm not losing my mind?"

"No," he said, and then, quickly and incoherently, "Damn it, no. Even the petrol—I told you the tank was almost empty and you saw him pushing it. Damn it, that was my jeep!"

"But here?" whispered Mrs. Pollifax. "*Here?*"

"It was Otto—I swear it—who jumped out and gave it a push," he said. "And that must have been your friend slumped in the back. Are you coming?" he demanded. He opened the door and jumped to the pavement.

"I certainly am," she said fervently. She could not imagine what kind of mix-up she had stumbled into. There had to be some reasonable explanation, but it would have to be delivered to her at a more appropriate moment. Stefan and Otto simply *couldn't* be working for Carstairs, too; not when Magda had virtually identified the two of them as her abductors. And they had killed Henry. But why were they *here?*

"Just a minute," said Colin, and reached into the compartment of the van to extract two lethal-looking guns. "Don't expect them to fire, they're made of wood," he whispered. "They're props Uncle Hu made for a short subject on Ataturk."

"But I'm delighted he did," she told him.

Props in hand they hurried down the driveway, moving from shadow to shadow until they came to the corner of the house. But

already it was too late. Mrs. Pollifax had hoped they might arrive in
the rear to find the jeep's motor still running, Stefan and Otto off
guard and Magda still accessible but the jeep had been abandoned.
The back door to the house stood wide open, the screened door
still swinging gently, but although a great deal of light and noise
came from the building there were no humans to be seen.

"Damn," said Colin. He looked intently at Mrs. Pollifax.
"You're not going to knock and ask for Dr. Belleaux." He might
have intended it as a question but it came out as a flat statement.

"No."

"Are you going to call the police?"

She said gently, "From what you've told me of Dr. Belleaux a
number of the police are probably inside at his party. And I don't
have a passport. No—I'm going to risk a look inside."

He looked shaken. "I say, that's rather dangerous."

She said steadily, "Perhaps it will be but I really don't know
what else to do. As you may have guessed, I came to Istanbul only
to meet and help Magda—and she's in there, and I'm responsible."

He nodded. "Then I'm going in with you."

She looked at him. "Colin, I can't let you become any more
involved, I really can't. I have to remind you that all I did was
deliver a message from your sister this afternoon—"

"Yesterday afternoon by now—"

"—and you'd never seen me before in your life. This is going
to be very illicit, I may get caught, and you've said yourself that
you're a physical coward."

He said fiercely, "Of course I'm a coward but I absolutely
loathe being pushed around—I told you that—and these men stole
my uncle's jeep, dumped a dead man in our garage and kidnapped
your friend. Now do let's stop talking—of course I'm going with
you!"

Mrs. Pollifax smiled faintly. "All right," and returned her
glance to the house. It was a two-storied rectangle of pale stucco
with blue shutters. She wondered if Stefan and Otto had gone
upstairs or down to the basement but there were no clues. She
tiptoed to the screen door and peered inside; directly opposite,
scarcely five feet away, a back staircase rose steeply toward the top
of the house. Her decision had been made for her: they would try
the upstairs first. "Look," she whispered, pointing.

To the right lay a long kitchen, brightly lit but empty of people although she could hear the sound of running water from a distant corner. Mrs. Pollifax slowly opened the screen door, testing for squeaks. Nothing happened and she slipped inside and across to the staircase with Colin directly behind her. She did not pause until she was halfway up the stairs. Here the rising sounds of the party proved an irritant: it was a very large party and the murmur of voices rose and fell in waves, but if they concealed any sounds that she and Colin made they had the disadvantage of concealing approaching footsteps as well. She felt trapped in noises, all of them confusing; still, she could not remain exposed on this stairway for any length of time and so she rallied, brought out her absurd wooden pistol and moved to the top of the stairs.

Here she met a wide carpeted hallway containing six doors, all of them closed. On her right, at the far end, the hall terminated in a stairwell and the carpet overflowed the stairs like a waterfall of gold; it was from this end of the house that music and conversation rose almost deafeningly. Mrs. Pollifax headed in the opposite direction, on the supposition that these rooms were farthest removed from people, and people would be what Stefan and Otto must avoid if they were here, and the thought of their being here—of all places!—still baffled and shocked Mrs. Pollifax.

The first door they opened was a bedroom but except for ornate hangings and baroque furniture it was empty. The second door proved to be a linen closet. With some impatience Mrs. Pollifax threw open the door to the third room, only to be reminded that impatience bred carelessness, for this time she had opened the door to a bedroom containing three people—the impact took her breath away—and in unison, also stunned, three people turned to stare at her.

It was as if she had abruptly cut the switch on an unwinding reel of film. Magda lay across a chaise lounge like a bundle that had been flung there, and Stefan, leaning over her, looked up in the act of withdrawing a hypodermic needle from her arm. Otto stood on guard a few feet from Mrs. Pollifax, his mouth open as he stared at her. He was the first to react: he moved so swiftly, so menacingly, that without a second to think about it Mrs. Pollifax lifted her right hand, flattened it as Lorvale had taught her, and dealt Otto a crisp karate chop to the side of his throat. He stared at her in astonish-

ment and then his eyes closed and he sank slowly to the floor.
Behind her Colin gasped, *"Mrs. Pollifax!"*

"Get his gun," said Mrs. Pollifax crisply.

Colin stooped and plucked it from the floor, pocketing his
own wooden prop. Holding the live gun he gestured Stefan away
from Magda. "Against the wall," he ordered, waving the gun with
growing enthusiasm.

Mrs. Pollifax, her flowered hat only a little askew, went at
once to Magda, who was trying to stand. "Can you walk?"

"I'm drugged," she said in an anguished voice. "Hurry!"

Mrs. Pollifax nodded, and, grasping her arm, led her to the
door. Colin followed, walking backward with his gun pointed at
Stefan. But Stefan refused to remain abjectly against the wall: he
took one step and then another, following Colin with a nasty grin
on his face.

"There's no lock on this door!" Colin said desperately, trying
to slam it in Stefan's face.

Mrs. Pollifax glanced back over her shoulder. Magda had already begun to sag and it was doubtful that she would remain
upright if Mrs. Pollifax withdrew her arm to help Colin. Obviously
Stefan was determined to follow them; he knew the gun was loaded
because it was Otto's, but he was not going to make it easy for
Colin, who was so patently an amateur. To hesitate for long would
risk their having to literally carry Magda out of the house in their
arms. "If he comes too close, shoot him," she said calmly, and
headed down the hall to the stairs.

But at the top of the rear staircase Mrs. Pollifax stopped in
dismay, for the downstairs hall and entrance that had been deserted
ten minutes ago was now aswarm with workers. The screen door
through which they had entered was propped wide open. Buckets
of ice were being carried in and empty trays wheeled out to a
waiting truck. A heavy-set butler stood at the bottom of the stairs
calling out orders and completely blocking the exit. He did not
look as if he would give ground easily, or let them through unchal-
lenged.

Mrs. Pollifax turned away. They had to get out of the house
quickly, before Magda lost consciousness, and there was no alternative now but to use the main staircase. Propping up Magda she
half-carried her to the stairwell, grasped the banister and began a

step-by-step descent. They made a ludicrous procession, she thought, herself and Magda clinging together in the vanguard, followed by Colin walking backward and brandishing a pistol at Stefan, who continued to leer and follow three paces behind. As they descended Mrs. Pollifax could look down and see the massive oak door at the foot of the stairs. She knew that beyond, parked in the street, stood Colin's van; if they could just get through that door . . .

The piano playing came to a sudden halt. Slowly the murmur of voices subsided into startled silence and Mrs. Pollifax found herself in full view of Dr. Belleaux's party; she was in fact staring down into dozens of gaping faces. She supposed that two women on the stairs might have gone unnoticed but that the sight of Colin holding a gun made for a certain conspicuousness. Rather wearily —it had been a long and violent evening—Mrs. Pollifax lifted her wooden gun and addressed the sea of faces below her. In her most imperious voice she said, "I will shoot the first person who tries to stop us." It was a phrase culled from the late late movies but it was the best that she could manage under the circumstances.

Someone said, "Get Dr. Belleaux!"

Mrs. Pollifax reached the bottom of the stairs and pulled open the door, holding it wide. As Colin backed into her, stepping painfully on her ankle, she said in a low voice, "Take Magda and run."

He nodded and pressed the functioning gun into her hand. "Thanks—I couldn't possibly shoot it," he admitted.

"I can," she said calmly. "Just get her out, she's going under."

It was now Colin who bore the sagging Magda into the night and down the path, and Mrs. Pollifax who faced Stefan. "I am going to shoot the first person who walks through this door after I leave," she called out, only a little embarrassed by her clichés. To her left, from a corner of her eye, she saw several people move apart, and for just one moment she allowed her glance to leave Stefan: she looked into the livingroom and into the eyes of the party's host who had suddenly appeared. She thought, *Dr. Belleaux, I presume,* and then her glance swerved back to Stefan, she saw him coiled to jump at her and she fired the gun at the ceiling above him. Slamming the door behind her, she ran.

Colin was bundling Magda into the van across the street but unfortunately Henry was already there, which had led to difficulties. When Mrs. Pollifax reached the van Colin was starting up the engine with a dead Henry at his elbow and an unconscious Magda in the passenger seat. "Jump in somewhere—anywhere," he cried in a harassed voice. "Try the floor or sit on Henry. Or Magda."

Mrs. Pollifax climbed in and fell across Magda just as the van began to move and a second before it raced down the street. "I'm heading for the ferry, I'm going to get you out of Istanbul right now, before all hell breaks loose," he said, and he turned on the van's lights as they reached the corner. "You can't go back to your hotel, and the first place Stefan will look for you is Ramsey Enterprises, and after that they'll begin watching the ferries and the airport. There's not a minute to lose; the ferries don't run as often at night."

"I'm a wanted citizen," Mrs. Pollifax said in a surprised voice.

Colin looked at her and grinned. "Well, look at the facts, Mrs. Pollifax," he suggested. "The police have your passport and will be looking for you, Stefan and Otto will be looking for you, you'll be wanted for burglarizing—not to mention kidnapping—and have you noticed the interesting passengers we've acquired? At the moment I can't think how to explain a dead man with a hole in his chest or a woman who's been heavily drugged."

Mrs. Pollifax looked at him. "Colin" she said accusingly, "you *enjoyed* it!"

"Good God, it was terrifying," he said. "What I am experiencing is the absolute relief at still being alive. Who would ever have believed we would get away with it! I say," he added, "shouldn't you do something about Henry before we reach the ferry?"

Mrs. Pollifax agreed; and as the van careened through the empty streets she alternately tugged and pulled Henry into the darkest shadows of the van.

Chapter Seven

At the Kabatas landing stage they encountered their first stroke of luck: a ferry was being readied to leave its slip. Ropes and chains were being cast off, but the gates had not yet closed. With a flourish Colin drove the van onto the ferry; only one more car followed and the gates swung shut. "But there are telephones?" pointed out Mrs. Pollifax bleakly.

"There are telephones, yes. Keep your fingers crossed that no one will be waiting for us on the other side!"

As they crossed the Bosporus they undertook a frenzied and certainly bizarre housecleaning of the van's rear, which had been casually equipped for living purposes. Under Colin's tutelage they set up a battered old army cot and chained it to the wall, placed a still heavily drugged Magda on it and covered her with a blanket. They rolled Henry under the one piece of built-in furniture in the van: a high workbench which Colin explained was used for developing photographs, cooking meals on a sterno and even, in emergencies, as a bed. "Do you think the people at Dr. Belleaux's party saw the van clearly enough to describe it?" asked Mrs. Pollifax, covering Henry with a blanket, too.

"From the window anyone could have seen the shape of it," Colin said. "But the license or its color, no. It was too dark—the nearest light was far down the street. But you know they need only inquire what vehicles belong to Ramsey Enterprises to learn the registry number and description. There's the jeep, and this van, and then the second van that Uncle Hu's taken to Erzurum. Do you think Stefan overheard Magda insisting on going to Yozgat?"

Mrs. Pollifax said in a dismal voice, "Probably." She sighed. "It does seem the most wretched luck that Magda's drugged again and can't explain more. My orders were to get her out of Turkey quickly—to save her life at any cost—and I don't *like* this Yozgat business. I've finally found her, and it would still be relatively simple to put her on a plane, whereas Yozgat—" Her voice trailed off uncertainly and she shook her head. "I don't even know where it is yet!"

"I don't mind dropping you off there," Colin said. "I've thought about it, you know. I can't go back to Istanbul until this blows over and I've decided to keep going and find Uncle Hu. He's the only person who can untangle all this—for me at least—and he should be starting back from Erzurum tomorrow morning."

"Colin—"

He smiled. "I know, I know, you hate to see me involved. It's purest chivalry, of course—I'm cursed with it. I was raised on King Arthur."

"I think that's rather charming," said Mrs. Pollifax thoughtfully, "but you're taking me on face value alone which alarms me."

"Rum, isn't it?" he said smiling, and shrugged. "I can't possibly explain it—call it a hunch or an instinct. Or put it this way: How can I possibly drop all this now and never know how it turns out? Good God, the thought appalls me. And do you realize that tonight—for the first time in my life—I've been involved in something I actually pulled off successfully? It's positively dazzling. In the meantime your friend Magda seems to attract the most unwholesome bunch of toughs I've ever seen, and I can't say very much for your other friend—I mean Dr. Belleaux, of course."

"I can't say very much for him, either," said Mrs. Pollifax with feeling. "I think that Mr. Carstairs would be extremely surprised by what we've seen tonight, too."

"Who?"

"Mr. Carstairs is the gentleman who—uh—arranged my coming here."

Colin said with a crooked smile, "To have sent you he must have a real sense of humor. There's the warning bell—come along to the front of the van, we're almost there."

"Oh," said Mrs. Pollifax in a hollow voice, turned off the flashlight and crept back into the passenger seat.

The ferry nudged its way into the slip, chains rattled, gates opened and engines warmed up. The cars ahead began to move, and Colin inched the van forward. Slowly they drove off the ferry and into the night: no police whistles shrilled, no one ran toward them shouting at them to halt. They had crossed the Bosporus and left the peninsula of Istanbul behind without incident. "Now where are we?" inquired Mrs. Pollifax and brought out her guide book.

"No need for that," said Colin. "This is Uskudar, formerly Chrysopolis, and noted mainly as a suburb and for its enormous Buyuk Mezaristan, or cemetery."

"Cemetery!" exclaimed Mrs. Pollifax thoughtfully.

Colin looked at her. "You can't possibly—"

"But we must find somewhere appropriate to leave Henry."

He groaned. "You look so extremely respectable, you know."

"I have a flexible mind—I believe it's one of the advantages of growing old," she explained. "I find youth quite rigid at times. Why *not* a cemetery?"

Colin sighed. "I daresay there's a certain logic there. You're not—uh—thinking of burying him as well?"

"That would be illegal," she told him reproachfully, "and scarcely kind to Henry."

"Sorry," he said. He peered out at a sign, and nodded. "This is the avenue—I think we're driving alongside the cemetery now. Watch for an entrance, will you?"

Several moments later they left the world of trams, lights and occasional automobiles and entered a subterranean night world of awesome silence. "This is the cemetery?" faltered Mrs. Pollifax.

"It's a cypress grove, quite huge. There's a sultan buried in the old part. I'd call the new part spooky enough."

"But what curious headstones!"

"They're Moslem, of course. The steles with knobs on the top represent women, the ones with turbans are men. Then there are variations—I've forgotten them—for priests and those who've gone to Mecca."

The van bumped to a jarring halt and he cut the motor. At once the silence was filled with an overwhelming drone of chirping grasshoppers and shrilling cicadas; the volume was incredible, as if they had entered a jungle. The headlights picked out tangles of sinister dark undergrowth and the silhouette of hundreds of headstones leaning in every conceivable direction. The moon, dimmer now and trailing clouds behind it, sailed over the forsaken scene and added a ghostly pallor to the tombs. When an owl hooted mournfully Mrs. Pollifax jumped.

"Well," said Colin, and flicked off the headlights.

"I suppose you had to turn off the lights?" said Mrs. Pollifax as both darkness and insect noises moved in on them.

"I really don't think we're supposed to be here," Colin pointed out reasonably.

"I can't think why not," she said bravely, and climbed down from her seat.

Clumsily, laboriously, they carried Henry from his hiding place and lifted him down to the damp grass. "Where do you want him?" asked Colin.

Mrs. Pollifax ignored the irony in his voice. "Over by that larger stone, I think. We want him to be noticed soon but not immediately. Do you think those horrid men took his identification?"

"Probably," gasped Colin as they carried Henry across a path that felt like a brook bed, up a small slope and to the larger, paler headstone that had caught Mrs. Pollifax's eye. "Don't show a light!" he said sharply.

"I'm writing his name and the name of his hotel on a slip of paper," she explained. "There! Henry Miles, care of Oteli Itep." She leaned over and tucked it into the pocket of his dark jacket. "I should like someone to do as much for me," she said firmly. She stood a moment looking into the eerie black shapes of gnarled tree trunks, creeping shrubbery and mooncast shadows. "He was a very nice man," she said at last. "Now, do let's leave."

"What did you do—roll 'im?" said a deep, lazy, amused voice from the darkness.

Mrs. Pollifax turned and saw a shadow detach itself from the darkness of the tomb. A giant of a man arose, stretched himself calmly, yawned and strolled nonchalantly toward them. In the dim light he looked seven feet tall but this was a trick of shadows— Colin turned on the flashlight, and he shrank to a more reasonable six feet. His face was swarthy, with dirty scraggly hair and a stubble of a beard. He wore filthy sailors' pants, a jacket that had once been white, a frayed turtle-neck sweater. His feet were shod in a pair of old sneakers with a hole in each toe.

Colin said bravely, "Who the devil are you, and what are you doing behind that gravestone?"

"Sleeping," said the man, looking down at them. "Til you drove in and woke me up." He put his hands on his hips and surveyed Mrs. Pollifax with interest, his eyes moving appreciatively over the flowered hat, lingering on her face, then smiling as they took in the navy blue suit, white blouse and shoes. He shook his head. "Now I seen everything!" He dropped to the ground and peered at Henry. "He's dead," he said. "You shoot him?"

"No."

"Then what the hell."

"Someone else shot him," Colin said crossly.

"We didn't know what else to do with him," explained Mrs. Pollifax. "Since we just happened to be passing by—why are you here?" she asked sternly.

"That's my business." He stood up and looked at them. "A couple of tourists dropping off a guy with a bullet hole in his chest!" He shook his head. "Now wouldn't the police like to hear about that?"

Mrs. Pollifax stiffened. "Nonsense. I very much doubt that you can afford to talk to the police."

He laughed; his guffaw threatened to awaken even the dead. "You got a suspicious mind. Okay, so I'm sleeping in a graveyard. So I'm broke. So you got a corpse, it makes us even. You also got a truck and you're gonna drive it out of here. I need to get out of here. I had it in mind we might make a deal." His voice caressed the last word. "Wotthehell, how about it? I'll take a lift if you're going in the right direction."

"Which direction is that?" asked Colin cautiously.

Cunningly the man replied, "Which direction you heading?"

Mrs. Pollifax realized that she wasn't certain of this herself. "How *do* we proceed?" she asked.

"Toward Ankara."

"Perfect!" said their new companion, beaming at them. "Got a friend there that owes me money."

"Have you a passport?"

"Of a sort."

"What's your name?"

"Sandor's enough. Just Sandor."

"Greek?"

"Of a sort."

"A sailor?"

The man was clearly laughing at them now. "Of a sort."

"Can you drive?" asked Mrs. Pollifax.

"I can drive."

Mrs. Pollifax exchanged glances with Colin. "An unholy alliance," commented Colin.

"Sheerest blackmail, of course," said Mrs. Pollifax cheerfully.

"But mutual," pointed out Colin with a faint smile. "All right, Sandor, we'll give you a lift."

"Of course," he said. "But on a condition."

Mrs. Pollifax stiffened. "Oh?"

"No monkey business—no stops. I don't want no welcoming committees in Ankara."

Mrs. Pollifax smiled. "That—uh—fits our plans quite well," she conceded graciously. "You know a way to Ankara that avoids—uh—welcoming committees?"

"Know the city like the back of my hand!"

"A veritable jewel," she murmured.

As they walked back to the van Colin said in a low voice, "Of course you realize he's wanted by the police."

"Then he's in good company," she pointed out in a kind voice. "What would you guess his crime to be?"

"Smuggling's big along the coast, and if he's been a sailor he's probably been involved in smuggling. Opium, probably."

"Opium," repeated Mrs. Pollifax, and smiled. "So now we have joined the underworld! How very surprising life can be . . . !"

Chapter Eight

They drove along nibbling at the grapes with which Sandor had equipped himself for his night in the graveyard. Following his initial shock at discovering they already had a passenger—"She dead, too?" he had asked with professional interest—Sandor announced that he was going to sleep before he did any driving. "But I'll know if you stop," he said, drawing a serviceable gun from a pocket. "I'll sleep on the floor. Any monkey tricks and I'll shoot."

"Why didn't you show your gun earlier?" asked Mrs. Pollifax curiously.

His glance was withering; obviously he felt that his wits and his tongue were sufficient for gullible foreigners. "Did I need to?" he asked with a shrug. "Now, drive." Whereupon he lay down on the floor of the van, curled up and began snoring.

The moon that had perversely haunted them hours earlier now disappeared just when it would have been the most appreciated, and to further depress Mrs. Pollifax the road to Izmit was bumpy. At first the Bay of Kadiköy cheered her with its cluster of lights, and later there were sustaining glimpses of the Sea of Marmora but presently a light rain began to fall, blurring all the lights and with it any hope of sightseeing. Mrs. Pollifax's thoughts darkened equally: she had neither slept nor eaten anything of substance since her arrival in Istanbul and she was beginning to feel the lack of both: lemonade and grapes served only as an appetizer for a dinner that moved increasingly out of reach. She was also beginning to feel the irregularity of her situation: having never in her life received so much as a parking ticket she was under suspicion by the police in this supposedly friendly country, and presently she might even become the subject of a nationwide alarm. She had arrived in this country with Henry, and Henry was dead. There was no one at

all to whom she could appeal—certainly not to Dr. Belleaux now—
and her companions in exile were a young British misfit and a
disreputable blackmailer acquired in a cemetery.

It was difficult to figure out just how it had all happened.
Perhaps I'm too flexible, she thought, and turned to scrutinize Colin
beside her. She was not a fool. There were high stakes involved in
this assignment, and many crosscurrents which she would probably
never know about. It had already occurred to her that Mia Ramsey
could have been artfully placed on the plane beside her to girlishly
suggest looking up Colin. But there had been no certainty that
Mrs. Pollifax would contact Colin at all, and several hours later it
was Colin who had saved Magda by concealing her from the police.
If he were part of a vast and sinister scheme it was doubtful that he
would have telephoned and left a message asking Mrs. Pollifax to
retrieve her lost friend; Magda would instead have disappeared
forever. No, she had to regard Colin as a small miracle.

The van's headlights picked out pretty little suburban villas
and strange place names: Kiziltoprak, Goztepe, Caddebostani Er-
enkoy, Saudiye, Bostanci. At a town called Maltepe the road met
the sea again and followed it on to the seaside port of Kartal. To
keep Colin awake Mrs. Pollifax read the road directions from the
small guide book she had purchased in London. When this palled
she read from the same book brief histories of the Ottoman and
then the Seljuk Empires until a listless Colin complained that
Sandor's snoring was more stimulating than ancient history. They
then argued whether, once past Izmit, they should drive to Ankara
by way of Bolu or Beyzapari.

"Which is the route people usually prefer?" she asked.

"Bolu. The road's excellent."

"Then I think we should go by way of Beyzapari."

They were still arguing this when they reached Izmit at half-
past three in the morning. As they crossed the railroad tracks to
leave the town they saw the first brightening of the horizon in the
east, and seeing it Colin nodded. "All right, Beyzapari. The
thought of getting to Ankara quickly is very tempting—after all,
it's 292 miles and we've gone only sixty—but if dawn's coming, and
the police will be looking for the van, then I concede we might not
get to Ankara at all if we go by Bolu. By the way, what exactly do

you expect—being an experienced undercover agent," he added dryly.

"I am not an undercover agent," said Mrs. Pollifax tartly. "I'm a courier. As to what I expect I would say just about anything, but that's because of Dr. Belleaux, you see."

Colin said wryly, "You've not yet found that rational explanation for Magda's being carried off to *his* house?"

"No I haven't," she said frankly, "and the really frightening part of it all is that he's a man whom everyone trusts. Carstairs told me he enjoys the confidence of the Turkish and American governments and you've described him as being a consultant to the police here and enjoying *everyone's* confidence. I seriously doubt that Carstairs would even remotely consider Dr. Belleaux's being involved in any treachery."

Colin said dryly, "Which leaves us the only two people who think otherwise? Damn it, that's a horrible thought!"

"Yes it is," said Mrs. Pollifax, and shivered. "But no matter how kind we try to be to Dr. Belleaux there's no getting around the fact that while he gives parties in his downstairs livingroom there are two chaps upstairs drugging a defenseless woman."

"Definitely a double standard there," agreed Colin.

She nodded. "His reputation makes it so patently unfair! There's no way to fight him—except to run, and I'm not sure that running is sensible, either, since it leaves him with an absolutely free hand. Just think of the possibilities open to him!"

"It's better you don't," Colin said gently.

Mrs. Pollifax nodded. He was quite right: they would be rendered helpless, like the tiger in a tiger hunt, with the police and Dr. Belleaux—separately or even together—beating the bushes in a steadily diminishing circle until they were isolated and then flushed out. "At least I have Magda," she said, but since she did not have the slightest idea of what to do with Magda, or how to get her safely out of the country before the police found them, this was not essentially comforting.

"Could you get word to your friend in Washington?" Colin asked.

"I don't know," she said slowly. "I was given strict orders not to. I was also given strict orders never to contact Henry; but then I did, you see, in order to warn him he was being followed, and you know what a monstrous mistake that was. I led Stefan straight back to Magda. A cable to Mr. Carstairs might do the same thing. Do you need to show a passport to send a cable?"

"Probably. I have mine with me but of course by the time we get to Ankara the police may very well be looking for me, too."

"Yes," said Mrs. Pollifax in a depressed voice, and resumed staring out of the window.

Beyond Izmit the road dipped down to Geyve and then wound up again through hills covered with fields of wheat and tobacco. Dawn found them on a high plateau beyond Goynuk, and then they reached a pass and coasted down into a plain. Beyond the town of Nallihan Colin suddenly pulled the van off to one side of the road and braked to a stop. "We've gone nearly a hundred and sixty miles and I'm tired," he said, mopping his forehead with his sleeve. "Sandor's going to have to pay his way now. Sandor," he called. "It's morning—half-past seven—and your turn to drive."

"What the hell," said Sandor, making a great deal of noise yawning. "This lady back here is staring at me," he complained. "Is there breakfast?"

"There's a camp stove somewhere," said Colin, "and the water jug is full, I filled it myself—Uncle Hu is always very fussy about that. And I believe there are bouillon cubes, dusty but soluble."

"But that's wonderful," said Mrs. Pollifax with feeling. She crawled back to Magda who was staring at the roof of the van with a puzzled expression. Seeing Mrs. Pollifax she said in a weak voice that bore a trace of irony, "Where am I now?"

"It's a little difficult to explain."

"Who was that man who snores so dreadfully?"

"That's even more difficult to explain. How are you feeling?"

"Weak and very thirsty. I have been drugged again?"

Mrs. Pollifax nodded. "It might be wise for you to get some fresh air now. It's very hot back here. Colin is making broth for you."

"Colin! That funny young man is still here?"

"The situation is extremely fluid and unconventional," Mrs. Pollifax told her, "but we *are* moving in the direction of Yozgat." She helped her to her feet, and out of the van to the roadside where Colin had set up his sterno.

Colin was saying, "Presently we'll be crossing the Anatolian plain and there will be even more sun, wind and dust." The water he was nursing came to a boil, he stirred bouillon into it and carefully divided it among four battered tin mugs. "Here you are," he said.

Never had Mrs. Pollifax tasted anything kinder to her palate: at first she rolled the broth on her tongue, savoring its wetness, and then she drank it greedily. "Purest nectar," she said with a sigh, and saw that color was coming back into Magda's white face for the first time. "At what hour do you think we will reach Ankara?" she asked.

Sandor was noisily smacking his lips. "With me driving we go like the wind. Another forty miles to Beysapari, beyond that sixty maybe." He was studying the van. "She has a Land Rover body?"

Colin nodded. "She's a rebuilt Land Rover, yes. Four-wheel drive and all that."

Sandor nodded. "Very good! By early afternoon we get there, or near enough. Then we go by back roads. They are very bad," he added regretfully, "but very very private."

"You are wanted by the police?" inquired Mrs. Pollifax companionably.

Sandor grinned. "You are a nice lady but you ask too many questions. In Ankara I have fine friends and I let you go free."

"Free?" said Mrs. Pollifax with amusement. "I didn't realize we'd been captured."

He patted his pocket with meaning. "I have you under guard, beware. Now wotthehell, let's go."

For some moments Mrs. Pollifax had been aware of a small piper cub plane drifting lazily along the horizon at a distance; she had watched it as Sandor talked. Now with one foot on the running board of the van she said in an alarmed voice, "Colin, look!" For the plane, having momentarily disappeared behind a ridge ahead of them, had suddenly reappeared now and was flying toward them at a shockingly low altitude. Colin stood behind her carrying the camp stove and squinting at the sky. The sound of the plane's engine grew frighteningly loud and for a moment Mrs. Pollifax wondered if they were going to be strafed: the plane passed so low that she could clearly see the face of the pilot, who in turn looked down at them; and then just as abruptly the plane's nose lifted, it climbed and began a long circle that carried it over the ridge again and away toward Ankara.

"Damn fool," Sandor shouted, shaking a fist at the horizon.

Colin said in a choked voice, "What the devil does that mean!"

"Reconnaissance, I think," said Mrs. Pollifax. "But by whom?" She was rather unnerved by the incident; until now she had felt safely removed from Istanbul, but she resolutely put aside her anxiety, helped Magda back to her cot and insisted that Colin have the dubious honor of napping on the floor because he was the more tired from driving. Again she took the passenger seat, this time beside Sandor, and they set off—or rather flew off, thought Mrs. Pollifax, clinging to the sides of the leather seat, for Sandor drove with abandon, swerving gaily around the holes in the road, swearing in Turkish and English at the holes he did not miss, and frequently taking both hands off the wheel to rub dust from his eyes or to light an evil-smelling cigar which almost immediately was extinguished.

The climbed now to a ravined and arid plateau, and the dust they raised all but obscured the sun. It was hot, the van captured and retained both the heat and the dust, and their water supply was gone. Since leaving Nallihan they had passed only one car and that one had been abandoned beside the road—probably with a broken axle, thought Mrs. Pollifax ominously. Nothing moved except the mountains on the horizon, which swam in the rising heat like mirages, until far ahead of them Mrs. Pollifax saw an approaching cloud of dust. "Dust storm?" she inquired—it was impossible to doze at all with Sandor at the wheel, and he had just finished telling her that dust storms were frequent in summer on the road to Ankara.

"Car," he said briefly.

Mrs. Pollifax nodded; she had begun to feel that if Sandor said it was a car it would be a car—and as it drew nearer it was indeed a car, a very old dusty touring car of 1920 vintage. The sun shone across its windshield, turning it opaque, so that as it approached them it appeared to be driven by remote control. It was therefore all the more startling to Mrs. Pollifax when she saw a hand and then an arm extend full-length from the passenger side of the car. When she saw the gun in that hand she stiffened. "Watch out—a gun!" she cried, and ducked her head just as the windshield in front of her splintered.

Sandor virtually stood on the brakes. "Wotthehell," he shouted, and fought the steering wheel to get them off the road.

Behind her Colin shouted, "Stay down, Mrs. Pollifax!"

Metal protested, tires squealed and Mrs. Pollifax's hat fell off as the van lurched across the ridge that contained the road; they bumped uncomfortably over untilled ground. Sandor was tugging at his belt with one hand; he brought out his gun but the car had already passed them: the sound of a second bullet rang *ping!* against the rear of the van.

In alarm Mrs. Pollifax turned and saw that Colin was reacting with astonishing efficiency; he had remembered that he had a gun, too, and now he was slashing at the glass in the round porthole window in the back; as she watched she saw him lift the gun he had taken from Stefan and push it through the window. She thought he fired it, but there was too much confusion to know. Sandor was swearing as he fought the wheel again, turning the van to head it back to the road.

"Look out!" screamed Mrs. Pollifax as the van swung around, for the ancient dust-ridden car had also turned and was heading toward them at accelerated speed, hoping to ram them if it couldn't shoot their tires first. For a second the van's wheels spun uselessly in a gully, then Sandor roared the engine and the van shot back on to the road just as the elderly Packard left it. A bullet zoomed over Sandor's head, again just missed Mrs. Pollifax and went out the open window. But Sandor had fired, too. He seemed to have three hands, one for the gearshift, one for the wheel, and one for firing. With a wrench of the wheel he turned and backed the van and tried to shoot down the car but the Packard swerved, circled and returned to the road to face them head-on.

They remained like this for several seconds, each car facing the other on the road with a distance of perhaps twenty yards between them, each driver revving his engine and waiting. Then with a burst of noise the Packard started down the road at full speed, heading directly toward them. "*Hooooweeeeee,*" shouted Sandor, his eyes shining—it was clearly a game to him—and he recklessly steered the van straight at the Packard, not giving an inch. Mrs. Pollifax screamed and slid from seat to floor. From here she looked up to see a familiar face—Otto's—almost at their window, saw the Packard hurtle past them, barely missing them. As the Packard passed from sight she heard Colin's gun begin firing from the rear window, heard the scream of tires, a terrifying sound of metal twisting and turning, twisting and rolling, and Mrs. Pollifax put her hands to her face. "They've turned over," cried Sandor, braking, and leaped out.

Mrs. Pollifax slid from her side of the van and jumped to the road. The Packard was lying upside down in the dust after rolling over several times. Mrs. Pollifax began to run. "We must help them," she cried, and then suddenly the silence was rent by a great explosion and flames turned the Packard into a funeral pyre. Mrs. Pollifax stepped back and covered her eyes. "Did anyone get out?" she gasped in horror.

Colin was beside her with a hand on her shoulder. He looked pale and shaken. "No," he said. "I watched. It was Otto driving, and a man I'd never seen before doing the shooting."

Sandor said belligerently, "What the hell goes on here, they maniacs? Nuts? They tried to kill us!" He looked incredulous. "What the hell they want?" he said, shaking a fist.

"Us," Mrs. Pollifax told him in a trembling voice.

He gaped at her. "Those jerks were gunning for *you?*"

Mrs. Pollifax nodded a little wearily. "Yes. First they sent the plane—there must have been radio communication, and then—"

Sandor looked from her to Colin and back again. "But why?" he demanded indignantly.

Mrs. Pollifax said weakly, "They apparently didn't want us to get to Ankara."

"That I could see for myself but what the hell's going on?"

Mrs. Pollifax hesitated and then recklessly took the plunge. "You might as well know, Sandor, that not only *those* men are after us but the police, too."

"Police!" He stared blankly. "You?"

"Yes."

His mouth dropped. "You *did* shoot the guy you was unloading in the cemetery!"

"No," she said patiently, "but Otto did—the man driving the Packard."

A light of comprehension dawned in Sandor's eyes. "I'll be

damned," he said, and to Mrs. Pollifax's surprise he gave her a look of grudging admiration. "I'll be damned," he said again, scratching his head, and then he began to laugh. "You're crooks too!" he cried delightedly.

Colin interrupted primly. "I say, I resent that very much!"

Sandor was wiping his eyes with a filthy handkerchief. "No offense, I know we're not in the same league." He grinned at them both. "So when I picked you up in the cemetery back there—and you let me come along like that—you was really picking me up!" He shook his head admiringly. "I thought I had you two scared to death of me."

Mrs. Pollifax said soberly, "I don't think we should stand here talking like this. I think we should leave before someone sees the smoke and comes to find out what's happened. Colin, do go back and reassure Magda." Still she remained standing and staring at the smoldering wreckage. "It could have been us," she said with a shudder. "They intended it to be us. Sandor, you did a remarkable job of driving."

He was still regarding her with amazement. "That guy Colin had a gun—he had it all the time. And you got gangsters after you —I picked a helluva bunch of people to hitch a ride with!" The expression in his eyes was one of infinite respect. "I know a guy could use you. You want to make some real money? I'll introduce you when we get to Ankara."

"I'm not sure Ankara's a good place for us to head," said Mrs. Pollifax sadly. "Not now. There may be roadblocks. And thank you but I don't need any 'real money,' I just want to get safely out of Turkey."

Sandor nodded wisely. "That bad then," he said, escorting her back to the van. After handing her up to the front he appeared to have reached a decision. "You come to Ankara," he said firmly. "Ankara's the place for you. I got good friends there, you hear? A little crooked"—he shrugged and grinned—"but wotthehell, you need help. If anybody can smuggle you into Ankara it's me, Sandor, and there my friends help you, wait and see."

Mrs. Pollifax looked into his face and was touched by his concern. "Thank you, Sandor," she said simply.

From the rear of the van Colin said bitterly, "He probably thinks he's bringing his pals two bona fide members of the Mafia."

Chapter Nine

In Langley, Virginia, it was Tuesday morning, just half-past eight and already over ninety degrees in the streets. Carstairs had arrived in his air-conditioned office high in the CIA building and was sipping a second cup of coffee as he read over dispatches that had come in during the night. He had just lighted a cigarette when Bishop walked in. "Sir," he said.

"Yes, Bishop, what is it?"

He held out a sheet of paper. "It's a routine report that arrived at the clearing office a few minutes ago from the State Department. They shipped it up here as fast as they could. It seems that during the night the State Department received an urgent request from Istanbul for the verification of one Mrs. Emily Pollifax, an alleged American traveling under an allegedly American passport."

"What the devil!" said Carstairs, scowling. He took the sheet of paper and stared at it. It was, as Bishop had said, one of the routine memos that circulated through a number of channels until it ended, heaven only knew where, as a fifth copy of what already had been filed in the Passport Division of the State Department. Its message was innocent enough but reading it Carstairs experienced his first uneasiness.

"I don't like it," he said.

"No, sir."

"I don't like it at all."

"No, sir."

"I see it's stamped five-fifteen A.M. upon arrival here. What time would that have been in Istanbul?"

"Nine-fifteen last night, sir."

Carstairs swore. "Only an hour following Mrs. Pollifax's first attempt to meet Ferenci-Sabo then." He didn't understand, of all the people moving in and out of Istanbul, what on earth could have drawn the attention of the police to Mrs. Pollifax? Her passport had been arranged on a top-priority basis and had been processed in less than an hour; had there been something important omitted in the processing? Had it appeared different or even forged to the police? No, that was impossible, he had double-checked it thoroughly himself.

"This is not calculated to induce calm," he said dryly. "When the police single out one person out of thousands—and that person happens to be an agent of ours—then a certain bleak note enters the picture." He shook his head. "We can't contact the Istanbul police, our interest would only produce a reaction that would be the despair of our diplomats—the right hand must never know what the left hand is doing," he added, and stubbed out one cigarette and lighted another.

But a possibility had occurred to him. "We can't do anything directly, Bishop, but we can be devious. Contact Barnes over in the State Department. Ask him if he'd mind cabling our consulate over there in Istanbul, in his name, to ask why the hell the Turkish police questioned the legal passport of one of our American citizens. I've got a meeting upstairs in five minutes but keep me posted if it lasts longer than I expect."

"Yes, sir. He's to make his inquiry routine but ask for immediate information?"

"Right. If the police have gone so far as to question Mrs. Pollifax the consulate ought to know about it. If they don't know, they'd jolly well better find out. I'm curious to say the least!"

"Right, sir."

When Carstairs returned from his meeting there was still no word. He sat back and reflected upon Mrs. Pollifax's schedule. She would have arrived in Istanbul about four yesterday afternoon—at least he knew now that she had arrived safely, he thought dryly. But at nine o'clock, or soon after, the Istanbul police had sent off a cable asking that her credentials be verified by the American government. Routine curiosity? Was the Hotel Itep under surveillance now? Had Mrs. Pollifax been injured, or even killed?

The reply, when it came in from the American consulate, was brief. The Istanbul police had questioned one Mrs. Emily Pollifax for half an hour during the preceding evening but they refused to say why they had taken her to central headquarters for questioning. They had retained her passport for twenty-four hours; upon receiving verification of her identity they were now prepared to return the passport to her. Mrs. Pollifax had not been located yet, however. She was registered at the Hotel Itep but had not been seen there since late Monday evening.

At this Carstairs swore again, briefly but savagely. "Not been seen! Not been located! And she doesn't have her passport?"

"No, sir," said Bishop. "They're still holding it for her."

"Thank God she's got Henry with her, but where the hell can she go without a passport?" demanded Carstairs. "Damn it, I'm helpless. I can't find out one blessed thing without endangering Ferenci-Sabo as well as Mrs. Pollifax, not to mention the goodwill of the Turkish government."

"There's Dr. Belleaux, sir."

He shook his head. "Not yet. I wanted absolute secrecy on Mrs. Pollifax—and I've got it, blast it, in fact I'm stuck with it. I'd contact Henry before I risked anyone else—but if Mrs. Pollifax is not in the hotel then it's not likely he'd be, either. Bishop, someone's knocking on the door."

"Yes, sir." Bishop opened it and returned bearing an interservice message. "From Barnes, sir, in the State Department. He's heard from the American consulate in Istanbul again."

"Again."

"Yes, sir. He's scrawled a note here saying he doesn't know what's up—or want to—and he's too much of a coward to phone you with this news."

"What news?" asked Carstairs in a hollow voice. "Read it, Bishop."

"Yes, sir. It's a cable: REGRET INFORM YOU BODY OF AMERICAN CITIZEN HENRY MILES—"

"*Body?*" echoed Carstairs in a stricken voice.

"Yes, sir. Shall I go on?"

Carstairs nodded, his face grim.

"—OF HENRY MILES DISCOVERED EARLY THIS MORNING IN USKUDAR CEMETERY STOP."

"Cemetery!"

"ONLY CLUE HANDWRITTEN NOTE APPENDED TO BODY QUOTE THIS IS HENRY MILES HOTEL ITEP STOP POLICE HAVE IDENTIFIED HANDWRIT-

ING AS BELONGING TO—" Bishop suddenly stopped and swallowed hard.

"They've got a lead?" broke in Carstairs savagely. "Get on with it, Bishop, for heaven's sake!"

—"BELONGING TO MRS. EMILY POLLIFAX, AMERICAN CITIZEN OF—"

"What?" exploded Carstairs.

—"OF NEW BRUNSWICK, NEW JERSEY, AND REGISTERED AT SAME HOTEL."

"Oh no," groaned Carstairs.

Bishop nodded. "Yes, sir. Emily is cutting quite a swath, isn't she? There's one more sentence, sir—"

"Then finish it," growled Carstairs.

"WARRANT ISSUED FOR HER ARREST."

"Good God," said Carstairs and slumped back into his chair. "Henry dead—our second agent killed inside of forty-eight hours over there; Mrs. Pollifax missing, and not a single word on Ferenci-Sabo." He sighed and shook his head. "It just about ends our attempt to contact Ferenci-Sabo, Bishop. If Mrs. Pollifax is still alive—and there's no certainty that they didn't get her, too—she's been rendered helpless without a passport. What can she do, where can she go? We'll have to proceed on the assumption that she can be of no more help to us."

"Yes, sir."

Carstairs rubbed his brow. "But we've still got to keep that lobby covered every evening until Friday—just in case. Is Hawkins still in London?"

Bishop nodded.

Carstairs sighed. "Apparently it's like dropping people into a bottomless well to send them to Istanbul, but we must keep trying. Fix up a telephone connection, will you Bishop? I'll give Hawkins the most superficial of briefings and if Ferenci-Sabo is still alive—the chances grow less every hour—he'll have to hide her in a cellar somewhere until we can think what to do next. Damn," he added.

"And Mrs. Pollifax, sir?"

Carstairs nodded. "I was coming to that. Send off a cable to Dr. Belleaux, Bishop. Alert him to the fact that Mrs. Emily Pollifax is one of our people, and may try to reach him, in which case we'd appreciate his giving her what help he can without bringing the roof down upon all our heads."

"Yes, sir."

Again he shook his head. "Not much else we can do for her, Bishop." He added irritably, "Oh, and add a full description of her for Dr. Belleaux so that he'll know precisely what she looks like, Bishop—and don't forget that damned flowered hat!"

Chapter Ten

Carefully Sandor inched the van through streets so narrow the houses could be touched on either side. Frequently their passage was halted by a donkey ambling ahead of them, or by women carrying jugs of water on their heads. There was no coolness in the shade. It was three o'clock in the afternoon and sun and dust lay heavy in the alleys, trapping smells of spices, charcoal, olive oil and manure. Mrs. Pollifax's impression of their entry into Ankara had been chaotic: they appeared to have approached the city by means of a dried-up river bed over which they had clattered and bumped, half-circling Ankara before darting furtively across one tree-lined boulevard to vanish into the old town. As they climbed higher now in this maze of streets Mrs. Pollifax glimpsed the top of the citadel ahead and then lost it. A moment later the van halted; Sandor wrestled furiously with the steering wheel and backed the van slowly, laboriously, through a hole in a crumbling wall. Bricks toppled and a fresh cloud of dust enveloped them.

They emerged in a courtyard, abandoned except for a solitary goat, tied to a ring in the wall, who lifted his head and brayed at them in protest. An old adobe building opened into the courtyard, its roof open to the sky, its walls giving shade to the few sparse tufts of grass on which the animal fed.

Sandor cut the engine. "We walk now but you wait first," he said firmly. "I go find Bengziz Madrali. He is receiver of stolen goods—I make sure he receive *you* now."

"How long will you be gone?" asked Mrs. Pollifax anxiously.

He shrugged. "I have to find him first, then I know how long I'll be gone. If anyone comes, hide in the old *khan*." He was gone before Mrs. Pollifax could protest.

"What's a *khan?*" she asked Colin.

"An inn." Staring at the gate through which Sandor had vanished he said, "I rather like him but I can't think why."

"That's very reassuring since we're completely dependent on him for the moment," Mrs. Pollifax pointed out. "Do you like Magda too?"

His gaze left the gate to sweep the courtyard. "She seems pleasant enough when she's not drugged. But then she nearly always is, isn't she?" He brightened. "I say, that looks like a Hittite frieze propping up that door. Hand me my camera, will you?" He began to prowl through the litter around the door, keeping a respectful distance from the goat, who watched him with suspicion.

"How nice to see you again!" Magda said cheerfully, crawling from the interior of the van to sit down beside Mrs. Pollifax on the top step. "Perhaps you can tell me where we are?"

"We've reached Ankara." She noted that Colin had disappeared with his camera into the ruins of the *khan* and she turned to Magda urgently. "We've not been able to talk and you must realize that from my point of view this journey to Yozgat is on faith alone. What *is* it that we go to Yozgat for?"

Magda hesitated. "I dare not say, not yet at least. But let me tell you this: I go to Yozgat to find the people who smuggled me out of Bulgaria and into Turkey." She was thoughtful for a moment and then she added quietly, "I do not know how you feel about gypsies. People hate and fear them. Perhaps you are not aware that in spite of—or because of—people's revulsion towards gypsies they were able to do a number of valuable things for the Allies during World War Two—those who were not wiped out by Hitler."

"Gypsies!" exclaimed Mrs. Pollifax in surprise.

"Yes. Some are nomadic and wander all over Europe while some have settled down, like the gypsies in Istanbul who live in what is called the Tin Village." She said almost shyly, "It is with them I hid when I first escaped Stefan and Otto and waited for you."

Mrs. Pollifax said in astonishment, "Do you mean it's the gypsies who got you across the border into Turkey?"

She nodded. "To be accepted by them is not easy, the Rom look on *gorgios* with deep contempt. But many years ago we worked together, I gained their trust, I learned their language, I know a few of them as true friends, and to know a few is to be accepted by them all. Yes, it was with them I crossed the border and it is to the Inglescus that I entrusted everything when I realized I was being followed. They promised to wait for me at Yozgat for a few days before they continued south to their rendezvous, a wedding later in the summer."

"But this is remarkable," said Mrs. Pollifax, delighted. "You have your own private underground!"

Magda's smile deepened. "You put it well. But please, you will remember the name Inglescu if anything goes wrong with me? Find them and say Magda sent you. They will understand."

"But can they be trusted with what you left them?"

"Yes," she said flatly.

"I can't help wondering why you suddenly left your old life. You understand that I was told the whole story about you. Did they find this out?"

Magda smiled. "No, they discovered nothing. I decided to retire."

"Retire!" cried Mrs. Pollifax.

"Yes, retire." At the expression on Mrs. Pollifax's face she burst out laughing. "But did you never think of people like me wishing to retire? I will no doubt be a shock to them—agents are not supposed to survive as long as I, they are supposed to die violently and early. But me, I have just gone on surviving—such an embarrassment!—and without even paying dues to the Social Security."

"What will you plan to do?" asked Mrs. Pollifax eagerly.

Magda shrugged. "I bring my own social security with me, as you will see. I have no plans except I wish to live a quiet life now, I want to plant flowers and watch them grow, feel sun on my face, think good thoughts, have real friends. I am tired of violence, of uncertainty and betrayals, of remaining always detached lest someone I grow to like must be betrayed, or betray me. Most, I am tired of acting the double part. This is how it began, I was an actress on the stage in Vienna, but who would guess I play the roles so long, day and night, on and on."

Mrs. Pollifax looked at her and was curiously touched. She thought of the *Times* biography which could not know or possibly describe—no one could—the complications or dangers which this woman must have met and mastered with intelligence and courage, and always alone. But she thought the story was written clearly in the lines of Magda's face: *Those are good lines,* she thought, *lines of humor and compassion and deep sadness. And I heard her laugh—how did she escape corruption from all this?* Her hand went out to touch Magda's hand and squeeze it. "There is one thing," she said quietly. "Something that complicates our getting to Yozgat and to the gypsies."

"Yes?"

"Before I left Washington I was given the name of a man in Istanbul to whom we could appeal for help if we needed it. A very reliable person whose name is Dr. Guillaume Belleaux."

"Yes?" said Magda with interest. "But that is reassuring."

Mrs. Pollifax shook her head. "The house in which you were drugged last night—the house to which Stefan and Otto took you —turned out to be the home of Dr. Guillaume Belleaux."

Magda's lips formed an O and her eyes widened. "*Mon dieu* but that is *not* reassuring! So this man is—but is he aware that you know this? Did he see you?"

"Yes to both questions." Mrs. Pollifax shook her head wryly as she recalled her exit from Dr. Belleaux's house and the face briefly glimpsed across the livingroom. "He may not have seen Colin, no, but he and I looked at each other across the room. Briefly but memorably."

"Then he is the one behind all this—he too plays the double game!" Magda reached out and gently touched Mrs. Pollifax. "It is a lonely business, this, is it not? I'm sorry. My God I'm sorry. But we must stay alive a little longer to annoy him, yes?"

"Yes," said Mrs. Pollifax but she winced a little as she reflected upon the odds: they did not speak Turkish and they were moving deeper and deeper into Turkey's interior; the police, Stefan and of course Dr. Belleaux were looking for them. She did not even know if Sandor would return, and without him they would be almost completely helpless. She thought that he would come back but he was, after all, a man of doubtful character. Still, it was his temperament, not his character, that was in their favor: she was trusting to his curiosity and to his Machiavellian nature to bring him back, if only to arrange what would happen next.

She looked up and waved at Colin who had wandered out of

the inn. He said dreamily, "Just think, these same walls were standing when Tamerlane came through this part of the country." He patted his camera. "I think I got a wonderful shot of that frieze, and the old walls inside; I'm absolutely certain I didn't muff it. No Sandor yet?"

"Here he comes," said Magda.

Mrs. Pollifax looked up to see him loping through the gateway and she had to control her gladness at seeing this disreputable, grinning, filthy man. She thought that even if he shaved and bathed she would recognize him because he would still exude the same boundless joy in living and in outwitting whatever forces resisted him. He had obviously been busy for his arms were full of bundles.

"I am back," he cried. "I have found Bengziz Madrali and he will help—there is much work to do, we go to meet him now but first—good Turkish peasant clothes so you will become incognito."

"Become what?" said Mrs. Pollifax, staring with distaste at what appeared to be a week's laundry that he held out to her.

Obviously he was conferring a great honor upon her. "For you ladies the baggy pants," he said. "Also the skirt, the shirt and the shawl that begins over your heads and goes everywhere—I show you its workings." He stuffed them into her arms without sympathy. "And for you," he cried happily to Colin, "the moustachio—a good sweep of one—and a cap and trousers with holes in them. You will look like me, eh? Could anything be better?"

"Oh nothing," Colin said dryly.

"Then wotthehell, change now in the truck and we go. Is better Madrali never see you in your own clothes, he has a feel for intrigue, that man, and the roadblocks are up."

Mrs. Pollifax had been halfway across the courtyard with her new clothes in her arms when he said this. She stopped. "Roadblocks?"

He nodded pleasantly. "Twenty minutes ago. *Pfut*—suddenly they are there. Police stopping everyone. Madrali hears everything, you understand? He says officially it is the new government study of traffic flow but he hears they look for specific peoples." Sandor beamed at them. "You do not wish to be specific peoples, do you? Incognito please—at once!"

* * *

Mrs. Pollifax thought the room looked exactly like a thieves'
den, and she discovered with some surprise that she felt delight-
fully at ease in such an atmosphere. Shadows leaped up the walls
and across the ceiling from candles burning in their sockets and
from the charcoal brazier on which their dinner of *tel kadayif* and
pilaf had been cooked. On one whitewashed wall hung a picture of
Ataturk in an unusually convivial, smiling pose. On the other side
of the brazier, seated cross-legged on the floor with a tray on his
lap, Bengziz Madrali squinted over the three cards of identity he
was forging for them. Occasionally he grunted expressively as he
examined his work through a jeweler's glass, and occasionally he
flashed Mrs. Pollifax a smile laden with warm reassurance and admiration.

"Your name is now Yurgadil Aziz," commented Sandor, eating noisily with his fingers from a platter and looking over
Madrali's shoulder. "The other lady is Nimet Aziz, and he"—
pointing a dripping finger at Colin—"is Nazmi Aziz."

Lost: one Emily Pollifax, she thought, and glanced ruefully at
the black baggy pants engulfing her legs.

From the corner Magda gave an amused laugh. Her hair had
been dyed brown from a bottle that Madrali had purchased in the
bazaar; and then it had been washed and set in fat steel curlers that
bristled gruesomely all over her head. She sat and smoked a Turkish cigarette with elegant fastidiousness, her hands moving gracefully but without any sign of being attached to her body, which had
become lost somewhere inside her voluminous Turkish disguise.
Near her sat Colin, loading his still camera with film for the passport photograph he was going to take of Magda when the curlers
were removed and her hair combed. Catching Mrs. Pollifax's
glance he said irritably, "Soon? You know I've got to develop the
picture and then it's got to dry!"

In appearance she thought he outdid them all. He wore
shabby pinstripe trousers tied with a belt of rope, a vest too tight
across his chest, a purple shirt and a pink bowtie. His sweeping
moustache left him almost mouthless and because he wasn't accustomed to it he kept trying to look down at it, which caused his eyes
to cross. He also complained that it itched. Yet in spite of all this he
had acquired a definite air of distinction. In some indescribable
manner his new identity brought out the fierceness in him that

Mrs. Pollifax had noticed when she first met him but which she had assumed was a defense against failure, and against taller and more successful men. But freed of any possible competitiveness, and wearing the most absurdly shabby clothes, Colin *was* fierce. There was no mistaking it: there was a look about him of a mountain brigand.

There is more of his family in him than he knows, thought Mrs. Pollifax with amusement. She stood up and walked over to Magda and felt her head. It was dry. Removing the curlers she said, "Mr. Madrali, you have the suntan make-up? You have the white backdrop for the passport picture?"

"*Evet, evet,*" he said, nodding. "Over there, pliss."

Colin shook his head. "I still can't imagine how you expect to get her out of the country when we can't even get out of Ankara."

"I go look into that now and make more questions," Sandor said, reluctantly putting aside his plate of food. "The new idea they come and go. Now I go."

"Good. The white blouse, please," said Mrs. Pollifax, helping Magda out of her Turkish clothes and into her own navy blue suit.

Sandor stopped and looked down at Magda. "Wotthehell she can't leave a country without a passport."

"She has a passport." Mrs. Pollifax said calmly as she began applying tan make-up to Magda's white face.

"Wotthehell, you forge those too?"

"It's a very respectable passport," she told him, "and very legal. There," she said, applying lipstick to Magda. "I think she looks rather like a poetess or an undernourished actress, don't you, Colin?"

Sandor went out, looking mystified. Colin said, "You're quite right, I wouldn't have believed it possible."

Flashbulbs illuminated the room several times before its native dimness returned, and then Magda lay down and promptly went to sleep. Colin at once became tiresomely cross and nervous about developing the film, and since Mr. Madrali's English was severely limited and he was still engrossed in his forgeries, Mrs. Pollifax opened the door and walked out.

The tiny house in which Mr. Madrali lived—or hid, as the case might be—leaned against the walls of the Citadel, even belonged to the wall of the Citadel, like something washed up against

the sides of an old ship. Mounting the tamped down earthen path
behind his house Mrs. Pollifax put back her head and looked up at
the wall that had withstood a thousand years of earthquakes, pillage
and armies, and then she looked down at the crooked, meandering
alleys below, with their rows of primitive hovels dropping to the
base of the hill. The sun was just disappearing behind the distant
mountains leaving a blaze of glorious color in the sky but on the
plains surrounding Ankara twilight had already fallen, and lights
were beginning to glitter along Ankara's streets and avenues.

As she stood transfixed the last notes of a muezzin's chant
reached her ears from below, sounding phantom in the high clear
air, and Mrs. Pollifax thought, *I must remember this moment*, and
then, *I shall have to come back and really see this country*. Yet she knew
that if she did come back it would be entirely different. It was the
unexpected that brought to these moments this tender, unname-
able rush of understanding, this joy in being alive. It was safety
following danger, it was food after hours of hunger, rest following
exhaustion, it was the astonishing strangers who had become her
friends. It was this and more, until the richness of living caught at
her throat, and all the well-meant security with which people surrounded themselves was exposed for what it truly was: a wall to
keep out life, a conceit, a mad delusion.

She was still standing there when Sandor walked up the steep
path. It had become quite dark; she realized with a start that she
had been standing there for a long time. "Is that you?" he said,
peering at her. Little squares and stripes of light lay behind him on
the path, formed by the shuttered and open windows of the surrounding houses.

"Yes," she said. "Where have you been?"

He said buoyantly, "I have biggest good luck! The twice-a-
week bus for Yozgat leaves at dawn. It will be hot, cheap, very
crowded. I went to Taksim Square to be sure—already the families
sleep there waiting."

"Bus?" said Mrs. Pollifax wonderingly. "But won't the police
be stopping the busses too?"

"When you see the busses you understand," he said cryptically. "Only Turks take them—tourists never!—and they buy tickets distantly ahead. But wotthehell, for big price I get four tickets
to Yozgat."

He said modestly, "For a little extra I come too. You need me for the translations."

She turned and looked at him gratefully. "Oh yes, we do need you, Sandor, but I scarcely dared hope—Aren't you wanted by the police too, Sandor? Who are you really?"

"A scoundrel," he said with a grin. "Who are *you*, really?"

She laughed. "Obviously I ask too many questions."

"That you do, yes." He shrugged. "Be comfortable, don't itch. It is like a story of Nasr-ed-Din Hodja who went through the East many hundreds of years ago. His stories live everywhere. One of them is that Nasr-ed-Din was walking a road one dark night when he saw three men coming toward him. 'Oho,' he thinks, 'they may be robbers' so he jumps over a wall and hides behind a rock. The three men see this and are curious and they too jump over the rock and go to him. 'What is wrong?' they ask. 'What are you doing here?' And Nasr-de-Din sees the truth of it—that they are not robbers—and he says, 'Oh gentlemen, I will tell you why we are all here. I am here because of *you*, and you are here because of *me*.' "

Mrs. Pollifax smiled. "A most philosophical parable. Are there more of them?"

"*Evet.* Another story is that Nasr-de-Din said he could see in the dark. Someone said to him, 'That may be so, Nasr-ed-Din but if this is true why then do you always carry a candle at night?' Nasr-ed-Din said, 'Why, to prevent other people from bumping into me!' "

Mrs. Pollifax laughed delightedly.

Sandor took her arm. "More I tell you another time. Please, go inside now before we are heard speaking English. Tomorrow at dawn we go to Yozgat."

Chapter Eleven

Having been officially hired as their guide, Sandor took them over with stern authority. He allowed them to sleep until three o'clock in the morning and then he prodded them awake. "For you to be real peasants you get up now. You will do rest of the sleeping in Taksim Square, please. Like others."

The three of them arose stiffly from their floormats. They would have to wash on their way down the hill, at the public well, Sandor told them; Madrali was bringing them tea and fruit for their breakfast. They would also be carrying their lunch on the bus with them—it was already packed in a basket: two jugs of water and the remains of their evening meal. He produced a small cardboard suitcase that looked as if it had been possessed by a dozen other people first. Into this Mrs. Pollifax packed her suit for Magda to wear, and Colin added a number of spare reels of film. His cameras he insisted upon carrying in a string bag. Mrs. Pollifax again checked her pantaloons for the wads of money and Magda's passport, all secured with large safety pins. Her flowered hat was presented to Mr. Madrali with instructions to dispose of it, as well as her useless, emptied purse.

They started out in the pale light of dawn, and at the base of the hill wrung Mr. Madrali's hands, thanked him and were once again on their own, a little more secure in their new identities but a little less secure at being on the street.

"I think I could get to like these baggy pants," said Mrs. Pollifax, lengthening her stride. "Is my headgear properly wrapped? Are you sure we're all right, with everything where it should be?"

"Good, very good," Sandor said gravely. "Except slower— please! You act like American. Dressed as you are dressed you come from a small village—do not walk so fast, so happy, and please—

stay behind us men!" He shrugged apologetically. "Not for myself, you understand, who know precisely who you are but for the role, the act. Anatolian women, they work hard, say nothing. And to wear the shawl pulled so across the mouth you must be very shy, very small village. You understand?"

"All right."

Sandor added, "You do not look so Turkish as the other lady, you see."

"Oh—sorry," she said contritely, falling still another pace behind him and Colin.

"And stop talking English," contributed Colin, delivering the final snub.

Magda's eyes were gleaming over her veil with amusement. "It worked," she said.

"What did?"

"You look properly cowed and snubbed now. Your shoulders droop, you look shamed and subservient."

Mrs. Pollifax said in a peevish undertone— she really had been feeling expansive—"It's all very well for you—he said you look the part."

"*Touché*," said Magda with a throaty little laugh that reminded Mrs. Pollifax she would be delightful company under more relaxed circumstances. They turned down a broad, tree-rimmed boulevard lined with buildings so modern that Mrs. Pollifax might have forgotten she was in the Near East but for the sight of goats being herded down a side street, and a flock of turkeys being driven screeching, wings flapping, across an intersection.

When they reached the square they learned what Sandor had meant about bus transportation to Yozgat. A bulging and ancient wooden vehicle stood beside the curb—"It's early," explained Sandor—and around it squatted dozens of families who looked as if they had been waiting all night long. Sandor reminded them they must not speak to anyone, not even to one another, but smile and keep smiling agreeably. They silently sat beside the others. After about an hour the driver of the bus came whistling across the boulevard, unlocked the bus and began shouting orders to the passengers to bring their suitcases to him for storage on top of the bus. A policeman wandered over and watched, then alarmed Mrs.

Pollifax by asking to see the cards of identity and the bus tickets of everyone waiting to leave.

"Do not panic," whispered Sandor. "Steady does it."

When the policeman reached Mrs. Pollifax she concentrated on looking as small and submissive as possible. "Yurgadil Aziz," he said musingly, as he examined her identity card. "Bilet?" he added, holding out his hand.

Sandor arose, spoke easily in Turkish and produced four bus tickets from his pocket. Mrs. Pollifax gathered that she had been asked for her ticket, and because the tickets had all been sold days earlier the possession of one precluded any of them being newly arrived Americans wanted by the police. The tickets were handed back, the policeman moved on, the bus driver shouted, passengers shouted, and like lemmings rushing to the sea they swarmed onto the bus. A child vomited. A pig squealed. Those without seats sat on the floor. Men and women laughed and congratulated themselves upon being there, and the trip to Yozgat was begun.

Seven hours and one hundred and thirty-eight miles later the bus jolted into Yozgat following innumerable stops to cool and refill an aging radiator, exercise children, revive fainting women and change a tire. After seven hours in such cramped quarters any disguises had become academic: everyone aboard knew that three of the passengers did not speak Turkish but no one appeared to even question the fact or to care. They were foreigners and therefore guests. Whether they were Yugoslavs or Rumanians or Bulgars —apparently no one even conceived of their being Americans— they were treated charmingly: smiled at, handed grapes, peaches and sweets and offered seats on the aisle several inches farther from the dust that billowed in through the open windows. Nevertheless the seven hours seemed endless and Mrs. Pollifax could feel only compassion for the majority of the passengers who were bound for Sivas. "When will they get there?" she asked Sandor.

He shrugged. "Six o'clock, eight o'clock, midnight, who knows? Only Allah. But do not worry, they are having the time of their lives."

"Magda isn't. She's looking horrible again."

"I will help her. Then I make discreet questions about the gypsies you seek," said Sandor. "There are always men in the square, and in a town like this everyone knows everybody else's business. I have thought further. In Yozgat there will not be many cars, and few gasolines. It will be less prominent to rent a horse and wagon. Whatthehell, okay?"

"What the hell okay," said Mrs. Pollifax with a smile, and as the bus halted in Yozgat square, honking its horn dramatically, she stood up and looked for Colin, who had become trapped in the aisle in back of her and could only wave and shrug.

Magda was helped from her seat by Sandor, and the three of them made their way to the front of the bus. Sandor jumped down first, followed by Magda, who almost fell into his arms, and Mrs. Pollifax stepped down behind them, lifted her head to look around her at Yozgat, and abruptly stiffened.

A man had separated himself from the cluster of people on the pavement, and had stepped forward to scrutinize each passenger as they dismounted. Now he was staring attentively into Mrs. Pollifax's half-concealed face; his glance moved to include Sandor and then fell upon Magda who swayed on Sandor's arm.

The man was easy to recognize because of his small pointed white goatee. She had in fact already exchanged glances with him once, across a crowded Istanbul livingroom. It was Dr. Guillaume Belleaux.

Now he stepped forward and spoke to Mrs. Pollifax in Turkish, his eyes a little amused as they rested on the wisps of hair that escaped her shawl. Before she had even faced the problem of replying his hand moved and he whipped back her scarves to expose her face. "Mrs. Pollifax, is it not?" he said cheerfully. "Precisely the woman Mr. Carstairs asked me to take care of—which I plan to do at once!"

Mrs. Pollifax stepped back in dismay.

"And your two companions would be Madame Ferenci-Sabo and Mr. Colin Ramsey of Ramsey Enterprises." He lifted an arm and waved to someone across the street. "I am aware that you know karate," he continued smoothly. "One move toward me and the gun that I hold under this newspaper will kill you."

"Wotthehell," said Sandor, but whether he was shocked at being mistaken for Colin, or by news of the gun, it was impossible to guess.

Mrs. Pollifax sighed. To get safely away from the searching Ankara police they had endured those seven uncomfortable hours on a bus only to walk into Dr. Belleaux's waiting arms. It did seem unfair, and exactly the sort of thing to blunt initiative.

"The car is coming—patience, please," said Dr. Belleaux. "We have only a few streets to go, and I advise you to enter the car quietly." He turned and looked at Colin, who stood paralyzed on the bottom step of the bus, gaping at him. He said sharply, *"Hareket etmek—cabucak!"*

Colin closed his mouth—he had looked singularly stupid with it open—and to Mrs. Pollifax's astonishment he snarled, *"Evet, evet,"* in a low surly voice and walked stiffly and angrily away.

For a moment Mrs. Pollifax was incredulous and then it dawned upon her that Dr. Belleaux had not recognized Colin; he had looked for two women and a man and he had found them without realizing that four of them traveled together now, or that Colin was also a member of the party. Colin, bless him, had understood this perfectly, and at once.

She and Sandor exchanged a long glance, and then the car drew up behind the bus and Dr. Belleaux said sharply, "Get in, please!" He held the door open. "No, Mr. Ramsey, sit in front, please, where I can shoot you if you prove difficult."

To enlighten confused Sandor Mrs. Pollifax said coldly, "Allow me to introduce you. I believe this is Dr. Guillaume Belleaux— you are, aren't you?—the leader of the gang who tried to kill us on the road to Ankara." The impact of this on Sandor was appreciable: she saw his eyes blaze before they went studiously blank. "The gentleman beside you," she added tartly, "is Stefan, who works with Dr. Belleaux and abducts people and drugs them, too."

Ignoring her Dr. Belleaux leaned forward. "Leave now, Stefan, the bus will remain here for sometime, I think. You know the way? That street over there, then left and a sharp right."

The car turned off the square, past a corner store whose signs read Cikolata—Sigara—Koka-Kola (*I can read that*, thought Mrs. Pollifax numbly) and down a cobbled street that soon turned into a solidly packed dirt road of the most primitive type. "Where are we going?" inquired Mrs. Pollifax.

"Not far," confided Dr. Belleaux; his voice was friendly and gracious; he was obviously a born host. "It seemed wisest to rent one of Yozgat's abandoned houses, while we waited for you. We have expected you, of course, and I guessed you would have to arrive in some kind of disguise, or not at all, with the police looking for you so assiduously. But of course the police have never known that you were coming to Yozgat. It gave Stefan and myself *such* a pleasant advantage!" He leaned forward. "To the right now, Stefan. When you reach the house drive the car around to the rear. I don't wish it seen from the road." To Mrs. Pollifax he said in a kindly voice, "I have a gun, you know. Several, to be exact. It is best if you understand now that there is nothing for you to do but relax and tell me all I wish to know. Then we shall understand one another—once you understand your situation."

They had pulled up beside a low, dusty stone house with a shuttered and empty look. The nearest house stood a quarter of a mile away. Stefan backed, and then drove up a rutted track to the back yard and cut the engine.

Dr. Belleaux said, "Assim is inside—blow the horn once, lightly. We will tie their hands tightly for the walk into the house."

When the door shut behind them it closed out all sunshine. Not even the shutters betrayed lines or threads of light. They stood in darkness until Dr. Belleaux lighted a candle, and then a lantern. "In here," he said and they were pushed into one of the two back rooms.

This was a room like a shed; obviously animals had once shared it with humans during cold winter nights. The floor was of beaten earth; a pile of old hay still filled one corner and there was a strong smell of must and manure. Once there had been a rear door but it had been bricked in but not whitewashed. Three straight wooden chairs occupied the center of the room; one by one they were tied to them, first their hands behind their backs and then their ankles. When this had been accomplished by Assim, whose face was sullen and cruel, Dr. Belleaux beckoned his helpmeets into the other room and Mrs. Pollifax could hear them speaking together in Turkish in low voices. She said softly, "Magda—you are all right?"

Magda lifted her head and wanly smiled. "For the moment, yes. But to come finally to Yozgat, to be so close—" She stopped.

Sandor said in a voice choked with rage. "You understand even I have heard of this Dr. Belleaux. I am still shocked, still in a daze. There must be the way to get free. Must!"

Mrs. Pollifax sighed. "Such as what?"

"There's Colin."

Mrs. Pollifax said gently, "What can he do? He doesn't even know where we are."

"Surely something!"

"What?"

Sandor was silent and then he said angrily, "I don't know!"

"He doesn't know where we've been taken," repeated Mrs. Pollifax, "and if he did, what could be done? He is alone, completely inexperienced and unaccustomed to violence."

"Since meeting you he has seen a little," pointed out Sandor dryly, and as the voices broke off in the other room he said, "We cannot just die like trussed pigs, there has to come a moment, just one—" He was silent as Dr. Belleaux re-entered the room.

"Ah there you are!" said Dr. Belleaux, as if he had absentmindedly misplaced them. "We have just been consulting on the arrangements. I have an interest in a small archaeological dig not far from here—you will be buried there tonight." He chuckled. "In a few years you may be dug up and acclaimed a real archaeological find!"

"Very amusing," said Mrs. Pollifax tartly. "And Mr. Carstairs? What will you tell him?"

Dr. Belleaux smiled charmingly. "Why, that I searched everywhere but that you and your little party had vanished from the face of the earth!"

"He really cabled you about me?" Mrs. Pollifax asked curiously.

Dr. Belleaux leaned against the wall and looked down at her in a friendly fashion. "Oh indeed yes, just last evening, and giving a very full description of you—which of course proved at once how dangerous you are to me! He had cabled me earlier about Henry Miles, naturally, but failed to mention you. It was fairly simple to dispose of Miles as well as the first chap whom I believed Miles was replacing, but I really had no idea who you worked for. When you stole Ferenci-Sabo from under my very nose—in full view of my friends—I still had no idea you worked for Carstairs, can you imagine?"

"How stupid you must feel," she agreed pleasantly. "For how many years have you been a double agent?"

"It scarcely matters," he said modestly. "Actually I've been what is usually referred to as a 'sleeper.' That is, held in abeyance for something truly worthwhile. Although I won't say I've not taken advantage of my privileged situation to cast a few stones," he confided charmingly. "An innuendo here, a lifted eyebrow there—" He obligingly lifted an eyebrow. "But Ferenci-Sabo's defection was big enough to bring orders for me to capture her at any cost, including my usefulness as a friend of the Americans and the Turks." He smiled. "However—happily for me—the cost looks very small indeed. By tomorrow I can look forward to resuming my *very* pleasant life in Istanbul again. For now, however," he concluded, his voice changing, "I must get to work."

"*Hain,*" growled Sandor.

"What does that mean?" asked Mrs. Pollifax.

"It means traitor," said Dr. Belleaux indifferently. He walked over to Magda and stared down at her. "Now what I should like to learn first," he said firmly, as if he were interviewing her for a job, "is just why the Americans have been brought into this, and how they were contacted. I find that—shall I say very suspicious?" He continued looking at Magda. "Lift your head!" he demanded sharply.

Slowly Magda lifted her head. "I want you to talk," he said in a suddenly cold and chilling voice. "You will tell me why and how you contacted Mr. Carstairs. You will tell me where are the papers you brought with you, and why you insisted on coming to Yozgat."

"No," said Magda.

Dr. Belleaux began to hit Magda across the cheekbones, methodically and viciously, and Mrs. Pollifax closed her eyes so that no one would see the tears she wept for Magda. Back and forth went the hand—one, two, one, two—but in his savagery Dr. Belleaux had miscalculated Magda's stamina. Her head suddenly went limp—she had mercifully fainted.

"Bastard," shouted Sandor.

Dr. Belleaux turned toward Mrs. Pollifax, and as she realized that her turn was next she closed her eyes again. A sudden picture

of her sunny apartment in New Brunswick, New Jersey, flashed
across her mind and she thought, *Is anything worth all this?* and then
she opened her eyes and met Dr. Belleaux's gaze steadily. He stood
over her, eyes narrowed, fist lifted, and she prayed for courage.

Chapter Twelve

Stepping down from the bus Colin was appalled at the sight of Dr. Belleaux in conversation with Mrs. Pollifax. It jarred all his senses; he had not glimpsed Dr. Belleaux at his house in Istanbul but he recognized him from newspaper pictures, and it was a shock to see him in the flesh, and here of all places. His second reaction was one of wild relief: everything had to be all right after all, Mrs. Pollifax had been wrong about Dr. Belleaux, and Dr. Belleaux had come to tell her so; and then he realized that this couldn't be so, the man had no business meeting them here in Yozgat, and as his eyes dropped to the newspaper that Dr. Belleaux held in such a peculiar position he instinctively realized there was a gun hidden there. It was all very disappointing and unnerving, and for a moment he thought he was going to be ill. He stood frozen to the bottom step of the bus while behind him voices rose in protest at his blocking the exit.

The protests inevitably drew Dr. Belleaux's attention; he turned, saw Colin staring and spoke sharply to him in Turkish, telling him to get moving, to go away. Colin was astonished to remember that he was in disguise, and was even more astonished to realize that he had not been recognized. He stammered, "*Evet—evet,*" and walked away from the bus and then across the street.

There he stopped, suddenly aware that he had nowhere to go. He realized that Mrs. Pollifax and Magda and Sandor had just been captured, and he felt an acute sense of loss. It seemed incredibly unjust after all they'd gone through. He thought dimly of shouting for the police and then he remembered that in joining Mrs. Pollifax he had placed himself beyond such conventional avenues of complaint. This was a chilling thought. There was no one at all to help—no one except himself, of course, and there was nothing he could do. Nothing at all. He saw Dr. Belleaux lift his arm and wave to a man seated in a parked car, saw the driver nod, turn the car and drive up behind the bus. Over the top of the car he saw the heads of his three friends as they climbed inside, and he heard the doors slam. Then the car pulled out and turned down the street next him. It passed quite near but the shades had been drawn in the rear and he saw only the driver. It was Stefan.

At that moment Colin understood that he was about to see his three friends vanish from sight—he would never know where they went, or see them again. He suddenly found this even less tolerable than his panic.

Furiously he glared at the people around him: wraith-like, ancient men slumped half-drowsing on benches in the shade; a woman dispiritedly sweeping with a twig broom; a boy pulling a loaded donkey across the road, the bus driver loading the bus with what looked like a sack of mail. At the corner he saw a narrow, fly-specked cafe open to the square—one sign said CIKOLATA—SIGARA; another advertised KOKA-KOLA. His glance fell to three old and dusty bicycles leaning against the wall, their owners apparently inside the shop. The car had just turned into the street beside that shop; a cloud of dust rose as it vanished.

Without thinking, and purely from instinct, Colin ran across the street, snatched up one of the fallen bicycles, mounted it and pedaled madly down the street into which the black car had turned. There were shouts behind him but he ignored them and pedaled faster. He couldn't see the car but he knew it was there because its dust filled his nostrils and chocked his throat. He had no idea where he was going, or even why, he knew only that he mustn't be separated from the group in the car.

He became increasingly aware that he was being pursued, and the shouts following him annoyed him. He pedaled past low rock walls, a dusty vineyard, little houses with peeling stucco until the cobbles came to an end and he faced two unpaved roads. As he hesitated his most immediate pursuer pedaled up beside him: it was, of all things, a girl, who proceeded to upbraid him in a flurry of noisy Turkish.

Despairingly, in English, he cried, "I can't understand you, I don't understand a word!"

The torrent went on and then suddenly, her lips open, the

girl stopped in mid-sentence, her eyes enormous. "But you speak English! You're not Turkish!"

"Yes, I'm English, and I've lost my friends, they're in that black car that drove down this street, and I'm terribly sorry to have—" He too stopped in mid-sentence. "But I say—you speak English too!"

She said impatiently, "I go to college in Istanbul. But what are you doing in such clothes? Are you a sociologist studying our customs? You are dressed like a peasant!"

"I must find that car!" he said urgently.

"The car went to the left, do you not see the dust?" she said calmly.

He pedaled a few feet and turned. "Look, I'll return your bicycle, I promise you. Or come along if you doubt me, but I have to follow that car!"

"I will go with you," she said firmly.

They pedaled together up the road to the left. Houses were set close together in a long row like small boxes; a rivulet of dirty water ran down one side of the road in a hollowed-out-trough. The street turned at an angle, displaying another length of soiled houses and dirt road and Colin had to swerve to avoid a goat. A donkey brayed from under a dusty tree. Here and there sat worn men; there were no women to be seen. The houses thinned, and he saw no car but at the last house on the road—isolated and at some distance away—there still lingered a faint cloud of dust.

"They are in that last house," the girl said. "Why are they staying there? It has been unoccupied for years. Are you sure they're in there? I will wait while you go to the door."

Colin climbed down from his bike. "It's not that simple," he said, turning to look at her and discovered that it was a mistake to look at her a second time. His first impression had been of a slightly plump and rounded young woman with a bland and candy-box sort of prettiness. Between first and second glance all clichés had vanished: she was exquisitely lovely. Her face *did* belong on a candy box: one of those fragile old Victorian boxes that dripped paper lace. Her skin was flawless, her lips full, sensual and pink, her eyes huge, round, heavily lashed and a curious shade of vivid blue that by contrast brought to life the very ordinary shade of brown hair. He frankly stared. "What's your name?" he asked.

"Sabahat Pasha. What is yours?"

"Nazim Aziz," he said absently.

She laughed. "What? But you are not Turkish!"

He flushed. "Actually it's Colin Ramsey but—oh hang it all, do go now," he said, parking his bicycle against a crumbling wall. "I'm going to walk the rest of the way."

"Go?" she said, and laughed. "How can I ride two bicycles back to town? And why do you not ride up to the door and make sure your friends are there?"

"Damn," he said, and looked at her helplessly, at her wide naïve eyes, and warm sympathetic mouth. How could he possibly explain the situation to her? It was impossible.

"Something is wrong," she said, watching him. "You are in some kind of trouble." The laughter had gone from her eyes, leaving them grave.

"Yes," he admitted. "But it's not a police matter," he added hastily. "They're all Americans, and calling the police would—well, prove very embarrassing."

"Americans!" she exclaimed. "Americans here in Yozgat? Oh but I would love to meet them! What brought them here to Yozgat? Are they also studying the customs?"

"We came to—" He stopped. With extraordinary clarity he suddenly remembered why they had come to Yozgat, and it occurred to him that help might be available after all. He said excitedly, "Sabahat, tell me. Are there gypsies camping in or near Yozgat?"

She looked startled and then thoughtful. "There were a number of them camped just outside of town for a few days. I know because they read the palms of many of my friends. But I hear they left yesterday, going south, and now there is only the man with the dancing bear."

"And is he a gypsy too?"

The girl laughed. "But of course—only the gypsies have dancing bears!" She looked at him, puzzled. "But he is very dirty, very soiled," she pointed out.

"Do you know where he stays?"

She nodded. "Beyond the mosque, on the road leaving town. I have seen his wagon. Also his dog." She shivered distastefully.

He said recklessly, "Please—if I ride the bicycle back to town with you, could you direct me to the road leading to the gypsy with the dancing bear?"

"You wish to *see* him?" she said in astonishment.

"I must."

She recoiled, obviously disturbed, and then she looked into his face and suddenly laughed. "Your moustache has slipped! It is crooked!"

He grinned. "I'm not surprised, the blasted thing itches, too." He felt for it with two fingers and began to peel it off, the girl watching gravely, as if the most important thing in the world at the moment was to learn how moustaches were removed.

But he had underestimated her intelligence, which had continued to assess and appraise him as they talked. She nodded suddenly, as if she had made up her mind. "Come—I will take you myself to the gypsy," she said. "You would not be able to speak to him if you found him, would you? I'm sure my friend won't mind if I borrow the bicycle a little while longer."

"I say—that's awfully kind of you," he said gratefully, and then heard himself ask, "Your friend—is it a girl or a boy?"

She glanced over her shoulder at him with amusement. "It is my girlfriend."

Colin turned his bike around and followed her back down the road into town. When they reached the square the bus had finally departed and in its place stood a small dingy cardboard suitcase and a string bag. "Good grief—my cameras! And Magda's suitcase!" he gasped. He had forgotten all about them. He stowed them away on the back of the bicycle, and with Sabahat in the lead they set out to look for the gypsy.

The gypsy's cart stood at some distance from the road, half-hidden within a grove of scrub and stunted trees. His campfire burned in a circle of stones, guarded by an ugly, ferocious-looking dog. "He must be at home because the bear is tied up to the wagon," Sabahat said, and added nervously, "But the dog is not tied."

"I'll go first," Colin told her. "Stay well behind, until I can get him to tie the dog. If he's there."

They didn't need to shout; they had no sooner left the road than the dog sprang up, growling, snarling, barking, baring his teeth in a terrifying manner, and when this did not send Colin into retreat the dog flew toward him as if to devour him. Colin stood still, his heart hammering. The gypsy appeared suddenly from the woods and stood watching, saying nothing, his gaze hostile, arms folded.

"I must talk to you," Colin shouted. "Call off your dog, will you?"

Behind him Sabahat bravely translated, her voice quivering only a little.

The gypsy spoke to the dog and the dog slunk away, head down, eyes still on Colin. Colin and Sabahat wheeled their bicycles nearer.

"Be careful," Sabahat said in a low voice, "I am sure he would like to steal the bicycles—see how he looks at them! Gypsies will steal anything."

"You'll translate?"

She nodded, eyes huge.

"Tell him I came to Yozgat to find the gypsies who were here yesterday. Ask if he knows them."

Sabahat translated and the man shrugged and replied. "He says if you give him money he will tell you anything you wish to hear."

Colin said sharply, "I don't want him to tell me anything I wish to hear, I want truth. I'm looking for a family of gypsies who were supposed to be here in Yozgat."

Sabahat and the gypsy exchanged words. "He says he wonders what you want of a gypsy family."

"I have a message from a friend of theirs."

"A friend of the *gypsies?*" faltered Sabahat.

"Yes. Tell him I came to Yozgat with that friend; she crossed the border into Turkey with them. Now she's in trouble and needs help."

The man's glance was sharp and inscrutable but when he had listened to Sabahat his face grew less closed. With much casualness he asked what the name of that lady might be who was a *gorgio* yet a friend of the Rom.

"Magda," said Colin, not daring to speak her well-publicized last name.

The man shrugged. He said he knew of no such person, nor anything of the gypsies who had been in this place.

"What you say is true?" whispered Sabahat.

Colin nodded. What could he produce to prove that he was speaking of Ferenci-Sabo, or had really known her? He suddenly remembered the passport photographs he had taken of Magda, and kneeling down beside the suitcase he burrowed through it. "Ah," he said triumphantly as he found two discarded pictures of Magda, and he carried one of them to the gypsy. "Magda," he said.

A flash of recognition lighted the man's eyes but as quickly as it arrived it was replaced by suspicion. Colin groaned. "Blast it, now he thinks I'm the police no doubt. Sabahat, I want you to tell him something very carefully, translating it for him sentence by sentence."

She nodded.

"Tell him Magda is in Yozgat. Tell him Magda was captured an hour ago. Abducted. Kidnapped."

Sabahat looked at him in astonishment. "Abducted?" she gasped.

"Please—tell him," Colin begged. "Tell him if he does not believe me then he can go and see for himself. You know the name of the street?" he asked Sabahat. "Tell him that, too. Tell him she is in an abandoned house, two men took her there."

The man's eyes had narrowed, and he looked at Colin so quickly that Colin wondered if the man did not know a little English after all. The man began to speak.

Sabahat said breathlessly, "He says the gypsies you look for left here late yesterday and began moving south on the road to Kayseri. And—" She gasped. "And he says he would like to see the house in Yozgat of which you speak."

Colin drew a sigh of relief. "Thank God—then he does know what I'm talking about!"

The gypsy began speaking again. "He asks you," said Sabahat, "to sit down with him on the steps of his caravan and tell him more clearly what has happened. He also wishes me to tell you that unfortunately he has no guns."

Colin said gravely, "Tell him I am a believer in nonviolence, anyway."

"Are you really?" cried Sabahat breathlessly. "Oh but so am I!

So are all my friends here and at college," she said with shining eyes. "Tell me, have you experienced any—what are they called—love-ins?"

Colin shook his head regretfully. "I'm sorry, no."

"You have spoken of such violent things—abductions, kidnappings—it is very difficult to imagine this. Who could do such a thing? Is it one of my own people who has done this to your friend?"

"Actually a Frenchman, I think," Colin said.

"So *many* foreigners in Yozgat?" she exclaimed. "Oh how my friends would love to know of this, you cannot imagine our hunger to speak to people from other lands. The summers in Yozgat are so very long, so very hot and tedious."

Colin abruptly halted on his way to the caravan. "How many friends have you in Yozgat?" he asked thoughtfully.

"Why, there are about twelve of us home from college." Her eyes suddenly slanted mischievously. "You are thinking of the same thing? You must be! I know you are!"

Colin looked at her and she looked at him, communication leaping between them. He thought he had never met anyone so perceptive unless it was his sister Mia.

The gypsy grunted—he had been waiting patiently for them. He spoke in a rush of Turkish to Sabahat, who leaned forward courteously to listen. When he had finished she nodded and smiled at Colin. "It's all right—he says he will trust you. He says he remained here, behind the others, to wait for the woman Magda and to guide her to the other gypsies. He says if you are the police then he will kill you with his knife. Otherwise he will help us."

"Us?" Colin said in surprise.

She smiled at him gravely. "If I abandon you now, how shall I ever learn if you succeed?"

Colin grinned. "Somewhere I've heard that before," he said dryly. "All right, let's make plans. This won't be easy but tell him I'm awfully glad to have him on my side."

"Me, too?" she asked boldly, her cheeks turning pink.

"You too," he said, smiling.

From where Colin and the gypsy crouched, the town seemed far away. They had crossed fields and then empty land to reach the

shed behind the house in which Magda, Mrs. Pollifax and Sandor
had been hidden. They had been taken here at twenty past one
o'clock; it was now half-past three in the afternoon. Ahead of them
nothing stirred, and they slipped around to the front of the shed
and inside. The darkness of its interior was welcome. They had
come to reconnoiter, to make certain that the three were still in the
house.

The gypsy pointed to the car and Colin nodded. They crept
from the shed across the barren yard to its shadows, where the
gypsy unsheathed his long knife and slashed each tire. When he
sheathed his knife again they moved to the wall of the house and
sat down under one of the two shuttered windows, pressing their
ears against the wall.

A moment later Colin was hearing Sandor's voice repeat over
and over, "*Ikiyuzlu . . . Ikiyuzlu . . .*" It was a word Colin had
heard his uncle use several times and so he was familiar with its
meaning, which was hypocrite, or more literally, his uncle had
explained, someone who wore two faces. Then Sandor abruptly
said, "*Canavar . . .*" and was silent. He at least was still alive.

The gypsy had begun sitting back on his heels to stare at the
wall above their heads, studying it fixedly with half-closed eyes, and
now he astonished Colin by running his hands lightly over the
surface. Colin saw that a seam ran up and then down the wall in the
shape of a doorway that had some time ago been bricked-over, but
clumsily. The gypsy's fingertips came together at one particular
brick, he braced himself, leaned a little, and lifted the brick out
with his hands. Just as quickly he put it back and turned to smile at
Colin. It was a smile of infinite triumph and satisfaction. At once
they both began to check the surface for other loosely mortared
bricks, and together found a dozen, all in the area that had once
been a door. Like all the houses in Anatolia, this one had been built
as a child would build a house of blocks: by simply placing one row
of sun-baked adobe bricks on top of the other without resorting to
beams or joists, and then at a later date a thin veneer of cement or
stucco had been added. The veneer had peeled away from most of
this abandoned house, exposing the crumbling mortar; sun and
wind had done the rest.

Having discovered the dozen bricks that were loose, the gypsy
brought out a knife for each of them and without a word spoken

they began to gently pry loose the mortar surrounding the other bricks. They worked for half an hour and then Colin glanced at his watch, touched the gypsy's arm and whispered, "Sabahat."

The man nodded, signaled that he would remain, and Colin crept away to hurry back into town and meet Sabahat.

After waiting fifteen minutes for Sabahat, Colin grew restless. She had instructed him to wait in the cafe, where he would be less vulnerable to curious passersby; on the other hand she had also pointed out that women never entered cafes in Anatolia, and so he must watch the window—grimy and fly-specked—for her face and her signal. He was reduced to sitting on a bench near the door and nervously fingering the identity card in his pocket and then his reapplied moustache.

The men seated around him in the cafe looked as if they had been turned into stone fifty years ago—he swore none of them had moved since he entered except the two men playing chess in the corner; twice they had reached forward to move a chesspiece. The others remained oblivious: unblinking, lips closed around hubble-bubble pipes, eyes blank. Colin felt he might have stumbled blindly into an opium den.

Two more men entered the cafe, followed by a third, and in fascination Colin watched to see how they would distribute themselves. The first to enter neither nodded nor spoke but moved to a corner and joined the silent ones. The second sat down and spread out a newspaper. The third said in a clear voice, "*Raki,*" and turned to survey the room.

Colin gasped. The man who had just violated the silence was his uncle Hu. There he stood in his usual faded blue work shirt and khaki shorts, looking around him for a face that interested him, his streaked hair and moustache bleached a shade closer to white after a week in the sun. Colin's first instinct was to dive under a table and hide, and then he remembered that he was in disguise. He met his uncle's gaze without flinching.

But this time he should have hidden. His uncle's trained photographer's eye slid over him, looked away and then slid back. A moment later, glass of raki in hand, Uncle Hu strolled over and sat down at the table nearest Colin.

From the corner of his mouth, very pleasantly, he said, "Do

you mind telling me what the devil you're doing here in Yozgat in that absurd moustache?"

Colin froze. He wished desperately he knew Turkish well enough so that he could get up, mutter something appropriate to an Anatolian peasant, and stalk away insulted.

"Of course I don't mean to trespass," his uncle continued in a mild voice, "but I have just spent one of the most horrible nights of my life in the local jail here. It seems that anyone driving a Ramsey Enterprises vehicle is being stopped by the police, searched and detained while the Istanbul police are consulted. I have been released—at last—because I don't answer to the description of the young sandy-haired chap they're looking for, who is traveling in the company of a woman wanted for questioning in some fiendish murder in Istanbul."

Colin said despairingly, "Let's go outside."

"Delighted," said his uncle. "I wondered at the time why I chose such a gloomy place to celebrate the end of my incarceration."

The sunlight was almost blinding. "How did you recognize me?" asked Colin miserably.

His uncle said witheringly, "My dear chap, you're my nephew. Oh, don't look so worried, I can't imagine anyone else recognizing you. I have a remarkable memory for faces, you know. When I saw you I thought, 'Those are Colin's cheekbones and eyes, in fact that looks precisely like Colin in peasant clothes and moustache.' And then—considering the circumstances, which have been somewhat jarring—I thought, 'Why *not* Colin in peasant clothes and moustache?' Now for heaven's sake tell me what the hell you've been up to while I've been in Erzurum. I don't mean to mix my metaphors—"

That was his uncle, thought Colin, concerned over metaphors in the midst of a trying situation. "Yes, sir," he said as they sat down on the bench outside the cafe. "Well, you see it's this way, sir —and I'll have to talk quickly—three friends of mine have been kidnapped here in Yozgat and are in a house about a mile away."

"I see," said his uncle. "Well, of course then you've got to get them out," he said without so much as a blink of the eye.

"Yes, sir," Colin agreed with a faint smile.

"One of these—er, friends—is the alleged murderess the police are looking for?" he inquired.

"Yes sir—but she didn't murder anyone, Uncle Hu. I was with her when Henry's body was left in the studio—your studio—" He stopped. He could not think of any possible way to explain the events of the past two days to his uncle. "It's all quite complicated," he added weakly. "Can't you just pretend you didn't see me and go on to Istanbul?"

His uncle considered this. "I could," he said reflectively, "but not without hearing your plans first. You have made plans, haven't you?" he said sharply.

"Yes, sir."

"Stop sir-ing me, I'm not your father." He frowned. "The thing is, I won't have you going to jail—horrid places, Turkish jails. I could volunteer. I'm not without experience in this kind of rescue operation—I was in the war, you know, and God knows these jails are to be avoided, your mother would never forgive me if—"

At that moment Sabahat hurried around the corner, gave a cry of relief at seeing him, and cried breathlessly, "We're ready—it's all settled! Yozgat's leading poet is going to read a poem of welcome—the same one he made up for the Premier's visit two years ago!—and the Greek Orthodox priest is going to say a prayer!"

"Poets? Priests?" said Uncle Hu with interest. He looked appreciatively at Sabahat and then at Colin. "I say—you do seem to be managing something rather well, do you mind terribly if I come along, too?"

Chapter Thirteen

Mrs. Pollifax sighed and opened her eyes. She had fallen or been pushed to the floor, still tied to the chair, so that her cheek rested on the hard earthen floor and any spontaneous movement was impossible. She heard Sandor say in a loud voice, "*Canavar . . .*" and she knew that something had happened to awaken her but she did not know what. From the other room—the door was open—she heard Dr. Belleaux say in a low voice, "Bring the serum out anyway. We'll have to risk its killing her, there's no other way . . ."

"*Magda,*" said Mrs. Pollifax in what she believed to be a loud clear voice, but realized a second later was only a whisper. She could not see Magda from where she lay—it must be Magda they had taken into the other room. She could see Sandor's feet not far away, the toes springing from his torn sneakers, but she could not see any more of him without lifting her head, and her head was on fire with a ribbon of pain that moved from cheekbone to brain. Concussion, she thought drowsily; could cheekbones have concussion? and then she drifted off again into unconsciousness.

When she next opened her eyes it was with the impression that she was in danger of being attacked by rats. She realized that she had been dreaming of rats gnawing their way through the wall, and for a moment, awakening, she thought she might still be within her nightmare because she distinctly heard rustling noises in the wall. *But that is definitely a rat in the wall,* she thought, listening. *I'm not losing my mind after all. I've regained consciousness!* There was not a great deal of reassurance in this thought because her circumstances had not changed. She remained huddled on the floor in the semi-darkness, her cheek pressed to the earth, the murmur of voices ebbing and rising from the other room. But she discovered that she was feeling better: still stiff and bruised but no longer aflame. She knew that it was blood she could taste when she licked her lips, and her nose ached, but it no longer throbbed, and the ribbon of pain had vanished. She dared to hope that no bones had been broken.

The voices from the other room were audible and she tried to make sense of them but she was still too blurred. She heard ". . . having gone to Bulgaria to help with security arrangements for the Festival of Youth. . . ." and then, "You had intended from the first to go to the British Consulate in Istanbul?"

"Not alone, no . . ." That was Magda's voice, oddly toneless. "But I had not expected to be looked for so quick or so—so accurately. I could not make trouble for my gypsy friends."

Gypsies, thought Mrs. Pollifax, frowning. Surely Magda ought not to be speaking about gypsies to Dr. Belleaux? She wondered what time it was, and as she licked her dry lips she wondered if she might call out for water. She felt very tired and dull. She tried to focus her eyes on Sandor's disreputable sneakers and then she tried to practice thinking very carefully. She supposed it was Thursday—no, no, it must still be Wednesday, late afternoon or early evening of their arrival day in Yozgat, and Dr. Belleaux had promised that presently they would be shot and carried off in the black car to an archaeological dig. That was not a very pleasant thought. She wondered if her body would ever be found and identified. Perhaps it was better if it wasn't, she reflected, since it would only prove extremely embarrassing to Mr. Carstairs and then of course there were her children. They were very nice children, Roger and Jane, but they would simply not understand how their mother came to be murdered in Turkey disguised as a native peasant woman. Nor would she be there to soften the explanation that between Garden Club meetings and her hospital work she had acquired this interesting little sideline as a CIA courier. It was not the sort of thing one could explain, certainly not to Jane at least.

But as her sluggishness diminished Mrs. Pollifax remembered that there was even more to be concerned about: there was Dr. Belleaux. The thought of Carstairs continuing to trust the man so appalled her that it jerked her to full consciousness at last, and in time to hear Dr. Belleaux say quite clearly. "You have been described as a defecting Communist agent, Madame Ferenci-Sabo. You are known to the Russians in this manner, too. But actually you have worked for the Americans all these years, is this not true?"

Mrs. Pollifax gasped, terrifyingly alert at last. It must have been drugs they had administered to Magda to force her to speak. Words overheard earlier came back to her . . . *we'll have to risk its killing her, there's no other way* . . . Not an ordinary drug then, but one of the truth serums.

No no no, she screamed, but no sound came from her throat and it was part of this nightmare that she could move her lips and her tongue yet make no sound. She began to struggle against the ropes that held her bound, frustrated by her helplessness to halt or delay Magda's confession to being a double agent.

"Yes, that is true," Magda said in reply, still in that cold, toneless voice. "I have been—am—a counteragent."

As Mrs. Pollifax sagged defeatedly she caught a glimpse of Sandor now, his head turned to listen. She noted the welt across his cheekbone and the gag stuffed into his mouth—he must have gone on shouting—and she thought, *Now he knows what Magda is, too.*

"I see," Dr. Belleaux said, and his voice shook a little, betraying his excitement at discovering that his wild suspicion was a literal fact. He drew a sharp breath and when he spoke again there was barely suppressed triumph in his voice, as if he knew he stumbled upon a masquerade so outrageous and so sinister that its ramifications would be felt everywhere—and especially on his own career, thought Mrs. Pollifax bitterly.

"Please tell me next how you notified the Americans after your extraordinary escape from my two men."

"I took money. Stefan had left some on the table, Turkish lira, and I took it. One of the gypsies in Istanbul sent a cable for me."

"And the address to which you sent it?"

Magda recited a cover address in Baltimore.

"Thank you!" said Dr. Belleaux cheerfully. "Thank you very much. Now I would like to discuss with you where you have hidden the missing document, the top secret paper you brought out of Russia with—"

He stopped abruptly. Mrs. Pollifax had heard it, too, an indefinable sound of movement outside, of something brushing the front door. Now she realized it had been a knock; it was repeated.

"What the devil!" exclaimed Dr. Belleaux. "Stefan!"

"*Evet,*" said Stefan calmly. "It is only a young girl, I saw her come. She has a notebook and pencil."

"She will have heard voices. Answer and get rid of her. Assim, hide the hypodermic. Cover the woman so she looks ill."

Mrs. Pollifax had been holding her breath. Now she expelled it and cleared her throat, testing it to see if her voice worked yet. If she could only scream—Practicing, she said in a small, hoarse, voice, "Someone—is—at—the—door."

She at least captured Sandor's attention; he made a frustrated rumbling noise in his throat and she saw him strain at his ropes. Stefan was unbolting and opening the front door. Mrs. Pollifax heard a clear young voice speak with a rush of enthusiasm and charm. But the words were Turkish—she had forgotten they would be. Mrs. Pollifax formed a scream in her throat. "Help!" she called out raspily. "Help! Help!"

Dr. Belleaux murmured something in Turkish in an amused voice, gave a little laugh and crossed the floor to close the door between the two rooms. With this act he blotted them out with finality.

Tears came to Mrs. Pollifax's eyes. "I'm sorry, Sandor," she said. "I would have liked to really scream but it's my voice. I can't."

Sandor rumbled again in reply. "I'm sorry you've been hurt and tied up and gagged," she told him, because it was important to practice speaking in case a second opportunity arose. "I'm sure you must be extremely sorry you ever joined us, but you must have overheard enough to realize this is something more important than any of us individually. It's the only attitude I can suggest," she added primly. The tears had run down her face to mingle with the dried blood on her cheeks. "I can only tell you—oh that rat in the wall is annoying," she cried furiously. "It's not enough that we're surrounded by human rats, there has to be—" She turned her head toward the outside wall.

Her gasp was almost as audible as her attempt to scream, for the wall was literally disappearing before her eyes. Sunshine was entering the dark room, inch by inch, as brick after brick was tidily, efficiently and very hastily removed by a pair of large brown human hands. Mrs. Pollifax could not believe it: either her vision or her mind had been seriously affected and she was hallucinating.

Within seconds a space appeared large enough for a pair of shoulders, and at once a pair of shoulders blocked off the light that had bruised and stabbed her swollen eyes. The words that slipped from Mrs. Pollifax's lips were entirely unpremeditated; she said incredulously, "Wotthehell!"

It had the effect of turning Sandor's head immediately, and as he saw the light, the opening, and the man's head his eyes widened in shock. Clearly he saw it too, and she was not hallucinating at all. The man's shoulders cleared the opening and he lifted his head. Mrs. Pollifax had never seen him before; his face was dark, tough, crafty. He lifted a finger to his lips, and after pulling his legs through the hole he tiptoed across the room. He was followed by a second man, and he too was a stranger to Mrs. Pollifax, so that she became certain that she must have lost consciousness again and was dreaming some happy, wishful fantasy of rescue.

The second man was tall, lanky and dusty. As if by prearrangement he went to Sandor. Neither man expected them to be capable of walking. Ropes were quickly slashed. Smoothly Mrs. Pollifax was picked up, carried to the opening in the wall and tilted forward on her knees. Hands reached in from outside and gently grasped Mrs. Pollifax's bleeding fingers. She was half-pushed and half-pulled through the aperture into the blinding brilliant sun of a late afternoon that contained—of all things—a smiling Colin Ramsey.

"Colin!" she gasped.

"Yes," he said, grinning. "Isn't it wonderful?" As Sandor was pushed out into the sunshine Colin raised both arms and waved at someone she could not see. The tall, sandy-haired man followed Sandor out of the hole and the dark, fierce-looking one began swiftly replacing the bricks.

"You'll have to walk several yards before you can rest," Colin said firmly. "We have to get you to the front corner of the house, and we have only three minutes to do it."

She understood nothing of this except that it was obviously not a dream, and that it was being managed with infinite precision so that she need do nothing at all. Nothing except walk, which was nearly impossible, but if Colin said it had to be done she would do it. Her feet felt like stumps, bloodless and lifeless, and her knees kept betraying her. Colin supported her, and the sandy-haired man supported Sandor, and slowly they reached the cover of a bedraggled grape vine at the corner of the house. Here the third man caught up with them and crouched down behind them as they waited.

A van drove slowly up the empty street. *Colin's van?* thought Mrs. Pollifax, bewildered, but that had been abandoned in Ankara. The van pulled up in front of the house. Half a dozen young people in western clothes leaped down from the rear and began unloading—it couldn't be possible—trays of fruit and food, jugs of water and huge armfuls of bright flowers. A man in the robes of a priest climbed down from the driver's seat and joined them; Mrs. Pollifax saw that they were going to walk up to the house in which she had been captive.

"Oh, stop them!" she whispered, and then, "Magda's in there!"

"We know that," Colin said calmly. "Sabahat knocked at the door a few minutes ago saying she was taking a census. She reported three men and an invalid woman in the front room."

"Sabahat? Census?" repeated Mrs. Pollifax dazedly.

"Now," Colin said to the sandy-haired man. The stranger nodded and walked down to the empty van and backed it up the cart track to Mrs. Pollifax and Sandor. "Get in quickly," Colin told her.

They fell clumsily into the rear, and then the van backed down into the street, this time pointing toward town, the motor kept running by the tall stranger. Colin and the dark gypsy-looking man moved toward the house, and incredulously Mrs. Pollifax leaned out to watch. The young people and the priest had absolutely vanished—into the house, realized Mrs. Pollifax disbelievingly—leaving the door wide open. Inside, it looked as if a party was in full bloom—and into this melee walked Colin and the gypsy.

A moment later they backed out carrying an unconscious Magda between them. A girl joined them, laughing and calling over her shoulder to the young people behind her. For one incredible moment Mrs. Pollifax saw Dr. Belleaux swim to the door like a salmon fighting his way upstream. A crowd of laughing youngsters accosted him and pulled him back. Furious, he stretched out his two hands toward Magda, face livid, and then someone placed a plate of grapes in those outstretched hands, a garland of flowers was lowered over his head and slowly he was sucked back into the livingroom, overwhelmed by currents too strong for him.

"What on earth—!" cried Mrs. Pollifax to Colin as the two men placed Magda in the rear of the van.

Colin grinned. "It's a love-in. Dr. Belleaux is being smothered with non-violence." He turned and grinned at the girl. "This is Sabahat, whose idea it was—Sabahat Pasha. Sabahat, ask Sebastien to sit up front and take us to the gypsies now, will you?"

"How do you do," Sabahat said, smiling at Mrs. Pollifax. "I'm so glad you are safe." She spoke to the gypsy in Turkish and then extended her hand to Colin. "I will make certain the three men do not get away for as long as is possible. I cannot promise much but it may help you a little," she told him gravely. "*Allaha ismarladik,* Colin Ramsey."

He shook his head. "Not for long, Sabahat," he said, firmly holding on to her hand. "You know I'll be back. In the meantime how can I thank you?"

She dimpled charmingly. "But my friends have always wished to meet such a scholar as Dr. Belleaux—there is no need to explain the situation to them. You are giving them a big day, and it is I who should thank you!"

He grinned. "Fair exchange then." He released her hand and shouted, "Okay, Uncle Hu, let's go!"

As the van roared into life and raced down the street Mrs. Pollifax exclaimed, "Did you call that man *Uncle Hu?*"

"Quite a lot has happened," Colin said modestly. "Yes, that's Uncle Hu. Letting him help seemed the least I could do, he's already spent one night in jail because of us, which places him beyond the pale. This is the van he drives—he was on his way back from Erzurum. The chap with him is a gypsy named Sebastien. I picked him up before I ran into Uncle Hu, he has a dancing bear and he stayed behind the other gypsies to wait for Magda."

Mrs. Pollifax looked at him in amazement. "Colin," she said, "you're an extraordinary young man."

He returned her glance, looked startled, and then a slow smile spread across his face. "Yes," he said with an air of discovery. "I believe I am."

Chapter Fourteen

Their precipitous flight from Yozgat was interrupted by Sebastien, who somewhat desperately reminded them that he had a horse, a dog, a wagon and a dancing bear to be retrieved. Colin crawled up front to the window and held a three-way conversation, the translations supplied by his uncle, but he crawled back to report that Sebastien was adamant: he could not go any further without his menage. They stopped briefly beside the road at the place where the gypsy had made camp; Sebastien looked for several moments at Uncle Hu's map, then marked a cross on the road, halfway between Yozgat and Kayseri.

Uncle Hu said, "He tells me the gypsies will be somewhere near the cross he's marked, and camping within sight of the road because they expect him to follow."

"And will he follow?"

"He'll hope to catch up with us by dawn."

They thanked Sebastien profusely for his help, Mrs. Pollifax gave him money from the wad pinned inside her baggy pants, and they resumed their breakneck trip south. Watching Mrs. Pollifax return the bills to their hiding place Sandor said with a weak grin, "The Bank of Pollifax, eh?"

"Hold still," Colin told him sharply, trying to wrap gauze around Sandor's bleeding wrists. "Uncle Hu always drives like this," he explained resignedly, "although I rather imagine he's trying to cover as much ground as possible before dark. You've no idea how black it gets out here on the plateau."

"No street lights," said Mrs. Pollifax brightly. "What time is it now?"

"Nearly eight. One hour until dark. There," he said, tying the last knot on Sandor's bandage and turning to Mrs. Pollifax.

"Hold out your wrists. I do hope you've had tetanus shots recently, they're a pulpy mess."

"Shouldn't you do Magda's first?"

He laughed shortly. "Why? She has an advantage over you she's unconscious. But her wrists aren't in such bad shape, they must have been untied when they drugged her." He looked soberly at Mrs. Pollifax and said, "By the way, I think it's time I ask how much Dr. Belleaux found out while he held you three captive."

Mrs. Pollifax sighed. "Nearly everything."

"Good God!"

She nodded. "This time they gave Magda a different sort of drug. They tried first to make her talk without it, but she wouldn't." To Sandor she said frankly, "You know who she is now, too."

He dropped his eyes. "*Evet.*"

"But does Dr. Belleaux know about the *gypsies?*" Colin asked. When Mrs. Pollifax nodded he shook his head. "What a foul piece of luck! That means he knows precisely where we're heading, or soon will. Everyone in Yozgat can tell him the gypsies have gone south."

Mrs. Pollifax felt it unnecessary to reply: The fresh air that had revived her was beginning to stupefy her now, and the wonder of being rescued was being replaced by fresh worries. She felt very weak, and a little nauseous—a reasonable reaction to what she had gone through but still inconvenient. If choice were given her she would without hesitation choose a hospital—even a nursing home would do, she thought wistfully—where she could bleed quietly between clean sheets, rouse only to sip nourishing liquids and to observe new ice packs being placed on bruises and swellings before drifting off into an exhausted sleep. Instead she was rocketing off across the bumpy Anatolian plain again, in a rather dirty van, while she sat on an extremely dirty floor holding on for dear life and adjusting to the realization that they were still in danger, and probably greater danger now because Dr. Belleaux knew everything about them.

Aloud she said, "Dr. Belleaux is going to be feeling very nasty, I think—he's just lost that elegant Istanbul life of his that he planned to get back to tomorrow, after burying us in some ruins."

"He almost did bury us," growled Sandor.

Mrs. Pollifax considered this and nodded. Yes, there was a great deal to be said for such an attitude: without Colin they would be dead now, in which case there would be no choice left them at all. *I'll feel sorry for myself later*, decided Mrs. Pollifax, and firmly put aside thoughts of rest to take charge again. "What weapons do we have, Colin?"

He looked amused. "You've gone professional again—I'm relieved. I still have Stefan's pistol, with three shots fired."

"They did not search me," Sandor said, bringing out the gun he had periodically waved at them. "But wotthehell, it's empty," he added sadly.

"Uncle Hu may have something," Colin said. "Of course he may no longer carry a gun because he's never been attacked on these trips by anything more than a goat. If he ever slows down I'll ask him."

But his uncle Hu gave no sign of slowing down, in fact as the road grew more atrocious his speed seemed to increase, as if he regarded the stones and gullies and potholes as an affront to an unblemished record. Magda had been rolled into a rug and braced against one wall; she was almost to be envied. If this was Wednesday, thought Mrs. Pollifax nostalgically—and she thought it was—she would be wheeling the hospital's bookcart at home, and tomorrow she would normally be having her karate lessons with Lorvale.

Except what was normalcy, she wondered; in Mr. Carstairs' world she was not even overdue yet, and certainly he had no idea that in cabling Dr. Belleaux her identity and description he had signed her death warrant for so long as she was in this country and at the mercy of Dr. Belleaux's considerable resources. She was neatly trapped indeed. Each new detail that Dr. Belleaux learned only inflamed his desperation as well as his ambitions: *he must* find them. They could escape him for the moment by going to the Turkish police and appealing for help, but this would at once cancel all hope of Magda fleeing the country; she would again become public property to be schemed over, fought over, questioned, requestioned and exploited. But even worse, Mrs. Pollifax suspected that by surrendering to the police they would become sitting targets for Dr. Belleaux instead of moving ones. It would take time and patience for their shocking charges against Dr. Belleaux to be investigated and proven, and while facts were checked they would be confined to some small area accessible only to the police, many of whom had already been charmed by that genius of criminology Dr. Belleaux. What would the headlines be then, she wondered: Mysterious Explosion Wipes Out Political Prisoners? or Fire Sweeps Wing of Prison, Five Dead? It was too risky to contemplate.

In any case, without passport and wanted for Henry's murder, Mrs. Pollifax could certainly not leave the country herself now. Her hopes had to be concentrated exclusively on Magda. If Magda could somehow be spirited beyond the border then she at least would be free—and she could communicate with Carstairs. . . .

She said, "How far are we from the nearest border, Colin?"

"Which one?"

"Any—except Russian," she amended.

Sandor answered. "From Greece about two hundred and fifty kilometers. From Syria maybe three hundred."

Mrs. Pollifax shook her head. "Too far. Where is the nearest airport then?"

Colin looked at her in dismay. "I believe there's one at Kayseri, about fifty miles south of us. But surely—"

"Do you think they'd dream of our risking an airport?"

Colin said, "No. Yes. Oh I don't know!"

She pointed out gently, "Every day that goes by will give Dr. Belleaux a better chance to find us. It's Time that's our worst enemy, but if we move boldly—"

Sandor turned and looked at her with interest.

"But that's such a reckless *gamble*," protested Colin. "What if it shouldn't work?"

Sandor grinned. "She's okay—she's got the crazy spirit. Except wotthehell I never expect it from such a person." He looked at Mrs. Pollifax appreciatively and his grin deepened.

Abruptly the van began a wild braking, jumped and came to a grinding halt. Uncle Hu slid open the window that in this van separated the cab from the rear. "Radiator," he said, gesturing ahead.

Thick clouds of vapor curled up from the hood of the van, obscuring the road. "She's boiled dry," he added unnecessarily.

"Oh dear," said Mrs. Pollifax, and she too crawled to the door of the van to follow Colin and Sandor outside.

"It will take time, maybe half an hour," Ramsey said, meeting them there. "Can't put cold water into a hot radiator or she'll crack, you know." He disappeared into the van and handed out sterno, pans and water jug. "Set it up, Colin," he said. Nodding pleasantly at Mrs. Pollifax he held out his hand. "How do you do. Hugh Ramsey's the name."

"Emily Pollifax," she said briskly, shaking his hand.

"That woman in there who was drugged—she hurt, too?"

"Bruised mainly. Still unconscious."

"Might as well leave her inside then. Turkish?"

"Uh—" Mrs. Pollifax opened her mouth and then closed it. "European," she said weakly.

Ramsey nodded and began pouring water carefully into two pans. "Damn nuisance, this," he said in his mild voice.

Colin drew out his gun. "I'll take a look at the road behind us," he said, and moved off toward a cluster of rocks and disappeared, soon to appear on top of the largest one. "No one on the road for miles," he called. "Where are we, Uncle Hu?"

His uncle shouted back, "We passed through Osmanpasa and crossed Kizil Irmak. Must be about forty miles out of Yozgat, sixty from Kayseri."

Mrs. Pollifax was looking at the sun that hung suspended over the range in the south, possibly the same mountain range she had seen from Ankara the evening before. A curious lavender and gold light bathed the wild land around them, the beginnings of a dusk that would suddenly terminate in darkness. They could ill afford this stop, she thought, and hoped the gypsies were not far ahead. "Do you see any signs of a gypsy camp?" she called to Colin.

He turned and looked in the other direction. "No."

The first two pans of water were boiling. Ramsey and Sandor carried them carefully to the front of the van, opened the hood and the radiator, and poured the hot water inside. Ramsey put his ear to the radiator. "So far so good," he said, returning to pour more water. "Drink some while we have it," he told Mrs. Pollifax, handing her a cup.

"Do *you* know about an airport at Kayseri?" she asked him hopefully.

"Oh yes, there's an aerodrome there. They've limited service, but in summer there are several flights a week to Ankara and Istanbul."

Colin had climbed down for a drink of water and he joined them now, explaining, "Mrs. Pollifax is determined to get our passenger"—he jerked his head toward the van,—"moving toward England."

"Yes," said Mrs. Pollifax firmly, and asked, "Is it true—absolutely true—that if we succeeded in getting her to Kayseri she would show her passport there, but *only* there, no matter how many changes she made enroute out of the country?"

Both Colin and his uncle nodded. "Quite right," Ramsey said. "She'd go through Passport Control and Customs at Kayseri, but at Istanbul she'd be considered *In Transit* and would be issued an In Transit card during her wait in the air terminal. This she'd give up as she boarded her plane for London or Paris or whatever."

Mrs. Pollifax's interest increased. This was it, of course—if it could be done. If they could get Magda to Kayseri. If she could walk through Customs without being challenged and stopped. There would be that one terrifying moment of inspection, but if she passed . . .

Watching her Colin said indignantly, "Mrs. Pollifax, you don't even know the plane schedules!"

His uncle Hu startled them both by saying, "I've got one in the van. I try to keep very up-to-date on plane, train and boat schedules, especially in summer when everything opens up in this part of the country. The water's hot—pour it in, will you? I'll go and look."

A fresh batch of water was on the fire when he returned carrying a shoebox stuffed with folders. "I've got it," he said, waving one. "It's the Van-Istanbul flight, Turkish airlines. Three days a week, Mondays, Wednesdays and Fridays departing Kayseri eight o'clock in the morning and arriving in Istanbul at eleven, with an asterisk denoting that this plane makes connections with the noon flights to Paris and London."

"Well!" said Mrs. Pollifax, delighted. "I believe I'll go inside and see if Magda's stirring yet."

"Take her some water," Colin suggested.

"You'll need a flashlight inside," contributed Ramsey, and

crawled in ahead of her. Colin and Sandor followed and they all surrounded Magda, who remained inert.

Mrs. Pollifax felt her pulse. "She seems all right," she said doubtfully. "She just doesn't wake up."

Colin said peevishly, "How you can even think of her taking a *plane* in a day or two!"

Uncle Hu said firmly, "If she can swallow water we must give her some before she becomes dehydrated. I'll hold her up. Give me the cup of water, and Colin shine the flashlight on her face."

Magda was lifted, still encased in her rug and still inert. The flashlight was turned on and Uncle Hu leaned over Magda with the cup.

The cup suddenly slipped from his fingers to the floor.

"What is it?" gasped Mrs. Pollifax, who could see Ramsey's face. "Colin, he's ill—do something!"

Uncle Hu shook his head; his face was white. *"Who is this woman?"* he demanded in a shaken voice.

"It's Magda," said Mrs. Pollifax, regarding him with astonishment. "We're taking her to the gypsies."

He shook his head violently. "Where did you find her? Where does she come from?"

They stared at him stupidly.

His voice rose. "Don't you understand I know this woman? She was supposed to have died in Buchenwald twenty-six years ago!"

Mrs. Pollifax said blankly, "Magda?"

"Not Magda!" He leaned forward and peered into the flashlit face. "I tell you she's Alice. Alice Blanche."

Something stirred in Mrs. Pollifax's jaded mind; a face, a recognition, a memory. Alice Blanche . . . but Blanche meant white in French, didn't it? Alice White—Alice Dexter White. . . . "You know her?" she faltered.

He nodded. "During World War Two, when I escaped from prison camp. She hid me for three months in Paris—occupied Paris. She—I—" He hesitated and then said simply, "She was very beautiful and very brave. Reckless, really. I thought she was captured and imprisoned. Charles said so. The Hawk said so. Red Queen said so. You must think I'm talking absolute gibberish," he said, looking up at Mrs. Pollifax. "She was an agent, you see."

Mrs. Pollifax nodded. She said quietly, "She still is. That's why you never found her."

He said in an appalled voice, "You can't be serious."

"I'm very serious. Surely you're aware that you've just helped rescue some rather controversial people from a house in Yozgat, and that we may be pursued even now?"

"Yes, but it's you, isn't it? Surely it's you who—"

Mrs. Pollifax said briskly, "Only superficially. It's this woman they're really after, and it's this woman we must get to Kayseri for a plane out of this country. If you've had time for newspapers on your trip you may have read about a certain Magda Ferenci-Sabo."

He nodded. "Yes, that defecting Communist agent."

Mrs. Pollifax glanced down at the still-unconscious Magda and said with a sigh, "Meet your defecting Communist, Mr. Ramsey. Now we really must leave before it grows any darker or we'll never find the gypsies. Is there enough water in the radiator now, Mr. Ramsey?"

"Yes," said Ramsey, still staring at Magda. "Good God!" he exclaimed again, incredulously, but he turned off the flashlight and followed them out without delay. They poured the last of the boiling water into the radiator. The sun had set with finality while they were inside the van, and twilight was rapidly replacing the long shadows. It would be dark in a matter of minutes.

Darkness came, and nothing existed for them except the twin beams of the van's headlights on the stony road ahead. Yet lacking darkness Mrs. Pollifax realized they would never have seen the gypsy camp, for it was the light of the campfire that drew their eyes: like an earthbound star it shone at some distance off the main road, made luminous by the opaque blackness surrounding it. Seeing it, Colin's uncle turned off the road and they bumped and jolted over a cart track of eroded earth and scrub.

"More dogs," groaned Colin as there mingled with the roar of the van the sound of howling cur dogs.

"Never mind, these are Magda's gypsies," Mrs. Pollifax told him warmly. "We've found them." Peering out she saw that there were two fires, one at either end of a camp laid out in a rectangle among rocks and a few stunted trees. Six or eight wagons had been drawn up to this rectangle, and Colin's uncle drove neatly into the middle before he brought the van to a halt.

"We're here," he shouted over his shoulder.

"Yes," said Mrs. Pollifax gratefully, and opened the rear door and stepped down.

Gypsies had appeared like shadows and formed a ring around the van. "Good evening," said Mrs. Pollifax eagerly. "We've brought you Magda, we're looking for—"

She stopped uncertainly. She realized that the gypsies formed a solid circle around her of folded arms, grim eyes and hostile faces. Not one of them moved but their eyes almost physically forced her to step back in retreat. For one nightmare moment Mrs. Pollifax wondered if they were going to stone her to death. She had never met with such an impenetrable wall of hatred. Something was terribly wrong.

Then from the shadows a voice said, "Good evening, Mrs. Pollifax!"

Dr. Belleaux strolled smiling into the circle of light followed by Stefan and Assim. "You mustn't expect a welcome here, Mrs. Pollifax. I arrived twenty minutes ago by helicopter and warned these people about you." He said softly, with a helpless shrug, "They already know that you've hidden Magda in the van, and that you've beaten and drugged her. I've told them they mustn't kill you but they are so very aroused, what is one to do?"

Chapter Fifteen

For a moment Mrs. Pollifax thought she was going to faint but that would have been too merciful; she did not faint. He had said what, *helicopter?* It smacked more of black magic against this wild, primitive backdrop of sky and stars and earth lighted by campfires. "It's not true!" she flung at the gypsies and looked into their high cheekboned, mahogany faces but her glance met no response. The frozen mute hostility did not waver; she felt whipped and shriveled by their bitter and accusing eyes.

"He lies!" she protested. "You mustn't believe him! We're Magda's friends!"

Behind her Colin said in a shaken voice, "I don't think they speak any English, Mrs. Pollifax."

"Not at all?" she cried passionately. She swung around. "They must know Turkish then! Sandor—Mr. Ramsey—translate, tell them quickly!"

"Good God, yes," murmured Uncle Hu, and stepped forward. He began to speak in Turkish, and had produced several sentences when Stefan calmly walked up to him and hit him with his fist, sending him unconscious to the ground. At the same moment Mrs. Pollifax heard a startled grunt from Sandor on her right —he ducked his head and ran.

The wall of gypsies shattered. With shouts the men took off after Sandor into the darkness while the women tightened the circle around Mrs. Pollifax, presumably to prevent her bolting too. "No no no!" cried Mrs. Pollifax, impatiently stamping her foot. "Do understand! Magda is our friend, that man lies!"

One of the women spat contemptuously.

"Inglis," said Mrs. Pollifax in case her baggy pants and shawls confused them. "You must listen to me! We're all in danger from that man!"

Half a dozen women climbed into the rear of the van. There were murmurs and gasps at the sight of Magda, and then little crooning sounds as she was lifted and brought out. Gently they carried her toward the more distant campfire, with Dr. Belleaux following and speaking to them, obviously pointing out each bruise and cut to them in an effort to whip them into a new fury of hatred.

Mrs. Pollifax looked at Stefan, who looked at her mockingly. She turned and looked at Colin, who was leaning over his uncle. She wondered if Sandor had been caught yet. She wondered how she could possibly make the gypsies understand that if they didn't act quickly they would all be killed, and their beloved Magda too. She wondered how long it would be before Magda regained consciousness. That was something only Dr. Belleaux knew, and he seemed very confident that Magda's ability to speak was not an imminent threat.

He was shouting to Stefan now, and to complete the irony he was shouting in English. "Tie them up," he called. "We can use the helicopter radio to contact the police. They can be here by dawn."

Police—dawn; what was he planning, she wondered as Stefan pushed them forward. Could Dr. Belleaux really afford to call in the police, or didn't he plan to be here when they came, or would they all be dead when the police arrived? Certainly by dawn he must expect to retrieve whatever document Magda had stolen from the Communists; if he already had this he would not be here. Now that he had established himself to the gypsies as Magda's protector was he counting on this to provide him with the gypsies' confidence? She was growing too tired to think.

Stefan led them past the second campfire where Magda had been placed between blankets. A dark, tousle-headed boy of nine or ten sat cross-legged beside Magda, watching a woman apply ointment to Magda's face wounds. The woman looked up at Mrs. Pollifax as she passed and hissed, *"Baulo-moosh!"* Clearly it was an epithet of the worst kind.

At some distance from the fires their bandaged hands were tied behind them again, and then to the trunk of a stunted, low-flying tree that looked curiously Japanese in its distortion. From here they could no longer see the van or Uncle Hu lying in the dust beside it. They could see one gypsy wagon and the silhouette of a horse grazing behind it in the shadows. They could see the fire and Magda's blanket-shrouded body, the woman and the boy. Beyond this circle of light the far-away cliffs were etched sharply against the deep blue night sky. The silence of the plain was almost complete except for the sound of the wind and an occasional muffled shout from the men who searched for Sandor.

"Well," said Mrs. Pollifax dispiritedly.

"Well," said Colin.

Stefan had disappeared. The boy who had been sitting beside Magda at the campfire arose and walked across the open space toward Mrs. Pollifax and Colin. He chose a position a few yards from them and sat down, cross-legged, to watch them now. He watched without expression, his face impassive. Two young men suddenly appeared and began to search Mrs. Pollifax and Colin. Their faces were dark, swarthy and leanly handsome, their hands expertly light. When they came upon Mrs. Pollifax's wad of money and unpinned it they shouted and held it high to show the boy, who laughed delightedly. The two young men added Colin's watch and pen to their treasure and happily walked away.

"A pretty kettle of fish," said Colin savagely.

Mrs. Pollifax said wearily, "I don't know how to make them understand. Surely someone here must have heard English spoken once or twice?"

Colin said doggedly, "They undoubtedly speak Bulgarian— no mean accomplishment—since they came from across the border. Of course they speak Romany, and probably some Hungarian as well, and a little Turkish. But even if they understood some English our dear old friend Dr. Belleaux got here first."

"But why would we come here to the gypsies at all—with Magda—if we'd beaten and drugged her?"

"For the same reason Dr. Belleaux came here: to get from the gypsies what Magda left here with them. In his case before she wakes up and calls him a bloody liar."

"If only she would—right now!" said Mrs. Pollifax with feeling. "She'd give one long loud scream at sight of him, and tell these people who he is in their own language, and—but will Dr. Belleaux *allow* her to wake up?"

"No, but he can't very well kill her in plain sight of her

friends." He added wryly, "At the moment I'm more worried about us. Nobody here would mind seeing *us* killed, and we haven't one single state secret up our sleeves to prolong our living. He can keep Magda drugged while he goes to work on the gypsies but we're only nuisances. I keep remembering Sebastien. He was going to hitch up his wagon, feed his dancing bear and follow us, remember?"

Mrs. Pollifax said gloomily, "But he didn't expect to find us before dawn, and it can't be midnight yet, can it? And it's more likely he fed his bear and then decided to curl up and sleep for a while. I'd rather put my money on Sandor, who at least—"

She stopped. The gypsies were bringing Sandor back into camp. One large and muscular gypsy carried him slung across his back like a slab of venison. In a long procession the men crossed their line of vision, passed the campfire and disappeared. "Unconscious," she said despairingly. "Not even capable of explaining in Turkish to the gypsies who we are!"

Colin said soberly, "What do you think Dr. Belleaux has in mind—that is, if you can enter that mind of his at all?"

Mrs. Pollifax considered. "I can at least guess. With Magda he has two possibilities: either he will fly her off to Russia with whatever papers he mentioned, or he will kill her and fly off to Russia himself with the mysterious papers. He has that helicopter. I daresay it's provided him by the Russians, and he need only radio ahead and cross the border at some prearranged spot with very little risk of being shot down."

"Either possibility disposes of his pleasant life in Istanbul at least!"

Mrs. Pollifax laughed. "Don't be naïve, my dear Colin. He can easily salvage his pleasant Istanbul life by saying that I murdered Magda."

"And risk a trial?" asked Colin. "Or am I being naïve again?"

"Yes, you are, really," Mrs. Pollifax told him. "Because by that time he will have seen to it that the gypsies kill *me*. Stone me to death, no doubt," she said tartly.

Stefan and Assim reappeared suddenly, carrying a trussed-up but still breathing Sandor. They knotted him to the tree as well—it was becoming heavily populated. Stefan said with a grin, "The gypsies hunt well for us, eh? We'll even let them kill you soon."

"Bring that other man here, too," said Dr. Belleaux, strolling in from the shadows. "The tall thin one. What is his name?" he asked Mrs. Pollifax.

"I don't think I'll tell you," she said coldly.

He shrugged. "It scarcely matters in any case." He regarded the tree with interest. "Perhaps this tree is the best solution of all for your demise, certainly less tedious than simulating knife murders for you all by the gypsies. A little kerosene sprinkled at the base of the tree, a match, a flaming tree and there would be no embarrassing traces left at all. The Turkish police," he added, "will be here by dawn. It is so very difficult to puzzle out how to dispose of so many of you."

Mrs. Pollifax said coldly, "You're very disappointing, Dr. Belleaux, you appear to have the mentality of a Neanderthal man—except I rather imagine I'm insulting the defenseless Neanderthal. I had expected something a little more imaginative, discriminating and subtle from a man of your obvious taste and background. You must be growing quite desperate."

Dr. Belleaux nodded. "It is a matter to which I must still give careful attention, Mrs. Pollifax," he admitted. "To me also it feels unpleasantly primitive. I naturally prefer the gypsies to kill you, as I think they will. But you have to be dealt with by dawn, which accelerates the pace. In any case you may rest assured that I will evolve a way of disposing of you all that will suit my own welfare—not yours," he added with a charming, if pointed smile. "Ah, you have the fourth one, Stefan—good! He is beginning to stir, and he speaks Turkish, so gag him as well, please. Check all the knots, Assim, and then back to the helicopter."

Mrs. Pollifax said indignantly, "You must realize that Magda will never give you what you want."

Dr. Belleaux smiled. "Of course not, but the gypsies will. They believe what I tell them."

"I find it rather depressing to have been right about that," Mrs. Pollifax said to Colin.

Dr. Belleaux glanced at his watch. "I advise you to say your prayers," he concluded. "I shall be speaking again now by radio to the police in Istanbul, and by dawn the police should be rendez-vousing here from all points of Anatolia."

"And you?" asked Mrs. Pollifax.

"I will be—elsewhere."

The three of them walked off into the darkness and vanished. The boy guarding them also got up suddenly and ran off into the shadows, leaving them alone.

"I'm terribly sorry, Colin," Mrs. Pollifax said with a sigh.

"If you're going to say what I think—don't," he told her coldly. "I was never—at any point—your responsibility, and you know that. I chose to come along, and I simply won't have you going all bleary and sentimental about me now."

She said gently, "And if I do, dear Colin, precisely what can you do about it?"

He said stiffly, "Well, I shall certainly think the less of you. I've no complaints—it's been a bit of a romp, you know."

She turned her head and looked at him. "I trust that you have the intelligence to realize that you're *not* a coward, and never have been!"

He grinned. "That's rather choice, isn't it? And how else would I have found out?"

The boy was returning. Again he came across the turf but this time he walked up to Mrs. Pollifax and looked into her face searchingly, and then from his pocket he drew out a small knife, leaned over her and cut the ropes at her ankles and wrists.

Colin said in astonishment, "I say—am I imagining things, or did he just—"

The boy fiercely shook his head, pressing one finger to his lips. As Mrs. Pollifax stared at him blankly he beckoned her to follow him.

"But the others!" protested Mrs. Pollifax, pointing to Colin and Sandor and Mrs. Ramsey.

The boy shook his head. His gestures grew more frantic.

"Go with him for heaven's sake," Colin said in a low voice. "You're not going to look a gift horse in the mouth, are you? If you make a scene he'll tie you up again!"

Torn between loyalty and curiosity Mrs. Pollifax followed him. Once she looked back, and at sight of her friends tied helplessly to the tree she would have gone back to them if the child had not tugged furiously at her baggy pants. What did he want, wondered Mrs. Pollifax and why was he doing this? She limped with him past the horses, around rocks and wagons—he was obviously hiding her from the other gypsies, and her curiosity had become almost intolerable when ahead of her she saw a tent pitched between two boulders. It was the only tent that she had seen in the camp. A light inside faintly illuminated its ragged edges and spilled out from its base. The boy pulled aside a curtain and gestured to Mrs. Pollifax to enter.

Mrs. Pollifax walked in. A lantern hung suspended from a tent pole, and seated cross-legged on a pillow beneath it was a square-shouldered gypsy woman. Hair threaded with silver hung to her shoulders, framing a square, high-cheekboned dark face. The eyes in the lantern light smoldered under heavy lids, and now they pierced Mrs. Pollifax like a laser beam.

The boy spoke rapidly to the woman, and she nodded. He beckoned Mrs. Pollifax to sit down in front of the gypsy, and Mrs. Pollifax stiffly lowered herself to the hard earth.

"Give me your hands," the woman said abruptly.

Mrs. Pollifax gasped. "You speak English!"

"Yes. The boy understands some but cannot speak it well."

Mrs. Pollifax's relief was infinite. "Thank heaven!" she cried. "I have tried—"

The woman shook her head. "Just give me your hands, please. Everything you wish to say is written in them, without lies or concealment."

"Without—" Mrs. Pollifax stretched out her hands, suppressing a desire to laugh hysterically. "If you insist," she said. "But there is so little time—"

"The boy tells me he has listened to you speak, and that my people have been lied to." She was gently examining the palms of the hands. "Your wrists are bandaged?"

"Yes. Like Magda's. The man in the white goatee did this."

"Hush." The woman closed her eyes, holding Mrs. Pollifax's hands in silence, as if they spoke a message to her. "You speak truth," she said abruptly, and opened her eyes. To the boy she said. "Bring Goru here at once—quickly! This woman does not lie, she lives under *koosti cherino*, the good stars." As the boy ran out she smiled at Mrs. Pollifax. "You are skeptical, I see."

"You can see this in a hand?"

"But of course—lips may lie but the lines in a hand never do, and I have the gift of *dukkeripen*. You are a widow, are you not?

Your hand tells me also that you have begun a second life—a second fate line has begun to parallel the first one."

"All widows begin second lives," pointed out Mrs. Pollifax gently.

The woman smiled into her eyes. "With so many marks of preservation on that second line, showing escape from dangers? And a cross on the mount of Saturn, foretelling the possibility of violent death at some future date?" She allowed Mrs. Pollifax to withdraw her hand. "But I am clairvoyant as well," she went on. "When I hold a hand I get pictures, as well as vibrations of good or evil. I feel that you have come to this country only days ago—by plane, I believe—and I get a very strong picture of you tied to a chair—this is very recent, is it not?—in a room where there is straw in one corner, and a door that has been bricked-over."

"How very astonishing!" said Mrs. Pollifax.

The woman's smile deepened. "You see the waste of words, then. But here is Goru."

Goru was enormous—it was he who had carried Sandor back to camp slung over his shoulder—and he was made even larger by the bulky sheepskin jacket he wore. As the woman talked to him he looked at Mrs. Pollifax with growing surprise, and then with humor. He made a magnificent shrug, snapped his fingers and grinned. With a bow to Mrs. Pollifax he hurried out.

The woman nodded. "We shall have some sport with that *gorgio*," she said in contempt. "The man descended on us like a bird in his machine, and spoke knowingly and urgently about Magda. He knew everything! How is that?"

"He drugged her earlier tonight, with the kind of drug that produces confession," explained Mrs. Pollifax. "You will help us now?"

The woman's lip curled. "Wars. Assassinations. Drugs that make even a Magda speak—" She shook her head. "I do not understand this civilization of yours. Do not look so anxious for your friends, my dear—trust Goru. You came to this country to help Magda?"

Mrs. Pollifax nodded. "But I can tell you nothing that Dr. Belleaux had not already said—except," she added with dignity, "that Magda was not drugged when she spoke to me of going to Yozgat to find the Inglescus."

The woman smiled. "I am Anyeta Inglescu."

"Are you?" Mrs. Pollifax was pleased, and put out her hand. "I'm Emily Pollifax."

"The name of Inglescu was not mentioned by the man with the goatee," the gypsy added. "But I do not understand why he goes to such trouble to speak lies, to try and fool us."

Mrs. Pollifax said bluntly, "He wants the document Magda escaped with."

"Document?" said the woman curiously.

Mrs. Pollifax nodded. "Whatever it is that Magda brought with her out of Bulgaria and entrusted to you." She gestured helplessly. "Microfilm. Microdots. Code. She has told me nothing except that she preferred risking death to abandoning it."

Anyeta Inglescu laughed. "I see." Lifting her voice she called out, and the boy who had brought Mrs. Pollifax to the tent came inside. "Come here," she told him gently, and taking his hand said to Mrs. Pollifax, "This is what Magda brought out of Bulgaria and left with us."

"I beg your pardon?" said Mrs. Pollifax blankly.

"You did not know that Magda has a grandchild? This is Dmitri Gurdjieff. She smuggled him out of Bulgaria, and entrusted him to us when she went to Istanbul to get help."

"Grandchild?" faltered Mrs. Pollifax. "Dmitri?" She stared incredulously at the boy and then she began to smile and the smile spread through her like warm wine until it merged in a laugh of purest delight. She understood perfectly: she was a grandmother herself. But what exquisite irony for Dr. Belleaux, she thought, that the treasure Magda had smuggled out from the iron curtain was her grandson! "But this is marvelous!" she cried. Gesturing toward the darkness beyond the tent she explained, "Out there secret agents are fighting, bribing, even killing in their greed to learn what Magda brought out with her—and it's a small boy! Nine or ten?" she asked.

"Actually he is eleven," Anyeta said.

Mrs. Pollifax nodded. "I have three grandchildren myself, and you?"

Anyeta laughed. "A dozen at least." They both regarded the boy tenderly, and he smiled at them. "His father is a high Communist official, very busy, scarcely known to the boy, and now he has remarried. Perhaps you did not know that Magda had a daughter born of her first marriage. The daughter died last year. Magda could not leave without the child."

The boy suddenly spoke. "Is not all so."

"What is not all so?" asked the gypsy.

"There is more." He had grown quite pale. Reaching inside his ragged shirt he said, "Is time maybe to speak, Anyeta. There is more."

He pulled out a blue stone tied to a coarse string around his neck. "This."

Anyeta smiled and shook her head. "That is your Evil Eye, Dmitri. It's only part of your disguise. Turkish children wear them to ward off evil."

The boy stubbornly shook his head. "It's more, Anyeta. Grandma gave it me in Sofia."

Anyeta's eyes narrowed. "In *Sofia?*" she said in a surprised voice.

"Da. Is hollow inside—for secrets."

Anyeta drew in her breath sharply. "Allah protect us!" she said in amazement. "I see, I begin to understand . . . but what can it be?"

Mrs. Pollifax smiled. "Her social security, I think," she said, and the last piece of the puzzle fell into place.

Chapter Sixteen

Suddenly Goru was back in the tent, speaking rapidly to Anyeta in an excited breathless voice. Anyeta's eyes narrowed, she nodded and turned to Mrs. Pollifax. "The man with the goatee has finished his work with the radio in the plane and is starting back to the camp. Goru asks you to return quickly to your friends and be tied up again."

In spite of Mrs. Pollifax's horror of being tied again she responded to the firmness and the urgency in the woman's voice. At the door of the tent she turned; Anyeta Inglescu had not stirred from her position. "You're not coming?" she asked.

The gypsy woman smiled. "I cannot walk," she said with a shrug of regret. "I have not walked in fifteen years."

"I'm sorry," said Mrs. Pollifax, surprised.

Goru had vanished; the boy Dmitri tugged at her arm nervously, and he guided her through the rocks back to the tree.

"What the devil!" cried Colin, seeing her. "Didn't you make a dash for it? Mrs. Pollifax, why the hell didn't you try to escape?"

She shook her head. "It's all right, Colin—really."

"All right? He's tying you up again!"

"Yes, I know." She turned and said carefully. "Listen but don't say anything, Colin, there isn't time. This boy understands English."

"*He* does?"

"Ssh," said Mrs. Pollifax as Dr. Belleaux came striding back.

He went first to the campfire and looked down at Magda, then he leaned over, felt her pulse, nodded and straightened. Seeing the gypsies emerge silently from their wagons he gestured them closer and began speaking to them. Eloquently he spread his arms, smiled, frowned, pointed to Magda, then to Mrs. Pollifax and Colin, his voice becoming increasingly edged with contempt and indignation. It was surprising, thought Mrs. Pollifax, how much could be communicated without a single word being understood.

"Born orator," growled Colin. "Real Hyde Park material."

"Can you catch any of it at all?"

"Just the word kill, which occurs with monotonous frequency," said Colin dryly.

Beckoning his audience closer Dr. Belleaux drew them away from the campfire toward the small group at the tree. Within minutes Mrs. Pollifax was surrounded closely and in danger of developing claustrophobia. At this point Dr. Belleaux suddenly drew out a knife; he seemed to be challenging one of the gypsies to use it, and to Mrs. Pollifax's surprise Goru stepped forward and grasped the knife, the gypsies cheering with approval at his move.

Goru ran his fingers over the knife's edge and tested it lovingly. The expression on his face made Mrs. Pollifax shiver. She looked up into the stolid faces of the gypsies and then at the triumphant smile on Dr. Belleaux's lips and she experienced the first chill of doubt. She realized that she had allowed herself to be tied up again, and that she was helpless. She remembered the money taken from her by the gypsy youths . . . it was so very *much* money. Now that Magda had been returned to the gypsies of what value really was she, or Colin, or his uncle or Sandor, compared to the wealth they had brought into the camp? It was wealth that would have to be given back if the gypsies chose to save them. She had trusted Anyeta but the woman was an invalid—had she really any influence? What if Goru chose to disbelieve or to ignore her? For the first time she realized that her being persuaded back to the tree could be a cunning trick, and she a fool to have trusted the persuaders.

Goru suddenly laughed and called out to one of his companions, who brought him a small jug. "*Icki,*" Goru said to Dr. Belleaux, and held out the jug to him. Dr. Belleaux sighed with exasperation as he accepted it. Another gypsy handed jugs to Stefan and to Assim, and at once jugs blossomed everywhere among the gypsies. Apparently a toast had been proposed by Goru—a toast to their murders, wondered Mrs. Pollifax?

"I don't like this," Colin said in a low voice.

Obviously Dr. Belleaux did not like it, either. Impatiently he lifted the jug to his lips, drained it, threw the empty vessel to the ground and spoke sharply to Goru. Goru, sipping his drink like a connoisseur, smiled back at him and smacked his lips appreciatively.

Angrily Dr. Belleaux seized the knife from Goru's hand. *"Budala,"* he snarled and turned to Mrs. Pollifax. "Enough delay!" he said, and looking down at her in a cold fury, he lifted the knife for its thrust into her heart.

Behind him no one stirred. The gypsies watched with a passive, detached interest, and Mrs. Pollifax realized they were not going to stop her murder. Dr. Belleaux's livid face came close and she gasped, bracing herself against his blow, and then she gasped again as he continued a headlong descent and pitched into her lap, the knife still in his hand, his body limp. He twitched once, and then was still.

"They will sleep for eight hours, they are not dead," Anyeta was explaining to Colin and Mrs. Pollifax. "We would be fools to kill a *gorgio*, the police are our enemies everywhere, like fleas forever on our backs."

An unbelievable amount of activity was taking place in the gypsy camp; Anyeta had been carried from her tent to a wagon where she sat on a cushion giving orders in a low husky voice. Her tent had been struck and packed away, and the two campfires extinguished and raked. Horses were being harnessed to the wagons, and the three casualties of the night—Magda, Sandor and Ramsey —had already been stowed carefully away in one of the wagons, wrapped in blankets and still unconscious.

"We have our own drugs, but kinder than theirs because they are herbs as old as time," she explained with a flash of a smile. "The three men will sleep dreamlessly for eight hours, and wake up refreshed. By then we must be far away."

"But where did your men carry them?" asked Colin.

"To the plane, where they have been strapped into the seats. They will make a peaceful picture when they are found. Now it is time to ask you an important question: You have found us, and you have found Magda's grandson, and soon she will open her eyes to see him, too. What do you plan to do with her?"

Mrs. Pollifax explained their hopes that Magda might be alert enough to be placed on the Friday plane at Kayseri.

"She has passport?"

"She has passport, ticket, money and clothes."

Anyeta smiled broadly. "Not money." She shook her head. "Yule!"

The youth who had robbed Mrs. Pollifax ran over, and Anyeta held out her palm. The young man grinned handsomely, brought the wad of bills from his pocket and bowed as he placed them in Anyeta's hand.

"He is very skillful, we are proud of him," Anyeta told Mrs. Pollifax. "But of course we do not steal from friends. Count it." She affectionately boxed his ears and he ran off to help with the loading. "So. You wish to take Magda to Kayseri. That is good— we head in that direction. What is more difficult is a place to hide for a day or two. You say Friday?"

"Yes. It must be Thursday by now. The plane leaves Friday morning at eight. The next plane is Monday, but who knows what could have happened by then?"

Anyeta nodded. "No hiding place is safe for that long! A place for us all to wait safely, then, during the daylight hours today. Yes I know of one, but far—we must go straight as the eagle flies toward the rock country near Ürgüp. From there it will take only hours to walk or ride to Kayseri, and it will be dark again when the time comes to get her to the airport." She nodded. "Very good."

A long shrill whistle broke the silence. "We are ready to go," Anyeta said. "We go cross-country, avoiding all roads."

Mrs. Pollifax took leave of her and hurried to the wagon in which her friends lay. Colin climbed into the van—he was to drive it a few miles from the scene and leave it hidden, to be found later. The wagons formed a line. From the lead wagon in which Anyeta and Goru rode there came a shout, and six wagons began to move into the night with only the stars to guide them south.

There was no tarpaulin over the wagon in which Mrs. Pollifax rode, and she could feel the softness of the cool night air on her cheeks. The wagon creaked and groaned over the untilled, rocky ground but the movement and the creaks were not unpleasant, and as her eyes adapted to the darkness Mrs. Pollifax could decipher rocks and boulders to left and right, and at last the silhouettes of her companions. Magda was beginning to stir at last, to fling out a hand and murmur occasional unintelligible words. The silhouette of dark curly hair beside her was Dmitri—her grandson, Mrs. Pollifax repeated to herself, still touched and amazed by the discovery. Colin drove the van that whined in low gear behind them while his uncle snored peacefully on the floor of the wagon, sharing a blanket with Sandor, who had also slipped into the exhausted sleep that still eluded Mrs. Pollifax.

Magda called out sharply, and Mrs. Pollifax crawled over Sandor and Ramsey to look at her. Dmitri was leaning over speaking to her, and Magda said, "It's you? It's really you, Dmitri?" in a wondering and astonished voice.

"Good morning," said Mrs. Pollifax. "I believe it's morning!"

Magda began to laugh. "And you too? No no, it is too much," she gasped, and reached for Mrs. Pollifax's hand. "Again you have rescued me. And found Dmitri!"

"It's been a long night," admitted Mrs. Pollifax, "but I had a great deal of help: Colin and Sandor, Colin's uncle, a girl named Sabahat and your gypsies."

Magda's laughter abruptly turned into tears, and then into exhausted, wrenching sobs.

"It's all right, Dmitri, let her cry," Mrs. Pollifax told the boy, patting his shoulder. "She'll feel better for it, she's been through so much."

Gradually Magda's tears subsided and she slept. She would need that sleep if she was to gain enough strength to board a plane within twenty-four hours—and that, thought Mrs. Pollifax as she crawled back to her corner of the wagon, was the one thing that mattered now. The seriousness of her own plight had dimmed once she had met Dmitri—and then the boy had pulled the Evil Eye from under his ragged shirt to show her, and Mrs. Pollifax had understood that she was of no importance at all to Dr. Belleaux, nor was Magda or her grandson. From the beginning he had been set upon recovering something more. What had Carstairs said? "The mystery is why Ferenci-Sabo's abductors didn't silence her on the spot by killing her—they certainly had no difficulties in gaining access to the consulate, damn it. Obviously Ferenci-Sabo still has more value to them alive."

But not because of Dmitri, Mrs. Pollifax realized. The kidnapped son of a high Bulgarian official would never bring about such a merciless pursuit. At most it would beget inquiries and protests at a government level, but not murder after murder, and certainly not the possible loss of Dr. Belleaux as a highly placed counteragent in Istanbul. Since Magda had not been killed following her abduction it was obvious that the knowledge Magda carried in her head was of less concern to the Communists than what she had carried out with her that was concrete, graspable, returnable and of an almost hysterical significance to them. Only after this had been recovered would Magda be silenced.

"A great deal changed with the invasion of Czechoslovakia," mused Mrs. Pollifax. "Perhaps even Russia's leadership changed, but certainly to the western world she turned suddenly irrational, paranoiac, unpredictable. As to what might be sealed inside that innocent-looking blue stone I can only guess, of course. What might it be to prove so threatening to the Communists? Transcripts of a terribly secret conversation? a photostatic copy of the minutes of a Politburo meeting? It would have to be an important clue as to what happened that August, and what can be expected in the future, and this would matter a great deal to NATO, to Yugoslavia and Rumania, to future nuclear pacts, to the balance of power."

Magda and her blue stone had to be gotten out of Turkey.

Not even Dmitri could be involved in the departure now. Perhaps Colin could look after the child until he had acquired the necessary papers to travel. She had no illusions as to what lay in store for herself, and jail would be no place for the boy.

The caravan halted, and Goru went to the rear of the line and spoke to Colin; the van was directed off the road, and several minutes later Colin jumped into the wagon beside Mrs. Pollifax carrying the van's battery in his arms. "Good lord what terrain!" he gasped. "Thought I'd have to abandon her long before this! No wonder roads are called the lifelines of civilization."

"Where did you leave the van?" asked Mrs. Pollifax curiously.

"There's a deserted village in there—Anatolia is pockmarked with them. A well runs dry, the people just move on and start a new village. I rammed the truck into one of the buildings that still has a roof." He glanced up at the sky. "It's just past three now, you know, it'll be dawn in an hour or so, and there's that damn helicopter to worry about as soon as it's light."

"Yes, the helicopter," sighed Mrs. Pollifax.

They dozed uncomfortably for another hour. Just as the country around them was growing visible in the cold first-light they crossed a main road, the first Mrs. Pollifax had seen since they left Yozgat. They crossed it wagon by wagon, with Goru waving each one on or back. Then they resumed their interminable procession southward. It must have been the Kayseri-Kirsehir road, Colin said drowsily, but Mrs. Pollifax only half-heard him.

When she opened her eyes again Magda was awake, propped up against the side of the wagon with one hand resting on Dmitri, who had fallen asleep with his head in her lap. The sun was rising with an explosion of colors that swept the sky like a wash of watercolor. Mrs. Pollifax looked at Magda and saw that her eyes were fastened almost hypnotically on Colin's sleeping uncle. Seeing Mrs. Pollifax sit up Magda lifted her free hand and waved at her, but it was with a puzzled frown that she said, "This man here—I do not understand where he came from."

"He—just arrived," said Mrs. Pollifax with humor.

"He so much resembles someone I once knew."

"He does?"

Magda nodded. "Someone I've not seen in—oh, twenty-five years at least. Many times I've wondered what happened to that man—one does, you know," she said with a faint smile. "Yet I believed I'd forgotten him until I saw this man. That same beak of a nose—"

Mrs. Pollifax looked at Uncle Hu buried in his blanket and said with a twinkle, "His nose is all one *can* see of him. Who is the man he reminds you of—a good sort, I hope?"

Magda nodded. "I have loved only two men in my life. There was my first husband Philippe—they called him the rich French playboy but it was the big performance with him because he too was an agent." She looked across the tangle of sleeping bodies at Mrs. Pollifax. "You understand he worked for his government—the French—in Intelligence. We had one year together before he was murdered."

"By whom?" asked Mrs. Pollifax.

"They were called Reds then," said Magda. "Only they did not just murder him, they arranged it to appear I had done their work. He was shot with my small pistol, still with my fingerprints on it, and there had been arranged false evidence of a lover." She shrugged. "It was blackmail. I would have preferred to kill myself but I was expecting a child, which revived my interest in living. And they did not know I already worked for my husband's people. I took my problem to French Intelligence."

"So that's when you became a double agent."

"Yes," Magda was silent, and then, "At least until World War Two when I work also with America and England." Her lips curved ruefully. "One does not expect to love a second time. I did not believe I had the heart left."

"But you did?" suggested Mrs. Pollifax with interest.

Magda sighed. "One cannot control such matters, eh? It was only an encounter, a passing thing, it was all it could mean with me because by then I was vulnerable, my daughter a hostage growing up in Russia." She frowned. "I have learned that one's life assumes a pattern—call it karma if you will. At every turning point in my life I am always thrust back into this work, as if a firm hand insists upon it. It has not been my karma to be either wife or mother for long."

Mrs. Pollifax said, "Perhaps it is now. As I understand karma —and the subject has interested me lately—a person can eventually work through to another level, isn't this true? There are karmic debts to be paid, but if one manages them well, and cheerfully, there comes a time when one moves on to a new level, a new beginning, a different karma."

"You speak as if you feel this," said Magda curiously.

Mrs. Pollifax laughed. "I can only tell you that suddenly— after quiet years of marriage and family life, and at my age, too!—I have entered a very dangerous profession. It's preposterous, as if the page of a book had been abruptly turned over by the wind. Mistake? Coincidence? Accident? There feels more to it than that. Perhaps I enter your kind of life just as you leave it for something else now."

"I could hope this for me," said Magda soberly.

"Do keep hoping," said Mrs. Pollifax, her gaze falling on Hu Ramsey with humor and a touch of mischief. She thought that just when life appeared to have no discernible pattern there could ar- rive a coincidence so startling that one could envision Forces tug- ging, arranging, balancing, contriving and contracting all the arrivals and departures of life. Magda and Colin's uncle had met once, years ago: now they met again through the most absurd of coincidences in the center of Turkish Anatolia. Mrs. Pollifax chuckled; it was so statistically impossible that she thought it had to be an act of cosmic humor, even of cosmic playfulness.

It was growing dangerously light when a shout came from a wagon up ahead. Goru stood up and waved, pointed, and Mrs. Pollifax understood that they were reaching their destination. She looked again at the high cliff that she had been examining from a distance for some time; now it rose sharply above them on their right, appearing to almost touch the sky. Here and there holes had been punched through the cliff by a giant hand, like a great wall with windows in it. Mrs. Pollifax sat up, alert and interested.

In the rubble that spilled down from the cliff like lava she could make out the shapes of crumbling houses; the hill running up to the cliff was honeycombed with caves, holes and the ruins of abandoned buildings. The wagons ahead had already begun to turn and head up the hill through the debris in a circling, ascending line. "What a wonderful hiding place!" said Mrs. Pollifax. "Unless —" She paused doubtfully. "Unless it's so good that it becomes the first place Dr. Belleaux looks for us."

Colin shook his head. "Not the first. I've driven through this part of the country with Uncle Hu, and it's even more dramatic further along. The rocks fairly jump out of the earth like weird stalactites. At Göreme they're called fairy tale chimneys—the early Christians hid in those rock chimneys centuries ago, hollowing them out inside and carving air holes and windows. They left behind fantastic Byzantine frescoes on their interior walls. The whole valley is full of surprises."

"Really? I wish I'd pinned the guidebook to my trousers."

"You ran out of pins," Colin reminded her.

The first wagon had reached the summit, and Goru had climbed out, looking small and doll-like against the great height of the wall behind him, and separated from the rest of them by the mountain of rubble. Their own wagon was lurching and slipping now as it followed the narrow rock-strewn path upward toward the top. Mrs. Pollifax clung to the sides of the wagon and prayed. Each time she looked ahead, a wagon in the line ahead had disappeared and she could only hope that it had safely reached Goru and been directed out of sight, and had not instead plunged into a hole or rolled back down the hill. They climbed higher and higher until Goru came into sight, suddenly his own size again. They had reached the top of the rubble, with the cliff above them.

By a curious freak of nature there was no rubble close to the cliff wall, and a kind of primitive, washed-out road curved up and down behind the houses that had once been built into the hill and inhabited. But as the wall had eroded over the decades—perhaps even centuries—the rocks and silt it sent down had fallen upon the houses, missing the small avenue directly under the wall, but leaving holes in the roofs that it did not completely demolish, and piling debris around the sinking homes. Along this primitive avenue the wagons had stopped, each in front of a ruin that still boasted a roof or half-roof while the men dug out rocks to allow their wagons inside. One by one Mrs. Pollifax saw the wagons backed out of view.

Their driver was Yule, who leaped down and began shouldering aside rocks—they were now the only wagon exposed. Colin jumped down to help, and behind her Mrs. Pollifax heard a startled voice say, "Wotthehell!"

"Sandor," she murmured, smiling, and turned.

Sandor was sitting erect rubbing his head but his eyes were on Magda and Ramsey. Mrs. Pollifax saw that these two were both awake and staring at each other with interest and astonishment; she had the impression that they must have been mutely observing one another for some time.

Colin's uncle said abruptly, "You're thinner. You never did care sufficiently about meals—no schedule at all. If you'd married me I should have insisted upon your eating. Why didn't you?"

"Why didn't I which—marry you, or eat?"

"You should have done both, you know. I've felt damnably juvenile not marrying all these years, but there's simply been no one to equal you. Why didn't you marry me?"

"I had a daughter in Russia."

"You could have told me, couldn't you?"

"Never," she said fondly. "You know you would have charged the Kremlin, Hugh, demanding she be brought to England—you would have gotten your head chopped off."

"It's France that has the guillotine, in Moscow I think it would be a firing squad," he reminded her.

Sandor was grinning broadly. He climbed past them to Mrs. Pollifax. "She knows him too!" he said.

At that moment someone shouted, and Goru came running toward them looking visibly alarmed. Ramsey spoke to him in Turkish and looked appalled. "It's the plane!" he shouted. "Get the wagon hidden! There's a plane on the horizon heading this way!"

Chapter Seventeen

Two men appeared from nowhere and took away the horse. Five more men raced from a hole in the rocks and actually lifted the wagon over a wall of tumbling stone and into the cellar of a house. The wagon sustained only one casualty—a wheel fell off—but the miracle was that it had not happened sooner.

Their hiding place was not unpleasant. The brilliant morning sun fell through the half-ruined floor in lattice-work squares and stripes. There were stone walls on three sides of them, and half a roof over their heads but the front of the house had long since vanished, and from the shadows Mrs. Pollifax had a breathtaking panoramic view across the valley. It was like hiding under a porch that had been swept to the top of a mountain.

From here Mrs. Pollifax could see the helicopter move slowly across the valley in the tilting, gliding, oddly tipsy fashion that to Mrs. Pollifax confounded all laws of air flight. It drew nearer, disappeared behind the cliff and then suddenly roared down over their heads. For a full moment it hung suspended over them, a giant eye searching for one tell-tale slip, one unexplained shadow, one sign of careless movement. It was frightening. When it lifted and began to beat its way slowly down to the other end of the cliff Mrs. Pollifax realized that she had been holding her breath. She expelled it slowly, realizing that this could happen again and again during the day. It was not a happy thought.

Magda said suddenly, angrily, "I cannot take a plane tomorrow morning and leave Dmitri to this. Never."

Mrs. Pollifax turned and looked into her face. The helicopter had affected her in the same way, delivering them all into a nightmare inhabited by birds of prey that swept down from the sky to look for them. "Yes, it's time to make plans," she said firmly. "Let's go and find Anyeta. The plane is gone?"

Colin nodded. "It disappeared southward."

"Good. We'll talk."

They formed a circle inside the cave in which Anyeta had taken refuge. "We move at dark," Anyeta said. "Goru says that will be about nine-thirty tonight. It will be necessary to move slowly in order to be careful, and because the way is not familiar. Goru does not know where the aerodrome is at Kayseri."

"I do," said Hu Ramsey. "Fortunately it's to the west of the town—on this side of it—so that there's no need to go through Kayseri. Look here, if I went back and got the van—"

"I used up nearly all of the spare gas last night," said Colin. "I'd calculate about ten more miles of gas are left in the tank. Twelve at most."

"Damn," said Uncle Hu mildly. "Colin, you know how far away the van is. Where would the nearest petrol station be?"

"Nearest to the van, you mean? Kirsehir definitely. But if you're thinking of retrieving it to get Magda to the aerodrome then you've got to remember that the search for the van may not have been called off yet. The license may still be on their lists. Someone's bound to stop you again, as they did at Yozgat, and that's perfectly all right if you're alone but if you ever had Magda and Mrs. Pollifax with you—" Colin shook his head. "Kaput. Finis!"

Mrs. Pollifax nodded. "He's quite right. I think Magda *must* get to the aerodrome by wagon, the van's too conspicuous."

Magda looked pensive. "I've no reservation for the eight o'clock flight, or even for the London flight. What if there is no room for me?"

Mrs. Pollifax nodded. "We must organize this very very carefully. Like generals plotting a battle."

"Gung ho and all that," suggested Colin, grinning.

"Exactly. Goru, you say you don't know where the aerodrome is. I think someone must go and find it—now, while it's daylight."

Anyeta translated this to Goru, who replied. "He will go himself," she said. "Alone. He will take a horse and find the best route for the wagons, also."

"There's another possibility," went on Mrs. Pollifax "Magda wants to know that Dmitri will not become involved in this. She also needs a reservation for the flight—it would certainly be reassuring to have one for Alice Dexter White clear through to London—and Mr. Ramsey has his van to retrieve, which has in it roughly enough gas to get to Kirsehir." She lifted her gaze. "Mr. Ramsey, if you could take Dmitri with you and reach that van sometime today, then you could drive it to Kirsehir for gas, and telephone the airport in Kayseri for Magda's flight reservations. You could also provide a—well, a diversion. Kirsehir looks quite removed from Kayseri on this map. If the police should stop the van you'd have with you only a small boy picked up on the road. You've already been checked out at Yozgat—it's possible you wouldn't be taken to jail again. You could then drive on to Ankara."

Ramsey shot her a quick glance. "Quite right, of course." He looked distinctly unhappy but it was to his credit, thought Mrs. Pollifax, that he did not protest leaving Magda. He was a man who could accept necessity.

"You would do that?" Magda said hopefully. "Hugh, I cannot tell you how grateful I would be."

"Of course I can do it," he said crisply. "Dmitri, you'll try me out next as a companion?"

"Must?" he said in a dispirited voice to Magda.

She spoke to him gently in Russian and he listened gravely, then with growing brightness. "Da," he told Ramsey, nodding. "I go. I am—how you say—gung ho?"

"Good boy," Ramsey said, ruffling his hair.

"You will need a horse and a guide," Anyeta told him. "Yule will go—he knows where the van is hidden, and he can bring the horse back before night. Anything else?"

They all leaned over the map to pinpoint their present location, the best route to Kirsehir for Ramsey, and the precise area of the Kayseri aerodrome. "Don't head south," Uncle Hu warned Goru. "The police have a station here"—he pointed—"at Inescu. As you can see, that's a little too near for comfort."

Goru nodded and stood up. "*Allaha ismarladik*," he said.

"*Gule, gule,*" said Uncle Hu, shaking his hand.

Mrs. Pollifax was busy thinking. "Magda will need sleep and food today," she told Anyeta. "Near the end of the day I'll fit her into my American clothes, which she can wear under her Turkish ones." Was there anything else, she wondered, mentally ticking off the plans. Magda would still be very weak. If they could reach the airport while it was still dark a wagon could deposit Magda very near to the air terminal without such unconventional arrival being noticed; she could peel off her Turkish clothes, leave them behind in the wagon and walk into the terminal as Alice Dexter White, American tourist. If her reservation had already been made by telephone then she need only pay for it—automatically Mrs. Pollifax felt for the wad of money pinned to her baggy pants and nodded—and then walk through Customs to the lounge.

"A suitcase," said Mrs. Pollifax. "She ought to have a suitcase like everyone else."

"Good thinking," said Colin, "but we've only that horrible cardboard thing Madrali fetched us. An American tourist carrying *that would* be frighteningly conspicuous."

Uncle Hu said, "Wait a minute, I can contribute one from the van—Yule can bring it back with him tonight. It's old and battered, I've kept film in it for years but it's definitely Bond Street and very British."

"Then that's it, isn't it?" announced Colin.

Anyeta produced a pair of crutches and joined them as they walked outside to see the horses saddled. Goru was just leaving, and she called out to him; he nodded and waved. "I told him to make his way to the end of the cliff, following the shade, so that if the plane should come back and see him there would be no sign of where he came from. You must do the same, Mr. Ramsey."

He nodded absently and turned to Magda. "You will be careful," he said flatly.

"I will be careful."

"It's not easy to leave you when I've just found you. You'll wait for me and Dmitri in Scotland?"

She nodded.

He leaned over and held her for a moment silently, and then he turned to Dmitri, smiled and said, "Well, Dmitri? We begin a long journey, you and I."

For a moment Dmitri and Magda clung to each other, and then he carefully removed the Evil Eye from around his neck and passed it over his grandmother's head. "Now is yours to guard," he said.

One of the men stationed above them on the cliffside shouted words down to Anyeta. "He says there is no sign of the plane, it is time you go quickly."

Lifting Dmitri to the saddle of his horse Ramsey said firmly, "We mustn't keep Yule waiting. Off we go, Dmitri. Gung ho, what?"

When they had disappeared along the cliff Mrs. Pollifax and Colin lingered outside to look out over the bright, sunlit, dusty valley. "Tomorrow at this time," began Mrs. Pollifax, seating herself on a crumbling wall.

"Yes?" said Colin, joining her.

She shook her head. "It's what makes sleep so impossible—the waiting," Mrs. Pollifax explained. "The not-knowing." She stared across the valley, her eyes narrowed against the brilliance of sun on whitened rock. "I love this part of the country," she said suddenly. "I've never seen anything quite like it. I had thought Turkey so dark—"

"Its history is dark."

"But look at it—everything sun-baked, the color of cream and old lace and ripe wheat and bleached rock and yellow grass, and then this brilliant blue sky and every now and then clumps of green the color of jade. I do wish I were an artist. What on earth are you scribbling?"

Colin grinned. "I intend to spend this endless day of ours shooting film, and I'm jotting down your adjectives. Uncle Hu could use them. He does his own narrations, you know."

"Would I get residuals?" asked Mrs. Pollifax with interest.

"Would you insist on it?"

"No."

"Good," said Colin briskly, "because I'm sure Uncle Hu doesn't even know what the word means, and the most you could expect would be a thank-you note."

He added firmly, with a confidence she'd not heard before, "I've decided there's something I can do to pay Uncle Hu back for his kindnesses, and that's to film the gypsies. You may not realize it, but in all his years in this country he's never been able to catch more than a passing shot of them from his car." He added dryly, "You can perhaps understand the difficulties in approaching them now. It's bothered him excessively. Now at last he has the opportunity to spend a day with them, film them, make friends with them, and damned if he's not off on an errand of mercy. The chance of a lifetime and he's missing it! I'm going to ask Anyeta if I can poke around filming her gypsies today."

"I'll come with you," said Mrs. Pollifax.

The hours of the day were long but not unpleasant. In mid-morning they ate warmed-over *domatesli pilaf* heated by Anyeta on a small, almost smokeless charcoal brazier. The horses were fed. Sandor took over the mending of the damaged wagon wheel and Colin roamed ubiquitously over the cliff with his camera, popping in and out of caves and cellars, following Magda and Mrs. Pollifax to the well when they drew water for Anyeta, filming the gypsy children at their play and the women at work.

The helicopter did not return but twice a small plane flew over, sending everyone into hiding until it was gone. "Police, I think," said Colin, squinting up at it through holes in the roof, and Anyeta sent out orders to double the lookouts posted on the cliff.

"She is a queen, you know—literally," Magda said during a moment when Anyeta ventured out on crutches to oversee the wagon's mending. "It is she who holds all the people together. Not only these, but many more."

"Queen of gypsies!" mused Mrs. Pollifax. "And now I have met one personally . . . She comes from Bulgaria?"

"Oh no," Magda said firmly. "No, I am not the only person she smuggled out. The gypsies in Bulgaria—it is a country very close to Russia ideologically—are being absorbed into Bulgarian life. They allow no nonsense, the Bulgars, and the gypsy children are made to go to school, to conform, to put aside their heritage and become good workers in the Bulgarian Communist life. It troubles the older ones. No, Anyeta and Goru also smuggled out illegally some of the Rom who wished to leave. Not many but a few."

"Not all of the eastern European countries are so rigid then?" asked Mrs. Pollifax.

"Oh no! Anyeta's roots are in Rumania, and from Rumania the gypsies wander freely into Yugoslavia over the mountains, and from there into Italy or western Germany."

"How did she lose the use of her legs—polio?" asked Mrs. Pollifax.

Magda laughed. "That is something not even I can discover! But it is said by the Rom that her gift for clairvoyance tripled when she lost the power to walk—as if all her strength went to this gift for the psychic." She shook her head admiringly. "She is an astonishing woman. When I first met her—"

"Where?" asked Mrs. Pollifax eagerly.

"It was in Budapest many years ago, in a cafe, and she was wearing pearls and diamonds. I was stunned to learn she was an Inglescu." Magda looked at Mrs. Pollifax and nodded. "Is this not amazing? Can you see her in diamonds? It is the wonder of life, such things. Perhaps you have heard of—?" She mentioned the name of a European concert violinist.

"Indeed I have," said Mrs. Pollifax. "I heard him play years ago in Carnegie Hall on one of his few American tours."

Magda nodded. "He was half-gypsy, you know. That was Anyeta's husband. But she is *all* gypsy, and grew sick from the *gorgio's* life. I hear that she became very thin, very pale, very sad, and nearly died. She had to come back to her people."

"To this," said Mrs. Pollifax reflectively, looking out at the sun and the white rocks. "I can only barely understand. Two days ago I wouldn't have understood at all."

Magda said softly, "The gypsies have a song—the words go like this:

> *Worldly goods that possess,*
> *Own and destroy you.*
> *Love must be like the blowing wind.*
> *Capture the wind between walls*
> *and it becomes stale.*
> *Open tents.*
> *Open hearts.*
> *Let the wind blow . . ."*

They were silent and then Mrs. Pollifax nodded. "Yes," she said quietly.

* * *

Magda slept, and seeing Anyeta watch her Mrs. Pollifax said curiously, "Does your gift for clairvoyance tell you anything?"

Anyeta was silent and then she said reluctantly, "I get no picture of Magda on a plane. Something is in the way, something intrudes. I am uneasy . . ."

Night came swiftly, like a blanket tossed over the plateau abruptly snuffing out the twilight. Yule had returned leading the spare horse. Yes, the Englishman and Dmitri had reached the van in midafternoon and he had watched while the battery was put in and he had seen the van leave. Its dust had been visible for some miles, and he was sure the two had reached the Kirsehir road successfully. Goru did not get back until dark; he had seen many police patroling the roads but he had avoided them and discovered the aerodrome. He had also found a valley through the mountains that would take them through the rock country without crossing any major roads. He looked exhausted, and Mrs. Pollifax guessed that he had combed the whole valley for the best route. He would have made a wonderful general, she thought, glad that he was on their side, but of course he was already Anyeta's guerrilla chieftain as he moved the gypsies over borders and through hostile countries. She watched him touch Magda on the shoulder and smile at her, and she realized the many years these people had known Magda, building a relationship that was tolerant and free and fiercely loyal.

Under her Turkish baggy pants Magda wore Mrs. Pollifax's knit suit and blouse. Now Mrs. Pollifax gave her passport and money. "In case we are separated," she said, trying not to remember Anyeta's uneasiness.

They moved out a little after ten o'clock. There had been some discussion of three wagons heading south to divert attention, but this had been quickly vetoed. Anyeta said flatly, "We Zingari stick together. We live, breathe, eat, die together. We also fight together." Mrs. Pollifax was inclined to be grateful for this. It was true that six wagons made more noise, were less mobile and more conspicuous but she too felt more secure with a full complement of gypsies around her. They were a formidable group to defy, as she knew personally from the previous evening.

They bypassed the town of Ürgüp and moved across the valley into the shadows of *Topuz Dagi* that unyieldingly guarded the eastern perimeter, its peak remote and sharp against the stars. The sky was brighter tonight. "There'll be a moon later," Colin said. "It must already be rising behind that mountain range."

"How far is it to Kayseri in miles?" asked Mrs. Pollifax.

He shook his head. "Too far for wagons moving this slowly, but perhaps Goru plans to camp at some point along the way and continue on horseback. Or perhaps this is a shortcut. It's hard to tell by the map."

Magda said firmly, "Trust Goru. He fought with Yugoslav partisans during the second world war, he can be very cunning." She turned to Mrs. Pollifax with a shy smile. "You have already trusted me—you have not asked why I go to Scotland. If I get away."

Mrs. Pollifax laughed softly. "But I knew you would explain if you chose to!"

Magda nodded. "Hugh has a hunting lodge there. If I succeed in getting to London I will send one cable to Washington from the airport and then I shall disappear again. You understand I shall be very stubborn until Dmitri is allowed to join me."

Mrs. Pollifax considered this and nodded. She supposed that one small boy could very easily be overlooked or ignored by governments once they were satisfied, and that even Carstairs could be rendered impotent by a government. "A little friendly persuasion," she said, nodding. "Yes, I understand. I won't ask for the address."

"Thank you."

The wagons jolted and bounced and creaked, it was very like their journey the night before, the cold following a day of heat, the same stars overhead, same sounds of muffled voices. But the radiance of the hidden moon gave an almost Biblical quality to the procession of primitive wagons moving across the austere, harsh countryside. The earth here was called *tuff*, Colin said, composed of ashes and mud and rock; there were no trees, its only fruit was the rocks, and there were so many of these that at times it became necessary to climb down from the wagons and lift them over boulders.

Sometime around two o'clock the line stopped and rough bread and jugs of water were distributed while Goru walked up and down the line checking wheels and axles on the carts. No one spoke above a whisper and the line moved on again soon. It was incredible country: the moonlight picked out whole forests of needle-shaped rock, a valley of rock chimneys arising white under the moon, a cluster of cone-shaped hovels like beehives.

It was four o'clock in the morning when word swept up and down the procession that they were being followed by a man on horseback. For the first time Mrs. Pollifax realized that Goru had scouts ahead and behind them but this realization came late to reassure her. The news of a pursuer struck her as inexplicable and ominous.

"It could be Sebastien," Colin said hopefully.

"Sebastien," repeated Mrs. Pollifax, remembering Yozgat. "Yes, it could be Sebastien," she said politely.

"One person on horseback is scarcely a threat to some thirty gypsies," Colin pointed out. "Why doesn't Goru stop and find out who it is?" He jumped down. "I'll walk ahead and ask."

He was back several minutes later wearing a frown. "Whoever it is he stays behind us at some distance. It was thought a coincidence at first—someone's trail crossing ours—but the rider takes the same turns, the same trails. Goru says there isn't time to stop, it's half-past four and the important thing is getting Magda to the aerodrome before eight."

"Quite so," Mrs. Pollifax said with feeling.

But uneasiness permeated the caravan. The line moved faster, and when a wagon needed help over the rocks there were sharp words exchanged. Yet whoever followed showed no sign of moving closer to them. Nothing changed except the sky, which was whitening with dawn, and the terrain which grew flatter as the rocks thinned. They were leaving the volcanic country behind them and returning to the flat and dusty Anatolian plateau. Somewhere on this plateau, between them and the foothills of the high mountains in the distance, lay Kayseri and the airport.

"How far now?" asked Mrs. Pollifax of Colin.

"I don't know," he said shortly.

"Then what time is it?"

"A few minutes after five."

As he said this Goru lifted his hand and called out a sharp command from the front, the sound of his voice startling after so many hours of caution. In the east the sky had turned into mother-of-pearl and the tip of an orange sun was lifting itself over the peak of the mountains. Goru was waving them to a halt because two men on horseback were approaching them from the north.

"They're in uniform," Mrs. Pollifax said as they drew closer, not hurrying but keeping their horses to a steady walk.

"The constabulary," Colin said shortly. "Rural police."

"Oh," said Mrs. Pollifax.

The two men rode up to Goru, their faces not unfriendly. They looked pleasant, relaxed, two men on normal patrol. For a few minutes they exchanged words with Goru and then, while one man continued idly conversing, the other rode slowly up and down the wagon line looking into the faces of the gypsies and glancing over and into the wagons. He rode back and the three-way conversation continued endlessly. Goru nodded and stood up, calling out to the gypsies.

Casually Sandor strolled back to them from Anyeta's wagon in which he was riding. He said, "They wish to see all identity cards."

"But this is going to take a long time!" said Mrs. Pollifax despairingly.

"Yes."

"Why the devil can't we just tie them up and take them along?" asked Colin irritably. "I still have Stefan's pistol!"

Sandor grinned. "What a lion you are! You wish them to know we have something to hide? When a police sees gypsies he either spits and rides on, or stops to see what they have stolen today. Please, a sense of dimension!"

"I think he means perspective," Magda said with a wry smile as she handed Sandor the card of *Nimet Aziz*. Mrs. Pollifax parted with *Yurgadil* and Colin with *Nazmi*, and Sandor carried them back to the police.

There followed an interminable wait, tense with anxiety lest the police ask to question each gypsy personally and discover that three of them were frauds. The police talked on and on while one of them shuffled through the pile of thirty cards, speaking sometimes to Goru or to Anyeta, sometimes to each other. Once they laughed—"Are they telling *jokes?*" whispered Colin indignantly— and then at last the papers were handed back to Goru and the wagons were waved ahead.

But they had been stopped for more than forty-five minutes, and it was now nearly six. Mrs. Pollifax was beginning to wonder if Magda could possibly reach the aerodrome in the two hours remaining to them. Her doubts were silent but she sensed that it was a question that hung suspended over the whole caravan as it moved forward. As for the two policemen, they had ridden off at a gallop and nothing could be seen of them but a cloud of dust.

"*Now* they hurry," said Colin bitterly. "Do you think we passed inspection?"

Mrs. Pollifax said tartly, "It depends on what they were looking for. If they were looking specifically for gypsies then they found them—and also did a brilliant job of slowing us down."

They were tired, hungry and dusty now, but they were apparently nearing a more civilized area: half an hour later they skirted a small village of a dozen buildings steaming in the early morning sun and threaded their way between vineyards into bare fields again. Sandor walked back to them with a new message from Anyeta.

"Goru wishes the wagons to go two-by-two now, one beside the other. This wagon will move next to his." He translated this to Yule, and their wagon bypassed the others and drew abreast of Anyeta and Goru.

Leaning over between wagons Anyeta said, "You must stay close to Magda now." There was a mute warning in her eyes for Mrs. Pollifax. "Very close, you understand?"

Mrs. Pollifax nodded. What did Anyeta see? Of what was she afraid? But it was not only Anyeta: Goru stood up, bracing himself, and tossed a club to Yule across the wagons and followed this with a string bag that contained—of all things—perfectly round, small rocks.

And then Mrs. Pollifax understood: she too heard the helicopter. As she looked up it came darting over the swelling hill ahead of them, delicate, small, yet monstrous, like a blown-up metallic dragonfly.

"So we are to meet the good doctor again," said Colin grimly. "But he's a fool this time! What can he do against so many of us?"

Mrs. Pollifax did not reply. Dr. Belleaux might be many things but he was not a fool. She looked around her thoughtfully. Behind them lay the vineyards. Ahead, to their right, a village graveyard populated a gently sloping, treeless hill. She could see nothing, but her skin prickled uneasily.

Into this the helicopter descended, sending clouds of dust into their eyes. Mrs. Pollifax coughed and ducked her head, drawing her shawl over her nose and eyes. When she peered through a slit of the shawl she saw the helicopter resting lightly on the ground some forty yards away, its blades still whirring, its dust almost blanketing them all. "Why the devil doesn't he turn that blasted machine off!" cried Colin, jumping down. "Get under the wagon or behind it or you'll be blinded by the dust!" he shouted, and held out a hand to Magda and Mrs. Pollifax.

Goru was shouting orders. Everyone seemed to be shouting to someone else. The door of the helicopter opened and Dr. Belleaux and Stefan jumped down with pistols. From somewhere on the right a gun was fired—it came from the graveyard on the hill, realized Mrs. Pollifax—and now she understood Dr. Belleaux's confidence: he had not come alone, he had at last joined forces with the Turkish police.

"*Mon dieu!*" cried Magda as the graveyard came to life and the police began pouring down the hill.

But they were still some distance away, and Mrs. Pollifax realized why Dr. Belleaux had left the engine alive on the helicopter: he had arrived but he was facing the gypsies for these few minutes with only his gun and Stefan's. She saw his uneasiness, his uncertainty, his determination to remain just beside the door of the helicopter lest a quick retreat prove necessary. Goru too, saw this and suddenly appeared from behind the plane. With a club he knocked the gun from Dr. Belleaux's hand.

Stefan whirled on him but at once other gypsies swept forward to surround them. Yule was knocked flat—Stefan was not an incompetent bodyguard—and a club flew into the air.

"To the vineyard! Hide in the vineyard!" shouted Anyeta from her wagon. "Quickly!"

"She's right—hurry!" cried Colin, tugging at her arm.

But Mrs. Pollifax shook her head. There was no future for them hiding in a vineyard, and the police had broken into a run as they crossed the fields. They would be here in a minute or two— three at the most—and it would be the finish for them. Magda would never reach the aerodrome, or her eight o'clock plane to freedom. Instead she was staring at the helicopter, momentarily abandoned and unguarded. It was a small miracle: how often did miracles such as this occur? She said, "Colin, can you fly a helicopter?"

He gaped at her. "God no!"

Magda threw back her head and laughed. "Mrs. Pollifax, you are irrepressible! Do you really think—"

"There's no other way," Mrs. Pollifax said firmly, and began to run, dragging Magda with her.

Colin hesitated, looked helplessly around him, then at the two fleeing women, and followed. Together they ran at break-neck speed around and through the melee of fist-fighters to reach the door of the helicopter. Mrs. Pollifax boosted Magda inside, pulled herself up and turned to give Colin a hand. At the same moment they were seen by the approaching police. A shot was fired and Colin fell back.

"Go!" he shouted. "Go!"

"Of course not!" cried Mrs. Pollifax, still clinging to his hand, and dragged him bodily over the threshold. "Bolt the doors!" she told Magda. "Keep everybody out!"

"But can you drive a helicopter?" asked Magda, leaning across Colin and bolting the doors.

Mrs. Pollifax snapped, "Of course not!" and sat down and looked at the levers. There were two of them, one jutting straight up from the floor, the other running parallel to her leg from behind the seat. She grasped the latter, closed her eyes, said a prayer, and pulled. The helicopter gave a little jump—they were still alive. Heartened, she grasped the second lever and thrust it forward and they hovered several feet from the ground, going nowhere but considerably frightening the people around the plane, who began to scatter. Mrs. Pollifax tackled the levers more sternly, and with a leap they began moving sideways, threatening to level gypsies as well as police. "Courage, Emily," she told herself, and returned to the first lever—and suddenly they were sailing over the heads of the gypsies and the police. "Well!" she gasped, and drew a breath of satisfaction. "Well!" she said, and only wished she could remember what she had done.

"Good God we're up," said Colin weakly.

"Be still, it's bloody but only a flesh wound," Magda told him. "Lie down!"

"Lie down?" Colin said. "Lie down when I've survived being shot only to be abducted in a helicopter flown by a madwoman? Mrs. Pollifax—"

"Ssh," she told him sternly. "Ssh—I'm driving this thing. Now where's the airport?" They were flying at low-level—in jumps, rather like a kangaroo—while Mrs. Pollifax tested levers, trying to find out which took them up, and which forward and sideways.

"Look out!" screamed Magda as they narrowly averted a tree.

The helicopter leaped, dropped, skimmed across a field almost on its side, turned, lifted and settled at a more conservative altitude. "I wish you would speak more quietly," Mrs. Pollifax said reprovingly. "When you shout in my ear I jump and so does my hand and so does the plane."

"Look—there's a highway!" Magda gasped, kneeling behind Mrs. Pollifax.

"Good—we'll follow it," said Mrs. Pollifax. "Colin, what time is it?"

He braced an arm, lifted it and scowled at his watch. "Seven-fifteen."

Magda said, "You're too low, Mrs. Pollifax, we're going to hit the cars." Forgetting to be quiet she screamed, "Look out!"

The plane jumped. Cars scattered to left and to right. Mrs. Pollifax tugged at the first lever that met her hand and they zoomed heavenward. Shakily she said, "We badly need an airport."

"I'm looking, believe me," said Magda.

They flew over Kayseri—it had to be Kayseri—and barely missed the top of a minaret that rose like a needle in their path. "Up!" screamed Magda.

"They build them too high!" shouted Mrs. Pollifax peevishly, pulled the wrong lever and sent them moving crablike back to the minaret. Furiously she tugged at another lever and they went skyward again.

"I see the airport!" cried Magda triumphantly, and there it was, a gloriously clear space a mile or two away decorated with runways and a control tower. "Watch those buildings!" Magda cried desparingly. "We're hovering!"

"I know we're hovering," cried Mrs. Pollifax, "but I can't seem to—" They shot abruptly forward, dropped low, then suddenly lower, the motor died and they came to rest on the ground. "I think we just ran out of gas," said Mrs. Pollifax. "Where are we?"

Magda said calmly, "We've just landed in the middle of Kayseri's public square, and barely missed a policeman directing traffic."

Mrs. Pollifax nodded and opened her eyes. "Yes, I see him," she said with a sigh. "A great many people seem to be looking at us, too."

From the floor of the helicopter Colin said. "Then get moving! Run! Grab a taxi! Leave the rest to me!"

He was quite right, of course. Mrs. Pollifax opened the door next to her, which was happily furthest from the policeman, slid out, extended a hand to Magda and they jumped down. For just a moment they stood hand in hand, blinking a little at the gathering crowd, then with pleasant nods and smiles they made their way to the sidewalk, allowed the crowd to stream past them, and casually slipped down a side street to look for a taxi.

"Head for the ladies room," Mrs. Pollifax told Magda. "Don't wait for me—two of us might draw attention. Go in, peel off your Turkish clothes and bundle them into a wastebasket."

It was precisely 7:35 as they entered the air terminal, and as she saw Magda escape into the ladies room Mrs. Pollifax looked around her and became aware of how they must look to the civilized world following their trip across Turkey by bus, car, wagon and helicopter. She moved humbly into a corner and waited.

Ten minutes later there emerged from the ladies room a thin, erect and distinguished-looking woman with head high, eyes alert and navy knit suit only slightly askew. Mrs. Pollifax smiled approvingly. Magda walked to the flight desk and with exquisite aplomb drew out bills from the shawl she carried over one arm. Several minutes later she reached Passport Control and held out her passport with confidence. The official took it, looked deeply into Magda's face, showed it to his companion officer, stamped it and with a nod returned it.

Not until she reached the door did Magda turn, her glance sweeping the lobby. When she saw Mrs. Pollifax in her dusty baggy pants and shawl her mouth curved slightly. They exchanged a long expressionless glance and then almost imperceptibly Magda lifted one hand in a gesture that could have been a wave or a salute.

It was now 7:55. Mrs. Pollifax moved to the window and watched Magda board the plane, watched the hands of the clock tick away five minutes, saw the stairs removed, the door closed, watched the plane begin to taxi down the runway. It stopped at the beginning of the long runway. "Go, go, go," whispered Mrs. Pollifax. The plane hesitated and then began to move again. As its wheels lifted Mrs. Pollifax slowly expelled her breath, and there were tears in her eyes.

Magda was airborne.

She turned and walked the length of the terminal to the front door. She did not falter when she saw the crowds gathering there, nor flinch at sight of police hurrying inside and barking out orders to the crowd of porters and tourists. As she drew nearer one of the police looked up and saw her and stepped forward.

"Mrs. Pollifax?" he said.

She sighed and nodded. Behind him she saw Dr. Belleaux stepping out of a car. He wore a strip of adhesive across one cheek but aside from this he looked his usual cool, authoritative self.

"You are wanted for questioning in the murder of Henry Miles," he said. "Come with us, please."

Chapter Eighteen

Her cell was small, made of stone and very old but not at all picturesque or pleasant. In fact it smelled. It had been cold and damp when she entered it at half-past eight, and then as the day progressed it became damp and hot with a sticky jungle humidity. There was a jug of water in one corner of the cell but no one brought food; no one came near her at all, for any purpose whatever, and this alarmed her because she had expected to tell her story to the police at once. Now she had no idea of what was happening, or of how much damage Dr. Belleaux might be doing while she was imprisoned here. She knew that Magda's plane had safely left—she had seen this for herself—but Magda could have been intercepted at Ankara or Istanbul, and might very easily be sitting in a cell now, too. The thought of such a defeat appalled her.

The hours crawled by, each of them bringing their own hell of doubt. Was Magda still on the plane? Was she even alive? Did Dr. Belleaux possess the Evil Eye by now? The very fact that no one came to her cell made her wonder if Dr. Belleaux was not exercising a great deal of authority; it was he who could least afford her communicating with anyone in charge here.

But if only *someone* would come! It was maddening to sit here charged with such a small, sad and truthless crime when she had news so explosive, and worries so alarming.

Toward noon she began to pace her cell, staring in exasperation at the tiny window high in the wall, or standing by the door in the hope of hearing footsteps outside. There was nothing. The day grew hotter and the walls of her cell began to literally sweat, the moisture running down and dropping with a soft *phfft* on the stones. Just in case her cell was wired she took to saying in a clear voice every thirty minutes, "I must talk to someone in charge, I

have information for the Turkish government." No one came, no
one listened, there was only heat and silence. After a number of
hours Mrs. Pollifax ceased her pacing and wearily sat down on the
metal bunk, feeling very depressed and extremely hungry.

She had completely lost track of time when the door to her
cell suddenly opened. The light had grown dimmer—it must be
late afternoon, she guessed—and it was difficult to see more than
the outline of the man, who said briskly, "I am sorry, Mrs. Pollifax!
There has been no time to interview you, and you have had a long
wait indeed. You will come with me please to a"—she heard him
sniff—"more agreeable place."

"Yes," she said in a dispirited voice.

He led her down a long, dimly lit dungeon of a corridor and
up worn stairs to a more civilized hall. At an open door he turned
to wait for her. "In here, please," he said. It was a beautiful door—
pure mahogany—and she realized that she was being ushered into
an office. It was a vast improvement. There was sunshine in the
room, as well as fresh air, and much more mahogany. Only the
bars across the windows reminded her that she was still in prison.

She sat down in a leather chair beside his desk and now that
her eyes were becoming accustomed to the light she examined the
man with some surprise. "We've met before," she said abruptly.

"Yes," he said, sitting down and smiling pleasantly at her. "In
Istanbul, at Central Headquarters. I am Mr. Piskapos."

"Of course," she said, recalling the man in plainclothes who
had remained beside the window, scarcely speaking. "May I ask
how Mr. Ramsey is? Mr. Colin Ramsey?"

"Oh yes, the young man found in the helicopter." He nodded. "Just a flesh wound, quite negligible."

"Has he—uh—spoken with you?"

Mr. Piskapos smiled at her with interest. "Now what would
he speak to me about, Mrs. Pollifax, eh?" He leaned over and
flicked on the switch of a tape recorder. "Have some figs," he said,
holding out to her a polished wooden bowl of fruit. "I must question you of many matters. Food will be brought you soon, but you
must be very hungry."

"Thank you," she said, and accepted a fig and held it—it was
a very sticky fig. She realized that after all these hours of waiting
she had finally acquired someone to speak to, and she no longer

had any idea of what to say. She could not think of any questions that might not provoke graver dangers for Magda—or Dmitri—or Colin and his uncle, or the gypsies, or even herself; nor of any answers that would not betray her connection with Mr. Carstairs and his organization.

"But let us get on with this," said Mr. Piskapos, and added calmly, "I am a member of the Turkish Intelligence, Mrs. Pollifax, and so you may speak frankly with me. You are an American agent, are you not?"

She shook her head. "You flatter me, Mr. Piskapos, I am an American tourist."

He nodded. "Then let us not pursue *that* detail any further."

"Thank you," she said with dignity. "Then may I ask—"

"Surely not why you've been incarcerated," he said with a mocking smile.

"On the contrary, I would like to ask what charges you plan to place against me."

"Any charges would be purely academic since your trial has already taken place," he said flatly.

"My trial?" she gasped. "Without me?"

He nodded. "Perhaps the word trial is a poor word, Mrs. Pollifax—the Intelligence department does not have trials. Let us say instead that a hearing has been held—it took a number of hours, which is why I am so late—and you were quite fairly represented, Mrs. Pollifax."

"Indeed?" she said coldly. "And by whom?"

"By Lieutenant Cevdet Suleiman."

She said indignantly, "I've never met a Lieutenant Suleiman, nor has any such man spoken to me, so that I fail to see how he could represent me. This was doubtless a recommendation of Dr. Belleaux?"

Mr. Piskapos beamed. "It is interesting to hear you mention Dr. Belleaux's name," he said. "Supposing you tell me how you happen to know Dr. Belleaux."

"What time is it?"

"Five o'clock." He leaned across the desk and displayed his wrist watch to her in case she doubted him.

Mrs. Pollifax hesitated and then nodded. If it was five o'clock in the afternoon then Magda was either safe or not safe, either landing in London or stalled hopelessly in Istanbul. In any case Carstairs could be left out of the picture: the important thing was to place Dr. Belleaux squarely *in* the picture. "Very well," she said, and began to speak of her arrival in Istanbul to help a friend who had appealed to her for aid by cablegram. "Her name," she said carefully, "was Magda Ferenci-Sabo."

If Mr. Piskapos was startled he did not show it; his eyes remained fixed inscrutably upon the blotter on his desk, he did not even blink.

Thus encouraged, Mrs. Pollifax plunged ahead to describe the events of the past four days. She left out very little except the names of Madrali, the Inglescus, and Sandor. When she had finished Mr. Piskapos flicked off the tape recorder.

"Thank you, Mrs. Pollifax," he said simply.

She found this annoyingly casual. She said, "Thank you for what? The truth? Lies? You don't believe what I've said about Dr. Belleaux?"

At her question he looked up, surprised. "Oh yes."

Jarred, she said, "Yes what?"

He smiled. "Perhaps I should tell you now that Dr. Belleaux is also in this prison—but not as a guest of our police this time. He was captured and booked only an hour after you arrived here, and he is here as a prisoner charged with espionage and treason." He smiled wryly. "At the hearing it was decided—because of this, and because of your work in exposing Dr. Belleaux—that Ferenci-Sabo be allowed to continue unmolested to London."

"Magda is safe?" gasped Mrs. Pollifax.

He said gravely, "We could have stopped her, you understand, but in this particular case the Biblical eye for an eye seemed just. In time, all of her information will be shared with my government, and in turn we have—Dr. Belleaux, as Lieutenant Suleiman pointed out to us."

"This lieutenant," began Mrs. Pollifax.

"However, for the safety of everyone concerned, continued Mr. Piskapos, "we have thought it best that if Alice Dexter White goes free, Magda Ferenci-Sabo must die. Die firmly, and publicly." He drew a sheet of paper from under his blotter. "Perhaps you would be interested in the news release we have prepared for the voice wire services?"

Mrs. Pollifax glanced impatiently at a report of Magda Ferenci-Sabo's death. Piskapos was saying, "You will of course wish to send a cable of reassurance to your superior, Mr. Carstairs, in Washington."

At hearing Carstairs' name spoken Mrs. Pollifax nearly choked on the fig that she had at last begun to eat. "You know—about Mr. Carstairs?" she gasped.

Piskapos laughed. "Obviously it is time that you met Cevdet," he said. He leaned back and smiled at Mrs. Pollifax. "I must explain to you that Lieutenant Suleiman had been lately involved in following a man who entered Turkey illegally, Mrs. Pollifax, and who took a job as valet in the employ of a most noted gentleman in Istanbul—to spy on that gentleman, we thought. The name of the man whom Lieutenant Suleiman was keeping under surveillance was Stefan Mihailic, and the gentleman who gave him employment is Dr. Guillaume Belleaux."

Mrs. Pollifax's eyes widened in surprise. "Dr. Belleaux!"

"Which may explain to you," continued Mr. Piskapos dryly, "how it was that Lieutenant Suleiman happened to be watching Dr. Belleaux's house last Monday night when two strangers rode up in a van containing a corpse, proceeded to burglarize Dr. Belleaux's house and then to carry out a half-conscious woman! Without consulting his superiors—but the man is a genius, of course—Lieutenant Suleiman decided that he must follow you in whatever conveyance he could put his hands on and discover what on earth you were up to. He had no idea who you or Ferenci-Sabo were until—alas—it was far too late." Piskapos smiled. "He seems to have acquired the utmost respect for you, Mrs. Pollifax, a respect, I might add, which my government now shares completely."

He leaned over and said into the intercom, "Send in Cevdet, please."

"I am bewildered," admitted Mrs. Pollifax. "I may be overtired but I simply don't understand."

Mr. Piskapos beamed at her reassuringly. "You will have plenty of time to understand. Lieutenant Suleiman has arranged a party for you all tonight in Ankara . . . for you, the young man Colin, Mr. Ramsey and Dmitri—who are already in Ankara now—and I believe something was mentioned of a pretty young woman from Yozgat. But Lieutenant Suleiman will tell you more of this. Ah, come in, Cevdet, come in!"

The door had opened. A figure in dazzling white linen stood there, a figure vaguely familiar and yet—paradoxically—utterly strange to Mrs. Pollifax. Black hair. A thin stripe of a moustache across the upper lip. Dazzling white teeth. Broad shoulders. This was an incredibly handsome man. Then he moved, and Mrs. Pollifax started. Dimly she remembered thinking—was it only a few days ago?—that even if he shaved and bathed she would recognize him because of his vitality, that bounding step and wonderful zest for life.

"Sandor!" she cried.

Mr. Piskapos stood up and said with a smile, "I would like you to meet Lieutenant Cevdet Suleiman, Mrs. Pollifax, of Turkish Intelligence."

Sandor laughed delightedly. "What the hell, eh, Mrs. Pollifax?" he said, and bounded forward to kiss her heartily on each cheek.

Chapter Nineteen

It was Saturday afternoon in Langley, Virginia, and in his office in the CIA building Carstairs had been staring at a small exhibit on his desk.

There was a hat that had been airmailed to him from Istanbul, discovered by the police on Wednesday in a street bazaar in Ankara. It was a veritable garden of a hat bearing the label of Mrs. Emily Pollifax of New Brunswick, New Jersey, but he had already known this: he had seen it himself on Mrs. Pollifax's head six days ago.

There was Bishop's memo from Pan American Airways stating that no Mrs. Emily Pollifax was aboard today's flight out of Istanbul for London.

There was the wire release torn from the teletype machine with the bulletin that would be tomorrow morning's headline. It was dated Kayseri July 10, and it reported the body of a woman identified as Magda Ferenci-Sabo discovered by a shepherd that morning, near Ürgüp in central Turkey.

And there was the cable that Bishop had handed him only a moment ago, and which Carstairs had just begun to read:

REGRET TO INFORM YOU MAGDA DEAD STOP ALICE DEXTER WHITE IN GOOD HEALTH AND RESUMING TRAVELS STOP PLEASE HAVE READY UPON ARRIVAL PASSPORT FOR DMITRI DEXTER WHITE AGE ELEVEN STOP DELAYING DEPARTURE TWENTY-FOUR HOURS FOR PARTY GIVEN MY HONOR ANKARA STOP HAVING WONDERFUL TIME EMILY POLLIFAX.

Carstairs read it again incredulously. "I don't believe it," he said in a stunned voice.

Bishop chuckled. "It leaves out so much, don't you think?

Such as where she's been for almost a week, and who killed Henry, and how she lost her hat, not to mention her rescuing Ferenci-Sabo—"

Carstairs said incredulously, "What did she do? How did she manage it? I thought she was dead. I thought they were both dead—"

" 'O ye of little faith,' " said Bishop with a grin.

Carstairs shook his head unbelievingly. "No word from Dr. Belleaux. Two agents already murdered. This hat turning up in Ankara of all places—and her passport. How did she get clear across Turkey without a passport?"

Bishop's grin broadened. "What interests me at the moment is who's giving the party in Mrs. Pollifax's honor. The Turkish government, do you suppose?"

"Don't be an idiot," snapped Carstairs, and then as his glance fell to the cable he began to smile. "I'll amend that," he said. "Anything's possible."

He read the cable a third time, and as it dawned upon him at last that Ferenci-Sabo and Pollifax were both safe—and he had lost a great deal of sleep over them the past several nights—he chuckled richly. "Bishop," he said, "find out what twenty-four hours' delay does to Mrs. Pollifax's arrival. She was booked on PanAm all the way, wasn't she? I believe I'll meet her plane personally on Monday."

"Yes, sir. There's one other matter, sir."

"What's that, Bishop?"

"May I come, too, sir?"

The Elusive
Mrs. Pollifax

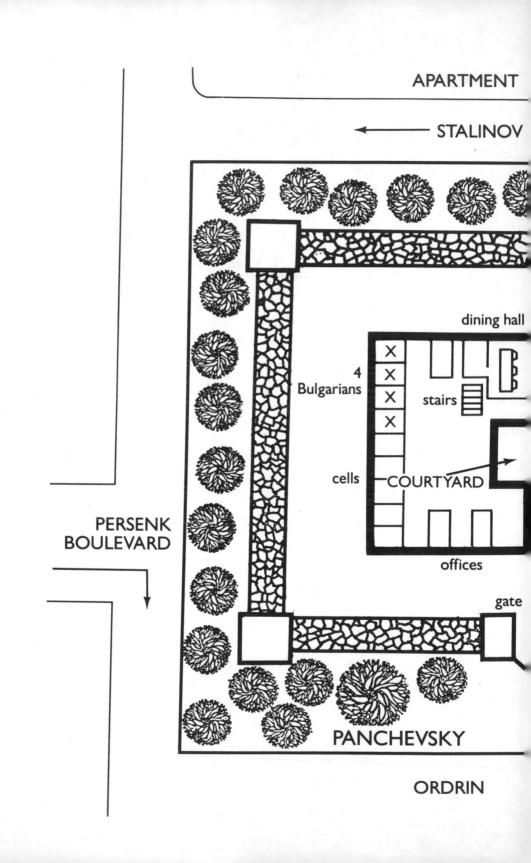

APARTMENT

STALINOV

dining hall

4
Bulgarians

stairs

cells

COURTYARD

PERSENK
BOULEVARD

offices

gate

PANCHEVSKY

ORDRIN

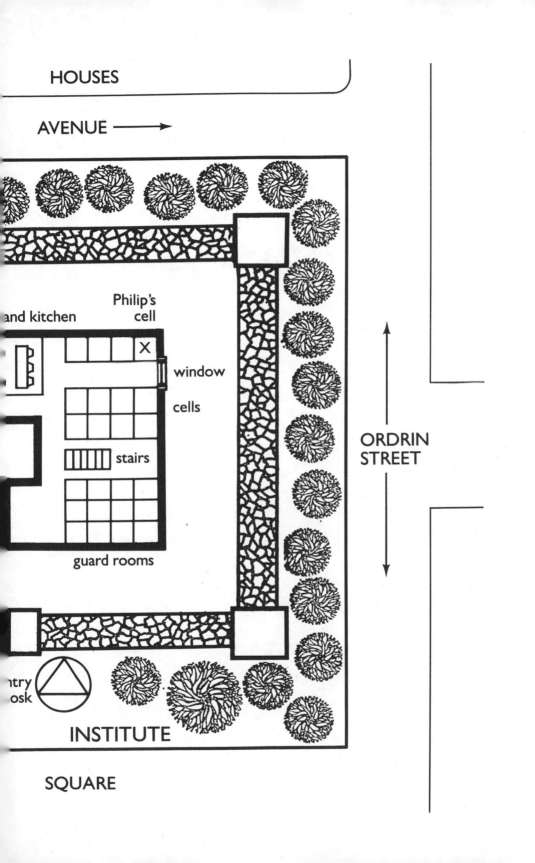

HOUSES

AVENUE ⟶

and kitchen

Philip's cell

X

window

cells

stairs

guard rooms

ORDRIN STREET

ntry osk

INSTITUTE

SQUARE

Chapter One

A small group of friends had assembled in Mrs. Pollifax's living room on this warm July evening. There was Miss Hartshorne from apartment 4-C across the hall; Professor Whitsun from the botany department of the university, and various loyal members of the Garden Club, led by Mrs. Otis, the president. For the last hour—without the slightest embarrassment—they had continued to check both their wristwatches and the clock on Mrs. Pollifax's wall. It was twenty minutes before midnight.

"Do you think *now*, Emily?" asked the president of the Garden Club anxiously.

"Yes, is it time?" asked Miss Hartshorne.

Mrs. Pollifax glanced at the professor for confirmation. He nodded. "Now or never I should say."

"Wonderful," breathed Mrs. Pollifax. "Lights out then, everyone!"

Flashlight in hand, she led the group into the kitchen. The window was open to the sultry night and the screen was already unlatched. Her flashlight played over the grillwork of the fire escape and came to rest on the box under the window. A reverent hush descended upon the group as they hung over Mrs. Pollifax's shoulder.

"It's bloomed," said Professor Whitsun in an awed voice. "I see it!"

"It's in bloom," called Mrs. Otis triumphantly over her shoulder to the others. "It's happened!"

"Turn on the lights and bring it inside," ordered Professor Whitsun. "Gently now. Are my cameras in place?"

Tenderly the window box was lifted to the sill, embraced and carried into the living room, where it was placed in the center of the rug.

"There are *three!*" cried Mrs. Pollifax, dropping to her knees beside a trio of delicate, spiky white flowers.

"So that's a night-blooming cereus," whispered Miss Hartshorne.

"They bloom just once a year, and then only for a few hours," said Professor Whitsun, adjusting the tripod for his camera.

"And Emily grew it on her fire escape," said Mrs. Otis. "Oh, Emily, it's *such* a coup for our Garden Club!"

"Speech," called the corresponding secretary.

"Yes, speech, Emily!"

"Hear! Hear!"

Beaming with pleasure Mrs. Pollifax rose to her feet and gently cleared her throat. "The night-blooming cereus . . ." she began.

At that same hour in New York City, Carstairs of the CIA and his assistant, Bishop, were sitting in a shabby Harlem hotel room under a single twenty-watt bulb suspended from the ceiling. The man they had come to see was slouched wearily on the edge of the unmade bed. His name was Shipkov, and he had just arrived from eastern Europe.

"I want the rest of this taken down in shorthand as well as taped," Carstairs told Bishop. To the man on the bed he added, "You're telling us that a stranger—a complete stranger—gave you accurate directions on just where and how to cross the Bulgarian border?"

The man nodded.

"Tell us again, slowly. Everything."

Shipkov closed his eyes in concentration. "It was in Sofia. I'd gone into a shop and he was waiting outside for me. He said 'Shipkov?' I turned. He began to speak to me in English—that was my first shock. He said, 'Your name is next on the List.'" Shipkov opened his eyes and made a face. "There is only one list in Bulgaria. It's not a healthy one."

"What did you say?" asked Carstairs, watching him closely.

Shipkov shrugged. "For how long have I lived in Sofia without a soul knowing I speak English? I was in shock. I can promise you it chilled the blood, a man calling me by name on the street and speaking to me in this language. I said nothing."

Carstairs nodded. "Go on."

"Next he told me, 'They're at your apartment now. If you go straight to Radzoi and cross the border at 11 P.M. tonight the border will be clear.' All I could think to reply was, 'Radzoi! That's the worst place of all to cross.' 'Not tonight,' he said. 'Not at eleven o'clock.'"

"Did he know you work for us?"

Shipkov laughed bleakly. "How can I even guess? The whole thing was wild."

"All right, go on."

"He said . . ." Shipkov closed his eyes, nodded and opened them. "*If you make it across the border get us help. Some of us care, do you understand? Right now we desperately need passports, identity papers. The arrests grow insane.'*"

"And that's when he gave you the piece of paper with the address and the instructions?"

"Yes. And then he simply walked away down the street."

"Amazing," said Carstairs thoughtfully. "And you'd never seen him before in your life?"

"Never," vowed Shipkov.

"Describe him."

"An educated man, well dressed but shabby. About sixty. Definitely an intellectual. As you can see, the instructions are typed, so he had access to an English typewriter. I'd guess a professor, but how many professors know how to cross the border?"

Carstairs said slowly, "But you would trust this man?"

"I didn't then, I do now," Shipkov answered promptly. "I hurried back to my apartment, as I told you. The police had already arrived. Two men were running up the steps, one stood in my window shouting down to them. Needless to say I bolted."

"And you met no guards at all crossing the border at Radzoi?"

"Not a soul," said Shipkov. "It was like a miracle."

Carstairs exchanged glances with Bishop. "The kind of miracle we like to hear about," he said quietly.

"You want me to go back into Bulgaria with passports?" Shipkov asked. "With a new identity I could do it."

Carstairs shook his head. "*Much* too risky. This will need a courier—a particular kind of courier." He frowned. "Have you any idea how the police got on to you?"

Shipkov sighed. "Too many questions about General Ignatov, I think. I confess to some carelessness there. I got carried away. But something's definitely up."

Carstairs leaned forward. "You discovered more?"

Shipkov nodded. "The general's been courting some of the younger members of the secret police. The new ones, the hero-worshipers. I've seen them going into his house late at night when he's in Sofia. Enough to make up a small cadre of loyal supporters if his ambitions grow any bigger."

Carstairs whistled.

"A dangerous man," Shipkov said, nodding. "Ruthless. A hero, too, after taking Bulgarian troops into Czechoslovakia in '68. The Soviets, they are very impressed with him."

"General Ignatov," mused Carstairs, and then with a glance at Shipkov he brought himself back to the moment. "You need rest, you look like hell," he said, and scrawling a few words on paper he added, "Go to this address, the people there will take care of you. On Tuesday I want to see you in Washington and we'll get the rest of this on tape." He drew bills from his pocket and handed them to Shipkov. "Get some clothes, too—and for God's sake be out of this place in an hour."

"Thanks," Shipkov said, pocketing money and papers. "Sorry I couldn't finish the job, Carstairs."

"Fortunes of war," Carstairs said, rising. "Bishop?"

Bishop finished locking the tape recorder. "Ready, sir."

With a nod to Shipkov they went out, descended dark, cluttered stairs and reached the street.

Chapter Two

When they had walked several blocks in silence Bishop said, "Shall I call a cab now, sir?"

Carstairs shook his head. "No, I don't think we'll be heading back to Washington yet. Get us a car and driver instead, Bishop. I believe we'll take a little drive into New Jersey."

"At this hour?"

Hands in his pockets, brows drawn, Carstairs said, "That was a wild story Shipkov brought us."

"It certainly was."

"What's wildest of all, I buy it," Carstairs said thoughtfully. "Which leaves us with the possibility that some kind of Underground may actually be forming in Bulgaria. And if they need a few passports—"

"Then you need a courier," finished Bishop.

"Exactly." Carstairs turned his face to Bishop and smiled; there was a twinkle in his eye. "Any suggestions?"

Without change of expression Bishop said, "You asked me to remind you, sir, never to use her again. You said she breaks all the rules—doesn't even *know* there are rules—and you age ten years while she's on assignment. In a word, sir, she's too much of a worry to you."

"Nonsense," retorted Carstairs, "it'll be different this time."

"I believe you said that before, too," Bishop pointed out.

Carstairs stopped and glared at him. "Damn it, if I want Mrs. Pollifax, then I'm damn well going to get Mrs. Pollifax. That is, if she can leave her karate and her geraniums," he amended.

"She's not growing geraniums this season," Bishop told him. "I believe she's trying her hand at the night-blooming cereus."

"Good God," said Carstairs, and then he glanced sharply at his assistant. "And how the hell do you know that?"

Bishop grinned. "Oh, we keep in touch, sir. She sent a fruit cake at Christmas—it made several members of the staff quite tipsy. There was a card at Easter, and she sent a knitted muffler in May. My birthday, you know."

"Good lord," said Carstairs, shaken. "Well, get a car and a driver for us and let's go. . . . Night-blooming cereus!" he repeated, and shook his head.

The car was equipped with telephones, and before they had even crossed the New Jersey marshes Carstairs was issuing orders and setting queries in motion. For a few minutes Bishop listened and watched, still fascinated after years of working with the man. He knew that by dawn they would be back in Washington—Carstairs was ordering a helicopter now to meet them at the New Brunswick airport—and the whole operation would be neatly under way and stored between file covers. And in Washington, thought Bishop, there would probably be a new crisis waiting—he closed his eyes and slept.

"Blast," he heard Carstairs say, and unwillingly Bishop opened his eyes.

"These damn budget cuts, this fiendish economy drive," sputtered Carstairs. "I've cleared this with Upstairs, but damned if they don't announce that if I'm sending a courier into Bulgaria with nothing but passports then my courier can jolly well smuggle in a few other items."

"Like what?" asked Bishop drowsily.

"Who knows? Something for that remaining agent we've got in Sofia, whatsisname, chap with the geese—"

"Radev," murmured Bishop. "Assen Radev."

"I'll fight it. I'll blast them. I refuse to share my couriers."

"Mmm," mumbled Bishop sympathetically.

"If you're going to sleep, Bishop," Carstairs told him coldly, "then for heaven's sake sleep and get it done with. I'll give you ten minutes and then let's buckle down to some *real* work."

Like a drowning man—how did Carstairs manage it, he wondered—Bishop clutched his proffered ten minutes and slept.

At two o'clock in the morning they were seated in Mrs. Pollifax's living room in New Brunswick, New Jersey, and she was looking at them as if they had just presented her with the Holy Grail.

"But I'd be delighted—absolutely delighted—to go to Bulgaria," she said, beaming at them, her face radiant.

Her appearance had immediately revived Bishop. She was wearing a voluminous robe of black and white stripes. It looked like a tent; it had probably once *been* a tent because there was a definitely rakish Arab look about it.

"But what an extraordinary story your Mr. Shipkov told!" She hesitated and looked at Carstairs reprovingly. "Should you have mentioned his name to me?"

Bishop grinned across the coffee table at his superior. "Yes, should you have?"

"It is not," said Carstairs pointedly, "his real name."

Mrs. Pollifax nodded. "I'm relieved. And will I travel under an assumed name, too?"

Carstairs shook his head. "No point in being unnecessarily devious. We'd like you to be a straightforward American tourist as usual. In fact this time you can make a public announcement to your friends and children that you'll be off to the Dalmatian coast, with a few days in Sofia. You'll have plenty of time to get ready because I'm scheduling you to leave in about ten days."

"Oh, how nice," said Mrs. Pollifax in a pleased voice. "You can't believe how frustrating it's been, nobody knowing where I go. Miss Hartshorne travels religiously on tours, and this year she's been urging me to visit Turkey—"

Carstairs broke into a laugh. "Turkey!"

"Yes," said Mrs. Pollifax, nodding. "How can I possibly tell her I've seen more of it than she has! There's Albania, too. I am probably the only person in New Brunswick to have visited Albania —even if I *was* in shackles," she admitted, "but my lips are sealed." Abruptly she asked, "But why ten days? Why not sooner?"

"Arrangements," said Carstairs. "They'll have to go by the conventional route. A visa. Letters to Balkantourist outlining what you'd like to see during your five or six days in Sofia."

"Balkantourist?"

"Yes, it's the only travel agency in Bulgaria, and it's run by the government. It *is* the government. They'll arrange your itinerary, they'll arrange everything, as well as watch over you with vast benevolence."

"That's clever."

"Yes, and you must never forget that it's the government watching over you. In fact Balkantourist is going to be your biggest problem, and we'll have to think of something to deflect their interest. Happily, this is their peak tourist season. They've not many English-speaking guides as yet so we'll hope and pray they won't be able to assign you a full-time guide. We'll see what we can come up with. You'll find the people themselves extremely friendly —the country's no larger than Kansas—and warm and nonpolitical, too. But not the government, Mrs. Pollifax. *Not* the government."

"I'll remember that," she said, nodding.

"Now about the passports—"

"Yes," said Mrs. Pollifax, leaning forward eagerly.

"I've always had the impression that you wear hats everywhere except to bed—an illusion I prefer to cherish," he said with a glance at her uncovered head. "I think we'll put them in your hat."

"How inventive!" she said warmly.

"A special hat," he went on. "Custom-made, with a false crown. Two crowns, actually. I've already set this in motion. A chap named Osmonde will call on you to consult about the design. Will Thursday morning at ten be convenient?"

"Perfect," she said.

"Good. . . . Bishop, have we covered the main points?"

Bishop glanced down at the memo beside his coffee cup. "Everything but the most important. The tailor shop."

Carstairs nodded and brought out the piece of paper Shipkov had given him. "Here it is—the original. I suggest you make a copy now."

Mrs. Pollifax looked at the wrinkled piece of paper that had been given to Shipkov on the streets of Sofia. She read:

> Durov, Tailor. Number 9 Vasil Levski Street.
> Brown sheepskin vest.
> Measurements: 40 long, 30 across back.
>   No buttons.

Give name and hotel.
Tsanko will contact you.

At the very bottom of the sheet, almost indecipherable, she read the words, *We beg help.* It was strangely poignant, this message scrawled in pencil on the soiled scrap of paper, and something of its urgency reached her as she sat in her comfortable living room thousands of miles away.

"How many passports can you send them?"

"We're going to manage eight if we can. That will take time, too, since they can't all be American. They'll probably have to be forged. Exquisitely, of course," he added with a smile.

She nodded. "Is the name Tsanko a first or a last name in Bulgaria?"

"First, I think, isn't it, Bishop?"

Bishop nodded.

"There is also . . ." Carstairs hesitated. "There is *always* the possibility that the message isn't authentic, Mrs. Pollifax. I want you to remember that. If you meet with unforeseen circumstances, you're to make a fast exit. Very fast."

"All right." She was copying the message on paper, and without glancing up she said, "I go to this shop and order a vest and then wait to be contacted. When I've given this man Tsanko the passports do I ask for anything from him?"

Carstairs frowned. "There's no bargain involved here, and he'd have every right to be affronted if we insist on anything in return. But if the occasion arises—I leave this entirely up to you—we certainly wouldn't mind learning more about a man named General Ignatov. What's his complete name, Bishop?"

"General Dimiter Kosta Ignatov," said Bishop promptly.

"You understand this Tsanko will probably know nothing. The press is state-controlled over there and the people aren't informed about much of anything," Carstairs explained. "But we'd appreciate your asking."

"I'll be glad to." Mrs. Pollifax completed her notes and handed Shipkov's message back to Carstairs, who stood up. "But you're leaving without finishing your coffee!" she told him.

"We have to. There'll be a helicopter waiting for us at your airport in"—he glanced at his watch—"ten minutes. But I must admit it's been a real experience meeting you in your natural habitat," he said with a grin. "As well as seeing your night-blooming cereus."

"Both the night-blooming cereus and I seem to bloom once a year," she said, smiling and rising, too. "Mr. Carstairs, I shall do my very best in Bulgaria, I really will. You can count on me."

Bishop saw Carstairs open his mouth to speak, wince and close it with a snap. "Yes," he said, and then, "We'll be in touch."

"What were you about to say?" asked Bishop curiously as they descended in the elevator to the street.

Carstairs said testily, "It wasn't anything I was going to say, damn it. I just experienced the most incredibly clear memory—it came over me in waves—of how I worry about that woman when she's away."

Bishop nodded. "Yes, I believe I pointed that out to you only a few—"

"If there's one thing I can't stand it's an 'I told you so' attitude," snapped Carstairs.

"Yes, sir," Bishop said, grinning.

Chapter Three

Mrs. Pollifax's preparations moved along smoothly. The next day she announced to friends and family that she would be flying to Europe soon for a visit to Yugoslavia and Bulgaria. Her daughter in Arizona was appalled. "Mother! Your first trip abroad and you're not going to visit Paris or London? You *must* visit Paris and London!" Jane tended to be somewhat managing, and Mrs. Pollifax braced herself for a long conversation.

Before telephoning her son, Roger, in Chicago, Mrs. Pollifax also braced herself, but for a different reason: Roger was a very intuitive young man.

"Bulgaria," he said now with interest. "You pick the most surprising places, Mother. Not Switzerland, France, Scotland or Belgium?"

"Bulgaria," she said firmly.

"We had the most interesting note from your neighbor Miss Hartshorne at Christmastime," he told her. "She seemed to think that you'd been here with us for a week last summer, and that Martha had been quite ill."

It was not the *non sequitur* that it sounded; Mrs. Pollifax understood him at once. "How very odd of her to think that," she said weakly.

"Wasn't it?" He chuckled. "Whatever you're up to, Mother, I hope it's fun." And with that he blithely hung up.

The gentleman named Osmonde arrived on Thursday at ten o'clock, and was thoroughly enjoyable. Mrs. Pollifax fed him tea and macaroons and was struck by his conscientiousness: he insisted first upon seeing, measuring and photographing the coat she would wear with the hat. "For the blending, the amalgamation," he said vaguely, and she obediently buttoned herself into the quilted brown travel coat that she intended to wear on the trip.

About the hat she was as doubtful as he. Every design that he sketched looked top-heavy and he agreed this would be a problem. "You'll be carrying almost fifteen ounces in the hat," he pointed out. "Distributed, of course. Pillbox? Derby?" He sighed. "It offends the aesthetics."

"What will you do?"

"The hat itself must be very light in weight, yet look heavy enough—complicated enough—to explain its odd bulk. Perhaps a wire structure with two-inch roses covering it?"

Mrs. Pollifax winced.

"A polyethylene motor helmet?" he suggested, pencil flying, and then after a glance at Mrs. Pollifax—her cheerful round face, bright eyes and unsubdued fly-away white hair—he sighed and discreetly put that idea aside. "Will you trust me?"

"I don't want to," Mrs. Pollifax told him frankly, "but I'm due at the Art Association lunch in half an hour. I shall have to trust you."

He left with relief, carrying measurements and notes.

On the following day there were fresh instructions from Carstairs—really Mrs. Pollifax had not felt so popular since she'd won a first prize for her geraniums.

"We've come up with something to help blunt Balkantourist's interest in you," he said. "At least we think it may if you can wangle it. There's a chap in Sofia you might try to hire as private guide on your arrival."

Mrs. Pollifax frowned. "I don't understand. Won't Balkantourist object to my doing this?"

Carstairs' voice was dry. "They'll probably find it amusing. This man has worked for them on a number of occasions, but he drinks too much to be reliable. Our newsmen often use him when they pass through Sofia. His name is Carleton Bemish."

"Bemish," repeated Mrs. Pollifax, writing it down.

"He's an Englishman—an expatriate—who's lived in Sofia for years and speaks the language fluently. He's even married to a Bulgarian. Technically he's a free-lance correspondent—does pieces for the London papers when there's a Balkan crisis—but actually he's one of those alcoholic hangers-on who can never go home again because of some tawdry scandal or another."

"He doesn't sound very appetizing," commented Mrs. Pollifax.

"Of course not. From what I'm told he'd sell his own mother, but he'll be a helluva lot easier to lose than Balkantourist when the time comes for you to make contact. By the way, we've decided you should rent a car for your stay in Sofia. That might entice Bemish, too—he doesn't have one. Is your license up to date?"

"Yes."

"Good. Try to get Bemish," he said, and rang off.

Mrs. Pollifax added his name to her list and continued her research on Bulgaria, impressed and surprised to learn that it had been free of Turkey's oppressive rule for only some eighty years. It was the Russians who had helped liberate Bulgaria from Turkey, and it was the Russians who had liberated them later from the Nazis. It suggested a much more congenial relationship than she'd expected, and a difference from other satellite countries that intrigued her.

There was one visitor to Mrs. Pollifax's apartment, however, that she had not expected. She came home one afternoon to find her door ajar and the lock so jammed that she could not turn the key in it. Yet so far as Mrs. Pollifax could discover nothing at all had been taken. "But just see the lock," she told the policeman when he arrived.

"You're sure nothing was stolen?" he said skeptically.

"I looked very carefully while I waited for you," she told him. "The only jewelry of any value is still in the box on my bureau. I have about thirty dollars in bills and small change lying here on the bookcase—in plain sight—in the Mexican pottery bowl. Even my television set's untouched, and it's portable."

"Odd," said the policeman, looking as baffled as Mrs. Pollifax felt. "Let's make a few inquiries. Maybe someone noticed a stranger on the premises. Your burglar may have been frightened away before he got inside."

The only person who had seen anyone at all in the hall that day was Miss Hartshorne, whose apartment lay across the hall. "Yes, I saw a stranger," she said. "I'd been downtown, and was having a little trouble finding the key in my purse. So I took longer than usual, and the elevator door opened and . . ."

Mrs. Pollifax was listening, as well as the policeman, and she smiled reassuringly at her friend. "But who was it?" she asked.

"Oh, he couldn't have been your burglar," Miss Hartshorne said flatly. "He had such a good face. Cheerful. He was even whistling as he came out of the elevator."

Mrs. Pollifax said firmly, "Grace, some of the most fiendish murderers have kind, cheerful faces. What man?"

"The young man who was delivering your cleaning. He held it up rather high as he came down the hall. It was on a hanger wrapped in that transparent plastic, you know. He said 'Good afternoon,' and I said 'Good afternoon' and then I found my key, unlocked my door and went in. He walked on to your door."

"What on earth made you think he went to *my* door?" asked Mrs. Pollifax. "Did you actually see him?"

Miss Hartshorne looked reproachful. "No, but I knew he was going there because he was carrying your coat, Emily. That quilted brown raincoat you wear. The new one. I could see it very clearly through the plastic."

Mrs. Pollifax looked at her thoughtfully, and then at the policeman, who had written all this down, and who now thanked Miss Hartshorne for her help. She did not say anything. She went back alone into her apartment to wait for the locksmith, but she remained thoughtful for a long time because she had not sent her quilted brown coat to the cleaner. She opened the closet door and looked inside. The coat hung there without any transparent wrappings. She took it out and examined it, then put her hand into each pocket. From one she drew out a wrinkled handkerchief with the initials EP, and from the other a bus token. She carried the coat to the window and studied it more carefully in the sunlight, but nothing appeared to be different. She put it on and observed it in the mirror. For a moment she thought it might be a shade longer than she remembered it, and then she chided herself for imagining things. She returned it to the closet.

But still it remained something of a mystery, not totally to be dismissed and apparently not to be solved until Miss Hartshorne changed her mind about its being this particular coat she'd seen.

A week later Mrs. Pollifax left for the Balkans wearing the

coat and her new custom-made hat. She had misjudged Osmonde. He had produced a marvelously imaginative hat, and just the kind that she enjoyed most. It was an inflated, cushiony bird's nest made out of soft woven straw with a small feathered bird perched at the peak. It was true that it had a tendency to tilt, but Mrs. Pollifax skewered it sternly in place with three stout hatpins.

"You *what?*" said Bishop incredulously. He had been on vacation for a week—his first vacation in five years—and he had returned only the day before. Now a cable had arrived from Bulgaria that was utterly mystifying to Bishop. It lay on the desk between them in Carstairs' office. It read:

COAT FOR 10573 CLEARED OKAY AND IN POSSESSION, WILL PROCEED AS DIRECTED.

10573 was Mrs. Pollifax's file number.

Carstairs sighed. "I told you, it's this damn economy drive. Upstairs insisted. Budgetwise, it took two experienced men a week to forge those passports, and then there were Mrs. Pollifax's travel expenses, not to mention Osmonde's bill for the hat. As they pointed out Upstairs, we get nothing but good will out of sending eight forged passports into Bulgaria. It's not enough to justify the expense. I was told this *flatly*. I had to share my courier."

Bishop said accusingly, "This cable is from Assen Radev."

"Yes, by way of Belgrade, Frankfurt, London and Baltimore. It came out with his weekly delivery of *pâté de foie gras.*"

Bishop's coldness turned glacial. "Radev's one of our nasties —you know that—and you've always sworn you'd keep Mrs. Pollifax out of the heavy stuff."

"I told you this was *not* my idea," Carstairs reminded him irritably. "They had to get some things to Radev, I had already engaged Mrs. Pollifax and briefed her for a simple courier job. What could I do? Radev has been sent Mrs. Pollifax's original coat. A duplicate coat was made—an exact copy, but fitted with the papers—and smuggled into Mrs. Pollifax's apartment. They're doubling up assignments everywhere."

"Then perhaps you can explain why the hell you didn't tell Mrs. Pollifax she's going into Bulgaria loaded for bear!"

Carstairs sighed. "Because she only goes through Customs 'loaded for bear,' as you call it, and as soon as she's entered Bulgaria, Radev will quietly exchange coats with her. She won't even know about it. I decided that was wisest. She's only an amateur, you know."

"I'm surprised you remember that," Bishop said bitterly. "I think it's shocking you didn't tell her. I suppose you've considered the possibility that Radev could have a heart attack before he can switch coats—or get clipped by a car?"

Carstairs said evenly, "Traffic is extremely light in Sofia, and I understand the rate of cardiac seizure in Bulgaria is very low. Something to do with all that yogurt they eat." He shook his head. "I'm afraid you're losing your usual sense of detachment, Bishop."

"Detachment! I don't even dare ask what's hidden in that coat—"

"It's better you not," Carstairs assured him gravely. "This isn't Sears Roebuck or Gimbels, you know. We're heels in the CIA, Bishop—outcasts and sinners and heels. Try to remember that."

Bishop's lips thinned. "Outcasts, yes. Sinners possibly. Heels obviously. But I thought we were at least *gentlemen*," he said coldly, and walked out, closing the door sharply behind him.

Chapter Four

Mrs. Pollifax sat in the Belgrade air terminal and waited patiently for TABSO to announce its flight to Sofia. She was quite ready for departure. The wild gray cliffs of Yugoslavia, its friendly people, the incredible blue of the Adriatic had relaxed and charmed her, but now there was work to do.

She had arrived early because she enjoyed watching departures. The planes for Frankfurt, Budapest, Dubrovnik and Brussels had been announced and had presumably left. Now she guessed all the remaining travelers were bound for Sofia, and her glance returned to a group of young people who occupied the corner of the lounge. She had been covertly observing them for some time, certain that two of them were Americans. She had expected them to leave on the plane for Brussels, but they were still here. They were bare-legged, tanned and long-haired—boys and girls alike—and instead of luggage they carried dusty packs on their backs.

They looked as though they were quarreling now, and as she watched, one of the girls lifted her voice and said furiously, "But I told you! All of us don't want to go to Bulgaria, can't you understand?"

"Debby, you're shouting."

"Why shouldn't I shout? I feel like shouting!"

Mrs. Pollifax frankly eavesdropped.

"Phil, for instance—and me, too," the American girl said. "And last night Andre admitted he wasn't all that interested either."

Her anger appeared to be directed at the stocky dark young man who seemed to be in charge of the group. He looked less a student than the others, older and harder. Now he gesticulated fiercely in reply. "We have the visas, yes? You think it easy to get visas to Bulgaria? Why the hell not?" His was an accent Mrs.

Pollifax found difficult to pinpoint—Yugoslavian, perhaps. In any case he sounded insulted by this revolt, and very angry indeed.

"But none of us really thought they'd give us visas!" flung out the American girl. "And Phil's got dysentery, and I just think it's—"

"We voted, didn't we?"

"Nikki and Debby, stop arguing," said the French girl flatly, and they all looked at her, and the ginger-haired English boy threw her a kiss and the third girl laughed and said something in German that caused them all to laugh.

All except the American boy named Phil, who picked up his knapsack and carried it to the bench beside Mrs. Pollifax and sat down.

"Trouble?" asked Mrs. Pollifax cheerfully.

He turned and stared at her and she in turn looked at him. He seemed a very *nice* young man. Disreputable, of course, in those filthy jeans and all that untidy black hair, but his eyes were a marvelous shade of intense blue and the height of his cheekbones gave his face an interesting shape.

The boy nodded; she had been approved. "We're getting damn sick of each other," he said bluntly.

Mrs. Pollifax smiled. "It happens. Have you been together long?"

He shrugged. "Some of us. But we were doing fine until Nikki came along. I'm beginning to hate his guts."

"That would be the bossy, dark young man?"

"Yeah, that's Nikki," he said, and they both stared across at Nikki, whose back was turned to them. "He showed up in Dubrovnik two weeks ago. Debby I met in Vienna—she's great—and she'd already met Ghislaine in Paris. Erika and Andre joined us on the road later, but Nikki—"

"Obviously the executive type," said Mrs. Pollifax sympathetically. Noting the expression on the young man's face she added sharply, "Are you all right?"

"Damn dysentery," he said. His face had gone white and he leaned over in pain, guarding himself by hugging his stomach with his arms.

"But haven't you medicine for it?"

He shook his head. "I lost it yesterday, but Nikki's feeding me his." He lifted his head and said with a little laugh, "Maybe I'll have to go along to Bulgaria with him just to stay with his pills. Actually I'm here only to see them off. I don't want to go to Bulgaria. No—I can't make up my mind." He laughed savagely. "Mind! I don't have any mind, it's gone all groggy."

Mrs. Pollifax said in alarm, "You poor boy, you look terribly pale and your speech is slurred. I think you're really ill."

"Dubrovnik," he said dreamily. "That's where we were and that's where I'd like to be."

"I've just come from there," Mrs. Pollifax told him, nodding. "It's magnificent, isn't it? I was there for the Music Festival."

He turned and looked at her. "You, too? Man, that was something, wasn't it? Those rock walls, the sea, the sky like velvet—" He abruptly yawned. "Damn it, now I'm sleepy—one extreme or the other, dysentery or stupor."

"The right medicine would cure both," she told him sternly.

He shook his head as if to clear it. "I'll get some. Do you have any idea what this says?" He pulled a piece of paper from his pocket and handed it to her. "I can't even tell what language it is."

Mrs. Pollifax glanced down at the wrinkled, narrow slip of paper on which several sentences had been printed, followed by a series of numbers. "That's the Cyrillic alphabet, isn't it?" she said, frowning over it. "It looks rather like a pass to a swimming pool, or a lottery ticket. Where did you get it?"

Phil laughed. "I picked somebody's pocket."

At that moment the loudspeaker system crackled with life and began to announce the departure of the TABSO flight for Sofia in four different languages, the voices echoing and re-echoing through the terminal. Further conversation became impossible and Mrs. Pollifax held out her hand to the young man. "Emily Pollifax," she shouted at him over the din. "Delighted to have met you. And please—do see a doctor about your dysentery."

He arose, too, blushed slightly and extended a hand in the manner of one remembering a nearly forgotten ritual. "Philip Trenda," he shouted as they shook hands. Abruptly a new spasm of pain crossed his face and he doubled up.

The American girl with the waist-length hair—they had

called her Debby—was suddenly at his side. "Phil, this is awful—you're really sick."

"I'll walk to the plane with you," he said.

"That's stupid. You ought to sit or lie down, not *walk.*"

His mouth tightened. "I'm not sick and I'm going to walk you to the plane."

"Your piece of paper," called Mrs. Pollifax.

He vaguely gestured it aside as he shouldered his pack and joined the girl. Mrs. Pollifax dropped the slip of paper into her purse, picked up her flight bag and followed the group of young people toward the gate. There she saw them re-group—yes, and resume their quarreling.

With a shake of her head Mrs. Pollifax gave up her ticket, received her seat number and boarded the plane. The young people arrived several minutes later and noisily made their way to the plane's rear. The young man named Philip was with them.

She thought, He shouldn't have let them talk him into coming. Not with dysentery. But that was the way travel was: a series of chance encounters, fleeting involvements, motives never explained, endings never known. Firmly she put aside all thought of the young American and fastened her seat belt. As they taxied down the runway for takeoff she opened a tattered copy of *Newsweek*.

But as the plane lifted, Mrs. Pollifax realized that printed words were lifeless to her at a moment when she was about to begin another courier assignment. She put down the magazine and gazed out of the window, wondering what she would be like when she finished this job because it seemed to her that each one left her changed. Now, once again, she was leaving behind friends, identity, children, possessions—everything secure—for another small adventure. At her age, too. But this was exactly the age, she thought, when life ought to be spent, not hoarded. There had been enough years of comfortable living, and complacency was nothing but delusion. One could not always change the world, she felt, but one could change oneself.

The plane had begun to decelerate. Glancing at her watch Mrs. Pollifax saw that it was much too early for them to be reaching Sofia. A voice began an announcement over the loudspeaker in Bulgarian, then in French, in German and at last in English: they were making an unscheduled stop in Rumania. The delay would be brief. No one was to leave the plane.

They landed. From her window Mrs. Pollifax could see a sign at some distance that said TRIASCA REPUBLIC SOCIALIST RUMANIA in huge red letters. Down the aisle an Englishman grumbled to his companion, "They never explain things in these countries. Or apologize."

"Police state, of course. I always wonder if they're going to arrest someone aboard or search our luggage. I say, it looks as if this stop's for someone special."

"Some high mucky-muck, eh?"

"Looks it."

"Isn't that General Ignatov? You were in Sofia last year. Bloody tiresome the way his picture was in the party newspaper week after week."

General Ignatov? Mrs. Pollifax turned to her window and saw a number of people making their way across the field to the plane. There was a comic-opera look about the procession. It was led by a tall, darkly handsome man wearing a uniform that fairly dripped medals. He was walking with long strides and cutting the air with a walking stick. Behind him two army officers had to break into a trot to keep up with him. Following them came a swarm of men in business suits.

Under Mrs. Pollifax's window the general halted, the others surrounded him and everyone shook hands. As the general moved slightly apart she saw him clearly. What a powerful face, she thought in surprise. He was laughing now, his teeth very white against his dark skin, his head thrown back in a posture of amusement, but she did not believe he was amused. She had the impression that he had taught himself to laugh because otherwise he would be all arrogance, cruelty, tension and energy.

A moment later he boarded the plane and she glimpsed him again as he paused in the space between tourist and first-class. He was issuing sharp orders now to the stewardess; the charm had vanished and he looked only brutal.

Mrs. Pollifax shivered. There was nothing comic-opera about this general. She suddenly understood that she was entering an iron curtain country, and that she was going to contact there a group that was defying all the power this man represented. She

realized that General Ignatov could squash that group under the
heel of one boot. He would squash her, too, if she crossed his line
of vision. And under the bird in her hat she carried eight very illicit
passports.

Chapter Five

No one was allowed to leave the plane in Sofia until General Ignatov and his two officers had disembarked. Mrs. Pollifax spent these minutes in anchoring her hat more securely and in trying to forget that she carried contraband. She remembered saying to Carstairs in her apartment, "I suppose in a country like Bulgaria these passports are the equivalent of gold."

"Not gold," he'd said. "Tell me first what the equivalent of a human life is, and perhaps then we can measure their value. Perhaps."

Once passengers were allowed to leave, Mrs. Pollifax descended from the plane and followed the others into the terminal. As she approached Customs she reminded herself that she was only a tourist, and fairly experienced at dissembling. She was also— thanks to retired police chief Lorvale Brown—moderately adept at karate, but still she could not remember when she had felt so nervous. She watched her suitcase opened and a pair of hands methodically sift its contents. The Customs man then looked at her, his eyes narrowing as they came to rest on the bird atop her hat. Mrs. Pollifax braced herself. A look of astonishment crossed his face, he smiled, nudged his companion and pointed to the bird. Two pairs of eyes regarded her hat in surprise, and then the first officer gave her an admiring grin and signaled her to move on. Happily she obeyed. She had passed Customs. There was only Balkantourist left to confront, and presumably in time her knees would stop trembling.

Carstairs had described Bulgarians as the realists among the Balkan people. "Also the most trustworthy," he had said crisply. "They'll never knife you in the back."

"That's reassuring," Mrs. Pollifax had said.

He had added gravely, "They'll wait instead for you to turn around first."

She was reminded of this by the Balkantourist representative who awaited her beyond Customs. The square, compact young woman greeted her with a hearty manner, but her eyes were surprisingly indifferent, almost contemptuous. Her face was high cheekboned and boyish and devoid of makeup; she wore a wrinkled khaki dress with insignia at each lapel. "I am Nevena," she said in a husky voice, heavily accented, and turning her back on Mrs. Pollifax she continued joking vivaciously with several of the Customs men. This left Mrs. Pollifax to cope with her luggage. She locked her suitcase, put away her passport and, luggage in hand, waited. Apparently Nevena was well known. Obviously she was in no hurry.

It was tiresome standing first on one foot and then the other. Mrs. Pollifax's glance strayed from Nevena and toward the dwindling line at Customs. Her eyes fell upon the group of young travelers from the Belgrade air terminal and she saw that again they appeared to be having problems, this time with Customs. Philip was propped against the counter smothering a yawn. Debby looked discouraged. Nikki, however, was still gesturing, his face livid as he argued with the man behind the counter. All of this Mrs. Pollifax noted in the flash of a second, just as a new official arrived to resolve the quarrel. He directed the group out of line and herded them to a far corner of the hall.

She interrupted Nevena firmly. "I'm going back through Customs," she announced. "I see that some friends of mine are having trouble over there, they may need help."

Nevena's frown was not encouraging. "Help?" she said gruffly.

Mrs. Pollifax pointed. "In the corner, see?"

Nevena's gaze followed her hand and then swerved back to give Mrs. Pollifax a quick, hard scrutiny. "Those peoples are known to you?"

"Yes."

Nevena shook her head. Her eyes rested again on Mrs. Pollifax, curious and a little startled. "The man speaking with them is not a Customs man. We go now."

"But I really think—"

"We go," Nevena said sharply, and tugged at Mrs. Pollifax's elbow, propelling her toward the door.

"I don't understand," said Mrs. Pollifax, resisting.

Nevena stopped just outside the building. "If they are in trouble you cannot help them."

"Why should they be in trouble?"

"That is a man from security questioning them. You wish to be in trouble, too?"

"Security?" echoed Mrs. Pollifax.

"The car is here," Nevena said sternly, pointing and opening the door. "Come—inside."   •

Mrs. Pollifax hesitated and then remembered that trouble was a luxury she couldn't afford and that security was a synonym for the secret police. With a sigh she climbed into the car. "What kind of trouble?" she persisted as Nevena joined her.

Nevena shrugged. "Maybe the visas are in disorder?"

Mrs. Pollifax relaxed. If that was the case then the group would be flown back to Yugoslavia and their squabbles over visiting Bulgaria would be ended. Nevertheless she had been reminded that it was not healthy to be singled out by the police here. She really *must* be cautious.

"Now," said Nevena as she started the car, "I speak to you of Sofia, which is some five thousand years old and is capital of Bulgaria. It is fourth Bulgarian capital after Pliska, Preslav and Tarnovo. The Thracians called it Serdika, the Slavs called it Sredets, the Byzantines, Triaditsa. Although destroyed and burned by Goths, Magyars, Huns, Patsinaks and Crusaders, Sofia is today a beautiful modern city. With its original historical and cultural monuments and numerous mineral springs our capital is a great attraction for tourists. . . ."

Oh dear, thought Mrs. Pollifax, suppressing a yawn, and in revolt she began her own assessment of Sofia, whose low silhouette lay stretched out ahead of her in the clear sparkling air. It was a sprawling city that encircled the foothill of a long high mountain range. The air was bracing and everything looked clean and fresh. Along the road grew clumps of Queen Anne's lace, oddly endearing to her after the brief chill that had visited her. She decided that she really must halt that droning, mechanical voice at her side. It was time to assert.

"There's a gentleman I would like to call on tomorrow," she told Nevena. "If you'll advise me how to find him."

Nevena's face tightened. "You *know* someone in my country?"

Mrs. Pollifax shook her head. Speaking each word slowly and clearly she explained, "I don't *know* this man. He's not even Bulgarian. His name was suggested to me by a friend, in case I wanted to learn more about your country. His name is Carleton Bemish."

"Oh—Mistair Beemish!" laughed Nevena, and her face sprang to life, gamine and suddenly pretty. "The funny one! Everyone knows Bemish." She said firmly, "He would be the good man for you if he is not busy. Maybe he have time. For myself I have not enough time, but you could join a group I begin tomorrow. At 1 P.M. sharp they tour Sofia in Balkantourist bus. Very *nice* bus."

"I'm renting a car while I'm here," pointed out Mrs. Pollifax.

"Oh—" Nevena slapped a hand to her forehead. "You are accurate! Eleven tomorrow." She slowed the car. "Mr. Bemish live there," she said, pointing to a narrow, modern cement building punctuated by very symmetrical balconies. "Only five squares from your hotel. I write the address for you in Bulgarian when you wish."

Mrs. Pollifax turned, affixing the look of the building in her mind. "Thank you," she said, and began to make a mental note of the corners they passed.

Within minutes they entered a plaza lined with modern shops and dominated by a towering granite and glass building. "Your hotel," pointed out Nevena proudly.

And despite the lettering across the front that in no way resembled Rila, it proved to be the Hotel Rila. Nevena parked at a side entrance with stairs leading into a small side lobby. "It is now 3 P.M.," she said with a stern glance at her wristwatch. "I register you at hotel and then there is time for me personally to show you Sofia. Maybe one and a half hours, very quick but—"

Very politely Mrs. Pollifax said, "Another day that would be pleasant, but I'd really prefer to rest now."

Nevena gave her a sharp glance. "You are old?"

"Very," said Mrs. Pollifax.

Nevena nodded. "You give me passport, I register you." At the desk she spoke severely in Bulgarian to the clerk and then turned to Mrs. Pollifax. "Okay, I go now. At 11 A.M. tomorrow sharp I meet you beside this desk when car arrives. The man who brings car speaks no English."

"That's very kind of you."

"This man who takes suitcase up for you, give him only a few *stotynki*, you understand? This is not a capitalist country."

Mrs. Pollifax nodded and watched her march out of the lobby. She wondered what someone like Nevena—so stolid, so efficient—would do with the two free hours she'd just been given. Certainly not rest, she thought, but then Mrs. Pollifax had no intention of resting either. Having just won herself a few hours of unexpected privacy, she thought it an excellent time to begin her sub rosa work. She would visit Durov's tailor shop.

Chapter Six

Nothing in this hotel district of Sofia was shabby. Everything was clean, bare, new, the boulevards almost empty
of traffic. Map in hand, Mrs. Pollifax crossed Vasil Levski
street to number nine and studied the word printed across the glass
window: it said **ШИВа4**. This was not particularly helpful. She
peered through the glass. Seeing the bolts of fabrics hanging along
the walls, she walked inside to find two men and a woman bent
over the hems and seams of fabric in their laps. The stolid-faced
woman with gray hair left her sewing machine and walked to the
counter. "Do you speak English?" asked Mrs. Pollifax.

The older man in the rear looked up suddenly. Without a
word the woman returned to her machine and the man came forward. "Pliss?" he said cautiously. "I speak the English."

"I would like to take home a man's sheepskin jacket or vest,"
she told him.

"Ah—we have fine skins," he said, nodding.

"Good." She met his eye before adding, "I want a brown vest
for a friend in America."

"A brown one!" he said with pleasure. "Not black?"

She shook her head. "Brown. Here are the measurements."
She offered them on a slip of paper.

The expression on his face remained totally unchanged. He
copied the measurements arduously, chewing on his underlip as he
labored. He lifted his head. "You stay at a hotel?"

"The Rila," she replied, and aware that the sign on her hotel
bore no resemblance to the word, she brought out the hotel's leaf-
let and showed him its picture.

"Yes. Your name?"

"Mrs. Pollifax."

"Pollifax." She noticed that he made no move to write down

either her name or the name of her hotel. "Excuse, pliss?" he said formally, and abruptly disappeared into the back room. Over the whirring of the sewing machines she could hear him speaking, perhaps on the telephone for she heard no answering voice. A few minutes later he returned. "The vest will cost"—he pursed his lips thoughtfully—"maybe twelve *leva*, maybe eighteen."

"Wonderful," exclaimed Mrs. Pollifax, quite carried away by the thought of paying only six or nine dollars for a sheepskin vest until she remembered it was an imaginary vest they discussed.

"We let you know. Maybe tomorrow, okay?" For the first time he gave her a glance that she could read as meaningful, and she nodded.

"Thank you," she said, and left.

Mrs. Pollifax walked slowly back to her hotel, pausing to look into a number of stores to prove that her interest was not limited to tailoring shops, should anyone be following her. When she reached the hotel and her room on the sixth floor, she discovered that she felt a great deal lighter: a grave responsibility had been lifted from her, she had found the shop and notified the Underground of her arrival. The rest would be up to the man named Tsanko now, and in the meantime she could relax and begin to enjoy Sofia.

After unpacking the top inch of her suitcase, she took a quick shower and then dressed. She felt quite stimulated by the brief exchange of words at number nine Vasil Levski. The man had reminded her of Mr. Omelianuk, the owner of the little delicatessen around the corner from her apartment in New Brunswick, and she reflected how alike people were, no matter where they lived. The problems changed, but people were the same. She wondered how she would be contacted, and when. Apparently not this evening; the man had implied tomorrow. That was disappointing, especially when she glanced at her watch and saw that it was only six o'clock. It seemed much too early for dinner, and in any case she wasn't hungry.

I'm feeling too efficient to be hungry, she thought, and it suddenly occurred to her that she might complete all of tomorrow's work today by calling upon Mr. Carleton Bemish. Perhaps she could persuade him to join her for dinner. Failing that, she could at least engage him for a sightseeing tour of Sofia tomorrow in her rented car.

Splendid idea, she decided, and putting on her hat she descended in the elevator to the small side lobby and walked outside to begin her search for Mr. Bemish's street and apartment house. One left turn, she remembered, and then four blocks to the Rila, which meant—turning it backward—that she walked four blocks away from the plaza and turned to the right. And there it was, giving her cause to congratulate herself on accomplishing so much during her first hours in Bulgaria.

But what a bleak-looking place the building was on closer scrutiny. It looked new, and very clean, but it had been constructed in the stark, concrete-modern style of the twenties that aimed at simplicity but succeeded only in looking utilitarian. Mrs. Pollifax entered a lobby that resembled a laundry room, with a drain placed squarely in the center of the floor; there were two couches, of tubular steel and hard plastic, at right angles along the wall. A directory of occupants gave Bemish's name, apartment 301, in both Bulgarian and English. A windowless staircase, also cement, led up to an unseen landing from which drifted the smell of cabbage. There was no elevator.

Mrs. Pollifax began to climb, and as she climbed the smell of cabbage grew stronger and the ill-placed ceiling lights grew more garish. At the door of apartment 301 she knocked and waited. The building was quiet, but from inside 301 came the sound of someone singing. It was a man's voice, overcharged, belligerent and rendered in a spirit that Mrs. Pollifax guessed did not come from any internal source of well-being. Mr. Bemish's cocktail hour had begun some hours ago.

The door opened and a cheerful, rotund man beamed at her.

"Mr. Bemish?" she said. "Mr. Carleton Bemish?"

He winked. "In the flesh."

And indeed her first impression was of flesh, rather a lot of it, and all of it arranged in circles: a plump round stomach, round face, round chins, small round eyes embedded in circles of flesh, and a small round mouth. He gave the impression of vast jovialness until Mrs. Pollifax looked directly into his eyes and found them curiously empty, like stones.

"I'm Mrs. Pollifax," she said. "May I come in? I was told that

. . ." She paused doubtfully. He stood blocking her entrance; she stopped and waited.

"Something nice, I hope?" he asked with a second wink.

"Told that I might talk with you," she said, and firmly walked past him into his living room. It was very bold of her, but she had already gained the impression that Mr. Bemish was not in full command of his faculties. "About a job," she said. "As my guide for several days."

Off to the right a door closed, but not before she had caught a glimpse of a drab, mouse-like little woman fleeing the room; a cleaning woman, perhaps, although the apartment did not look as if it had been cleaned in years.

"I couldn't be less interested," said Carleton Bemish, following her into the room. "I'm otherwise occupied. Busy. Very busy."

And very prosperous, too, noticed Mrs. Pollifax as her glance fell on a heavily draped round table in the center of the room. On it stood a silver bucket with a bottle of champagne protruding from it. It was a startling sight in such a shabby room. She said mechanically, "I'm sorry, you're expecting someone?"

"My dear woman, of course I'm expecting someone," he said pompously, rocking a little on his heels. "A man like myself has many important friends. Many."

Her glance fell to the couch near the table and she saw long white cardboard boxes piled there. From one of them spilled the shimmering folds of a brocade dressing gown. His glance followed hers and he beamed. "Not bad, hmm?" he said, walking over to the couch. He pulled the robe from the box and held it up. "They're not underestimating Carleton Bemish any more! Look at it—pure silk!"

"Ah, you've inherited money," suggested Mrs. Pollifax.

He draped the robe across his shoulders and winked at her. "What I've inherited is a news story—the biggest—and I've made the news story myself. I feel surprisingly like God!" He came near to Mrs. Pollifax, the robe streaming behind him like a train, his breath suffocatingly alcoholic. With intense scorn, and breathing heavily at her, he said, "They're no longer saying 'Good old Bemish, nice old Bemish' . . . They treat me with respect now, I can tell you." He tapped his right temple meaningfully. "Brains. Wit. That's what it takes to survive, Mrs.—what's your name?"

"Pollifax."

"The thing is," he said defiantly, "I'm not up for hire. Carleton Bemish is no longer a has-been. You understand?"

Mrs. Pollifax sighed. "I understand. You're no longer a has-been."

He peered suspiciously into her face. "That sounds damn impertinent."

"You're standing on my right foot," said Mrs. Pollifax frankly.

He jumped back. "Oh—sorry."

She nodded. "I quite understand now that you're not available, and so I'll just run along. In the meantime I'll be looking forward to reading your news story."

He beamed appreciatively. "*With* by-line. Already posted—to London, Paris, New York. But not," he added, owlishly, "in Sofia. Not in this country. Pity about that."

Thoroughly tired of this, Mrs. Pollifax moved to the door; he was suddenly there before her, his mood changed again. "Wait a minute," he said suspiciously. "Who did you say you are?"

"Mrs. Pollifax," she sighed. "I came to see you about guiding—"

He relaxed. "Oh yes, I remember."

Someone else had arrived at Mr. Bemish's door and was knocking. "My guest!" said Carleton Bemish happily, and threw open the door, exclaiming in Bulgarian to the man who stood there illuminated by the overhead hall light. His face was clearly outlined and Mrs. Pollifax stared at him in surprise. She knew him. He in turn glanced at her with barely concealed impatience and addressed himself to Bemish, the two of them speaking in rapid Bulgarian.

She knew him, but from where? He was young, very dark, square and broad-shouldered. "The Belgrade air terminal!" she said aloud.

The young man turned and looked at her. "I beg your pardon?"

"You're Nikki," she said in surprise. "You were in Philip's group. What was his name, Philip Trenda?"

Carleton Bemish's mouth dropped open. He turned to look incredulously at Nikki.

"Oh?" said Nikki, heavy brows lifting. "You were there, perhaps?" he added smoothly.

"Yes indeed," she told him warmly. "And later I saw your group led away from the Customs line by the police, and I wanted to come over and . . ." She stopped. The atmosphere almost crackled with shocks. Carleton Bemish's eyes were growing larger and rounder while Nikki's eyes were growing narrower. She added limply, "But you're—all right? They didn't bother you?"

Nikki bowed stiffly. "A small misunderstanding, no more." He looked at her curiously. "You say that you knew Philip?"

"I didn't say so," she pointed out. "We had a brief but very interesting chat in the air terminal, that's all. Now I really must leave," she said. "Please remember me to Philip when you see him," she told Nikki, and over her shoulder to them both, "Good night."

Neither man responded. She had the feeling that she left them dazed, but she couldn't honestly attribute it to the force of her personality. She wondered what she'd said that so took them by surprise.

The smell of cabbage was stronger in the hall, reminding Mrs. Pollifax of her own hunger and of the increasing lateness of the hour. She hurried back to her hotel.

Mrs. Pollifax dined alone with a small sense of letdown that aborted her appetite. First of all the food in the hotel restaurant was imitation American, the peas straight from a can, and yet—perversely—no one, not even the headwaiter, knew the English language; a contact with Tsanko appeared impossible for another twelve or fifteen hours, and Carleton Bemish was not available at all. She told herself that she was experiencing the effects of her first hours in a strange country far from home, although this was of small consolation to her frame of mind, which was gloomy.

It was not until she was in the middle of dessert that it suddenly struck her how very odd it was that Bemish's guest had turned out to be Nikki. How it did happen that a hitchhiking Yugoslavian student was on such friendly terms with a man who lived in Sofia?

I know many, many important people, Bemish had said defiantly.

The thought so startled her that she looked up in astonishment to meet the eye of a small gray-haired man in a gray suit who was watching her closely from a table near the entrance. He glanced away so swiftly that she gave him a second look, at once curious and alerted. He was short and stolid, his suit badly cut and his whole appearance so remarkably anonymous that she would never have noticed him except for his stare. She had the impression that he had only recently arrived, and this was confirmed by a glance at his table, still empty of food.

Perhaps it was Tsanko, she thought hopefully, and perhaps contact would be made soon, after all.

She paid her bill and went upstairs, but no one knocked on her door and no messages were slipped under the rug. Rather sadly, she retired at half-past ten.

Chapter Seven

S ometime during the night Mrs. Pollifax experienced a nightmare in which she was lying helplessly in bed at home and
being observed by a burglar who had entered her room. She
was not accustomed to nightmares and as she fought her way back
to consciousness she discovered that she was indeed in bed, it was
night and a man was standing at the foot of the bed looking down
at her. He was clearly silhouetted against the window.

Mrs. Pollifax waited, breath suspended, for the man to identify himself as Tsanko. He did not. He moved stealthily away from
the foot of the bed and went toward the closet, where he turned on
a small flashlight. He leaned over the lock, his back to her.

If he wasn't Tsanko, she thought indignantly, then he must be
a plain, old-fashioned burglar, and without stopping to consider
the risks Mrs. Pollifax slid out of her bed and stood up. Carefully
tiptoeing along the wall she came up behind the man, flattened her
right hand and delivered a medium karate chop to the side of his
neck—at least she hoped it was only a medium blow—and watched
him sink to the floor.

Switching on the lights she saw there was no doubt at all that
the man was a thief because he held her brown quilted coat in his
arms. He lay on his side, half of the coat trapped under him, a
relatively young man wearing a black suit and black tie. Stepping
over him she went to the telephone and picked up the receiver. "I
have a burglar in my room," she told the desk clerk coldly.

The reply was depressing and sounded like, *"Murdekoochinko
lesso razenum."*

"Burglar. Thief!" she said. "Does anyone speak English?"

"Anglichanin? Amerikanski?"

Mrs. Pollifax grimly put down the phone, stepped again over
the man and opened the door. She peered outside; the halls were

deserted. Leaving her door open she walked down to the elevator, but there was no one there either. With a sigh she stepped into it and descended to the lobby.

There were two men at the desk, and it was a full two minutes before they were able to control their surprise at seeing Mrs. Pollifax emerge from the elevator in flowered pajamas. It was at least another several minutes before they understood that she wanted them to return to her room with her, and this appeared to induce in them an even deeper state of shock. Neither of them spoke English and it was necessary for them to identify her by their desk records. When this had been done they telephoned Balkantourist.

A peevish Nevena was reached at last. "It is 3 A.M.," she announced furiously.

"I have a burglar lying on the floor of my hotel room," Mrs. Pollifax told her.

This was translated by Nevena to the room clerk, who stared at Mrs. Pollifax incredulously.

The phone was handed back to Mrs. Pollifax. "We do not have thieves in Bulgaria," Nevena said coldly, and then with outrageous illogic, "You should not encourage such matters by not locking your closet and your door."

"I locked both the door to the closet and the door to my room," said Mrs. Pollifax crisply. "I placed the key to the closet under my pillow and slept on it. But the man had already broken into the closet because he had my brown quilted coat in his arms. I saw it."

Orders were given to the hotel clerks, one of whom gestured Mrs. Pollifax to the elevator and returned with her to the sixth floor. He accompanied her to her room, where the door remained open. He first looked inside, cautiously.

Mrs. Pollifax followed him in. The room was empty.

"He's gone," she said indignantly. "He's gotten away."

The desk clerk pointed to the door of the closet and looked at her questioningly. For a moment Mrs. Pollifax didn't understand, and then she saw that the door was locked. She went to her pillow. The key had not been touched, and removing it she returned to the closet. With the desk clerk watching she unlocked and opened the door.

Her coat was hanging in the closet, as well as her clothes. The hat was on the shelf. Nothing had been touched.

In open-mouthed astonishment—for she had just seen her coat *out* of the closet—she turned to the desk clerk. It needed only one glance to understand what he thought. "Amerikanski," he muttered indignantly, and left.

What Nevena's reaction would be to the locked closet taxed Mrs. Pollifax's imagination. This time before retiring, however, she placed two chairs in front of her door and hid the key to the closet under the mattress.

On first encounter Nevena gave no indication of her anger during the night. She was delighted to find Mrs. Pollifax waiting. "You still wish to advance by yourself, on the wheels?"

"Yes indeed, and I've decided to drive to the TV tower on Mount Vitosha. It'll be easiest to find because I can see it ahead of me while I drive."

"Good! You may also wish to try the cable car—it goes down, then up—splendid views! For lunch the Kopitoto is good, very good. Here is the driver." She waved to him vigorously and ushered Mrs. Pollifax outside to the door of a trim little green Volkswagen. "You are certain?" she demanded.

Mrs. Pollifax looked at the car and felt a wave of doubt. Then, "I'm certain," she said and climbed in, turned the key in the ignition and heard the purring of the engine.

But Nevena insisted upon having the last word. She leaned over the window, her eyes suddenly brimming with glee. "Be certain nobody steals the pretty brown coat again, eh, Mrs. Pollifax?" she shouted into her ear.

Chapter Eight

An hour later Mrs. Pollifax was seated triumphantly on the terrace of the Kopitoto restaurant, a mountain breeze ruffling the bird on her hat and Sofia lying at her feet. Marvelous, she thought, gazing around her appreciatively, and as her glance roamed the terrace with its bright little tables she saw that either Sofia was a very small town indeed, or she was beginning to know a surprising number of people. She saw first of all the small gray man from the hotel dining room the evening before. He was just seating himself, and she thought his arrival four minutes after her own was an interesting development. It was of course a very scenic place in which to lunch; it was also possible that he was a fellow tourist, perhaps visiting Sofia from another Balkan country, but she was not inclined to think so: he looked so particularly joyless.

The second person she recognized on the terrace was the American girl Debby, from the group at the Belgrade air terminal. Although Philip was missing, it was otherwise the same group of young people. One of them arose—it was Nikki, still talking aggressively, with gestures. He was abruptly cut off from view by the arrival of her waiter.

Mrs. Pollifax ordered and ate her lunch. Finished, she gathered up coat and purse and looked across the terrace. Phil had still not rejoined the group and Nikki was just leaving, smiling and formally shaking hands with each member of the party. Mrs. Pollifax watched him go and then crossed the terrace.

"Good afternoon," she said cheerfully. "We traveled together here on the same plane from Belgrade. Are you enjoying Sofia?"

Five faces turned blankly to her.

"It was Phil I spoke with," she explained, dropping into the chair Nikki had vacated. "Is he with you today?"

The American girl promptly burst into tears.

"*Mon cheri*," said the pale young man softly, grasping her wrist.

"Is she ill?" asked Mrs. Pollifax anxiously.

"It's Phil," explained the other girl. "You mentioned Phil."

"Yes, I was concerned about his dysentery. How is he? Or rather, where is he?"

"In prison—here in Sofia," blurted out Debby with a sob. "They've arrested him."

"Arrested him!" cried Mrs. Pollifax.

The ginger-haired British boy nodded. "The idiots seem to think he's some kind of spy."

"Phil a spy," Debby repeated angrily. She drew a sodden handkerchief from her pocket and wiped her eyes. "I remember you," she said abruptly. "You did talk to Phil and now he's—and in Bulgaria of all places!" She burst into tears again.

"But I don't understand," protested Mrs. Pollifax. "What on earth happened?"

The young Frenchman turned to her and in precise English and a soft voice explained. "First they questioned us at Customs—"

"Who did?" asked Mrs. Pollifax, wondering if they shared Nevena's knowledge of uniforms.

He shrugged. "The uniforms were different. We do not know since we don't speak their language. Nikki was upset—"

"In what language was he upset?" asked Mrs. Pollifax quickly.

Again he shrugged. "Who knows? He is—Yugoslavian, isn't he?" he asked the others. "In any case he was very angry—in what language I don't know," he added with a soft smile for Mrs. Pollifax, "and they took him away, into another room. A few minutes later he came and said okay, it was a small misunderstanding."

She nodded; that sounded familiar.

"Then we decided to be stoppers—"

"That's what they call hitchhikers here," put in the girl.

"Except no one picked us up so we kept walking, stopping only once—"

"To take a picture—"

"Phil took it," added the girl. "But of nothing but flowers."

"And then *they* drove up, two new men in a car, no uniforms, and said Phil would have to be questioned. They said this to us in French. And they just—took him away."

"But that's incredible," cried Mrs. Pollifax. "Does the Embassy know?"

"We went there at once. It was a big shock to them. This morning they say he has been charged with espionage, and the Embassy suggests we leave this country at once," he said in a melancholy voice. "Because we were with him."

"Which we will do," added the French boy, "on the six o'clock plane out of Sofia this afternoon."

Debby said suddenly, "I think it's terrible just going off and leaving Phil. It could have been any of us, and he's here all alone—"

"You heard Nikki. He's going to stay a few days and keep doing everything possible."

"Nikki's not leaving with you?" asked Mrs. Pollifax sharply.

She thought Debby looked at her appraisingly. "No," the girl said quietly. "How do you happen to know who Nikki is?"

"Philip complained about him."

"Yes," said Debby, looking abstracted.

The French boy had glanced at his watch. "We must go," he said. "We must be certain we catch that plane. It's nearly three o'clock now and we want to stop again at the Embassy for news." He looked politely at Mrs. Pollifax. "You have been kind to ask."

"But I'm so terribly sorry," she said. "For all of you, but especially for Philip. You're quite sure you'll be allowed to leave safely?"

"Reasonably sure, madam," said the French boy. "We have the assurances of your Embassy."

Mrs. Pollifax nodded. "I'm glad."

Debby said politely, "We hope your stay is a pleasanter one than ours. You're at the Hotel Pliska?"

Mrs. Pollifax shook her head. "The Rila."

Debby nodded. "Good-bye. You've been nice to ask."

One by one they shook hands with her, and Mrs. Pollifax watched them move across the terrace trailing their packs behind them. She thought about Philip Trenda, remembering his thick black hair, the level blue eyes, his dysentery and his indecision over staying or going, and she felt very alarmed for him. A Bulgarian prison was hardly a fitting experience for such a young person. He probably didn't even know that his Embassy was trying to reach him. He would be feeling very alone, very frail, and of course almost no Bulgarians spoke English, which would make it all the more frustrating.

But espionage! Despite the warmth of the sun across her shoulders, Mrs. Pollifax shivered. There but for the grace of God, she reminded herself, and at that moment she glanced up and met the eyes of the little gray man in the gray suit. He looked hastily away, but his interest was no longer coincidence. *He's following me,* she thought. The bright terrace seemed dimmer and the breeze cold.

After a trip down and back on Mount Vitosha's cable car—it would have been exhilarating if she had not just learned of Philip's arrest—Mrs. Pollifax drove her rented car slowly back through the environs of Sofia and to her hotel. It was four o'clock when she picked up her key at the desk. She ascended in the elevator carrying half a dozen picture postcards to write, and was just settling down to them at the desk when she heard a light knocking at her door.

Tsanko at last! thought Mrs. Pollifax with relief, and hurried across the room to fling open the door.

A teary-eyed Debby stood in the hall.

"But—oh dear!" faltered Mrs. Pollifax.

The girl said defiantly, "I want to talk to you. I *have* to talk to you."

"But your plane—good heavens! Aren't you missing your plane?"

"I'm not taking the plane."

A chambermaid down the hall was watching them. Mrs. Pollifax said, "Come inside."

"They can arrest me if they want. I'm not leaving," stormed Debby as she followed Mrs. Pollifax into the room. "Not until Phil's free. I know Nikki said we all *must* get out quickly, but I can't. Phil's my friend, he's the nicest boy I ever met."

"But this isn't America, you know," Mrs. Pollifax said, closing the door and then locking it. "It may take weeks to free your young man." She looked at Debby, who had thrown herself into the chair by the window, and after one glance at the girl's clenched jaw she added quietly, "There isn't anything you can *do*, you know."

"I can be suspicious," she said indignantly. "I tried to talk to the others, Andre especially, but they told me I was imagining things. They didn't *want* to listen."

Mrs. Pollifax said with interest, "Imagining what things?"

"You'll say the same thing," the girl cried accusingly. "You will, I know you will. But I won't get on the plane—I won't."

"Then why did you come here?" asked Mrs. Pollifax. "I remember how very casually you asked at what hotel I was staying. You knew even then that you were going to stay behind in Sofia and come here to see me. Why?"

"Because all of a sudden—for no reason at all—you said, 'Nikki isn't leaving with you?' And you looked surprised. And that's it, you see—Nikki."

Mrs. Pollifax abruptly sat down on the edge of the bed. "Nikki. . . . Go on."

Leaning forward, the girl said earnestly, "It's Nikki who insisted we come to Bulgaria. Nobody—but nobody—had the slightest intention of coming here, or even wanted to. 'Let's go to Bulgaria' he said day after day, like brainwashing, and it was Nikki who got the visas for us, he handled everything. Phil didn't want to come. He said Bulgaria was the last place he wanted to go. He had every intention of not coming—"

"Yes, I know. Why did he let you all persuade him?"

Debby looked helplessly at Mrs. Pollifax. "It's crazy, I know it is, but I think Phil was drugged."

Mrs. Pollifax started. "Drugged!"

She nodded. "Yes. From all that Phil said, he planned to see the rest of us off on the plane and either wait for us in Belgrade or go back to Dubrovnik. I mean, he really wasn't going to *go* to Bulgaria."

"Yes," said Mrs. Pollifax in a startled voice, remembering.

"Nikki gave him a pill at breakfast that day—he said it was a dysentery pill. All I know is that Phil did get on that plane and he slept. He slept so hard that nobody could rouse him, nobody could talk to him and when we got to Sofia the stewardess had to help us wake him. And then . . ."

"Yes?"

Debby scowled. "That's only part of it. When we got to Customs, Nikki acted so strangely. It happened because he couldn't find something, some paper or other—it must have been paper because he kept turning his wallet inside out, and what will fit in a wallet except paper? The Customs man got very uptight about it all, and he called some other man in uniform, who took us out of line, and he took Nikki away to question him. The other kids were afraid for Nikki, except . . ."

"Yes?"

She shook her head. "I got a different feeling. There was something wrong about it all. I don't know how to explain it except I've noticed in these communist countries how quiet people get when they meet a uniform. They're afraid of drawing attention to themselves, you know? It's spooky. But Nikki acted so—so arrogant. As if the Customs man was a peasant. Nikki wasn't afraid, he was *furious.*"

Mrs. Pollifax was silent; it was not until Debby spoke again that she realized how far her thoughts had gone.

"Well?" asked Debby angrily. "You're going to tell me I'm crazy now, aren't you?"

Mrs. Pollifax looked at her and smiled. "Foolhardy, perhaps. Reckless to stay, yes. Crazy, no. You think Philip was persuaded into Bulgaria for just this purpose? To be arrested?"

Debby looked startled. "Is that what I think? I hadn't followed it that far. I just don't think Nikki is what he appears to be."

Mrs. Pollifax nodded absently. She was thinking that this was clearly her moment of truth and that she had a decision to make. The sensible thing, of course, was to place Debby in a taxi and send her off at once, alone, to the American Embassy. There she would be listened to by a minor clerk, told that she had a lively imagination and shipped out of Sofia with dispatch.

That was the sensible course. Debby would be upset, but she would survive; Mrs. Pollifax would remain at leisure to carry out her courier assignment with no complications; Philip Trenda would eventually be released because surely American citizens couldn't be imprisoned forever on trumped-up charges? But the drawback to taking the sensible course, reflected Mrs. Pollifax, was that it so frequently diminished the people involved. Debby would survive but certainly not without suffering a deep loss of faith. She herself would remain at leisure, but at the cost of a lively quarrel with her conscience, and there was no one to guarantee Philip Trenda's freedom, or even his future. Not yet.

Mrs. Pollifax made the only decision that was possible for her. "If we hurry I think we can get to the Embassy before it closes," she said, and stood up. "I'll go with you. I think your doubts about Nikki are quite sound, for reasons which I'll explain when we get there."

"You mean you're listening?" gasped the girl.

"I'm listening," said Mrs. Pollifax. "You've already missed your plane. Have you money? Have you a room for tonight?"

"Money, yes," said Debby. "No room, because we bunked in a place Nikki found for us and I didn't want him to know I was staying behind."

"Very shrewd of you," said Mrs. Pollifax, placing her hat squarely on her head. "If the Rila has no space for you, you can share this room, but you really must promise to leave Sofia in the morning," she told her sharply. "You simply can't go around expressing yourself in a country like this without getting into a great deal of trouble."

"I'm already in trouble," Debby said forlornly.

"Then promise, and let's go."

Chapter Nine

It was almost six o'clock before they were ushered into the office of a Mr. Benjamin Eastlake at the Embassy. "I want you to listen to this young friend of Philip Trenda's," Mrs. Pollifax said, adding tartly, "if only because we've had to talk to so many people before reaching you. I shouldn't care to try finding you again."

"My apologies," Eastlake said. "I've been running late all day and now I'm overdue at a tiresome cocktail party. I'm well protected by secretaries," he added wryly. "A most serious business, this, the Bulgarians arresting an American and charging him with espionage. I've been in touch with Washington all day and I can tell you that a formal complaint has already been lodged with the Bulgarian government."

"Will that help?" asked Debby eagerly.

Eastlake shrugged. "It depends entirely on why the Bulgarians arrested him. Or why they *think* they arrested him."

"Perhaps what Debby would like to tell you may add a piece to the puzzle," suggested Mrs. Pollifax.

Eastlake smiled at Debby. "You look familiar. You were here yesterday?"

Debby smiled back shyly. "Yes, except I didn't say anything. Nikki did all the talking."

He nodded. "Very well. Talk."

Debby explained her suspicions to Mr. Eastlake, beginning with Belgrade and ending with her visit to Mrs. Pollifax at the Hotel Rila.

"Who quite wisely felt I should hear this," he said judiciously. "But you know it's very difficult to believe this young Nikki can be quite as sinister as you paint him. He was properly outraged about the whole situation, and extremely concerned."

Mrs. Pollifax said quietly, "I wonder if you know what passport he travels under?"

"Passport? You mean his nationality?" Eastlake rang a buzzer. "Bogen, could you get me that list of young people traveling with Trenda?" It was given him and as he glanced down the sheet he frowned. "Odd."

"What is?"

"He had a German passport. He didn't have a German accent."

"He told us he was Yugoslavian," Debby said indignantly.

Eastlake's scowl lightened. "Then he's probably a transplanted Yugoslavian. Yugoslavs are allowed to leave their country, you know. Theirs is the only communist government that allows immigration, free access and egress, et cetera." He smiled. "Very possible, you know, for him to be both German and Yugoslavian."

Mrs. Pollifax was not to be diverted. She said firmly, "Last night I went to the apartment of a gentleman I'd been told might become my guide around Sofia. Do you know a Mr. Carleton Bemish?"

Eastlake winced. "I've met him. I shouldn't care to *know* him."

"Mr. Bemish appeared to have met with a windfall," she continued quietly. "Champagne on the table. Boxes of new clothes on his couch. He wasn't at all interested in becoming my guide. He was far more interested in the guest he was expecting."

Eastlake looked bored but polite.

"As I was about to leave," she went on crisply, "his guest arrived at the door and they greeted one another effusively, like very old friends. His guest," she added, "was Nikki."

"Nikki!" echoed Eastlake.

"Nikki?" said Debby in a startled voice and turned to stare at Mrs. Pollifax in astonishment. "But Nikki's never been to Bulgaria before. He said so."

"Can you be certain it was Nikki?" asked Eastlake with a frown.

"I was so certain that I reminded him I'd seen him in the Belgrade air terminal, and had traveled on the same plane. He made no attempt to deny it. In fact we spoke of . . ." She stopped in mid-sentence.

"What?" asked Debby, leaning forward.

Mrs. Pollifax frowned. "I'd quite forgotten. I told him I'd seen you all being questioned at Customs, and I told Nikki I hoped there had been no trouble."

"Yes?" said Eastlake, no longer looking bored.

"Nikki said it had been nothing, only a small misunderstanding, but *he didn't mention that Philip had been arrested.*"

"This was last night?"

Mrs. Pollifax nodded.

"But that was hours after Phil had been arrested," gasped Debby. "What time?"

"About seven."

"Only an hour after Nikki was here in this office wanting to know what was being done to release Phil," said Eastlake. "You think Nikki could be Bulgarian?"

"It's an interesting possibility, don't you think?" suggested Mrs. Pollifax.

Eastlake whistled. "It would certainly put a different light on the subject."

Debby was looking excited. "Oh, I'm so glad we came!"

Mrs. Pollifax looked at her. "But none of this begins to free Philip, you know. It may only make it . . . more difficult."

"But why?"

It was Eastlake who replied. "She means that there may be some purpose behind Phil's arrest that we don't know and can't guess." He regarded Debby thoughtfully.

"What are you thinking?" asked Mrs. Pollifax, watching him. "What will you do?"

He lifted both hands helplessly. "Report this at once to Washington, of course."

"But why Phil?" asked Debby.

"Exactly. Why not you, or that young Andre? Why anybody at all?" asked Eastlake. "Above all, why a young American student? If they're trying to provoke an incident . . ." His lips tightened. "Now that you've reported this, Debby, I want your promise to be on the morning plane out of Sofia."

Debby sighed. "I already promised Mrs. Pollifax."

"Then if you'll wait in the corridor I'd like to speak to Mrs. Pollifax alone."

When she had gone Eastlake shook his head and stood up. He walked to the window, stared out and then turned. "A damnable situation," he growled. "That girl absolutely must be gotten out of Bulgaria tomorrow."

"You think she's in danger?"

He looked at her in surprise. "Danger? Not very likely. Why should she be?"

"I thought—"

"It has other ramifications," he said curtly. "I wish like hell this girl had left with the others. The Bulgarians are very strait-laced about their young people. I've been trying all day—before I heard these new details—to find out who on earth allowed these kids into this country."

"I don't understand," said Mrs. Pollifax.

"They're virtually hippies," he said bluntly. "Oh, nice enough kids, of course, but not representative of our best American youth. The propaganda value of their appearance alone is enough to turn my hair white. I understand they were seen walking barefooted in Sofia—and not a one of the young men has had a haircut in months."

"I see," said Mrs. Pollifax. "I suppose it's your job to consider things like this, but I would have thought you might be more concerned about—"

"Naturally I'm concerned," he snapped. "But I happen to officially represent the United States here and this means thinking in terms of image." He leaned forward. "I'm talking about public-ity, Mrs. Pollifax. Photographs. Make sure that girl leaves tomor-row, and wearing shoes and a clean dress."

"I'm not sure she has a dress," said Mrs. Pollifax tartly. "She's waiting outside, do you want to ask her?"

He looked at her. "Just get her out before the news story heats up."

"In the meantime," said Mrs. Pollifax, rising, "I assume that you'll keep in mind that Philip Trenda, no matter what length his hair, is still an American citizen?"

Eastlake gave her a long, level scrutiny. "Oh yes, Mrs. Pol-lifax, we will," he said dryly. "We do our best for distressed Ameri-can citizens even if they turn out to be criminals or bona fide spies.

But it would be infinitely simpler if it was someone like yourself who had been arrested yesterday."

"Even if I turned out to be a spy?" asked Mrs. Pollifax with a pleasant smile.

He looked at her pityingly, as if the poverty of her humor overtaxed his patience, and Mrs. Pollifax left with the feeling that she had delivered the last word, even if her audience didn't realize it.

At nine she and Debby dined together in the hotel restaurant. They had no sooner ordered when a waiter emerged who spoke primitive English—Mrs. Pollifax wondered where the management had been hiding him—and announced that Balkantourist was calling her on the telephone at the front desk.

"That will be Nevena," she said with a sigh, and left Debby to follow the man upstairs to the lobby. "Mrs. Pollifax," she said into the phone.

But it was not Balkantourist. "How do you do," said a man's voice, lightly accented. "This is the man from the shop you visited yesterday. About the brown sheepskin vest?"

"Oh—yes," gasped Mrs. Pollifax. "Yes indeed." She was aware of two desk clerks at her elbow and she inched unobtrusively away from them. "I'm very glad to hear," she said, but of one thing she was certain: this was not the same man she had spoken with in the tailor shop—the voice and the accent were different.

"Our mutual friend has been called away," continued the voice smoothly. "It is suggested you meet him in Tarnovo."

"Where?"

"It is some distance. You have a car? It is suggested you leave tomorrow, Wednesday morning. It is a drive in miles of some one hundred fifty. A reservation has been made for you at the Hotel Yantra tomorrow night."

"Those two names," said Mrs. Pollifax, fumbling for a pencil. "Again, please?"

"Tarnovo. T-a-r-n-o-v-o. The Hotel Yantra."

"Yes," said Mrs. Pollifax, baffled by such unexpected instructions. "But why?" she asked. "Is this really necessary? I don't understand—"

The voice was cold. "Quite necessary." A gentle click at the other end of the line told her that she was no longer in contact with her mysterious caller. She placed the receiver back on the hook. With a polite smile for the two young desk clerks, she made her way quickly to the ladies' room, locked the door behind her and removed a map of Bulgaria from her purse. Eventually she found Tarnovo—it was in the center of the country.

But why? she thought indignantly. Why must she leave Sofia and go driving halfway across Bulgaria, even if the country *was* only three hundred miles from west to east?

She could think of only two reasons at the moment. The small gray man might *not* be one of Tsanko's people. Or Shipkov's message and this telephone call were both a trap and there was no Tsanko at all.

Neither possibility was heartening. But she had come to Bulgaria to carry out an assignment and this was the first communication she'd received. If it was a trap, she was going to have to discover it for herself by following it through to the end.

Carefully she tore up her written notes on Tarnovo and flushed them down the toilet. Returning to Debby she said, "I'll be leaving Sofia too, tomorrow. I'm going to do a little touring of the countryside."

"Oh," said Debby, startled.

Mrs. Pollifax reached out and patted her hand. "But I won't forget about Philip. I'll keep in touch with the Embassy for as long as I'm in Bulgaria and if you'll give me your address I'll write every piece of news I hear."

But even as she reassured Debby she was thinking, Why Tarnovo? Why so far?

It was upsetting, and she admitted to a distinct uneasiness.

Chapter Ten

A change of plan was not casually accomplished. The hotel had collected Mrs. Pollifax's passport upon her arrival and in order to recover it she had to explain her plans to leave the next day. Balkantourist was telephoned, and an irate Nevena summoned again to demand what on earth she wanted.

"I want to drive into the country tomorrow and remain away for a few days," explained Mrs. Pollifax.

"You arrived only yesterday in Sofia."

"That's true. Now I want to leave."

"Why?"

Mrs. Pollifax sighed and embarked upon a story about meeting tourists that day who had told her Sofia was not the real Bulgaria.

"They said *that?*" Nevena said suspiciously. "Who were they?"

"I haven't the slightest idea. But in any case you know I want to see the real Bulgaria and I was planning anyway to drive into the country before I leave. Now I want to go tomorrow."

"Yes? Well, then, Borovets would be good, very good. It is south of Sofia, they ski there big in winter. I make a reservation at Hotel Balkantourist in Borovets for your arrival there tomorrow."

Mrs. Pollifax opened her mouth to protest and then closed it. There was obviously no point in mentioning Tarnovo to Nevena if Nevena wanted her to go to Borovets. If she persisted, the reservation at the Hotel Yantra might be accidentally uncovered, too. At this moment Mrs. Pollifax clearly understood the frustration that caused small children to lie through their teeth in the face of authority.

"Give me the manager, I speak with him," Nevena said, and Mrs. Pollifax gladly handed the phone to him. At length he prom-

ised to have her passport for her in the morning when she checked
out.

"Thank you—nine o'clock," emphasized Mrs. Pollifax, and
decided that it would be infinitely simpler if she did not mention
that Debby would be staying the night with her.

Mrs. Pollifax set her alarm for a seven o'clock rising, determined to see that her young charge arrived at the airport on time;
she wanted nothing to interfere with her new rendezvous in
Tarnovo. She was pleased to note that at sight of a proper bathroom Debby made happy feminine sounds and dug out shampoo,
soap and creams from her pack. It was possible, thought Mrs. Pollifax, that she would even wear a dress for the flight.

On this pleasant note Mrs. Pollifax fell asleep.

She awoke suddenly, with a rapidly beating heart. But this is
growing tiresome, she thought, staring up at a man silhouetted
beside her bed. He had half turned away from her and was holding
an object up to the dim light from the window. He held it with one
hand and with the other hand he stroked it. Eyes wide open now,
Mrs. Pollifax saw that it was a knife he held. He was touching it,
testing it, with a concentration that turned her cold.

He moved with infinite grace. His speed was incredible. Mrs.
Pollifax barely had time to roll to the edge of the bed. As she
dropped to the floor she heard the ugly ripping sound of the knife
slicing the pillow where only a second before her head had lain.
Then with a second swift movement he turned toward Debby's
bed.

Mrs. Pollifax screamed.

It was a small scream, but it was effective. In the other bed
Debby sat upright and turned on the bedside light in one fluid,
competent motion that amazed Mrs. Pollifax. The light showed
her assailant half-crouched between the beds, his eyes blinking at
the sudden light.

Debby didn't scream. To Mrs. Pollifax's astonishment she
stood up in bed and with a wild shout threw herself at the man and
carried him to the floor with her. It was the most surprising tackle
that Mrs. Pollifax had ever seen. The young, she thought, must feel
so very un-used.

She stumbled to her feet to help. As Debby and the man

rolled out into the middle of the room she saw the knife flash in the man's hand and abruptly he jumped to his feet. Debby clung to his legs. He viciously kicked away her grasp, brushed past Mrs. Pollifax, opened the door and fled.

Mrs. Pollifax had never seen him before. Since she was unlikely to see him again tonight she turned to Debby, who sat on the floor rocking back and forth in pain, her left hand cradled between her knees and blood streaming down her face from a scalp wound.

"Oh, my dear," gasped Mrs. Pollifax after one glance at the bone pushing its way through the skin of Debby's thumb, and she hurried to the telephone. There she stopped, remembering that no one would understand her cry for help and that she'd already had a burglar the night before. She turned back. "Debby, we're going to have to get you downstairs to the lobby," she said fiercely. "Can you walk? Your scalp wound needs stitches, and your thumb needs a splint."

"I'll be okay," Debby said in a dazed voice.

"Lean on me. And tell them you fell into a mirror, do you understand?"

"But he tried to kill me!" cried Debby.

Mrs. Pollifax nodded. "Yes," she said, and for just a moment allowed herself to remember what it had felt like to be inches away from his knife. But what troubled her most of all in remembering was that the man had known Debby was in the room with her. There'd been no hesitation at all—and no light shown—before he'd turned from Mrs. Pollifax to the next bed.

He had planned to murder them both.

"I don't think we can afford the police," she explained. "Trust me, will you?" Releasing Debby she hurried into the bathroom. The mirror lining the sink was impossible to fall into, but there was a full-length mirror attached to the back of the door. Mrs. Pollifax grabbed Debby's hairbrush and after several attacks succeeded in shattering the glass. "Let's go," she told Debby and they moved slowly out into the hall, a trail of blood taking shape behind them. The self-service elevator bore them down to the lobby, the doors slid open and Mrs. Pollifax carried her bloody companion into the lobby.

The picture they made abolished any need for translations. The desk clerk shouted, rang bells, pressed buzzers; a potential hotel scandal provoked the same reaction in any language and any country. Debby was delivered into the hands of a doctor who arrived breathless and beltless and still in bedroom slippers. The manager of the hotel followed, and then at last a representative of Balkantourist—but not Nevena, for which Mrs. Pollifax could be grateful.

It was daylight before it was all over: the setting and bandaging of Debby's thumb, the stitching of the scalp wound and the questions. It no longer mattered to Mrs. Pollifax how it had all happened. What began to matter very much was her departure for Tarnovo in several hours; this was, after all, the whole point of her being in Bulgaria. "I want to speak," she told the Balkantourist representative firmly.

"Yes?"

"I am due to leave Sofia this morning in my car."

"Yes, yes, they have your passport ready to give you," he said.

"And the girl is to leave Sofia by plane this morning—"

"No," said the Balkantourist representative flatly.

"I beg your pardon?"

"The doctor says *no*. The doctor is firm. The girl cannot take flight alone. She must be looked after twenty-four hours. She is tired—spent, you know? There is some shock. To wander alone"— he shook his head disapprovingly—"she would cry, maybe faint, go unconscious. She needs the comfort of a presence, you understand?"

Mrs. Pollifax considered this; he was only too right, of course, but she couldn't possibly delay her own departure. Yet if she couldn't leave Debby here alone then there was only one alternative, and this dismayed her because she had no idea what lay ahead of her in Tarnovo. "Is she well enough to do a little driving in a car? In my *presence?*"

This was queried of the doctor, who smiled warmly, nodding. Mr. Eastlake wouldn't like this, she thought, but then Mr. Eastlake could be prevented from knowing about it. Tsanko wouldn't like it either—if they ever made contact—and she was sure that Carstairs would be appalled.

But she could scarcely abandon the child to a lonely hotel room for several days, and she could certainly not insist that Debby fly off to another lonely hotel room in another strange country.

Her limitations as a ruthless agent had never been so pressing. Mrs. Pollifax sighed over them even as she said, "Good. She'll go with me then."

Everyone looked extremely relieved, and Mrs. Pollifax realized that the hotel would be delighted to be rid of her. Just to be sure of this she asked that a basket of fruit be packed for their drive, and two breakfasts be sent to her room.

It was exactly half-past nine when they drove away from the hotel, and considering the obstacles they'd encountered, Mrs. Pollifax congratulated herself on their leaving at all. Debby was curled up in the rear seat with orders to read road signs, remain quiet and stay warm. In any case Mrs. Pollifax had to concentrate for the first half an hour on getting them out of Sofia, with its maze-like streets leading into broad boulevards whose names all seemed to end in *ev* or *iski*. It was made more difficult by the fact that she wanted to go east on Route One toward Tarnovo, but she had been given detailed directions south, into artery number five, which would take her to Borovets. She was aware by this time of how few people spoke English in Bulgaria—and the perils of getting lost under such conditions—and so she simply followed her printed directions out of Sofia and then detoured north to Route One through a town called—incongruously—Elin Pelin. But all of this added miles to their excursion.

"There—we have reached Route One at last," she announced as they bounced onto a paved road. "Thank heaven that route numbers look the same in any language."

"Route One doesn't *feel* any better," Debby said, sitting up and looking around her. "What are these roads built of?"

Poplars lined the road, and beyond them stretched fields that carried the eye to the mountains on either side, still clouded by morning haze. The valley was green and rolling, punctuated by tidy haystacks at symmetrical intervals, and here and there low-lying walls of intricately worked stone. They passed a hay wagon and a farm truck and then no one.

"Of stone," said Mrs. Pollifax in reply. "Rather like those farm walls. You can see it here and there where the macadam's missing—a parquet affect." Waving a hand toward the mountains on their left, she added, "We cross that range further along, at

Shipka Pass, where something like twenty-eight thousand Bulgarians died fighting the Turks."

"Twenty-eight *thousand?*" repeated Debby disbelievingly.

"You'll find it on the back of the map, translated into French,
German and English. It says there's a monument and a restaurant
there. They fought in the dead of winter and when they ran out of
ammunition they threw rocks and boulders down the slopes at the
Turks. There were eighteen survivors."

Debby whistled. "That beats Custer's last stand. Twenty-
eight thousand and they didn't even *win?*"

"I don't think they're on the winning side very often in Bulgaria," said Mrs. Pollifax tartly.

Debby said, "That's dramatic, you know? I never thought
about the places I hiked through this summer."

"Rather a waste. What *did* you think about?"

"Finding other kids. Looking for a piece of the action. That
sort of thing."

"Do your parents know you just wander about picking up
rides and people?"

Debby emitted a sound like *"Ech."*

"Do they even know you're in *Bulgaria?*" she asked in a startled voice.

This time Debby's comment sounded like *"Aaaah."*

Mrs. Pollifax sighed. "Debby, if we're going to be traveling
together I really think you'll have to enlarge your vocabulary. I'm
sure you'd much prefer to be with people your own age, but for a
few days we'll have to accept this situation and lay down some
ground rules. Later you can explain what '*aaaah*' means, but what
on earth is '*ech*'?"

Debby looked resentful. "Dr. Kidd doesn't ask things like
that. He's my psychiatrist and he wants me to be spontaneous."

"Well, I've nothing against psychiatrists or spontaneity," retorted Mrs. Pollifax, "but I do think clear communication simpli-
fies life a great deal. Now. What does *ech* mean?"

Debby laughed. "It sounds so funny when you say it."

"It sounds funny when you say it, too. What took you to a
psychiatrist, by the way?"

"I run away a lot," Debby said vaguely. "And I get attached to too many boys. It upsets my parents. Dr. Kidd says I get devoted to people because *they're* not. Dr. Kidd says they are, but I don't believe it. How *can* they be when they never say no and are scared of me?"

Mrs. Pollifax deftly supplied her own translation. "You mean you haven't written your parents at all since you left America?"

"That's right," said Debby. "I'm giving them a restful summer."

"But don't they mind not hearing? Don't they worry?"

"You know," she said a little wistfully, "I wish they did sometimes. Just once in a while. They really don't know what to do with me and they always want me to be *happy*. I'm too old for summer camps now so they said I could go to Europe on my own. Dr. Kidd said maybe I'll find myself by doing it."

Mrs. Pollifax was silent and then she said lightly, dryly, "I see. Rather like a lost-and-found department."

But Debby had grown tired of the subject. "I wonder how Phil is today. What's at this Borovets place we're going to visit, or are you going to say I'll find out soon enough?"

"You would if we were going there," Mrs. Pollifax told her. "But we're not, we're going to Tarnovo."

"For pete's sake why?"

"Because I've never had any intention of going anywhere else," said Mrs. Pollifax reasonably. "Debby, look at the map and see if there's a gas station at Zlatica, will you? You'll find tiny red automobiles printed on the map wherever one can buy gas."

Debby rustled the map. "Yes, there's one at Zlatica. Isn't it weird? There aren't many in the whole country. Or cars either."

Mrs. Pollifax said without expression, "There's been a black Renault behind us on the road for some time. I think we'll have the gas tank filled and let it pass us." She'd first noted the car as far back as Elin Pelin, because of the clouds of dust it had raised behind them on that particular stretch of dusty countryside. Now, some miles later, it was still there and the coincidence made her uneasy.

Near Zlatica she pulled into the neat cement and grass compound decorated with flower beds and Nempon signs, and two husky women in blue overalls emerged.

"Oh, wow," said Debby, collapsing into giggles.

"Sssh," said Mrs. Pollifax sternly, and after a clumsy exchange of sign language and a great number of titters and smiles, the gas tank was filled, the oil checked and bills counted. More important, the black Renault passed them and disappeared ahead.

The road carried them along the floor of the valley, the mountains on either side growing sharper as the haze cleared. They passed tiny thatch-roofed farmhouses, each with its yard neatly enclosed by fences made of woven twigs. Sometimes an old woman sat on a bench by the door, a spindle in one hand, a bundle of flax in the other. Once they saw a shepherd standing at a distance on a hill, his watchtower behind him, a marvelous leather cape across his shoulders. "He actually carries a *crook*," Debby said in awe.

And then the fields turned into acre after acre of roses, entire hillsides dotted with extravagant pinks and yellows and scarlets. "This must be the Valley of Roses," Debby announced after a look at the map.

"Debby, I'm thinking about that horrid man with the knife last night," said Mrs. Pollifax abruptly. "Where did you learn to tackle like that, by the way? You were marvelous."

"Oh that was nothing," Debby said eagerly. "You should see me on the parallel bars and the ropes. I adore phys. ed., it's the only subject I pass in school. What about that man? Do you think he had anything to do with Phil's arrest?"

"I don't know," said Mrs. Pollifax honestly. "Debby, have you any idea at all why it should have been Philip who was arrested?"

"Of course not," said Debby. "I wish we could stop at one of those rose places. Want a grape from the basket?"

"No, and you answered my question much too quickly," she said. "Of course the answer wouldn't be obvious. Tell me what you know about him."

"About Phil?" Debby was smiling. "Nothing much except I think he's just great. He digs Simon and Garfunkel—and Leonard Cohen—and he's gentle and he *listens*."

"Debby."

"Hmm?"

"I didn't ask how you *feel* about him, I'm trying to find out why he was arrested for espionage an hour after he arrived in Bulgaria. Facts."

"Facts?" echoed Debby blankly.

"Yes. For instance, where does Philip come from? Where does he live? What do his parents do?" Mrs. Pollifax glanced into the rearview mirror at Debby's face and saw its bewilderment.

"Oh. Well . . ." Debby began, and floundered. "I only met him three weeks ago," she said indignantly. "*Those* things don't matter."

"They matter now," said Mrs. Pollifax firmly. "Think. Concentrate."

"If you want *labels*," Debby said scornfully, "he's a sophomore at the University of Illinois."

"Good! An excellent beginning." She realized that she was asking Debby to violate an unspoken code and she added very gently, "It's this sort of thing, Debby, that could solve the riddle. More, it could help free him."

Debby said promptly, "Well, I've got some of his books in my pack. Maybe he scribbled his address in one of them."

Mrs. Pollifax heard rustlings and clankings and smiled as she saw Debby toss out a tin drinking cup, a hairbrush and an assortment of paperbacks. Debby said, "This one's his—and this—and the Kahlil Gibran. Hey," she shouted, "I found something."

"Hooray," said Mrs. Pollifax.

"It was stuck in the pages as a bookmark." She handed Mrs. Pollifax a pocket calendar the size of a playing card, a familiar plasticized type distributed by banks and corporations at Christmastime.

Mrs. Pollifax handed it back. "Read it to me," she said. "I can't read it without stopping the car."

"It says"—Debby held it up to the light—"in large letters it says TRENDA-ARCTIC OIL COMPANY, and under this in small letters, *President, Peter F. Trenda. Headquarters Chicago, Illinois; Fairbanks, Alaska, and St. John's, Newfoundland.*"

Mrs. Pollifax nodded. "Good for you. I feel better."

Debby's voice was disappointed. "All it means is that Phil's parents are rich. Filthy rich, probably."

Mrs. Pollifax glanced into the rearview mirror at Debby. "Even that's a help," she told her, and then her glance went beyond Debby to the road. A black Renault sedan had just drawn out of a side road and was driving at some distance behind them.

Chapter Eleven

They reached Shipka Pass shortly after noon, having stopped a few minutes to marvel at the Shipka Monastery, with its gold onion domes gleaming softly in the sun like an enchanted fairy-tale palace.

Once at the summit they parked the car in the broad flat parking area and Mrs. Pollifax stood a minute listening to the wind. "It sounds like the sea," she said. "As if it's swept thousands and thousands of miles without meeting any resistance." She realized that she was also listening for the sound of an engine behind them, and when no black Renault appeared she sighed with relief. Turning toward the low stone buildings she said, "Let's treat ourselves to a really Bulgarian lunch, shall we?"

"Great," said Debby. "How far are we from that place you want to go?"

"About twenty or thirty miles. Not far."

They lunched on cuzek patladjan and mishmash and misquette grapes under dark murals of the Battle of Shipka Pass. Mrs. Pollifax produced aspirin from her bag for Debby, whose thumb was beginning to throb, and they bought a few postcards in the lobby. While Debby lingered in the ladies' room Mrs. Pollifax wandered outside just in time to see a black Renault sedan drive out of the parking expanse and head down the mountain toward Gabrovo and Tarnovo.

She watched it vanish with a worried frown. It was possible that another tourist might drive from Sofia to Shipka Pass along this same route, and at precisely the same hour, but it struck her as exceedingly odd that they reached Shipka Pass at the same time. She had stopped for gas at Zlatica, and had seen the Renault pass them, and then they had stopped at the monastery and had again seen the Renault pass. Yet the Renault had not reached the summit before they did, and now it was just leaving.

If that's the same Renault, then we're being followed, she thought, naming her fear. But by whom? There had been the small gray man in the gray suit, her mysterious burglar of the first evening, the man with the knife last night, and there was the remote possibility that Tsanko could be keeping them under surveillance. She couldn't imagine Balkantourist going to such lengths to make sure that she reached Borovets. Remembering Nevena's character, she thought that Balkantourist would have flagged her down two miles out of Sofia and sternly forced her back on the road southward.

I don't like it, she thought, remembering that she was here on nothing but faith and a telephone call from a stranger. It was extraordinary, this abrupt order to leave Sofia and drive halfway across Bulgaria. Could Tsanko really be trusted?

She felt acutely lonely as she stood listening to the sound of the wind. Her only companion was a charming, waif-like child who was more likely to prove a liability in case of untoward circumstances. She herself felt unaccountably frail. She thought it must stem from the odd juxtaposition of the familiar and the sinister; no country so foreign in nature had the right to look so much like the American countryside of New England, with Queen Anne's lace growing along the roads, poplar trees and spruces thickly lining the slopes, and mountains scalloping the horizon at a distance. It was *not* New England, but its very familiarity blunted all sense of real danger. She had to struggle to remember that this was a police state and a country where almost no English was spoken. What was most provoking of all, the words were so cluttered with consonants that one couldn't even guess their meaning. What *could* one do with a word spelled **СВЯТ?**

"Hey—what's the matter?" asked Debby, joining her. "You look spooky."

"I *feel* spooky," admitted Mrs. Pollifax with a frown. "I don't know why, either, except I have the feeling we shouldn't have stopped here for lunch."

"It must be the ghosts of Shipka Pass," Debby said. "You know—those twenty-eight thousand Bulgarians killed here fighting the Turks."

"Of course," said Mrs. Pollifax lightly. "Shall we go now?"

*   *   *

They had traveled only a few miles down the mountainside when the brakes failed. The road was steep and curving, with a precipitous drop on the right and a precipitous slope on the left. As Mrs. Pollifax stamped helplessly on the brake pedal again and again the car only gathered momentum. Furiously she tugged at the emergency brake; for just a second it caught, lessening their speed, and then the emergency snapped under the strain and came away in her hand.

"What is it?" cried Debby.

"Brakes," gasped Mrs. Pollifax, and clung to the wheel as they gathered speed and wildly careened around a hairpin curve. Out of the corner of her eye she saw the sheer, cliff-like drop on their right. Nothing on earth could hold their wheels on the road if they met a second curve like this. They would fly off the mountain into space and plummet to the depths of the ravine.

"We've got to crash," she shouted. "Get down!"

The road briefly straightened. With all of her strength Mrs. Pollifax leaned on the steering wheel, pulling it toward the mountain side of the road. Every instinct in her body fought a crash. The wall of the mountain loomed near to the windshield and for just one second she stared straight into rich black soil lightly covered over with low evergreens, grass, the stunted trunk of a tree in a crevice, and then came the impact of metal against earth, terrible grinding noises, the splintering of glass and silence.

She opened her eyes to discover that she was still alive. "Debby?" she gasped.

From somewhere behind her Debby mumbled something unintelligible and her head lifted from the floor of the car. "I'm okay," she said in a surprised voice. A second later she added with still more surprise, "But I think I'm going to scream if we don't get out of here. Are we trapped?"

Mrs. Pollifax looked around her. The car had tunneled its way several feet into the steep hillside—she shuddered to think how fast they'd been going—and she was staring into a wall of earth. "We'll break the back window," she announced. "Open up the rear seat, they said the tools are under it." Her hat was on the floor; she picked it up and placed it on her head again.

A few minutes later the last surviving window of the car had been broken with a lug, and Debby threw out her pack and crawled after it. Mrs. Pollifax followed less gracefully with her suitcase and sat down beside her next to the road. She realized that her hands were trembling badly, and she pressed them together in her lap. I hope I'm not going to faint, she thought.

"Well, are you going to sue the Volkswagen people or Balkantourist?" asked Debby indignantly. "We could have been *killed!*"

A dozen replies occurred to Mrs. Pollifax, all of which she discarded. It didn't seem the kindest moment to tell Debby that their brakes must have been tampered with while they lunched at Shipka Pass. It was a miracle they were still alive.

She thought, I'll tell her later, and she wished with surprising savagery that Debby had left on the plane this morning, broken thumb or no, for it was even less pleasant to realize it might be Debby someone was determined to murder.

Within the hour they caught a lift with a farmer who spoke no English but who nevertheless managed to express his genuine horror over their plight. He placed them in his battered truck, offered them peaches and cigarettes and drove them into Gabrovo. But not to a Nempon station; he took them to the police.

Well, thought Mrs. Pollifax philosophically, in for a penny, in for a pound.

The houses in Gabrovo were the same dun-colored stucco boxes they had seen along the way, the roofs of clay tile or thatch, the windows curtained with yellowing newspapers. The police, however, were quartered behind a wall with a gate, over which was suspended a neat black sign. From the main building just inside the gate jutted long low buildings forming a perfect square around a compound of grass and flowers in the center. Their Bulgarian friend went inside and came out with two policemen in uniforms of dark trousers and apple-green Eisenhower jackets. Presumably he had explained the condition of their car and its abandonment. Passports were shown, and after a brief interval another farmer was summoned who spoke some English—he had once worked a year in Kansas, he said—and he reported that the police were heartbroken at the situation of the American tourists. The proper authorities would be notified, the car towed to the nearest Nempon station and a message conveyed to them in Tarnovo when repairs had been made.

In the meantime—with the apologies of everyone concerned—there was nothing in town for them with wheels except a motorcycle.

"Motorcycle?" said Mrs. Pollifax doubtfully.

"Oh beautiful," cried Debby ecstatically. "I know how to drive a motorcycle, I ride one lots of times at home."

It was in this way that Mrs. Pollifax and Debby roared into Tarnovo on a motorcycle with Debby at the handlebars, the luggage roped to the rear and Mrs. Pollifax squashed between them, one hand inside of Debby's belt, the other clinging to her hat.

Chapter Twelve

Nothing had prepared Mrs. Pollifax for Tarnovo. It was built all over six hilltops of the Balkan mountain range and then repeatedly severed by the knife-cut wound of the Yantra's deep gorges. Houses tilted absurdly on the edge of the cliffs, and at the base—far below—trickled the Yantra, reduced by time and drought until its stream barely covered the bones of its riverbed. The old town, isolated, seemed to brush the sky and the clouds. It had once been the capital of an ancient kingdom—the Second Bulgarian Kingdom—and the remains of its fortress still crenelated the top of Tsaravets Hill. A stone entrance gate connected Tsaravets Hill to the main street of the town. This gate had stood since A.D. 1185, the only means of reaching a fortress rendered almost inviolate by the river encircling its hill half a mile below.

The Hotel Yantra was a modest building on a steep, cobblestoned street. Inside the open front door of the hotel lay a dusty lobby with a dusty leather couch and a glass-fronted display case of souvenirs: costumed dolls; postcards; a few tubes of toothpaste, and cigarettes, including a dusty package of Camels.

"Pollifax," she said to the woman behind the desk.

The woman offered pencil and paper with which Mrs. Pollifax obligingly wrote her name. The woman studied it and gave a sharp cry of recognition. She rang a bell, reached for a key and handed it to her along with a large white envelope.

Mrs. Pollifax opened the envelope and drew out a sheet of unsigned notepaper. On it was typed:

Tsaravets Hill is charming by moonlight. About 10 P.M. this evening, somewhere between gate and fortress.

Her heart beat a little faster at the message; she crushed the paper into her purse and turned back to the woman, who had reverted to sign language. Matching her gestures, Mrs. Pollifax described Debby's need for lodging, too. Passports were submitted and they were shown to a room with two beds on the second floor.

"Again no screens," commented Mrs. Pollifax, standing at the open window. Their room was directly over the front door and the cobblestoned street. She could understand why defenestration was the most customary form of assassination in the Balkans—there had been no screens in Sofia, either, and her room had been on the sixth floor.

"There's no water," called Debby from the bathroom.

"Nonsense, there has to be water," said Mrs. Pollifax, joining her. The floor of the tiny bathroom was painted a bilious green. There was neither tub nor shower stall, but high on one wall hung a shower spray with a drain under it. But none of the faucets yielded water. "I'll go and tell them," she said, and turned on her heel.

This challenge Mrs. Pollifax met by standing in front of the woman at the desk, wrenching open imaginary faucets and lifting her hands in dismay. The woman smiled and went to the telephone. A moment later she handed the receiver across the counter, gesturing to her to speak. "Hello?" Mrs. Pollifax said doubtfully.

"Yes," answered a voice at the other end of the wire. "You the English speak?"

"I certainly do," cried Mrs. Pollifax. "To whom am I speaking?"

"To Herr Vogel at Balkantourist hotel the street down. I visit here, some English I speak. The problem is what, *bitte?*"

"The problem is no water. Can you explain this to them here?"

"Ah . . ." The sigh was long and heavy. "But water there is nowhere at this hour, Fraulein. Between six and eight at night flows the water, you understand? Six and eight. In the morning flows the water seven to ten."

"Let me write that down," said Mrs. Pollifax despairingly. "But why the water flows—I mean, why?"

"A mountain town is Tarnovo, very high. Scarce is the water here. Did you see the jugs in the bathroom?"

"Jugs—yes."

"You the water fill with them, *bitte?* Six o'clock."

Mrs. Pollifax profusely thanked him, congratulated the clerk on her resourcefulness and went back to explain the situation to Debby, who was incredulous.

"It's ten minutes before six now," Mrs. Pollifax said. "I suggest we wait."

Precisely at six there issued from the bathroom an assortment of hollow noises, belches, rumbles and at last a trickling of water. Ten minutes later the toilet could be flushed. By that time Debby was at the sink washing a shirt and Mrs. Pollifax filling jugs of water, after which they took turns showering. They dined downstairs, below street level on an open balcony overlooking the gorge, and after this strolled briefly through the streets of the old town.

Shortly after nine o'clock Debby went to bed pleading exhaustion, and after reading a little while in the lobby Mrs. Pollifax left the hotel to enter Tsaravets Gate.

Debby awoke reluctantly from her sleep and for a moment had no idea where she was. Oh yes, Bulgaria, she remembered, and then, Tarnovo, and then she remembered Mrs. Pollifax. What had awakened her was the sound of men talking under her window, and since the window was wide open, and the entrance to the hotel directly below her, the voices rang out loud and clear. She thought what a queer, primitive place it was: no air conditioning, no screens and water only a few hours a day. It was like entering another world through a time capsule.

She had not been asleep for long because it was still not dark —twilight, actually. Debby crawled out of bed and went to the window and stood there, wishing she dared lean out, perhaps even to ask the men below to tell their local jokes somewhere else. But she didn't feel particularly venturesome. She was tired and her thumb ached and it was pleasant to stand there looking out and feel a faint breeze enter the stifling room. There was a streetlamp across the cobblestoned pavement and under it a flower stand that was closing for the night. The old woman placed the flowers carefully in baskets—there were not many—and simply walked away. She thought it must be peaceful to live in a place like this and know who you were, know your roots and feel them grow deep. It was almost ten o'clock by Debby's travel clock and she wondered where Mrs. Pollifax had gone.

About Mrs. Pollifax Debby felt wary and a little threatened; wary because she didn't understand her and threatened because she was in danger of liking her very much. Such a thought appalled her. Debby had long ago stopped trusting adults and it followed that they had long since given up trusting her. Nor was she trustworthy in the least—Debby was the first to concede this—except with those of her own age, and her trust here was ardent, inviolate and usually misplaced, as Dr. Kidd made a point of reminding her.

But then Dr. Kidd was adult, too, and just a shade phony, his hair worn too self-consciously long, his clothes carefully mod.

Her problem with Mrs. Pollifax was that she couldn't find anything phony about her yet. She said exactly what she thought. She didn't make the slightest pretense at entertaining Debby or deferring to her. *We have to accept the situation and lay down some ground rules,* she'd said, and that was that. There seemed to be something infinitely *reliable* about her; it was incredible in anyone so Establishment. There was also the matter of the motorcycle, ridden without any trauma at all, and after the burglary Mrs. Pollifax had actually broken the mirror in the bathroom, which implied a cooler head than one might expect from a woman who wore a bird's nest on her head.

Now she was out walking somewhere instead of fussing over Debby and her broken thumb. It upset all of Debby's conclusions that adults lived dreary lives pleasing everyone except themselves and never having any fun.

The men under her window suddenly broke into loud laughter and departed. Twilight was slipping level by level into darkness and the solitary streetlamp brightened as the natural light retreated. A large open farm truck drove down the street, its brakes squealing. It was filled with women seated motionless all around the open sides, black silhouettes in shawls, patient stoic figures being taken off to work in the fields. There was something sinister about their stillness.

Hearing footsteps outside in the hall, Debby jumped back into bed and closed her eyes, not wanting Mrs. Pollifax to know she'd been missed. Her haste proved unnecessary, however, because Mrs. Pollifax seemed to be having a great deal of trouble with the lock and the key.

The door opened. Debby closed her eyes again and feigned sleep. This was a mistake because just as it dawned upon her that Mrs. Pollifax didn't wear heavy boots or smell of onions a pair of rough hands had stuffed a gag into her mouth. There wasn't even time to roll over and kick, or jump up and flail with her fists, because she found herself being rolled into a coarse, smelly rug— over and over—and then she was lifted up and—it was incredible but there was no other explanation—lifted to the open window and dropped into another pair of hands waiting below in the street.

It had grown abruptly dark as Mrs. Pollifax began her walk toward the fortress and she hugged her coat against the dampness and the mountain breeze. Crossing the bridge, she left behind the pleasant, companionable sounds of the town and entered a strange world of country silence. There were no lights along the narrow road. Ahead of her the moon rose over Tsaravets Hill outlining the lonely towers of the old fortress and for just a moment time turned itself upside down so that Mrs. Pollifax could imagine this same scene eight centuries ago: the wind blowing through the river gorge and up across the hills; the night watch on Baldwin Tower ready to challenge her approach; lanterns like fireflies moving through the distant fortress; the sound of horses' hoofs on cobbles, the sentry singing out the hour in whatever language they spoke in Byzantine days, and over it all the same timeless moon dusting the same dark feudal hills where tsars and patriarchs and boyars sharpened their swords and prayed to their saints for protection.

Ahead an owl hooted, and Mrs. Pollifax jumped. From among the shrubs and bushes on the hill came a girl's coquettish laugh followed by a small delighted scream. She was not entirely alone, realized Mrs. Pollifax, but still she turned and uneasily looked behind her.

A car was inching its way through Tsaravets Gate. In the darkness it looked like a dark, moving slug with dim eyes. Its presence surprised her because she'd assumed the ancient gate was closed to traffic, and certainly not many cars existed that were small enough to drive through it. On the other hand she supposed that the officials involved in restoring the fortress had to have some means of entering. She stood back against the retaining wall that hugged the hill, and waited for the car to pass.

The car did not pass. It slowed as it neared her and then stopped. A door was opened, pinning her against the stone wall, and a voice said, "Get in, Mrs. Pollifax."

The voice astonished Mrs. Pollifax. "Mr.—*Bemish?*" she gasped, peering into the dark car. Surely Mr. Bemish couldn't be Tsanko! "Is that your voice, Mr. Bemish?" she asked uncertainly.

From the rear seat came sounds of movement, a stifled groan and then a shout: "Mrs. Pollifax! Run!"

"Debby?" gasped Mrs. Pollifax.

Before she could make sense of this—Debby being in the car when less than an hour ago she had been sound asleep in the hotel, and of Mr. Bemish being here when he ought to be in Sofia—an arm reached out from the back seat and roughly pulled Mrs. Pollifax inside. The motor was gunned and the car jerked forward.

"How dare you!" cried Mrs. Pollifax, pummeling the driver's shoulders with her fists.

"Get her off me! Gag the girl!" shouted Bemish, and spoke sharply in Bulgarian to his companion, who caught Mrs. Pollifax's arms and pressed a revolver to the back of her neck. At the same time what had seemed to be a rolled-up rug on the floor of the car began to move, clumsily kicking Mrs. Pollifax. She lifted her feet.

"How did you get Debby?" she demanded of Bemish.

He chuckled. "Very simple, really. Yugov picked the lock of your room, rolled her into a rug and dropped her out of the window into my arms. These things are very casually done in the Balkans."

"But what on earth do you want of us?"

"You have made so much trouble, the two of you," he said simply. "It has to stop."

"What trouble?" she demanded. "You're kidnapping us and we don't even know why. I don't understand." Apparently no one cared to explain further and when she spoke again it was in a different voice. "May I ask where we're going?"

"To the fortress," said Bemish. "There are a number of excavations and pits honey-combing the area."

Excavations, pits—she did not like the sound of such words; they had a lonely, hollow ring to them. Nor did Debby apparently, either, for she made a renewed effort to roll herself out of the rug. "Does Debby *have* to be tied up like an animal?" she asked quietly.

"Yes—like an animal," Bemish said. The hatred in his voice was almost a physical assault.

The car's headlights picked out an end to the retaining wall and a widening of the road into a cleared section. Above them the horizon was occupied by the outline of the fortress's tower and she realized they were almost under it. The car's lights were switched off and Mr. Bemish climbed out and turned. He held a gun in his hand; this much the moon illuminated. "Out," he said, waving the gun.

"I don't want to get out," said Mrs. Pollifax.

"Out, or I'll shoot the girl here and now."

Mrs. Pollifax climbed out.

"This way," Bemish said, prodding her. His companion followed, carrying Debby wrapped in the rug over his shoulder. After walking a few paces Bemish drew apart a clump of bushes and descended rock steps into a hole that was half cellar, half excavation. The man behind Mrs. Pollifax trod on her heel and then shoved her down as well. She entered what appeared to be the corner of an ancient, half-buried room.

Bemish was lighting a candle. "Over there," he said curtly, his face washed clean of friendliness. He brought a smaller gun from his jacket and began attaching a silencer to it, taking his time.

Mrs. Pollifax thought, There must be something I can do or say. She felt curiously mesmerized, completely unable to come to grips with their seizure. It had all happened so quickly. She had faced death before on her other assignments, but her protestations of innocence had never been so genuine as they were now. The moment seemed totally unreal—insane—because of its senselessness. "Why?" she said aloud to Bemish, and then as his companion unrolled Debby from the rug and propped her up beside Mrs. Pollifax, she said furiously, "You've made a terrible mistake! It's unspeakable, your murdering an innocent girl like this!"

"Orders," Bemish said, tight-lipped.

"From whom? And why?"

He looked at her closely. "You make nothing but trouble, Mrs. Pollifax, and now you make questions. You think I risk your speaking just once more with Mr. Eastlake?"

"Eastlake!" she gasped. "But that was about Philip!"

His lips trembled; drops of sweat shone on his forehead. "Bulgaria is my home now—my home, do you know what that means?" he shouted at her. "There's nowhere left for me to go, and you stick your silly American noses into my business. There's big money at stake, months of arrangements—months, do you hear?—and you come along and blunder into my business."

"*What* arrangements?" cried Mrs. Pollifax. "*What* money? *What* business?"

"Nikki understood," he shouted furiously. "Nikki saw right away that it's not fair. I've nothing, and Stella's brother has everything. If Petrov hadn't emigrated to America he'd have to share all his money, wouldn't he? He'd be forced to—this is a socialist country!"

He was plainly on the verge of hysteria. She felt pity for the violence in him that was driving him toward madness. Very quietly, for she had to understand, Mrs. Pollifax said, "Who is Stella, Mr. Bemish?"

"Stella? My wife, of course. And he sends her only hand-outs —his own sister!—when he has millions. Think of it, millions, and all in American dollars. Nikki understood, he saw immediately how unjust it is." Desperately he cried, "You think I want to kill you in cold blood like this? Don't you understand I have to, that it's orders? I must!"

His eyes widened in sudden astonishment. He said "orders" in a dazed voice, and then "must." His lips formed a silent O from which a trickle of blood emerged. Slowly, gently, he sank to the earth, his eyes fixed upon Mrs. Pollifax uncomprehendingly. His companion gasped and jumped for Bemish's fallen gun. As he reached it Mrs. Pollifax heard a soft *plop* and he, too, sank to the earth.

She stared in astonishment. They were both dead. Incredulous, she turned toward the entrance—to the gaping hole in the stone wall—and saw movement. Two men slid feet first into the cellar carrying rifles. One was young, dark and swarthy, wearing heavy corduroys and a gray sweater. The other man was Mrs. Pollifax's age, broad and bulky-shouldered with curling ironic brows. He said sharply to her, "You are Mrs. Pollifax?"

"Thank God," she gasped, suddenly weak.

"I'm Tsanko."

"Tsanko," she repeated numbly. "I'd almost forgotten. It wasn't a wild goose chase after all, then—you really are Tsanko."

"*Da.*" He was kneeling beside the two men, searching them, and as he opened the wallet of Bemish's companion he whistled. "This one is a member of the secret police." He looked at Mrs. Pollifax questioningly and then his glance fell on Debby. "Your friend is still with gag," he said. "You wish this?"

Mutely, Mrs. Pollifax shook her head. She tugged at Debby's gag and at once the girl burst into tears. "I want to go home," she cried indignantly. "I don't like this country. Burglars, lousy brakes, Phil's arrest, people rolling me into rugs and dropping me out of windows." Her voice rose hysterically. "Are those two men *dead?*"

"Yes," Tsanko said curtly, standing up, "and there is no time to bury them, we will have to use a little dynamite and bury the cellar instead. Kosta . . ." He turned and spoke to the young man in Bulgarian. Kosta nodded and climbed out of the cellar.

Debby said accusingly, "This man knows your name, I heard him!"

"Yes," said Mrs. Pollifax gently, "I came to Bulgaria to meet him. I do hope you're not going to have hysterics, because we're still in great danger."

Debby stared at her and suddenly quieted. "No, I won't have hysterics. *Why* did you come to Bulgaria to meet him, Mrs. Pollifax?"

"Later," she told her.

They climbed together out of the crumbling cellar, bushes tearing at their faces, and after several minutes Tsanko followed and gestured them toward a hill some distance away. Here they waited in silence. Presently Kosta joined them, as well as a second young man, and as they walked over and down the hill Mrs. Pollifax heard the sound of a small, muffled explosion behind them, like very faint thunder.

Mr. Carleton Bemish had just been buried. *Requiescat in pace*, thought Mrs. Pollifax sadly.

Chapter Thirteen

We are nearly there," said Tsanko.

Ahead of them stood a wall silhouetted against the moonlit sky, a solitary, abandoned wall holding back a hill grown over with grass. "We go inside this hill," he explained. "It hides a secret tunnel that once led to the fortress."

Kosta leaned over, pulling aside bushes to reveal a gap in the huge stones along the base of the wall. One by one they crawled into a narrow earthen tunnel, made an abrupt turn and emerged into a cave. Mrs. Pollifax heard Tsanko striking matches and suddenly light flared from a lantern. They were in a large room laced with roots, its ceiling braced by ancient timbers.

"You have given us much trouble, Amerikanski," Tsanko said, blowing out his match and turning up the wick of the lantern. Shaggy white brows completely shadowed his eyes. He looked tough, shrewd and weathered. Studying her face with equal frankness, he said, "Please—sit down, you are exhausted." From a corner he brought her a three-legged stool. From his pocket he removed a small vial, uncapped it and, leaning over the lantern, held it under her nose. "Smelling salts," he explained. "No, please—you look very faint."

"It's been a long day," confessed Mrs. Pollifax.

He carried the vial to Debby, the sharp smell of ammonia lingering behind him. He said dryly, "I believe this. I have observed you once in Sofia from a car. At that time the color of your face was surely five times brighter than at this minute." He sat down across from her and said bluntly, "On that occasion in Sofia I thought you a foolish American lady. Now I am not so sure. Do you know you have been followed by the secret police since the night you arrived in Sofia? We have had severe doubts about you."

"I'm sorry," she said, nodding. "That's why you wanted to get me out of Sofia—I understand that now."

"Not for *your* safety," he pointed out harshly. "For ours. We began to fear that Shipkov had betrayed us."

"Oh no, Shipkov reached New York safely, thanks to you," she said warmly. "Are you the man who warned him on the street?"

Tsanko shook his head. "That was Boris."

"You have a marked talent for saving lives," she said gratefully.

He was watching her intently; now he shook his head. "You still have no idea of the danger you have been in, Amerikanski—from us—especially after you came to Tarnovo with two men still following you. I can assure you it was only the utmost good luck—for you!—that I hear you speak with the two men on the road, and hear this young lady scream. Until then I am sure you are friends with these men, and arranging big trap for me."

"But I thought I was the one walking into a trap," she told him in surprise.

He lifted his shoulders in a large and eloquent shrug. "Touché. But we begin to see that you are in trouble, Amerikanski, you have blundered into something we know nothing about. How is this?"

"Philip Trenda," said Mrs. Pollifax, "Does that name mean anything to you?"

"It might," he said evasively and turned to Kosta, who had dropped in a corner with both hands across his eyes. "What is it?" he asked sharply, and then broke into Bulgarian.

"Is he all right?"

"He has never killed a man before," Tsanko explained. "He will feel better soon."

"You didn't answer my question about Philip Trenda, you know."

He shrugged. "One does not like to confess one listens to Radio Skolje, it is forbidden in my country. Yes, his arrest has caused a great noise in the Western world. But does this explain your being followed in Sofia by"—he removed a piece of paper from his pocket and read from it—"by one Mincho Kolarov, also one Assen Radev—"

"*Two?*" said Mrs. Pollifax blankly.

"And now these men."

"I don't understand," she said, puzzled. "I noticed a short gray-haired man in a gray suit—"

"That was Mincho Kolarov of the secret police. The other party, Assen Radev, we know nothing about. Late last night he returned to a collective farm outside of Sofia. He appears to raise geese."

"Geese!" echoed Mrs. Pollifax in astonishment.

"Yes. And now we have this Bemish, in company with a man never before seen by us."

"He's a man I've never seen before, either. Back in the cellar you said he was from the secret police. How could you know?"

"You saw me remove the wallet from his body. His papers carry the name of Titko Yugov, and this particular kind of identity card is carried only by members of our secret police."

He handed her the narrow card of plastic and she gave a start. "*It looks like a lottery ticket or a swimming pass,*" she heard herself say aloud, and she began to dig into her purse, dumping papers out all around her. "Here it is," she said in amazement. "I'd completely forgotten. What does this say? You see, it's exactly the same kind of card except it carries a different name. I've had it in my purse since Belgrade."

Tsanko took it, glanced it over and looked at her questioningly. He said quietly, "This one identifies its bearer as one Nikolai F. Dzhagarov, serial number 3891F in the Secret Security Police of the People's Republic of Bulgaria."

Debby, who had been leaning wearily against the wall, suddenly straightened. "That's *Nikki!*"

"Nikki," repeated Mrs. Pollifax. "So there it is—the proof. Nikki's not only Bulgarian, but he's a member of your police." The knowledge saddened her because it removed all hope that Philip's arrest had been an accident. "I think I'd better tell you the whole story," she said to Tsanko. "If I begin at the beginning, leaving out nothing, perhaps you can tell us what we've fallen into."

"I beg that you explain," Tsanko said with some relief.

Mrs. Pollifax began to talk, her glance occasionally falling upon Debby, whose face grew more and more incredulous. When she had finished it was Debby who broke the silence. "But you're one of those nasty CIA spies!" she wailed. "And those brakes were fixed to *kill* us? And our coming to Bulgaria was all part of a *plot?*"

"It is no wonder you needed smelling salts," Tsanko said, regarding Mrs. Pollifax with curiosity. "It becomes very simple upon hearing this. You know too much. In Bulgaria it is not wise to know too much, especially about something in which the secret police are involved."

"But what do I know?" protested Mrs. Pollifax.

"Let us consider—perhaps you are too near to see it. Certainly the luxuries in Bemish's apartment suggest a liberal reward for something, and Bemish himself has spoken of months of planning."

"Yes," said Mrs. Pollifax, nodding vigorously.

"This paper the Trenda boy gave to you in the air terminal" —he tapped it with a finger—"it would explain the trouble Nikki had at the border. Without it he could no longer prove he was secret police and his special privileges are denied him at Customs."

"All right," agreed Mrs. Pollifax.

"Your visit to Mr. Eastlake would have been observed, too— the walls of an Embassy are all ears. Tell me again what Bemish spoke to you in those last minutes in the cellar. He was about to kill you, and he was opening up. He believed he was explaining everything, even if it made no sense."

Mrs. Pollifax frowned, remembering. "He was very angry, very bitter," she said. "It was something about Stella having a brother, Petrov, who emigrated to America and made millions, but if he'd stayed in Bulgaria he would have had to share his money."

"Presumably with Bemish," said Tsanko with a quick smile.

"Yes. I asked him who Stella was, and he explained she was his wife. They received only 'hand-outs,' as he put it . . ." She stopped because Tsanko looked so startled.

"But there begins something," he said in surprise. "Bemish married a Bulgarian, you know. It is the habit here that when a woman marries a foreigner she is still identified—referred to—by her Bulgarian name. In Sofia, Mrs. Bemish is still known as Stella Trendafilov."

"Trendafilov!" repeated Mrs. Pollifax. "But that name sounds very much like—"

"Exactly," said Tsanko, nodding. "If a Trendafilov emigrated to America is it not possible he might shorten the name?"

"Good heavens," said Mrs. Pollifax.

Debby gasped, "But if you shorten Trendafilov it comes out Trenda! That would make Phil a relative—a nephew!"

"Well, well," murmured Mrs. Pollifax.

"But why would Mr. Bemish want to see his nephew in jail for espionage? I don't get it," Debby said helplessly.

"It is not necessary we 'get it,' " Tsanko told her firmly. "To draw conclusions so quickly would be very foolish. We must collect facts. To put them together must come later."

Mrs. Pollifax said dryly, "It's a little difficult not to put them together now. We've discovered that Philip is probably the son of a man named Peter Trenda, who's president of Trenda-Arctic Oil Company. Presumably that makes him a man of some wealth. Bemish, over here, has a rich brother-in-law in America named Petrov Trendafilov, and Bemish appears to have been quite in-volved in Philip's arrest. Perhaps it was even his idea."

"Wow, yes," said Debby eagerly.

"Do you think Mr. Bemish could have been a member of the secret police, like Nikki?"

Tsanko shook his head. "He would never be trusted. No, he is more likely an informer to the police—that is more his character and it would explain better his relationship with Nikki." He sighed. "There have always been bad rumors about Bemish, that he picks up money in strange ways, that he is cruel to his wife. She was very beautiful once, I am told. A pity."

Mrs. Pollifax said slowly, "Then it must begin with Bemish and Nikki—Philip's arrest, I mean. *That's* what Debby and I know that we shouldn't."

The lantern sputtered and the flame began streaming, its light unbelievably golden. Tsanko leaned over and adjusted the wick, dimming the light, and they became hollow-eyed ghosts again. "But it has become something much bigger now," he said with narrowed eyes. "Do not forget, Amerikanski, you have been under surveillance by genuine members of the secret police. How they became involved, and why . . ." Tsanko was thoughtful. "I smell something very rotten here, I experience deep curiosity. My inquiries must be very discreet, however, because of what happened tonight."

"But they're both dead, even buried," pointed out Debby.

Mrs. Pollifax looked at her. "There's still Nikki back in Sofia."

"Oh God, yes," she said, tears springing to her eyes. "You *will* find out something?" she asked Tsanko.

"Yes, we'll want to know," Mrs. Pollifax told him soberly.

"I keep trying to remember back to Yugoslavia," Debby said in an anguished voice. "Before all this happened. Phil never mentioned having relatives in Bulgaria, but he did act uptight about his reasons for not coming here with us. He just kept saying 'I can't go'—very firmly—but once he said his father would be furious if he went. Except he didn't say why."

Tsanko nodded. "His father was sensible. If he is Bulgarian and once fled the country there is always the fear of something. One never knows of what, but the Intelligence here is very excellent." He sighed. "However, all of this is conjecture, which I dislike. We must next verify."

Mrs. Pollifax was removing hatpins from her hat, which she now handed to him. "The passports are in the crown," she explained. "I'm told there are eight of them for you inside."

"Inside the *hat?*" he said in astonishment.

"Passports?" echoed Debby, wide-eyed. "So that's why you're meeting him!"

Tsanko turned the hat over with amusement. "We will be most interested to examine this construction. Ah, American technology. We hear of it even here." He looked up as a second young man entered; his voice warmed as he greeted him. "This is Encho," he explained. "He has driven the black Renault back into Tarnovo and left it parked on the main street. If the car was seen coming in to Tsaravets then it has now been seen leaving as well. If you go back now"—he pulled out a heavy old-fashioned gold watch and glanced at it—"I think you must. Your absence will be noted."

"But the inquiries?" insisted Mrs. Pollifax. "You said you'd make inquiries. When will we hear what you learn about Philip?"

He looked surprised. "But you have given me the hat, which

you tell me contains passports. Your job is complete, you can be out of Bulgaria by tomorrow noon."

She shook her head. "That's impossible, absolutely impossible."

"Why?"

She thought what a *lived* man he looked, square and shaggy, his lined face burned dark by sun and wind. "I don't like people trying to kill me," she said quietly. "I liked Philip Trenda and he's Debby's friend. He's very young, and I don't believe anyone else in Bulgaria—including, perhaps, the American Embassy—really cares."

"But you do?"

"Someone *must*," she said fiercely.

"Then we will meet again," Tsanko told her, and he picked up the bird's nest hat and returned it to her. It was a gesture that completely took Mrs. Pollifax aback. He was handing her the passports—the lives of his friends—as a promise. "We will meet in the morning, I hope. If possible, Encho will come to the hotel for you. Encho lives here in Tarnovo, he drives a government taxi for tourists. He also speaks a little English.

"But now it is past midnight," he said, rising. "Balkantourist will be upset enough with your being in Tarnovo instead of Borovets, and two men have been killed tonight, wiped off the face of the earth. This is dangerous in any country. It will be a busy night for us."

Mrs. Pollifax held out the hat to him. "You've just given me back what I was assigned to deliver to you. Surely it's not professional for me to accept this?"

He smiled faintly and there was the hint of a twinkle in his eyes. "I am not sure either of us is professional, is this not possible?"

She looked at him in astonishment, and something like recognition arose between them.

"It is a long walk back," he said, escorting her to the cave's entrance. "When you have seen the Bulgarian mountains in moonlight you see my country at its best. Sleep well, Amerikanski," he added.

She nodded, and she and Debby followed Kosta from the cave.

Chapter Fourteen

At CIA headquarters in Langley Field, Virginia, it had been a trying Thursday. An ambassador had been abducted in South America the night before, and this morning an agent was missing in Hong Kong. There was also the continuing puzzle of young Philip Trenda, whose arrest was filling the front pages of the newspapers. Yesterday the State Department had asked Carstairs to see what he could discover about the situation through less conventional channels. It was a nuisance being called in on the job. Carstairs had already been summoned Upstairs twice for conferences and his routine work was piling up on the desk.

Having been involved in this crisis for only twenty-four hours Carstairs admitted to almost no progress and no new leads at all. He glanced now over a routine report on the affair from a B. Eastlake at the United States Embassy in Sofia. It was an abbreviated memo, a digest of the hour-by-hour reports coming from Sofia. Halfway down the first page Carstairs noticed a reference by Eastlake to two American tourists who had come to the Embassy on Tuesday. They had managed to suggest that Philip had been lured into Bulgaria by a young Yugoslavian traveling under a German passport.

There were always people to suggest this sort of thing and Carstairs noted that quite rightly Eastlake placed small faith in the story. He had given it only three lines in the report.

But Eastlake's job was judicial and diplomatic; Carstairs, on the other hand, lived and worked in a world of improbabilities, fantasies and the completely irrational. He pressed the buzzer for Bishop and handed him the report.

"Get me detailed information about these two tourists

Eastlake talked to in Sofia. Exactly what was said, and why, and what sort of people they are. I want to know today."

"Right, sir," said Bishop, and went out.

Carstairs sighed. Nothing about Trenda's arrest made the slightest sense so far. The State Department couldn't figure out what the Bulgarians were up to, or what they planned to do. The Embassy in Sofia had still not been allowed to contact young Trenda. There were no details at all about the espionage charges, and none of this boded well for Philip. So far as Carstairs had been able to discover, the boy had no connection with political or subversive groups. He'd gone to public schools and then to the University of Illinois. He was the only child of a rich man. He wrote poetry, and the nearest he'd come to revolt against any system at all was a short article in his school paper on the current injustices of the draft. If he'd been engaged in suspicious activities they surely must have begun after he reached Europe in June. At this moment his being accused of espionage seemed utterly far-fetched, but of course it had to be checked out, and thoroughly.

Carstairs realized he felt desperately sorry for the boy. In only one area of his arrest had he been lucky: someone had caught the story at once, and it had captured the attention of newspapers all over Europe. This was an enormous help to him, although Carstairs knew how fickle such publicity could be, too. If Trenda wasn't freed soon—by the sheer weight of that publicity—a fresh crisis would move him off the front pages and the story would gradually die. He'd seen it happen. That would leave the State Department in charge, and sometimes the diplomatic exchanges went on ad infinitum. Three or four years from now Trenda might emerge from prison in Bulgaria and rate a small story on page two. Readers would say with a frown, "Familiar name, Trenda . . . good God, has he been in prison all these *years?*"

Bishop knocked and walked in, his usually cheerful face clouded. "Something new from Sofia?" asked Carstairs.

"From Sofia, yes," said Bishop stiffly. "Nothing to do with the Trenda affair, however. It's the weekly *pâté de foie gras* report from Assen Radev. It's just been decoded."

Carstairs' glance sharpened. "Is Mrs. Pollifax all right? Did he switch the coats?"

Bishop only looked disapproving as he handed over the report.

He read: WHO IS THIS 10573 YOU SENT STOP ANY EXCHANGE OF COATS IMPOSSIBLE STOP REPEAT IMPOSSIBLE STOP EVEN BURGLARY FAILED STOP NEVER STAYS IN ONE PLACE STOP NOW GONE TO BOROVETS BUT ISN'T THERE STOP AM RETURNING TO WORK STOP WHY ARE SECRET POLICE TRAILING 10573 STOP.

When he had finished reading it Carstairs began to slowly, softly swear. When he ran out of expletives he added in an exhausted voice, "Those damn fools Upstairs. And Radev certainly has a neat way of planting bombshells, hasn't he? Why are the secret police trailing Mrs. Pollifax indeed!"

Bishop's face softened. "It could be Tsanko's men trailing her, couldn't it? Radev may have misunderstood the situation."

"Do you really think so?" asked Carstairs bitterly.

Bishop shook his head.

When he'd gone Carstairs lit a cigarette and considered this new complication. It wasn't only the reference to secret police that troubled him, he didn't like the sound of Mrs. Pollifax going off to Borovets and not arriving there. Had she been arrested? And why Borovets? She had a car, it was true, but nothing had been said about her leaving Sofia. The tailor shop was in Sofia, and Tsanko was in Sofia. He didn't like it. Damn it, he thought, he'd told her to make a fast exit if anything looked suspicious. Why the hell hadn't she bolted?

He thought furiously, She trusts too many people.

He'd told Bishop this wasn't Sears Roebuck and it wasn't Gimbels they worked for, but he knew that he'd meant it for himself. He loathed worrying like this about one of his people. He considered putting through a transatlantic call to the Hotel Rila to check on her, and then he discarded the idea as idiotic. His call would be monitored. Even if he reached Mrs. Pollifax he couldn't possibly say, "Get rid of the coat you're wearing—burn it, hide it, cut it up, give it to somebody." She wouldn't have the slightest idea what he meant—it was the hat she'd been assigned to protect, not her coat—and the people monitoring his call would have only *too* clear an idea of what he meant.

Damn, he thought, and as Bishop walked in again he snapped, "Well?"

There was a twinkle in Bishop's eye. What was more alarming, he'd brought Carstairs a cup of steaming hot coffee. Bishop never volunteered coffee unless it was for purposes of fortification during a difficult moment.

Almost cheerfully Bishop said, "The State Department has been in touch with Eastlake at the U.S. Embassy in Sofia, sir. You remember you asked for details on the two tourists who suggested Trenda might have been deliberately brought into Bulgaria?"

"Of course," Carstairs said.

"Here's the report. You might like to take a look at the names of those tourists first—they're at the bottom of the page. Names and passport numbers."

Carstairs grasped the paper and allowed his glance to drop to the bottom. He read: Mrs. Virgil Pollifax, Apt. 4B, Hemlock Arms, New Brunswick, N.J., U.S.A.

He exploded. "What the hell! Bishop," he demanded furiously, "can you tell me what the devil Mrs. Pollifax is doing mixing into something that's none of her business? Doesn't she realize she has eight passports in her hat, not to mention that blasted coat Radev's been incapable of switching?"

"She doesn't know about the coat, sir," Bishop reminded him silkily.

"But doesn't she realize she's not in New Brunswick, New Jersey? Doesn't she understand she's not supposed to *meddle?* Bishop, what the hell are you grinning about?"

"You, sir. Mrs. Pollifax is so much like you."

"What?" snapped Carstairs.

Bishop nodded. "She goes off on tangents. Operates on impulse and trusts her intuition. When she stops upsetting you, sir, it'll be because she's turned into a well-behaved, well-trained and completely predictable operator. You'll sleep nights and stop swearing. And then she'll be like all your professional agents, and of no use to you at all, will she?"

Carstairs glared at him. "Are you suggesting I run this department on nothing but impulse and intuition, Bishop?"

"I have never known you to follow the book, sir," said Bishop serenely. "That's why you're so successful, isn't it? Incidentally, your telephone's buzzing, sir."

Angrily, Carstairs flipped switches and barked into the receiver. He listened and his expression changed. Hanging up he said, "Something's happening. The Bulgarian Embassy's going to make an important announcement in ten minutes."

Chapter Fifteen

Mrs. Pollifax was awakened at nine o'clock the next morning in Tarnovo by an urgent hammering on the door and a message—acted out in pantomime—that she was wanted at once on the telephone in the lobby. Mrs. Pollifax threw her coat over her pajamas and hurried downstairs.

She had expected it to be Nevena, and braced herself. But it was not Nevena, it was the American Embassy in Sofia, and after being told to wait she at last heard the faint but unmistakable voice of Mr. Eastlake.

"However did you find me!" she exclaimed.

Eastlake's voice sounded tired. "With difficulty. Have you heard from Balkantourist this morning?"

"No."

"You will," he said dryly. "They told me where you are. They seem rather angry, though. There was some kind of accident?"

"Among other things," she said. He couldn't have called about the accident and she told him so.

"Quite true," he said. "I recall your concern about young Trenda, and knowing that you're still in the country I thought you might enjoy your vacation more if you knew he's being released this afternoon. At two o'clock, at the Embassy."

"Released?" echoed Mrs. Pollifax incredulously.

"Released. You sound surprised."

"Surprised but delighted," she said hastily. She wondered how she could possibly explain her intense surprise, when Philip's confinement had brought three attempts on her life, the latest of them last night. "At two o'clock, you said?"

"Yes. If you have that young Debby's address you might like to reassure her as well, although she's bound to be reading it in the major western Europe newspapers."

"Yes," said Mrs. Pollifax, and then, "What made them . . . that is . . ."

"Diplomatic pressure, I imagine," Eastlake said crisply. "I suspect the Kremlin intervened as well. Because of Bemish's early dispatches the news has been headlined since Tuesday morning in London, Paris, New York, Oslo. . . . But all's well that ends well, eh, Mrs. Pollifax? Happy journeying."

"Yes . . . and thank you so much," she said, hung up and hurried upstairs to tell Debby. "Philip's being released at two this afternoon in Sofia."

Debby sat bolt upright. "Great!" she shouted and rolled to her feet in that same beautifully fluid athletic manner that had so dazzled Mrs. Pollifax on the night of the burglary.

"Breakfast first, and then packing," said Mrs. Pollifax hurriedly, but even so she was summoned to her second telephone call while still in bare feet.

This time it was Nevena, a very excited and aggrieved Nevena, who wanted to know what Mrs. Pollifax was doing in Tarnovo when she was supposed to be in Borovets.

"Well," said Mrs. Pollifax, drawing a deep breath, "I met some people who told me Tarnovo was too beautiful to be missed. I met them only a block from the hotel when I took a wrong turning—"

"How could you take a wrong turning?" demanded Nevena. "The directions were plain, very clear. I saw them. They said—"

"I took this wrong turning," continued Mrs. Pollifax blandly, "and I met these people."

"What people?"

"English, I think, or Canadian. The man was quite tall and had a scar. On his left cheek," she added artistically. "And so I decided to go to Tarnovo instead."

She could almost hear Nevena's foot stamping. "You Americans," she said indignantly. "You see what happens now, your car is wrecked. They wake me up to say it will take very long to fix the car and you will need a new car in Tarnovo when all the time you are supposed to be in Borovets. First you come to Sofia and are to stay, and then you meet some people who tell you Sofia is not the real Bulgaria—"

She has an excellent memory, thought Mrs. Pollifax.

"And now you meet some other peoples—"

"I'm truly sorry," said Mrs. Pollifax, wearying of the joke. "In America, you see, we're quite free to—"

She had made her point; Nevena interrupted, but her voice was reproachful now rather than angry. "It is very difficult for me when you change the itinerary. How can I give you the idyllic service when you jump so? There will be another car for you at 1 P.M., leaving Sofia soon to reach you, and the driver will personally return you to the Hotel Rila."

"I'd rather leave earlier," said Mrs. Pollifax. "I could take the train?"

"There will be the car," Nevena said flatly, and then as a dutiful afterthought she added, "You are not hurt by the accident, Mrs. Pollifax?"

"I was not hurt," said Mrs. Pollifax and hung up. She had just seen Encho enter the lobby, catch sight of her and quietly jerk his head toward the street.

She and Debby sat primly upright in the rear seat of Encho's battered and dusty taxi. Encho had said in his broken English that Tsanko had news for them, and Mrs. Pollifax had said, "Yes, and I have news for him, too." But it was necessary for Encho to drive them first through Tarnovo, slowing and pointing at houses of historical distinction to establish the fact that they were tourists in case they were being watched. At last he stopped in front of a small wooden house that clung to the side of a hill. "My house," he said proudly. "Tsanko waits." When Debby started to climb out, too, he gestured her back. "Tsanko say you take pictures," he said and handed her a camera. "To explain the stop."

Inside the house Tsanko was pacing up and down the dark, slant-floored living room, and at sight of the expression on his face Mrs. Pollifax was jolted. She had expected this to be a happy meeting, and although it was true that he must have gone without sleep and done a great deal of work since they'd seen him, she was not prepared for such a grim, drawn face. "Something is the matter?" she said breathlessly.

His voice was harsh. "I have made the inquiries about your young American and it is not good."

She stared at him in disbelief. "Not good! But I've just heard —whatever do you mean?"

"They have all gone mad, insane. I cannot foresee how he comes out of this alive."

"But he must, he's going to!" gasped Mrs. Pollifax.

Tsanko ceased his pacing and turned to her. "I beg your pardon—sit down," he said. "Please." But he did not sit down, he resumed his restless pacing instead. "It is like this—please listen carefully. My government was taken completely by surprise with this Trenda's arrest. Madness!" he said in an aside, both hands to his head. "The government knew nothing! It was confronted with the *fait accompli*."

"Well, then," said Mrs. Pollifax hopefully.

He savagely interrupted her. "In Bulgaria such matters lead to blood baths, Amerikanski. You are a government—think a moment —and you discover this situation has brought the world down on your head. It makes grave conditions internationally, this arrest of an American student. Headlines. Protests. *And you knew nothing about it.* This is embarrassing, you understand?"

"Very," she said, nodding.

"As the government, you cannot afford to say you know nothing, it loses the face, it implies no power. But you cannot publicly sanction it, either. You are stuck. You must find a way out, eh?"

"Yes, and—"

His hand cut the air. "Heads have rolled. The chief of the security police has been taken mysteriously ill and has resigned. He has been replaced by General Ignatov."

"General Ignatov!"

He halted, peering at her from under his thick brows. "You know this name?"

"I was asked to question you about him if possible. We came to Sofia on the same plane, too—there was an unscheduled stop in Rumania to pick him up."

"Well, I can tell you now that he has just become head of our secret security." He shook his head. "I fear for my country. He is in charge personally of this mess, and he has announced suddenly to the foreign press that at two o'clock this afternoon Philip Trenda will be released and flown out of the country to Belgrade."

Mrs. Pollifax nodded happily. "Yes, isn't that wonderful? Mr. Eastlake phoned me about it, it was so terribly kind of him."

Tsanko said grimly, "I do not believe it. Something will intervene—a last minute cancellation, a delay—because the ransom has not yet been paid."

"The *what?*" gasped Mrs. Pollifax.

Tsanko nodded, his eyes narrowed. "Money. A million dollars in hard currency from the Trenda fortune. Money in American dollars."

"A million!" whispered Mrs. Pollifax.

"Yes. To be paid by Philip Trenda's father personally into a Swiss bank in Zurich on Monday morning at ten o'clock."

"But this is only Thursday, and if Philip is freed today—"

"Exactly. Why would he pay this great ransom if his son is safe?"

Mrs. Pollifax stared at him, appalled. "You think this announcement is a fraud? Something made up by General Ignatov to placate the press, to stall until Monday?"

Tsanko abruptly sat down and looked into her face. "I will be frank with you, Amerikanski. I am deeply disturbed over this General Ignatov's involvement in the matter. There are details to this situation I do not like. Always it is interesting to me to see who swims to the top at such a time. I find most interesting that it is General Ignatov who offers instant solutions to my government in this crisis."

She understood at once. "Does he know Nikki?" she asked.

"You are very quick," he acknowledged with a smile. "Yes, it happens that he does. My informant tells me General Ignatov knows quite a number of young members of the secret police. Is this not a surprising coincidence?"

Mrs. Pollifax said slowly, "Carleton Bemish knew Nikki, and Nikki—"

"Is a protégé of General Ignatov," finished Tsanko for her.

"They were both on the same plane with me—at least from Rumania to Sofia," said Mrs. Pollifax. "There was no point of contact, though."

"Yet this Nikki was allowed a passport to leave Bulgaria and go to Yugoslavia to bring back young Trenda. He could have managed this only with powerful backing," pointed out Tsanko. "This I

have found astonishing from the start. Please note as well that
although my government knew nothing of this plot there were
bona fide members of the secret police keeping you under surveillance. Someone with influence is behind all this."

"You think it's General Ignatov," she said, nodding.

Tsanko said dryly, "I always think. The coincidences begin to
grow surprising."

"There's more?"

He nodded. "The arrests began at once last night. Included
among them are some members of secret security. Our friend
Nikki, however, was given promotion at once."

Mrs. Pollifax's lips formed an O of comprehension.

"Out of hundreds of secret police it is Nikki that is singled
out. The arrests are of much interest as well. Each person arrested
has been severe critic of General Ignatov, or is out-and-out enemy,
and several are men to whom he owes much money. Creditors, in a
word."

"He's planning to overthrow the government," said Mrs. Pollifax flatly.

Tsanko nodded. "I think so. Not immediately, but soon—and
my government is too blind at this moment, too upset to see. All
that General Ignatov has needed is to have the secret police in his
pocket. And last night he was given this like a gift."

"Oh dear," said Mrs. Pollifax.

"My informant is among his enemies," he added sadly. "He,
too, is member of the secret police, an old friend. He fears now for
his life."

"I'm sorry," she said. "He's one of your group?"

Tsanko shook his head. "No, but he has given us much valued
information. It is he who told us the man Shipkov was to be arrested." He smiled wryly. "He and Shipkov shared an interest in
General Ignatov, they nearly met one night watching General
Ignatov's home. Each one occupied—I am told—a different
flowerbed."

Mrs. Pollifax smiled. "That must have been funny. But
Tsanko, why the ransom? If General Ignatov now has what he
wanted from the beginning—"

"Why not?" said Tsanko with a shrug. "Doubtless he will use
the ransom as evidence against his enemies. He will say, 'Look at

the plot—all this for Western currency!' Each dollar will be a nail in their coffins. He can impound the money and present it to his government—that will earn him another medal. And there is nothing like a million in American dollars to make oneself popular." He shook his head sadly. "Poor Bemish. He wanted only a little money for wine and women and cigarettes, and see how he has been used by these two."

"And Philip?" she asked quietly.

He nodded. "Exactly. That is why I beseech Encho to take you to Sofia at once, in his taxi—you can pay him a little something for it?—so that you can be at the Embassy at two. Myself, I must go back also, but alone."

"Balkantourist is sending . . ." Mrs. Pollifax stopped and shook her head. "We'll go with Encho," she said. "I'm very alarmed about this." Removing her bird's nest hat, again she gave it to him. "Please—these are the passports I was sent to give you."

He nodded. "I will accept them now, although—alas—three of the people these would have rescued were taken to Panchevsky Institute last night. At General Ignatov's orders."

"Taken where?" she asked.

"That is the name of a mental institute in Sofia, now filled with political prisoners—who may be the sanest of us all," he added with a sigh.

She said swiftly, "You doubt your government."

"I would protect my government against General Ignatov with my *life*." His fierceness startled her.

Forgetting discretion, she asked bluntly, "Tsanko, who are you? All this information, and you've collected it in hours. And Tarnovo," she persisted. "You're free to travel here without question?"

He laughed. "I have a summer home here in the hills, which is why I come to Tarnovo. As to who I am—I'm a good communist, a patriot and also—God help me—a humanist."

"But are you against the Russians?"

His brows shot up. "Please—not at all! They protect us from the wolves, they give us years of peace, some prosperity." He hesitated and then he said soberly, "But before I die I would like to see my country move, have direction. We go nowhere in Bulgaria, and our young people deserve better. They grow bitter, despondent, strangled by bureaucracy—"

"You're a nationalist!" she cried triumphantly.

He laughed. "Please—such words are very dangerous. It is best we not talk political, Amerikanski. Allow me the pleasure to enjoy my first American, like a good wine, eh?"

On the ride back to Sofia, Debby said suddenly, "I don't *want* to like you, Mrs. Pollifax, and I shall keep trying not to like you, but I do want you to know that I'm grateful to be alive today."

"I confess to a certain pleasure in it myself," said Mrs. Pollifax, startled.

Debby said, "My parents give me everything." She said it as though she were reciting something too important to be given significance. "They say they want me to have everything because they had such a hard time when they were young. But when I ask for something *I* want they tell me I'm spoiled and ungrateful. My mother always wants me to confide in her," she said. "Girl stuff. The one time I did tell her something important she was shocked and called my father and they punished me. My father spends all his time making money and my mother spends all her time spending it, shopping with her friends or playing bridge. They're bored and miserable and they want me to grow up to be just like them. And I can't—I won't, I won't, I *won't*."

A boil is being lanced, thought Mrs. Pollifax, and said without expression, "I see."

"Phil's parents are different. I think it's why I like him so much. Do you know he had to earn every cent he's spending on this trip to Europe?" Her voice was awed.

Mrs. Pollifax glanced at her with interest.

"Of course you can now start explaining my parents," Debby pointed out. "Don't you want to?"

"Not at all," said Mrs. Pollifax truthfully.

"You're not going to tell me they mean well?"

"I don't know whether they mean well or not," said Mrs. Pollifax tartly. "I've never met them."

"Don't you even want to give advice?"

Mrs. Pollifax laughed. "No, because you'll work it out for yourself. You strike me as being a very intelligent young person.

And also," she added thoughtfully, "because you came very, *very* near to losing your life last night."

"What's that have to do with it?" asked Debby indignantly.

"Everything, I think," said Mrs. Pollifax musingly. "It's the greatest revolution of all. But not recommended in large doses," she added firmly, "and now we must keep it from ever happening again."

They were late in reaching Sofia, and there was no time to go first to the hotel and leave their suitcases. It was already five minutes past the hour when Encho deposited them at the Embassy; they had time only to wave good-bye to him as they flew across the pavement. Now it was Debby who was in command as she went to the desk and asked if Philip Trenda was really being released today.

"The group is in the library," said the clerk stiffly.

"Group?"

"Mr. Trenda is meeting with foreign reporters."

"Then he's really *here?*" cried Debby excitedly.

"But of course," said the clerk, looking at them in surprise.

A feeling of deep relief filled Mrs. Pollifax: miracles did happen, and Tsanko had been wrong.

"Wonderful," Debby cried. "Oh, Mrs. Pollifax, isn't this a beautiful, beautiful day? He's here, he's free, he's *out*. Where's the library?"

The clerk patiently ushered them down the hall and into the library. It was a large sunny room, half filled with people and cameras. Unfortunately the twenty or thirty men present—as well as cameras—were all in one corner of the room, forming a tight, almost inviolate circle around two people who stood against the wall.

"We really are late," murmured Mrs. Pollifax, standing on tiptoe.

"Oh blast, I can't see him," Debby said, jumping up and down.

Mrs. Pollifax looked about for a chair, found one and stood on it. "I can see his head," she told Debby, peering between and over the newsmen. "He's grown a small beard. Try a chair, Debby. There, do you see him?"

"I can't—yes! There he is."

Phil stood next to Eastlake, his shoulders slouched; he was wearing dark glasses against the popping of the flashbulbs. He looked thinner, weary, lacking in animation. I wonder if he was drugged while in prison, thought Mrs. Pollifax.

"Please, gentlemen," Eastlake was saying, "he has a plane to catch, and we've very little time. But as you can see, he's been released and that's the important thing. Keep your questions very brief, please."

"Were you treated well?" called someone from the rear row. Philip replied in a low husky voice.

"We can't hear him back here," called out a man with a British accent.

"He said he was treated well and is looking forward to getting home now," Eastlake said. "He has a slight cold, a touch of laryngitis."

"Is he aware that his arrest made sensational headlines all over the world?"

Eastlake answered for him, smiling. "I don't think he realizes anything, he's been completely out of touch and we've had little time to talk."

"Does he hold it against the Bulgarian government that he was arrested like this?"

Eastlake looked pained. "Gentlemen, please, I refer you to the written statement which has been distributed among you all. He says he holds no personal animosity toward the Bulgarian government, he's only glad to be free and going home. And now I think we really must leave for the airport. If you will excuse us, gentlemen . . ."

There was a fresh storm of flashbulbs and then a path was made for Eastlake and Philip. They passed very near to Mrs. Pollifax, who stood back. Debby, on the other hand, moved forward. "Phil?" she said as he passed by.

His head turned slightly—Mrs. Pollifax could no longer see his face—and then he followed Eastlake out of the room and down the hall. The newsmen pressed forward, separating Mrs. Pollifax from Debby.

In a matter of seconds the room had emptied and Mrs. Pollifax turned to see Debby leaning against the nearest wall, her eyes closed and both of her hands pressed to her stomach. She looked as if she were about to be very ill.

"Debby?" faltered Mrs. Pollifax.

Through clenched teeth Debby said, "It wasn't Phil. Do you understand—*that wasn't Phil.*"

Mrs. Pollifax stared at her. "Wasn't Phil," she echoed, and suddenly sat down because she realized at once that Debby was right: there had been no sense of recognition, of familiarity when she'd glimpsed him. The height and build and general characteristics were the same, but it was someone else—an impostor—with laryngitis to disguise the voice, a stubble of beard to confuse the jawline and dark glasses to conceal the eyes.

Tsanko had said that there would be a last-minute cancellation, some kind of delay—but this was worse, this was far more ominous because in the eyes of the world it had been Philip Trenda who had just walked out with Eastlake, and that meant . . .

"Oh God," Debby said, covering her face with her hands. "Phil's still in prison—and *nobody knows?*"

Mrs. Pollifax nodded.

Debby uncovered her face and looked at Mrs. Pollifax. "I'm scared," she said. "I've never been so scared in my life."

"It's better to be angry," said Mrs. Pollifax thoughtfully. "This is why they tried to kill us last night—*they* knew."

"But how can they get away with it? There'll be Phil's parents . . ."

Mrs. Pollifax said sadly, "I don't think we have to speculate—I'm sure they'll have thought of everything." But what that *everything* might be was too chilling for her to name yet. "I wish you'd screamed in front of everyone as soon as you saw it wasn't Philip," she added forlornly.

"I couldn't," Debby said. "I'm inhibited. I am. I really am. All those people, and then I wasn't absolutely sure until they were walking out." She shivered.

"Well, we've certainly got to tell Mr. Eastlake as soon as he returns from the airport."

Debby shook her head. "You can, but not me. He'd only insist I leave the country again."

"But you just said you were frightened."

"For Phil, not for myself. Actually I'm terrified for him if you want the truth."

Mrs. Pollifax believed her. How oddly quixotic the child was! Filled with prickly hostilities and impulsive bursts of warmth, deeply troubled and only half formed but unquestioningly generous. "I'll see Mr. Eastlake alone," she said, and then reconsidered. She could hear herself explaining all that she knew to Eastlake and she could hear his protestations. "My dear Mrs. Pollifax, what an outrageous story you tell! Can you substantiate just one of these wild accusations?"

And she couldn't. She couldn't produce Tsanko, and she couldn't reveal her own role in this or even prove what lay behind the series of accidents. Was there anything she *could* prove? Yes, there was.

"Dry your eyes, Debby," she said, and stood up. "I've an idea —let's go."

"Go where?"

"To see Mrs. Bemish before she learns she's a widow."

Debby's reaction was forthright: "Ech," she said distastefully.

The smell of cooked cabbage competed today with the odor of a very strong antiseptic. Mrs. Pollifax reached the third landing of the apartment house with Debby close behind her, and knocked on the door of 301. She wondered if she was drawn here by guilt, because if she had not interfered with Bemish's greedy plans he would still be alive. Even more pertinent, however, she felt a need to share this crisis with someone who might care about Philip. Carstairs would be appalled at her coming here, and Tsanko might be shocked, but it was time to prove beyond doubt that a relationship existed between the Bemishes in Sofia and the Trendas in America.

The door opened a few inches to frame a stoic, browned face. "Mrs. Bemish?"

"*Da.*" The door opened wider and Mrs. Pollifax recognized the drab little woman she had glimpsed on her earlier visit. This was a peasant's face, shuttered, proud, seamed and crisscrossed with lines. On the left cheekbone a bruise was turning purple; Bemish's legacy, no doubt. What an odious man!

She said, "Do you speak English? May we come in and talk to you?"

The door opened wider and Mrs. Pollifax and Debby entered the dreary, cluttered apartment. "I speak small English," the woman admitted. "But—my husband not here. He left with business and is not back yet."

"I know he's not here," said Mrs. Pollifax. "We came to see *you.*"

"Yes?" The woman had sat down opposite them in a chair, her hands slack in her lap. Now she looked startled and uneasy.

"We came to ask about your brother in America."

"Petrov! Oh yes, yes," she said eagerly, nodding her head.

"You do have a brother in America, then," said Mrs. Pollifax, exchanging a quick glance with Debby.

"*Da,*" the woman cried excitedly, and jumped to her feet and hurried into the next room. When she returned she carried pictures with her. "Petrov," she said proudly. "Very good man. He is called Peter now."

"Peter Trenda?" asked Mrs. Pollifax.

"Here's *Phil!*" cried Debby, leaning over the pictures. "See?"

"You know Philip?" said Mrs. Bemish in an astonished voice. "You know Petrov's son?"

"We're friends," Debby told her, nodding.

"You and Philip!" The woman's eyes fed hungrily on Debby's face. "This is much honor," she whispered.

Leaning forward, Mrs. Pollifax said, "And do you know that Petrov's son—your nephew—is here in Sofia?"

The woman drew in her breath harshly. "*Here? Bora,* how is this?"

"He's in Sofia in jail. In prison."

Mrs. Bemish looked bewildered. "Why should Petrov's son be in prison?"

"Dzhagarov and your husband arranged this."

"Dzhagarov and—" She bit off her words abruptly, looking frightened and angry. "I do not believe this."

"Do you know the word 'ransom'? They want a great deal of money from your brother Petrov. You must know your nephew was visiting Yugoslavia?"

"*Da,*" the woman said. "His first trip to Europe. Yugoslavia."

"Nikki was there, too, and persuaded him to come here to Bulgaria."

The woman looked from one face to another, studying each of them. "Philip never come to Bulgaria," she said, shaking her head. "Never. Not good."

"But he did come," Debby told her. "I think Nikki drugged him to get him here. And he was arrested at once here in Sofia—I was with him when it happened. He was charged with espionage."

"What is this word 'espionage'?"

"Spying," said Mrs. Pollifax.

Mrs. Bemish said sharply, "I cannot believe. There are no Americans at Panchevsky Institute. You lie."

"Where?"

"Panchevsky Institute. I work there," said Mrs. Bemish. "I know. Every night I work there, eight o'clock to six in morning. I work there in kitchens. No Americans." She shook her head fiercely.

"You mean the prison here is called that," Mrs. Pollifax said, remembering Tsanko's words. "But working in the kitchens, would you *know*?" She leaned forward. "They say it's in newspapers all over Europe that Philip Trenda has been arrested on charges of espionage. Your husband sent out the early news stories, but it's not in the papers here because—" She stopped.

Something she said had triggered a response. Mrs. Bemish looked suddenly chilled and old. "When?" she whispered.

"Monday," Debby told her.

They waited while the woman wrestled with some fact or piece of gossip overheard or guessed; it must have been this because her refusal to believe had been replaced by doubt. She was silent a long time and then her eyes narrowed and she stood up and walked over to the window, pulled back the curtains and stood there staring out. "So," she said at last and turned, her eyes hard. "So."

Mrs. Pollifax saw that she was trembling, and then, as she watched, Mrs. Bemish threw back her head and with her lips shut tight in a grimace there came from her throat a harsh animal cry of pain. It was terrible. In her cry was expressed all the anguish and the humiliation of years, suffered stoically and in private. It was indecent to watch, and Mrs. Pollifax looked away.

After several minutes, regaining control, Mrs. Bemish said in a lifeless voice, "At Panchevsky Institute—high up—there is special room for ШПИОН. Spies," she explained. "On Monday they say young boy—very young—is brought in. He is foreigner. The guards say how young he is, with much black hair, very Bulgarian but speaking no Bulgarian." She looked pleadingly at Mrs. Pollifax. "If this is Philip . . ."

"Can you find out? Could you at least find out what language he does speak? Or what he's done?"

The woman looked frightened. "I *try*," she said, and then, "My husband kill me if he find out."

Debby started to speak, but Mrs. Pollifax shook her head. "You may have to choose," she said. "You may have to choose between your husband and your nephew." It did not feel the right moment to tell her that her husband was dead.

"For Petrov I do this," said Mrs. Bemish simply. "He is good brother, always. He write letters. Every month he send two hundred *leva* to help us." She lifted her eyes to Mrs. Pollifax and said fiercely, "For Petrov I would die."

Somewhat taken aback by her passion, Mrs. Pollifax nodded; she believed her. Rising she said, "We'd better leave now, but we'll see you again, Mrs. Bemish. Tomorrow, I think. Friday."

Mrs. Bemish only nodded.

They tiptoed out of the apartment, quietly closing the door behind them. "That poor woman," Debby said in a hushed voice.

But a startling idea had just occurred to Mrs. Pollifax and she was turning it over speculatively in her mind. Its simplicity dazzled her. As they reached the ground floor she asked of herself, "Why not?"

"Why not what?" said Debby. "Mrs. Pollifax, you're looking spooky again."

"It's so tempting," confided Mrs. Pollifax thoughtfully. "We have an Underground, and a woman who would die for her brother . . ." Caution intruded and she shook her head. "No, no, impossible." But caution held no appeal. "Let's make another call," she suggested, and felt suddenly rejuvenated.

Chapter Sixteen

Number nine Vasil Levski had already locked its doors, but a solitary woman remained working under a strong light behind the counter. Mrs. Pollifax knocked and then rattled the door. "Is the man who speaks English here?" she asked when the woman opened the door.

"Englis?" The woman shrugged and went to the rear and shouted.

Presently Mrs. Pollifax's friend peered out from the rear, lifted his brows in surprise at seeing her and walked grudgingly toward her. "Yes?" he asked curtly.

"The vest," said Mrs. Pollifax. "I ordered a brown sheepskin vest." She fumbled in her purse for paper.

"I know, I know," he said flatly. "I remember."

But Mrs. Pollifax nevertheless handed him the sales slip. "This one," she explained, moving to his side and pointing to the order. "I find I must have it sooner than I expected."

On it she had printed in pencil: MUST SEE TSANKO AT ONCE. URGENT.

The man looked at her sharply.

"Something has come up," she said clearly. "Can you rush the order?"

He handed the slip of paper back to her. "I see what can be done. You are lady at the hotel?"

"The Rila, yes."

"How soon do you leave?"

"As soon as I have the vest."

He nodded. "I will let you know," he said, and she left.

This time Debby submitted her passport at the hotel and registered legally, receiving a room of her own down the hall, which she left as quickly as possible to rejoin Mrs. Pollifax. It was she who opened the door to the tailor a few hours later. He carried a handsome vest on a hanger, unwrapped so that Mrs. Pollifax could see that it was brown. He handed her the bill, bowed and quickly walked away down the hall.

But it was not a bill, it was a note. BE AT SIDE ENTRANCE 7:15, WATCH FOR BLUE CAR. To this had been added in script, *Why does a man who raises geese carry in a valise a coat identical to yours?*

"Well, that's a punch line," Debby said when Mrs. Pollifax passed the message to her. "What does it mean? And—good heavens, what's the matter?"

Mrs. Pollifax had abruptly sat down on the edge of the bed. "An exact duplicate," she said in a startled voice. She was remembering her first night in Sofia, and the burglar who had arrived in the middle of her nightmare. She had discovered him with her quilted brown coat in his arms, yet at the same time her coat had been locked away securely in the closet. Supernatural powers indeed! There were *two* coats, and the burglar had brought the second coat into the room *with* him.

But why?

At that moment—with dizzying clarity—Mrs. Pollifax found her thoughts going back to Miss Hartshorne and a jammed door lock. *Of course he was heading for your apartment, Emily, he was carrying your brown quilted coat with him. I could see it plainly through the cellophane wrapping.*

Very softly Mrs. Pollifax said, "I have a distinct feeling that Mr. Carstairs wasn't frank with me this time. Debby—hand me those scissors on the bureau, will you?" Reaching for her coat, she looked it over, turned it inside out and stared at the lining.

"What are you going to do?" Debby asked in an alarmed voice, handing her the scissors.

"Operate," said Mrs. Pollifax and, grasping the lining of the coat, she began snipping the threads of one of the plump quilted squares.

"Are you out of your skull?" gasped Debby.

"I'm solving a mystery. You like mysteries, don't you?"

"I used to until I came to Bulgaria."

"Well, here's a new one for you." From her coat she drew a folded piece of paper and held it up.

"Money?" said Debby in a shocked voice.

"Some kind of foreign money." She turned over the note, frowning. "Not Bulgarian. Russian, do you suppose?"

Debby brought out a Bulgarian *lev* and compared them. "Not Bulgarian. Mrs. Pollifax, you didn't *know* about this? Do you suppose every single quilted square in your coat has a bill like this?"

"I think we can count on it," she said, and was silent, considering the situation.

"But why? And what are you going to do with the money now that you've found it?"

A faint smile tugged at Mrs. Pollifax's lips. "Since Mr. Carstairs didn't enlighten me, I see no need to do anything at all. I think I shall regard it as 'found money.' Finders keepers, you know."

"But there could be a small fortune here!"

Mrs. Pollifax nodded. "It's almost the hand of Providence intervening, isn't it?" she said cheerfully. "I always say it's an ill wind that doesn't blow someone good."

"Mrs. Pollifax, you're being mysterious."

"Yes, I am," she acknowledged truthfully. "But now it's time to go and meet Tsanko, and we mustn't keep the blue car waiting."

As Mrs. Pollifax and Debby advanced from the hotel steps to the curb the small blue car drew up, a young man leaned over to open the door for them and they climbed quickly into the rear seat. For fifteen minutes they toured the streets of Sofia and Mrs. Pollifax noted how frequently their driver checked his rearview mirror. Once he parked on a side street to allow cars to pass before he maneuvered out again to resume driving. It was half an hour before he abruptly pulled into a long alley, drove the length of it to an inside court, cut the engine and gestured toward a door ahead of them.

It was a rear door to a low, concrete-block warehouse. There were other warehouses and other doors emptying into the yard, all of them dark. Their escort unlocked the drab metal door with his own key and beckoned them to follow. They descended broad cement stairs and walked across an echoing expanse of floor piled high with wooden crates in neat rows. At the far end a door opened, emitting light, and Tsanko observed their arrival.

"Well, Amerikanski," he said humorously.

"Well, Tsanko," she said warmly.

"I was not sure I would see you again. I know that bad news brings you, but still I am delighted."

"Very bad news," Debby interrupted breathlessly. "They released Phil—cameras and newsmen and everything—and it wasn't Phil at all."

Tsanko nodded. "Yes, I learn this as soon as I returned to Sofia this afternoon. I learn more, too. Georgi—you have met Georgi? He is student at our university."

"Hi," Debby said.

Tsanko gave the young man instructions that sent him ahead into the room from which he'd emerged. Yet when they followed him inside the room was empty, which startled Mrs. Pollifax.

"We talk here, please." He pulled out wooden crates and they each claimed one.

"We meet in strange places," observed Mrs. Pollifax. "A cave, a furnace room—"

"About Phil," said Debby impatiently.

Tsanko began speaking, but without looking at Debby, which Mrs. Pollifax thought ominous. "As I told you this morning, General Ignatov is in charge of this nasty situation now, and General Ignatov is a man of much resource. He has produced another Trenda—a stroke of genius, is it not?"

"But how?" asked Mrs. Pollifax.

"There is this young man, of a same physiological character, a promising young man highly trained in the Soviet Union to speak English, to accomplish various matters, but with the great misfortune to have become addicted to cocaine. You understand? A grave embarrassment." Tsanko glanced at his watch. "He is just now landing in Belgrade to meet your press. He will be taken to a hotel. Tomorrow morning he will have performed usefully for his country—he will be found dead in his bed of a heart seizure."

"Oh no," she said sadly.

"Thus Philip Trenda will have been disposed of—*but not in Bulgaria.* Already it has been suggested to the senior Mr. Trenda in your United States that this is not his son. He knows, you understand? He will announce his departure for Europe to recover the body of his son. In truth he will proceed to Zurich to deposit the ransom money in a number account on Monday morning." He stopped, still not looking at Debby.

"And Phil? They'll release Phil then?" she asked in a hopeless voice.

Tsanko met her glance squarely at last, and after a terrible moment Debby covered her face with her hands.

"How did you find out all this?" asked Mrs. Pollifax quietly.

He didn't reply; he said instead, "You see the situation. To free your friend would make too many Philip Trendas."

There was silence, and then Mrs. Pollifax said in a stifled voice, "He'll never see America again, then. He'll die here?"

"Yes."

"But he's alive *now?*"

"Until Monday, when the ransom has been paid."

He had never wanted to come to Bulgaria and now he would meet his death here. He couldn't be more than twenty, she thought, and by Monday night he would be another statistic, another human being sacrificed to an insane political end. She thought of Philip's father preparing to leave for Zurich, understanding the odds but praying that somehow his son might be allowed to live. She said, "His father will be hoping for a miracle."

"There are no miracles in Bulgaria," Tsanko told her. "Someone has said that in my country a happy ending is a battle where only five thousand Bulgars are sacrificed to save a hundred Turks or Russians."

"Then we must make a miracle," said Mrs. Pollifax fiercely. "Surely we can make a miracle? Just to stand by and let this happen . . ." She looked at Tsanko. "Your Underground group is somewhere nearby, aren't they? Would you let me speak to them?"

Tsanko gave her a quick, startled glance. "You are always a surprise to me, Amerikanski. Yes, they are in the next room. They expect a report from me tonight about the passports."

"I have a proposition to make to them."

"Proposition? I do not know this word."

"Let me put it this way. You mentioned a mental hospital in Sofia."

"Panchevsky Institute, yes."

"You said that several of your friends are there now. I happen to believe Philip's there, too. That gives us a mutual interest in that prison, doesn't it? And you have an Underground."

His jaw dropped. "My dear Amerikanski, if you mean what I think you mean—"

"There's the other factor, the political one," she continued determinedly. "You don't approve of General Ignatov—you said so—but if he succeeds with the ransom and with Philip's murder then there'll be no stopping him, isn't that true?"

Tsanko stared at her from under his heavy brows. "You continue to surprise me, Amerikanski!"

Debby said, "Mrs. Pollifax, he seems to know, but I don't. *What are you talking about?*"

Neither of them answered her. With an effort Tsanko wrenched his gaze from Mrs. Pollifax's face. "You had better meet my 'Underground' before you develop ideas," he said dryly, and he arose and moved behind the furnace. There he opened a small steel door and led them into a room that resembled a ship's boiler room, its walls an abstract of crisscrossing pipes.

Four people turned to look at them in surprise. There was Kosta, whom they had last seen in Tarnovo, and Georgi, who had brought them here, and two other men, both of Tsanko's vintage. "This is all?" said Mrs. Pollifax, startled.

"We are only amateurs—concerned citizens," explained Tsanko. "We have never been militant revolutionists. It simply grew too much for us, seeing innocent friends threatened, misunderstood and sent to prison. Allow me to introduce you, putting aside last names, please. First I would like you to meet my old friend, Volko."

Volko arose, beaming at her. He was very tall, a charmingly pear-shaped gentleman whose narrow shoulders sloped down to a swelling stomach hung with a gold watch chain. He wore a black suit and a stiff white collar. She'd not seen anyone dressed like that since her childhood, and then it had been a costume shared by bank presidents and morticians. He looked very proper, very dignified, but there was a sardonic glint to his black eyes that promised a sense of the absurd. "I am so much honored," he said, very nearly clicking his heels as he bowed.

"Volko is the businessman in our group," Tsanko explained gravely. "As a matter of fact this is his warehouse."

"Volko," she murmured, smiling and shaking his hand.

"And this is Boris."

"Boris! The man who warned Shipkov on the street?"

Boris, too, arose, but languidly. He looked like a man who nursed a chronic case of exhaustion—once erect he slouched as if the effort of standing had depleted him. Every line of his face dropped with irony and her exclamation of pleasure at meeting him caused him to flinch, as if he'd been met by an unexpectedly strong wind. But the grasp of his hand was surprisingly firm.

"Kosta you have already met," concluded Tsanko. "He has driven my car for me for many years." If he had expected comment on the smallness of his group he was disappointed; Mrs. Pollifax was the more intrigued by the fact that in a socialist state Tsanko had his own personal driver.

"Hi," said Debby, with a smile for Kosta.

"Does everyone speak English?" asked Mrs. Pollifax.

"All except Kosta."

"Perhaps then you could explain to them what I've just suggested to you?"

"What *have* you suggested?" asked Tsanko bluntly.

Everyone had sat down and now they all looked at her expectantly. It was not quite the same as addressing the Garden Club at home, thought Mrs. Pollifax, and she anxiously cleared her throat. "I have an idea. A dangerous one," she admitted frankly. "I've brought you eight passports from America which you can't use because your friends have been taken to Panchevsky Institute. And there's Philip Trenda—only a pawn, you know, a young American student who's going to be murdered next week so that General Ignatov will keep his power. I think Philip's at Panchevsky Institute, too. Here are all these people imprisoned in the same building. I think we should get them out."

"Out?" echoed Debby in an awed voice.

"Out?" cried Georgi eagerly. "Oh—splendid!"

"Out," mused Volko thoughtfully. "Hmmmm."

"I have never heard such simplicity," murmured Boris. "Just —out?" He snapped his fingers.

"Yes."

Tsanko said, "Naturally we'd all enjoy very much rescuing

our friends. Unfortunately none of us are magicians. No one escapes from Panchevsky Institute."

"Then perhaps it's time someone did," she said. "What on earth is an Underground for if you don't do things like that? I've never heard of an Underground just sitting around. They're supposed to . . ."

"To what?"

She gestured helplessly. "I don't know. *Do* things. Blow up trains, rescue people. That's what they do in movies."

"But this is not a movie," pointed out Tsanko logically.

"But who else can get them out? What *will* you do with your group?"

"Rescue people when possible, yes, but not blow up trains."

Mrs. Pollifax said, "I don't see why you can't rescue them while they're *in* prison. If we all put our heads together—"

"You are naïve," Tsanko told her bluntly.

"Not at all—I'm well aware of the risks and I'd insist upon sharing them. I've not come here empty-handed, either," she told him heatedly. "Did you know that Mrs. Bemish works at Panchevsky Institute? She works nights in the kitchen from eight o'clock to six in the morning, and don't forget that Philip is her nephew. She was utterly appalled to hear that he's here in prison because of her husband."

Tsanko said in astonishment, "You've seen her? You've told her?"

Mrs. Pollifax nodded. "Yes, of course, and I have every reason to believe she'll help us. I think I can also promise you the help of Assen Radev."

Tsanko looked at her in horror. "You know this Radev who followed you?"

"You explained him when you told me about the coat," she said. "I think he's a professional agent for the CIA."

The reaction to this was rewarding to say the least. Tsanko said incredulously, "How is this?"

"I at once opened up the lining of my coat to see why it's of such interest," she told him, and brought out the sample bill, handing it to him. "This is what I found. It seems I've brought rather a lot of money into your country without knowing it. I think Assen

Radev was supposed to exchange coats with me very quickly and quietly. He certainly tried—he must have been my burglar."

Georgi said eagerly, "It is I who searched the valise. He walk around Sofia all the time carrying this bag. What a surprise, a coat so explicitly like yours."

"It was a surprise for me, too," said Mrs. Pollifax frankly.

"But this is Russian money," Tsanko said in surprise.

She nodded.

He was considering this with a frown. "And even if Radev is a CIA agent it doesn't promise his help."

Mrs. Pollifax smiled at him forgivingly. "You might leave that to me," she suggested gently.

Tsanko turned to the others and they began speaking excitedly together in Bulgarian. When he turned back to Mrs. Pollifax he said, "Georgi is eager, as only young people can be. Kosta is gloomy, Volko interested and Boris—"

"Dismayed," said Boris heavily.

"Why?" asked Mrs. Pollifax.

He sighed. "I beg you to look at us, are we a group for violence? We have not even a gun among us. Have we?" he asked the others.

Volko said with a smile, "No, Boris."

"You see?"

Volko added pleasantly, "But you forget, comrade, that my factory makes Very pistols, parachute flares and fireworks. Such things are made of explosives."

"Splendid!" said Mrs. Pollifax, beaming at him.

Georgi said, "Boris, in class you teach us of violence, how is it you speak so negative now? You teach us how we fight the Turks and the Nazis—"

"But did I never point out we lose each time?" said Boris sarcastically.

Volko held up a hand. "Please, I would like to hear more of the Amerikanski's plan."

"Plan? How can there be a plan yet?" asked Mrs. Pollifax. "First we have to enlist Assen Radev and Mrs. Bemish, and then gather information about this Panchevsky Institute."

Tsanko said grimly, "This last I give you now. It is impregnable, an ancient building, a castle. The Turks did their torturing in it. It is a large, square, stone building in the middle of the city. Around it has been built a high stone wall with sentry boxes and lights at each corner of the wall. Streets go right past it . . ."

Mrs. Pollifax said thoughtfully, "Why don't we go and take a look at it right now? Is there a car available?"

The men exchanged glances. "Certainly not in a car," Tsanko murmured. "We must not be seen together."

"One of the trucks, perhaps?" said Volko. "There is one in the alley, a closed-up—how do you say, *van?* Georgi, you could wear coveralls and drive."

"*Ypa,*" he said, grinning.

"It will be dangerous," said Boris. "My God, if we are stopped . . ."

Tsanko laughed and patted him on the shoulder. "Then the Amerikanski will rescue you, too, from Panchevsky Institute, my friend. Come, shall we go?"

Chapter Seventeen

Crouched in the rear of the van, Mrs. Pollifax watched their progress over Georgi's shoulder. It was early twilight. The lights of the cafes in the tourist district spilled out across the cobblestones along with the sound of strident nasal folk songs shouted into microphones that distorted the sound. A few people strolled along the pavement glancing into shop windows, but once they left the hotel area behind them all attempt at night life was abandoned and the streets were almost deserted.

They had driven for about ten minutes when Georgi said, "There it is ahead of us. The wall."

It loomed in the distance, an anachronism in this newly created suburban boulevard, an ugly Chinese wall cutting across their path, bisecting the road and forcing it to split to right and to left. The boulevard had a mild downhill grade. At the bottom Georgi braked in the shadow of the wall and turned, following it to the right. They came out in a broad square—"This is the front, the entrance," said Georgi—and Mrs. Pollifax peered over his shoulder at an expanse of flood-lit cobblestones, two shabby stone pillars embracing the iron gate, and a sentry's kiosk. Then the van passed, turning left to follow the wall down a narrow side street. On the opposite side from which they had entered the square, Georgi braked the van to a stop and they parked.

They were silent. The whole neighborhood was silent, as if crushed by this monstrosity of stone. Across this street on which they had parked, Mrs. Pollifax could look up at the wall as it rose fifteen or twenty feet above them. No actual light could be seen anywhere, yet an illumination like marsh mist hung over the compound, as though on the other side of the wall the sun had risen and it was noon.

"Damn," said Debby in a stifled, angry voice.

Mrs. Pollifax realized that Tsanko and the others were waiting for her to speak, their faces turned toward her, and she could think of nothing to say. Her eyes followed the wall down the street, picking out the silhouette of the sentry box mounted on the wall at the corner, where it turned at right angles. It was a relatively primitive sentry box, no more than an enclosure against rain or snow, its windows glassless and open; as far as she could see there were no sentries inside. "Drive around the corner, Georgi, let's look at the sentry box," she said.

Volko said, "We should not go around all the way again, we have been the only traffic on the square."

She nodded. "Once will do, surely."

The car moved, and now other heads peered to look at the sentry station, too; Mrs. Pollifax could still see no men inside, although as they continued slowly along the last side of the square they met a guard ambling along the top of the wall, a machine gun strapped to his back. Then they were again on the boulevard from which they had entered the square; Georgi accelerated the car and they sped up the boulevard.

"Well?" said Tsanko, leaning over, and his eyes were kind. "You are ready to give it up now?"

Mrs. Pollifax looked at him and then looked away, not answering. The sight of the wall had sobered her; she was still stricken by the visual impact of its height, length, solidity, but above all by its officialness. Nor was this lessened by the knowledge that it was only a wall. There was nothing rational about a wall, whether it encircled Berlin, San Quentin or the ghettos of Warsaw. A wall was a symbol, fortified as much by the idea behind it as by bricks and guns.

But she also remembered that inside this wall lived Philip Trenda, who was going to be killed in a few days. He was young and far from home and he had never wanted to come to Bulgaria, and Debby had said he liked Leonard Cohen and Simon and Garfunkel.

She angrily, "I like Simon and Garfunkel, too. No, I'm not ready to give up, do you understand?"

They returned to the warehouse and sat down with cups of weak tea. The hot water was drawn from one of the furnace boilers by Volko, and Mrs. Pollifax shared three tea bags she carried in her purse. The silence proved oddly companionable. It was broken at last by Volko.

"This is not impossible, you know," he said thoughtfully. "The spirit counts for most. You recall, Tsanko and Boris, some of the tricks we play on the Nazis?"

"Twenty-eight years ago," put in Boris.

"*Da.* We have fewer muscles, but the more brains," pointed out Tsanko.

"You really have access to explosives?" Mrs. Pollifax asked Volko.

He made a gesture that encompassed the basement and the entire warehouse. "Access?" he said modestly. "Is all here. Mostly fireworks this month, enough for May Day in every socialist country."

"Well, now," said Mrs. Pollifax, her eyes brightening. "For myself, I know a little karate. Debby, what could you contribute?"

Debby looked astonished. "You mean you'd let me help?"

"You'd have to," pointed out Mrs. Pollifax.

Debby considered this with great seriousness. "I wish I could think of something," she confessed. "I can drive a motorcycle. And I'm good on the parallel bars and the ropes, and come to think of it I know a lot about knots. All those years of summer camp, you know? Maybe I could tie up a guard."

Knots, motorcycle, wrote Mrs. Pollifax, pencil in hand.

They glanced next at Boris, who sat beside Debby looking glum. "Please," he said. "For this I know nothing."

"Come, come, Boris," said Tsanko, "you were once a champion at shooting. I see the gold medals on your wall."

"Really?" said Georgi eagerly.

Boris gave him a dark look. "What I shoot, Georgi, was the bow and the arrows."

"Oh," said Georgi dispiritedly.

"I am wondering," said Mrs. Pollifax thoughtfully, "if Panchevsky Institute's reputation may not be our greatest asset. In my experience this sort of thing induces carelessness." Fixing Boris with a stern eye, she said, "After all, if *you* had a reputation like that —terrifying—what else would you need? You could relax."

"Already you are terrifying *me,*" Boris said. He smiled and the effect upon his gloomy features was dazzling. "I think you must be like one of our witches in the Balkan mountains."

"She thinks in a straight line," said Tsanko. "There are no detours in this woman. So. She has made a point—Panchevsky Institute may be impregnable, but human nature is not."

Volko glanced at his watch. "It grows late. I suggest lists of what is available to us, and much careful thinking of this idea."

"And then when we've contacted Mrs. Bemish and Radev we can put them all together!" finished Mrs. Pollifax triumphantly. "In the meantime I'll volunteer to visit Assen Radev tomorrow. I can try to persuade Balkantourist to arrange a tour of his goose farm. You can tell me where it is and how to find it?" she asked Tsanko.

"It is the Dobri Vapcarow Collective farm, in the village of Dobri Vapcarow. You understand it is not *his* geese, this is socialist state. The geese are raised for their livers, which are one of our most successful exports to the Western world. For the making of *pâté de foie gras*," he explained.

"How very capitalistic," murmured Mrs. Pollifax. "But I mustn't visit this goose farm with the money still in my coat. Is there a way to remove it overnight?"

"There is our tailor comrade," put in Volko.

"Good! And if the coat could be returned to me in the morning, quite early, at the Rila?"

"You give us a busy night again," said Tsanko, handing her a piece of paper. "This is the name of the collective. I have written it in Bulgarian and in English."

"What about Mrs. Bemish?" asked Debby. "She said she'd die for her brother."

"A momentary aberration, perhaps," commented Mrs. Pollifax. "But yes—what about Mrs. Bemish?"

"I know where she lives," said Georgi eagerly. "I could telephone her tomorrow to say I have message for her. Does she know yet her husband has been killed?"

Tsanko shook his head. "How can she know when he is buried in the rocks of Tsaravets Hill? Only Nikki will guess. But of course she will be alarmed by the absence, it has been twenty-four hours now."

Boris said, "You go and see this woman, Georgi, and she will tell the police about you and I will lose my best student."

"I'll take the chance," Georgi said fiercely. "Someone has to be liaison, like army."

Tsanko intervened with a sigh. "This is a problem for all of us. I have no desire to be seen by these two people, this Radev and Mrs. Bemish. You understand the danger for us if we can be identified?"

Debby said joyously, "Stocking masks!"

Mrs. Pollifax clapped her hands. "Bravo, Debby!" Seeing the others look blank, she explained, "This is what was first used in our Brink's holdups. The silk stocking over the head blurs the features completely. I can contribute several pairs, and you'll see."

"Holdups?" said Volko, puzzled. "Brink?"

Boris said firmly, "James Cagney, Volko. You recall the American movies we enjoy much?"

Mrs. Pollifax checked her watch and stood up. "It's getting late," she said regretfully. "Debby and I should go back to the hotel before anyone wonders where we've gone. In any case, if I'm going to request a visit to a goose farm I'll have to telephone Balkantourist at once." She added sadly, "They don't seem to like sudden jolts."

It was agreed that the blue car would call for them at the hotel at five o'clock tomorrow. "Do not be discouraged, Amerikanski," Tsanko told her. "We are neither fools nor cowards. You give us hope."

It had been a long day and Mrs. Pollifax was looking forward to her first night of uninterrupted sleep since arriving in Bulgaria. She and Debby said good night in the hall and Mrs. Pollifax waited, watching, while Debby unlocked the door of her room, gave her a peace sign and went inside. Disguising a yawn—it was only half-past nine—she unlocked her own door.

The lights were on. Seated opposite the door in a chair was Nevena.

"Why, Nevena," said Mrs. Pollifax warmly, "Just the person I wanted to see!"

"So, Mrs. Pollifax," said Nevena grimly.

It was at that moment that Mrs. Pollifax remembered the long list of her indiscretions with Balkantourist and the number of necessary apologies that had accumulated. She was relieved that Debby—whose presence in Bulgaria was still on tenuous grounds, as yet unrealized by both Eastlake and Balkantourist—was safely out of sight. "I was about to telephone Balkantourist," Mrs. Pollifax said truthfully.

"You were not in Tarnovo when the driver called for you at one o'clock this afternoon," said Nevena.

"No—I wasn't," admitted Mrs. Pollifax.

"He waited."

"I left a message—"

"He had orders to wait for you. He waited. Where were you?"

"I was offered a ride back to Sofia. Mr. Eastlake at my Embassy had telephoned—"

Nevena bluntly interrupted. "That we know. But"—she fixed her eyes sternly on Mrs. Pollifax—"Mr. Eastlake telephone you before I do."

Mrs. Pollifax blinked at this; Balkantourist had been doing some thorough detective work during the course of the day. Obviously she was in trouble here, which, with so many other things to think about, seemed tiresome indeed. "I offered to go by train," pointed out Mrs. Pollifax. "I expressed an interest in getting back to Sofia earlier than you suggested."

Nevena threw up her hands. "I never tour anybody like you. Balkantourist is angry, very angry. You do whatever you please, it is most insulting."

"I'm sorry."

"You are sorry, but you continue to do what you please. You not behave nicely. It is too much, we have no choice."

"No choice?" echoed Mrs. Pollifax, very alert now suddenly.

"You must go," Nevena said coldly, rising. "You go first plane tomorrow."

Mrs. Pollifax sat very still. She understood at last that her first battle was being fought here, in this room, and if she lost there would be no other battles at all. She felt a deep chill rising in her and she knew that she must use this cold to become ruthless, not for herself but for the thin hope of rescuing Philip Trenda. "I'm sorry," she said quietly to Nevena. "I'm really very sorry, Nevena.

I was about to telephone you my apologies and ask if I might visit one of your great collectives, of which I've been hearing such splendid things. But of course if I must leave . . ." She sighed. "If Balkantourist says I must leave then of course I must. My daughter, Jane, will be disappointed, of course. She raises geese."

"She what?" said Nevena, startled.

"She raises geese," Mrs. Pollifax said firmly. "I have just heard this afternoon, Nevena, that your country is becoming well known for its *pâté de foie gras*. I had no idea. My daughter would be so interested in learning what your country . . ."

Nevena stared at her. "You never mention this in your letter to Balkantourist of what you wish to see."

Mrs. Pollifax shrugged. "I had no idea—I thought the French were the *pâté de foie gras* people. The Strasbourg *pâté de foie gras* is so . . . so . . ."

"French!" Nevena's lip curled. "French?" She tossed her head. "We excel the French, they are bourgeois. We export much goose livers for the best *pâté de foie gras*—"

"So I've just heard," murmured Mrs. Pollifax. "And I was looking forward—"

"The *French*," Nevena repeated contemptuously. She was silent a moment and then she said cautiously, "It is possible that if your apology is acceptable—I can see."

"It would certainly be merciful," said Mrs. Pollifax truthfully.

"Okay, I see," said Nevena. "If this is so, someone take you tomorrow, which is Friday, and you leave Saturday morning."

"Without a tour of Sofia," said Mrs. Pollifax, nodding.

Nevena said sharply, "Without tour of Sofia? You have seen Sofia!"

Mrs. Pollifax shook her head. "Only Mount Vitosha, and then I became tired, you see, and returned to the hotel. I've not seen the Nefesky Cathedral, or your monument to the Soviet Army, or the Georgi Dimitrov Mausoleum. Or Lenin Square, for that matter."

Nevena's lips thinned. "You cannot be trusted with a car again." But she had not said no. A lengthy silence followed, which heartened Mrs. Pollifax because Nevena was frowning thoughtfully. After a moment she lifted her gaze and regarded Mrs. Pollifax sternly. "You have no sense," she said. "You come, you go, we cannot find you."

"True, Nevena," she said contritely.

"But you are old woman. I believe you when you say you are sorry. I make with you a compromise. If you behave very nice we take you tomorrow to collective farm. On Saturday ten o'clock you join organized tour—many peoples—of my city. Then you leave Saturday night seven o'clock sharp to reach airport nine o'clock plane."

Soberly Mrs. Pollifax nodded. She had at least gained forty-eight hours; it might be enough time, it had to be enough time.

"And," added Nevena severely, "you report to Balkantourist all the time. On such terms—"

"I'm on probation," suggested Mrs. Pollifax.

"Pro-bation? I not know such word."

"It means," explained Mrs. Pollifax, "that I have behaved very rudely and am being given a second opportunity for which I am most grateful, Nevena."

Nevena's face softened. "You are not *bad*," she explained, as though she had considered this already in some depth. "But you are careless, lazy. In Bulgaria peoples are not careless and lazy."

Mrs. Pollifax nodded; she believed her.

"We give you forty-eight hours, no more. But I—how you call it?—intercede for you because you are not bad, only without sense. But you make sense now, you understand? Be very, very good or you go."

"Thank you, Nevena," said Mrs. Pollifax.

"You see? We are reasonable peoples, we Bulgarians," Nevena said, touching her almost affectionately on the shoulder. "In our anger we can be kind."

"Very kind," said Mrs. Pollifax firmly, and hoped she would leave soon.

"The Dobri Vapcarow Collective raises geese for the *pâté de foie gras*," Nevena said. "At nine sharp be in lobby."

When she had gone Mrs. Pollifax fumbled for the slip of paper Tsanko had given her upon which he had written the name of the collective at which Radev worked: it was the Dobri Vapcarow Collective, and Mrs. Pollifax decided that her fortune, however mixed so far, was at least for the moment on the ascendency.

Chapter Eighteen

D ebby was in Mrs. Pollifax's room at seven. "I thought I'd want to sleep all day, but there's too much going on," she explained. "Mrs. Pollifax, were you serious last night? I mean, do you think there's the slightest *possibility?*"

Mrs. Pollifax groped for pencil and paper and wrote, *Room may be bugged. Wait.* Handing it to Debby, she said casually, "My Balkantourist guide, Nevena, was waiting for me here last night. Balkantourist feels I've behaved very irresponsibly toward them—as of course I have," she added piously. "Nevena had come to suggest I leave Bulgaria at once."

"They're expelling you?" gasped Debby.

"That word was not mentioned, fortunately—it sounds a little strong. However, she's graciously given me another forty-eight hours—if I behave myself—so that I can visit a collective farm today, and tour Sofia tomorrow."

"Well, wow," Debby said, making congratulatory gestures.

Mrs. Pollifax nodded. "And now I shall take a bath."

"I just might write a postcard to Dr. Kidd," said Debby. "I'll tell him I've eloped with a Bulgarian sheepherder."

Mrs. Pollifax closeted herself in the bathroom and blessed the sufficiency of hot water in Sofia: she had a great deal of thinking to do, mainly about Debby, who had been so conveniently overlooked by everyone for the moment. Debby's thumb was healing now, they were back in Sofia, but somehow, through circumstances beyond anyone's control, Debby had become more and more involved during the last twenty-four hours. The problem was, how much more involved should she become?

Her being here in Sofia was dangerous. There was Nikki, who by this time would have guessed something untoward had happened to Mr. Bemish on Wednesday night. Nikki would be asking

questions. Inquiries in Tarnovo would take time; they would, however, establish the fact that not only had Mrs. Pollifax survived her
trip to Tarnovo but that she had left Tarnovo alive yesterday and
accompanied by a young American girl with long brown hair.

Of course there was no way to link them with Bemish in
Tarnovo. The black Renault would be discovered parked on a main
street in town, and the bodies of Bemish and Titko Yugov would
probably never be found. But there would remain the unalterable
coincidence that all of them had been in Tarnovo the same night,
and that Bemish had disappeared while Mrs. Pollifax was still very
much alive. It would also prove very dismaying for Nikki to learn
that Debby was her companion; he wouldn't like this. He would
look for them in Sofia and place them under surveillance again. By
tonight at the latest, she mused; we've had a day's respite, that's all.

But Nikki was such an angry young man that it was unpleasant to contemplate his reactions. Their unexpected survival would
certainly curb his delight at how smoothly his plot was moving
toward its climax in Zurich on Monday morning.

And if he ever learned that both she and Debby had been at
the Embassy yesterday to witness the release of Philip's impersona-
tor—she shuddered. It could become very difficult for them to
remain alive in Bulgaria.

Should she suggest that Debby leave, then? She thought that
if she insisted upon it Debby might consent to go as far as Belgrade
and wait for news, but she would certainly rebel at going any farther. The trouble here was that Debby might talk too much in a
changed environment. Belgrade would still be buzzing with gossip
about Philip Trenda's release and Debby would be eager to find
other young companions again. The temptation to tell what she
knew would be very strong indeed.

But the worst of it, reflected Mrs. Pollifax, would be Debby's
terrible vulnerability in Belgrade. Nikki had already found his way
there once and he presumably still owned a valid passport for
travel. Who would there be to watch over Debby?

This last realization settled it: it might be dangerous for
Debby here in Sofia; it could prove equally dangerous for her to be
banished to a nearby capital where Mrs. Pollifax could no longer
keep an eye on her. *I'll ask Tsanko about hiding her for the next forty-*

eight hours, she thought, and made a mental note to see that Debby recovered her passport from the hotel today.

"The tailor delivered your coat," Debby announced as Mrs. Pollifax emerged from her thoughts and her bath. "The receipt's on the bed."

Mrs. Pollifax picked up the receipt and read *Money in coat is counterfeit.* "What on earth!" she exclaimed.

Debby nodded. "Your—uh—employers are certainly weirdos."

"Devious," said Mrs. Pollifax. "Rather shocking, too, I might add." She wondered if Assen Radev knew the Russian rubles were counterfeit. Probably. Counterfeit money did upsetting things to a country's economy, didn't it? If enough counterfeit Russian money circulated through a devoted satellite country it could cause some rather hard feelings toward Russia, couldn't it? The bills would move steadily out from Sofia into the villages and among the peasants, who distrusted paper money anyway, and if a hard-working peasant sold a precious cow and found his currency was worthless it would prove quite a blow. In fact it would be heartbreaking, she thought with a shake of her head. She would have to speak very sternly to Carstairs about this when they met again. Then she remembered that Carstairs would probably have a number of biting comments to make about her involving the Underground in unauthorized activities and she decided not to think about it now and began looking for a clean pair of gloves.

"And what kind of mash have we here?" asked Mrs. Pollifax in a depressed voice as she peered into still another tub at the Dobri Vapcarow Collective.

She and Debby had been at the collective for nearly two hours and had not so much as glimpsed Assen Radev. They had seen a great number of geese, and rather too much of their substitute guide. He was a young man named Slavko, who sweated heavily over his translations, but she supposed it was not every day that a guide was forced into translating words like force-fed, *foie gras*, liver, mash and gaggles of geese.

"This mixture has more corn than rye or wheat," said Slavko after conferring with the foreman. He had already explained that the Dobri Vapcarow Collective was such a success that it was now a model for other collectives, and a laboratory for small experiments. "They eat our *foie gras* in all the capitals of Europe," Slavko said proudly. "It brings much praise, much money."

The foreman, who spoke no English, listened impassively. He was a huge, ruddy-faced man in overalls and muddy hip boots who seemed to regard Slavko with the amusement he would accord a three-legged goose or some other colorful mutation of animal life; he smiled occasionally at Mrs. Pollifax, frequently at Debby and not at all at Slavko.

But of Assen Radev they had seen nothing, and Mrs. Pollifax began to fear that she had miscalculated. She'd had no real, graspable idea of what a collective farm was, vaguely assuming it to resemble a New Jersey truck farm, intimate and on a small scale. This collective was like an open sea of land with a small island of barns on it. The cluster of barns and outbuildings was separated by smaller seas of trampled mud, and totally surrounded by pens of geese, but beyond this nothing could be seen on the horizon except clouds, and field after field of growing corn and wheat: the collective incorporated three villages and mile after mile of land. Assen Radev could be anywhere; he was certainly not here.

"The land belongs to the workers," Slavko was reciting. "After the crops are harvested, twenty percent of the profits go to the state, ten percent to the planting and ten percent to new machinery and repairs. The remaining sixty percent is divided among the workers according to workdays they have given—for two hundred workdays one thousand *leva*, for two hundred and fifty workdays, fifteen hundred *leva*."

"That's five hundred American dollars," Debby announced triumphantly.

"In this room," continued Slavko after consulting with the foreman, "there is compared the feeding by the hand with the feeding by machine."

Debby peered into the room and stepped back. "Ech," she said. She had barely survived watching the geese fed by machine. She had fled outside, where Mrs. Pollifax had heard her retching. "I won't," she said. "I can't."

Mrs. Pollifax nodded. "Quite sensible. Wait outside."

Four healthy-looking young women in overalls looked up as they entered the next room of the barn. Each was engaged in inserting a funnel down the throat of a goose, emptying mash into the funnel and then forcing it down the goose's throat with a milking motion of the hands. They worked quickly, contentedly, like laboratory workers moving from test tube to test tube.

"It's only if you don't think about it, I suppose," said Mrs. Pollifax vaguely, and Slavko looked at her questioningly. "Forcing the food into them like that," she explained.

"It makes beautiful livers—big, big," Slavko said, reverently sketching dimensions with his hands.

Mrs. Pollifax looked away quickly, certain that she would never be able to eat *pâté de foie gras* again.

"Now we have the big surprise for you," Slavko said as they emerged into the sunlight again. "Please—across these ditches—step high!—to last building."

"Another surprise?" said Debby wearily, catching up with them.

They mounted the wooden steps of a building with curtains at its windows, and entered a large bare room. "Please—you relax now if you please," said Slavko. "This is building of collective meetings and keeping of books. Please sit, remove the coats if you will and relax."

"I will," said Mrs. Pollifax, and shrugged off her coat and hung it over a chair, sitting down next to it to guard it.

But when the foreman arrived, moving more slowly than they, Slavko hurried them all into a second room. "See—for you!" he cried with pleasure.

Mrs. Pollifax exclaimed aloud. A long trestle table had been set up in this room and on it had been spread for them the fruits of the farm: bowls of fat red raspberries still glistening with dew; platters of delicate honeydew, chunks of cantaloupe and red juicy watermelon, a small loaf of *pâté* and several jugs of colorless liquor. At once Slavko slipped into the role of host and handed Debby and Mrs. Pollifax tiny glasses into which he poured the liquid.

"*Slivowicz,*" he said, beaming.

"How very hospitable of you all," she said. Over his shoulder Mrs. Pollifax met the interested gaze of Lenin mounted on the wall: the picture was the only decorative note in the bare meeting room. "To peace," she added, lifting her glass, and suddenly remembered that she had left her coat in the other room. "My coat," she said. "Debby, could you . . . ?"

"Right," said Debby, and promptly left, but when she returned she was empty-handed and obviously puzzled. She mutely shook her head, shrugging, and Mrs. Pollifax had to continue listening to the statistics that Slavko was earnestly reciting, as though by sheer volume he could persuade her of Bulgaria's superiority.

At last she turned to Debby and said bluntly, "Not there?"

"Absolutely vanished."

Slavko pressed more *slivowicz* on them, but Mrs. Pollifax demurred, her mind now on the missing coat. "Liquid fire," she told Slavko, smiling, and then, "I do think we must leave, Slavko. We're growing tired." And late, she added silently, noting that already it was two o'clock. Thanking them all with enthusiasm, she made her retreat to the anteroom and on the threshold stopped short because her coat was hanging over the chair where she had left it.

She and Debby exchanged glances. Without any change of expression Mrs. Pollifax picked up her coat and put it on; her heart was beating faster. She had filled its pockets before coming here and she was not surprised to find her handkerchief still in the left pocket and a handful of coins in the right. What her fingers searched for now were the small knots of thread that she had sewn into the lining of the left pocket: five of them, thick enough to be felt but not seen. And they were no longer there.

"What is it?" asked Debby in a low voice as they walked toward the car.

Mrs. Pollifax was smiling. "I'm daring to hope that our trip here hasn't been in vain."

"Even though you didn't see him?"

"Not a glimpse," she said, "but I think I'm wearing the other coat."

They had not seen Radev at the collective, but when Mrs. Pollifax unlocked the door of her hotel room her burglar of the first evening was sitting in a chair by the window. "You certainly made good time," she congratulated him, closing and locking the door behind her.

His brows lifted. "You are not surprised?"

514   Dorothy Gilman

"No, of course not. I do hope I didn't hurt you too badly the other night?"

His gaze was stony. "I have come for the money—it was not in the coat. I will have it now, please."

"If the money had been in the coat," she said reasonably, "you wouldn't have come and I would never have met you. I want to talk to you. By the way, the room may be bugged."

"The hell it is," said Radev. "I checked." He regarded her with curiosity, his eyes hostile. "You're not the amateur I first thought, but this is bad, very bad, this meeting. Against all orders."

"I first met you as a burglar," she retorted, "and that wasn't *my* idea."

"You give me helluva shock. In fact you give me helluva lot of shocks. How can I get near you when the secret police stay on your tail—and I mean really on your tail—from seven o'clock Monday on? I never have a chance. Then you go off to Borovets but are not at Borovets at all. Now I am waiting for my money." He brought a small pistol from his pocket and rested it casually on one knee.

"Did you know the Russian rubles are counterfeit?" she asked, sitting on the bed opposite him.

"Sure I know they're counterfeit. How did *you* know they're counterfeit?"

"I think that gun is extremely bad manners," said Mrs. Pollifax, glancing at it. "Do you mind pointing it in another direction? We're supposed to be allies, you know."

"It's so you don't get any ideas, and don't be too sure we're allies, either," he said. "I got no allies, I work for cash. And I want that money."

"And we want *you*," Mrs. Pollifax told him cheerfully. "You're a professional, you see, and we need one badly." Operation sounded like a professional word. "We have an operation planned."

He said savagely, "Appendix or tonsils? Look, lady, I'm in a hurry and I want that money. Do I have to kill you to get it?"

Mrs. Pollifax shrugged. "Possibly. Have you heard of Philip Trenda?"

"Sure I've heard of Philip Trenda. He's dead. They found him dead today in Belgrade."

"So soon?" murmured Mrs. Pollifax. "That poor boy. Except

it wasn't Philip Trenda who died in Belgrade, you see, it was an imposter. Philip Trenda's still alive and in Sofia."

Radev sighed. "Lady, I couldn't care less. I'm not paid to worry about Trenda, I'm paid to get that money you brought in."

Mrs. Pollifax said tactfully, "But you see, I have it and you don't."

He stared at her in astonishment. "You're blackmailing me?"

"I wondered how long it would take you to understand," she said happily. "Of course I'm blackmailing you. I have what you want, and you have what I want. That's the way blackmail works, isn't it? But I'll be very glad to give you the rubles after you've volunteered to help."

"Volunteered?" he said mockingly.

"Yes, volunteered."

"And if I take my lumps and just leave?"

"Why should you?" she asked. "We only want to borrow your professional services for a few days. You'll have the rubles by Sunday." If we're still alive, she added silently.

"Christ," he muttered. "Maybe I just ought to shoot you and forget the whole thing."

"The others, of course, would know that you shot me. I wouldn't give a nickel for your chances of survival."

"Others?"

"The people I'm working with," she told him. "The Underground that I'm allied with here."

"You're kidding me. In Bulgaria?"

"It's my assignment, contacting them. It's they who identified you when you were following me, and they who searched your bag and found the duplicate coat. They know all about you. Name, address and—uh—affiliations."

"Christ," he groaned. "All right, help do what?"

"Free Philip Trenda, of course, as well as a few friends of the Underground."

He considered, scowling. "And then I'd get the rubles?"

"Then you'd get the rubles."

"And where are these people?"

"In Panchevsky Institute."

He sprang to his feet. "For chrissake, why not choose something easy? Like assassinating the Premier, for instance."

"Please—I do not like profanity," begged Mrs. Pollifax.

"Are you out of your mind? Panchevsky Institute?"

"Since that's where he is—and since we want to get him out,"
she said tartly, "then naturally that's the place from which we will
have to recover him."

"Insane," he said. "When?"

"This weekend."

"For chrissake."

"Mr. Radev—"

"Okay, sorry, but I tell you it's impossible, you're mad. I got a
contact at Panchevsky who tells me about security and it's tight,
it's—"

"Contact?" said Mrs. Pollifax quickly. "A prisoner?"

"Of course not, a guard," he snapped. "What do you think I
am, an amateur? He tells me who goes in, who comes out—for a
price, of course, but he also tells me—"

"Mr. Radev, I love you," said Mrs. Pollifax impulsively, and
leaned over and kissed him. "You see? You know a guard. I *knew*
you'd be able to help us."

Radev recoiled. "Keep your hands off me, lady. For chrissake."

"I'm just so pleased," she confessed. "The others lack a certain toughness, a certain experience—and you even have a gun."

He looked alarmed. "You mean they *don't?*"

"It's almost five o'clock," she said, consulting her watch. "I
suggest you come along and meet them now. We've very little
time, and final plans simply have to be made tonight."

Still he stood, not moving. "I have one thing to say," he
announced. "You look like a nice old lady. Really nice. Really kind,
sweet, gentle. You are not nice," he added.

"Now *that*," said Mrs. Pollifax, "is one of the nicest compliments I've had from a professional. Thank you, Mr. Radev."

"Oh for chrissake," he said bitterly.

Chapter Nineteen

This time when the small blue car drew up to the Hotel Rila, Mrs. Pollifax directed Georgi to the hotel's service entrance. "Assen Radev is joining us by way of the rear door. He's just been enlisted," she told him.

"*Bora*," murmured Georgi, impressed. "You really are like a witch. But he will have to wear bandage over the eyes or he will know to find us again. Your scarf, please?"

"All right. What about Mrs. Bemish?"

"She has been with us all day giving much information. This lady has much courage. Last night she go to third floor at Panchevsky Institute—very illegitimate, you understand—and looks. She make guards very angry, but she says, 'This is Petrov's son.' "

"I'm so glad we went to see her," said Debby.

Radev climbed in and grudgingly suffered the scarf to be tied over his eyes. When they arrived at the warehouse, their steps echoing again through the basement, Georgi whispered, "You have face stockings?"

Mrs. Pollifax handed him four pairs of stockings and he hurried ahead. When she and Debby and Radev entered the room behind the furnace they found the faces of their Underground friends unrecognizably blurred: the noses flattened, mouths distorted and chins obscured by the gauzy stockings. Mrs. Pollifax removed Radev's blindfold and he swore heavily. "Goons!" he cried despairingly.

"Bring in Mrs. Bemish," said Tsanko. He was lifting a large sheet of cardboard to the wall. When he had propped it among the pipes he stood back and Mrs. Pollifax saw that it was a large diagram of Panchevsky Institute. "Good evening," he said, bowing. "I look sinister? As you can see, we have been busy."

"Good evening, Tsanko. We've been busy, too. This is Assen Radev, who knows a guard at Panchevsky Institute."

"Someone's missing," she said, counting the shrouded heads. "Capital!"

"Volko—he has been taking apart fireworks today and working out formulas. Is most important. Ah, Mrs. Bemish," he said.

Georgi had brought in Mrs. Bemish, looking frightened, although her face brightened at sight of Mrs. Pollifax and Debby. "They think I do something," she whispered to Mrs. Pollifax. "Is this possible?"

"Ah—here is Volko, we begin now," said Tsanko. "Please, everyone sit? Please, the meeting is to come to order," he said sternly. "We are about to consider the storming of Panchevsky."

Boris said sourly, "What a pity we not forget whole thing and go to big tourist nightclub for evening."

Tsanko leaned over and affectionately gripped his shoulder. Straightening, he said, "Perhaps I say now that Boris has twice been to prisons for slips of the tongue. He has spent eight of past sixteen years in jails for mention of history not in our Republic of Bulgaria textbooks. Yet still he risks himself by helping us."

"I am behaving so badly you must say this?" asked Boris gloomily.

"Very badly," Tsanko told him gravely.

Boris smiled, and again his face lighted up. "Then I be quiet —if only someone tell me how to silence my stomach, which growls at thought of prisons. Never mind, as history professor I have always the longing to see history made. Please continue."

Tsanko nodded. "Mrs. Bemish has brought much news for us tonight, both good and bad. In return we have had only bad news for her. We have told her that her husband is dead. Because his death is on our heads it is only fair we give her passport to leave country if this experience is survived. It is agreed? . . . Now here is diagram made from her very helpful description."

After swift glances at Mrs. Bemish they turned to the diagram. "The bad news is this," continued Tsanko. "Our Bulgarian friends are here"—he pointed to the first floor of the south side. "Philip Trenda is at opposing end of Panchevsky, and high up, on third floor."

"Ouch," said Debby, wincing.

Glances swerved reproachfully to Mrs. Pollifax. "And the good news?" she asked, ignoring the others.

Mrs. Bemish spoke. "The wall is not busy," she said. "Only one man walk round and round. This is vacation season, workers go free to Varna and Golden Sands. Seven guards gone this week."

"Do you mean there aren't sentries in each box?"

Mrs. Bemish nodded.

"A touch of carelessness," murmured Mrs. Pollifax happily.

"What are the plans?" asked Assen Radev, speaking for the first time.

Mrs. Pollifax said, "We make the plans now. To begin with, because it does look so frightful—the diagram—I suggest we forget it's a prison with a wall around it and look at it as though it's two boxes, one inside the other."

Assen Radev made a rude sound.

Boris said, "We are attacking *boxes?*"

"But she's right," Debby said, jumping to her feet. "Look where Phil is, his cell is high up but directly across from the wall."

"Three stories high," pointed out Boris.

"Yes, but don't you see? We wouldn't have to enter the prison at all to rescue Phil if we could get across the courtyard from the wall to a window."

Boris sighed. "And which of us has wings? Who is an angel? What windows would be open in a prison?"

Debby said impatiently, "I don't know about windows, but I do know you can get across space like that with ropes. I told you I know about ropes. Last summer at camp we learned how to cross white water—that's rapids—on a rope. It was a survival course, only our parents heard about it and the instructor got fired and we all went back to beadwork. But what's the difference between crossing rapids or a prison courtyard by rope?"

"Did you do it personally?" asked Mrs. Pollifax. "Can you remember how it worked?"

Debby nodded. "Yes to both."

Tsanko shook his head. "You are forgetting something. Doubtless your instructor swam the rapids first to secure the rope at the other side. How would you achieve this across a courtyard?"

With a heavy sigh Boris uncrossed his legs. Almost crossly he said, "Do not obliterate the child. I hesitate to encourage this mad-

ness, but the solution is there—the rope could be shot across with
the bow and the arrow." He sat back and glared at them all.

"Hey," said Debby, looking with a fresh eye at Boris.

"Wild," said Assen Radev disgustedly.

"Of course it's wild," Mrs. Pollifax told him indignantly.
"What else have we to work with but imagination?"

"Okay, you want wild ideas? I have the wild idea," said Volko,
getting up and walking to the diagram. "Here on first floor you see
our countrymen, our friends. Let us look at them a minute. You
recall this is hill here, on Persenk Boulevard. If one of my trucks is
stolen, with explosives in it, and is parked here on Persenk Boulevard, at top of hill, and brakes happen to be bad, very bad, and the
truck begin rolling . . ."

There was silence.

Georgi said, "It would roll down the hill and explode the
outer wall but go no farther. It would never touch the walls of
Panchevsky."

"Explosives? You have explosives?" said Assen Radev. "Me, I
have only geese and one pistol. If you have dynamite here is what
could be done."

As Assen rose from his chair Mrs. Pollifax wrote down *geese—
one pistol.*

"You need two explosions, two separate ones, you understand? One for outside wall, one for Institute. What kind of explosives you have?"

"Fireworks," said Boris gloomily.

"You're kidding. What about detonators?"

"A small amount of pentolite," said Volko. "But not enough
for two big explosions."

Radev frowned. "On collective there is PETN for clearing of
rocks. But what do I get from this?" he demanded. "For me this is
very dangerous, I know none of you, but you all know who I am.
Anytime it pleases, you need just finger me, telling identity, what I
do."

Tsanko nodded. "He has a point there."

Mrs. Pollifax realized that to her growing list of indiscretions
she had added the lifting of an agent's cover. She sighed.

Radev said, "You give this lady here, this Mrs. Bemish, passport out of country. I think I prefer passport to counterfeit Russian rubles."

The members of the Underground exchanged glances. "We have only eight passports," pointed out Tsanko. "We've promised Mrs. Bemish safe-conduct to her brother and we reserve one for this young Trenda, who will not have a passport any more, and there are four of our countrymen who must not remain in Bulgaria."

"That's six," Radev said. "Give me one and you keep fifty thousand counterfeit Russian rubles in trade."

Tsanko and Volko exchanged amused glances. Volko said, "We might have a use for those counterfeit rubles, eh, my friend?"

"But it leaves us with only one passport." Tsanko turned to Radev. "You would have to earn it. Let us hear first what you can do to earn it."

Radev laughed. "You get money's worth from me—I know explosives. I learn in America before they deport me. I am real hood, and frankly do not care to see another goose in my life again. I know also the guard at Panchevsky named Miroslav. You give me some counterfeit rubles and I pay him well for whatever you wish him to do. Maybe he even let me into Panchevsky, yes? A little explosive wrapped in plastic, a fuse, and I maybe break locks here or there. All this I do for passport."

His words brought a distinct change to the atmosphere. Radev was just what they needed. Mrs. Pollifax could sense doubts being replaced by eagerness.

Even Mrs. Bemish was affected. Leaning forward, she said with bright eyes, "I go to work now, but first, you do this at night when I am there and I put out electric boxes if you show me how. In room off kitchen, big room. Electric switches run lights and siren."

"Sirens—*bora!*" muttered Georgi.

"*Da*, sirens."

"They have a generator for emergencies, I suppose," Tsanko said.

Mrs. Bemish nodded. "When electric go off—snowstorm or power kaput—big machine start. Generator."

"How long before they can start it?"

"I think," she said, and closed her eyes. "Two, maybe three

years back. I am making mishmash. Elena bring candle and I cut maybe ten eggplants. Then I peel and take out seeds before generator bring lights again." She opened her eyes. "Ten, maybe fifteen minutes."

Georgi said, "You mean we have only ten minutes—fifteen at most—to get prisoners out?"

"You want to spend any longer in Panchevsky Institute?" said Boris dryly. "You hear her, we have ten eggplants' time."

Mrs. Pollifax intervened. "Another point. Difficult as it may be, I strongly urge that we do this tomorrow night or Sunday morning. I've been asked by Balkantourist to leave."

"How is this?" said Tsanko.

She told him of Nevena and her anger. "So I shall have to tour Sofia tomorrow and behave very well, which means assignments really must be distributed tonight."

"We prefer not to use women," Tsanko told her.

"Nonsense," she said flatly. "Everyone involved in this can't wear stocking masks over their faces. You're going to have to use people who have passports and can leave the country."

Radev said, "This is true. If you give me passport I risk myself big. This lady leave, too, and the girl. If this is success there will be investigation later."

Tsanko threw up his hands helplessly. "Then we must get to work—serious work!"

"Exactly," said Volko. "Let us hear more talk."

As everyone began to speak at once Mrs. Pollifax thought, Brainstorming! and settled back contentedly in her chair, knowing they were involved now, knowing that each of them was ready to make something happen.

It was midnight before they reached a tentative plan and broke up, but only because they needed sleep for the hours ahead. During her day as a tourist Mrs. Pollifax was to purchase nine Bulgarian wristwatches—one for each member of the group—so that the ten or fifteen minutes allotted them could be plotted precisely by the hands of identical watches. Debby was to drop out of sight, hidden by Georgi in an abandoned hut on the outskirts of the city. In that same hut in the country Volko and Radev would spend most of the day designing their explosives. Assen Radev was to contact the guard at Panchevsky Institute who was on his payroll and discover what could be worked out, and Mrs. Bemish had promised to alert the four Bulgarian prisoners to the possibility of rescue, and try to learn more about the third floor that housed Philip's cell.

The attack on Panchevsky Institute had been set for three o'clock Sunday morning, just before dawn.

On this note they parted, each of them with a sense of astonishment at the events of the evening.

Chapter Twenty

T he next morning Nevena strode into the lobby of the Rila
exuding cheerfulness. "The bus is outside filled with peoples," she told Mrs. Pollifax. "Very nice peoples, all western Europeans. You like Slavko yesterday? You like goose farm?
Please recall at seven tonight I come and take you to airport for
nine o'clock plane."

"I recall," said Mrs. Pollifax meekly.

"You come now for tour of Sofia."

It was the beginning of a long day, thought Mrs. Pollifax as
she seated herself on the Balkantourist bus. It was a luxurious vehicle, with a driver who spoke no English, a small chair beside him
for Nevena and a microphone into which she spoke. If Mrs. Pollifax had expected to be bored by Nevena's deluxe tour, she was
soon pleasantly surprised.

All along the boulevards flags were flying in the breeze. "You
see Sofia in unique moment," announced Nevena, breathing heavily into the microphone, her eyes sparkling. "Tomorrow Comrade
Brezhnev, Party Chairman of our great Soviet comrades, come to
visit with our leaders. There will be procession and many talks
spoken here."

The bus drew to a halt before the National Assembly building
so they might observe the wooden stands, the workers installing
microphones. "Across, down avenue, consider Georgi Dimitrov
Mausoleum," she continued. "There will be ceremony there, too,
in morning, the Changing of the Guard for Chairman Brezhnev."

As the tour progressed, Mrs. Pollifax noticed that Nevena
showed a definite preference for the new and the Soviet-inspired.
Not for her St. George's Church, which had been built in the third
century; she was visibly bored. She allowed them an hour to examine the ikons and the Thracian exhibits in the crypt of the Nev-

sky Cathedral, but plainly what impressed her most was the number of people who came to Bulgaria to see them. However, about the Monument to the Red Army she waxed poetic, and her voice fairly sang as she pointed out the new Pliska and Rila hotels and the apartment complexes on the outskirts of the city. Apparently Nevena was not one of the young people about whom Tsanko worried. Over thirty, probably, thought Mrs. Pollifax.

In the middle of the day they lunched on Mount Vitosha, at the restaurant where Mrs. Pollifax had first learned of Philip's arrest. They descended the mountain in cable cars and met the Balkantourist bus at the bottom, and were whisked off to Boyana to see the church's medieval art. At half-past two Mrs. Pollifax was deposited back at her hotel. "I shall do a little shopping for souvenirs now," she told Nevena reassuringly. "At the Tzum department store."

"But at seven o'clock be in lobby, please," instructed Nevena.

"Yes," said Mrs. Pollifax, and made her way around the corner and down the street to the Tzum, where she confounded the clerks by purchasing nine watches. Following this she spent an hour in her room setting and checking the watches and then on impulse she brought out a stamped postcard and wrote to her neighbor Miss Hartshorne, *Dear Grace, If I should be late in returning—detained for any reason* (such as going to either prison or the firing squad, she thought) *please deliver my night-blooming cereus to Professor Whitsun.* This sounded pessimistic and so she added with a flourish, *Having lovely time, Emily.* And then she tore the postcard up and dropped it into the wastebasket.

At half-past four she put the watches carefully back into the paper shopping bag, locked the door behind her and went downstairs through the lobby to the front entrance. Presently the familiar blue car drew up, she climbed inside and she and Georgi drove away.

The hut in the country had once been a stone house with a thatch roof until a fire had destroyed the roof and blackened the interior. Timbers leaned crazily against the stone walls and sunflowers had begun to weave a new roof of vines. It was charming and pastoral. Above all it was hidden from sight at the edge of a wood and isolated from the nearest tiny village.

"But where is everyone?" asked Mrs. Pollifax as Georgi parked the car under a linden tree.

"Ah, Boris is in the forest rehearsing his fifty-pound hunting bow. You know—he is good, very good? Volko and Radev are in hole under house packing explosives."

"And Debby? Tsanko?"

"Tsanko come to us later. Debby? She is no doubt with Boris rehearsing ropes." He added proudly, "We have long, long rope, very strong, used by men to clean windows very high."

"Scaffolding rope?" suggested Mrs. Pollifax. "I wonder how you found *that*."

Georgi said eagerly, "You must not think small of our group. Is true Volko and Tsanko and Boris are not young, but they much knowledge, much history. I myself enjoyed much cynicism in beginning, wanting only young people. Now I am different. We join together like sky and clouds, you know? They see the way to get things, they have great knowledge."

Experienced scavengers, thought Mrs. Pollifax with a smile.

"Radev has visited guard he knows. He was gone long time. He brings news this guard Miroslav will go on wall midnight to dawn. At 3 A.M. sharp this man will stop at gate to smoke the cigarette and talk. He will not be on wall. But Radev pay much money—oh, wow!"

"Oh, wow?" Mrs. Pollifax laughed. "You've been with Debby!"

"You see that?" he said, grinning. "She is good girl, we become friends today."

"And Mrs. Bemish? Has anyone seen her today?"

"*Da*. As liaison I go visit her 8 A.M. this morning. She observe and make pictures of windows on Trenda side of Institute. Radev and Boris go over these very very slowly."

"So all the equipment, and all the information, is here," said Mrs. Pollifax as they walked from car to hut.

Georgi nodded. "We gain much experience for Underground. Come—inside."

"I'm curious, Georgi," she said. "You're very young. Why do *you* do all this?"

Georgi looked surprised. "They not tell you? My brother is one of prisoners in Panchevsky."

"Oh—I'm sorry."

"Life imprisonment," said Georgi, nodding. "He is good communist, too, but he disagree with wrong party official, they search apartment and find notebook in which he records the correctness of our becoming freer, like Yugoslavia. They say this very bad, very revisionist." He sighed. "He will not want to leave his beloved Bulgaria, but if he go—maybe things change a little in five, ten years, and he return. Already my country is better now than before. No more—how you call it—bloodlettings? Purges?"

They descended a ladder into the cellar under the house. It was very primitive, no more than a large hole dug out of the earth for storing food. A few scorched herbs still hung from the ceiling. Under them Volko and Radev were checking off small shapeless packages like two earnest storekeepers taking inventory.

"Ah, Amerikanski," said Volko, turning to smile at her. "Welcome! Come see what is done today."

"I'd love to!"

"This Radev is very expert. Radev, tell her."

"Not bad," acknowledged Radev. "Here is ingenious short fuse, two minutes. This is for Tsanko, very powerful, but in small package, you see? We test two of these, they are so perfect maybe I go into business." He grinned. "Here you see six gentler packages of explosive, also for pockets, almost no fuse, maybe five seconds. Two of them delivered today to Mrs. Bemish, two for you and me, four for Georgi and Kosta."

"And the largest one?" she asked.

"Already it is wired to inside of truck. Heaven preserve the accidents, it is to go off with contact."

Mrs. Pollifax drew a deep sigh of relief. "Well, then," she said, looking around her, "everything appears to be going splendidly." She beamed at them. She supposed that guns would have made their plan simpler; Tsanko's hunting rifles had remained in Tarnovo and only Radev had a gun. She had expressed the hope that this would be a nonviolent raid, to which Boris had drawled, "For them or us?" "Both," she'd replied, and he had snorted derisively.

At seven o'clock Volko quietly left—no one explained why— and Georgi spread a large square of cloth on the floor of the hut. There they ate dinner, literally breaking bread together from a huge loaf and washing it down with red wine. Across the tablecloth Debby caught her eye and said, "Isn't this great, Mrs. Pollifax?" She was eating with her fingers, her face healthily pink from the sun. There was nothing waif-like about her today. She's using herself, she's needed, thought Mrs. Pollifax, and wondered why so many people insisted upon happiness being a matter of ease.

Tsanko had still not arrived. "He and Volko go to big gathering," Boris explained when she inquired about them both. "What you call party?"

"Party!" It seemed a most extraordinary time to go partying.

"We decide today—you are not here—that Volko not be with us tonight. We insist he preserve himself because he supply truck and explosives and needs the good story."

"An alibi!" supplied Mrs. Pollifax.

"*Da*. Already he risk much. The police will learn in time where truck come from and they will be harsh. We have arranged for warehouse to be attacked, the locks broken, wooden boxes entered. By who nobody will know, but when they speak with Volko he will be very innocent. All night he will be at ceremony. Given," he added with a grin, "for General Ignatov."

Mrs. Pollifax laughed. "How clever of you all!"

"*Da*. How can head of security doubt the man who drinks with him, eh?" He glanced at his watch. "But Tsanko be here by midnight. You are nervous, Amerikanski?"

"Very," she said.

He nodded. "None of us know, eh? One asks, is this to be died for?"

"And what's your answer?" asked Mrs. Pollifax.

He smiled. "Is not worth dying for, no, but worth being alive to do."

She nodded. "I like you, Boris. I like your skepticism, too."

He shrugged, amused. "It keeps me alive, it entertains me. One must have entertainments, eh?"

It grew slowly dark, and then cold. They could show no lights except in the cellar and after an hour Mrs. Pollifax felt stifled by the smallness of the room and by the single candle that illuminated them. Debby and Georgi talked earnestly in one corner about their countries and their friends. Kosta, Boris and Radev were arguing heatedly in Bulgarian. Watching them, Mrs. Pollifax had too much time to recall her rashnesses, and the many people she had involved in this assault on the Institute, as well as the terrible risks they would all be taking before dawn. Yet given just one small opportunity to save a human life—and the factor of being in the right place at the right time—was there anything to do except try? One made a decision with the mind, she thought—with the cool logic of a chess player—and then it became necessary to grow to it, to curb the emotional protests, resist the longing to give up, to doubt, to flee. The real enemy was fear.

"I believe I shall go out and sit under a tree," she told them.

"Don't go far," Debby called to her.

She was seated under the tree when Tsanko arrived, driving the van without lights across the untilled earth. He did not see her until she called out to him. He walked over and sat down beside her on the rough bench. "It is gravest concern to me how you are tonight," he said. "You are well?"

"Anxious but well," she said.

He nodded. In the darkness his face was dim, without dimension. "No moon, we are fortunate," he said.

They sat quietly together, the sounds of the night encircling them: the shrilling of cicadas, the call of a whippoorwill, a murmur of rustling leaves from the forest. It was extraordinary how fond she had become of this man, thought Mrs. Pollifax, and she reflected upon how few persons there were with whom she felt an instinctive rapport. There was never anything tangible about this. It was composed of humor, attitude, spirit—all invisible—and it made words completely unnecessary between them.

He said abruptly, "You have good life in America? Tell me of this. A *Cpeda*—Wednesday—for instance. What do you do on a Wednesday?"

"Wednesday," repeated Mrs. Pollifax thoughtfully. "I wake up in my apartment in New Brunswick, New Jersey—I have one bedroom, one large, sunny living room and a kitchen with dining space. The New York *Times* is on my doorstep and I read it with my breakfast." It seemed incredibly far away and unreal. "On Wednesdays I wheel the bookcart at the hospital. It's a very *quiet* life," she admitted. "Except on Fridays when I have my karate lessons. And lately I've considered flying lessons."

He looked at her, smiling. "For you this would be good, very good."

"And I have grown a night-blooming cereus on my fire escape," she added almost shyly.

He said quietly, "This is important. Why?"

She hesitated. "Because lately I've had the feeling we rush toward something—some kind of Armageddon—set into motion long ago. There are so many people in the world, and so much destructiveness. I was astonished when I first heard that a night-blooming cereus blooms only once a year, and always at midnight. It implies such *intelligence* somewhere."

"And did it bloom?" he asked.

She nodded triumphantly. "At twenty minutes before midnight, the week before I left for your country."

"Then there are still mysteries left in this world," he said with relief.

"And your Wednesdays?" she asked. "I'm not allowed to ask about your Wednesdays? This is not a dialogue?"

He sighed heavily. "I wish you may, but no, I cannot, even to you. This is sad because you have become very dear to me, Amerikanski."

She said softly, "It's like a problem in mathematics, I think. For me so much has been added by knowing you, and when I leave —if I am so fortunate," she added wryly, "it will be with a sense of loss, of subtraction."

"At such an age," mused Tsanko, and chuckled. "As if the affections count years! But for me there has been a long time without feeling. My first wife and my little daughter die in 1928—no, not die, they are shot against the wall by the Orim. Murdered. There were three thousand people killed that night, arrested as suspected communists. My daughter had high fever, you see, and despite curfew Adriana wrapped our child in blankets and hurried to find doctor." He shook his head. "My son survived, he is forty now. It was madness, we were not even communists then. But it made one of me," he added.

"How terrible that must have been for you."

"It was. Later I married again, when my son, Vasil, was a

grown man—1945, that was. I was most political, and my wife was also political." He shrugged. "That was bad mistake, we have been divorced many years, she is an engineer in Varna. Alas, the climate of Bulgaria is not good for love. But good for peaches," he added with humor, bringing a peach from his pocket. "Please? For you."

They sat eating peaches until Georgi came to the door and said, "There you are—it's time to begin preparing for Panchevsky Institute."

"Suddenly the clock moves too fast," mused Tsanko. "Early in morning I have appointment I cannot avoid. I will not see you again. Everything has been said but this—please do not be killed tonight, Amerikanski."

"Nor you, Tsanko," she said, and they stood silently together for a moment.

"We are of different cultures on the outside," he said slowly, "but inside we are alike. If only you were born Bulgarian, Amerikanski, we could change the world! You will remember, eh?"

"On Wednesdays," said Mrs. Pollifax gravely.

He laughed. "On Wednesdays, yes," he said, and very formally leaned over and kissed her on each cheek.

Chapter Twenty-One

It was dark and silent in the vicinity of Panchevsky Institute. Only the building itself glowed with light. At five minutes before three o'clock Mrs. Pollifax sat in Assen Radev's farm truck that was filled with honking geese in the rear. She was wearing a shapeless cotton dress, a shabby sweater and over her head a bandanna tied at the nape of her neck. On her shoulder was pinned a card bearing unintelligible letters that supposedly read: I AM A MUTE. "Well, Mrs. Pollifax?" said Radev cheerfully.

She was not quite so cheerful, but she guessed that he was a man who thrived on danger, and therefore his interest in life increased in proportion to the nearness of death. On the whole it was not a bad way to approach Panchevsky Institute, she thought. She glanced at her watch; Radev glanced at his and nodded. "We go," he said, and headed the truck down the street and around the corner into Ordrin Square. Ahead of them, a block away, she could see the walls and the front gate of Panchevsky Institute.

At the top of the hill on Persenk Boulevard, Georgi checked his watch. "One minute to go," he said to Kosta in Bulgarian. "You think we come out of this alive, comrade?"

"Who knows?" said Kosta with a shrug. "It's better to be all dead than half dead."

On the opposite side of the wall, on narrow Ordrin Street, Debby sat beside Boris in the van and shivered from cold and nervousness. "I feel a little sick," she told Boris.

He said very gently, "It's the waiting, you understand. It grows better when there is something to do, you will see."

"It's one minute before three o'clock, Boris," she said, looking at her watch. He nodded, climbed out and began to unlock the rear door of the van where the ladder was hidden.

Tsanko had crossed Persenk Boulevard and now he strolled along beside the high wall, one hand in his pocket fingering the bundle there. Reaching the middle of the wall, he checked his watch, kneeled as if to tie a shoelace and inserted the bundle tightly against the wall. A match flared. When he straightened he began to walk very swiftly, almost running, toward a van parked diagonally across the road, near Stalinov Avenue. He appeared not to notice the large truck soundlessly moving toward him down Persenk Boulevard on his left; it gained momentum as it neared the bottom of the hill. Tsanko had just opened the door to the van when the outer wall of Panchevsky Institute erupted, a portion of it bursting into fragments. The sound of the explosion followed a second later, just as the massive truck rolled through the broken wall and entered the courtyard.

Half a minute later came the sound of the truck's crash, followed by a second, louder explosion.

At the gate Assen Radev was saying, "You may not be expecting two dozen geese for your kitchens, but they are your dinner today. Hell, what do you want done with them? Who's in charge? I tell you they are ordered for this morning."

The guard pointed to Mrs. Pollifax, and Radev said carelessly, "She belongs at the collective, I'm taking her back. She can't speak, she's a mute."

A second man casually joined them and with a wink at Radev spoke persuasively to his companion; it was Miroslav, earning his bribe. The guard fingered the papers with annoying slowness and then nodded. "Take them into the inside court, they can kill the geese there, idiot. But be fast."

Slowly the truck from the collective inched through the gates and then through the second iron gate into the courtyard. "You see the stairs?" said Radev in a low voice to Mrs. Pollifax. "On the right. The door to each floor is kept locked, but the stairs are clear and go up to the top floor."

Mrs. Pollifax nodded. She climbed out and opened the tailgate at the back of the truck. Two dozen geese stared at her, and with a furious motion she gestured them outside, scattering them as they fluttered to the ground honking in outrage. A moment later came the sound of the first explosion.

Boris and Debby heard the sound of the first explosion as they waited in Ordrin Street, the ladder half out of the van. It was dark on the street, but noonday on the top of the wall, and Debby was thinking about Mrs. Bemish and the lights. If Mrs. Bemish couldn't reach them—or damaged them too late—what on earth could they do?

"Set up the ladder," Boris told her. "I'll go first and you follow. Watch the ropes—nothing must tangle them! Do it as we practiced all day."

"I will."

They heard the second explosion and then, abruptly, the sound of a siren began to shrill and was just as suddenly cut off as the lights all over the Institute died. Mrs. Bemish had reached the fuse box. "Now," said Boris, and they hurried up the ladder.

Georgi and Kosta were bent low in the truck as it rolled through the gaping hole in the outer wall and continued, on momentum alone, through the Institute courtyard. As it neared the brick wall of the Institute, Georgi shouted, "Jump, my friend!"

They threw themselves out of the truck, rolling over and over until they crouched under the walls of the building. The truck roared through the wall, setting off the explosives wired under its hood; bricks and stones rained down all around them. "Now," shouted Georgi, and they leaped over the rubble and ran into the cellblock. They were hailed by cheers from the cells and Georgi was grinning as he made his way through the dust. There was plenty of dynamite, he was thinking. He would first free their four friends, among them his brother, but while Kosta hurried the four out to Tsanko there would be time to release a few others as well. They might not get far, but what the hell, he thought; they could have a taste of freedom, smell the free air, feel like men again. He could give them choice at least.

He was opening the door of his brother's cell when the lights went out.

* * *

In the inner courtyard Radev and Mrs. Pollifax were busy directing the geese consistently toward the stairs leading up into the higher cellblocks. Before the echo of the first explosion had died away at least six of the frightened geese had settled on the stair. As the second explosion took place Mrs. Pollifax and Radev each seized a goose and ran up the stairs, driving the dozen others before them. They had reached the second-floor landing when the lights went out. Someone came running down the staircase, tripped over the geese and brushed past Mrs. Pollifax with an oath. With the goose under her arm Mrs. Pollifax continued to climb. A dark shape suddenly careened into her, almost knocking her over; a man grasped her arm, a match flared, a guard spoke sharply and Mrs. Pollifax lifted the goose, making noises in her throat and pointing skyward. The guard disgustedly gestured her aside, blew out the match and hurried on down the stairs.

She had lost Radev; the goose she carried had just learned that by arching his long neck he could peck at her chin and draw blood. With considerable relief Mrs. Pollifax reached the third floor and paused. The door stood open, knocked from its hinges, and she could hear the fluttering of wings ahead of her in the darkness.

She went in quietly, disoriented and suddenly without direction. She faced a long dark hall with a window at the far end; to her left lay another window. Between these stood cellblocks, line after line of them. She stood there, lost, until a light flared at the window on her left. The light sputtered like a Fourth of July sparkler, made a small sound and then she saw Radev lean forward, silhouetted against the sky, and lift out the bars of the window. She dropped the goose and joined him just in time to help him pick up the rope Boris had shot across the yard and secure it to the bars of a cell.

Geese were honking. All over the building men were shouting. She called out, "Philip? Philip Trenda?"

"I have to be dreaming," said an American voice from the cell next to the window.

"Over here," she told Radev, and he lighted a match. In its glow they saw a white face with hollow eyes staring at them from behind bars, a face Mrs. Pollifax had last seen at Customs, on

Monday. She said inadequately, tears in her eyes, "Hello there," and then: "We've come to get you out."

Debby kneeled on the wall next to Boris, her teeth chattering. Once in a while they had gently tested the rope, but it remained slack and without support. It was awful, waiting, thought Debby. She tried to picture Mrs. Pollifax and Radev climbing the stairs to the third floor, tried to live it with them. She wished she could have gone with Radev; Tsanko had said no, a pretty young girl would draw too much attention at the gate.

They ought to be there now, she thought, and staring at the window she was rewarded by the sight of a small flicker of light. She whispered to Boris, "They've reached the window."

Crouched low, Boris said, "*Da*, thank God!" He leaned over and tested the rope, tugging gently. Triumphantly he said, "It is anchored, we get ready now. Say your prayers!"

Now Mrs. Pollifax and Radev would have found Phil, the last bundle of dynamite would be applied to the lock of his cell and any moment he would be at the window, ready to cross. "How much more time?" she asked Boris.

He glanced down at his illuminated watch. "It is now 3:11."

"He ought to be crossing," she whispered, "Radev and Mrs. Pollifax ought to be going downstairs to the truck."

"Patience," said Boris.

Debby strained her eyes trying to peer through the darkness. She leaned over and felt the rope; it was secure, but there was no weight on it. She thought, I won't panic, but he ought to be crossing. I'm not scared, I'm not. She realized that never before had she cared or felt so much about two people as she did at this moment. It was insane, it was as though her whole life had begun only a week ago. She was suddenly terrified for everyone involved in this, but she was the most frightened for Phil and Mrs. Pollifax.

"Boris," she said, her voice trembling.

He turned and she saw him nod. "*Da*—something is wrong," he said heavily.

"I know," she said, and stood up.

On the third floor of the Institute, Radev had stuffed dynamite into the lock of Philip's cell and applied a match to it. As the light flared for a brief second Philip Trenda said to Mrs. Pollifax in astonishment, "I've seen you before! I know I've seen you before!"

"Ssh," hissed Radev.

The fuse ignited and Mrs. Pollifax stepped back. There was the sound of a muffled *crack!* and they were in darkness again, but in that darkness Mrs. Pollifax felt someone breathing down her neck from behind. She said in a low voice, "Assen?"

But Radev was opening the door to the cell. She said, "Who . . . ?" but before she could turn around she felt a gun pressed into the small of her back.

Radev had not noticed. The person behind Mrs. Pollifax suddenly spoke to Radev roughly, in Bulgarian, and Radev growled in his throat and turned.

"What is it?" asked Mrs. Pollifax. "Who is it?"

"It's Miroslav, the guard."

"He has a gun in my back," protested Mrs. Pollifax.

Radev spoke sharply to the man and the gun was removed. In the darkness Miroslav and Radev shifted positions cautiously. Miroslav backed to the window to stand outlined against it, gun in hand. Radev moved away from Philip's cell in order to conceal the rope tied to its bars. They stood like this in silence and then Radev spoke to the man in anger.

It was torture not knowing what they said. Radev's voice was biting; Miroslav's was calm. The man had been well paid—and not even in counterfeit rubles, after all, but in authentic Bulgarian *leva* —but still he stood with his gun directed at them, not willing to let them go.

"What *is* it?" cried Mrs. Pollifax impatiently.

"The dog," said Radev, and spat on the floor. "The *dog*. He took the bribe, now he says he gets more money turning us in and getting a medal. He didn't know I was going to release the American capitalist spy."

Mrs. Pollifax heard Philip say, "Oh God."

"He's barricading the window," went on Radev, "and he says in a few minutes both lights and guards will return. He has only to wait."

"Does he speak English?"

"No."

"Have you any dynamite left?"

"No."

"He hasn't noticed the rope yet. If one of us could just reach him and hold him long enough for Philip to get to the window . . ."

Radev's voice was cynical. "You wish to volunteer? That's exactly what he's waiting for." Then in a peculiar voice he added, "Wait. Something is happening."

"What?" demanded Mrs. Pollifax.

"Ssh," he said, and then: "Pray God the lights do not come on. The rope is tight, do you understand?"

"Tight," echoed Mrs. Pollifax uncomprehendingly and then she realized that in concealing the rope Radev stood where he could also touch it, and her heart began to beat very fast. "Talk to him," she said in a low voice. "Keep him talking, Radev."

"*Da.*"

Mrs. Pollifax fixed her eyes on the barless window behind Miroslav. She saw a hand grasp the window sill and then the silhouette of a slim body drag itself up to the sill. In a clear conversational voice Mrs. Pollifax addressed the shadow. "The guard stands with a gun, and with his back to the window. *His back to the window!*" The figure was crouched there now, black against the sky. It was Debby.

Tackle, she thought silently. Tackle, Debby, *tackle!*

Debby stood up, remained poised for a second on the sill and then hurled herself toward the floor of the cellblock, taking Miroslav with her. With trembling fingers Mrs. Pollifax lighted a match. It was enough for Radev; he found Miroslav, bent over him and wrested the gun from his hands. A moment later Debby stood up. Behind her there was the sound of bone hitting bone, a groan and then Radev said, "He's out cold."

"Debby—oh thank God you made it," gasped Mrs. Pollifax.

"Debby?" repeated Philip incredulously. "Debby's here?"

"I'm here," Debby said in a steady voice. "Phil, there's a rope attached to the window and you have to go quickly, hand over hand, so the rest of us can follow. Can you?"

"With pleasure," he said fervently.

Radev said, "We can't all go by rope, there isn't time. I have Miroslav's gun. How about it, Mrs. Pollifax? Shall we make a fast retreat by the stairs into hell knows what?"

"Yes," said Mrs. Pollifax. She reached out, grasped Debby's hand and squeezed it. "You won't wait too long?"

"I won't," promised Debby.

Mrs. Pollifax and Radev walked down the hall to the staircase. A goose rushed at them and Radev scooped it up and pushed it into Mrs. Pollifax's arms. They descended as quickly as they dared in the darkness, braced for discovery at any minute. They reached the last landing and then the inner courtyard and now they saw why they had not been challenged yet: fires had broken out following the explosions and the courtyard was filled with black smoke. They jumped into the truck and Radev backed and turned it and they drove through the first gate. At the second gate Radev called out to the solitary guard at the sentry box.

The guard came running. To Mrs. Pollifax's surprise Radev cut the guard's questions short with a laugh, reached over and took the goose from her and tossed it into the man's arms. A moment later the guard opened the gates for them.

"He wanted only to ask about the fire," said Radev. "I told him he will have roast geese for dinner."

As they drove through the gates the lights and the siren of Panchevsky Institute came on simultaneously. Mrs. Pollifax looked down at her watch: it was precisely 3:27. She said blankly, "It's over. It's over, Radev, and we're still alive!"

"Beginner's luck, eh, Comrade Pollifax?" said Radev.

Minutes later they reached the appointed rendezvous in a park at the edge of Sofia, and what was most satisfying of all, Debby and Boris and Philip were in the car behind them.

Chapter Twenty-Two

Outside the Hotel Rila a man was sweeping the street with a broom of thick twigs tied around a crooked stick. The sky brightened during the past hour and there was a suffusion of pink in the east where the sun was rising. As Mrs. Pollifax mounted the steps of the hotel she turned and saw Georgi and the small blue car disappear for the last time and then she entered the lobby, properly dressed as a tourist again, her purse over her arm. A dozing desk clerk jerked awake and stared at her reproachfully. She wrote the number of her room on his memo pad and he handed her the key. He also handed over her passport, which had been placed in the box, and she tucked it into her purse.

As she ascended in the elevator to the sixth floor she felt a sense of sadness. It was completely illogical, she reminded herself, because the sacking of Panchevsky Institute had been accomplished without bloodshed and with a success beyond all expectation. What was more, the passports she had delivered to Tsanko were about to save five lives as well as give new lives to Mrs. Bemish and Assen Radev.

I'm just very tired, she thought.

She tried to remember that she and Debby, Philip and Mrs. Bemish would be meeting on Monday in Zurich, in front of the bank to which Petrov Trendafilov would bring the ransom, but even this didn't lift her sagging spirits.

She tried also to remember Philip's astonishment at meeting her again, or the flash of Assen Radev's grin as he said, "Beginner's luck, eh, Comrade Pollifax?" But another voice blotted them out, a voice that she would remember for the rest of her life: *I am not sure either of us is professional, is this not so? . . . I am good communist, a patriot and also—God help me—a humanist. . . . You have become very dear to me, Amerikanski.*

The elevator opened at the sixth floor and she walked down the hall to her room and inserted the key into the lock. She already missed Debby, but Debby would be making her way to the airport alone after she had helped to change Philip into Anton Schoenstein, a German with German credentials and clothes. She opened the door and flicked on the lights and brought her suitcase from the closet and carried it to the bed. Moving to the bureau, she picked up comb, brush and cold cream. She glanced at herself in the mirror and was startled to see how little changed she looked after twenty-seven minutes inside Panchevsky Institute. Perhaps one day next year—very suddenly—new lines would etch themselves on her face and she could say, *Those are Panchevsky lines.*

Suddenly in the mirror she saw the door to the bathroom open silently. A foot—a black boot—inserted itself against the door and Nikolai Dzhagarov moved into the doorway and stood watching her. Their glances met in the mirror.

"You have perhaps forgotten me," he said, bringing out a gun. "My name is Nikki."

"Yes, I *had* forgotten you," she admitted. "Foolishly," she added in a low voice.

"You may turn around now—slowly, hands up," he said. "You will forget the suitcase, Mrs. Pollifax, you are my prisoner and before I let you go I must know how to find my friend Debby and my friend Carleton Bemish."

Slowly Mrs. Pollifax turned, hands lifted.

"Now. First you will tell me where Karlo Bemish and Titko Yugov are to be found."

Mrs. Pollifax's first reaction was one of relief: Nikki was still twenty-four hours behind them, he didn't know about the prison raid, his mind was stubbornly fixed on Tarnovo, which felt to her like a century ago. Her second reaction was the more realistic. Dzhagarov had all the time in the world, and a gun, and he was a dangerous man. She might have to die tonight.

"I didn't think you cared about Mr. Bemish," she said lightly. "You certainly exploited him rather cruelly, didn't you?"

Nikki shrugged. "He asked for it. What a bore, that man,

always talking of his millionaire brother-in-law in America! An obsession. When he learned Phil would be visiting Yugoslavia in July he had the audacity to try and bribe me so that he might go to Belgrade and collect a few dollars from the boy." He laughed savagely. "A few thousand was all he wanted, can you imagine? What a small mind!"

"I wonder if I might lower my hands," said Mrs. Pollifax hopefully.

"No." He left the doorway and moved across the room toward her. As he passed the bed he reached out and shoved her suitcase on the floor, kicking it viciously across the room. "So much for your departure," he said contemptuously. "I want to know where Bemish can be found. I want to know where Debby is. She's been in Bulgaria all this time, she did not leave with the others. Why?"

"Debby left Bulgaria last night," she told him. "If you ask at the desk you'll discover she picked up her passport late yesterday afternoon. She's gone."

"No one by that name flew out of Sofia yesterday or last night or early this morning. She is still here." He moved behind her and placed the point of his pistol at the back of her neck. It felt cold against her flesh. "Where is she?"

"I don't know," said Mrs. Pollifax.

"Where is Bemish?"

"I don't know," repeated Mrs. Pollifax.

The pistol burrowed deeper. "I will count to four," he said. "If you do not speak I will kill you."

"Yes," she said numbly.

"One," said Nikki.

Mrs. Pollifax closed her eyes. She remembered that Tsanko was safe and that he had taken to safety the four men who had been rescued. The four would presently be leaving Bulgaria by bus, car and boat. Assen Radev had been given his well-earned passport and perhaps—knowing Radev—was already across the border.

"Two," said Nikki.

But they all needed time, she thought: Debby and Philip, especially.

"Try Bemish first," suggested Nikki smoothly. "You were in

Tarnovo that same night he disappeared. You saw him—of course you saw him."

She shook her head. "I didn't see him."

"Three," said Nikki, and waited.

Mrs. Pollifax also waited. It would be a sudden and clean death, she thought, and she had always known the odds were against her dying in bed at home in New Brunswick, New Jersey.

Suddenly Nikki laughed and removed the gun from her neck. "You have strong nerves. You think I kill you so quickly—here of all places—without learning what I wish to know? Pick up the suitcase on the floor and close it."

Mrs. Pollifax sighed, crossed the room and placed the suitcase on the bed.

"Put the coat on and pick up the purse," he directed. When she had done this he added, "Now carry the suitcase out the door ahead of me. You will proceed down the hall to the elevator, then to the lobby, out of the lobby to my car. Walk!"

She picked up the empty suitcase and went to the door. "Where are we going?" she asked quietly.

"Headquarters. They will know how to deal with you there. The new head of security, General Ignatov, will see that you talk— he knows all the ways. Don't turn around!" he said sharply. "I shall be directly behind you, gun in pocket."

Mrs. Pollifax walked steadily down the hall to the elevator. If there was a long wait for the elevator, she thought, it might be possible to draw close enough to Dzhagarov to catch him off balance with a kick and a shin strike.

Unfortunately the elevator was standing at the sixth floor, depressingly empty, its doors wide open.

"In," said Nikki, and joined her only when she had walked to the rear.

They descended, facing each other. When the elevator stopped he said, "Walk out now. Speak to no one and cross the lobby. A car is outside, the safety catch is off my gun. No tricks."

The doors of the elevator slid open and Mrs. Pollifax walked out into the lobby. She realized that she was about to enter a Bulgaria that no tourists were allowed to see, and the lobby was her last glimpse of the familiar.

"So there you are, Mrs. Pollifax!" cried an indignant and familiar voice. Nevena stood beside the desk, hands on hips. "How insulting you are, Mrs. Pollifax! I am here at 7 P.M. sharp last night and you are not here, now they call from the hotel to say you are back, and again I must leave my work to find you! *Bora!* It is too much."

Mrs. Pollifax stopped uncertainly, the gun at her back.

"You have your suitcase—good," continued Nevena, walking toward her. "They tell me you have been given passport as well. You will come at once, please, this is gravest dishonor for you. Yes, yes, what is it, Comrade Dzhagarov?" she asked impatiently.

"She is mine," Nikki told her coldly, and began speaking to her rapidly in Bulgarian.

"Nonsense—she is mine," Nevena interrupted sharply. "Speak in English, Comrade Dzhagarov, or you will make the scandal. People are listening, you understand? This woman is not yours, she is to leave country at once, she is *persona non grata*. Balkantourist is *finis* with her. Kaput!"

Nikki said icily, "I tell you she is mine, Comrade Chernokolev. I have orders she must go to headquarters for interrogation."

"Show me the orders," Nevena said angrily.

Nikki shrugged. "They are not written. You wish to cross General Ignatov?"

"General Ignatov!" Nevena laughed. "Idiot—he was arrested only a few hours ago. By now he is on his way to Panchevsky Institute."

"Arrested?" repeated Nikki. "I do not believe you. What a liar you are!"

She shrugged. "Please yourself, comrade, but you would do well not to speak his name. I will be kind and forget you spoke of him."

Nikki looked shaken. "This is not possible. On what charges?"

Nevena looked at him scornfully. "His home is searched last night while he is at celebration. Big fortune in Russian rubles is found there."

"So?"

"The rubles were counterfeit," Nevena said curtly, and grasping Mrs. Pollifax firmly by the arm she led her out of the door to a waiting car.

"You see the trouble you make," Nevena continued as she pushed her into the car. "It is Sunday, I do not work on Sunday." She started the motor and they hurtled forward. "I anticipate viewing of Party Chairman Brezhnev's arrival from Moscow and now you make the work for me, *more* work."

Mrs. Pollifax turned her head and looked at her wordlessly.

"They already begin the ropes along the street," went on Nevena hotly, "and I doubt gravely we get to aerodrome in time for the early plane to Belgrade. Soon they stop cars."

"Yes," said Mrs. Pollifax, testing her voice and surprised to find that she could still speak.

"Dzhagarov is arrogant," said Nevena. "As for you, Mrs. Pollifax—please. You are too old for travel. Go home to your children, your grandchildren, you understand?"

Mrs. Pollifax drew a deep breath; it was beginning to dawn upon her that she was going to survive this day, after all. The cool, early morning air was reviving her; it occurred to her that she had been very near to a state of collapse back at the hotel. She realized that Nevena had no idea at all that she had just saved her life, and this struck her as incredible and wonderful and a little hilarious, and this, too, revived her. "Yes," she said to Nevena, and her eyes turned to Mount Vitosha and then to the sun spilling gold across the road and to the clusters of vivid blue asters.

"Do me the favor of staying in your home," went on Nevena, driving very fast, her profile stern. "You have not the gift for coordination."

"No," Mrs. Pollifax said humbly.

Nevena swerved to avoid a flock of sheep crossing the road. *"Nahot,"* she said under her breath, and sent the car racing down still another country road. "You Americans must learn the purpose, the punctualness. I forgive much because you are old, but never come back to my country, you understand?"

"I understand," said Mrs. Pollifax, clinging to her seat.

They emerged on a broad boulevard. "You see the police collecting," pointed out Nevena reproachfully. "Chairman Brezhnev must already be landing at the aerodrome, we may be cut off. I drive quick, but I do not know. When the glorious leader of the Soviet Union comes to our country it is great honor."

"It's going to be a lovely day," ventured Mrs. Pollifax. "For his arrival," she added quickly as Nevena gave her a suspicious glance.

"We make good time—there is entrance to aerodrome," Nevena announced, and with a quick glance at her watch added, "We have ten minutes to get you to Customs, half an hour to plane departure." But as they began the long drive into the terminal Nevena clucked suddenly and with exasperation. "We are to be stopped," she said.

A barricade had been set up just this side of the terminal, and uniformed police were standing around it. They gestured the car to the side and Nevena handed one of the guards her credentials, speaking vivaciously and pointing ahead. The guard shook his head.

Nevena said with a shrug, "Well, we must stop, but not for long, and it is gravest honor for you, Mrs. Pollifax—you also will observe the Chairman Brezhnev pass by. The procession is just leaving the air terminal." She parked the car and climbed out. "Come if you please," she said indifferently. "For me this is happy moment, I see the Chairman after all."

Mrs. Pollifax climbed out of the car and joined Nevena by the side of the road—it seemed a very small way in which to repay Nevena for saving her life. She stood quietly as the procession of cars slowly approached: first the uniformed men on motorcycles, then one long, black, closed limousine—"There is Chairman Brezhnev with our Premier!" cried Nevena, stiffening in a salute— and following this came three open limousines filled with wooden-faced men in black suits.

How stiff and Slavic they looked, thought Mrs. Pollifax, amused, and then her glance rested upon one of the men in the second limousine and she stared in astonishment. There was no mistaking that profile, that square jaw, those shaggy brows. She said, "Who . . ." and then she stopped and cleared her throat and said, "Who are the men in the cars following your Premier, Nevena?"

"Members of our Politburo," said Nevena, not turning. "High officials of our government."

I have an appointment early in the morning, Tsanko had said.

The heads remained fixed, like statues—he did not see her—and standing behind Nevena, unseen by her, Mrs. Pollifax lifted a hand and gravely saluted, too.

Chapter Twenty-Three

It was early Monday morning in Langley Field, Virginia, and just six o'clock as Carstairs entered his office. With the Trenda affair so tragically ended by the boy's death there was a great deal of back work to clear away. It was all very well to begin a day at the leisurely hour of nine if dealing with American affairs, but at that hour in America it was already 2 P.M. in Europe.

As Carstairs sat down at his desk Bishop suddenly appeared in the doorway of the adjacent room, yawning and shaking his head. Carstairs said in astonishment, "Good God, what on earth are you doing here at this hour?"

Bishop peered at him through glazed eyes. "Sleeping. I had a date. Seemed a hell of a lot simpler to come here at four o'clock in the morning than go all the way back to my apartment."

"You look like death itself," Carstairs told him with a shudder. "Go and wash your face and get us some coffee."

"Adrenalin would be better," Bishop said bleakly and went out rubbing his eyes.

Carstairs returned to the pile of reports on his desk from South America, Iraq, Helsinki and Vienna. There was still nothing from Bulgaria and this began to be alarming. He'd sent an urgent message to Assen Radev through emergency channels demanding that Radev track down and recover both Mrs. Pollifax and her coat. That message had gone off four days ago, on Wednesday night, with instructions that its arrival be verified at once—and no verification had come through. He didn't like it, he didn't like any part of the summing up: nothing from Radev since the last routine message reporting the secret police tailing Mrs. Pollifax, and nothing from Mrs. Pollifax, who should have left Bulgaria yesterday, on Sunday.

What did it mean—betrayal? . . . God, it was hard not knowing.

Bishop reappeared carrying a pot of coffee and looking decently shaved and alert again. "Morning," he said cheerfully. "The medical records on young Trenda have just come through from his family doctor." He tossed them on the desk.

"I suppose there's absolutely no history of rheumatic fever or heart deficiency?"

"None at all, sir."

"Just as we all thought," said Carstairs gloomily, his eyes scanning the records. "I assume his father will agree to an autopsy as soon as he's brought back the body?"

Bishop hesitated. "I understand not, sir."

"What?" Bishop was shocked and incredulous. "Why the hell not?"

"He left for Europe Saturday night, you know, after refusing to speak to reporters at the airport. Earlier, in Chicago—just after the announcement of his son's death—he said very flatly 'no autopsy.'"

The desk was suddenly too confining for Carstairs and he sprang to his feet and began pacing. "There's something horribly wrong here," he said, "and I'm not seeing where yet."

"About Philip's death, you mean?"

Carstairs brushed this aside impatiently. "Of course about Trenda's death—we can *all* smell the convenience of it, but I doubt that murder can ever be proven. No, I mean there's something horribly wrong about *everything*. Mrs. Pollifax is hell knows where with the secret police tailing her. Radev's silent. And Mr. Trenda says 'no autopsy.' Why? What does he know that we don't? What do they know in Bulgaria that we don't?"

"The telephone, sir."

Carstairs whirled and glared at him, saw the orange light flashing at his desk and swore. "Damn, I came in early to escape telephone calls. All right, acknowledge the blasted thing, Bishop."

Bishop leaned over and flicked off the light. "Carstairs' office, Bishop speaking . . ." He was silent and then he shouted, "*What?*" He swiveled in his chair and signaled Carstairs. "Yes, we certainly *will* accept a collect call from Mrs. Emily Pollifax in Zurich, Switzerland."

Carstairs' jaw dropped. "She's safe? She's calling?" He
crossed the room in two strides. "Hello?" he barked into the telephone. "Hello? Connection's not through yet," he growled to
Bishop. "Get this on tape, will you? And what the hell's she doing
in Switzerland?"

Bishop switched on the tape recorder and took the liberty of
plugging in the headset jack and adjusting the headset to his ears.
At the other end of the line he heard a familiar voice say, "Mr.
Carstairs? Is that you, Mr. Carstairs?"

Bishop grinned. It was extraordinary how lighthearted he
suddenly felt.

"Go ahead, please," the overseas operator said.

"Thank God!" cried Carstairs. "You're all right, Mrs. Pollifax?"

"I'm just fine," said Mrs. Pollifax happily. "I hope you are,
too? Mr. Carstairs, I realize this is ruinously expensive for the
taxpayers, my calling you from Europe—"

"They've borne worse," said Carstairs savagely. "Mrs. Pollifax, we heard the secret police were trailing you. Were you able to
meet Tsanko?"

"Oh yes—a marvelous man," she told him warmly. "But I'm
not calling about that, I'm calling about a passport. There's a
young American student with me who's had his passport confiscated—"

"You say you *did* meet Tsanko," said Carstairs with relief.

"Yes, he has the hat and its contents, Mr. Carstairs. But you
didn't tell me about the coat. Or Assen Radev." Her voice was
mildly reproachful.

"Radev?" echoed Carstairs. "You know his name? You met
him? That was expressly forbidden, Mrs. Pollifax, I'll have his head
for that."

"If you can find him," replied Mrs. Pollifax pleasantly. "He
flew out with us yesterday and I hope you'll be kind to him, he was
so *very* helpful."

"What do you mean, 'flew out'?" Carstairs said ominously.
"He belongs in Bulgaria. He's paid to *stay* in Bulgaria."

"Oh well, he couldn't possibly stay after the trouble began,
you know. I think you'll find him on the French Riviera, he said

something about a vacation. But Mr. Carstairs, I'm calling about this young American—"

"What trouble?" he demanded. "Mrs. Pollifax, did Radev catch up with your coat and exchange it or didn't he?"

"You mean the counterfeit rubles," said Mrs. Pollifax pleasantly. "No, I don't believe he ever saw them, but in any case it scarcely matters because General Ignatov has them now, and he—"

Carstairs said slowly, "Mrs. Pollifax, I thought I heard you say General Ignatov, but the connection's poor. *Who* has the rubles?"

Mrs. Pollifax sighed. "General Ignatov, but he's gone to prison so that scarcely matters either. Mr. Carstairs I'm *not* telephoning about Assen Radev or General Ignatov, I'm calling about this young American whose passport was confiscated. It's very important, he wants to return tomorrow and I know that a word from you will restore his passport."

"My dear Mrs. Pollifax," he said irritably, "I can't possibly interfere in such matters, that's strictly State Department business. It's naïve of you even to ask, because you can't be certain at all that he's American."

"But of course he is," said Mrs. Pollifax indignantly. "I entered Bulgaria with him and he was American when he was arrested. Perhaps you've read about him in the newspapers, his name is Philip Trenda."

There was a baffled silence. "Philip Trenda?" repeated Carstairs.

"Yes, you've read about him?"

"Read about him! He's been the major headline for a week. But he's dead, Mrs. Pollifax. He died in Belgrade on Friday."

Mrs. Pollifax sighed. "No, he didn't die, Mr. Carstairs, that's what I'm trying to explain. He's here in Zurich with me, in fact we're all here at the Grand Hotel, his father, too. It was someone else they sent to Belgrade, and that's why his passport is gone, you see, but we were able to get him out."

"Out?"

"Yes, out of Panchevsky Institute."

"Nonsense," Carstairs said flatly. "Nobody gets out of Panchevsky Institute."

"Well, I'm sorry to disillusion you. We got him out of Panchevsky Institute and then out of Bulgaria."

"And who the hell's we?" demanded Carstairs.

"The Underground. But Philip's traveling under the name of Anton Schoenstein, you see, and since it's one of your forged passports I'm not at all sure that he'll be allowed into the United States, and—"

Carstairs interrupted in a dazed voice. "Mrs. Pollifax, are you trying to tell me that Philip Trenda's *alive?*"

"Of course," she said cheerfully. "It's why I called, but I do think I must hang up now because they're waiting for me on the balcony. We're having a champagne breakfast, you see, because we're all safe and because the ransom wasn't paid, so if you'll excuse me—"

"*Ransom!*" shouted Carstairs. "What ransom? Mrs. Pollifax!"

"Yes?"

"I'm taking the next plane over! Don't move from that hotel and don't let Philip Trenda or his father speak to a soul, do you hear? Good God, this sounds like State Department business at the highest level."

He hung up. In a hollow voice he said, "Did you get that on tape, Bishop? Every word?"

"I certainly did, sir. And eavesdropped as well."

"I sent her to Bulgaria to deliver eight passports," Carstairs said, looking stunned. "How in the hell did she end up putting General Ignatov in prison, corrupting our last agent in Sofia and resurrecting a dead American?"

"Definitely a meddler," Bishop said, grinning. "Now shall I call the State Department first or the air lines, sir?"

At the other end of the line, in Zurich, Mrs. Pollifax hung up the telephone, crossed the room and opened the glass doors to the balcony. On the threshold she paused a minute to admire the scene in front of her, the long table heaped with flowers, waiters hovering, the Trendas and Debby seated and waiting for her. A motley group, she thought with a smile. There was Peter Trenda, nee Petrov Trendafilov, a delightful little man with a shock of hair as white as his linen suit. To his right sat Philip, his eyes a shade less haunted today, although his face was still pale and tired. Mrs. Bemish sat on his left, looking already younger and straighter as she beamed at her brother. And there was Debby, her hair swept high on her head today and her eyes like stars.

Survivors of a strange week, thought Mrs. Pollifax.

"Champagne for breakfast!" Debby was saying in an awed voice as the waiter leaned over and filled her glass. "Not to mention breakfast at noon. It's so rococo, like one of those late late movies starring Carole Lombard."

"Well, after all, Dad's sitting here with a million bucks in that attaché case. Hey," Phil said, looking up and seeing Mrs. Pollifax, "come and join us, the party's ready to begin and there's so much to tell Dad. Did your phone call go through?"

Nodding, she crossed the balcony to the table. "Yes, but it was *such* a difficult conversation—Mr. Carstairs didn't seem to have the slightest idea what I was talking about."

Debby laughed. "That's because he hasn't been with you for the past week!"

"He's taking the next plane over," Mrs. Pollifax told Mr. Trenda. "You and Philip aren't to speak to anyone until he arrives. Something about the State Department."

Peter Trenda nodded. "I quite approve. They will not want to embarrass Bulgaria about this. We are both incognito anyway," he added with a smile, "since I am registered here as Petrov Trendafilov, and my son is still Anton Schoenstein. My son," he repeated, smiling at Philip. "My son who is risen from the dead. Mrs. Pollifax . . . Debby . . ." His voice broke. "How can I ever express what I feel this morning when I approach the bank and find you all waiting for me? You have returned to me my son and my sister."

Mrs. Pollifax smiled. Lightly, to cover the emotion of the moment, she said, "I think some toasts are in order, don't you? So much champagne!"

Trenda nodded. "You are very wise—the joy and the tears are very near to us just now. Well, Philip? To you I give the first toast because you are truly the host today."

Philip looked about him at their faces. He said soberly, "All right. I think I'll go back to the beginning of all this and propose a toast to a chance meeting in the Belgrade air terminal. That's where it all began, isn't it?"

"But is anything chance, I wonder?" mused Mrs. Pollifax.

Peter Trenda smiled. "You feel that, too?" he asked. Lifting his glass, he said, "Then let us drink next—very seriously—to the arrivals and departures of life, that they may never be careless."

Debby suddenly shivered.

"What is it, Deb?" asked Phil. "Cold?"

"No." There were tears in her eyes. "I don't know, I really don't. Except—for a whole week I've been tired and frightened, I nearly got murdered three times and my thumb was broken and—I've never felt so good. Will you let me make the next toast? If anyone will lend me a handkerchief, that is."

"Handkerchief!" exclaimed Mr. Trenda, laughing. "Please—I would give you my life, young lady, a handkerchief is nothing."

"Thanks," Debby said, and wiped her eyes. Lifting her glass, she stared at it for so long and so thoughtfully that Mrs. Pollifax wondered what she was seeing in its golden contents.

We have each returned a little bemused and enchanted, she thought.

Debby said soberly, "This toast can only be to one person, a very brave man named Tsanko."

Mrs. Pollifax became suddenly still and alert.

"We don't know who he was," she went on with a scowl. "I don't suppose anyone will ever know. But he saved our lives in Tarnovo and we wouldn't be here now if it weren't for him. But also this toast is to him because . . ." She blushed and darted a quick, apologetic glance at Mrs. Pollifax. "Because someday I hope a man will look at me the way he looked at Mrs. Pollifax."

"Hear, hear," said Phil softly.

"I like this girl," Mr. Trenda said, smiling at Mrs. Pollifax. "Shall we drink our next toast to this man, then?"

"To Tsanko," Debby said, nodding. "Whoever he is."

"To Tsanko," echoed Mrs. Pollifax, smiling, and for just a moment—but there would be many such moments—her thoughts traveled back to a moonlit fortress in Tarnovo, to a bench outside a country hut, and from there at last to a procession of passing limousines. *And may no one ever learn who he is,* she added silently, like a prayer.